TRIAL
AND
ERROR

TRIAL
AND
ERROR

AN OXFORD ANTHOLOGY OF LEGAL STORIES

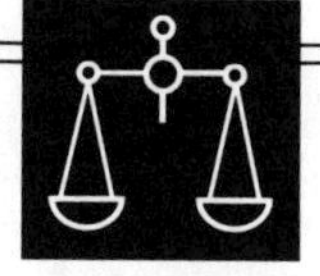

EDITED BY

Fred R. Shapiro and Jane Garry

New York Oxford
Oxford University Press
1998

Oxford University Press

Oxford New York
Athens Auckland Bangkok Bombay
Calcutta Cape Town Dar es Salaam Delhi
Florence Hong Kong Istanbul Karachi
Kuala Lumpur Madras Madrid Melbourne
Mexico City Nairobi Paris Singapore
Taipei Tokyo Toronto Warsaw

and associated companies in
Berlin Ibadan

Published by Oxford University Press, Inc.
198 Madison Avenue, New York, New York 10016

Library of Congress Cataloging-in-Publication Data

Trial and error : an Oxford anthology of legal stories /
edited by Fred R. Shapiro and Jane Garry.
p. cm. Includes index.
ISBN 0-19-509547-2
1. Legal stories, English. 2. Legal stories, American. 3. Law—
Great Britain—Fiction. 4. Law—United States—Fiction.
5. English fiction. 6. American fiction. I. Shapiro, Fred R. II. Garry, Jane.
PR1309.L43T75 1997 823.008'0355—dc21 97–19789

1 3 5 7 9 8 6 4 2

Printed in the United States of America
on acid-free paper

CONTENTS

PREFACE

> *Our seniors at the Bar, within the Bar, and even at the Bench, read novels; and, if not belied, some of them have written novels into the bargain.*
> —SIR WALTER SCOTT

What did Ovid, Seneca, Giovanni Boccaccio, Petrarch, Michel de Montaigne, Francis Bacon, John Donne, Henry Fielding, Voltaire, James Boswell, Johann Wolfgang von Goethe, Washington Irving, Walter Scott, Honoré de Balzac, Benjamin Disraeli, Victor Hugo, Thomas Carlyle, Henry Wadsworth Longfellow, William Makepeace Thackeray, Charles Dickens, Gustave Flaubert, Robert Louis Stevenson, Henry James, Marcel Proust, John Galsworthy, Franz Kafka, Wallace Stevens, and Louis Auchincloss have in common? All of these authors—and they are only the best-known of a much longer list—either practiced or studied law. The roster of literary figures who were the children of lawyers is similarly impressive.

Since literature has historically been the province of the upper middle classes, it is not surprising that so many authors should have been trained in the solid profession of law. But that other respectable profession, medicine, has counted far fewer writers among its ranks. Surely one reason for the powerful attraction of lawyers to literature is that law is a quintessentially verbal vocation. In the words of the great torts scholar William L. Prosser, law is "one of the principal literary professions. One might hazard the supposition that the average lawyer in the course of a lifetime does more writing than a novelist."

While a few of these luminaries, such as Scott and Auchincloss, were remarkably successful in pursuing dual careers as writers and lawyers, many who originally embarked on a legal career eventually aborted their studies or ceased practicing in order to pursue writing full-time; others continued with both professions but felt a strong tension between the two. (Disraeli is said to have remarked that the law depressed him, while literature exalted him.) In *Law and Letters in American Culture* (1984), Robert A. Ferguson sketches the biography of Charles Brockden Brown, one of America's first significant novelists, whose career epitomized the tension between a devotion to literature and the practice of law. After six miserable years in a Philadelphia law office, Brown stopped practicing in 1793 and became a professional writer, to the dismay of his family and friends and his own resulting depression and loss of self-esteem.

In Brown's *Memoirs of Stephen Calvert* (1799–1800) the protagonist, Stephen Calvert, is torn between two women who personify the conflict between law and literature. Ferguson notes that Stephen's cousin, Louisa Calvert, who represents law, is "tedious, ugly, and boring. . . . As a companion for the artist, the good Louisa is particularly hopeless. . . . Calvert is ready to marry [her] anyway to improve his financial situation and to avoid the rebukes of family and friends." Louisa is juxtaposed with Brown's symbol of literature, Clelia Neville, who "appears so beautiful that Calvert's senses are temporarily overpowered."

Since ancient times law has found its way into literature as the backdrop against which human beings wrestle with a vast array of moral, psychological, and political issues. Transgressions ranging in scale from the organized horror of the Holocaust to the breaking of a wedding troth have been presented before formal legal bodies in the pursuit of justice. The law court is the forum in which intensely private actions and motives are subjected to public scrutiny; it is a stage upon which past deeds enacted in the grip of fear, sexual passion, or rage—or just in cold blood—are reconstructed in order to arrive at the truth of what happened and to ensure that justice is done. Yet, as the critic Dwight MacDonald has said, great writers who have been attracted to the subject of law have demonstrated that sometimes "truth is too small a fish to be caught in the law's coarse meshes." Thus a theme of Stevenson's *Weir of Hermiston* (1894) is the exquisite difficulty of judging another human being. The private agony of Melville's Captain Vere in condemning Billy Budd is another study of this dilemma.

The strong connection between the legal and the literary has been recognized by a rapidly growing "law and literature" movement. Law schools increasingly offer classes both on legal themes in literature and legal texts as literature, some taught by prominent humanists such as Stanley Fish, Carolyn Heibrun, and Robert Coles. There are two journals devoted to law and literature: *Yale Journal of Law and the Humanities* and *Cardozo Studies in Law and Literature*. Outside the academy, the success of John Grisham, Scott Turow, and other authors of "legal thrillers" attest to the considerable interest in law-related fiction among general readers.

Trial and Error presents thirty-two of the most outstanding English-language stories treating the human dimension of the law: individuals caught up in the legal system as practitioners, participants, and sometimes victims. Peopling these pages are lawyers, criminal defendants, litigants, clients, judges, police officers, jurors, and witnesses. The selections range topically over criminal law, law enforcement, military justice, international law, civil rights, property, wills and estates, contract, marriage, divorce and custody, abortion, and the legal profession.

While previous anthologies of law and literature have included stories broadly relating to crime and punishment, morality, psychological guilt, or divine justice, we have instead selected stories focused squarely on legal institutions, legal rules, or legal actors. So, for example, Edgar Allen Poe's "The Tell-Tale Heart" (1843) will not be found here, nor will Anthony Burgess's *A Clockwork Orange* (1962), because they do not focus on trials, on the substantive or procedural rules of the law, or the roles individuals assume in the legal process.

It was extremely tempting to include such penetrating Continental commentators as Gogol, Balzac, Hugo, Flaubert, Dostoyevsky, Tolstoy, Maupassant, France, Kafka, and Camus, among others. We chose, however, the more coherent plan of limiting this book to English-language works. The English-speaking nations share not only a language and a literary tradition, but also the tradition of the common law. A collection embracing literature from Continental Europe or beyond would require a great deal more explication of the legal systems involved, and would risk losing its intelligibility in a welter of different cultures and legal regimes. American and English writers predominate here, but stories from Scotland, Ireland, South Africa, and Australia are also included.

In two significant respects we have gone beyond the usual coverage of anthologies. First, we have included chapters or passages from novels. Doing so has enabled us to consider a wealth of great fiction encompassing some of the most powerful writing about law, since many more novels than short stories deal with legal themes. However, not all such novels could be successfully excerpted. There are a number that we were unable to include because of the difficulty of extracting an excerpt that would stand on its own (for example, Scott's *Heart of Midlothian*, Dickens's *Great Expectations*, Dreiser's *An American Tragedy*, Wright's *Native Son*, and Gaddis's *A Frolic of His Own*).

Perhaps a more unusual presence in an anthology of legal stories is nonfiction. But as Scott wrote, "in the State Trials or in the Books of Adjournal . . . you read new pages of the human heart and turns of fortune far beyond what the boldest novelist ever attempted to produce from the coinage of his brain." We have included here three purely nonfictional selections: Rebecca West's account of the Nuremberg trials from *A Train of Powder*; Quentin Crisp's description of his legal harassment as a homosexual in 1940s London (*The Naked Civil Servant*); and Charles Reich's portrayal of life as a corporate lawyer (*The Sorcerer of Bolinas Reef*). At least two other selections straddle the boundary between fiction and nonfiction (the "tall tale" by Mark Twain from *Roughing It* is grounded in fact, and "Shooting an Elephant," an anecdote by George Orwell, may or may not have actually happened).

As in literature generally, a number of the fictional selections were inspired by real-life legal incidents (*Adam Bede, Bleak House, Billy Budd,* "The Letter," "A Jury of Her Peers"). The boundaries among works of this type, factual stories that have been embellished by the author, and nonfictional accounts of literary merit seem artificial to us. In pursuing a broader definition of a "story," we hope to suggest a broader vision of legal storytelling. Though we acknowledge that literary forms besides narrative—especially drama—are rich in legal material, we have omitted them from this volume in the interests of coherence.

Of the familiar "chestnuts" of law and literature, we have included two magnificent selections indispensable to the field. These are excerpts from Charles Dickens's *Bleak House* and Herman Melville's *Billy Budd*. However, we have passed over many of the most frequently reprinted law-and-literature stories, such as Dickens's *Pickwick Papers* and Stephen Vincent Benét's "The Devil and Daniel Webster." In their place we have found fresher, more unexpected material, much of it never before anthologized, such as Nadine Gordimer's "Happy Event," Philip Roth's "Eli, the Fanatic," James McPherson's "An Act of Prostitution," and Tom Wolfe's *The Bonfire of the Vanities*.

Twentieth-century stories predominate, with nine of the thirty-two selections from 1968 or later. Literature from before the nineteenth century does not appear here because it predates the maturity of the short story and the novel, and because early legal references tend to be more obscure to modern audiences. Our starting point is the first modern short story in English, Scott's "The Two Drovers" (1827), a tale about a murder culminating in a trial.

We have made a special effort to give voice to two groups who have until recently been largely excluded from the ranks of lawyers, judges, and litigants in British and American society: African Americans and women. (Dickens's Sally Brass of *The Old Curiosity Shop*, "a kind of amazon at common law," was an exception in nineteenth-century literature and life.) Because of their exclusion, women and blacks have tended to write from an outsider's vantage point, and their stories sharpen the critical focus of the anthology.

African Americans and women may have especially ample reason to criticize the legal system, but a critical or satirical perspective toward law animates the majority of stories included here. Many of the writers direct a reformer's zeal at specific injustices within the system; some come close to condemning law as a whole. In the writings of literary artists, criticism of law can take a sharp and potent form. It was a novelist, not a politician or a legal scholar, who penned the timeless comment: "The majestic equality of the law . . . forbids the rich as well as the poor to sleep under bridges, to beg in the streets, and to steal bread" (Anatole France).

We have taken care to reprint the most authoritative texts of the selections. Preceding each story is a headnote offering context and clarification on the story, details of original publication, and biographical information about the author, particularly his or her experience with the law. For excerpts from novels, basic plot and character descriptions are provided. When a story is based on an actual trial or legal incident, we describe the real-life events and personalities. Although in most instances the authors treat law on a general enough level so that elucidation of legal technicalities is not required, we have explained obscure or archaic points of law when necessary.

TRIAL
AND
ERROR

SIR WALTER SCOTT
(1771–1832)

Walter Scott was born in Edinburgh and was the son of a lawyer, in whose office he was apprenticed in 1786 after studying at the University of Edinburgh. In 1792 he was admitted to the bar, and although he thought law "an irksome and even hateful profession," Scott had a successful legal career. He became sheriff of Selkirkshire and, in 1806, clerk of the Court of Session. Edward Wagenknecht has noted that "His legal training furnished him with much material used directly in his fictions. It may also well have reinforced the consciousness of tradition that was such an important part of his stock in trade, and it certainly disciplined the exuberant imagination that was at the outset both his blessing and his handicap as a writer."

After gaining great renown as a poet, Scott turned to novel writing. In 1814 he published *Waverley, or, 'Tis Sixty Years Since*, virtually inventing the historical novel. Many books followed in the *Waverley* series, including *The Heart of Midlothian* (1818), today regarded as his greatest.

"The Two Drovers" was one of three tales collected under the title *Chronicles of the Canongate*, after first having been pirated in the pages of the *London Weekly Review*, October 20, 1827. It is often called the first modern short story in English literature.

In its introduction, Scott wrote that he had learned the story of a friend murdering his friend from the late George Constable, Esq.: "He had been present, I think, at the trial at Carlisle, and seldom mentioned the venerable judge's charge to the jury, without shedding tears. . . ." However, the Record Office in the Castle, Carlisle, has no files of murder cases. The story was most likely not based on an actual case; the theme of a friend killing a friend as a matter of honor is found in at least one of the traditional ballads that Scott had collected in *The Minstrelsy of the Scottish Border* (1802–1803). In his notes to "Graeme and Bewick," he had written that "the custom of drinking deep and taking deadly revenge for slight offenses produced very tragical events on the border."

Scott was steeped in the manners and customs of Scotland and used them for dramatic effect in his fiction. A powerful example in "The Two Drovers" is the foretelling of Harry Wakefield's death by Robin Oig's aunt, who sees her nephew's dirk (a short knife) covered with blood and begs him not to take it on his journey. The doctrine of second sight was widely believed in Scotland, especially in the Highlands.

THE TWO DROVERS

— 1827 —

CHAPTER I.

It was the day after Doune Fair when my story commences. It had been a brisk market, several dealers had attended from the northern and midland counties in England, and English money had flown so merrily about as to gladden the hearts of the Highland farmers. Many large droves were about to set off for England, under the protection of their owners, or of the topsmen whom they employed in the tedious, laborious, and responsible office of driving the cattle for many hundred miles, from the market where they had been purchased to the fields or farm-yards where they were to be fattened for the shambles.

The Highlanders in particular are masters of this difficult trade of driving, which seems to suit them as well as the trade of war. It affords exercise for all their habits of patient endurance and active exertion. They are required to know perfectly the drove-roads, which lie over the wildest tracts of the country, and to avoid as much as possible the highways, which distress the feet of the bullocks, and the turnpikes, which annoy the spirit of the drover; whereas on the broad green or grey track, which leads across the pathless moor, the herd not only move at ease and without taxation, but, if they mind their business, may pick up a mouthful of food by the way. At night, the drovers usually sleep along with their cattle, let the weather be what it will; and many of these hardy men do not once rest under a roof during a journey on foot from Lochaber to Lincolnshire. They are paid very highly, for the trust reposed is of the last importance, as it depends on their prudence, vigilance, and honesty, whether the cattle reach the final market in good order, and afford a profit to the grazier. But, as they maintain themselves at their own expense, they are especially economical in that particular. At the period we speak of, a Highland drover was victualled for his long and toilsome journey with a few handfuls of oatmeal and two or three onions, renewed from time to time, and a ram's horn filled with whisky, which he used regularly, but sparingly, every night and morning. His dirk, or *skene-dhu (i.e.*, black-knife), so worn as to be concealed beneath the arm or by the folds of the plaid, was his only weapon, excepting the cudgel with which he directed the movements of the cattle. A Highlander was never so happy as on these occasions. There was a variety in the whole journey which exercised the Celt's natural curiosity and love of motion; there were the constant change of place and scene, the petty adventures incidental to the traffic, and the intercourse with the various farmers, graziers, and traders, intermingled with occasional merry-makings, not the less acceptable to Donald that they were void of expense; and there was the consciousness of superior skill, for the Highlander, a child amongst flocks, is a prince amongst herds, and his natural habits induce him to disdain the shepherd's slothful life, so that he feels himself nowhere more at home than when following a gallant drove of his country cattle in the character of their guardian.

Of the number who left Doune in the morning, and with the purpose we have described, not a *glunamie* of them all cocked his bonnet more briskly, or gartered his tartan hose under knee over a pair of more promising *spiogs* (legs), than did Robin Oig M'Combich, called familiarly Robin Oig—that is, Young, or the Lesser, Robin. Though small of stature, as the epithet Oig implies, and not very strongly limbed, he was as light and alert as one of the deer of his mountains. He had an elasticity of step, which in the course of a long march made many a stout fellow envy him; and the manner in which he busked his plaid and adjusted his bonnet argued a consciousness that so smart a John Highlandman as himself would not pass unnoticed among the Lowland lasses. The ruddy cheek, red lips, and white teeth set off a countenance which had gained by exposure to the weather a healthful and hardy rather than a rugged hue. If Robin Oig did not laugh, or even smile frequently, as indeed is not the practice among his countrymen, his bright eyes usually gleamed from under his bonnet with an expression of cheerfulness ready to be turned into mirth.

The departure of Robin Oig was an incident in the little town, in and near which he had many friends, male and female. He was a topping person in his way, transacted considerable business on his own behalf, and was entrusted by the best farmers in the Highlands, in preference to any other drover in that district. He might have increased his business to any extent had he condescended to manage it by deputy; but except a lad or two, sister's sons of his own, Robin rejected the idea of assistance, conscious, perhaps, how much his reputation depended upon his attending in person to the practical discharge of his duty in every instance. He remained, therefore, contented with the highest premium given to persons of his description, and comforted himself with the hopes that a few journeys to England might enable him to conduct business on his own account, in a manner becoming his birth. For Robin Oig's father, Lachlan M'Combich (or *son of my friend*, his actual clan-surname being M'Gregor), had been so called by the celebrated Rob Roy, because of the particular friendship which had subsisted between the grandsire of Robin and that renowned cateran. Some people even say that Robin Oig derived his Christian name from one as renowned in the wilds of Loch Lomond as ever was his namesake Robin Hood in the precincts of merry Sherwood. "Of such ancestry," as James Boswell says, "who would not be proud?" Robin Oig was proud accordingly; but his frequent visits to England and to the Lowlands had given him tact enough to know that pretensions which still gave him a little right to distinction in his own lonely glen might be both obnoxious and ridiculous if preferred elsewhere. The pride of birth, therefore, was like the miser's treasure, the secret subject of his contemplation, but never exhibited to strangers as a subject of boasting.

Many were the words of gratulation and good-luck which were bestowed on Robin Oig. The judges commended his drove, especially Robin's own property, which were the best of them. Some thrust out their snuff-mulls for the parting pinch—others tendered the *doch-an-dor-rach*, or parting cup. All cried—"Good-luck travel out with you and come home with you.—Give you luck in the Saxon market—brave notes in the *leabhar-dhu*" (black pocket-book), "and plenty of English gold in the *sporran*" (pouch of goat-skin).

The bonny lasses made their adieus more modestly, and more than one, it was said, would have given her best brooch to be certain that it was upon her that his eye last rested as he turned towards the road.

Robin Oig had just given the preliminary "*Hoo-hoo!*" to urge forward the loiterers of the drove, when there was a cry behind him.

"Stay, Robin—bide a blink. Here is Janet of Tomahourich—auld Janet, your father's sister."

"Plague on her, for an auld Highland witch and spae-wife," said a farmer from the Carse of Stirling; "she'll cast some of her cantrips on the cattle."

"She canna do that," said another sapient of the same profession—"Robin Oig is no the lad to leave any of them, without tying St. Mungo's knot on their tails, and that will put to her speed the best witch that ever flew over Dimayet upon a broomstick."

It may not be indifferent to the reader to know that the Highland cattle are peculiarly liable to be *taken*, or infected, by spells and witchcraft, which judicious people guard against by knitting knots of peculiar complexity on the tuft of hair which terminates the animal's tail.

But the old woman who was the object of the farmer's suspicion seemed only busied about the drover, without paying any attention to the drove. Robin, on the contrary, appeared rather impatient of her presence.

"What auld-world fancy," he said, "has brought you so early from the ingle-side this morning, Muhme? I am sure I bid you good-even, and had your god-speed, last night."

"And left me more siller than the useless old woman will use till you come back again, bird of my bosom," said the sibyl. "But it is little I would care for the food that nourishes me, or the fire that warms me, or for God's blessed sun itself, if aught but weal should happen to the grandson of my father. So let me walk the *deasil* round you, that you may go safe out into the far foreign land, and come safe home."

Robin Oig stopped, half embarrassed, half laughing, and signing to those around that he only complied with the old woman to soothe her humour. In the meantime she traced around him, with wavering steps, the propitiation, which some have thought has been derived from the Druidical mythology. It consists, as is well known, in the person who makes the *deasil* walking three times round the person who is the object of the ceremony, taking care to move according to the course of the sun. At once, however, she stopped short, and exclaimed, in a voice of alarm and horror, "Grandson of my father, there is blood on your hand."

"Hush, for God's sake, aunt," said Robin Oig; "you will bring more trouble on yourself with this Taishataragh" (second sight) "than you will be able to get out of for many a day."

The old woman only repeated, with a ghastly look, "There is blood on your hand, and it is English blood. The blood of the Gael is richer and redder. Let us see—let us"———

Ere Robin Oig could prevent her, which, indeed, could only have been by positive violence, so hasty and peremptory were her proceedings, she had drawn from his side the dirk which lodged in the folds of his plaid, and held it up, exclaiming, although the weapon gleamed clear and bright in the sun, "Blood, blood—Saxon blood again. Robin Oig M'Combich, go not this day to England!"

"Prutt, trutt," answered Robin Oig, "that will never do neither—it would be next thing to running the country. For shame, Muhme—give me the dirk. You cannot tell by the colour the difference betwixt the blood of a black bullock and a white one, and you speak of knowing Saxon from Gaelic blood. All men have their blood from Adam, Muhme. Give me my skene-dhu, and let me go on my road. I should have been halfway to Stirling brig by this time—Give me my dirk, and let me go."

"Never will I give it to you," said the old woman—"Never will I quit my hold on your plaid, unless you promise me not to wear that unhappy weapon."

The women around him urged him also, saying few of his aunt's words fell to the ground; and as the Lowland farmers continued to look moodily on the scene, Robin Oig determined to close it at any sacrifice.

"Well, then," said the young drover, giving the scabbard of the weapon to Hugh Morrison, "you Lowlanders care nothing for these freats. Keep my dirk for me. I cannot give it you, because it was my father's; but your drove follows ours, and I am content it should be in your keeping, not in mine.—Will this do, Muhme?"

"It must," said the old woman—"that is, if the Lowlander is mad enough to carry the knife."

The strong westlandman laughed aloud.

"Goodwife," said he, "I am Hugh Morrison from Glenae, come of the Manly Morrisons of auld langsyne, that never took short weapon against a man in their lives. And neither needed they: they had their broad-swords, and I have this bit supple," showing a formidable cudgel—"for dirking ower the board, I leave that to John Highlandman.—Ye needna snort, none of you Highlanders, and you in especial, Robin. I'll keep the bit knife, if you are feared for the auld spaewife's tale, and give it back to you whenever you want it."

Robin was not particularly pleased with some part of Hugh Morrison's speech; but he had learned in his travels more patience than belonged to his Highland constitution originally, and he accepted the service of the descendant of the Manly Morrisons, without finding fault with the rather depreciating manner in which it was offered.

"If he had not had his morning in his head, and been but a Dumfries-shire hog into the boot, he would have spoken more like a gentleman. But you cannot have more of a sow than a grumph. It's shame my father's knife should ever slash a haggis for the like of him."

Thus saying (but saying it in Gaelic), Robin drove on his cattle, and waved farewell to all behind him. He was in the greater haste, because he expected to join at Falkirk a comrade and brother in profession, with whom he proposed to travel in company.

Robin Oig's chosen friend was a young Englishman, Harry Wakefield by name, well known at every northern market, and in his way as much famed and honoured as our Highland driver of bullocks. He was nearly six feet high, gallantly formed to keep the rounds at Smithfield, or maintain the ring at a wrestling-match; and although he might have been overmatched, perhaps, among the regular professors of the Fancy, yet, as a yokel or rustic, or a chance customer, he was able to give a bellyful to any amateur of the pugilistic art. Doncaster races saw him in his glory, betting his guinea, and generally successfully; nor was there a main fought in Yorkshire, the feeders being persons of celebrity, at which he was not to be seen, if business permitted. But though a *sprack* lad, and fond of pleasure and its haunts, Harry Wakefield was steady, and not the cautious Robin Oig M'Combich himself was more attentive to the main chance. His holidays were holidays indeed; but his days of work were dedicated to steady and persevering labour. In countenance and temper Wakefield was the model of Old England's merry yeomen, whose clothyard shafts, in so many hundred battles, asserted her superiority over the nations, and whose good sabres, in our own time, are her cheapest and most assured defence. His mirth was readily excited; for, strong in limb and constitution, and fortunate in circumstances, he was disposed to be pleased with everything about him; and such difficulties as he might occasionally encounter were, to a man of his energy, rather matter of amusement than serious annoyance. With all the merits of a sanguine temper, our young English drover was not without his defects. He was irascible, sometimes to the verge of being quarrelsome; and perhaps not the less inclined to bring his disputes to a pugilistic decision, because he found few antagonists able to stand up to him in the boxing-ring.

It is difficult to say how Harry Wakefield and Robin Oig first became intimates; but it is certain a close acquaintance had taken place betwixt them, although they had apparently few common subjects of conversation or of interest, so soon as their talk ceased to be of bullocks. Robin Oig, indeed, spoke the English language rather imperfectly upon any other topics but stots and kyloes, and Harry Wakefield could never bring his broad Yorkshire tongue to utter a single word of Gaelic. It was in vain Robin spent a whole morning, during a walk over Minch Moor, in attempting to teach his companion to utter, with true precision, the shibboleth *Llhu*, which is the Gaelic for a calf. From Traquair to Murder-cairn the hill rang with the discordant attempts of the Saxon upon the unmanageable monosyllable, and the heartfelt laugh which followed every failure. They had, however, better modes of awakening the echoes; for Wakefield could sing many a ditty to the praise of Moll, Susan, and Cicely, and Robin Oig had a particular gift at whistling interminable pibrochs through all their involutions, and—what was more agreeable to his companion's southern ear—knew many of the northern airs, both lively and pathetic, to which Wakefield learned to pipe a bass. Thus, though Robin could hardly have comprehended his companion's stories about horse-racing and cock-fighting or fox-hunting, and although his own legends of clan-fights and *creaghs*, varied with talk of Highland goblins and fairy folk, would have been caviare to his companion, they contrived nevertheless to find a degree of pleasure in each other's company, which had for three years back induced them to join company and travel together, when the direction of their journey permitted. Each, indeed, found his advantage in this companionship; for where could the Englishman have found a guide through the Western Highlands like Robin Oig M'Combich? and when they were on what Harry called the *right* side of the Border, his patronage, which was extensive, and his purse, which was heavy, were at all times at the service of his Highland friend, and on many occasions his liberality did him genuine yeoman's service.

CHAPTER II.

Were ever two such loving friends!
How could they disagree?
Oh, thus it was, he loved him dear,
And thought how to requite him,
And having no friend left but he,
He did resolve to fight him.
Duke upon Duke.

The pair of friends had traversed with their usual cordiality the grassy wilds of Liddesdale, and crossed the opposite part of Cumberland, emphatically called the Waste. In these solitary regions the cattle under the charge of our drovers derived their subsistence chiefly by picking their food as they went along the drove road, or sometimes by the tempting opportunity of a *start and owerloup*, or invasion of the neighbouring pasture, where an occasion presented itself. But now the scene changed before them; they were descending towards a fertile and enclosed country, where no such liberties could be taken with impunity, or without a previous arrangement and bargain with the possessors of the ground. This was more especially the case, as a great northern fair was upon the eve of taking place, where both the Scotch and English drover expected to dispose of a part of their cattle, which it was desirable to produce in the market rested and in good order. Fields were therefore difficult to be obtained, and only upon high terms. This necessity occasioned a temporary separation betwixt the two friends, who went to bargain, each as he could, for the separate accommodation of his herd. Unhappily it chanced that both of them, unknown to each other, thought of bargaining for the ground they wanted on the property of a country gentleman of some fortune, whose estate lay in the neighbourhood. The English drover applied to the bailiff on the property, who was known to him. It chanced that the Cumbrian Squire, who had entertained some suspicions of his manager's honesty, was taking occasional measures to ascertain how far they were well founded, and had desired that any inquiries about his enclosures, with a view to occupy them for a temporary purpose, should be referred to himself. As, however, Mr. Ireby had gone the day before upon a journey of some miles' distance to the northward, the bailiff chose to consider the check upon his full powers as for the time removed, and concluded that he should best consult his master's interest, and perhaps his own, in making an agreement with Harry

Wakefield. Meanwhile, ignorant of what his comrade was doing, Robin Oig, on his side, chanced to be overtaken by a good-looking smart little man upon a pony, most knowingly hogged and cropped, as was then the fashion, the rider wearing tight leather breeches and long-necked bright spurs. This cavalier asked one or two pertinent questions about markets and the price of stock. So Robin, seeing him a well-judging civil gentleman, took the freedom to ask him whether he could let him know if there was any grass-land to be let in that neighbourhood, for the temporary accommodation of his drove. He could not have put the question to more willing ears. The gentleman of the buckskins was the proprietor, with whose bailiff Harry Wakefield had dealt, or was in the act of dealing.

"Thou art in good luck, my canny Scot," said Mr. Ireby, "to have spoken to me, for I see thy cattle have done their day's work, and I have at my disposal the only field within three miles that is to be let in these parts."

"The drove can pe gang two, three, four miles very pratty weel indeed," said the cautious Highlander; "put what would his honour pe axing for the peasts pe the head, if she was to tak the park for twa or three days?"

"We won't differ, Sawney, if you let me have six stots for winterers, in the way of reason."

"And which peasts wad your honour pe for having?"

"Why—let me see—the two black—the dun one—yon doddy—him with the twisted horn—the brockit—How much by the head?"

"Ah," said Robin, "your honour is a shudge—a real shudge—I couldna have set off the pest six peasts petter mysell, me that ken them as if they were my pairns, puir things."

"Well, how much per head, Sawney," continued Mr. Ireby.

"It was high markets at Doune and Falkirk," answered Robin.

And thus the conversation proceeded, until they had agreed on the *prix juste* for the bullocks, the squire throwing in the temporary accommodation of the enclosure for the cattle into the boot, and Robin making, as he thought, a very good bargain, provided the grass was but tolerable. The squire walked his pony alongside of the drove, partly to show him the way and see him put into possession of the field, and partly to learn the latest news of the northern markets.

They arrived at the field, and the pasture seemed excellent. But what was their surprise when they saw the bailiff quietly inducting the cattle of Harry Wakefield into the grassy Goshen which had just been assigned to those of Robin Oig M'Combich by the proprietor himself! Squire Ireby set spurs to his horse, dashed up to his servant, and, learning what had passed between the parties, briefly informed the English drover that his bailiff had let the ground without his authority, and that he might seek grass for his cattle wherever he would, since he was to get none there. At the same time he rebuked his servant severely for having transgressed his commands, and ordered him instantly to assist in ejecting the hungry and weary cattle of Harry Wakefield, which were just beginning to enjoy a meal of unusual plenty, and to introduce those of his comrade, whom the English drover now began to consider as a rival.

The feelings which arose in Wakefield's mind would have induced him to resist Mr. Ireby's decision; but every Englishman has a tolerably accurate sense of law and justice, and John Fleecebumpkin, the bailiff, having acknowledged that he had exceeded his commission, Wakefield saw nothing else for it than to collect his hungry and disappointed charge, and drive them on to seek quarters elsewhere. Robin Oig saw what had happened with regret, and hastened to offer to his English friend to share with him the disputed possession. But Wakefield's pride was severely hurt, and he answered disdainfully, "Take it all, man—take it all—never make two bites of a cherry—thou canst talk over the gentry, and blear a plain man's eye—Out upon you, man—I would not kiss any man's dirty latchets for leave to bake in his oven."

Robin Oig, sorry but not surprised at his comrade's displeasure, hastened to entreat his friend to wait but an hour till he had gone to the squire's house to receive payment for the cattle he had sold, and he would come back and help him to drive the cattle into some convenient place of rest, and explain to him the whole mistake they had both of them fallen into. But the Englishman continued indignant: "Thou hast been selling, hast thou? Ay, ay—thou is a cunning lad for kenning the hours of bargaining. Go to the devil with thyself, for I will ne'er see thy fause loon's visage again—thou should be ashamed to look me in the face."

"I am ashamed to look no man in the face," said Robin Oig, something moved; "and, moreover, I will look you in the face this blessed day, if you will bide at the clachan down yonder."

"Mayhap you had as well keep away," said his comrade; and, turning his back on his former friend, he collected his unwilling associates, assisted by the bailiff, who took some real and some affected interest in seeing Wakefield accommodated.

After spending some time in negotiating with more than one of the neighbouring farmers, who could not, or would not, afford the accommodation desired, Harry Wakefield at last, and in his necessity, accomplished his point by means of the landlord of the alehouse at which Robin Oig and he had agreed to pass the night, when they first separated from each other. Mine host was content to let him turn his cattle on a piece of barren moor, at a price little less than the bailiff had asked for the disputed enclosure; and the wretchedness of the pasture, as well as the price paid for it, were set down as exaggerations of the breach of faith and friendship of his Scottish crony. This turn of Wakefield's passions was encouraged by the bailiff (who had his own reasons for being offended against poor Robin, as having been the unwitting cause of his falling into disgrace with his master), as well as by the innkeeper, and two or three chance guests, who stimulated the drover in his resentment against his quondam associate—some from the ancient grudge against the Scots, which, when it exists anywhere, is to be found lurking in the Border countries, and some from the general love of mischief which characterises mankind in all ranks of life, to the honour of Adam's children be it spoken. Good John Barleycorn, also, who always heightens and exaggerates the prevailing passions, be they angry or kindly, was not wanting in his offices on this occasion; and confusion to false friends and hard masters was pledged in more than one tankard.

In the meanwhile Mr. Ireby found some amusement in detaining the northern drover at his ancient hall. He caused a cold round of beef to be placed before the Scot in the butler's pantry, together with a foaming tankard of home-brewed, and took pleasure in seeing the hearty appetite with which these unwonted edibles were discussed by Robin Oig M'Combich. The squire himself, lighting his pipe, compounded between his patrician dignity and his love of agricultural gossip by walking up and down while he conversed with his guest.

"I passed another drove," said the squire, "with one of your countrymen behind them—they were something less beasts than your drove, doddies most of them—a big man was with them—none of your kilts though, but a decent pair of breeches—D'ye know who he may be?"

"Hout aye—that might, could, and would be Hughie Morrison—I didna think he could hae peen sae weel up. He has made a day on us; but his Argyleshires will have wearied shanks. How far was he pehind?"

"I think about six or seven miles," answered the squire, "for I passed them at the Christenbury Crag, and I overtook you at the Hollan Bush. If his beasts be leg-weary, he will be maybe selling bargains."

"Na, na, Hughie Morrison is no the man for pargains—ye maun come to some Highland body like Robin Oig hersell for the like of these—put I maun pe wishing you goot night, and twenty of them let alane ane, and I maun down to the clachan to see if the lad Harry Waakfelt is out of his humdudgeons yet."

The party at the alehouse were still in full talk, and the treachery of Robin Oig still the theme of conversation, when the supposed culprit entered the apartment. His arrival, as usually happens in such a case, put an instant stop to the discussion of which he had furnished the subject, and he was received by the company assembled with that chilling silence which, more than a thousand exclamations, tells an intruder that he is unwelcome. Surprised and offended, but not appalled by the reception which he experienced, Robin entered with an undaunted and even a haughty air, attempted no greeting, as he saw he was received with none, and placed himself by the side of the fire, a little apart from a table, at which Harry Wakefield, the bailiff, and two or three other persons, were seated. The ample Cumbrian kitchen would have afforded plenty of room, even for a larger separation.

Robin, thus seated, proceeded to light his pipe, and call for a pint of twopenny.

"We have no twopence ale," answered Ralph Heskett, the landlord; "but as thou find'st thy own tobacco, it's like thou mayst find they own liquor too—it's the wont of they country, I wot."

"Shame, goodman," said the landlady, a blithe bustling housewife, hastening herself to supply the guest with liquor—"Thou knowest well enow what the strange man wants, and it's thy trade to be civil, man. Thou shouldst know that if the Scot likes a small pot he pays a sure penny."

Without taking any notice of this nuptial dialogue, the Highlander took the flagon in his hand, and, addressing the company generally, drank the interesting toast of "Good markets" to the party assembled.

"The better that the wind blew fewer dealers from the north," said one of the farmers, "and fewer Highland runts to eat up the English meadows."

"Saul of my pody, put you are wrang there, my friend," answered Robin, with composure; "it is your fat Englishmen that eat up our Scots cattle, puir things."

"I wish there was a summat to eat up their drovers," said another; "a plain Englishman canna make bread within a kenning of them."

"Or an honest servant keep his master's favour, but they will come sliding in between him and the sunshine," said the bailiff.

"If these pe jokes," said Robin Oig, with the same composure, "there is ower mony jokes upon one man."

"It is no joke, but downright earnest," said the bailiff. "Harkye, Mr. Robin Ogg, or whatever is your name, it's right we should tell you that we are all of one opinion, and that is, that you, Mr. Robin Ogg, have behaved to our friend Mr. Harry Wakefield here like a raff and a blackguard."

"Nae doubt, nae doubt," answered Robin, with great composure; "and you are a set of very pretty judges, for whose prains or pehaviour I wad not gie a pinch of sneeshing. If Mr. Harry Waakfelt kens where he is wranged, he kens where he may be righted."

"He speaks truth," said Wakefield, who had listened to what passed, divided between the offence which he had taken at Robin's late behaviour and the revival of his habitual feelings of regard.

He now rose and went towards Robin, who got up from his seat as he approached and held out his hand.

"That's right, Harry—go it—serve him out," resounded on all sides—"tip him the nailer—show him the mill."

"Hold your peace all of you, and be—," said Wakefield; and then, addressing his comrade, he took him by the extended hand, with something alike of respect and defiance. "Robin," he said, "thou hast used me ill enough this day; but if you mean, like a frank fellow, to shake hands, and take a tussle for love on the sod, why, I'll forgie thee, man, and we shall be better friends than ever."

"And would it not pe petter to pe cood friends without more of the matter?" said Robin. "We will be much petter friendships with our panes hale than proken."

Harry Wakefield dropped the hand of his friend, or rather threw it from him.

"I did not think I had been keeping company for three years with a coward."

"Coward pelongs to none of my name," said Robin, whose eyes began to kindle, but keeping the command of his temper. "It was no coward's legs or hands, Harry Waakfelt, that drew you out of the fords of Frew, when you was drifting ower the plack rock, and every eel in the river expected his share of you."

"And that is true enough, too," said the Englishman, struck by the appeal.

"Adzooks!" exclaimed the bailiff. "Sure Harry Wakefield, the nattiest lad at Whitson Tryste, Wooler Fair, Carlisle Sands, or Stagshaw Bank, is not going to show white feather? Ah, this comes of living so long with kilts and bonnets—men forget the use of their daddles."

"I may teach you, Master Fleecebumpkin, that I have not lost the use of mine," said Wakefield, and then went on. "This will never do, Robin. We must have a turn-up, or we shall be the talk of the country side. I'll be d—d if I hurt thee—I'll put on the gloves, gin thou like. Come, stand forward like a man."

"To be peaten like a dog," said Robin. "Is there any reason in that? If you think I have done you wrong, I'll go before your shudge, though I neither know his law nor his language."

A general cry of "No, no—no law, no lawyer! a bellyful and be friends," was echoed by the bystanders.

"But," continued Robin, "if I am to fight, I have no skill to fight like a jackanapes, with hands and nails."

"How would you fight, then?" said his antagonist; "though I am thinking it would be hard to bring you to the scratch anyhow."

"I would fight with proadswords, and sink point on the first plood drawn—like a gentlemans."

A loud shout of laughter followed the proposal, which indeed had rather escaped from poor Robin's swelling heart than been the dictate of his sober judgment.

"Gentleman, quotha!" was echoed on all sides, with a shout of unextinguishable laughter; "a very pretty gentleman, God wot—Canst get two swords for the gentlemen to fight with, Ralph Heskett?"

"No, but I can send to the armoury at Carlisle, and lend them two forks to be making shift with in the meantime."

"Tush, man," said another, "the bonny Scots come into the world with the blue bonnet on their heads, and dirk and pistol at their belt."

"Best send post," said Mr. Fleecebumpkin, "to the Squire of Corby Castle, to come and stand second to the *gentleman*."

In the midst of this torrent of general ridicule, the Highlander instinctively griped beneath the folds of his plaid.

"But it's better not," he said in his own language. "A hundred curses on the swine-eaters, who know neither decency nor civility!"

"Make room, the pack of you," he said, advancing to the door.

But his former friend interposed his sturdy bulk, and opposed his leaving the house; and when Robin Oig attempted to make his way by force, he hit him down on the floor, with as much ease as a boy bowls down a nine-pin.

"A ring, a ring!" was now shouted, until the dark rafters, and the hams that hung on them, trembled again, and the very platters on the *bink* clattered against each other. "Well done, Harry"—"Give it him home, Harry"—"Take care of him now—he sees his own blood!"

Such were the exclamations, while the Highlander, starting from the ground, all his coldness and caution lost in frantic rage, sprang at his antagonist with the fury, the activity, and the vindictive purpose of an incensed tiger-cat. But when could rage encounter science and temper? Robin Oig again went down in the unequal contest; and as the blow was necessarily a severe one, he lay motionless on the floor of the kitchen. The landlady ran to offer some aid, but Mr. Fleecebumpkin would not permit her to approach.

"Let him alone," he said; "he will come to within time, and come up to the scratch again. He has not got half his broth yet."

"He has got all I mean to give him, though," said his antagonist, whose heart began to relent towards his old associate; "and I would rather by half give the rest to yourself, Mr. Fleecebumpkin, for you pretend to know a thing or two, and Robin had not art enough even to peel before setting to, but fought with his plaid dangling about him.—Stand up, Robin, my man! all friends now; and let me hear the man that will speak a word against you, or your country, for your sake."

Robin Oig was still under the dominion of his passion, and eager to renew the onset; but being withheld on the one side by the peace-making Dame Heskett, and on the other aware that Wakefield no longer meant to renew the combat, his fury sank into gloomy sullenness.

"Come, come, never grudge so much at it, man," said the brave-spirited Englishman, with the placability of his country; "shake hands, and we will be better friends than ever."

"Friends!" exclaimed Robin Oig with strong emphasis—"friends!—Never. Look to yourself, Harry Waakfelt."

"Then the curse of Cromwell on your proud Scots stomach, as the man says in the play, and you may do your worst, and be d—d; for one man can say nothing more to another after a tussle than that he is sorry for it."

On these terms the friends parted. Robin Oig drew out, in silence, a piece of money, threw it on the table, and then left the alehouse. But turning at the door, he shook his hand at Wakefield, pointing with his forefinger upwards, in a manner which might imply either a threat or a caution. He then disappeared in the moonlight.

Some words passed after his departure between the bailiff, who piqued himself on being a little of a bully, and Harry Wakefield, who, with generous inconsistency, was now not indisposed to begin a new combat in defence of Robin Oig's reputation, "although he could not use his daddles like an Englishman, as it did not come natural to him." But Dame Heskett prevented this second quarrel from coming to a head by her peremptory interference. "There should be no more fighting in her house," she said; "there had been too much already.—And you, Mr. Wakefield, may live to learn," she added, "what it is to make a deadly enemy out of a good friend."

"Pshaw, dame! Robin Oig is an honest fellow, and will never keep malice."

"Do not trust to that—you do not know the dour temper of the Scots, though you have dealt with them so often. I have a right to know them, my mother being a Scot."

"And so is well seen on her daughter," said Ralph Heskett.

This nuptial sarcasm gave the discourse another turn; fresh customers entered the tap-room or kitchen, and others left it. The conversation turned on the expected markets, and the report of prices from different parts both of Scotland and England—treaties were commenced, and Harry Wakefield was lucky enough to find a chap for a part of his drove, and at a very considerable profit; an event of consequence more than sufficient to blot out all remembrances of the unpleasant scuffle in the earlier part of the day. But there remained one party from whose mind that recollection could not have been wiped away by the possession of every head of cattle betwixt Esk and Eden.

This was Robin Oig M'Combich.—"That I should have had no weapon," he said, "and for the first time in my life!—Blighted be the tongue that bids the Highlander part with the dirk—the dirk—ha! the English blood!—My Muhme's word—when did her word fall to the ground?"

The recollection of the fatal prophecy confirmed the deadly intention which instantly sprang up in his mind.

"Ha! Morrison cannot be many miles behind; and if it were a hundred, what then?"

His impetuous spirit had now a fixed purpose and motive of action, and he turned the light foot of his country towards the wilds, through which he knew, by Mr. Ireby's report, that Morrison was advancing. His mind was wholly engrossed by the sense of injury—injury sustained from a friend; and by the desire of vengeance on one whom he now accounted his most bitter enemy. The treasured ideas of self-importance and self-opinion, of ideal birth and quality, had become more precious to him (like the hoard to the miser), because he could only enjoy them in secret. But that hoard was pillaged, the idols which he had secretly worshipped had been desecrated and profaned. Insulted, abused, and beaten, he was no longer worthy, in his own opinion, of the name he bore, or the lineage which he belonged to—nothing was left to him—nothing but revenge; and, as the reflection added a galling spur to every step, he determined it should be as sudden and signal as the offence.

When Robin Oig left the door of the alehouse, seven or eight English miles at least lay betwixt Morrison and him. The advance of the former was slow, limited by the sluggish pace of his cattle; the last left behind him stubble-field and hedge-row, crag and dark heath, all glittering with frost-rime in the broad November moonlight, at the rate of six miles an hour. And now the distant lowing of Morrison's cattle is heard; and now they are seen creeping like moles in size and slowness of motion on the broad face of the moor; and now he meets them—passes them, and stops their conductor.

"May good betide us," said the Southlander—"Is this you, Robin M'Combich," or your wraith?"

"It is Robin Oig M'Combich," answered the Highlander, "and it is not.—But never mind that, put pe giving me the skene-dhu."

"What! you are for back to the Highlands—The devil!—Have you selt all off before the fair? This beats all for quick markets!"

"I have not sold—I am not going north—May pe I will never go north again.—Give me pack my dirk, Hugh Morrison, or there will pe words petween us."

"Indeed, Robin, I'll be better advised before I gie it back to you—it is a wanchancy weapon in a Highlandman's hand, and I am thinking you will be about some barns-breaking."

"Prutt, trutt! let me have my weapon," said Robin Oig impatiently.

"Hooly and fairly," said his well-meaning friend. "I'll tell you what will do better than these dirking doings—Ye ken Highlander, and Lowlander, and Border-men are a' ae man's bairns when you are over the Scots dyke. See, the Eskdale callants, and fighting Charlie of Liddesdale, and the Lockerbie lads, and the four Dandies of Lustruther, and a wheen mair grey plaids, are coming up behind; and if you are wranged, there is the hand of a Manly Morrison, we'll see you righted, if Carlisle and Stanwix baith took up the feud."

"To tell you the truth," said Robin Oig, desirous of eluding the suspicions of his friend, "I have enlisted with a party of the Black Watch, and must march off tomorrow morning."

"Enlisted! Were you mad or drunk?—You must buy yourself off—I can lend you twenty notes, and twenty to that, if the drove sell."

"I thank you—thank ye, Hughie; but I go with good will the gate that I am going—so the dirk—the dirk!"

"There it is for you, then, since less wunna serve. But think on what I was saying.—Waes me, it will be sair news in the braes of Balquhidder, that Robin Oig M'Combich should have run an ill gate, and ta'en on."

"Ill news in Balquhidder, indeed!" echoed poor Robin: "but Cot speed you, Hughie, and send you good marcats. Ye winna meet with Robin Oig again, either at tryste or fair."

So saying, he shook hastily the hand of his acquaintance, and set out in the direction from which he had advanced, with the spirit of his former pace.

"There is something wrang with the lad," muttered the Morrison to himself; "but we will maybe see better into it the morn's morning."

But long ere the morning dawned the catastrophe of our tale had taken place. It was two hours after the affray had happened, and it was totally forgotten by almost every one, when Robin Oig returned to Heskett's inn. The place was filled at once by various sorts of men, and with noises corresponding to their character. There were the grave low sounds of men engaged in busy traffic, with the laugh, the song, and the riotous jest of those who had nothing to do but to enjoy themselves. Among the last was Harry Wakefield, who, amidst a grinning group of smockfrocks, hobnailed shoes, and jolly English physiognomies, was trolling forth the old ditty,

> What though my name be Roger,
> Who drives the plough and cart—

when he was interrupted by a well-known voice saying in a high and stern voice, marked by the sharp Highland accent, "Harry Waakfelt—if you be a man stand up!"

"What is the matter? What is it?" the guests demanded of each other.

"It is only a d—d Scotsman," said Fleecebumpkin, who was by this time very drunk, "whom Harry Wakefield helped to his broth to-day, who is now come to have *his could kail* het again."

"Harry Waakfelt," repeated the same ominous summons, "stand up, if you be a man!"

There is something in the tone of deep and concentrated passion which attracts attention and imposes awe, even by the very sound. The guests shrank back on every side, and gazed at the Highlander as he stood in the middle of them, his brows bent and his features rigid with resolution.

"I will stand up with all my heart, Robin, my boy, but it shall be to shake hands with you, and drink down all unkindness. It is not the fault of your heart, man, that you don't know how to clench your hands."

By this time he stood opposite to his antagonist; his open and unsuspecting look strangely contrasted with the stern purpose which gleamed wild, dark, and vindictive in the eyes of the Highlander.

"'Tis not thy fault, man, that, not having the luck to be an Englishman, thou canst not fight more than a school-girl."

"I *can* fight," answered Robin Oig sternly, but calmly, "and you shall know it. You, Harry Waakfelt, showed me to-day how the Saxon churls fight—I show you now how the Highland dunniewassel fights."

He seconded the word with the action, and plunged the dagger, which he suddenly displayed, into the broad breast of the English yeoman, with such fatal certainty and force that the hilt made a hollow sound against the breast-bone, and the double-edged point split the very heart of his victim. Harry Wakefield fell and expired with a single groan. His assassin next seized the bailiff by the collar, and offered the bloody poniard to his throat, whilst dread and surprise rendered the man incapable of defence.

"It were very just to lay you beside him," he said, "but the blood of a base pickthank shall never mix on my father's dirk with that of a brave man."

As he spoke, he cast the man from him with so much force that he fell on the floor, while Robin, with his other hand, threw the fatal weapon into the blazing turf-fire.

"There," he said, "take me who likes—and let fire cleanse blood if it can."

The pause of astonishment still continuing, Robin Oig asked for a peace-officer, and, a constable having stepped out, he surrendered himself to his custody.

"A bloody night's work you have made of it," said the constable.

"Your own fault," said the Highlander. "Had you kept his hands off me twa hours since, he would have been now as well and merry as he was twa minutes since."

"It must be sorely answered," said the peace-officer.

"Never you mind that—death pays all debts; it will pay that too."

The horror of the bystanders began now to give way to indignation; and the sight of a favourite companion murdered in the midst of them, the provocation being, in their opinion, so utterly inadequate to the excess of vengeance, might have induced them to kill the perpetrator of the deed even upon the very spot. The constable, however, did his duty on this occasion, and, with the assistance of some of the more reasonable persons present, procured horses to guard the prisoner to Carlisle, to abide his doom at the next assizes. While the escort was preparing, the prisoner neither expressed the least interest nor attempted the slightest reply. Only, before he was carried from the fatal apartment, he desired to look at the dead body, which, raised from the floor, had been deposited upon the large table (at the head of which Harry Wakefield had presided but a few minutes before, full of life, vigour, and animation), until the surgeons should examine the mortal wound. The face of the corpse was decently covered with a napkin. To the surprise and horror of the bystanders, which displayed itself in a general *Ah!* drawn through clenched teeth and half-shut lips, Robin Oig removed the cloth, and gazed with a mournful but steady eye on the lifeless visage, which had been so lately animated that the smile of good-humoured confidence in his own strength, of conciliation at once, and contempt towards his enemy, still curled his lip. While those present expected that the wound, which had so lately flooded the apartment with gore, would send forth fresh streams at the touch of the homicide, Robin Oig replaced the covering, with the brief exclamation, "He was a pretty man!"

My story is nearly ended. The unfortunate Highlander stood his trial at Carlisle. I was myself present, and as a young Scottish lawyer, or barrister at least, and reputed a man of some quality, the politeness of the Sheriff of Cumberland offered me a place on the bench. The facts of the case were proved in the manner I have related them; and whatever might be at first the prejudice of the audience against a crime so un-English as that of assassination from revenge, yet when the rooted national prejudices of the prisoner had been explained, which made him consider himself as stained with indelible dishonour, when subjected to personal violence; when his previous patience, moderation, and endurance were considered, the generosity of the English audience was inclined to regard his crime as the wayward aberration of a false idea of honour rather than as flowing from a heart naturally savage, or perverted by habitual vice. I shall never forget the charge of the venerable judge to the jury, although not at that time liable to be much affected either by that which was eloquent or pathetic.

"We have had," he said, "in the previous part of our duty" (alluding to some former trials) "to discuss crimes which infer disgust and abhorrence, while they call down the well-merited vengeance of the law. It is now our still more melancholy task to apply its salutary though severe enactments to a case of a very singular character, in which the crime (for a crime it is, and a deep one) arose less out of the malevolence of the heart than the error of the understanding—less from any idea of committing wrong than from an unhappily perverted notion of that which is right. Here we have two men, highly esteemed, it has been stated, in their rank of life, and attached, it seems, to each other as friends, one of whose lives has been already sacrificed to a punctilio, and the other is about to prove the vengeance of the offended laws; and yet both may claim our commiseration at least, as men acting in ignorance of each other's national prejudices, and unhappily misguided rather than voluntarily erring from the path of right conduct.

"In the original cause of the misunderstanding we must in justice give the right to the prisoner at the bar. He had acquired possession of the enclosure, which was the object of competition, by a legal contract with the proprietor, Mr. Ireby; and yet, when accosted with reproaches undeserved in themselves, and galling doubtless to a temper at least sufficiently susceptible of passion, he offered notwithstanding to yield up half his acquisition, for the sake of peace and good neighbourhood, and his amicable proposal was rejected with scorn. Then follows the scene at Mr. Heskett the publican's, and you will observe how the stranger was treated by the deceased, and, I am sorry to observe, by those around, who seem to have urged him in a manner which was aggravating in the highest degree. While he asked for peace and for composition, and offered submission to a magistrate, or to a mutual arbiter, the prisoner was insulted by a whole company, who seem on this occasion to have forgotten the national maxim of 'fair play'; and while attempting to escape from the place in peace, he was intercepted, struck down, and beaten to the effusion of his blood.

"Gentlemen of the Jury, it was with some impatience that I heard my learned brother, who opened the case for the crown, give an unfavourable turn to the prisoner's conduct on this occasion. He said the prisoner was afraid to encounter his antagonist in fair fight, or to submit to the laws of the ring; and that therefore, like a cowardly Italian, he had recourse to his fatal stiletto, to murder the man whom he dared not meet in manly encounter. I observed the prisoner shrink from this part of the accusation with the abhorrence natural to a brave man; and as I would wish to make my words impressive, when I point his real crime, I must secure his opinion of my impartiality, by rebutting everything that seems to me a false accusation. There can be no doubt that the prisoner is a man of resolution—too much resolution—I wish to Heaven that he had less, or rather that he had a better education to regulate it.

"Gentlemen, as to the laws my brother talks of, they may be known in the bull-ring, or the bear-garden, or the cockpit, but they are not known here. Or, if they should be so far admitted as furnishing a species of proof that no malice was intended in this sort of combat, from which fatal accidents do sometimes arise, it can only be so admitted when both parties are *in pari casu*, equally acquainted with, and equally willing to refer themselves to, that species of arbitrament. But will it be contended that a man of superior rank and education is to be subjected, or is obliged to subject himself, to this coarse and brutal strife, perhaps in opposition to a younger, stronger, or more skilful opponent? Certainly even the pugilistic code, if founded upon the fair play of Merry Old England, as my brother alleges it to be, can contain nothing so preposterous. And, gentlemen of the jury, if the laws would support an English gentleman, wearing, we will suppose, his sword, in defending himself by force against a violent personal aggression of the nature offered to this prisoner, they will not less protect a foreigner and a stranger, involved in the same unpleasing circumstances. If, therefore, gentlemen of the jury, when thus pressed by a *vis major*, the object of obloquy to a whole company, and of direct violence from one at least, and, as he might reasonably apprehend, from more, the panel had produced the weapon which his countrymen, as we are informed, generally carry about their persons, and the same unhappy circumstance had ensued which you have heard detailed in evidence, I could not in my conscience have asked from you a verdict of murder. The prisoner's personal defence might indeed, even in that case, have gone more or less beyond the *moderamen inculpatae tutelae*, spoken of by lawyers, but the punishment incurred would have been that of manslaughter, not of murder. I beg leave to add that I should have thought this milder species of charge was demanded in the case supposed, notwithstanding the statute of James I. cap. 8, which takes the case of slaughter by stabbing with a short weapon, even without malice prepense, out of the benefit of clergy. For this statute of stabbing, as it is termed, arose out of a temporary cause; and as the real guilt is the same, whether the slaughter be committed by the dagger or by sword or pistol, the benignity of the modern law places them all on the same, or nearly the same, footing.

"But, gentlemen of the jury, the pinch of the case lies in the interval of two hours interposed betwixt the reception of the injury and the fatal retaliation. In the heat of affray and *chaude mêlée*, law, compassionating the infirmities of humanity, makes allowance for the passions which rule such a stormy moment—for the sense of present pain, for the apprehension of further injury, for the difficulty of ascertaining with due accuracy the precise degree of violence which is necessary to protect the person of the individual, without annoying or injuring the assailant more than is absolutely necessary. But the time necessary to walk twelve miles, however speedily performed, was an interval sufficient for the prisoner to have recollected himself; and the violence with which he carried his purpose into effect, with so many circumstances of deliberate determination, could neither be induced by the passion of anger, nor that of fear. It was the purpose and the act of predetermined revenge, for which law neither can, will, nor ought to have sympathy or allowance.

"It is true, we may repeat to ourselves, in alleviation of this poor man's unhappy action, that his case is a very peculiar one. The country which he inhabits was, in the days of many now alive, inaccessible to the laws, not only of England, which have not even yet penetrated thither, but to those to which our neighbours of Scotland are subjected, and which must be supposed to be, and no doubt actually are, founded upon the general principles of justice and equity which pervade every civilised country. Amongst their mountains, as among the North American Indians, the various tribes were wont to make war upon each other, so that each man was obliged to go armed for his own protection. These men, from the ideas which they entertained of their own descent and of their own consequence, regarded themselves as so many cavaliers or men-at-arms, rather than as the peasantry of a peaceful country. Those laws of the ring, as my brother terms them, were unknown to the race of warlike mountaineers; that decision of quarrels by no other weapons than those which nature has given every man must to them have seemed as vulgar and as preposterous as to the noblesse of France. Revenge, on the other hand, must have been as familiar to their habits of society as to those of the Cherokees or Mohawks. It is indeed, as described by Bacon, at bottom a kind of wild untutored justice; for the fear of retaliation must withhold the hands of the oppressor where there is no regular law to check daring violence. But though all this may be granted, and though we may allow that, such having been the case of the Highlands in the days of the prisoner's fathers, many of the opinions and sentiments must still continue to influence the present generation, it cannot, and ought not, even in this most painful case, to alter the administration of the law, either in your hands, gentlemen of the jury, or in mine. The first object of civilisation is to place the general protection of the law, equally administered, in the room of that wild justice which every man cut and carved for himself according to the length of his sword and the strength of his arm. The law says to the subjects, with a voice only inferior to that of the Deity, 'Vengeance is mine.' The instant that there is time for passion to cool and reason to interpose, an injured party must become aware that the law assumes the exclusive cognisance of the right and wrong betwixt the parties, and opposes her inviolable buckler to every attempt of the private party to right himself. I repeat that this unhappy man ought personally to be the object rather of our pity than our abhorrence, for he failed in his ignorance, and from mistaken notions of honour. But his crime is not the less that of murder, gentlemen, and, in your high and important office, it is your duty so to find. Englishmen have their angry passions as well as Scots; and should this man's action remain unpunished, you may unsheath, under various pretences, a thousand daggers betwixt the Land's-end and the Orkneys."

The venerable judge thus ended what, to judge by his apparent emotion, and by the tears which filled his eyes, was really a painful task. The jury, according to his instructions, brought in a verdict of guilty; and Robin Oig M'Combich, *alias* M'Gregor, was sentenced to death, and left for execution, which took place accordingly. He met his fate with great firmness, and acknowledged the justice of his sentence. But he repelled indignantly the observations of those who accused him of attacking an unarmed man. "I give a life for the life I took," he said, "and what can I do more?"

CHARLES DICKENS
(1812–1870)

Charles John Huffam Dickens was born in Portsea, England, the son of a navy clerk who was later imprisoned for debt. At age fifteen Dickens worked as a clerk to a Gray's Inn solicitor, then became one of the best shorthand court reporters in London. Although he was never admitted to the bar, he entertained the idea of becoming a barrister for twenty years. Dickens published sketches of contemporary life in the city, culminating in the extraordinarily popular serial *Pickwick Papers* (1836–37). Other serialized novels brought him unprecedented acclaim.

With a breadth of vision that is scarcely conceivable today, Dickens commented in his fiction on the injustices of his society. The legal world fell within his purview; lawyers and litigants, law courts and law offices, and the law of debtors, divorce, married women's property, child welfare, and criminal justice are all prominent topics in his writings. *Pickwick Papers,* for example, contains perhaps the greatest comic trial in literature, and *Great Expectations* features Mr. Jaggers, who Cardozo Law School professor Richard Weisberg has called "a paradigm for all subsequent Anglo-American fictional lawyers."

The Dickens novel most closely identified with the law is *Bleak House* (1853), the first chapter of which is reprinted here. In this powerfully written passage (and book) about Court of Chancery procedure, Hamlet's classic denunciation of "the law's delay" is expanded into a powerful critique of a system of litigation in which "(t)he little plaintiff or defendant, who was promised a new rocking-horse when Jarndyce and Jarndyce should be settled, has grown up, possessed himself of a real horse, and trotted away into the other world."

By the early 1850s the need for reform of the Court of Chancery, which dealt with disputes over wills and trusts, had reached scandalous proportions because of understaffing and antiquated rules. An actual suit concerning a contested fortune, the *Jennens* case, had begun in 1798 and was still unsettled in the 1850s (as it was to remain as late as 1915, when costs had reached a total of £250,000). This suit was the immediate inspiration for *Bleak House*'s *Jarndyce and Jarndyce.* Also informing the novel was Dickens's personal experience of Chancery: in 1844 he had been victorious plaintiff in five actions to restrain breaches of copyright of *A Christmas Carol.* His biographer John

Forster reported that "after infinite vexation and trouble, he had himself to pay the costs incurred on his own behalf."

A reform movement was already underway before *Bleak House* appeared, but the novel's depiction of Chancery abuses stirred even the most complacent interests. In no small part due to the book's influence, the court was finally overhauled by the Judicature Act of 1873.

from BLEAK HOUSE

— 1853 —

In Chancery

London. Michaelmas Term lately over, and the Lord Chancellor sitting in Lincoln's Inn Hall. Implacable November weather. As much mud in the streets, as if the waters had but newly retired from the face of the earth, and it would not be wonderful to meet a Megalosaurus, forty feet long or so, waddling like an elephantine lizard up Holborn Hill. Smoke lowering down from chimney-pots, making a soft black drizzle, with flakes of soot in it as big as full-grown snow-flakes—gone into mourning, one might imagine, for the death of the sun. Dogs, undistinguishable in mire. Horses, scarcely better; splashed to their very blinkers. Foot passengers, jostling one another's umbrellas, in a general infection of ill-temper, and losing their foot-hold at street-corners, where tens of thousands of other foot passengers have been slipping and sliding since the day broke (if this day ever broke), adding new deposits to the crust upon crust of mud, sticking at those points tenaciously to the pavement, and accumulating at compound interest.

Fog everywhere. Fog up the river, where it flows among green aits and meadows; fog down the river, where it rolls defiled among the tiers of shipping, and the waterside pollutions of a great (and dirty) city. Fog on the Essex marshes, fog on the Kentish heights. Fog creeping into the cabooses of collier-brigs; fog lying out on the yards, and hovering in the rigging of great ships; fog drooping on the gunwales of barges and small boats. Fog in the eyes and throats of ancient Greenwich pensioners, wheezing by the firesides of their wards; fog in the stem and bowl of the afternoon pipe of the wrathful skipper, down in his close cabin; fog cruelly pinching the toes and fingers of his shivering little 'prentice boy on deck. Chance people on the bridges peeping over the parapets into a nether sky of fog, with fog all round them, as if they were up in a balloon, and hanging in the misty clouds.

Gas looming through the fog in divers places in the streets, much as the sun may, from the spongy fields, be seen to loom by husbandman and ploughboy. Most of the shops lighted two hours before their time—as the gas seems to know, for it has a haggard and unwilling look.

The raw afternoon is rawest, and the dense fog is densest, and the muddy streets are muddiest, near that leaden-headed old obstruction, appropriate ornament for the threshold of a leaden-headed old corporation: Temple Bar. And hard by Temple Bar, in Lincoln's Inn Hall, at the very heart of the fog, sits the Lord High Chancellor in his High Court of Chancery.

Never can there come fog too thick, never can there come mud and mire too deep, to assort with the groping and floundering condition which this High Court of Chancery, most pestilent of hoary sinners, holds, this day, in the sight of heaven and earth.

On such an afternoon, if ever, the Lord High Chancellor ought to be sitting here—as here he is—with a foggy glory round his head, softly fenced in with crimson cloth and curtains, addressed by a large advocate with great whiskers, a little voice, and an interminable brief, and outwardly directing his contemplation to the lantern in the roof, where he can see nothing but fog. On such an afternoon, some score of members of the High Court of Chancery bar ought to be—as here they are—mistily engaged in one of the ten thousand stages of an endless cause, tripping one another up on slippery precedents, groping knee-deep in technicalities, running their goat-hair and horse-hair warded heads against walls of words, and making a pretence of equity with serious faces, as players might. On such an afternoon, the various solicitors in the cause, some two or three of whom have inherited it from their fathers, who made a fortune by it, ought to be—as are they not?—ranged in a line, in a long matted well (but you might look in vain for Truth at the bottom of it), between the registrar's red table and the silk gowns, with bills, cross-bills, answers, rejoinders, injunctions, affidavits, issues, references to masters, masters' reports, mountains of costly nonsense, piled before them. Well may the court be dim, with wasting candles here and there: well may the fog hang heavy in it, as if it would never get out; well may the stained glass windows lose their colour, and admit no light of day into the place; well may the uninitiated from the streets, who peep in through the glass panes in the door, be deterred from entrance by its owlish aspect, and by the drawl languidly echoing to the roof from the padded dais where the Lord High Chancellor looks into the lantern that has no light in it, and where the attendant wigs are all stuck in a fog-bank! This is the Court of Chancery; which has its decaying houses and its blighted lands in every shire; which has its worn-out lunatic in every madhouse, and its dead in every churchyard; which has its ruined suitor, with his slipshod heels and threadbare dress, borrowing and begging through the round of every man's acquaintance; which gives to monied might, the means abundantly of wearying out the right; which so exhausts finances, patience, courage, hope; so overthrows the brain and breaks the heart; that there is not an honourable man among its practitioners who would not give—who does not often give—the warning, 'Suffer any wrong that can be done you, rather than come here!'

Who happen to be in the Lord Chancellor's court this murky afternoon besides the Lord Chancellor, the counsel in the cause, two or three counsel who are never in any cause, and the well of solicitors before mentioned? There is the registrar below the Judge, in wig and gown; and there are two or three maces, or petty-bags, or privy purses, or whatever they may be, in legal court suits. These are all yawning; for no crumb of amusement ever falls from JARNDYCE AND JARNDYCE (the cause in hand), which was squeezed dry years upon years ago. The short-hand writers, the reporters of the court, and the reporters of the newspapers, invariably decamp with the rest of the regulars when Jarndyce and Jarndyce comes on. Their places are a blank. Standing on a seat at the side of the hall, the better to peer into the curtained sanctuary, is a little mad old woman in a squeezed bonnet, who is always in court, from its sitting to its rising, and always expecting some incomprehensible judgment to be given in her favour. Some say she really is, or was, a party to a suit; but no one knows for certain, because no one cares. She carries some small litter in a reticule which she calls her documents; principally consisting of paper matches and dry lavender. A sallow prisoner has come up, in custody, for the half-dozenth time, to make a personal application 'to purge himself of his contempt;' which, being a solitary surviving executor who has fallen into a state of conglomeration about accounts of which it is not pretended that he had ever any knowledge, he is not at all likely ever to do. In the meantime his prospects in life are ended. Another ruined suitor, who periodically appears from Shropshire, and breaks out into efforts to address the Chancellor at the close of the day's business, and who can by no means be made to understand that the Chancellor is legally ignorant of his existence after making it desolate for a quarter of a century, plants himself in a good place and keeps an eye on the Judge, ready to call out 'My Lord!' in a voice of sonorous complaint, on the instant of his rising. A few lawyers' clerks and others who know this suitor by sight, linger, on the chance of his furnishing some fun, and enlivening the dismal weather a little.

Jarndyce and Jarndyce drones on. This scarecrow of a suit has, in course of time, become so complicated, that no man alive knows what it means. The parties to it understand it least; but it has been observed that no two Chancery lawyers can talk about it for five minutes, without coming to a total disagreement as to all the premises. Innumerable children have been born into the cause; innumerable young people have married into it; innumerable old people have died out of it. Scores of persons have deliriously found themselves made parties in Jarndyce and Jarndyce, without knowing how or why; whole families have inherited legendary hatreds with the suit. The little plaintiff or defendant, who was promised a new rocking-horse when Jarndyce and Jarndyce should be settled, has grown up, possessed himself of a real horse, and trotted away into the other world. Fair wards of court have faded into mothers and grandmothers; a long procession of Chancellors has come in and gone out; the legion of bills in the suit have been transformed into mere bills of mortality; there are not three Jarndyces left upon the earth perhaps, since old Tom Jarndyce in despair blew his brains out at a coffee-house in Chancery Lane; but Jarndyce and Jarndyce still drags its dreary length before the Court, perennially hopeless.

Jarndyce and Jarndyce has passed into a joke. That is the only good that has ever come of it. It has been death to many, but it is a joke in the profession. Every master in Chancery has had a reference out of it. Every Chancellor was 'in it,' for somebody or other, when he was counsel at the bar. Good things have been said about it by blue-nosed, bulbous-shoed old benchers, in select port-wine committee after dinner in hall. Articled clerks have been in the habit of fleshing their legal wit upon it. The last Lord Chancellor handled it neatly when, correcting Mr. Blowers, the eminent silk gown who said that such a thing might happen when the sky rained potatoes, he observed, 'or when we get through Jarndyce and Jarndyce, Mr. Blowers;'—a pleasantry that particularly tickled the maces, bags, and purses.

How many people out of the suit, Jarndyce and Jarndyce has stretched forth its unwholesome hand to spoil and corrupt, would be a very wide question. From the master, upon whose impaling files reams of dusty warrants in Jarndyce and Jarndyce have grimly writhed into many shapes; down to the copying-clerk in the Six Clerks' Office, who has copied his tens of thousands of Chancery-folio-pages under that eternal heading; no man's nature has been made better by it. In trickery, evasion, procrastination, spoliation, botheration, under false pretences of all sorts, there are influences that can never come to good. The very solicitors' boys who have kept the wretched suitors at bay, by protesting time out of mind that Mr. Chizzle, Mizzle, or otherwise, was particularly engaged and had appointments until dinner, may have got an extra moral twist and shuffle into themselves out of Jarndyce and Jarndyce. The receiver in the cause has acquired a goodly sum of money by it, but has acquired too a distrust of his own mother, and a contempt for his own kind. Chizzle, Mizzle, and otherwise, have lapsed into a habit of vaguely promising themselves that they will look into that outstanding little matter, and see what can be done for Drizzle—who was not well used—when Jarndyce and Jarndyce shall be got out of the office. Shirking and sharking, in all their many varieties, have been sown broadcast by the ill-fated cause; and even those who have contemplated its history from the outermost circle of such evil, have been insensibly tempted into a loose way of letting bad things alone to take their own bad course, and a loose belief that if the world go wrong, it was, in some off-hand manner, never meant to go right.

Thus, in the midst of the mud and at the heart of the fog, sits the Lord High Chancellor in his High Court of Chancery.

'Mr. Tangle,' says the Lord High Chancellor, latterly something restless under the eloquence of that learned gentleman.

'Mlud,' says Mr. Tangle. Mr. Tangle knows more of Jarndyce and Jarndyce than anybody. He is famous for it—supposed never to have read anything else since he left school.

'Have you nearly concluded your argument?'

'Mlud, no—variety of points—feel it my duty tsubmit—ludship,' is the reply that slides out of Mr. Tangle.

'Several members of the bar are still to be heard, I believe?' says the Chancellor, with a slight smile.

Eighteen of Mr. Tangle's learned friends, each armed with a little summary of eighteen hundred sheets, bob up like eighteen hammers in a pianoforte, make eighteen bows, and drop into their eighteen places of obscurity.

'We will proceed with the hearing on Wednesday fortnight,' says the Chancellor. For the question at issue is only a question of costs, a mere bud on the forest tree of the parent suit, and really will come to a settlement one of these days.

The Chancellor rises; the bar rises; the prisoner is brought forward in a hurry; the man from Shropshire cries, 'My lord!' Maces, bags, and purses, indignantly proclaim silence, and frown at the man from Shropshire.

'In reference,' proceeds the Chancellor, still on Jarndyce and Jarndyce, 'to the young girl——'

'Begludship's pardon—boy,' says Mr. Tangle, prematurely.

'In reference,' proceeds the Chancellor, with extra distinctness, 'to the young girl and boy, the two young people,'

(Mr. Tangle crushed.)

'Whom I directed to be in attendance to-day, and who are now in my private room, I will see them and satisfy myself as to the expediency of making the order for their residing with their uncle.'

Mr. Tangle on his legs again.

'Begludship's pardon—dead.'

'With their,' Chancellor looking through his double eyeglass at the papers on his desk, 'grandfather.'

'Begludship's pardon—victim of rash action—brains.'

Suddenly a very little counsel, with a terrific bass voice, arises, fully inflated, in the back settlements of the fog, and says, 'Will your lordship allow me? I appear for him. He is a cousin, several times removed. I am not at the moment prepared to inform the Court in what exact remove he is a cousin; but he *is* a cousin.'

Leaving this address (delivered like a sepulchral message) ringing in the rafters of the roof, the very little counsel drops, and the fog knows him no more. Everybody looks for him. Nobody can see him.

'I will speak with both the young people,' says the Chancellor anew, 'and satisfy myself on the subject of their residing with their cousin. I will mention the matter to-morrow morning when I take my seat.'

The Chancellor is about to bow to the bar, when the prisoner is presented. Nothing can possibly come of the prisoner's conglomeration, but his being sent back to prison; which is soon done. The man from Shropshire ventures another demonstrative 'My lord!' but the Chancellor, being aware of him, has dexterously vanished. Everybody else quickly vanishes too. A battery of blue bags is loaded with heavy charges of papers and carried off by clerks; the little mad old woman marches off with her documents; the empty court is locked up. If all the injustice it has committed, and all the misery it has caused, could only be locked up with it, and the whole burnt away in a great funeral pyre,—why so much the better for other parties than the parties in Jarndyce and Jarndyce!

GEORGE ELIOT

(1819–1880)

Mary Ann Evans, who assumed the pen name George Eliot, was born in Warwickshire in the English Midlands in the first quarter of the nineteenth century, and her novels contain vivid portrayals of that world. As a child Eliot was intellectually precocious; in young adulthood she joined a literary circle and published a number of philosophical translations. In 1850 she became an assistant editor and contributor to the *Westminster Review.* With the encouragement of her life companion, George Henry Lewes, she began writing fiction. *Scenes of a Clerical Life* (1858) was followed by *Adam Bede,* which won her literary acclaim.

In *Adam Bede,* milkmaid Hetty Sorrel is loved by the main character but becomes the lover of Captain Arthur Donnithorne, the heir to the local estate. After Arthur leaves to join his regiment, Hetty discovers she is pregnant and travels to Windsor, where he is stationed, only to learn that his regiment has left for Ireland. This excerpt depicts Hetty's trial for the murder of her baby, whom, in her despair and confusion, she hid under a bush shortly after its birth.

Hetty's plight was inspired by a true story told to Eliot around 1840 by her aunt, a Methodist preacher and the model for the novel's preacher, Dinah Morris. Eliot's aunt had visited a girl who was in prison for the death of her baby but who had refused to confess until, after a night of prayer, she broke down and admitted the crime. Similarly, Hetty confesses to Dinah in her prison cell that she abandoned her baby. Unlike her prototype, however, Hetty does not die on the gallows; Eliot contrives to save her at the last moment by having Arthur Donnithorne ride up with a paper commuting Hetty's sentence to transportation.

Historically, illegitimate babies have been at greater risk of dying than legitimate ones, especially in the babies' first year of life. In England the "poor law" of 1576 (18 Eliz. I, c. 3) was designed to punish parents of bastard children who were a financial burden on their parish. (In practice, this almost always meant mothers.) The poor law increased an unwed mother's motivation to conceal an illegitimate pregnancy and to commit infanticide. In fact, in the years after the passage of this law, the rate of conviction for infanticide rose sharply. Parliament responded to this situation by passing another law in 1624 that guided juries in suspected cases of newborn murder, directing that a mother's concealment of pregnancy and of her neonate's body created automatic presumption of murder. The burden of proof of innocence was upon the mother, who had to show that her baby was stillborn or had died naturally. (This law applied only to unmarried women.) After the law's passage, there was another rise in the prosecution of infanticide cases due to heightened enforcement by magistrates.

Adam Bede is set in 1799. In 1803 the law on concealment was repealed and indictments for infanticide declined; thereafter, indictments continued to decline as social tolerance of illegitimacy grew. Juries that did convict were more likely to return a verdict of manslaughter than of murder.

from ADAM BEDE

— 1859 —

The Verdict

The place fitted up that day as a court of justice was a grand old hall, now destroyed by fire. The mid-day light that fell on the close pavement of human heads, was shed through a line of high pointed windows, variegated with the mellow tints of old painted glass. Grim dusty armour hung in high relief in front of the dark oaken gallery at the farther end; and under the broad arch of the great mullioned window opposite was spread a curtain of old tapestry, covered with dim melancholy figures, like a dozing indistinct dream of the past. It was a place that through the rest of the year was haunted with the shadowy memories of old kings and queens, unhappy, discrowned, imprisoned; but to-day all those shadows had fled, and not a soul in the vast hall felt the presence of any but a living sorrow, which was quivering in warm hearts.

But that sorrow seemed to have made itself feebly felt hitherto, now when Adam Bede's tall figure was suddenly seen, being ushered to the side of the prisoner's dock. In the broad sunlight of the great hall, among the sleek shaven faces of other men, the marks of suffering in his face were startling even to Mr. Irwine, who had last seen him in the dim light of his small room; and the neighbours from Hayslope who were present, and who told Hetty Sorrel's story by their firesides in their old age, never forgot to say how it moved them when Adam Bede, poor fellow, taller by the head than most of the people round him, came into court and took his place by her side.

But Hetty did not see him. She was standing in the same position Bartle Massey had described, her hands crossed over each other, and her eyes fixed on them. Adam had not dared to look at her in the first moments, but at last, when the attention of the court was withdrawn by the proceedings, he turned his face towards her with a resolution not to shrink.

Why did they say she was so changed? In the corpse we love, it is the *likeness* we see—it is the likeness, which makes itself felt the more keenly because something else *was* and *is not*. There they were—the sweet face and neck, with the dark tendrils of hair, the long dark lashes, the rounded cheek and the pouting lips: pale and thin—yes—but like Hetty, and only Hetty. Others thought she looked as if some demon had cast a blighting glance upon her, withered up the woman's soul in her, and left only a hard despairing obstinacy. But the mother's yearning, that completest type of the life in another life which is the essence of real human love, feels the presence of the cherished child even in the debased, degraded man; and to Adam, this pale, hard-looking culprit was the Hetty who had smiled at him in the garden under the apple-tree boughs—she was that Hetty's corpse, which he had trembled to look at the first time, and then was unwilling to turn away his eyes from.

But presently he heard something that compelled him to listen, and made the sense of sight less absorbing. A woman was in the witness-box, a middle-aged woman, who spoke in a firm distinct voice. She said—

"My name is Sarah Stone. I am a widow, and keep a small shop licensed to sell tobacco, snuff, and tea, in Church Lane, Stoniton. The prisoner at the bar is the same young woman who came, looking ill and tired, with a basket on her arm, and asked for a lodging at my house on Saturday evening, the 27th of February. She had taken the house for a public, because there was a figure against the door. And when I said I didn't take in lodgers, the prisoner began to cry, and said she was too tired to go anywhere else, and she only wanted a bed for one night. And her prettiness, and her condition, and something respectable about her clothes and looks, and the trouble she seemed to be in, made me as I couldn't find in my heart to send her away at once. I asked her to sit down, and gave her some tea, and asked her where she was going, and where her friends were. She said she was going home to her friends: they were farming folks a good way off, and she'd had a long journey that had cost her more money than she expected, so as she'd hardly any money left in her pocket, and was afraid of going where it would cost her much. She had been obliged to sell most of the things out of her basket; but she'd thankfully give a shilling for a bed. I saw no reason why I shouldn't take the young woman in for the night. I had only one room, but there were two beds in it, and I told her she might stay with me. I thought she'd been led wrong, and got into trouble, but if she was going to her friends, it would be a good work to keep her out of further harm."

The witness then stated that in the night a child was born, and she identified the baby-clothes then shown to her as those in which she had herself dressed the child.

"Those are the clothes. I made them myself, and had kept them by me ever since my last child was born. I took a deal of trouble both for the child and the mother. I couldn't help taking to the little thing and being anxious about it. I didn't send for a doctor, for there seemed no need. I told the mother in the daytime she must tell me the name of her friends, and where they lived, and let me write to them. She said, by-and-by she would write herself, but not to-day. She would have no nay, but she would get up and be dressed, in spite of everything I could say. She said she felt quite strong enough; and it was wonderful what spirit she showed. But I wasn't quite easy what I should do about her, and towards evening I made up my mind I'd go, after Meeting was over, and speak to our minister about it. I left the house about half-past eight o'clock. I didn't go out at the shop door, but at the back door which opens into a narrow alley. I've only got the ground-floor of the house, and the kitchen and bedroom both look into the alley. I left the prisoner sitting up by the fire in the kitchen with the baby on her lap. She hadn't cried or seemed low at all, as she did the night before. I thought she had a strange look with her eyes, and she got a bit flushed towards evening. I was afraid of the fever, and I thought I'd call and ask an acquaintance of mine, an experienced woman, to come back with me when I went out. It was a very dark night. I didn't fasten the door behind me; there was no lock: it was a latch with a bolt inside, and when there was nobody in the house I always went out at the shop door. But I thought there was no danger in leaving it unfastened that little while. I was longer than I meant to be, for I had to wait for the woman that came back with me. It was an hour and a half before we got back, and when we went in, the candle was standing burning just as I left it, but the prisoner and the baby were both gone. She'd taken her cloak and bonnet, but she'd left the basket and the things in it. . . . I was dreadful frightened, and angry with her for going. I didn't go to give information, because I'd no thought she meant to do any harm, and I knew she had money in her pocket to buy her food and lodging. I didn't like to set the constable after her, for she'd a right to go from me if she liked."

The effect of this evidence on Adam was electrical; it gave him new force. Hetty could not be guilty of the crime—her heart must have clung to her baby—else why should she have taken it with her? She might have left it behind. The little creature had died naturally, and then she had hidden it: babies were so liable to death—and there might be the strongest suspicions without any proof of guilt. His mind was so occupied with imaginary arguments against such suspicions, that he could not listen to the cross-examination by Hetty's counsel, who tried, without result, to elicit evidence that the prisoner had shown some movements of maternal affection towards the child. The whole time this witness was being examined, Hetty had stood as motionless as before: no word seemed to arrest her ear. But the sound of the next witness's voice touched a chord that was still sensitive; she gave a start and a frightened look towards him, but immediately turned away her head and looked down at her hands as before. This witness was a man, a rough peasant. He said—

"My name is John Olding. I am a labourer, and live at Tedd's Hole, two miles out of Stoniton. A week last Monday, towards one o'clock in the afternoon, I was going towards Hetton Coppice, and about a quarter of a mile from the coppice I saw the prisoner, in a red cloak, sitting under a bit of a haystack not far off the stile. She got up when she saw me, and seemed as if she'd be walking on the other way. It was a regular road through the fields, and nothing very uncommon to see a young woman there, but I took notice of her because she looked white and scared. I should have thought she was a beggar-woman, only for her good clothes. I thought she looked a bit crazy, but it was no business of mine. I stood and looked back after her, but she went right on while she was in sight. I had to go to the other side of the coppice to look after some stakes. There's a road right through it, and bits of openings here and there, where the trees have been cut down, and some of 'em not carried away. I didn't go straight along the road, but turned off towards the middle, and took a shorter way towards the spot I wanted to get to. I hadn't got far out of the road into one of the open places, before I heard a strange cry. I thought it didn't come from any animal I knew, but I wasn't for stopping to look about just then. But it went on, and seemed so strange to me in that place, I couldn't help stopping to look. I began to think I might make some money of it, if it was a new thing. But I had hard work to tell which way it came from, and for a good while I kept looking up at the boughs. And then I thought it came from the ground; and there was a lot of timber-choppings lying about, and loose pieces of turf, and a trunk or two. And I looked about among them, but could find nothing; and at last the cry stopped. So I was for giving it up, and I went on about my business. But when I came back the same way pretty nigh an hour after, I couldn't help laying down my stakes to have another look. And just as I was stooping and laying down the stakes, I saw something odd and round and whitish lying on the ground under a nut-bush by the side of me. And I stooped down on hands and knees to pick it up. And I saw it was a little baby's hand."

At these words a thrill ran through the court. Hetty was visibly trembling: now, for the first time, she seemed to be listening to what a witness said.

"There was a lot of timber-choppings put together just where the ground went hollow, like, under the bush, and the hand came out from among them. But there was a hole left in one place, and I could see down it, and see the child's head; and I made haste and did away the turf and the choppings, and took out the child. It had got comfortable clothes on, but its body was cold, and I thought it must be dead. I made haste back with it out of the wood, and took it home to my wife. She said it was dead, and I'd better take it to the parish and tell the constable. And I said, 'I'll lay my life it's that young woman's child as I met going to the coppice.' But she seemed to be gone clean out of sight. And I took the child on to Hetton parish and told the constable, and we went on to Justice Hardy. And then we went looking after the young woman till dark at night, and we went and gave information at Stoniton, as they might stop her. And the next morning another constable came to me, to go with him to the spot where I found the child. And when we got there, there was the prisoner sitting against the bush where I found the child; and she cried out when she saw us, but she never offered to move. She'd got a big piece of bread on her lap."

Adam had given a faint groan of despair while this witness was speaking. He had hidden his face on his arm, which rested on the boarding in front of him. It was the supreme moment of his suffering: Hetty was guilty: and he was silently calling to God for help. He heard no more of the evidence, and was unconscious when the case for the prosecution had closed—unconscious that Mr. Irwine was in the witness-box, telling of Hetty's unblemished character in her own parish, and of the virtuous habits in which she had been brought up. This testimony could have no influence on the verdict, but it was given as part of that plea for mercy which her own counsel would have made if he had been allowed to speak for her—a favour not granted to criminals in those stern times.

At last Adam lifted up his head, for there was a general movement round him. The judge had addressed the jury, and they were retiring. The decisive moment was not far off. Adam felt a shuddering horror that would not let him look at Hetty, but she had long relapsed into her blank hard indifference. All eyes were strained to look at her, but she stood like a statue of dull despair.

There was a mingled rustling, whispering, and low buzzing throughout the court during this interval. The desire to listen was suspended, and every one had some feeling or opinion to express in under-tones. Adam sat looking blankly before him, but he did not see the objects that were right in front of his eyes—the counsel and attorneys talking with an air of cool business, and Mr. Irwine in low earnest conversation with the judge: did not see Mr. Irwine sit down again in agitation, and shake his head mournfully when somebody whispered to him. The inward action was too intense for Adam to take in outward objects until some strong sensation roused him.

It was not very long, hardly more than a quarter of an hour, before the knock which told that the jury had come to their decision, fell as a signal for silence on every ear. It is sublime—that sudden pause of a great multitude, which tells that one soul moves in them all. Deeper and deeper the silence seemed to become, like the deepening night, while the jurymen's names were called over, and the prisoner was made to hold up her hand, and the jury were asked for their verdict.

"Guilty."

It was the verdict every one expected, but there was a sigh of disappointment from some hearts, that it was followed by no recommendation to mercy. Still the sympathy of the court was not with the prisoner: the unnaturalness of her crime stood out the more harshly by the side of her hard immovability and obstinate silence. Even the verdict, to distant eyes, had not appeared to move her; but those who were near saw her trembling.

The stillness was less intense until the judge put on his black cap, and the chaplain in his canonicals was observed behind him. Then it deepened again, before the crier had had time to command silence. If any sound were heard, it must have been the sound of beating hearts. The judge spoke—

"Hester Sorrel. . . ."

The blood rushed to Hetty's face, and then fled back again, as she looked up at the judge, and kept her wide-open eyes fixed on him, as if fascinated by fear. Adam had not yet turned towards her: there was a deep horror, like a great gulf, between them. But at the words—"and then to be hanged by the neck till you be dead," a piercing shriek rang through the hall. It was Hetty's shriek. Adam started to his feet and stretched out his arms towards her; but the arms could not reach her: She had fallen down in a fainting-fit, and was carried out of court.

MARK TWAIN
(1835–1910)

Samuel Langhorne Clemens, writing under the name Mark Twain, bestrides nineteenth-century American literature, indeed nineteenth-century American culture, like a colossus. He seems to have done everything and seen everything in his long and colorful life as a steamboat pilot, Confederate soldier, prospector, Wild West journalist, humorist, novelist, and businessman. Born in the town of Florida, Missouri, in 1835, he died seventy-five years later an international celebrity and a literary artist of the highest renown.

In *Roughing It,* Twain wrote, ''I had studied law an entire week, and then given it up because it was so prosy and tiresome.'' His father, John Marshall Clemens, had been a lawyer and later became a judge of the Monroe County Court in Florida (Missouri) and a justice of the peace in Missouri.

Twain's career and writings intersected with the legal world at many points. He may have been the most litigious author in American history: according to one biographer, ''Mark Twain was the lawyer's best friend and severest critic . . . About once a week he wanted a lawsuit against somebody.'' The suits were primarily attempts to prevent pirating of his books. Prompted by his personal experiences, Twain (who once declared that ''only one thing, is impossible for God: to find any sense in any copyright law on the planet'') became a leading advocate of international copyright protection.

As critic of the legal system, Twain had two favorite targets: he repeatedly lampooned the insanity defense, and he ridiculed the system of jury selection, calling it ''the most ingenious and infallible agency for *defeating* justice that human wisdom could contrive.'' In addition to these satirical themes, Twain's other major legal interest was criminal trials. Dozens of trials figure in his books, including *The Gilded Age, Tom Sawyer, Pudd'nhead Wilson,* and *Joan of Arc.*

The trial story here is excerpted from *Roughing It,* Twain's 1872 narrative of his Western travels. Earlier versions of this ''Great Landslide Case'' appeared in the *San Francisco Morning Call,* August 30, 1863, and the *Buffalo Express,* April 2, 1870. The tale is based on an actual practical joke that took place in Carson City, Nevada, in February 1862. ''General Buncombe'' 's real name was Benjamin B. Bunker, United States Attorney for the Nevada Territory; ''Dick Hyde'' was rancher Richard D. Sides; ''Hal Brayton'' was Twain's friend, attorney Hal Clayton; and ''ex-Governor Roop'' was former territorial governor Isaac N. Roop. In calling the Sides character ''Hyde,'' Twain may have been lampooning Mormon judge Orson Hyde, who invoked a divine curse on Sides in the course of a property dispute between them.

from ROUGHING IT

— 1872 —

The mountains are very high and steep about Carson, Eagle and Washoe Valleys—very high and very steep, and so when the snow gets to melting off fast in the spring and the warm surface-earth begins to moisten and soften, the disastrous land-slides commence. The reader cannot know what a land-slide is, unless he has lived in that country and seen the whole side of a mountain taken off some fine morning and deposited down in the valley, leaving a vast, treeless, unsightly scar upon the mountain's front to keep the circumstance fresh in his memory all the years that he may go on living within seventy miles of that place.

Gen. Buncombe was shipped out to Nevada in the invoice of Territorial officers, to be U.S. Attorney. He considered himself a lawyer of parts, and he very much wanted an opportunity to manifest it—partly for the pure gratification of it and partly because his salary was Territorially meagre (which is a strong expression). Now the older citizens of a new territory look down upon the rest of the world with a calm, benevolent compassion, as long as it keeps out of the way—when it gets in the way they snub it. Sometimes this latter takes the shape of a practical joke.

One morning Dick Hyde rode furiously up to Gen. Buncombe's door in Carson City and rushed into his presence without stopping to tie his horse. He seemed much excited. He told the General that he wanted him to conduct a suit for him and would pay him five hundred dollars if he achieved a victory. And then, with violent gestures and a world of profanity, he poured out his griefs. He said it was pretty well known that for some years he had been farming (or ranching as the more customary term is,) in Washoe District, and making a successful thing of it, and furthermore it was known that his ranch was situated just in the edge of the valley, and that Tom Morgan owned a ranch immediately above it on the mountain side. And now the trouble was that one of those hated and dreaded land-slides had come and slid Morgan's ranch, fences, cabins, cattle, barns and everything down on top of *his* ranch and exactly covered up every single vestige of his property, to a depth of about thirty-eight feet. Morgan was in possession and refused to vacate the premises—said he was occupying his own cabin and not interfering with anybody else's—and said the cabin was standing on the same dirt and same ranch it had always stood on, and he would like to see anybody make him vacate.

"And when I reminded him," said Hyde, weeping, "that it was on top of my ranch and that he was trespassing, he had the infernal meanness to ask me why didn't I *stay* on my ranch and hold possession when I see him a coming! Why didn't I *stay* on it, the blathering lunatic—by George, when I heard that racket and looked up that hill it was just like the whole world was a ripping and a tearing down that mountain side—splinters, and cord-wood, thunder and lightning, hail and snow, odds and ends of hay stacks, and awful clouds of dust!—trees going end over end in the air, rocks as big as a house jumping 'bout a thousand feet high and busting into ten million pieces, cattle turned inside out and a coming head on with their tails hanging out between their teeth!—and in the midst of all that wrack and destruction sot that cussed Morgan on his gate-post, a wondering why I didn't *stay and hold possession!* Laws bless me, I just took one glimpse, General, and lit out'n the country in three jumps exactly.

"But what grinds me is that that Morgan hangs on there and won't move off'n that ranch—says it's his'n and he's going to keep it—likes it better'n he did when it was higher up the hill. Mad! Well, I've been so mad for two days I couldn't find my way to town—been wandering around in the brush in a starving condition—got anything here to drink, General? But I'm here *now*, and I'm a going to law. You hear *me*!"

Never in all the world, perhaps, were a man's feelings so outraged as were the General's. He said he had never heard of such high-handed conduct in all his life as this Morgan's. And he said there was no use in going to law—Morgan had no shadow of right to remain where he was—nobody in the wide world would uphold him in it, and no lawyer would take his case and no judge listen to it. Hyde said that right there was where he was mistaken—everybody in town sustained Morgan; Hal Brayton, a very smart lawyer, had taken his case; the courts being in vacation, it was to be tried before a referee, and ex-Governor Roop had already been appointed to that office and would open his court in a large public hall near the hotel at two that afternoon.

The General was amazed. He said he had suspected before that the people of that Territory were fools, and now he knew it. But he said rest easy, rest easy and collect the witnesses, for the victory was just as certain as if the conflict were already over. Hyde wiped away his tears and left.

At two in the afternoon referee Roop's court opened, and Roop appeared throned among his sheriffs, the witnesses, and spectators, and wearing upon his face a solemnity so awe-inspiring that some of his fellow-conspirators had misgivings that maybe he had not comprehended, after all, that this was merely a joke. An unearthly stillness prevailed, for at the slightest noise the judge uttered sternly the command:

"Order in the court!"

And the sheriffs promptly echoed it. Presently the General elbowed his way through the crowd of spectators, with his arms full of law-books, and on his ears fell an order from the judge which was the first respectful recognition of his high official dignity that had ever saluted them, and it trickled pleasantly through his whole system:

"Way for the United States Attorney!"

The witnesses were called—legislators, high government officers, ranchmen, miners, Indians, Chinamen, negroes. Three-fourths of them were called by the defendant Morgan, but no matter, their testimony invariably went in favor of the plaintiff Hyde. Each new witness only added new testimony to the absurdity of a man's claiming to own another man's property because his farm had slid down on top of it. Then the Morgan lawyers made their speeches, and seemed to make singularly weak ones—they did really nothing to help the Morgan cause. And now the General, with exultation in his face, got up and made an impassioned effort; he pounded the table, he banged the law-books, he shouted, and roared, and howled, he quoted from everything and everybody, poetry, sarcasm, statistics, history, pathos, bathos, blasphemy, and wound up with a grand war-whoop for free speech, freedom of the press, free schools, the Glorious Bird of America and the principles of eternal justice! [Applause.]

When the General sat down, he did it with the conviction that if there was anything in good strong testimony, a great speech and believing and admiring countenances all around, Mr. Morgan's case was killed. Ex-Governor Roop leant his head upon his hand for some minutes, thinking, and the still audience waited for his decision. Then he got up and stood erect, with bended head, and thought again. Then he walked the floor with long, deliberate strides, his chin in his hand, and still the audience waited. At last he returned to his throne, seated himself, and began, impressively:

"Gentlemen, I feel the great responsibility that rests upon me this day. This is no ordinary case. On the contrary it is plain that it is the most solemn and awful that ever man was called upon to decide. Gentlemen, I have listened attentively to the evidence, and have perceived that the weight of it, the overwhelming weight of it, is in favor of the plaintiff Hyde. I have listened also to the remarks of counsel, with high interest—and especially will I commend the masterly and irrefutable logic of the distinguished gentleman who represented the plaintiff. But gentlemen, let us beware how we allow mere human testimony, human ingenuity in argument and human ideas of equity to influence us at a moment so solemn as this. Gentlemen, it ill becomes us, worms as we are, to meddle with the decrees of Heaven. It is plain to me that Heaven, in its inscrutable wisdom, has seen fit to move this defendant's ranch for a purpose. We are but creatures, and we must submit. If Heaven has chosen to favor the defendant Morgan in this marked and wonderful manner; and if Heaven, dissatisfied with the position of the Morgan ranch upon the mountain side, has chosen to remove it to a position more eligible and more advantageous for its owner, it ill becomes us, insects as we are, to question the legality of the act or inquire into the reasons that prompted it. No—Heaven created the ranches and it is Heaven's prerogative to reärrange them, to experiment with them, to shift them around at its pleasure. It is for us to submit, without repining. I warn you that this thing which has happened is a thing with which the sacrilegious hands and brains and tongues of men must not meddle. Gentlemen, it is the verdict of this court that the plaintiff, Richard Hyde, has been deprived of his ranch by the visitation of God! And from this decision there is no appeal."

Buncombe seized his cargo of law-books and plunged out of the court room frantic with indignation. He pronounced Roop to be a miraculous fool, an inspired idiot. In all good faith he returned at night and remonstrated with Roop upon his extravagant decision, and implored him to walk the floor and think for half an hour, and see if he could not figure out some sort of modification of the verdict. Roop yielded at last and got up to walk. He walked two hours and a half, and at last his face lit up happily and he told Buncombe it had occurred to him that the ranch underneath the new Morgan ranch still belonged to Hyde, that his title to the ground was just as good as it had ever been, and therefore he was of opinion that Hyde had a right to dig it out from under there and—

The General never waited to hear the end of it. He was always an impatient and irascible man, that way. At the end of two months the fact that he had been played upon with a joke had managed to bore itself, like another Hoosac Tunnel, through the solid adamant of his understanding.

ANTHONY TROLLOPE
(1815–1882)

Although Trollope never studied law, he was the son and father of barristers and his novels are filled with lawyers—by one count, he invented about a hundred. Among his novels with strong legal plots are *Orley Farm* (1862), *Lady Anna* (1874), and *Mr. Scarborough's Family* (1883); in these he was preoccupied almost to the point of obsession with themes of inheritance, land, and property.

Born in London, Trollope was educated at Harrow and Winchester, and at age nineteen he embarked on a career in the Post Office. He published his first novel in 1847 and thereafter wrote industriously, rising early every morning to write before going to work. After the success of the Barchester novels he resigned his post and devoted himself to writing; by the end of his life he had authored sixty novels.

In his *Autobiography* Trollope wrote that his father, a talented but troubled Chancery lawyer, ''kept dingy, almost suicidal chambers, at No. 23 Old Square, Lincoln's Inn'' and was ''plagued with so bad a temper that he drove the attorneys from him.'' Perhaps because of this model, Trollope's depictions of lawyers would be predominantly negative. The leading exception is the Solicitor-General, Sir William Patterson, in *Lady Anna*. Sir William at first appears to be a typically savage Trollopian barrister, but he soon emerges as a humane and imaginative apostle of compromise.

The action of *Lady Anna* is set in the 1830s. According to the novel, ''in 181-'' Josephine Murray had married Earl Lovel, a rake twice her age, who informed her six months after the wedding that he was married to an Italian woman and that the child Josephine was carrying would not be heir to his title. After providing the erstwhile Countess with an income, the Earl left for Italy, and their daughter, Anna, was born. Josephine instituted a prosecution for bigamy, but the Earl was acquitted because the Italian marriage could not be proved.

The excerpt printed here begins with the return of the old Earl and his Italian mistress who may or may not have been his wife. When the Earl dies, Josephine presents her claim to the inheritance, a claim that hinges on her being able to establish that her marriage was valid. Meanwhile, the title has descended on a young cousin of the Earl's who contests Josephine's claim.

The Countess and her daughter are represented by Sergeant Bluestone, ''a very violent man, taking up all his cases as though the very holding of a brief opposite to his was an insult to himself.'' Counsel for the young Earl is the forementioned Sir William Patterson, who persuades his client to propose marriage to Lady Anna so that the two can share the inheritance. Anna, however, remains true to her fiancé, a tailor, even though by marrying the Earl she would make a more prestigious and advantageous match.

Trollope consulted his friend Charles Merewether, Q.C., to ensure legal accuracy, and the record of that consultation is now among the Trollope Papers in the Bodleian Library. Trollope outlined legal plot details in the left-hand column and noted Merewether's replies in the right.

from LADY ANNA

— 1874 —

The Earl's Will

Not a word had been heard in Keswick of the proposed return of the old lord—for the Earl was now an old man—past his sixtieth year, and in truth with as many signs of age as some men bear at eighty. The life which he had led no doubt had had its allurements, but it is one which hardly admits of a hale and happy evening. Men who make women a prey, prey also on themselves. But there he was, back at Lovel Grange, and no one knew why he had come, nor whence, nor how. To Lovel Grange in those days, now some forty years ago, there was no road for wheels but that which ran through Keswick. Through Keswick he had passed in the middle of the night, taking on the post-horses which he had brought with him from Grassmere, so that no one in the town should see him and his companion. But it was soon known that he was there, and known also that he had a companion. For months he resided thus, and no one saw him but the domestics who waited upon him. But rumors got abroad as to his conduct, and people through the country declared that Earl Lovel was a maniac. Still his property was in his own control, and he did what it listed him to do.

As soon as men knew that he was in the land, claim after claim was made upon him for money due on behalf of his wife, and loudest among the claimants was Thomas Thwaite, the tailor. He was loudest and fiercest among the claimants, but was loud and fierce not in enmity to his old friend the Countess, but with a firm resolve to make the lord pay the only price of his wickedness which could be exacted from him. And if the Earl could be made to pay the claims against him which were made by his wife's creditors, then would the law, so far, have decided that the woman was his wife. No answer was made to any letter addressed to the Earl, and no one calling at the Grange could obtain speech or even sight of the noble owner. The lord's steward at the Grange referred all comers to the lord's attorneys in London, and the lord's attorneys simply repeated the allegation that the lady was not the lord's wife. At last there came tidings that an inquiry was to be made as to the state of the lord's health and the state of the lord's mind, on behalf of Frederic Lovel, the distant heir to the title. Let that question of the lord's marriage with Josephine Murray go as it might, Frederic Lovel, who had never seen his far-away cousin, must be the future earl. Of that there was no doubt—and new inquiries were to be made. But it might well be that the interest of the young heir would be more deeply involved in the marriage question than in other matters concerning the family. Lovel Grange and the few mountain farms attached to the Cumberland estate must become his, let the frantic Earl do what damage he might to those who bore his name; but the bulk of the property, the wealth of the Lovels, the great riches which had enabled this mighty lord to live as a beast of prey among his kind, were at his own disposal. He had one child certainly, the Lady Anna, who would inherit it all were the father to die intestate, and were the marriage proved. The young heir and those near to him altogether disbelieved the marriage—as was natural. They had never seen her who now called herself the Countess, but who for some years after her child was born had called herself Mrs Murray—who had been discarded by her own relations, and had taken herself to live with a country tailor. As years had rolled by the memory of what had really occurred in Applethwaite Church had become indistinct; and, though the reader knows that that marriage was capable of easy proof—that there would have been but little difficulty had the only difficulty consisted in proving that—the young heir and the distant Lovels were not assured of it. Their interest was adverse, and they were determined to disbelieve. But the Earl might, and probably would, leave all his wealth to a stranger. He had never in any way noticed his heir. He cared for none that bore his name. Those ties in the world which we call love, and deem respectable, and regard as happy, because they have to do with marriage and blood relationship as established by all laws since the days of Moses, were odious to him and ridiculous in his sight, because all obligations were distasteful to him—and all laws, except those which preserved to him the use of his own money. But now there came up the great question whether he was mad or sane. It was at once rumoured that he was about to leave the country, and fly back to Sicily. Then it was announced that he was dead.

And he was dead. He had died at the age of sixty-seven, in the arms of the woman he had brought there. His evil career was over, and his soul had gone to that future life for which he had made it fit by the life he had led here. His body was buried in Applethwaite churchyard, in the further corner of which long, straggling valley parish Lovel Grange is situated. At his grave there stood no single mourner—but the young lord was there, of his right, disdaining even to wear a crape band round his hat. But the woman remained shut up in her own chamber—a difficulty to the young lord and his lawyer, who could hardly tell the foreigner to pack and begone before the body of her late—lover had been laid in the grave. It had been simply intimated to her that on such a date—within a week from the funeral—her presence in the house could not longer be endured. She had flashed round upon the lawyer, who had attempted to make this award known to her in broken French, but had answered simply by some words of scorn, spoken in Italian to her waiting-maid.

Then the will was read in the presence of the young Earl—for there was a will. Everything that the late lord had possessed was left, in one line, to his best-beloved friend, the Signorina Camilla Spondi; and it was stated, and very fully explained, that Camilla Spondi was the Italian lady living at the Grange at the date on which the will was made. Of the old lord's heir, the now existing Earl Lovel, no mention was made whatever. There were, however, two other clauses or parts in the will. There was a schedule giving in detail the particulars of the property left to Camilla Spondi; and there was a rambling statement that the maker of the will acknowledged Anna Murray to be his illegitimate daughter—that Anna Murray's mother had never been the testator's legitimate wife, as his real wife, the true Countess Lovel, for whom he had separately made adequate provision, was still alive in Sicily at the date of that will—and that by a former will now destroyed he had made provision for Anna Murray, which provision he had revoked in consequence of the treatment which he had received from Josephine Murray and her friends. They who believed the statements made in this will afterwards asserted that Anna had been deprived of her inheritance by the blow with which the tailor had felled the Earl to the earth.

To Camilla Spondi intimation was given of the contents of the Earl's will as far as they concerned her; but she was told at the same time that no portion of the dead man's wealth would be placed in her hands till the courts should have decided whether or no the old lord had been sane or insane when he signed the document. A sum of money was, however, given her, on condition that she should take her immediate departure—and she departed. With her personally we need have no further concern. Of her cause and of her claim some mention must be made; but in a few pages she will drop altogether from our story.

A copy of the will was also sent to the lawyers who had hitherto taken charge of the interests of the repudiated Countess, and it was intimated that the allowance hitherto made to her must now of necessity cease. If she thought fit to prosecute any further claim, she must do so by proving her marriage—and it was explained to her, probably without much of legal or precise truth in the explanation, that such proof must include the disproving of the assertion in the Earl's will. As it was the intention of the heir to set aside that will, such assurance was, to say the least of it, disingenuous. But the whole thing had now become so confused that it could hardly be expected that lawyers should be ingenuous in discussing it.

The young Earl clearly inherited the title and the small estate at Lovel Grange. The Italian woman was prima facie heiress to everything else—except to such portion of the large personal property as the widow could claim as widow, in the event of her being able to prove that she had been a wife. But in the event of the will being no will, the Italian woman would have nothing. In such case the male heir would have all if the marriage were no marriage—but would have nothing if the marriage could be made good. If the marriage could be made good, the Lady Anna would have the entire property, except such portion as would be claimed of right by her mother, the widow. Thus the Italian woman and the young lord were combined in interest against the mother and daughter as regarded the marriage; and the young lord and the mother and daughter were combined against the Italian woman as regarded the will—but the young lord had to act alone against the Italian woman, and against the mother and daughter whom he and his friends regarded as swindlers and impostors. It was for him to set aside the will in reference to the Italian woman, and then to stand the brunt of the assault made upon him by the soi-disant wife.

In a very short time after the old Earl's death a double compromise was offered on behalf of the young Earl. The money at stake was immense. Would the Italian woman take £10,000, and go her way back to Italy, renouncing all further claim; and would the soi-disant Countess abandon her title, acknowledge her child to be illegitimate, and go her way with another £10,000—or with £20,000, as was soon hinted by the gentlemen acting on the Earl's behalf? The proposition was one somewhat difficult in the making, as the compromise, if made with both, would be excellent, but could not be made to any good effect with one only. The young Earl certainly could not afford to buy off the Italian woman for £10,000, if the effect of such buying off would only be to place the whole of the late lord's wealth in the hands of his daughter and of his daughter's mother.

The Italian woman consented. She declared with Italian energy that her late loving friend had never been a day insane; but she knew nothing of English laws, and but little of English money. She would take the £10,000—having had a calculation made for her of the number of lire into which it would run. The number was enormous, and she would take the offer. But when the proposal was mentioned to the Countess, and explained to her by her old friend, Thomas Thwaite, who had now become a poor man in her cause, she repudiated it with bitter scorn—with a scorn in which she almost included the old man who had made it to her. 'Is it for that, that I have been fighting?' she said.

'For that in part,' said the old man.

'No, Mr Thwaite, not for that at all; but that my girl may have her birth allowed and her name acknowledged.'

'Her name shall be allowed and her birth shall be acknowledged,' said the tailor, in whose heart there was nothing base. 'She shall be the Lady Anna, and her mother shall be the Countess Lovel.' The estate of the Countess, if she had an estate, then owed the tailor some five or six thousand pounds, and the compromise offered would have paid the tailor every shilling and have left a comfortable income for the two women.

'For myself I care but little,' said the mother, taking the tailor's hand in hers and kissing it. 'My child is the Lady Anna, and I do not dare to barter away her rights.' This took place down at the cottage in Cumberland, and the tailor at once went up to London to make known the decision of the Countess—as he invariably called her.

Then the lawyers went to work. As the double compromise could not be effected, the single compromise could not stand. The Italian woman raved and stamped, and swore that she must have her half million of lire. But of course no right to such a claim had been made good to her, and the lawyers on behalf of the young Earl went on with their work. Public sympathy as a matter of course went with the young Earl. As against the Italian woman he had with him every English man and woman. It was horrible to the minds of English men and English women that an old English Earldom should be starved in order that an Italian harlot might revel in untold riches. It was felt by most men and protested by all women that any sign of madness, be it what it might—however insignificant—should be held to be sufficient against such a claimant. Was not the fact that the man had made such a will in itself sufficient proof of his madness? There were not a few who protested that no further proof could be necessary. But with us the law is the same for an Italian harlot and an English widow; and it may well be that in its niceties it shall be found kinder to the former than to the latter. But the Earl had been mad, and the law said that he was mad when he had made his will—and the Italian woman went away, raging, into obscurity.

The Italian woman was conquered, and now the battle was open and free between the young Earl and the claimant Countess. Applications were made on behalf of the Countess for funds from the estate wherewith to prove the claim, and to a certain limited amount they were granted. Such had been the life of the late Earl that it was held that the cost of all litigation resulting from his misdeeds should be paid from his estate—but ready money was wanted, immediate ready money, to be at the disposal of the Countess to any amount needed by her agent, and this was hardly to be obtained. By this time public sympathy ran almost entirely with the Earl. Though it was acknowledged that the late lord was mad, and though it had become a cause of rejoicing that the Italian woman had been sent away penniless, howling into obscurity, because of the old man's madness, still it was believed that he had written the truth when he declared that the marriage had been a mock marriage. It would be better for the English world that the young Earl should be a rich man, fit to do honour to his position, fit to marry the daughter of a duke, fit to carry on the glory of the English peerage, than that a woman, ill reputed in the world, should be established as a Countess, with a daughter dowered with tens of thousands, as to whom it was already said that she was in love with a tailor's son. Nothing could be more touching, more likely to awaken sympathy, than the manner in which Josephine Murray had been carried away in marriage, and then roughly told by the man who should have protected her from every harshly blowing wind of heaven that he had deceived her and that she was not his wife. No usage to which woman had ever been subjected, as has been said before, was more adapted to elicit compassion and energetic aid. But nineteen years had now passed by since the deed was done, and the facts were forgotten. One energetic friend there still was—or we may say two, the tailor and his son Daniel. But public belief ran against the Countess, and nobody who was anybody in the world would give her her title. Bets were laid, two and three to one against her; and it was believed that she was an impostor. The Earl had all the glory of success over his first opponent, and the loud boasting of self-confident barristers buoyed up his cause.

But loud-boasting barristers may nevertheless be wise lawyers, and the question of a compromise was again mooted. If the lady would take thirty thousand pounds and vanish, she should have the money clear of deduction, and all expenses should be paid. The amount offered was thought to be very liberal, but it did not amount to the annual income that was at stake. It was rejected with scorn. Had it been quadrupled, it would have been rejected with equal scorn. The loud-boasting barristers were still confident; but—. Though it was never admitted in words still it was felt that there might be a doubt. What if the contending parties were to join forces, if the Countess-ship of the Countess were to be admitted and the heiress-ship of the Lady Anna, and if the Earl and the Lady Anna were to be united in holy wedlock? Might there not be a safe solution from further difficulty in that way?

Lady Anna

The idea of this further compromise, of this something more than compromise, of this half acknowledgment of their own weakness, came from Mr Flick, of the firm of Norton and Flick, the solicitors who were employed in substantiating the Earl's position. When Mr Flick mentioned it to Sir William Patterson, the great barrister, who was at that time Solicitor-General and leading counsel on behalf of Lord Lovel, Sir William Patterson stood aghast and was dismayed. Sir William intended to make mincemeat of the Countess. It was said of him that he intended to cross-examine the Countess off her legs, right out of her claim, and almost into her grave. He certainly did believe her to be an impostor, who had not thought herself to be entitled to her name when she first assumed it.

'I should be sorry, Mr Flick, to be driven to think that anything of that kind could be expedient.'

'It would make sure of the fortune to the family,' said Mr Flick.

'And what about our friend, the Countess?'

'Let her call herself Countess Lovel, Sir William. That will break no bones. As to the formality of her own marriage, there can be no doubt about that.'

'We can prove by Grogram that she was told that another wife was living,' said Sir William. Grogram was an old butler who had been in the old Earl's service for thirty years.

'I believe we can, Sir William; but—. It is quite clear that we shall never get the other wife to come over and face an English jury. It is of no use blinking it. The gentleman whom we have sent over doubts her altogether. That there was a marriage is certain, but he fears that this woman is not the old Countess. There were two sisters, and it may be that this was the other sister.'

Sir William was a good deal dismayed, but he recovered himself. The stakes were so high that it was quite possible that the gentleman who had been sent over might have been induced to open his eyes to the possibility of such personation by overtures from the other side. Sir William was of opinion that Mr Flick himself should go to Sicily. He was not sure that he, Sir William, Her Majesty's Solicitor-General, would not make the journey in person. He was by no means disposed to give way. 'They tell me that the girl is no better than she should be,' he said to Mr Flick.

'I don't think so bad as that of her,' said Mr Flick.

'Is she a lady—or anything like a lady?'

'I am told she is very beautiful.'

'I dare say—and so was her mother before her. I never saw a handsomer woman of her age than our friend the Countess. But I could not recommend the young lord to marry an underbred, bad girl, and a bastard who claims to be his cousin—and support my proposition merely on the ground of her looks.'

'Thirty-five thousand a year, Sir William!' pleaded the attorney.

'I hope we can get the thirty-five thousand a year for our client without paying so dear for them.'

It had been presumed that the real Countess, the original Countess, the Italian lady whom the Earl had married in early life, would be brought over, with properly attested documentary evidence in her pocket, to prove that she was the existing Countess, and that any other Countess must be either an impostor or a deluded dupe. No doubt the old Earl had declared, when first informing Josephine Murray that she was not his wife, that his real wife had died during the few months which had intervened since his mock marriage; but it was acknowledged on all sides that the old Earl had been a villain and a liar. It was no part of the duty of the young Earl, or of those who acted for him, to defend the character of the old Earl. To wash that blackamoor white, or even to make him whity-brown, was not necessary to anybody. No one was now concerned to account for his crooked courses. But if it could be shown that he had married the lady in Italy—as to which there was no doubt—and that the lady was still alive, or that she had been alive when the second marriage took place, then the Lady Anna could not inherit the property which had been freed from the grasp of the Italian mistress. But it seemed that the lady, if she lived, could not be made to come. Mr Flick did go to Sicily, and came back renewing his advice to Sir William that Lord Lovel should be advised to marry the Lady Anna.

At this time the Countess, with her daughter, had moved their residence from Keswick up to London, and was living in very humble lodgings in a small street turning out of the New Road, near the Yorkshire Stingo. Old Thomas Thwaite had accompanied them from Cumberland, but the rooms had been taken for them by his son, Daniel Thwaite, who was at this time foreman to a somewhat celebrated tailor who carried on his business in Wigmore Street; and he, Daniel Thwaite, had a bedroom in the house in which the Countess lodged. The arrangement was not a wise one, as reports had already been spread abroad as to the partiality of the Lady Anna for the young tailor. But how should she not have been partial both to the father and to the son, feeling as she did that they were the only two men who befriended her cause and her mother's? As to the Countess herself, she, perhaps, alone of all those who interested themselves in her daughter's cause, had heard no word of these insinuations against her child. To her both Thomas and Daniel Thwaite were dear friends, to repay whom for their exertions with lavish generosity—should the means to do so ever come within their reach—was one of the dreams of her existence. But she was an ambitious woman, thinking much of her rank, thinking much even of the blood of her own ancestors, constantly urgent with her daughter in teaching her the duties and privileges of wealth and rank. For the Countess never doubted that she would at last attain success. That the Lady Anna should throw herself away upon Daniel Thwaite did not occur to her as a possibility. She had not even dreamed that Daniel Thwaite would aspire to her daughter's hand. And yet every shop-boy and every shop-girl in Keswick had been so saying for the last twelvemonth, and rumours which had hitherto been confined to Keswick and its neighborhood were now common in London. For the case was becoming one of the celebrated causes of the age, and all the world was talking of the Countess and her daughter. No momentary suspicion had crossed the mind of the Countess till after their arrival in London; and then when the suspicion did touch her it was not love that she suspected—but rather an unbecoming familiarity which she attributed to her child's ignorance of the great life which awaited her. 'My dear,' she said one day when Daniel Thwaite had left them, 'you should be less free in your manner with that young man.'

'What do you mean, mamma?' said the daughter, blushing.

'You had better call him Mr Thwaite.'

'But I have called him Daniel ever since I was born.'

'He always calls you Lady Anna.'

'Sometimes he does, mamma.'

'I never heard him call you anything else,' said the Countess, almost with indignation. 'It is all very well for the old man, because he is an old man and has done so much for us.'

'So has Daniel—quite as much, mamma. They have both done everything.'

'True; they have both been warm friends; and if ever I forget them may God forget me. I trust that we may both live to show them that they are not forgotten. But it is not fitting that there should exist between you and him the intimacy of equal positions. You are not and cannot be his equal. He has been born to be a tailor, and you are the daughter and heiress of an Earl.'

These last words were spoken in a tone that was almost awful to the Lady Anna. She had heard so much of her father's rank and her father's wealth—rank and wealth which were always to be hers, but which had never as yet reached her, which had been a perpetual trouble to her, and a crushing weight upon her young life, that she had almost learned to hate the title and the claim. Of course it was a part of the religion of her life that her mother had been duly married to her father. It was beyond a doubt to her that such was the case. But the constant battling for denied rights, the assumption of a position which could not be attained, the use of titles which were simply ridiculous in themselves as connected with the kind of life which she was obliged to lead—these things had all become odious to her. She lacked the ambition which gave her mother strength, and would gladly have become Anna Murray or Anna Lovel, with a girl's ordinary privilege of loving her lover, had such an easy life been possible to her.

In person she was very lovely, less tall and robust than her mother had been, but with a sweeter, softer face. Her hair was less dark, and her eyes were neither blue nor bold. But they were bright and soft and very eloquent, and when laden with tears would have softened the heart, almost, of her father. She was as yet less powerful than her mother, both in body and mind, but probably better calculated to make a happy home for a husband and children. She was affectionate, self-denying, and feminine. Had that offer of compromise for thirty, twenty, or for ten thousand pounds been made to her, she would have accepted it willingly—caring little for her name, little even for fame, so that she might have been happy and quiet, and at liberty to think of a lover as are other girls. In her present condition, how could she have any happy love? She was the Lady Anna Lovel, heir to a ducal fortune—but she lived in small close lodgings in Wyndham Street, New Road. She did not believe in the good time coming as did her mother. Their enemy was an undoubted Earl, undoubtedly owner of Lovel Grange of which she had heard all her life. Would it not be better to take what the young lord chose to give them and to be at rest? But she did not dare to express such thoughts to her mother. Her mother would have crushed her with a look.

'I have told Mr Thwaite', the mother said to her daughter, 'what we were saying this morning.'

'About his son?'

'Yes—about his son.'

'Oh, mamma!'

'I was bound to do so.'

'And what did he say, mamma?'

'He did not like it, and told me that he did not like it—but he admitted that it was true. He admitted that his son was no fitting intimate for Lady Anna Lovel.'

'What should we have done without him?'

'Badly indeed; but that cannot change his duty, or ours. He is helping us to struggle for that which is our own; but he would mar his generosity if he put a taint on that which he is endeavouring to restore to us.'

'Put a taint, mamma!'

'Yes—a taint would rest upon your rank if you as Lady Anna Lovel were familiar with Daniel Thwaite as with an equal. His father understands it, and will speak to him.'

'Mamma, Daniel will be very angry.'

'Then he will be very unreasonable—but, Anna, I will not have you call him Daniel any more.'

The Tailor of Keswick

Old Thomas Thwaite was at this time up in London about the business of the Countess, but had no intention of residing there. He still kept his shop in Keswick, and still made coats and trousers for Cumberland statesmen. He was by no means in a condition to retire from business, having spent the savings of his life in the cause of the Countess and her daughter. Men had told him that, had he not struck the Earl in the yard of the Crown at Keswick, as horses were being brought out for the lord's travelling carriage, ample provision would have been made by the rich old sinner for his daughter. That might have been so, or might not, but the saying instigated the tailor to further zeal and increased generosity. To oppose an Earl, even though it might be on behalf of a Countess, was a joy to him; to set wrong right, and to put down cruelty and to relieve distressed women was the pride of his heart—especially when his efforts were made in antagonism to one of high rank. And he was a man who would certainly be thorough in his work, though his thoroughness should be ruinous to himself. He had despised the Murrays, who ought to have stuck to their distant cousin, and had exulted in his heart at thinking that the world would say how much better and truer had been the Keswick tailor than the well-born and comparatively wealthy Scotch relations. And the poets of the lakes, who had not as yet become altogether Tories, had taken him by the hand and praised him. The rights of the Countess and the wrongs of the Countess had become his life. But he still kept on a diminished business in the north, and it was now needful that he should return to Cumberland. He had heard that renewed offers of compromise were to be made—though no idea of the proposed marriage between the distant cousins had been suggested to him. He had been discussing the question of some compromise with the Countess when she spoke to him respecting his son; and had recommended that certain terms should, if possible, be effected. Let the money be divided, on condition that the marriage were allowed. There could be no difficulty in this if the young lord would accede to such an arrangement, as the marriage must be acknowledged unless an adverse party should bring home proof from Italy to the contrary. The sufficiency of the ceremony in Applethwaite Church was incontestable. Let the money be divided, and the Countess be Countess Lovel, and Lady Anna be the Lady Anna to all the world. Old Thomas Thwaite himself had seemed to think that there would be enough of triumph in such a settlement. 'But the woman might afterwards be bribed to come over and renew her claim,' said the Countess. 'Unless it be absolutely settled now, they will say when I am dead and gone that my daughter has no right to her name.' Then the tailor said that he would make further inquiry how that might be. He was inclined to think that there might be a decision which should be absolute, even though that decision should be reached by compromise between the now contending parties.

Then the Countess had said her word about Daniel Thwaite the son, and Thomas Thwaite the father had heard it with ill-concealed anger. To fight against an Earl on behalf of the Earl's injured wife had been very sweet to him, but to be checked in his fight because he and his were unfit to associate with the child of that injured wife was very bitter. And yet he had sense to know that what the Countess said to him was true. As far as words went, he admitted the truth; but his face was more eloquent than his words, and his face showed plainly his displeasure.

'It is not of you that I am speaking,' said the Countess, laying her hand upon the old man's sleeve.

'Daniel is, at any rate, fitter than I,' said the tailor. 'He has been educated, and I never was.'

'He is as good as gold. It is not of that I speak. You know what I mean.'

'I know very well what you mean, Lady Lovel.'

'I have no friend like you, Mr Thwaite—none whom I love as I do you. And next to you is your son. For myself, there is nothing that I would not do for him or you—no service, however menial, that I would not render you with my own hands. There is no limit to the gratitude which I owe you. But my girl is young, and if this burden of rank and wealth is to be hers—it is proper that she do honour to it.'

'And it is not honourable that she should be seen speaking—to a tailor?'

'Ah—if you choose to take it so!'

'How should I take it? What I say is true. And what you say is true also. I will speak to Daniel.' But she knew well, as he left her, that his heart was bitter against her.

The old man did speak to his son, sitting with him up in the bedroom over that which the Countess occupied. Old Thomas Thwaite was a strong man, but his son was in some respects stronger. As his father had said of him, he had been educated—or rather instructed; and instruction leads to the power of thinking. He looked deeper into things than did his father, and was governed by wider and greater motives. His father had been a Radical all his life, guided thereto probably by some early training, and made steadfast in his creed by feelings which induced him to hate the pretensions of an assumed superiority. Old Thwaite could not endure to think that one man should be considered to be worthier than another because he was richer. He would admit the riches, and even the justice of the riches—having been himself, during much of his life, a rich man in his own sphere; but would deny the worthiness; and would adduce, in proof of his creed, the unworthiness of certain exalted sinners. The career of the Earl Lovel had been to him a sure proof of the baseness of English aristocracy generally. He had dreams of a republic in which a tailor might be president or senator, or something almost noble. But no rational scheme of governance among mankind had ever entered his mind, and of pure politics he knew no more than the journeyman who sat stitching upon his board.

But Daniel Thwaite was a thoughtful man who had read many books. More's *Utopia* and Harrington's *Oceana*, with many a tale written in the same spirit, had taught him to believe that a perfect form of government, or rather of policy, under which all men might be happy and satisfied, was practicable on earth and was to be achieved not merely by the slow amelioration of mankind under God's fostering ordinances, but by the continued efforts of good and wise men who, by their goodness and wisdom, should be able to make the multitude believe in them. To diminish the distances, not only between the rich and the poor but between the high and the low, was the grand political theory upon which his mind was always running. His father was ever thinking of himself and of Earl Lovel; while Daniel Thwaite was considering the injustice of the difference between ten thousand aristocrats and thirty million of people, who were for the most part ignorant and hungry. But it was not that he also had not thoughts of himself. Gradually he had come to learn that he need not have been a tailor's foreman in Wigmore Street had not his father spent on behalf of the Countess Lovel the means by which he, the son, might already have become a master tradesman. And yet he had never begrudged it. He had been as keen as his father in the cause. It had been the romance of his life, since his life had been capable of romance—but with him it had been no respect for the rank to which his father was so anxious to restore the Countess, no value which he attached to the names claimed by the mother and the daughter. He hated the Countess-ship of the Countess, and the ladyship of the Lady Anna. He would fain that they should have abandoned them. They were to him odious signs of iniquitous pretensions. But he was keen enough to punish and to remedy the wickedness of the wicked Earl. He reverenced his father because he assaulted the wicked Earl and struck him to the ground. He was heart and soul in the cause of the injured wife. And then the one thing on earth that was really dear to him was the Lady Anna.

It had been the romance of his life. They had grown up together as playmates in Cumberland. He had fought scores of battles on her behalf with those who had denied that she was the Lady Anna—even though he had then hated the title. Boys had jeered him because of his noble little sweetheart, and he had exulted at hearing her so called. His only sister and his mother had died when he was young, and there had been none in the house but his father and himself. As a boy he had ever been at the cottage of the Countess, and he had sworn to Lady Anna a thousand times that he would do and die in her service. Now he was a strong man, and was more devoted to her than ever. It was the great romance of his life. How could it be brought to pass that the acknowledged daughter of an Earl, dowered with enormous wealth, should become the wife of a tailor? And yet such was his ambition and such his purpose. It was not that he cared for her dower. It was not, at any rate, the hope of her dower that had induced him to love her. His passion had grown and his purpose had been formed before the old Earl had returned for the last time to Lovel Grange—when nothing was known of the manner in which his wealth might be distributed. That her prospect of riches now joined itself to his aspirations it would be an affectation to deny. The man who is insensible to the power which money brings with it must be a dolt; and Daniel Thwaite was not a dolt, and was fond of power. But he was proud of heart, and he said to himself over and over again that should it ever come to pass that the possession of the girl was to depend on the abandonment of the wealth, the wealth should be abandoned without a further thought.

It may be imagined that with such a man the words which his father would speak to him about the Lady Anna, suggesting the respectful distance with which she should be approached by a tailor's foreman, would be very bitter. They were bitter to the speaker and very bitter to him who heard them. 'Daniel,' said the father, 'this is a queer life you are leading with the Countess and Lady Anna just beneath you, in the same house.'

'It was a quiet house for them to come to—and cheap.'

'Quiet enough, and as cheap as any, I dare say—but I don't know whether it is well that you should be thrown so much with them. They are different from us.' The son looked at his father, but made no immediate reply. 'Our lot has been cast with theirs because of their difficulties,' continued the old man, 'but the time is coming when we had better stand aloof.'

'What do you mean, father?'

'I mean that we are tailors, and these people are born nobles.'

'They have taken our help, father.'

'Well; yes, they have. But it is not for us to say anything of that. It has been given with a heart.'

'Certainly with a heart.'

'And shall be given to the end. But the end of it will come soon now. One will be a Countess and the other will be the Lady Anna. Are they fit associates for such as you and me?'

'If you ask me, father, I think they are.'

'They don't think so. You may be sure of that.'

'Have they said so, father?'

'The Countess has said so. She has complained that you call her daughter simply Anna. In future you must give her a handle to her name.' Daniel Thwaite was a dark brown man, with no tinge of ruddiness about him, a thin spare man, almost swarthy, whose hands were as brown as a nut, and whose cheeks and forehead were brown. But now he blushed up to his eyes. The hue of the blood as it rushed to his face forced itself through the darkness of his visage, and he blushed, as such men do blush—with a look of indignation of his face. 'Just call her Lady Anna,' said the father.

'The Countess had been complaining of me then?'

'She has hinted that her daughter will be injured by your familiarity, and she is right. I suppose that the Lady Anna Lovel ought to be treated with deference by a tailor—even though the tailor may have spent his last farthing in her service.'

'Do not let us talk about the money, father.'

'Well; no. I'd as lief not think about the money either. The world is not ripe yet, Daniel.'

'No—the world is not ripe.'

'There must be earls and countesses.'

'I see no must in it. There are earls and countesses as there used to be mastodons and other senseless, overgrown brutes roaming miserable and hungry through the undrained woods—cold, comfortless, unwieldy things, which have perished in the general progress. The big things have all to give way to the intellect of those which are more finely made.'

'I hope men and women will not give way to bugs and fleas,' said the tailor, who was wont to ridicule his son's philosophy.

The son was about to explain his theory of the perfected mean size of intellectual created beings, when his heart was at the present moment full of Anna Lovel. 'Father,' he said, 'I think that the Countess might have spared her observations.'

'I thought so too—but as she said it, it was best that I should tell you. You'll have to marry some day, and it wouldn't do that you should look there for your sweetheart.' When the matter was thus brought home to him, Daniel Thwaite would argue it no further. 'It will all come to an end soon,' continued the old man, 'and it may be that they had better not move till it is settled. They'll divide the money, and there will be enough for both in all conscience. The Countess will be the Countess, and the Lady Anna will be the Lady Anna; and then there will be no more need of the old tailor from Keswick. They will go into another world, and we shall hear from them perhaps about Christmas time with a hamper of game and maybe a little wine, as a gift.'

'You do not think that of them, father.'

'What else can they do? The lawyers will pay the money, and they will be carried away. They cannot come to our house, nor can we go to theirs. I shall leave tomorrow, my boy, at six o'clock; and my advice to you is to trouble them with your presence as little as possible. You may be sure that they do not want it.'

Daniel Thwaite was certainly not disposed to take his father's advice, but then he knew much more than did his father. The above scene took place in the evening, when the son's work was done. As he crept down on the following morning by the door of the room in which the two ladies slept, he could not but think of his father's words, 'It wouldn't do that you should look there for your sweetheart.' Why should it not do? But any such advice as that was now too late. He had looked there for his sweetheart. He had spoken, and the girl had answered him. He had held her close to his heart, and had pressed her lips to his own, and had called her his Anna, his well-beloved, his pearl, his treasure; and she—she had only sighed in his arms, and yielded to his embrace. She had wept alone when she thought of it, with a conscious feeling that as she was the Lady Anna there could be no happy love between herself and the only youth whom she had known. But when he had spoken, and had clasped her to his heart, she had never dreamed of rebuking him. She had known nothing better than he, and desired nothing better than to live with him and to be loved by him. She did not think that it could be possible to know anyone better. This weary, weary title filled her with dismay. Daniel, as he walked along thinking of her embrace, thinking of those kisses, and thinking also of his father's caution, swore to himself that the difficulties in his way should never stop him in his course.

The Solicitor-General makes a Proposition

When Mr Flick returned from Sicily he was very strongly in favour of some compromise.

He had seen the so-called Italian Countess—who certainly was now called Contessa by everybody around her—and he did not believe that she had ever been married to the old Earl. That an Italian lady had been married to the old lord now twenty-five years ago, he did believe—probably the younger sister of this woman—and he also believed that this wife had been dead before the marriage at Applethwaite. That was his private opinion. Mr Flick was, in his way, an honest man—one who certainly would have taken no conscious part in getting up an unjust claim; but he was now acting as legal agent for the young Earl, and it was not his business to get up evidence for the Earl's opponents. He did think that were he to use all his ingenuity and the funds at his disposal he would be able to reach the real truth in such a manner that it should be made clear and indubitable to an English jury; but if the real truth were adverse to his side, why search for it? He understood that the English Countess would stand her ground on the legality of the Applethwaite marriage, and on the acquittal of the old Earl as to the charge of bigamy. The English Countess being firm, so far as that ground would make her firm, it would in reality be for the other side—for the young Earl—to prove a former marriage. The burden of the proof would be with him, and not with the English Countess to disprove it. Disingenuous lawyers—Mr Flick, who though fairly honest could be disingenuous, among the number—had declared the contrary. But such was the case; and, as money was scarce with the Countess and her friends, no attempt had been made on their part to bring home evidence from Sicily. All this Mr Flick knew, and doubted how far it might be wise for him further to disturb that Sicilian romance. The Italian

Countess, who was a hideous, worn-out old woman, professing to be forty-four, probably fifty-five, and looking as though she were seventy-seven, would not stir a step towards England. She would swear and had sworn any number of oaths. Documentary evidence from herself, from various priests, from servants, and from neighbours there was in plenty. Mr Flick learned through his interpreter that a certain old priest ridiculed the idea of there being a doubt. And there were letters—letters alleged to have been written by the Earl to the living wife in the old days, which were shown to Mr Flick. Mr Flick was an educated man, and knew many things. He knew something of the manufacture of paper, and would not look at the letters after the first touch. It was not for him to get up evidence for the other side. The hideous old woman was clamorous for money. The priests were clamorous for money. The neighbours were clamorous for money. Had not they all sworn anything that was wanted, and were they not to be paid? Some moderate payment was made to the hideous, screeching, greedy old woman; some trivial payment—as to which Mr Flick was heartily ashamed of himself—was made to the old priest; and then Mr Flick hurried home, fully convinced that a compromise should be made as to the money, and that the legality of the titles claimed by the two English ladies should be allowed. It might be that that hideous hag had once been the Countess Lovel. It certainly was the case that the old Earl in latter years had so called her, though he had never once seen her during his last residence in Sicily. It might be that the clumsy fiction of the letters had been perpetrated with the view of bolstering up a true case with false evidence. But Mr Flick thought that there should be a compromise, and expressed his opinion very plainly to Sir William Patterson. 'You mean a marriage,' said the Solicitor-General. At this time Mr Hardy, Q.C., the second counsel acting on behalf of the Earl, was also present.

'Not necessarily by a marriage, Sir William. They could divide the money.'

'The girl is not of age,' said Mr Hardy.

'She is barely twenty as yet,' said Sir William.

'I think it might be managed on her behalf,' said the attorney.

'Who could be empowered to sacrifice her rights?' said Mr Hardly, who was a gruff man.

'We might perhaps contrive to tide it over till she is of age,' said the Solicitor-General, who was a sweet-mannered, mild man among his friends, though he could cross-examine a witness off his legs—or hers—if the necessity of the case required him to do so.

'Of course we could do that, Sir William. What is a year in such a case as this?'

'Not much among lawyers, is it, Mr Flick? You think that we shouldn't bring our case into court.'

'It is a good case, Sir William, no doubt. There's the woman—Countess, we will call her—ready to swear, and has sworn, that she was the old Earl's wife. All the people round call her the Countess. The Earl undoubtedly used to speak of her as the Countess, and send her little dribbles of money, as being his Countess, during the ten years and more after he left Lovel Grange. There is the old priest who married them.'

'The devil's in it if that is not a good case,' said Mr Hardy.

'Go on, Mr Flick,' said the Solicitor-General.

'I've got all the documentary evidence of course, Sir William.'

'Go on, Mr Flick.' Mr Flick scratched his head. 'It's a very heavy interest, Sir William.'

'No doubt it is. Go on.'

'I don't know that I've anything further to say, except that I'd arrange it if I could. Our client, Sir William, would be in a very pretty position if he got half the income which is at stake.'

'Or the whole with the wife,' said the Solicitor-General.

'Or the whole with the wife, Sir William. If he were to lose it all, he'd be—so to say, nowhere.'

'Nowhere at all,' said the Solicitor-General. 'The entailed property isn't worth above a thousand a year.'

'I'd make some arrangement,' said Mr Flick, whose mind may perhaps have had a not unnatural bend towards his own very large venture in this concern. That his bill, including the honorarium of the barristers, would sooner or later be paid out of the estate, he did not doubt—but a compromise would make the settlement easy and pleasant.

Mr Hardy was in favour of continued fighting. A keener, honester, more enlightened lawyer than Mr Hardy did not wear silk at that moment, but he had not the gift of seeing through darkness which belonged to the Solicitor-General. When Mr Flick told them of the strength of their case, as based on various heads of evidence in their favour, Mr Hardy believed Mr Flick's words and rejected Mr Flick's opinion. He believed in his heart that the English Countess was an impostor, not herself believing in her own claim; and it would be gall and wormwood to him to give such a one a moiety of the wealth which should go to support the ancient dignity and aristocratic grace of the house of Lovel. He hated compromise and desired justice—and was a great rather than a successful lawyer. Sir William had at once perceived that there was something in the background on which it was his duty to calculate, which he was bound to consider—but with which at the same time it was inexpedient that he should form a closer or more accurate acquaintance. He must do the best he could for his client. Earl Lovel with a thousand a year, and that probably already embarrassed, would be a poor, wretched creature, a mock lord, an earl without the very essence of an earldom. But Earl Lovel with fifteen or twenty thousand a year would be as good as most other earls. It would be but the difference between two powdered footmen and four, between four hunters and eight, between Belgrave Square and Eaton Place. Sir William, had he felt confident, would of course have preferred the four footmen for his client, and the eight hunters, and Belgrave Square; even though the poor English Countess should have starved, or been fed by the tailor's bounty. But he was not confident. He began to think that that wicked old Earl had been too wicked for them all. 'They say she's a very nice girl,' said Sir William.

'Very handsome indeed, I'm told,' said Mr Flick.

'And in love with the son of the old tailor from Keswick,' said Mr Hardy.

'She'll prefer the lord to the tailor for a guinea,' said Sir William.

And thus it was decided, after some indecisive fashion, that their client should be sounded as to the expedience of a compromise. It was certain to them that the poor woman would be glad to accept, for herself and her daughter, half of the wealth at stake, which half would be to her almost unlimited riches, on the condition that their rank was secured to them—their rank and all the privileges of honest legitimacy. But as to such an arrangement the necessary delay offered no doubt a serious impediment, and it was considered that the wisest course would be to propose the marriage. But who should propose it, and how should it be proposed? Sir William was quite willing to make the suggestion to the young lord or the young lord's family, whose consent must of course be first obtained; but who should then break the ice to the Countess? 'I suppose we must ask our friend, the Serjeant,' said Mr Flick. Serjeant Bluestone was the leading counsel for our Countess, and was vehemently energetic in this case. He swore everywhere that the Solicitor-General hadn't a leg to stand upon, and that the Solicitor-General knew that he hadn't a leg. Let them bring that Italian Countess over if they dared. He'd countess her, and discountess her too! Since he had first known the English courts of law there had been no case hard as this was hard. Had not the old Earl been acquitted of the charge of bigamy, when the unfortunate woman had done her best to free herself from her position? Serjeant Bluestone, who was a very violent man, taking up all his cases as though the very holding of a brief opposite to him was an insult to himself, had never before been so violent. 'The Serjeant will take it as a surrender,' and Mr Flick.

'We must get round the Serjeant,' said Sir William. 'There are ladies in the Lovel family; we must manage it through them.' And so it was arranged by the young lord's lawyers that an attempt should be made to marry him to the heiress.

The two cousins had never seen each other. Lady Anna had hardly heard of Frederic Lovel before her father's death; but, since that, had been brought up to regard the young lord as her natural enemy. The young lord had been taught from his youth upwards to look upon the soi-disant Countess and her daughter as impostors who would some day strive to rob him of his birthright—and, in these latter days, as impostors who were hard at work upon their project. And he had been told of the intimacy between the Countess and the old tailor—and also of that between the so-called Lady Anna and the young tailor. To these distant Lovels—to Frederic Lovel who had been brought up with the knowledge that he must be the Earl, and to his uncle and aunt by whom he had been brought up—the women down at Keswick had been represented as vulgar, odious, and disreputable. We all know how firm can be the faith of a family in such matters. The Lovels were not without fear as to the result of the attempt that was being made. They understood quite as well as did Mr Flick the glory of the position which would attend upon success, and the wretchedness attendant upon a pauper earldom. They were nervous enough, and in some moods frightened. But their trust in the justice of their cause was unbounded. The old Earl, whose memory was horrible to them, had purposely left two enemies in their way. There had been the Italian mistress backed up by the will; and there had been this illegitimate child. The one was vanquished; but the other—! Ah—it would be bad with them indeed if that enemy could not be vanquished too! They had offered £30,000 to the enemy; but the enemy would not accept the bribe. The idea of ending all their troubles by a marriage had never occurred to them. Had Mrs Lovel been asked about it, she would have said that Anna Murray—as she always studiously called the Lady Anna—was not fit to be married.

The young lord, who a few months after his cousin's death had been old enough to take his seat in the House of Peers, was a gay-hearted, kindly young man, who had been brought home from sea at the age of twenty on the death of an elder brother. Some of the family had wished that he should go on with his profession in spite of the earldom; but it had been thought unfit that he should be an earl and a midshipman at the same time, and his cousin's death while he was still on shore settled the question. He was a fair-haired, well-made young lad, looking like a sailor, and every inch a gentleman. Had he believed that the Lady Anna was the Lady Anna, no earthly consideration would have induced him to meddle with the money. Since the old lord's death, he had lived chiefly with his uncle Charles Lovel, having passed some two or three months at Lovel Grange with his uncle and aunt. Charles Lovel was a clergyman, with a good living at Yoxham, in Yorkshire, who had married a rich wife, a woman with some two thousand a year of her own, and was therefore well to do in the world. His two sons were at Harrow, and he had one other child, a daughter. With them also lived a Miss Lovel, Aunt Julia—who was supposed of all the Lovels to be the wisest and most strong-minded. The parson, though a popular man, was not strong-minded. He was passionate, loud, generous, affectionate and indiscreet. He was very proud of his nephew's position as head of the family—and very full of his nephew's wrongs arising from the fraud of those Murray women. He was a violent Tory, and had heard much of the Keswick Radical. He never doubted for a moment that both old Thwaite and young Thwaite were busy in concocting an enormous scheme of plunder by which to enrich themselves. To hear that they had both been convicted and transported was the hope of his life. That a Radical should not be worthy of transportation was to him impossible. That a Radical should be honest was to him incredible. But he was a thoroughly humane and charitable man, whose good qualities were as little intelligible to old Thomas Thwaite, as were those of Thomas Thwaite to him.

To whom should the Solicitor-General first break the matter? He had already had some intercourse with the Lovels, and had not been impressed with a sense of the parson's wisdom. He was a Whig Solicitor-General, for there were still Whigs in those days, and Mr Lovel had not much liked him. Mr Flick had seen much of the family—having had many interviews with the young lord, with the parson, and with Aunt Julia. It was at last settled by Sir William's advice that a letter should be written to Aunt Julia by Mr Flick, suggesting that she should come up to town.

'Mr Lovel will be very angry,' said Mr Flick.

'We must do the best we can for our client,' said Sir William. The letter was written, and Miss Lovel was informed in Mr Flick's most discreet style that, as Sir William Patterson was anxious to discuss a matter concerning Lord Lovel's case in which a woman's voice would probably be of more service than that of a man, perhaps Miss Lovel would not object to the trouble of a journey to London. Miss Lovel did come up, and her brother came with her.

The interview took place in Sir William's chambers, and no one was present but Sir William, Miss Lovel, and Mr Flick. Mr Flick had been instructed to sit still and say nothing unless he were asked a question; and he obeyed his instructions. After some apologies, which were perhaps too soft and sweet—and which were by no means needed, as Miss Lovel herself, though very wise, was neither soft nor sweet—the great man thus opened his case. 'This is a very serious matter, Miss Lovel.'

'Very serious indeed.'

'You can hardly perhaps conceive how great a load of responsibility lies upon a lawyer's shoulders, when he has to give advice in such a case as this, when perhaps the prosperity of a whole family may turn upon his words.'

'He can only do his best.'

'Ah yes, Miss Lovel. That is easy to say; but how shall he know what is the best?'

'I suppose the truth will prevail at last. It is impossible to think that a young man such as my nephew should be swindled out of a noble fortune by the intrigues of two such women as these. I can't believe it, and I won't believe it. Of course I am only a woman, but I always thought it wrong to offer them even a shilling.' Sir William smiled and rubbed his head, fixing his eyes on those of the lady. Though he smiled she could see that there was real sadness in his face. 'You don't mean to say you doubt?' she said.

'Indeed I do.'

'You think that a wicked scheme like this can succeed before an English judge?'

'But if the scheme be not wicked? Let me tell you one or two things, Miss Lovel—or rather my own private opinion on one or two points. I do not believe that these two ladies are swindlers.'

'They are not ladies, and I feel sure that they are swindlers,' said Miss Lovel very firmly, turning her face as she spoke to the attorney.

'I am telling you, of course, merely my own opinion, and I will beg you to believe of me that in forming it I have used all the experience and all the caution which a long course of practice in these matters has taught me. Your nephew is entitled to my best services, and at the present moment I can perhaps do my duty to him most thoroughly by asking you to listen to me.' The lady closed her lips together, and sat silent. 'Whether Mrs Murray, as we have hitherto called her, was or was not the legal wife of the late Earl, I will not just now express an opinion; but I am sure that she thinks that she was. The marriage was formal and accurate. The Earl was tried for bigamy, and acquitted. The people with whom we have to do across the water, in Sicily, are not respectable. They cannot be induced to come here to give evidence. An English jury will be naturally averse to them. The question is one simply of facts for a jury, and we cannot go beyond a jury. Had the daughter been a son, it would have been in the House of Lords to decide which young man should be the peer—but as it is, it is simply a question of property, and of facts as to the ownership of the property. Should we lose the case, your nephew would be—a very poor man.'

'A very poor man, indeed, Sir William.'

'His position would be distressing. I am bound to say that we should go into court to try the case with very great distrust. Mr Flick quite agrees with me.'

'Quite so, Sir William,' said Mr Flick.

Miss Lovel again looked at the attorney, closed her lips tighter than ever, but did not say a word.

'In such cases as this prejudices will arise, Miss Lovel. It is natural that you and your family should be prejudiced against these ladies. For myself, I am not aware that anything true can be alleged against them.'

'The girl has disgraced herself with a tailor's son,' almost screamed Miss Lovel.

'You have been told so, but I do not believe it to be true. They were, no doubt, brought up as children together; and Mr Thwaite has been most kind to both the ladies.' It at once occurred to Miss Lovel that Sir William was a Whig, and that there was in truth but little difference between a Whig and a Radical. To be at heart a gentleman, or at heart a lady, it was, to her thinking, necessary to be a Tory. 'It would be a thousand pities that so noble a property should pass out of a family which, by its very splendour and ancient nobility, is placed in need of ample means.' On hearing this sentiment, which might have become even a Tory, Miss Lovel relaxed somewhat the muscles of her face. 'Were the Earl to marry his cousin—'

'She is not his cousin.'

'Were the Earl to marry the young lady who, it may be, will be proved to be his cousin, the whole difficulty would be cleared away.'

'Marry her!'

'I am told that she is very lovely, and that pains have been taken with her education. Her mother was well born and well bred. If you would get at the truth, Miss Lovel, you must teach yourself to believe that they are not swindlers. They are no more swindlers than I am a swindler. I will go further—though perhaps you, and the young Earl, and Mr Flick, may think me unfit to be entrusted any longer with this case, after such a declaration—I believe, though it is with a doubting belief, that the elder lady is the Countess Lovel, and that her daughter is the legitimate child and the heir of the late Earl.'

Mr Flick sat with his mouth open as he heard this—beating his breast almost with despair. His opinion tallied exactly with Sir William's. Indeed, it was by his opinion, hardly expressed, but perfectly understood, that Sir

William had been led. But he had not thought that Sir William would be so bold and candid.

'You believe that Anna Murray is the real heir?' gasped Miss Lovel.

'I do—with a doubting belief. I am inclined that way—having to form my opinion on very conflicting evidence.' Mr Flick was by this time quite sure that Sir William was right in his opinion—though perhaps wrong in declaring it—having been corroborated in his own belief by the reflex of it on a mind more powerful than his own. 'Thinking as I do,' continued Sir William—'with a natural bias towards my own client—what will a jury think, who will have no such bias? If they are cousins—distant cousins—why should they not marry and be happy, one bringing the title, and the other the wealth? There could be no more rational union, Miss Lovel.'

Then there was a long pause before anyone spoke a word. Mr Flick had been forbidden to speak, and Sir William, having made his proposition, was determined to await the lady's reply. The lady was aghast, and for a while could neither think nor utter a word. At last she opened her mouth. 'I must speak to my brother about this.'

'Quite right, Miss Lovel.'

'Now I may go, Sir William?'

'Good morning, Miss Lovel.' And Miss Lovel went.

'You have gone farther than I thought you would, Sir William,' said Mr Flick.

'I hardly went far enough, Mr Flick. We must go farther yet if we mean to save any part of the property for the young man. What should we gain, even if we succeeded in proving that the Earl was married in early life to the old Sicilian hag that still lives? She would inherit the property then—not the Earl.'

HERMAN MELVILLE

(1819–1891)

At the age of twenty, Herman Melville commenced a seafaring career that included such adventures as jumping ship in the Marquesas Islands and being taken captive by the Typee cannibals. He wrote of his South Seas experiences in the sensationally popular novels *Typee* and *Omoo.* In 1847 Melville married Elizabeth Shaw and returned to his native New York City. Four years later, he published *Moby-Dick,* a sprawling parable now regarded as his masterpiece. In his lifetime, however, Melville's later books (including *Moby-Dick*) failed to secure popularity or critical esteem; the author sank into obscurity as a customs inspector. His reputation soared in the twentieth century following the belated publication (in 1924) of the novella *Billy Budd, Sailor,* which Melville had written shortly before his death.

Billy Budd is set in 1797, a time of war between Great Britain and Revolutionary France. The British merchant ship *Rights of Man* is stopped by the warship *H.M.S. Bellipotent,* which impresses into military service the merchant vessel's best sailor, Billy Budd. Billy is a ``Handsome Sailor'' and a symbol of goodness to whom the *Bellipotent*'s diabolical master-at-arms, John Claggart, takes an unjustified dislike. Claggart's minions persecute Billy and unsuccessfully attempt to enlist Billy in a mutiny. The excerpt included here follows these events.

One element of the legal background of *Billy Budd* is the regime of military statutes, familiar to Melville from his naval service. Among these statutes, the Articles of War of 1749 and the Mutiny Act underlie the actions of the warship's Captain Edward Vere. Another element is a famous 1842 case, ``the *Somers* affair.'' The *U.S.S. Somers* was a naval training vessel on which three sailors were summarily hanged for mutiny. The ship's captain, Alexander Mackenzie, and lieutenant, Guert Gansevoort, were court-martialed after their return from sea and acquitted. Melville, who was Gansevoort's first cousin and who mentions the *Somers* in *Billy Budd,* may have patterned Vere, Billy, and Claggart on counterparts in this real-life incident.

Also in the background of the story is Melville's father-in-law, Lemuel Shaw, Chief Justice of the Massachusetts Supreme Court and one of the most important American jurists of the nineteenth century. Robert Cover, in his book *Justice Accused,* has suggested that Shaw may have been a model for Captain Vere. The Chief Justice's duties required him to return fugitive slaves in violation of his personal conscience, just as Vere's position requires him to apply the Articles of War to Billy even though he knows Billy to be morally innocent.

from BILLY BUDD

— 1891 —

Elsewhere it has been said that in the lack of frigates (of course better sailers than line-of-battle ships) in the English squadron up the Straits at that period, the *Bellipotent 74* was occasionally employed not only as an available substitute for a scout, but at times on detached service of more important kind. This was not alone because of her sailing qualities, not common in a ship of her rate, but quite as much, probably, that the character of her commander, it was thought, specially adapted him for any duty where under unforeseen difficulties a prompt initiative might have to be taken in some matter demanding knowledge and ability in addition to those qualities implied in good seamanship. It was on an expedition of the latter sort, a somewhat distant one, and when the *Bellipotent* was almost at her furthest remove from the fleet, that in the latter part of an afternoon watch she unexpectedly came in sight of a ship of the enemy. It proved to be a frigate. The latter, perceiving through the glass that the weight of men and metal would be heavily against her, invoking her light heels crowded sail to get away. After a chase urged almost against hope and lasting until about the middle of the first dogwatch, she signally succeeded in effecting her escape.

Not long after the pursuit had been given up, and ere the excitement incident thereto had altogether waned away, the master-at-arms, ascending from his cavernous sphere, made his appearance cap in hand by the mainmast respectfully waiting the notice of Captain Vere, then solitary walking the weather side of the quarter-deck, doubtless somewhat chafed at the failure of the pursuit. The spot where Claggart stood was the place allotted to men of lesser grades seeking some more particular interview either with the officer of the deck or the captain himself. But from the latter it was not often that a sailor or petty officer of those days would seek a hearing; only some exceptional cause would, according to established custom, have warranted that.

Presently, just as the commander, absorbed in his reflections, was on the point of turning aft in his promenade, he became sensible of Claggart's presence, and saw the doffed cap held in deferential expectancy. Here be it said that Captain Vere's personal knowledge of this petty officer had only begun at the time of the ship's last sailing from home, Claggart then for the first, in transfer from a ship detained for repairs, supplying on board the *Bellipotent* the place of a previous master-at-arms disabled and ashore.

No sooner did the commander observe who it was that now deferentially stood awaiting his notice than a peculiar expression came over him. It was not unlike that which uncontrollably will flit across the countenance of one at unawares encountering a person who, though known to him indeed, has hardly been long enough known for thorough knowledge, but something in whose aspect nevertheless now for the first provokes a vaguely repellent distaste. But coming to a stand and resuming much of his wonted official manner, save that a sort of impatience lurked in the intonation of the opening word, he said "Well? What is it, Master-at-arms?"

With the air of a subordinate grieved at the necessity of being a messenger of ill tidings, and while conscientiously determined to be frank yet equally resolved upon shunning overstatement, Claggart at this invitation, or rather summons to disburden, spoke up. What he said, conveyed in the language of no uneducated man, was to the effect following, if not altogether in these words, namely, that during the chase and preparations for the possible encounter he had seen enough to convince him that at least one sailor aboard was a dangerous character in a ship mustering some who not only had taken a guilty part in the late serious troubles, but others also who, like the man in question, had entered His Majesty's service under another form than enlistment.

At this point Captain Vere with some impatience interrupted him: "Be direct, man; say *impressed men.*"

Claggart made a gesture of subservience, and proceeded. Quite lately he (Claggart) had begun to suspect that on the gun decks some sort of movement prompted by the sailor in question was covertly going on, but he had not thought himself warranted in reporting the suspicion so long as it remained indistinct. But from what he had that afternoon observed in the man referred to, the suspicion of something clandestine going on had advanced to a point less removed from certainty. He deeply felt, he added, the serious responsibility assumed in making a report involving such possible consequences to the individual mainly concerned, besides tending to augment those natural anxieties which every naval commander must feel in view of extraordinary outbreaks so recent as those which, he sorrowfully said it, it needed not to name.

Now at the first broaching of the matter Captain Vere, taken by surprise, could not wholly dissemble his disquietude. But as Claggart went on, the former's aspect changed into restiveness under something in the testifier's manner in giving his testimony. However, he refrained from interrupting him. And Claggart, continuing, concluded with this: "God forbid, your honor, that the *Bellipotent*'s should be the experience of the ——"

"Never mind that!" here peremptorily broke in the superior, his face altering with anger, instinctively divining the ship that the other was about to name, one in which the Nore Mutiny had assumed a singularly tragical character that for a time jeopardized the life of its commander. Under the circumstances he was indignant at the purposed allusion. When the commissioned officers themselves were on all occasions very heedful how they referred to the recent events in the fleet, for a petty officer unnecessarily to allude to them in the presence of his captain, this struck him as a most immodest presumption. Besides, to his quick sense of self-respect it even looked under the circumstances something like an attempt to alarm him. Nor at first was he without some surprise that one who so far as he had hitherto come under his notice had shown considerable tact in his function should in this particular evince such lack of it.

But these thoughts and kindred dubious ones flitting across his mind were suddenly replaced by an intuitional surmise which, though as yet obscure in form, served practically to affect his reception of the ill tidings. Certain it is that, long versed in everything pertaining to the complicated gun-deck life, which like every other form of life has its secret mines and dubious side, the side popularly disclaimed, Captain Vere did not permit himself to be unduly disturbed by the general tenor of his subordinate's report.

Furthermore, if in view of recent events prompt action should be taken at the first palpable sign of recurring insubordination, for all that, not judicious would it be, he thought, to keep the idea of lingering disaffection alive by undue forwardness in crediting an informer, even if his own subordinate and charged among other things with police surveillance of the crew. This feeling would not perhaps have so prevailed with him were it not that upon a prior occasion the patriotic zeal officially evinced by Claggart had somewhat irritated him as appearing rather supersensible and strained. Furthermore, something even in the official's self-possessed and somewhat ostentatious manner in making his specifications strangely reminded him of a bondsman, a perjurous witness in a capital case before a court-martial ashore of which when a lieutenant he (Captain Vere) had been a member.

Now the peremptory check given to Claggart in the matter of the arrested allusion was quickly followed up by this: "You say that there is at least one dangerous man aboard. Name him."

"William Budd, a foretopman, your honor."

"William Budd!" repeated Captain Vere with unfeigned astonishment. "And mean you the man that Lieutenant Ratcliffe took from the merchantman not very long ago, the young fellow who seems to be so popular with the men—Billy, the Handsome Sailor, as they call him?"

"The same, your honor; but for all his youth and good looks, a deep one. Not for nothing does he insinuate himself into the good will of his shipmates, since at the least they will at a pinch say—all hands will—a good word for him, and at all hazards. Did Lieutenant Ratcliffe happen to tell your honor of that adroit fling of Budd's, jumping up in the cutter's bow under the merchantman's stern when he was being taken off? It is even masked by that sort of good-humored air that at heart he resents his impressment. You have but noted his fair cheek. A mantrap may be under the ruddy-tipped daisies."

Now the Handsome Sailor as a signal figure among the crew had naturally enough attracted the captain's attention from the first. Though in general not very demonstrative to his officers, he had congratulated Lieutenant Ratcliffe upon his good fortune in lighting on such a fine specimen of the *genus homo*, who in the nude might have posed for a statue of young Adam before the Fall. As to Billy's adieu to the ship *Rights-of-Man*, which the boarding lieutenant had indeed reported to him, but, in a deferential way, more as a good story than aught else, Captain Vere, though mistakenly understanding it as a satiric sally, had but thought so much the better of the impressed man for it; as a military sailor, admiring the spirit that could take an arbitrary enlistment so merrily and sensibly. The foretopman's conduct, too, so far as it had fallen under the captain's notice, had confirmed the first happy augury, while the new recruit's qualities as a "sailor-man" seemed to be such that he had thought of recommending him to the executive officer for promotion to a place that would more frequently bring him under his own observation, namely, the captaincy of the mizzentop, replacing there in the starboard watch a man not so young whom partly for that reason he deemed less fitted for the post. Be it parenthesized here that since the mizzentopmen have not to handle such breadths of heavy canvas as the lower sails on the mainmast and foremast, a young man if of the right stuff not only seems best adapted to duty there, but in fact is generally selected for the captaincy of that top, and the company under him are light hands and often but striplings. In sum, Captain Vere had from the beginning deemed Billy Budd to be what in the naval parlance of the time was called a "King's bargain": that is to say, for His Britannic Majesty's navy a capital investment at small outlay or none at all.

After a brief pause, during which the reminiscences above mentioned passed vividly through his mind and he weighed the import of Claggart's last suggestion conveyed in the phrase "mantrap under the daisies," and the more he weighed it the less reliance he felt in the informer's good faith, suddenly he turned upon him and in a low voice demanded: "Do you come to me, Master-at-arms, with so foggy a tale? As to Budd, cite me an act or spoken word of his confirmatory of what you in general charge against him. Stay," drawing nearer to him; "heed what you speak. Just now, and in a case like this, there is a yardarm-end for the false witness."

"Ah, your honor!" sighed Claggart, mildly shaking his shapely head as in sad deprecation of such unmerited severity of tone. Then, bridling—erecting himself as in virtuous self-assertion—he circumstantially alleged certain words and acts which collectively, if credited, led to presumptions mortally inculpating Budd. And for some of these averments, he added, substantiating proof was not far.

With gray eyes impatient and distrustful essaying to fathom to the bottom Claggart's calm violet ones, Captain Vere again heard him out; then for the moment stood ruminating. The mood he evinced, Claggart—himself for the time liberated from the other's scrutiny—steadily regarded with a look difficult to render: a look curious of the operation of his tactics, a look such as might have been that of the spokesman of the envious children of Jacob deceptively imposing upon the troubled patriarch the blood-dyed coat of young Joseph.

Though something exceptional in the moral quality of Captain Vere made him, in earnest encounter with a fellow man, a veritable touchstone of that man's essential nature, yet now as to Claggart and what was really going on in him his feeling partook less of intuitional conviction than of strong suspicion clogged by strange dubieties. The perplexity he evinced proceeded less from aught touching the man informed against—as Claggart doubtless opined—than from considerations how best to act in regard to the informer. At first, indeed, he was naturally for summoning that substantiation of his allegations which Claggart said was at hand. But such a proceeding would result in the matter at once getting abroad, which in the present stage of it, he thought, might undesirably affect the ship's company. If Claggart was a false witness—that closed the affair. And therefore, before trying the accusation, he would first practically test the accuser; and he thought this could be done in a quiet, undemonstrative way.

The measure he determined upon involved a shifting of the scene, a transfer to a place less exposed to observation than the broad quarter-deck. For although the few gun-room officers there at the time had, in due observance of naval etiquette, withdrawn to leeward the moment Captain Vere had begun his promenade on the deck's weather side; and though during the colloquy with Claggart they of course ventured not to diminish the distance; and though throughout the interview Captain Vere's voice was far from high, and Claggart's silvery and low; and the wind in the cordage and the wash of the sea helped the more to put them beyond earshot; nevertheless, the interview's continuance already had attracted observation from some topmen aloft and other sailors in the waist or further forward.

Having determined upon his measures, Captain Vere forth-with took action. Abruptly turning to Claggart, he asked, "Master-at-arms, is it now Budd's watch aloft?"

"No, your honor."

Whereupon, "Mr. Wilkes!" summoning the nearest midshipman. "Tell Albert to come to me." Albert was the captain's hammock-boy, a sort of sea valet in whose discretion and fidelity his master had much confidence. The lad appeared.

"You know Budd, the foretopman?"

"I do, sir."

"Go find him. It is his watch off. Manage to tell him out of earshot that he is wanted aft. Contrive it that he speaks to nobody. Keep him in talk yourself. And not till you get well aft here, not till then let him know that the place where he is wanted is my cabin. You understand. Go.—Master-at-arms, show yourself on the decks below, and when you think it time for Albert to be coming with his man, stand by quietly to follow the sailor in."

Now when the foretopman found himself in the cabin, closeted there, as it were, with the captain and Claggart, he was surprised enough. But it was a surprise unaccompanied by apprehension or distrust. To an immature nature essentially honest and humane, forewarning intimations of subtler danger from one's kind come tardily if at all. The only thing that took shape in the young sailor's mind was this: Yes, the captain, I have always thought, looks kindly upon me. Wonder if he's going to make me his coxswain. I should like that. And may be now he is going to ask the master-at-arms about me.

"Shut the door there, sentry," said the commander; "stand without, and let nobody come in.—Now, Master-at-arms, tell this man to his face what you told of him to me," and stood prepared to scrutinize the mutually confronting visages.

With the measured step and calm collected air of an asylum physician approaching in the public hall some patient beginning to show indications of a coming paroxysm, Claggart deliberately advanced within short range of Billy and, mesmerically looking him in the eye, briefly recapitulated the accusation.

Not at first did Billy take it in. When he did, the rose-tan of his cheek looked struck as by white leprosy. He stood like one impaled and gagged. Meanwhile the accuser's eyes, removing not as yet from the blue dilated ones, underwent a phenomenal change, their wonted rich violet color blurring into a muddy purple. Those lights of human intelligence, losing human expression, were gelidly protruding like the alien eyes of certain uncatalogued creatures of the deep. The first mesmeristic glance was one of serpent fascination; the last was as the paralyzing lurch of the torpedo fish.

"Speak, man!" said Captain Vere to the transfixed one, struck by his aspect even more than by Claggart's. "Speak! Defend yourself!" Which appeal caused but a strange dumb gesturing and gurgling in Billy; amazement at such an accusation so suddenly sprung on inexperienced nonage; this, and, it may be, horror of the accuser's eyes, serving to bring out his lurking defect and in this instance for the time intensifying it into a convulsed tongue-tie; while the intent head and entire form straining forward in an agony of ineffectual eagerness to obey the injunction to speak and defend himself, gave an expression to the face like that of a condemned vestal priestess in the moment of being buried alive, and in the first struggle against suffocation.

Though at the time Captain Vere was quite ignorant of Billy's liability to vocal impediment, he now immediately divined it, since vividly Billy's aspect recalled to him that of a bright young schoolmate of his whom he had once seen struck by much the same startling impotence in the act of eagerly rising in the class to be foremost in response to a testing question put to it by the master. Going close up to the young sailor, and laying a soothing hand on his shoulder, he said, "There is no hurry, my boy. Take your time, take your time." Contrary to the effect intended, these words so fatherly in tone, doubtless touching Billy's heart to the quick, prompted yet more violent efforts at utterance—efforts soon ending for the time in confirming the paralysis, and bringing to his face an expression which was as a crucifixion to behold. The next instant, quick as the flame from a discharged cannon at night, his right arm shot out, and Claggart dropped to the deck. Whether intentionally or but owing to the young athlete's superior height, the blow had taken effect full upon the forehead, so shapely and intellectual-looking a feature in the master-at-arms; so that the body fell over lengthwise, like a heavy plank tilted from erectness. A gasp or two, and he lay motionless.

"Fated boy," breathed Captain Vere in tone so low as to be almost a whisper, "what have you done! But here, help me."

The twain raised the felled one from the loins up into a sitting position. The spare form flexibly acquiesced, but inertly. It was like handling a dead snake. They lowered it back. Regaining erectness, Captain Vere with one hand covering his face stood to all appearance as impassive as the object at his feet. Was he absorbed in taking in all the bearings of the event and what was best not only now at once to be done, but also in the sequel? Slowly he uncovered his face; and the effect was as if the moon emerging from eclipse should reappear with quite another aspect than that which had gone into hiding. The father in him, manifested towards Billy thus far in the scene, was replaced by the military disciplinarian. In his official tone he bade the foretopman retire to a stateroom aft (pointing it out), and there remain till thence summoned. This order Billy in silence mechanically obeyed. Then going to the cabin door where it opened on the quarter-deck, Captain Vere said to the sentry without, "Tell somebody to send Albert here." When the lad appeared, his master so contrived it that he should not catch sight of the prone one. "Albert," he said to him, "tell the surgeon I wish to see him. You need not come back till called."

When the surgeon entered—a self-poised character of that grave sense and experience that hardly anything could take him aback—Captain Vere advanced to meet him, thus unconsciously intercepting his view of Claggart, and, interrupting the other's wonted ceremonious salutation, said, "Nay. Tell me how it is with yonder man," directing his attention to the prostrate one.

The surgeon looked, and for all his self-command somewhat started at the abrupt revelation. On Claggart's always pallid complexion, thick black blood was now oozing from nostril and ear. To the gazer's professional eye it was unmistakably no living man that he saw.

"Is it so, then?" said Captain Vere, intently watching him. "I thought it. But verify it." Whereupon the customary tests confirmed the surgeon's first glance, who now, looking up in unfeigned concern, cast a look of intense inquisitiveness upon his superior. But Captain Vere, with one hand to his brow, was standing motionless. Suddenly, catching the surgeon's arm convulsively, he exclaimed, pointing down to the body, "It is the divine judgment on Ananias! Look!"

Disturbed by the excited manner he had never before observed in the

Bellipotent's captain, and as yet wholly ignorant of the affair, the prudent surgeon nevertheless held his peace, only again looking an earnest interrogatory as to what it was that had resulted in such a tragedy.

But Captain Vere was now again motionless, standing absorbed in thought. Again starting, he vehemently exclaimed, "Struck dead by an angel of God! Yet the angel must hang!"

At these passionate interjections, mere incoherences to the listener as yet unapprised of the antecedents, the surgeon was profoundly discomposed. But now, as recollecting himself, Captain Vere in less passionate tone briefly related the circumstances leading up to the event. "But come; we must dispatch," he added. "Help me to remove him" (meaning the body) "to yonder compartment," designating one opposite that where the foretopman remained immured. Anew disturbed by a request that, as implying a desire for secrecy, seemed unaccountably strange to him, there was nothing for the subordinate to do but comply.

"Go now," said Captain Vere with something of his wonted manner. "Go now. I presently shall call a drumhead court. Tell the lieutenants what has happened, and tell Mr. Mordant" (meaning the captain of marines), "and charge them to keep the matter to themselves."

Full of disquietude and misgiving, the surgeon left the cabin. Was Captain Vere suddenly affected in his mind, or was it but a transient excitement, brought about by so strange and extraordinary a tragedy? As to the drumhead court, it struck the surgeon as impolitic, if nothing more. The thing to do, he thought, was to place Billy Budd in confinement, and in a way dictated by usage, and postpone further action in so extraordinary a case to such time as they should rejoin the squadron, and then refer it to the admiral. He recalled the unwonted agitation of Captain Vere and his excited exclamations, so at variance with his normal manner. Was he unhinged?

But assuming that he is, it is not so susceptible of proof. What then can the surgeon do? No more trying situation is conceivable than that of an officer subordinate under a captain whom he suspects to be not mad, indeed, but yet not quite unaffected in his intellects. To argue his order to him would be insolence. To resist him would be mutiny.

In obedience to Captain Vere, he communicated what had happened to the lieutenants and captain of marines, saying nothing as to the captain's state. They fully shared his own surprise and concern. Like him too, they seemed to think that such a matter should be referred to the admiral.

Who in the rainbow can draw the line where the violet tint ends and the orange tint begins? Distinctly we see the difference of the colors, but where exactly does the one first blendingly enter into the other? So with sanity and insanity. In pronounced cases there is no question about them. But in some supposed cases, in various degrees supposedly less pronounced, to draw the exact line of demarcation few will undertake, though for a fee becoming considerate some professional experts will. There is nothing namable but that some men will, or undertake to, do it for pay.

Whether Captain Vere, as the surgeon professionally and privately surmised, was really the sudden victim of any degree of aberration, every one must determine for himself by such light as this narrative may afford.

That the unhappy event which has been narrated could not have happened at a worse juncture was but too true. For it was close on the heel of the suppressed insurrections, an aftertime very critical to naval authority, demanding from every English sea commander two qualities not readily interfusable—prudence and rigor. Moreover, there was something crucial in the case.

In the jugglery of circumstances preceding and attending the event on board the *Bellipotent*, and in the light of that martial code whereby it was formally to be judged, innocence and guilt personified in Claggart and Budd in effect changed places. In a legal view the apparent victim of the tragedy was he who had sought to victimize a man blameless; and the indisputable deed of the latter, navally regarded, constituted the most heinous of military crimes. Yet more. The essential right and wrong involved in the matter, the clearer that might be, so much the worse for the responsibility of a loyal sea commander, inasmuch as he was not authorized to determine the matter on that primitive basis.

Small wonder then that the *Bellipotent*'s captain, though in general a man of rapid decision, felt that circumspectness not less than promptitude was necessary. Until he could decide upon his course, and in each detail; and not only so, but until the concluding measure was upon the point of being enacted, he deemed it advisable, in view of all the circumstances, to guard as much as possible against publicity. Here he may or may not have erred. Certain it is, however, that subsequently in the confidential talk of more than one or two gun rooms and cabins he was not a little criticized by some officers, a fact imputed by his friends and vehemently by his cousin Jack Denton to professional jealousy of Starry Vere. Some imaginative ground for invidious comment there was. The maintenance of secrecy in the matter, the confining all knowledge of it for a time to the place where the homicide occurred, the quarter-deck cabin; in these particulars lurked some resemblance to the policy adopted in those tragedies of the palace which have occurred more than once in the capital founded by Peter the Barbarian.

The case indeed was such that fain would the *Bellipotent*'s captain have deferred taking any action whatever respecting it further than to keep the foretopman a close prisoner till the ship rejoined the squadron and then submitting the matter to the judgment of his admiral.

But a true military officer is in one particular like a true monk. Not with more of self-abnegation will the latter keep his vows of monastic obedience than the former his vows of allegiance to martial duty.

Feeling that unless quick action was taken on it, the deed of the foretopman, so soon as it should be known on the gun decks, would tend to awaken any slumbering embers of the Nore among the crew, a sense of the urgency of the case overruled in Captain Vere every other consideration. But though a conscientious disciplinarian, he was no lover of authority for mere authority's sake. Very far was he from embracing opportunities for monopolizing to himself the perils of moral responsibility, none at least that could properly be referred to an official superior or shared with him by his official equals or even subordinates. So thinking, he was glad it would not be at variance with usage to turn the matter over to a summary court of his own officers, reserving to himself, as the one on whom the ultimate accountability would rest, the right of maintaining a supervision of it, or formally or informally interposing at need. Accordingly a drumhead court was summarily convened, he electing the individuals composing it: the first lieutenant, the captain of marines, and the sailing master.

In associating an officer of marines with the sea lieutenant and the sailing master in a case having to do with a sailor, the commander perhaps deviated from general custom. He was prompted thereto by the circumstance that he took that soldier to be a judicious person, thoughtful, and not altogether incapable of grappling with a difficult case unprecedented in his prior experience. Yet even as to him he was not without some latent misgiving, for withal he was an extremely good-natured man, an enjoyer of his dinner, a sound sleeper, and inclined to obesity—a man who though he would always maintain his manhood in battle might not prove altogether reliable in a moral dilemma involving aught of the tragic. As to the first lieutenant and the sailing master, Captain Vere could not but be aware that though honest natures, of approved gallantry upon occasion, their intelligence was mostly confined to the matter of active seamanship and the fighting demands of their profession.

The court was held in the same cabin where the unfortunate affair had taken place. This cabin, the commander's, embraced the entire area under the poop deck. Aft, and on either side, was a small stateroom, the one now temporarily a jail and the other a dead-house, and yet smaller compartment, leaving a space between expanding forward into a goodly oblong of length coinciding with the ship's beam. A skylight of moderate dimension was overhead, and at each end of the oblong space were two sashed porthole windows easily convertible back into embrasures for short carronades.

All being quickly in readiness, Billy Budd was arraigned, Captain Vere necessarily appearing as the sole witness in the case, and as such temporarily sinking his rank, though singularly maintaining it in a matter apparently trivial, namely, that he testified from the ship's weather side, with that object having caused the court to sit on the lee side. Concisely he narrated all that had led up to the catastrophe, omitting nothing in Claggart's accusation and deposing as to the manner in which the prisoner had received it. At this testimony the three officers glanced with no little surprise at Billy Budd, the last man they would have suspected either of the mutinous design alleged by Claggart or the undeniable deed he himself had done. The first lieutenant, taking judicial primacy and turning toward the prisoner, said, "Captain Vere has spoken. Is it or is it not as Captain Vere says?"

In response came syllables not so much impeded in the utterance as might have been anticipated. They were these: "Captain Vere tells the truth. It is just as Captain Vere says, but it is not as the master-at-arms said. I have eaten the King's bread and I am true to the King."

"I believe you, my man," said the witness, his voice indicating a suppressed emotion not otherwise betrayed.

"God will bless you for that, your honor!" not without stammering said Billy, and all but broke down. But immediately he was recalled to self-control by another question, to which with the same emotional difficulty of utterance he said, "No, there was no malice between us. I never bore malice against the master-at-arms. I am sorry that he is dead. I did not mean to kill him. Could I have used my tongue I would not have struck him. But he foully lied to my face and in presence of my captain, and I had to say something, and I could only say it with a blow, God help me!"

In the impulsive aboveboard manner of the frank one the court saw confirmed all that was implied in words that just previously had perplexed them, coming as they did from the testifier to the tragedy and promptly following Billy's impassioned disclaimer of mutinous intent—Captain Vere's words, "I believe you, my man."

Next it was asked of him whether he knew of or suspected aught savoring of incipient trouble (meaning mutiny, though the explicit term was avoided) going on in any section of the ship's company.

The reply lingered. This was naturally imputed by the court to the same vocal embarrassment which had retarded or obstructed previous answers. But in main it was otherwise here, the question immediately recalling to Billy's mind the interview with the afterguardsman in the forechains. But an innate repugnance to playing a part at all approaching that of an informer against one's own shipmates—the same erring sense of uninstructed honor which had stood in the way of his reporting the matter at the time, though as a loyal man-of-war's man it was incumbent on him, and failure so to do, if charged against him and proven, would have subjected him to the heaviest of penalties; this, with the blind feeling now his that nothing really was being hatched, prevailed with him. When the answer came it was a negative.

"One question more," said the officer of marines, now first speaking and with a troubled earnestness. "You tell us that what the master-at-arms said against you was a lie. Now why should he have so lied, so maliciously lied, since you declare there was no malice between you?"

At that question, unintentionally touching on a spiritual sphere wholly obscure to Billy's thoughts, he was nonplussed, evincing a confusion indeed that some observers, such as can readily be imagined, would have construed into involuntary evidence of hidden guilt. Nevertheless, he strove some way to answer, but all at once relinquished the vain endeavor, at the same time turning an appealing glance towards Captain Vere as deeming him his best helper and friend. Captain Vere, who had been seated for a time, rose to his feet, addressing the interrogator. "The question you put to him comes naturally enough. But how can he rightly answer it?—or anybody else, unless indeed it be he who lies within there," designating the compartment where lay the corpse. "But the prone one there will not rise to our summons. In effect, though, as it seems to me, the point you make is hardly material. Quite aside from any conceivable motive actuating the master-at-arms, and irrespective of the provocation to the blow, a martial court must needs in the present case confine its attention to the blow's consequence, which consequence justly is to be deemed not otherwise than as the striker's deed."

This utterance, the full significance of which it was not at all likely that Billy took in, nevertheless caused him to turn a wistful interrogative look toward the speaker, a look in its dumb expressiveness not unlike that which a dog of generous breed might turn upon his master, seeking in his face some elucidation of a previous gesture ambiguous to the canine intelligence. Nor was the same utterance without marked effect upon the three officers, more especially the soldier. Couched in it seemed to them a meaning unanticipated, involving a prejudgment on the speaker's part. It served to augment a mental disturbance previously evident enough.

The soldier once more spoke, in a tone of suggestive dubiety addressing at once his associates and Captain Vere: "Nobody is present—none of the ship's company, I mean—who might shed lateral light, if any is to be had, upon what remains mysterious in this matter."

"That is thoughtfully put," said Captain Vere; "I see your drift. Ay, there is a mystery; but, to use a scriptural phrase, it is a 'mystery of iniquity,' a matter for psychologic theologians to discuss. But what has a military court to do with it? Not to add that for us any possible investigation of it is cut off by the lasting tongue-tie of—him—in yonder," again designating the mortuary stateroom. "The prisoner's deed— with that alone we have to do."

To this, and particularly the closing reiteration, the marine soldier, knowing not how aptly to reply, sadly abstained from saying aught. The first lieutenant, who at the outset had not unnaturally assumed primacy in the court, now overrulingly instructed by a glance from Captain Vere, a glance more effective than words, resumed that primacy. Turning to the prisoner, "Budd," he said, and scarce in equable tones, "Budd, if you have aught further to say for yourself, say it now."

Upon this the young sailor turned another quick glance toward Captain Vere; then, as taking a hint from that aspect, a hint confirming his own instinct that silence was now best, replied to the lieutenant, "I have said all, sir."

The marine—the same who had been the sentinel without the cabin door at the time that the foretopman, followed by the master-at-arms, entered it—he, standing by the sailor throughout these judicial proceedings, was now directed to take him back to the after compartment originally assigned to the prisoner and his custodian. As the twain disappeared from view, the three officers, as partially liberated from some inward constraint associated with Billy's mere presence, simultaneously stirred in their seats. They exchanged looks of troubled indecision, yet feeling that decide they must and without long delay. For Captain Vere, he for the time stood—unconsciously with his back toward them, apparently in one of his absent fits—gazing out from a sashed porthole to windward upon the monotonous blank of the twilight sea. But the court's silence continuing, broken only at moments by brief consultations, in low earnest tones, this served to arouse him and energize him. Turning, he to-and-fro paced the cabin athwart; in the returning ascent to windward climbing the slant deck in the ship's lee roll, without knowing it symbolizing thus in his action a mind resolute to surmount difficulties even if against primitive instincts strong as the wind and the sea. Presently he came to a stand before the three. After scanning their faces he stood less as mustering his thoughts for expression than as one inly deliberating how best to put them to well-meaning men not intellectually mature, men with whom it was necessary to demonstrate certain principles that were axioms to himself. Similar impatience as to talking is perhaps one reason that deters some minds from addressing any popular assemblies.

When speak he did, something, both in the substance of what he said and his manner of saying it, showed the influence of unshared studies modifying and tempering the practical training of an active career. This, along with his phraseology, now and then was suggestive of the grounds whereon rested that imputation of a certain pedantry socially alleged against him by certain naval men of wholly practical cast, captains who nevertheless would frankly concede that His Majesty's navy mustered no more efficient officer of their grade than Starry Vere.

What he said was to this effect: "Hitherto I have been but the witness, little more; and I should hardly think now to take another tone, that of your coadjutor for the time, did I not perceive in you—at the crisis too—a troubled hesitancy, proceeding, I doubt not, from the clash of military duty with moral scruple—scruple vitalized by compassion. For the compassion, how can I otherwise than share it? But, mindful of paramount obligations, I strive against scruples that may tend to enervate decision. Not, gentlemen, that I hide from myself that the case is an exceptional one. Speculatively regarded, it well might be referred to a jury of casuists. But for us here, acting not as casuists or moralists, it is a case practical, and under martial law practically to be dealt with.

"But your scruples: do they move as in a dusk? Challenge them. Make them advance and declare themselves. Come now; do they import something like this: If, mindless of palliating circumstances, we are bound to regard the death of the master-at-arms as the prisoner's deed, then does that deed constitute a capital crime whereof the penalty is a mortal one. But in natural justice is nothing but the prisoner's overt act to be considered? How can we adjudge to summary and shameful death a fellow creature innocent before God, and whom we feel to be so?—Does that state it aright? You sign sad assent. Well, I too feel that, the full force of that. It is Nature. But do these buttons that we wear attest that our allegiance is to Nature? No, to the King. Though the ocean, which is inviolate Nature primeval, though this be the element where we move and have our being as sailors, yet as the King's officers lies our duty in a sphere correspondingly natural? So little is that true, that in receiving our commissions we in the most important regards ceased to be natural free agents. When war is declared are we the commissioned fighters previously consulted? We fight at command. If our judgments approve the war, that is but coincidence. So in other particulars. So now. For suppose condemnation to follow these present proceedings. Would it be so much we ourselves that would condemn as it would be martial law operating through us? For that law and the rigor of it, we are not responsible. Our vowed responsibility is in this: That however pitilessly that law may operate in any instances, we nevertheless adhere to it and administer it.

"But the exceptional in the matter moves the hearts within you. Even so too is mine moved. But let not warm hearts betray heads that should be cool. Ashore in a criminal case, will an upright judge allow himself off the bench to be waylaid by some tender kinswoman of the accused seeking to touch him with her tearful plea? Well, the heart here, sometimes the feminine in man, is as that piteous woman, and hard though it be, she must here be ruled out."

He paused, earnestly studying them for a moment; then resumed.

"But something in your aspect seems to urge that it is not solely the heart that moves in you, but also the conscience, the private conscience. But tell me whether or not, occupying the position we do, private conscience should not yield to that imperial one formulated in the code under which alone we officially proceed?"

Here the three men moved in their seats, less convinced than agitated by the course of an argument troubling but the more the spontaneous conflict within.

Perceiving which, the speaker paused for a moment; then abruptly changing his tone, went on.

"To steady us a bit, let us recur to the facts.—In wartime at sea a man-of-war's man strikes his superior in grade, and the blow kills. Apart from its effect the blow itself is, according to the Articles of War, a capital crime. Furthermore——"

"Ay, sir," emotionally broke in the officer of marines, "in one sense it was. But surely Budd purposed neither mutiny nor homicide."

"Surely not, my good man. And before a court less arbitrary and more merciful than a martial one, that plea would largely extenuate. At the Last Assizes it shall acquit. But how here? We proceed under the law of the Mutiny Act. In feature no child can resemble his father more than that Act resembles in spirit the thing from which it derives—War. In His Majesty's service—in this ship, indeed—there are Englishmen forced to fight for the King against their will. Against their conscience, for aught we know.

Though as their fellow creatures some of us may appreciate their position, yet as navy officers what reck we of it? Still less recks the enemy. Our impressed men he would fain cut down in the same swath with our volunteers. As regards the enemy's naval conscripts, some of whom may even share our own abhorrence of the regicidal French Directory, it is the same on our side. War looks but to the frontage, the appearance. And the Mutiny Act, War's child, takes after the father. Budd's intent or non-intent is nothing to the purpose.

"But while, put to it by those anxieties in you which I cannot but respect, I only repeat myself—while thus strangely we prolong proceedings that should be summary—the enemy may be sighted and an engagement result. We must do; and one of two things must we do—condemn or let go."

"Can we not convict and yet mitigate the penalty?" asked the sailing master, here speaking, and falteringly, for the first.

"Gentlemen, were that clearly lawful for us under the circumstances, consider the consequences of such clemency. The people" (meaning the ship's company) "have native sense; most of them are familiar with our naval usage and tradition; and how would they take it? Even could you explain to them—which our official position forbids—they, long molded by arbitrary discipline, have not that kind of intelligent responsiveness that might qualify them to comprehend and discriminate. No, to the people the foretopman's deed, however it be worded in the announcement, will be plain homicide committed in a flagrant act of mutiny. What penalty for that should follow, they know. But it does not follow. *Why?* they will ruminate. You know what sailors are. Will they not revert to the recent outbreak at the Nore? Ay. They know the well-founded alarm—the panic it struck throughout England. Your clement sentence they would account pusillanimous. They would think that we flinch, that we are afraid of them—afraid of practicing a lawful rigor singularly demanded at this juncture, lest it should provoke new troubles. What shame to us such as a conjecture on their part, and how deadly to discipline. You see then, whither, prompted by duty and the law, I steadfastly drive. But I beseech you, my friends, do not take me amiss. I feel as you do for this unfortunate boy. But did he know our hearts, I take him to be of that generous nature that he would feel even for us on whom in this military necessity so heavy a compulsion is laid."

With that, crossing the deck he resumed his place by the sashed porthole, tacitly leaving the three to come to a decision. On the cabin's opposite side the troubled court sat silent. Loyal lieges, plain and practical, though at bottom they dissented from some points Captain Vere had put to them, they were without the faculty, hardly had the inclination, to gainsay one whom they felt to be an earnest man, one too not less their superior in mind than in naval rank. But it is not improbable that even such of his words as were not without influence over them, less came home to them than his closing appeal to their instinct as sea offices: in the forethought he threw out as to the practical consequences to discipline, considering the unconfirmed tone of the fleet at the time, should a man-of-war's man's violent killing at sea of a superior in grade be allowed to pass for aught else than a capital crime demanding prompt infliction of the penalty.

Not unlikely they were brought to something more or less akin to that harassed frame of mind which in the year 1842 actuated the commander of the U.S. brig-of-war *Somers* to resolve, under the so-called Articles of War, Articles modeled upon the English Mutiny Act, to resolve upon the execution at sea of a midshipman and two sailors as mutineers designing the seizure of the brig. Which resolution was carried out though in a time of peace and within not many days' sail of home. An act vindicated by a naval court of inquiry subsequently convened ashore. History, and here cited without comment. True, the circumstances on board the *Somers* were different from those on board the *Bellipotent*. But the urgency felt, well-warranted or otherwise, was much the same.

Says a writer whom few know, "Forty years after a battle it is easy for a noncombatant to reason about how it ought to have been fought. It is another thing personally and under fire to have to direct the fighting while involved in the obscuring smoke of it. Much so with respect to other emergencies involving considerations both practical and moral, and when it is imperative promptly to act. The greater the fog the more it imperils the steamer, and speed is put on though at the hazard of running somebody down. Little ween the snug card players in the cabin of the responsibilities of the sleepless man on the bridge."

In brief, Billy Budd was formally convicted and sentenced to be hung at the yardarm in the early morning watch, it being now night. Otherwise, as is customary in such cases, the sentence would forthwith have been carried out. In wartime on the field or in the fleet, a mortal punishment decreed by a drumhead court—on the field sometimes decreed by but a nod from the general—follows without delay on the heel of conviction, without appeal.

It was Captain Vere himself who of his own motion communicated the finding of the court to the prisoner, for that purpose going to the compartment where he was in custody and bidding the marine there to withdraw for the time.

Beyond the communication of the sentence, what took place at this interview was never known. But in view of the character of the twain briefly closeted in that stateroom, each radically sharing in the rarer qualities of our nature—so rare indeed as to be all but incredible to average minds however much cultivated—some conjectures may be ventured.

It would have been in consonance with the spirit of Captain Vere should he on this occasion have concealed nothing from the condemned one—should he indeed have frankly disclosed to him the part he himself had played in bringing about the decision, at the same time revealing his actuating motives. On Billy's side it is not improbable that such a confession would have been received in much the same spirit that prompted it. Not without a sort of joy, indeed, he might have appreciated the brave opinion of him implied in his captain's making such a confidant of him. Nor, as to the sentence itself, could he have been insensible that it was imparted to him as to one not afraid to die. Even more may have been. Captain Vere in end may have developed the passion sometimes latent under an exterior stoical or indifferent. He was old enough to have been Billy's father. The austere devotee of military duty, letting himself melt back into what remains primeval in our formalized humanity, may in end have caught Billy to his heart, even as Abraham may have caught young Isaac on the brink of resolutely offering him up in obedience to the exacting behest. But there is no telling the sacrament, seldom if in any case revealed to the gadding world, wherever under circumstances at all akin to those here attempted to be set forth two of great Nature's nobler order embrace. There is privacy at the time, inviolable to the survivor; and holy oblivion, the sequel to each diviner magnanimity, providentially covers all at last.

The first to encounter Captain Vere in act of leaving the compartment was the senior lieutenant. The face he beheld, for the moment one expressive of the agony of the strong, was to that officer, though a man of fifty, a startling revelation. That the condemned one suffered less than he who mainly had effected the condemnation was apparently indicated by the former's exclamation in the scene soon perforce to be touched upon.

Of a series of incidents within a brief term rapidly following each other, the adequate narration may take up a term less brief, especially if explanation or comment here and there seem requisite to the better understanding of such incidents. Between the entrance into the cabin of him who never left it alive, and him who when he did leave it left it as one condemned to die; between this and the closeted interview just given, less than an hour and a half had elapsed. It was an interval long enough, however, to awaken speculations among no few of the ship's company as to what it was that could be detaining in the cabin the master-at-arms and the sailor; for a rumor that both of them had been seen to enter it and neither of them had been seen to emerge, this rumor had got abroad upon the gun decks and in the tops, the people of a great warship being in one respect like villagers, taking microscopic note of every outward movement or non-movement going on. When therefore, in weather not at all tempestuous, all hands were called in the second dogwatch, a summons under such circumstances not usual in those hours, the crew were not wholly unprepared for some announcement extraordinary, one having connection too with the continued absence of the two men from their wonted haunts.

There was a moderate sea at the time; and the moon, newly risen and near to being at its full, silvered the white spar deck wherever not blotted by the clear-cut shadows horizontally thrown of fixtures and moving men. On either side the quarter-deck the marine guard under arms was drawn up; and Captain Vere, standing in his place surrounded by all the wardroom officers, addressed his men. In so doing, his manner showed neither more nor less than that properly pertaining to his supreme position aboard his own ship. In clear terms and concise he told them what had taken place in the cabin: that the master-at-arms was dead, that he who had killed him had been already tried by a summary court and condemned to death, and that the execution would take place in the early morning watch. The word *mutiny* was not named in what he said. He refrained too from making the occasion an opportunity for any preachment as to the maintenance of discipline, thinking perhaps that under existing circumstances in the navy the consequence of violating discipline should be made to speak for itself.

Their captain's announcement was listened to by the throng of standing sailors in a dumbness like that of a seated congregation of believers in hell listening to the clergyman's announcement of his Calvinistic text.

At the close, however, a confused murmur went up. It began to wax. All but instantly, then, at a sign, it was pierced and suppressed by shrill whistles of the boatswain and his mates. The word was given to about ship.

To be prepared for burial Claggart's body was delivered to certain petty officers of his mess. And here, not to clog the sequel with lateral matters, it may be added that at a suitable hour, the master-at-arms was committed to the sea with every funeral honor properly belonging to his naval grade.

In this proceeding as in every public one growing out of the tragedy strict adherence to usage was observed. Nor in any point could it have been at all deviated from, either with respect to Claggart or Billy Budd, without begetting undesirable speculations in the ship's company, sailors, and more particularly men-of-war's men, being of all men the greatest sticklers for usage. For similar cause, all communication between Captain Vere and the condemned one ended with the closeted interview already given, the latter being now surrendered to the ordinary routine preliminary to the end. His transfer under guard from the captain's quarters was effected without unusual precautions—at least no visible ones. If possible, not to let the men so much as surmise that their officers anticipate aught amiss from them is the tacit rule in a military ship. And the more that some sort of trouble should really be apprehended, the more do the officers keep that apprehension to themselves, though not the less unostentatious vigilance may be augmented. In the present instance, the sentry placed over the prisoner had strict orders to let no one have communication with him but the chaplain. And certain unobtrusive measures were taken absolutely to insure this point.

In a seventy-four of the old order the deck known as the upper gun deck was the one covered over by the spar deck, which last, though not without its armament, was for the most part exposed to the weather. In general it was at all hours free from hammocks; those of the crew swinging on the lower gun deck and berth deck, the latter being not only a dormitory but also the place for the stowing of the sailors' bags, and on both sides lined with the large chests or movable pantries of the many messes of the men.

On the starboard side of the *Bellipotent*'s upper gun deck, behold Billy Budd under sentry lying prone in irons in one of the bays formed by the regular spacing of the guns comprising the batteries on either side. All these pieces were of the heavier caliber of that period. Mounted on lumbering wooden carriages, they were hampered with cumbersome harness of breeching and strong side-tackles for running them out. Guns and carriages, together with the long rammers and shorter linstocks lodged in loops overhead—all these, as customary, were painted black; and the heavy hempen breechings, tarred to the same tint, wore the like livery of the undertakers. In contrast with the funereal hue of these surroundings, the prone sailor's exterior apparel, white jumper and white duck trousers, each more or less soiled, dimly glimmered in the obscure light of the bay like a patch of discolored snow in early April lingering at some upland cave's black mouth. In effect he is already in his shroud, or the garments that shall serve him in lieu of one. Over him but scarce illuminating him, two battle lanterns swing from two massive beams of the deck above. Fed with the oil supplied by the war contractors (whose gains, honest or otherwise, are in every land an anticipated portion of the harvest of death), with flickering splashes of dirty yellow light they pollute the pale moonshine all but ineffectually struggling in obstructed flecks through the open ports from which the tampioned cannon protrude. Other lanterns at intervals serve but to bring out somewhat the obscurer bays which, like small confessionals or side-chapels in a cathedral, branch from the long dim-vistaed broad aisle between the two batteries of that covered tier.

Such was the deck where now lay the Handsome Sailor. Through the rose-tan of his complexion no pallor could have shown. It would have taken days of sequestration from the winds and the sun to have brought about the effacement of that. But the skeleton in the cheekbone at the point of its angle was just beginning delicately to be defined under the warm-tinted skin. In fervid hearts self-contained, some brief experiences devour our human tissue as secret fire in a ship's hold consumes cotton in the bale.

But now lying between the two guns, as nipped in the vice of fate, Billy's agony, mainly proceeding from a generous young heart's virgin experience of the diabolical incarnate and effective in some men—the tension of that agony was over now. It survived not the something healing in the closeted interview with Captain Vere. Without movement, he lay as in a trance, that adolescent expression previously noted as his taking on something akin to the look of a slumbering child in the cradle when the warm hearth-glow of the still chamber at night plays on the dimples that at whiles mysteriously form in the cheek, silently coming and going there. For now and then in the gyved one's trance a serene happy light born of some wandering reminiscence or dream would diffuse itself over his face, and then wane away only anew to return.

The chaplain, coming to see him and finding him thus, and perceiving no sign that he was conscious of his presence, attentively regarded him for a space, then slipping aside, withdrew for the time, peradventure feeling that even he, the minister of Christ though receiving his stipend from Mars, had no consolation to proffer which could result in a peace transcending that which he beheld. But in the small hours he came again. And the prisoner, now awake to his surroundings, noticed his approach, and civilly, all but cheerfully, welcomed him. But it was to little purpose that in the interview following, the good man sought to bring Billy Budd to some godly understanding that he must die, and at dawn. True, Billy himself freely referred to his death as a thing close at hand; but it was something in the way that children will refer to death in general, who yet among their other sports will play a funeral with hearse and mourners.

Not that like children Billy was incapable of conceiving what death really is. No, but he was wholly without irrational fear of it, a fear more prevalent in highly civilized communities than those so-called barbarous ones which in all respects stand nearer to unadulterate Nature. And, as elsewhere said, a barbarian Billy radically was—as much so, for all the costume, as his countrymen the British captives, living trophies, made to march in the Roman triumph of Germanicus. Quite as much so as those later barbarians, young men probably, and picked specimens among the earlier British converts to Christianity, at least nominally such, taken to Rome (as today converts from lesser isles of the sea may be taken to London), of whom the Pope of that time, admiring the strangeness of their personal beauty so unlike the Italian stamp, their clear ruddy complexion and curled flaxen locks, exclaimed, "Angles" (meaning *English*, the modern derivative), "Angles, do you call them? And is it because they look so like angels?" Had it been later in time, one would think that the Pope had in mind Fra Angelico's seraphs, some of whom, plucking apples in gardens of the Hesperides, have the faint rosebud complexion of the more beautiful English girls.

If in vain the good chaplain sought to impress the young barbarian with ideas of death akin to those conveyed in the skull, dial, and crossbones on old tombstones, equally futile to all appearance were his efforts to bring home to him the thought of salvation and a Savior. Billy listened, but less out of awe or reverence, perhaps, than from a certain natural politeness, doubtless at bottom regarding all that in much the same way that most mariners of his class take any discourse abstract or out of the common tone of the workaday world. And this sailor way of taking clerical discourse is not wholly unlike the way in which the primer of Christianity, full of transcendent miracles, was received long ago on tropic isles by any superior *savage*, so called—a Tahitian, say, of Captain Cook's time or shortly after that time. Out of natural courtesy he received, but did not appropriate. It was like a gift placed in the palm of an outreached hand upon which the fingers do not close.

But the *Bellipotent*'s chaplain was a discreet man possessing the good sense of a good heart. So he insisted not in his vocation here. At the instance of Captain Vere, a lieutenant had apprised him of pretty much everything as to Billy: and since he felt that innocence was even a better thing than religion wherewith to go to Judgment, he reluctantly withdrew; but in his emotion not without first performing an act strange enough in an Englishman, and under the circumstances yet more so in any regular priest. Stooping over, he kissed on the fair cheek his fellow man, a felon in martial law, one whom though on the confines of death he felt he could never convert to a dogma; nor for all that did he fear for his future.

Marvel not that having been made acquainted with the young sailor's essential innocence the worthy man lifted not a finger to avert the doom of such a martyr to martial discipline. So to do would not only have been as idle as invoking the desert, but would also have been an audacious transgression of the bounds of his function, one as exactly prescribed to him by military law as that of the boatswain or any other naval officer. Bluntly put, a chaplain is the minister of the Prince of Peace serving in the host of the God of War—Mars. As such, he is as incongruous as a musket would be on the altar at Christmas. Why, then, is he there? Because he indirectly subserves the purpose attested by the cannon; because too he lends the sanction of the religion of the meek to that which practically is the abrogation of everything but brute Force.

The night so luminous on the spar deck, but otherwise on the cavernous ones below, levels so like the tiered galleries in a coal mine—the luminous night passed away. But like the prophet in the chariot disappearing in heaven and dropping his mantle to Elisha, the withdrawing night transferred its pale robe to the breaking day. A meek, shy light appeared in the East, where stretched a diaphanous fleece of white furrowed vapor. That light slowly waxed. Suddenly *eight bells* was struck aft, responded to by one louder metallic stroke from forward. It was four o'clock in the morning. Instantly the silver whistles were heard summoning all hands to witness punishment. Up through the great hatchways rimmed with racks of heavy shot the watch below came pouring, overspreading with the watch already on deck the space between the mainmast and foremast including that occupied by the capacious launch and the black booms tiered on either side of it, boat and booms making a summit of observation for the powder-boys and younger tars. A different group comprising one watch of topmen leaned over the rail of that sea balcony, no small one in a seventy-four, looking down on the crowd below. Man or boy, none spake but in whisper, and few spake at all. Captain Vere—as before, the central figure among the assembled commissioned officers—stood nigh the break of the poop deck facing forward. Just below him on the quarter-deck the marines in full equipment were drawn up much as at the scene of the promulgated sentence.

At sea in the old time, the execution by halter of a military sailor was generally from the foreyard. In the present instance, for special reasons the mainyard was assigned. Under an arm of that yard the prisoner was presently brought up, the chaplain attending him. It was noted at the time, and remarked upon afterwards, that in this final scene the good man evinced little or nothing of the perfunctory. Brief speech indeed he had with the condemned one, but the genuine Gospel was less on his tongue than in his aspect and manner towards him. The final preparations personal to the latter being speedily brought to an end by two boatswain's mates, the consummation impended. Billy stood facing aft. At the penultimate moment, his words, his only ones, words wholly unobstructed in the utterance, were these: "God bless Captain Vere!" Syllables so unanticipated coming from one with the ignominious hemp about his neck—a conventional felon's benediction directed aft towards the quarters of honor; syllables too delivered in the clear melody of a singing bird on the point of launching from the twig—had a phenomenal effect, not unenhanced by the rare personal beauty of the young sailor, spiritualized now through late experiences so poignantly profound.

Without volition, as it were, as if indeed the ship's populace were but the vehicles of some vocal current electric, with one voice from alow and aloft came a resonant sympathetic echo: "God bless Captain Vere!" And yet at that instant Billy alone must have been in their hearts, even as in their eyes.

At the pronounced words and the spontaneous echo that voluminously rebounded them, Captain Vere, either through stoic self-control or a sort of momentary paralysis induced by emotional shock, stood erectly rigid as a musket in the ship-armorer's rack.

The hull, deliberately recovering from the periodic roll to leeward, was just regaining an even keel when the last signal, a preconcerted dumb one, was given. At the same moment it chanced that the vapory fleece hanging low in the East was shot through with a soft glory as of the fleece of the Lamb of God seen in mystical vision, and simultaneously therewith, watched by the wedged mass of upturned faces, Billy ascended; and, ascending, took the full rose of the dawn.

In the pinioned figure arrived at the yard-end, to the wonder of all no motion was apparent, none save that created by the slow roll of the hull in moderate weather, so majestic in a great ship ponderously cannoned.

ROBERT LOUIS STEVENSON

(1850–1894)

Robert Louis Stevenson, born in Edinburgh, was the son of a lighthouse engineer. His father and uncle were the third generation of engineers in his family, and Stevenson was expected to follow suit, but he switched his studies at the University of Edinburgh from engineering to law. In 1872 he passed his preliminary examination for the Scottish Bar, and from May to July he worked as a law clerk. In July of 1875 he passed his written papers and was admitted as an advocate. But Stevenson, who knew from an early age that he wanted to be a writer, had studied law merely to mollify his overbearing father after he had abandoned engineering. One of his biographers notes that ``In his short and undistinguished legal career he earned just four guineas.'' Instead of practicing law, he began publishing essays and short stories. As late as 1881 Stevenson's father told a friend that he was still disappointed that his son was not practicing law.

Stevenson's most famous works were published within a six-year period: *Treasure Island* (1883), *A Child's Garden of Verses* (1885), *The Strange Case of Dr. Jekyll and Mr. Hyde* (1886), *Kidnapped* (1886), and *The Master of Ballantrae* (1889). He was working on *Weir of Hermiston* when he died suddenly at the age of forty-four. Two years earlier Stevenson had written that he expected this novel to be his masterpiece, and although it is unfinished, critics generally concur.

Adam Weir, Lord Hermiston, the intimidating Lord Justice-Clerk of the novel, is closely modeled on Robert MacQueen, Lord Braxfield (1722–99), who was Lord Justice-Clerk during the famous sedition trials of 1793–94 in Edinburgh. (The Justice-Clerk was the head of the criminal court of Scotland.) Stevenson had read about Braxfield in Lord Cockburn's *Memorial of His Time* (1856), which proclaims Braxfield's conduct as a criminal judge ``a disgrace to the age. . . . It may be doubted if he was ever so much in his element as when tauntingly repelling the last despairing claim of a wretched culprit, and sending him to Botany Bay or to the gallows with an insulting jest.''

The emotional power of *Weir of Hermiston* derives from the tension between Adam Weir and his son Archie, which mirrors, to some extent, Stevenson's troubled relationship with his own father. As a child, Archie is disturbed by his father's reputation as the ``Hanging Judge.'' The excerpt opens after the death of Archie's mother. Archie, now a law student at the University of Edinburgh, sees his father sentence a pitiful common criminal to death. He attends the execution and is moved to publicly denounce what he perceives to be his father's cruelty. Afterward, the Lord Justice-Clerk tells his son, "It's impossible you should think any longer of coming to the Bar," and banishes him to Hermiston, the family estate outside Edinburgh. Before he leaves, Archie has an emotional discussion with Lord Glenalmond about his father, the practice of law, and the burden of judgment.

from WEIR OF HERMISTON

— 1894 —

Father and Son

My Lord Justice-Clerk was known to many; the man Adam Weir perhaps to none. He had nothing to explain or to conceal; he sufficed wholly and silently to himself; and that part of our nature which goes out (too often with false coin) to acquire glory or love, seemed in him to be omitted. He did not try to be loved, he did not care to be; it is probable the very thought of it was a stranger to his mind. He was an admired lawyer, a highly unpopular judge; and he looked down upon those who were his inferiors in either distinction, who were lawyers of less grasp or judges not so much detested. In all the rest of his days and doings, not one trace of vanity appeared; and he went on through life with a mechanical movement, as of the unconscious, that was almost august.

He saw little of his son. In the childish maladies with which the boy was troubled, he would make daily inquiries and daily pay him a visit, entering the sick-room with a facetious and appalling countenance, letting off a few perfunctory jests, and going again swiftly, to the patient's relief. Once, a Court holiday falling opportunely, my lord had his carriage, and drove the child himself to Hermiston, the customary place of convalescence. It is conceivable he had been more than usually anxious, for that journey always remained in Archie's memory as a thing apart, his father having related to him from beginning to end, and with much detail, three authentic murder cases. Archie went the usual round of other Edinburgh boys, the high school and the college; and Hermiston looked on, or rather looked away, with scarce an affectation of interest in his progress. Daily, indeed, upon a signal after dinner, he was brought in, given nuts and a glass of port, regarded sardonically, sarcastically questioned. "Well, sir, and what have you donn with your book to-day?" my lord might begin, and set him posers in law Latin. To a child just stumbling into Corderius,

Papinian and Paul proved quite invincible. But papa had memory of no other. He was not harsh to the little scholar, having a vast fund of patience learned upon the Bench, and was at no pains whether to conceal or to express his disappointment. "Well, ye have a long jaunt before ye yet!" he might observe, yawning, and fall back on his own thoughts (as like as not) until the time came for separation, and my lord would take the decanter and the glass, and be off to the back chamber looking on the Meadows, where he toiled on his cases till the hours were small. There was no "fuller man" on the Bench; his memory was marvellous, though wholly legal; if he had to "advise" extempore, none did it better; yet there was none who more earnestly prepared. As he thus watched in the night, or sat at table and forgot the presence of his son, no doubt but he tasted deeply of recondite pleasures. To be wholly devoted to some intellectual exercise is to have succeeded in life; and perhaps only in law and the higher mathematics may this devotion be maintained, suffice to itself without reaction, and find continual rewards without excitement. This atmosphere of his father's sterling industry was the best of Archie's education. Assuredly it did not attract him; assuredly it rather rebutted and depressed. Yet it was still present, unobserved like the ticking of a clock, an arid ideal, a tasteless stimulant in the boy's life.

But Hermiston was not all of one piece. He was, besides, a mighty toper; he could sit at wine until the day dawned, and pass directly from the table to the Bench with a steady hand and a clear head. Beyond the third bottle, he showed the plebeian in a larger print; the low, gross accent, the low, foul mirth, grew broader and commoner; he became less formidable, and infinitely more disgusting. Now, the boy had inherited from Jean Rutherford a shivering delicacy, unequally mated with potential violence. In the playing-fields, and amongst his own companions, he repaid a coarse expression with a blow; at his father's table (when the time came for him to join these revels) he turned pale and sickened in silence. Of all the guests whom he there encountered, he had toleration for only one: David Keith Carnegie, Lord Glenalmond. Lord Glenalmond was tall and emaciated, with long features and long delicate hands. He was often compared with the statue of Forbes of Culloden in the Parliament House; and his blue eye, at more than sixty, preserved some of the fire of youth. His exquisite disparity with any of his fellow-guests, his appearance as of an artist and an aristocrat stranded in rude company, riveted the boy's attention; and as curiosity and interest are the things in the world that are the most immediately and certainly rewarded, Lord Glenalmond was attracted to the boy.

"And so this is your son, Hermiston?" he asked, laying his hand on Archie's shoulder. "He's getting a big lad."

"Hout!" said the gracious father, "just his mother over again—daurna say boo to a goose!"

But the stranger retained the boy, talked to him, drew him out, found in him a taste for letters, and a fine, ardent, modest, youthful soul; and encouraged him to be a visitor on Sunday evenings in his bare, cold, lonely dining-room, where he sat and read in the isolation of a bachelor grown old in refinement. The beautiful gentleness and grace of the old Judge, and the delicacy of his person, thoughts, and language, spoke to Archie's heart in its own tongue. He conceived the ambition to be such another; and, when the day came for him to choose a profession, it was in emulation of Lord Glenalmond, not of Lord Hermiston, that he chose the Bar. Hermiston looked on at this friendship with some secret pride, but openly with the intolerance of scorn. He scarce lost an opportunity to put them down with a rough jape; and, to say truth, it was not difficult, for they were neither of them quick. He had a word of contempt for the whole crowd of poets, painters, fiddlers, and their admirers, the bastard race of amateurs, which was continually on his lips. "Signor Feedle-eerie!" he would say. "Oh, for Goad's sake, no more of the Signor!"

"You and my father are great friends, are you not?" asked Archie once.

"There is no man that I more respect, Archie," replied Lord Glenalmond. "He is two things of price. He is a great lawyer, and he is upright as the day."

"You and he are so different," said the boy, his eyes dwelling on those of his old friend, like a lover's on his mistress's.

"Indeed so," replied the Judge; "very different. And so I fear are you and he. Yet I would like it very ill if my young friend were to misjudge his father. He has all the Roman virtues: Cato and Brutus were such; I think a son's heart might well be proud of such an ancestry of one."

"And I would sooner he were a plaided herd," cried Archie, with sudden bitterness.

"And that is neither very wise, nor I believe entirely true," returned Glenalmond. "Before you are done you will find some of these expressions rise on you like a remorse. They are merely literary and decorative; they do not aptly express your thought, nor is your thought clearly apprehended, and no doubt your father (if he were here) would say 'Signor Feedle-eerie!' "

With the infinitely delicate sense of youth, Archie avoided the subject from that hour. It was perhaps a pity. Had he but talked—talked freely—let himself gush out in words (the way youth loves to do and should), there might have been no tale to write upon the Weirs of Hermiston. But the shadow of a threat of ridicule sufficed; in the slight tartness of these words he read a prohibition; and it is likely that Glenalmond meant it so.

Besides the veteran, the boy was without confidant or friend. Serious and eager, he came through school and college, and moved among a crowd of the indifferent, in the seclusion of his shyness. He grew up handsome, with an open, speaking countenance, with graceful, youthful ways; he was clever, he took prizes, he shone in the Speculative Society.* It should seem he must become the centre of a crowd of friends; but something that was in part the delicacy of his mother, in part the austerity of his father, held him aloof from all. It is a fact, and a strange one, that among his contemporaries Hermiston's son was thought to be a chip of the old block. "You're a friend of Archie Weir's?" said one to Frank Innes; and Innes replied, with his usual flippancy and more than his usual insight: "I know Weir, but I never met Archie." No one had met Archie, a malady most incident to only sons. He flew his private signal, and none heeded it; it seemed he was abroad in a world from which the very hope of intimacy was banished; and he looked round about him on the concourse of his fellow-students, and forward to the trivial days and acquaintances that were to come, without hope or interest.

As time went on, the tough and rough old sinner felt himself drawn to the son of his loins and sole continuator of his new family, with softnesses of sentiment that he could hardly credit and was wholly impotent to express. With a face, voice, and manner trained through forty years to terrify and repel, Rhadamanthus may be great, but he will scarce be engaging. It is a fact that he tried to propitiate Archie, but a fact that cannot be too lightly taken; the attempt was so unconspicuously made, the failure so stoically supported. Sympathy is not due to these steadfast iron natures. If he failed to gain his son's friendship, or even his son's toleration, on he went up the great, bare staircase of his duty, uncheered and undepressed. There might have been more pleasure in his relations with Archie, so much he may have recognised at moments; but pleasure was a by-product of the singular chemistry of life, which only fools expected.

An idea of Archie's attitude, since we are all grown up and have forgotten the days of our youth, it is more difficult to convey. He made no attempt whatsoever to understand the man with whom he dined and breakfasted. Parsimony of pain, glut of pleasure, these are the two, alternating ends of youth; and Archie was of the parsimonious. The wind blew cold out of a certain quarter—he turned his back upon it; stayed as little as was possible

*A famous debating society of the students of Edinburgh University.

in his father's presence; and when there, averted his eyes as much as was decent from his father's face. The lamp shone for many hundred days upon these two at table—my lord ruddy, gloomy, and unreverent; Archie with a potential brightness that was always dimmed and veiled in that society; and there were not, perhaps, in Christendom two men more radically strangers. The father, with a grand simplicity, either spoke of what interested himself, or maintained an unaffected silence. The son turned in his head for some topic that should be quite safe, that would spare him fresh evidences either of my lord's inherent grossness or of the innocence of his inhumanity; treading gingerly the ways of intercourse, like a lady gathering up her skirts in a by-path. If he made a mistake, and my lord began to abound in matter of offence, Archie drew himself up, his brow grew dark, his share of the talk expired; but my lord would faithfully and cheerfully continue to pour out the worst of himself before his silent and offended son.

"Well, it's a poor hert that never rejoices," he would say, at the conclusion of such a nightmare interview. "But I must get to my plew-stilts." And he would seclude himself as usual in the back room, and Archie go forth into the night and the city, quivering with animosity and scorn.

In the Matter of the Hanging of Duncan Jopp

It chanced in the year 1813 that Archie strayed one day into the Justiciary Court. The macer made room for the son of the presiding judge. In the dock, the centre of men's eyes, there stood a whey-coloured, mis-begotten caitiff, Duncan Jopp, on trial for his life. His story, as it was raked out before him in that public scene, was one of disgrace and vice and cowardice, the very nakedness of crime; and the creature heard and it seemed at times as though he understood—as if at times he forgot the horror of the place he stood in, and remembered the shame of what had brought him there. He kept his head bowed and his hands clutched upon the rail; his hair dropped in his eyes and at times he flung it back; and now he glanced about the audience in a sudden fellness of terror, and now looked in the face of his judge and gulped. There was pinned about his throat a piece of dingy flannel; and this it was perhaps that turned the scale in Archie's mind between disgust and pity. The creature stood in a vanishing point; yet a little while, and he was still a man, and had eyes and apprehension; yet a little longer, and with a last sordid piece of pageantry, he would cease to be. And here, in the meantime, with a trait of human nature that caught at the beholder's breath, he was tending a sore throat.

Over against him, my Lord Hermiston occupied the Bench in the red robes of criminal jurisdiction, his face framed in the white wig. Honest all through, he did not affect the virtue of impartiality; this was no case for refinement; there was a man to be hanged, he would have said, and he was hanging him. Nor was it possible to see his lordship, and acquit him of gusto in the task. It was plain he gloried in the exercise of his trained faculties, in the clear sight which pierced at once into the joint of fact, in the rude, unvarnished gibes with which he demolished every figment of defence. He took his ease and jested, unbending in that solemn place with some of the freedom of the tavern; and the rag of man with the flannel round his neck was hunted gallowsward with jeers.

Duncan had a mistress, scarce less forlorn and greatly older than himself, who came up, whimpering and curtseying, to add the weight of her betrayal. My lord gave her the oath in his most roaring voice, and added an intolerant warning.

"Mind what ye say now, Janet," said he. "I have an e'e upon ye; I'm ill to jest with."

Presently, after she was tremblingly embarked on her story, "And what made ye do this, ye auld runt?" the Court interposed. "Do ye mean to tell me ye was the panel's mistress?"

"If you please, ma loard," whined the female.

"Godsake! ye made a bonny couple," observed his lordship; and there was something so formidable and ferocious in his scorn that not even the galleries thought to laugh.

The summing up contained some jewels.

"These two peetiable creatures seem to have made up thegither, it's not for us to explain why."—"The panel, who (whatever else he may be) appears to be equally ill set-out in mind and boady."—"Neither the panel nor yet the old wife appears to have had so much common sense as even to tell a lie when it was necessary." And in the course of sentencing, my lord had this *obiter dictum*: "I have been the means, under God, of haanging a great number, but never just such a disjaskit rascal as yourself." The words were strong in themselves: the light and heat and detonation of their delivery, and the savage pleasure of the speaker in his task, made them tingle in the ears.

When all was over, Archie came forth again into a changed world. Had there been the least redeeming greatness in the crime, any obscurity, any dubiety, perhaps he might have understood. But the culprit stood, with his sore throat, in the sweat of his mortal agony, without defence or excuse; a thing to cover up with blushes; a being so much sunk beneath the zones of sympathy that pity might seem harmless. And the judge had pursued him with a monstrous, relishing gaiety, horrible to be conceived, a trait for nightmares. It is one thing to spear a tiger, another to crush a toad; there are æsthetics even of the slaughter-house; and the loathsomeness of Duncan Jopp enveloped and infected the image of his judge.

Archie passed by his friends in the High Street with incoherent words and gestures. He saw Holyrood in a dream, remembrance of its romance awoke in him and faded; he had a vision of the old radiant stories, of Queen Mary and Prince Charlie, of the hooded stag, of the splendour and crime, the velvet and bright iron of the past; and dismissed them with a cry of pain. He lay and moaned in the Hunter's Bog, and the heavens were dark above him and the grass of the field an offence. "This is my father," he said. "I draw my life from him; the flesh upon my bones is his, the bread I am fed with is the wages of these horrors." He recalled his mother, and ground his forehead in the earth. He thought of flight, and where was he to flee to? of other lives, but was there any life worth living in this den of savage and jeering animals?

The interval before the execution was like a violent dream. He met his father; he would not look at him, he could not speak to him. It seemed there was no living creature but must have been swift to recognise that imminent animosity; but the hide of the Lord Justice-Clerk remained impenetrable. Had my lord been talkative, the truce could never have subsisted; but he was by fortune in one of his humours of sour silence; and under the very guns of his broadside Archie nursed the enthusiasm of rebellion. It seemed to him, from the top of his nineteen years' experience, as if he were marked at birth to be the perpetrator of some signal action, to set back fallen Mercy, to overthrow the usurping devil that sat, horned and hoofed, on her throne. Seductive Jacobin figments, which he had often refuted at the Speculative, swam up in his mind and startled him as with voices; and he seemed to himself to walk accompanied by an almost tangible presence of new beliefs and duties.

On the named morning he was at the place of execution. He saw the fleering rabble, the flinching wretch produced. He looked on for a while at a certain parody of devotion, which seemed to strip the wretch of his last claim to manhood. Then followed the brutal instant of extinction, and the paltry dangling of the remains like a broken jumping-jack. He had been prepared for something terrible, not for this tragic meanness. He stood a moment silent, and then—"I denounce this God-defying murder," he shouted; and his father, if he must have disclaimed the sentiment, might have owned the stentorian voice with which it was uttered.

Frank Innes dragged him from the spot. The two handsome lads followed the same course of study and recreation, and felt a certain mutual attraction, founded mainly on good looks. It had never gone deep; Frank was by nature a thin, jeering creature, not truly susceptible whether of feeling or inspiring friendship; and the relation between the pair was altogether on the outside, a thing of common knowledge and the pleasantries that spring from a common acquaintance. The more credit to Frank that he was appalled by Archie's outburst, and at least conceived the design of keeping him in sight, and, if possible, in hand, for the day. But Archie, who had just defied—was it God or Satan?—would not listen to the word of a college companion.

"I will not go with you," he said. "I do not desire your company, sir; I would be alone."

"Here, Weir, man, don't be absurd," said Innes, keeping a tight hold upon his sleeve. "I will not let you go until I know what you mean to do with yourself; it's no use brandishing that staff." For indeed at that moment Archie had made a sudden—perhaps a war-like—movement. "This has been the most insane affair; you know it has. You know very well that I'm playing the good Samaritan. All I wish is to keep you quiet."

"If quietness is what you wish, Mr. Innes," said Archie, "and you will promise to leave me entirely to myself, I will tell you so much, that I am going to walk in the country and admire the beauties of nature."

"Honour bright?" asked Frank.

"I am not in the habit of lying, Mr. Innes," retorted Archie. "I have the honour of wishing you good-day."

"You won't forget the Spec.?" asked Innes.

"The Spec.?" said Archie. "Oh, no, I won't forget the Spec."

And the one young man carried his tortured spirit forth of the city and all the day long, by one road and another, in an endless pilgrimage of misery; while the other hastened smilingly to spread the news of Weir's access of insanity, and to drum up for that night a full attendance at the Speculative, where further eccentric developments might certainly be looked for. I doubt if Innes had the least belief in his prediction: I think it flowed rather from a wish to make the story as good and the scandal as great as possible; not from any ill-will to Archie—from the mere pleasure of beholding interested faces. But for all that his words were prophetic. Archie did not forget the Spec.; he put in an appearance there at the due time, and, before the evening was over, had dealt a memorable shock to his companions. It chanced he was the president of the night. He sat in the same room where the Society still meets—only the portraits were not there; the men who afterwards sat for them were then but beginning their career. The same lustre of many tapers shed its light over the meeting; the same chair, perhaps, supported him that so many of us have sat in since.

At times he seemed to forget the business of the evening, but even in these periods he sat with a great air of energy and determination. At times he meddled bitterly and launched with defiance those fines which are the precious and rarely used artillery of the president. He little thought, as he did so, how he resembled his father, but his friends remarked upon it, chuckling. So far, in his high place above his fellow-students, he seemed set beyond the possibility of any scandal; but his mind was made up—he was determined to fulfil the sphere of his offence. He signed to Innes (whom he had just fined, and who had just impeached his ruling) to succeed him in the chair, stepped down from the platform, and took his place by the chimney-piece, the shine of many wax tapers from above illuminating his pale face, the glow of the great red fire relieving from behind his slim figure. He had to propose, as an amendment to the next subject in the casebook, "Whether capital punishment be consistent with God's will or man's policy?"

A breath of embarrassment, of something like alarm, passed round the room, so daring did these words appear upon the lips of Hermiston's only son. But the amendment was not seconded; the previous question was promptly moved and unanimously voted, and the momentary scandal smuggled by. Innes triumphed in the fulfilment of his prophecy. He and Archie were now become the heroes of the night; but whereas every one crowded about Innes, when the meeting broke up, but one of all his companions came to speak to Archie.

"Weir, man! that was an extraordinary raid of yours!" observed this courageous member, taking him confidentially by the arm as they went out.

"I don't think it a raid," said Archie grimly. "More like a war. I saw that poor brute hanged this morning, and my gorge rises at it yet."

"Hut-tut!" returned his companion, and, dropping his arm like something hot, he sought the less tense society of others.

Archie found himself alone. The last of the faithful—or was it only the boldest of the curious?—had fled. He watched the black huddle of his fellow-students draw off down and up the street, in whispering or boisterous gangs. And the isolation of the moment weighed upon him like an omen and an emblem of his destiny in life. Bred up in unbroken fear of himself, among trembling servants, and in a house which (at the least ruffle in the master's voice) shuddered into silence, he saw himself on the brink of the red valley of war, and measured the danger and length of it with awe. He made a détour in the glimmer and shadow of the streets, came into the back stable lane, and watched for a long while the light burn steady in the Judge's room. The longer he gazed upon that illuminated window-blind, the more blank became the picture of the man who sat behind it, endlessly turning over sheets of process, pausing to sip a glass of port, or rising and passing heavily about his book-lined walls to verify some reference. He could not combine the brutal judge and the industrious, dispassionate student; the connecting link escaped him; from such a dual nature, it was impossible he should predict behaviour; and he asked himself if he had done well to plunge into a business of which the end could not be foreseen; and presently after, with a sickening decline of confidence, if he had done loyally to strike his father. For he had struck him—defied him twice over and before a cloud of witnesses—struck him a public buffet before crowds. Who had called him to judge his father in these precarious and high questions? The office was usurped. It might have become a stranger; in a son—there was no blinking it—in a son, it was disloyal. And now, between these two natures so antipathetic, so hateful to each other, there was depending an unpardonable affront: and the providence of God alone might foresee the manner in which it would be resented by Lord Hermiston.

These misgivings tortured him all night and arose with him in the winter's morning; they followed him from class to class, they made him shrinkingly sensitive to every shade of manner in his companions, they sounded in his ears through the current voice of the professor; and he brought them home with him at night unabated and indeed increased. The cause of this increase lay in a chance encounter with the celebrated Dr. Gregory. Archie stood looking vaguely in the lighted window of a book shop, trying to nerve himself for the approaching ordeal. My lord and he had met and parted in the morning as they had now done for long, with scarcely the ordinary civilities of life; and it was plain to the son that nothing had yet reached the father's ears. Indeed, when he recalled the awful countenance of my lord, a timid hope sprang up in him that perhaps there would be found no one bold enough to carry tales. If this were so, he asked himself, would he begin again? and he found no answer. It was at this moment that a hand was laid upon his arm, and a voice said in his ear, "My dear Mr. Archie, you had better come and see me."

He started, turned around, and found himself face to face with Dr. Gregory. "And why should I come to see you?" he asked, with the defiance of the miserable.

"Because you are looking exceeding ill," said the doctor, "and you very evidently want looking after, my young friend. Good folk are scarce, you know; and it is not every one that would be quite so much missed as yourself. It is not every one that Hermiston would miss."

And with a nod and a smile, the doctor passed on.

A moment after, Archie was in pursuit, and had in turn, but more roughly, seized him by the arm.

"What do you mean? what did you mean by saying that? What makes you think that Hermis—my father would have missed me?"

The doctor turned about and looked him all over with a clinical eye. A far more stupid man than Dr. Gregory might have guessed the truth; but ninety-nine out of a hundred, even if they had been equally inclined to kindness, would have blundered by some touch of charitable exaggeration. The doctor was better inspired. He knew the father well; in that white face of intelligence and suffering, he divined something of the son; and he told, without apology or adornment, the plain truth.

"When you had the measles, Mr. Archibald, you had them gey and ill; and I thought you were going to slip between my fingers," he said. "Well, your father was anxious. How did I know it? says you. Simply because I am a trained observer. The sign that I saw him make ten thousand would have missed; and perhaps—*perhaps*, I say, because he's a hard man to judge of—but perhaps he never made another. A strange thing to consider! It was this. One day I came to him: 'Hermiston,' said I, 'there's a change.' He never said a word, just glowered at me (if ye'll pardon the phrase) like a wild beast. 'A change for the better,' said I. And I distinctly heard him take his breath."

The doctor left no opportunity for anti-climax; nodding his cocked hat (a piece of antiquity to which he clung) and repeating "Distinctly" with raised eyebrows, he took his departure, and left Archie speechless in the street.

The anecdote might be called infinitely little, and yet its meaning for Archie was immense. "I did not know the old man had so much blood in him." He had never dreamed this sire of his, this aboriginal antique, this adamantine Adam, had even so much of a heart as to be moved in the least degree for another—and that other himself, who had insulted him! With the generosity of youth, Archie was instantly under arms upon the other side: had instantly created a new image of Lord Hermiston, that of a man who was all iron without and all sensibility within. The mind of the vile jester, the tongue that had pursued Duncan Jopp with unmanly insults, the unbeloved countenance that he had known and feared for so long, were all forgotten; and he hastened home, impatient to confess his misdeeds, impatient to throw himself on the mercy of this imaginary character.

He was not to be long without a rude awakening. It was in the gloaming when he drew near the doorstep of the lighted house, and was aware of the figure of his father approaching from the opposite side. Little day-light lingered; but on the door being opened, the strong yellow shine of the lamp gushed out upon the landing and shone full on Archie, as he stood, in the old-fashioned observance of respect, to yield precedence. The Judge came without haste, stepping stately and firm; his chin raised, his face (as he entered the lamplight) strongly illumined, his mouth set hard. There was never a wink of change in his expression; without looking to the right or left, he mounted the stair, passed close to Archie, and entered the house. Instinctively, the boy, upon his first coming, had made a movement to meet him; instinctively, he recoiled against the railing, as the old man swept by him in a pomp of indignation. Words were needless; he knew all—perhaps more than all—and the hour of judgment was at hand.

It is possible that, in this sudden revulsion of hope and before these symptoms of impending danger, Archie might have fled. But not even that was left to him. My lord, after hanging up his cloak and hat, turned round in the lighted entry, and made him an imperative and silent gesture with his thumb, and with the strange instinct of obedience, Archie followed him into the house.

All dinner time there reigned over the Judge's table a palpable silence, and as soon as the solids were despatched he rose to his feet.

"M'Killop, tak' the wine into my room," said he; and then to his son: "Archie, you and me has to have a talk."

It was at this sickening moment that Archie's courage, for the first and last time, entirely deserted him. "I have an appointment," said he.

"It'll have to be broken, then," said Hermiston, and led the way into his study.

The lamp was shaded, the fire trimmed to a nicety, the table covered deep with orderly documents, the backs of law books made a frame upon all sides that was only broken by the window and the doors.

For a moment Hermiston warmed his hands at the fire, presenting his back to Archie; then suddenly disclosed on him the terrors of the Hanging Face.

"What's this I hear of ye?" he asked.

There was no answer possible to Archie.

"I'll have to tell ye, then," pursued Hermiston. "It seems ye've been skirling against the father that begot ye, and one of His Maijesty's Judges in this land; and that in the public street, and while an order of the Court was being executit. Forbye which, it would appear that ye've been airing your opeenions in a Coallege Debatin' Society;" he paused a moment: and, then, with extraordinary bitterness, added: "Ye damned eediot."

"I had meant to tell you," stammered Archie. "I see you are well informed."

"Muckle obleeged to ye," said his lordship, and took his usual seat. "And so you disapprove of Caapital Punishment?" he added.

"I am sorry, sir, I do," said Archie.

"I am sorry, too," said his lordship. "And now, if you please, we shall approach this business with a little more parteecularity. I hear that at the hanging of Duncan Jopp—and, man! ye had a fine client there—in the middle of all the riffraff of the ceety, ye thought fit to cry out, 'This is a damned murder, and my gorge rises at the man that haangit him.' "

"No, sir, these were not my words," cried Archie.

"What were yer words, then?" asked the Judge.

"I believe I said, 'I denounce it as a murder!' " said the son, "I beg your pardon—a God-defying murder. I have no wish to conceal the truth," he added, and looked his father for a moment in the face.

"God, it would only need that of it next!" cried Hermiston. "There was nothing about your gorge rising, then?"

"That was afterwards, my lord, as I was leaving the Speculative. I said I had been to see the miserable creature hanged, and my gorge rose at it."

"Did ye, though?" said Hermiston. "And I suppose ye knew who haangit him?"

"I was present at the trial; I ought to tell you that, I ought to explain. I ask your pardon beforehand for any expression that may seem undutiful. The position in which I stand is wretched," said the unhappy hero, now fairly face to face with the business he had chosen. "I have been reading some of your cases. I was present while Jopp was tried. It was a hideous business. Father, it was a hideous thing! Grant he was vile, why should you hunt him with a vileness equal to his own? It was done with glee—that is the word—and you did it with glee, and I looked on, God help me! with horror."

"You're a young gentleman that doesna approve of Caapital Punishment," said Hermiston. "Weel, I'm an auld man that does. I was glad to get Jopp haangit, and what for would I pretend I wasna? You're all for honesty, it seems; you couldna even steik your mouth on the public street. What for should I steik mines upon the Bench, the King's officer, bearing the sword, a dreid to evil-doers, as I was from the beginning, and as I will be to the end! Mair than enough of it! Heedious! I never gave twa thoughts to heediousness, I have no call to be bonny. I'm a man that gets through with my day's business, and let that suffice."

The ring of sarcasm had died out of his voice as he went on; the plain words became invested with some of the dignity of the Justice-seat.

"It would be telling you if you could say as much," the speaker resumed. "But ye cannot. Ye've been reading some of my cases, ye say. But it was not for the law in them, it was to spy out your faither's nakedness, a fine employment in a son. You're splairging; you're running at lairge in life like a wild nowt. It's impossible you should think any longer of coming to the Bar. You're not fit for it; no splairger is. And another thing: son of mines or no son of mines, you have flung fylement in public on one of the Senators of the Coallege of Justice, and I would make it my business to see that ye were never admitted there yourself. There is a kind of a decency to be observit. Then comes the next of it—what am I to do with ye next? Ye'll have to find some kind of a trade, for I'll never support ye in idleset. What do ye fancy ye'll be fit for? The pulpit? Na, they could never get diveenity into that bloackhead. Him that the law of man whammles is no' likely to do muckle better by the law of God. What would ye make of hell? Wouldna your gorge rise at that? Na, there's no room for splairgers under the fower quarters of John Calvin. What else is there? Speak up. Have ye got nothing of your own?"

"Father, let me go to the Peninsula," said Archie. "That's all I'm fit for—to fight."

"All? quo' he!" returned the Judge. "And it would be enough too, if I thought it. But I'll never trust ye so near the French, you that's so Frenchifeed."

"You do me injustice there, sir," said Archie. "I am loyal; I will not boast; but any interest I may have ever felt in the French——"

"Have ye been so loyal to me?" interrupted his father.

There came no reply.

"I think not," continued Hermiston. "And I would send no man to be a servant of the King, God bless him! that has proved such a shauchling son to his own faither. You can splairge here on Edinburgh street, and where's the hairm? It doesna play buff on me! And if there were twenty thousand eediots like yourself, sorrow a Duncan Jopp would hang the fewer. But there's no splairging possible in a camp; and if you were to go to it, you would find out for yourself whether Lord Well'n'ton approves of caapital punishment or not. You a sodger!" he cried, with a sudden burst of scorn. "Ye auld wife, the sodgers would bray at ye like cuddies!"

As at the drawing of a curtain, Archie was aware of some illogicality in his position, and stood abashed. He had a strong impression, besides, of the essential valour of the old gentleman before him, how conveyed it would be hard to say.

"Well, have ye no other proposeetion?" said my lord again.

"You have taken this so calmly, sir, that I cannot but stand ashamed," began Archie.

"I'm nearer voamiting, though, than you would fancy," said my lord.

The blood rose to Archie's brow.

"I beg your pardon, I should have said that you had accepted my affront. . . . I admit it was an affront; I did not think to apologise, but I do, I ask your pardon; it will not be so again, I pass you my word of honour. . . . I should have said that I admired your magnanimity with—this—offender," Archie concluded with a gulp.

"I have no other son, ye see," said Hermiston. "A bonny one I have gotten! But I must just do the best I can wi' him, and what am I to do? If ye had been younger, I would have wheepit ye for this rideeculous exhibeetion. The way it is, I have just to grin and bear. But one thing is to be clearly understood. As a faither, I must grin and bear it; but if I had been the Lord Advocate instead of the Lord Justice-Clerk, son or no son, Mr. Erchibald Weir would have been in a jyle the night."

Archie was now dominated. Lord Hermiston was coarse and cruel; and yet the son was aware of a bloomless nobility, an ungracious abnegation of the man's self in the man's office. At every word, this sense of the greatness of Lord Hermiston's spirit struck more home; and along with it that of his own impotence, who had struck—and perhaps basely struck—at his own father, and not reached so far as to have even nettled him.

"I place myself in your hands without reserve," he said.

"That's the first sensible word I've had of ye the night," said Hermiston. "I can tell ye, that would have been the end of it, the one way or the other; but it's better ye should come there yourself, than what I would have had to hirstle ye. Weel, by my way of it—and my way is the best—there's just the one thing it's possible that ye might be with decency, and that's a laird. Ye'll be out of hairm's way at the least of it. If ye have to rowt, ye can rowt amang the kye; and the maist feck of the caapital punishment ye're like to come across'll be guddling trouts. Now, I'm for no idle lairdies; every man has to work, if it's only at peddling ballants; to work, or to be wheepit, or to be haangit. If I set ye down at Hermiston, I'll have to see you work that place the way it has never been workit yet; ye must ken about the sheep like a herd; ye must be my grieve there, and I'll see that I gain by ye. Is that understood?"

"I will do my best," said Archie.

"Well, then, I'll send Kirstie word the morn, and ye can go yourself the day after," said Hermiston. "And just try to be less of an eediot!" he concluded, with a freezing smile, and turned immediately to the papers on his desk.

Opinions of the Bench

Late the same night, after a disordered walk, Archie was admitted into Lord Glenalmond's dining-room where he sat, with a book upon his knee, beside three frugal coals of fire. In his robes upon the bench, Glenalmond had a certain air of burliness: plucked of these, it was a may-pole of a man that rose unsteadily from his chair to give his visitor welcome. Archie had suffered much in the last days, he had suffered again that evening; his face was white and drawn, his eyes wild and dark. But Lord Glenalmond greeted him without the least mark of surprise or curiosity.

"Come in, come in," said he. "Come in and take a seat. Carstairs" (to his servant), "make up the fire, and then you can bring a bit of supper," and again to Archie, with a very trivial accent: "I was half expecting you," he added.

"No supper," said Archie. "It is impossible that I should eat."

"Not impossible," said the tall old man, laying his hand upon his shoulder, "and, if you will believe me, necessary."

"You know what brings me?" said Archie, as soon as the servant had left the room.

"I have a guess, I have a guess," replied Glenalmond. "We will talk of it presently—when Carstairs has come and gone, and you have had a piece of my good Cheddar cheese and a pull at the porter tankard: not before."

"It is impossible I should eat," repeated Archie.

"Tut, tut!" said Lord Glenalmond. "You have eaten nothing to-day, and, I venture to add, nothing yesterday. There is no case that may not be made worse; this may be a very disagreeable business, but if you were to fall sick and die, it would be still more so, and for all concerned—for all concerned."

"I see you must know all," said Archie. "Where did you hear it?"

"In the mart of scandal, in the Parliament House," said Glenalmond. "It runs riot below among the Bar and the public, but it sifts up to us upon the Bench, and rumour has some of her voices even in the divisions."

Carstairs returned at this moment, and rapidly laid out a little supper; during which Lord Glenalmond spoke at large and a little vaguely on indifferent subjects, so that it might be rather said of him that he made a cheerful noise, than that he contributed to human conversation; and Archie sat upon the other side, not heeding him, brooding over his wrongs and errors.

But so soon as the servant was gone, he broke forth again at once. "Who told my father? Who dared to tell him? Could it have been you?"

"No, it was not me," said the Judge; "although—to be quite frank with you, and after I had seen and warned you—it might have been me. I believe it was Glenkindie."

"That shrimp!" cried Archie.

"As you say, that shrimp," returned my lord; "although really it is scarce a fitting mode of expression for one of the Senators of the College of Justice. We were hearing the parties in a long, crucial case, before the fifteen; Creech was moving at some length for an infeftment; when I saw Glenkindie lean forward to Hermiston with his hand over his mouth and make him a secret communication. No one could have guessed its nature from your father; from Glenkindie, yes, his malice sparked out of him a little grossly. But your father, no. A man of granite. The next moment he pounced upon Creech. 'Mr. Creech,' says he, 'I'll take a look of that sasine,' and for thirty minutes after," said Glenalmond, with a smile, "Messrs. Creech and Co. were fighting a pretty uphill battle, which resulted, I need hardly add, in their total rout. The case was dismissed. No, I doubt if ever I heard Hermiston better inspired. He was literally rejoicing *in apicibus juris*."

Archie was able to endure no longer. He thrust his plate away and interrupted the deliberate and insignificant stream of talk. "Here," he said, "I have made a fool of myself, if I have not made something worse. Do you judge between us—judge between a father and a son. I can speak to you; it is not like. . . . I will tell you what I feel and what I mean to do; and you shall be the judge," he repeated.

"I decline jurisdiction," said Glenalmond, with extreme seriousness. "But, my dear boy, if it will do you any good to talk, and if it will interest you at all to hear what I may choose to say when I have heard you, I am quite at your command. Let an old man say it, for once, and not need to blush: I love you like a son."

There came a sudden sharp sound in Archie's throat. "Ay," he cried, "and there it is! Love! Like a son! And how do you think I love my father?"

"Quietly, quietly," says my lord.

"I will be very quiet," replied Archie. "And I will be baldly frank. I do not love my father; I wonder sometimes if I do not hate him. There's my shame; perhaps my sin; at least, and in the sight of God, not my fault. How was I to love him? He has never spoken to me, never smiled upon me; I do not think he ever touched me. You know the way he talks? You do not talk so, yet you can sit and hear him without shuddering, and I cannot. My soul is sick when he begins with it; I could smite him in the mouth. And all that's nothing. I was at the trial of this Jopp. You were not there, but you must have heard him often; the man's notorious for it, for being—look at my position! he's my father and this is how I have to speak of him—notorious for being a brute and cruel and a coward. Lord Glenalmond, I give you my word, when I came out of that Court, I longed to die—the shame of it was beyond my strength: but I—I——" he rose from his seat and began to pace the room in a disorder. "Well, who am I? A boy, who have never been tried, have never done anything except this twopenny impotent folly with my father. But I tell you, my lord, and I know myself, I am at least that kind of a man—or that kind of a boy, if you prefer it—that I could die in torments rather than that any one should suffer as that scoundrel suffered. Well, and what have I done? I see it now. I have made a fool of myself, as I said in the beginning; and I have gone back, and asked my father's pardon, and placed myself wholly in his hands—and he has sent me to Hermiston," with a wretched smile, "for life, I suppose—and what can I say? he strikes me as having done quite right, and let me off better than I had deserved."

"My poor, dear boy!" observed Glenalmond. "My poor, dear and, if you will allow me to say so, very foolish boy! You are only discovering where you are; to one of your temperament, or of mine, a painful discovery. The world was not made for us; it was made for ten hundred millions of men, all different from each other and from us; there's no royal road there, we just have to sclamber and tumble. Don't think that I am at all disposed to be surprised; don't suppose that I ever think of blaming you; indeed I rather admire! But there fall to be offered one or two observations on the case which occur to me and which (if you will listen to them dispassionately) may be the means of inducing you to view the matter more calmly. First of all, I cannot acquit you of a good deal of what is called intolerance. You seem to have been very much offended because your father talks a little sculduddery after dinner, which it is perfectly licit for him to do, and which (although I am not very fond of it myself) appears to be entirely an affair of taste. Your father, I scarcely like to remind you, since it is so trite a commonplace, is older than yourself. At least, he is *major* and *sui juris*, and may please himself in the matter of his conversation. And, do you know, I wonder if he might not have as good an answer against you and me? We say we sometimes find him *coarse*, but I suspect he might retort that he finds us always dull. Perhaps a relevant exception."

He beamed on Archie, but no smile could be elicited.

"And now," proceeded the Judge, "for 'Archibald on Capital Punishment.' This is a very plausible academic opinion; of course I do not and I cannot hold it; but that's not to say that many able and excellent persons have not done so in the past. Possibly, in the past, also, I may have a little dipped myself in the same heresy. My third client, or possibly my fourth, was the means of a return in my opinions. I never saw the man I more believed in; I would have put my hand in the fire, I would have gone to the cross for him; and when it came to trial he was gradually pictured before me, by undeniable probation, in the light of so gross, so cold-blooded, and so black-hearted a villain, that I had a mind to have cast my brief upon the table. I was then boiling against the man with even a more tropical temperature than I had been boiling for him. But I said to myself: 'No, you have taken up his case; and because you have changed your mind it must not be suffered to let drop. All that rich tide of eloquence that you prepared last night with so much enthusiasm is out of place, and yet you must not desert him, you must say something.' So I said something, and I got him off. It made my reputation. But an experience of that kind is formative. A man must not bring his passions to the Bar—or to the Bench."

This story had slightly rekindled Archie's interest. "I could never deny," he began—"I mean I can conceive that some men would be better dead. But who are we to know all the springs of God's unfortunate creatures? Who are we to trust ourselves where it seems that God Himself must think twice before He treads, and to do it with delight? Yes, with delight. *Tigris ut aspera*."

"Perhaps not a pleasant spectacle," said Glenalmond. "And yet, do you know, I think somehow a great one."

"I've had a long talk with him to-night," said Archie.

"I was supposing so," said Glenalmond.

"And he struck me——I cannot deny that he struck me as something very big," pursued the son. "Yes, he is big. He never spoke about himself; only about me. I suppose I admired him. The dreadful part——"

"Suppose we did not talk about that," interrupted Glenalmond. "You know it very well, it cannot in any way help that you should brood upon it, and I sometimes wonder whether you and I—who are a pair of sentimentalists—are quite good judges of plain men."

"How do you mean?" asked Archie.

"*Fair* judges, I mean," replied Glenalmond. "Can we be just to them? Do we not ask too much? There was a word of yours just now that impressed me a little when you asked me who we were to know all the springs of God's unfortunate creatures. You applied that, as I understood, to capital cases only. But does it—I ask myself—does it not apply all through? Is it any less difficult to judge of a good man or of a half-good man, than of the worst criminal at the bar? And may not each have relevant excuses?"

"Ah, but we do not talk of punishing the good," cried Archie.

"No, we do not talk of it," said Glenalmond. "But I think we do it. Your father, for instance."

"You think I have punished him?" cried Archie.

Lord Glenalmond bowed his head.

"I think I have," said Archie. "And the worst is, I think he feels it! How much, who can tell, with such a being? But I think he does."

"And I am sure of it," said Glenalmond.

"Has he spoken to you, then?" cried Archie.

"Oh, no," replied the Judge.

"I tell you honestly," said Archie, "I want to make it up to him. I will go, I have already pledged myself to go, to Hermiston. That was to him. And now I pledge myself to you, in the sight of God, that I will close my mouth on capital punishment and all other subjects where our views may clash, for—how long shall I say? when shall I have sense enough?—ten years. Is that well?"

"It is well," said my lord.

"As far as it goes," said Archie. "It is enough as regards myself, it is to lay down enough of my conceit. But as regards him, whom I have publicly insulted? What am I to do to him? How do you pay attentions to a—an Alp like that?"

"Only in one way," replied Glenalmond. "Only by obedience, punctual, prompt, and scrupulous."

"And I promise that he shall have it," answered Archie. "I offer you my hand in pledge of it."

"And I take your hand as a solemnity," replied the Judge. "God bless you, my dear, and enable you to keep your promise. God guide you in the true way, and spare your days, and preserve to you your honest heart." At that, he kissed the young man upon the forehead in a gracious, distant, antiquated way; and instantly launched, with a marked change of voice, into another subject. "And now, let us replenish the tankard; and I believe, if you will try my Cheddar again, you would find you had a better appetite. The Court has spoken, and the case is dismissed."

"No, there is one thing I must say," cried Archie. "I must say it in justice to himself. I know—I believe faithfully, slavishly, after our talk—he will never ask me anything unjust. I am proud to feel it, that we have that much in common, I am proud to say it to you."

The Judge, with shining eyes, raised his tankard. "And I think perhaps that we might permit ourselves a toast," said he. "I should like to propose the health of a man very different from me and very much my superior—a man from whom I have often differed, who has often (in the trivial expression) rubbed me the wrong way, but whom I have never ceased to respect and, I may add, to be not a little afraid of. Shall I give you his name?"

"The Lord Justice-Clerk, Lord Hermiston," said Archie, almost with gaiety; and the pair drank the toast deeply.

It was not precisely easy to re-establish, after these emotional passages, the natural flow of conversation. But the Judge eked out what was wanting with kind looks, produced his snuff-box (which was very rarely seen) to fill in a pause, and at last, despairing of any further social success, was upon the point of getting down a book to read a favourite passage, when there came a rather startling summons at the front door, and Cartairs ushered in my Lord Glenkindie, hot from a midnight supper. I am not aware that Glenkindie was ever a beautiful object, being short, and gross-bodied, and with an expression of sensuality comparable to a bear's. At that moment, coming in hissing from many potations, with a flushed countenance and blurred eyes, he was strikingly contrasted with the tall, pale, kingly figure of Glenalmond. A rush of confused thought came over Archie—of shame that this was one of his father's elect friends; of pride, that at the least of it Hermiston could carry his liquor; and last of all, of rage, that he should have here under his eye the man that had betrayed him. And then that, too, passed away; and he sat quiet, biding his opportunity.

The tipsy senator plunged at once into an explanation with Glenalmond. There was a point reserved yesterday, he had been able to make neither head nor tail of it, and seeing lights in the house, he had just dropped in for a glass of porter—and at this point he became aware of the third person. Archie saw the cod's mouth and the blunt lips of Glenkindie gape at him for a moment, and the recognition twinkle in his eyes.

"Who's this?" said he. "What? is this possibly you, Don Quickshot? And how are ye? And how's your father? And what's all this we hear of you? It seems you're a most extraordinary leveller, by all tales. No king, no parliaments, and your gorge rises at the macers, worthy men! Hoot, toot! Dear, dear me! Your father's son, too! Most rideeculous!"

Archie was on his feet, flushing a little at the reappearance of his unhappy figure of speech, but perfectly self-possessed. "My lord—and you, Lord Glenalmond, my dear friend," he began, "this is a happy chance for me, that I can make my confession and offer my apologies to two of you at once."

"Ah, but I don't know about that. Confession? It'll be judeecial, my young friend," cried the jocular Glenkindie. "And I'm afraid to listen to ye. Think if ye were to make me a coanvert!"

"If you would allow me, my lord," returned Archie, "what I have to say is very serious to me; and be pleased to be humorous after I am gone!"

"Remember, I'll hear nothing against the macers!" put in the incorrigible Glenkindie.

But Archie continued as though he had not spoken. "I have played, both yesterday and to-day, a part for which I can only offer the excuse of youth. I was so unwise as to go to an execution; it seems I made a scene at the gallows; not content with which, I spoke the same night in a college society against capital punishment. This is the extent of what I have done, and in case you hear more alleged against me, I protest my innocence. I have expressed my regret already to my father, who is so good as to pass my conduct over—in a degree, and upon the condition that I am to leave my law studies." . . .

O. HENRY
(1862–1910)

William Sydney Porter (his middle name was originally spelled Sidney) was born in Greensboro, North Carolina, and later moved to Texas, where he worked as a draftsman and a bank teller. In 1894 he had to quit his job at the First National Bank of Austin when money was found to be missing from his accounts. Porter was indicted, but a grand jury found the evidence insufficient; then bank examiners reopened the case. On his way to stand trial in Austin, Porter fled to Honduras, returning only when his wife became terminally ill. In 1898 he was tried and convicted of embezzlement and sentenced to three years in the Ohio federal penitentiary.

While in prison, Porter devoted himself to writing and published fourteen stories in national magazines. Following his release, he went to New York City, where he adopted the pen name O. Henry and achieved international fame as a short-story writer specializing in surprise endings. Porter died of cirrhosis and diabetes at the age of forty-seven.

Porter vowed not to write about crime and punishment after leaving prison. Inevitably, however, his experiences with the law and with incarceration influenced his work. His stories draw extensively upon anecdotes gleaned from his fellow prisoners. Recurring characters in his fiction include the "gentle grafter" and a variety of other outlaws and criminals.

"The Cop and the Anthem" first appeared in the New York *Sunday World*, December 4, 1904, and was reprinted in O. Henry's highly popular second book, *The Four Million* (1906). The story's protagonist, Soapy, is the best-known of another of Porter's stock character types, the tramp. This ironic tale of pursuit of a jail cell has been adapted as drama, comedy, and even opera up to the present day.

THE COP AND THE ANTHEM
— 1904 —

On his bench in Madison Square Soapy moved uneasily. When wild geese honk high of nights, and when women without sealskin coats grow kind to their husbands, and when Soapy moves uneasily on his bench in the park, you may know that winter is near at hand.

A dead leaf fell in Soapy's lap. That was Jack Frost's card. Jack is kind to the regular denizens of Madison Square, and gives fair warning of his annual call. At the corners of four streets he hands his pasteboard to the North Wind, footman of the mansion of All Outdoors, so that the inhabitants thereof may make ready.

Soapy's mind became cognizant of the fact that the time had come for him to resolve himself into a singular Committee of Ways and Means to provide against the coming rigor. And therefore he moved uneasily on his bench.

The hibernatorial ambitions of Soapy were not of the highest. In them were no considerations of Mediterranean cruises, of soporific Southern skies or drifting in the Vesuvian Bay. Three months on the Island was what his soul craved. Three months of assured board and bed and congenial company, safe from Boreas and blue-coats, seemed to Soapy the essence of things desirable.

For years the hospitable Blackwell's had been his winter quarters. Just as his more fortunate fellow New Yorkers had bought their tickets to Palm Beach and the Riviera each winter, so Soapy had made his humble arrangements for his annual hegira to the Island. And now the time was come. On the previous night three Sabbath newspapers, distributed beneath his coat, about his ankles and over his lap, had failed to repulse the cold as he slept on his bench near the spurting fountain in the ancient square. So the Island loomed big and timely in Soapy's mind. He scorned the provisions made in the name of charity for the city's dependents. In Soapy's opinion the Law was more benign than Philanthropy. There was an endless round of institutions, municipal and eleemosynary, on which he might set out and receive lodging and food accordant with the simple life. But to one of Soapy's proud spirit the gifts of charity are encumbered. If not in coin you must pay in humiliation of spirit for every benefit received at the hands of philanthropy. As Cæsar had his Brutus, every bed of charity must have its toll of a bath, every loaf of bread its compensation of a private and personal inquisition. Wherefore it is better to be a guest of the law, which, though conducted by rules, does not meddle unduly with a gentleman's private affairs.

Soapy, having decided to go to the Island, at once set about accomplishing his desire. There were many easy ways of doing this. The pleasantest was to dine luxuriously at some expensive restaurant; and then, after declaring insolvency, he handed over quietly and without uproar to a policeman. An accommodating magistrate would do the rest.

Soapy left his bench and strolled out of the square and across the level sea of asphalt, where Broadway and Fifth Avenue flow together. Up Broadway he turned, and halted at a glittering café, where are gathered together nightly the choicest products of the grape, the silkworm, and the protoplasm.

Soapy had confidence in himself from the lowest button of his vest upward. He was shaven, and his coat was decent and his neat black, ready-tied four-in-hand had been presented to him by a lady missionary on Thanksgiving Day. If he could reach a table in the restaurant unsuspected success would be his. The portion of him that would show above the table would raise no doubt in the waiter's mind. A roasted mallard duck, thought Soapy, would be about the thing—with a bottle of Chablis, and then Camembert, a demi-tasse and a cigar. One dollar for the cigar would be enough. The total would not be so high as to call forth any supreme manifestation of revenge from the café management; and yet the meat would leave him filled and happy for the journey to his winter refuge.

But as Soapy set foot inside the restaurant door the head waiter's eye fell upon his frayed trousers and decadent shoes. Strong and ready hands turned him about and conveyed him in silence and haste to the sidewalk and averted the ignoble fate of the menaced mallard.

Soapy turned off Broadway. It seemed that his route to the coveted Island was not to be an epicurean one. Some other way of entering limbo must be thought of.

At a corner of Sixth Avenue electric lights and cunningly displayed wares behind plate-glass made a shop window conspicuous. Soapy took a cobblestone and dashed it through the glass. People came running around the corner, a policeman in the lead. Soapy stood still, with his hands in his pockets, and smiled at the sight of brass buttons.

"Where's the man that done that?" inquired the officer, excitedly.

"Don't you figure out that I might have had something to do with it?" said Soapy, not without sarcasm, but friendly, as one greets good fortune.

The policeman's mind refused to accept Soapy even as a clue. Men who smash windows do not remain to parley with the law's minions. They take to their heels. The policeman saw a man halfway down the block running to catch a car. With drawn club he joined in the pursuit. Soapy, with disgust in his heart, loafed along, twice unsuccessful.

On the opposite side of the street was a restaurant of no great pretensions. It catered to large appetites and modest purses. Its crockery and atmosphere were thick; its soup and napery thin. Into this place Soapy took his accusive shoes and telltale trousers without challenge. At a table he sat and consumed beefsteak, flapjacks, doughnuts and pie. And then to the waiter he betrayed the fact that the minutest coin and himself were strangers.

"Now, get busy and call a cop," said Soapy. "And don't keep a gentleman waiting."

"No cop for youse," said the waiter, with a voice like butter cakes and an eye like the cherry in a Manhattan cocktail. "Hey, Con!"

Neatly upon his left ear on the callous pavement two waiters pitched Soapy. He arose joint by joint, as a carpenter's rule opens, and beat the dust from his clothes. Arrest seemed but a rosy dream. The Island seemed very far away. A policeman who stood before a drug store two doors away laughed and walked down the street.

Five blocks Soapy travelled before his courage permitted him to woo capture again. This time the opportunity presented what he fatuously termed to himself a "cinch." A young woman of a modest and pleasing guise was standing before a show window gazing with sprightly interest at its display of shaving mugs and ink-stands, and two yards from the window a large policeman of severe demeanor leaned against a water plug.

It was Soapy's design to assume the rôle of the despicable and execrated "masher." The refined and elegant appearance of his victim and the contiguity of the conscientious cop encouraged him to believe that he would soon feel the pleasant official clutch upon his arm that would insure his winter quarters on the right little, tight little isle.

Soapy straightened the lady missionary's ready-made tie, dragged his shrinking cuffs into the open, set his hat at a killing cant and sidled toward the young woman. He made eyes at her, was taken with sudden coughs and "hems," smiled, smirked and went brazenly through the impudent and contemptible litany of the "masher." With half an eye Soapy saw that the policeman was watching him fixedly. The young woman moved away a few steps, and again bestowed her absorbed attention upon the shaving mugs. Soapy followed, boldly stepping to her side, raised his hat and said:

"Ah there, Bedelia! Don't you want to come and play in my yard?"

The policeman was still looking. The persecuted young woman had but to beckon a finger and Soapy would be practically en route for his insular haven. Already he imagined he could feel the cozy warmth of the station-house. The young woman faced him and, stretching out a hand, caught Soapy's coat sleeve.

"Sure, Mike," she said, joyfully, "if you'll blow me to a pail of suds. I'd have spoke to you sooner, but the cop was watching."

With the young woman playing the clinging ivy to his oak Soapy walked past the policeman overcome with gloom. He seemed doomed to liberty.

At the next corner he shook off his companion and ran. He halted in the district where by night are found the lightest streets, hearts, vows and librettos. Women in furs and men in greatcoats moved gaily in the wintry air. A sudden fear seized Soapy that some dreadful enchantment had rendered him immune to arrest. The thought brought a little of panic upon it, and when he came upon another policeman lounging grandly in front of a transplendent theatre he caught at the immediate straw of "disorderly conduct."

On the sidewalk Soapy began to yell drunken gibberish at the top of his harsh voice. He danced, howled, raved, and otherwise disturbed the welkin.

The policeman twirled his club, turned his back to Soapy and remarked to a citizen.

" 'Tis one of them Yale lads celebratin' the goose egg they give to the Hartford College. Noisy; but no harm. We've instructions to lave them be."

Disconsolate, Soapy ceased his unavailing racket. Would never a policeman lay hands on him? In his fancy the Island seemed an unattainable Arcadia. He buttoned his thin coat against the chilling wind.

In a cigar store he saw a well-dressed man lighting a cigar at a swinging light. His silk umbrella he had set by the door on entering. Soapy stepped inside, secured the umbrella and sauntered off with it slowly. The man at the cigar light followed hastily.

"My umbrella," he said, sternly.

"Oh, is it?" sneered Soapy, adding insult to petit larceny. "Well, why don't you call a policeman? I took it. Your umbrella! Why don't you call a cop? There stands one on the corner."

The umbrella owner slowed his steps. Soapy did likewise, with a presentiment that luck would again run against him. The policeman looked at the two curiously.

"Of course," said the umbrella man—"that is—well, you know how these mistakes occur—I—if it's your umbrella I hope you'll excuse me—I picked it up this morning in a restaurant——If you recognize it as yours, why—I hope you'll——"

"Of course it's mine," said Soapy, viciously.

The ex-umbrella man retreated. The policeman hurried to assist a tall blonde in an opera cloak across the street in front of a street car that was approaching two blocks away.

Soapy walked eastward through a street damaged by improvements. He hurled the umbrella wrathfully into an excavation. He muttered against the men who wear helmets and carry clubs. Because he wanted to fall into their clutches, they seemed to regard him as a king who could do no wrong.

At length Soapy reached one of the avenues to the east where the glitter and turmoil was but faint. He set his face down this toward Madison

Square, for the homing instinct survives even when the home is a park bench.

But on an unusually quiet corner Soapy came to a standstill. Here was an old church, quaint and rambling and gabled. Through one violet-stained window a soft light glowed, where, no doubt, the organist loitered over the keys, making sure of his mastery of the coming Sabbath anthem. For there drifted out to Soapy's ears sweet music that caught and held him transfixed against the convolutions of the iron fence.

The moon was above, lustrous and serene; vehicles and pedestrians were few; sparrows twittered sleepily in the eaves—for a little while the scene might have been a country churchyard. And the anthem that the organist played cemented Soapy to the iron fence, for he had known it well in the days when his life contained such things as mothers and roses and ambitions and friends and immaculate thoughts and collars.

The conjunction of Soapy's receptive state of mind and the influences about the old church wrought a sudden and wonderful change in his soul. He viewed with swift horror the pit into which he had tumbled, the degraded days, unworthy desires, dead hopes, wrecked faculties and base motives that made up his existence.

And also in a moment his heart responded thrillingly to this novel mood. An instantaneous and strong impulse moved him to battle with his desperate fate. He would pull himself out of the mire; he would make a man of himself again; he would conquer the evil that had taken possession of him. There was time; he was comparatively young yet: he would resurrect his old eager ambitions and pursue them without faltering. Those solemn but sweet organ notes had set up a revolution in him. To-morrow he would go into the roaring downtown district and find work. A fur importer had once offered him a place as driver. He would find him to-morrow and ask for the position. He would be somebody in the world. He would——

Soapy felt a hand laid on his arm. He looked quickly around into the broad face of a policeman.

"What are you doin' here?" asked the officer.

"Nothin'," said Soapy.

"Then come along," said the policeman.

"Three months on the Island," said the Magistrate in the Police Court the next morning.

JOHN GALSWORTHY
(1867–1933)

John Galsworthy was born in Kingston, Surrey, attended Harrow, and studied law at Oxford. He was admitted to Lincoln's Inn and called to the bar in 1890, although he practiced for only two years: "I read in various Chambers, practiced almost not at all, and disliked my profession thoroughly." In 1897 he published his first collection of stories, *From the Four Winds*. He used the pen name John Sinjohn for this collection and for his first three novels.

Galsworthy wrote plays, essays, and poetry in addition to fiction and was interested in a wide range of social issues, including prison reform. His play *Justice* (1910) moved Winston Churchill to enact immediate reform measures, including reduction of the hours of solitary confinement. In 1932 Galsworthy was awarded the Nobel Prize for Literature.

Galsworthy's most famous novels, collectively titled *The Forsyte Saga* (1906–1922), are a brilliant portrait of an upper-middle-class London family over forty years beginning in 1886. Like Galsworthy, the central character, Soames Forsyte, is a solicitor and the son of a solicitor. Soames is complexly drawn, at once inspiring pity and contempt. His unrequited love for his wife, Irene, fuels much of the drama and plot of the long story: "He had married this woman, conquered her, made her his own, and it seemed to him contrary to the most fundamental of all laws, the law of possession, that he could do no more than own her body—if indeed he could do that, which he was beginning to doubt."

Concern with law and middle-class propriety runs throughout the novel; indeed Galsworthy invented a number of legal situations in both this novel and the later novels. For example, when Soames realizes that Irene and his architect are in love, he sues the architect for breach of contract for overspending on the construction of his house. The courtroom scene in this excerpt is from Soames's sister Winifred's suit for restitution of conjugal rights, begun, under Soames's direction, as preliminary to a divorce. Winifred's husband, Montague Dartie, a womanizer and ne'er-do-well, has absconded to Buenos Aires with another woman. If he does not return to Winifred after being ordered to do so by the Court, she will be able to legally establish desertion and thus divorce him. (Until 1923 a woman could not divorce her husband for adultery alone; she had to prove the additional ground of either cruelty or desertion.)

When "Monty" does return in response to the judicial order, Soames exclaims to Winifred: "Hoist with our own petard. Why the deuce didn't you let me try cruelty?" In time, Soames will sue Irene for divorce, charging adultery (which was sufficient ground for a man to gain a divorce) and naming his cousin as co-respondent.

from THE FORSYTE SAGA

— 1906 —

Odd that one whose life was spent in bringing to the public eye all the private coils of property, the domestic disagreements of others, should dread so utterly the public eye turned on his own; and yet not odd, for who should know so well as he the whole unfeeling process of legal regulation.

He worked hard all day. Winifred was due at four o'clock; he was to take her down to a conference in the Temple with Dreamer, Q.C., and waiting for her he re-read the letter he had caused her to write the day of Dartie's departure, requiring him to return.

"DEAR MONTAGUE,

"I have received your letter with the news that you have left me for ever and are on your way to Buenos Aires. It has naturally been a great shock. I am taking this earliest opportunity of writing to tell you that I am prepared to let bygones be bygones if you will return to me at once. I beg you to do so. I am very much upset, and will not say any more now. I am sending this letter registered to the address you left at your Club. Please cable to me.

"Your still affectionate wife,

"WINIFRED DARTIE."

Ugh! What bitter humbug! He remembered leaning over Winifred while she copied what he had pencilled, and how she had said, laying down her pen, "Suppose he comes, Soames!" in such a strange tone of voice, as if she did not know her own mind. "He won't come," he had answered, "till he's spent his money. That's why we must act at once." Annexed to the copy of that letter was the original of Dartie's drunken scrawl from the Iseeum Club. Soames could have wished it had not been so manifestly penned in liquor. Just the sort of thing the Court would pitch on. He seemed to hear the Judge's voice say: "You took this seriously! Seriously enough to write him as you did? Do you think he meant it?" Never mind! The fact was clear that Dartie had sailed and had not returned. Annexed also was his cabled answer: "Impossible return. Dartie." Soames shook his head. If the whole thing were not disposed of within the next few months the fellow would turn up again like a bad penny. It saved a thousand a year at least to get rid of him, besides all the worry to Winifred and his father. 'I must stiffen Dreamer's back,' he thought; 'we must push it on.'

Winifred, who had adopted a kind of half-mourning which became her fair hair and tall figure very well, arrived in James' barouche drawn by James' pair. Soames had not seen it in the City since his father retired from business five years ago, and its incongruity gave him a shock. 'Times are changing,' he thought; 'one doesn't know what'll go next!' Top hats even were scarcer. He enquired after Val. Val, said Winifred, wrote that he was going to play polo next term. She thought he was in a very good set. She added with fashionably disguised anxiety: "Will there be much publicity about my affair, Soames? *Must* it be in the papers? It's so bad for him, and the girls."

With his own calamity all raw within him, Soames answered:

"The papers are a pushing lot; it's very difficult to keep things out. They pretend to be guarding the public's morals, and they corrupt them with their beastly reports. But we haven't got to that yet. We're only seeing Dreamer to-day on the restitution question. Of course he understands that it's to lead to a divorce; but you must seem genuinely anxious to get Dartie back—you might practice that attitude to-day."

Winifred sighed.

"Oh! What a clown Monty's been!" she said.

Soames gave her a sharp look. It was clear to him that she could not take her Dartie seriously, and would go back on the whole thing if given half a chance. His own instinct had been firm in this matter from the first. To save a little scandal now would only bring on his sister and her children real disgrace and perhaps ruin later on if Dartie were allowed to hang on to them, going downhill and spending the money James would leave his daughter. Though it *was* all tied up, that fellow would milk the settlements somehow, and make his family pay through the nose to keep him out of bankruptcy or even perhaps goal! They left the shining carriage, with the shining horses and the shining-hatted servants on the Embankment, and walked up to Dreamer Q.C.'s Chambers in Crown Office Row.

"Mr. Bellby is here, sir," said the clerk; "Mr. Dreamer will be ten minutes."

Mr. Bellby, the junior—not as junior as he might have been, for Soames only employed barristers of established reputation; it was, indeed, something of a mystery to him how barristers ever managed to establish that which made him employ them—Mr. Bellby was seated, taking a final glance through his papers. He had come from Court, and was in wig and gown, which suited a nose jutting out like the handle of a tiny pump, his small shrewd blue eyes, and rather protruding lower lip—no better man to supplement and stiffen Dreamer.

The introduction to Winifred accomplished, they leaped the weather and spoke of the war. Soames interrupted suddenly:

"If he doesn't comply we can't bring proceedings for six months. I want to get on with the matter, Bellby."

Mr. Bellby, who had the ghost of an Irish brogue, smiled at Winifred and murmured: "The Law's delays, Mrs. Dartie."

"Six months!" repeated Soames; "it'll drive it up to June! We shan't get the suit on till after the long vacation. We must put the screw on, Bellby"—he would have all his work cut out to keep Winifred up to the scratch.

"Mr. Dreamer will see you now, sir."

They filed in, Mr. Bellby going first, and Soames escorting Winifred after an interval of one minute by his watch.

Dreamer Q.C., in a gown but divested of wig, was standing before the fire, as if this conference were in the nature of a treat: he had the leathery, rather oily complexion which goes with great learning, a considerable nose with glasses perched on it, and little greyish whiskers; he luxuriated in the perpetual cocking of one eye, and the concealment of his lower with his upper lip, which gave a smothered turn to his speech. He had a way, too, of coming suddenly round the corner on the person he was talking to; this, with a disconcerting tone of voice, and a habit of growling before he began to speak—had secured a reputation second in Probate and Divorce to very few. Having listened, eye cocked, to Mr. Bellby's breezy recapitulation of the facts, he growled, and said:

"I know all that;" and coming round the corner at Winifred, smothered the words:

"We want to get him back, don't we, Mrs. Dartie?"

Soames interposed sharply:

"My sister's position, of course, is intolerable."

Dreamer growled. "Exactly. Now, can we rely on the cabled refusal, or must we wait till after Christmas to give him a chance to have written—that's the point, isn't it?"

"The sooner——" Soames began.

"What do you say, Bellby?" said Dreamer, coming round his corner.

Mr. Bellby seemed to sniff the air like a hound.

"We won't be on till the middle of December. We've no need to give um more rope than that."

"No," said Soames, "why should my sister be incommoded by his choosing to go——"

"To Jericho!" said Dreamer, again coming round his corner; "quite so. People oughtn't to go to Jericho, ought they, Mrs. Dartie?" And he raised his gown into a sort of fantail. "I agree. We can go forward. Is there anything more?"

"Nothing at present," said Soames meaningly; "I wanted you to see my sister."

Dreamer growled softly: "Delighted. Good evening!" And let fall the protection of his gown.

They filed out. Winifred went down the stairs. Soames lingered. In spite of himself he was impressed by Dreamer.

"The evidence is all right, I think," he said to Bellby. "Between ourselves, if we don't get the thing through quick, we never may. D'you think *he* understands that?"

"I'll make um," said Bellby. "Good man though—good man."

Soames nodded and hastened after his sister. He found her in a draught, biting her lips behind her veil, and at once said:

"The evidence of the stewardess will be very complete."

Winifred's face hardened; she drew herself up, and they walked to the carriage. And, all through that silent drive back to Green Street, the souls of both of them revolved a single thought: 'Why, oh! why should I have to expose my misfortune to the public like this? Why have to employ spies to peer into my private troubles? They were not of my making." . . .

Dartie Versus Dartie

The suit—Dartie *versus* Dartie—for restitution of those conjugal rights concerning which Winifred was at heart so deeply undecided, followed the laws of subtraction towards day of judgment. This was not reached before the Courts rose for Christmas, but the case was third on the list when they sat again. Winifred spent the Christmas holidays a thought more fashionably than usual, with the matter locked up in her low-cut bosom. James was particularly liberal to her that Christmas, expressing thereby his sympathy, and relief, at the approaching dissolution of her marriage with that 'precious rascal,' which his old heart felt but his old lips could not utter.

The disappearance of Dartie made the fall in Consols a comparatively small matter; and as to the scandal—the real animus he felt against that fellow, and the increasing lead which property was attaining over reputation in a true Forsyte about to leave this world, served to drug a mind from which all allusions to the matter (except his own) were studiously kept. What worried him as a lawyer and a parent was the fear that Dartie might suddenly turn up and obey the Order of the Court when made. That would be a pretty how-de-do! The fear preyed on him in fact so much that, in presenting Winifred with a large Christmas cheque, he said: "It's chiefly for that chap out there; to keep him from coming back." It was, of course, to pitch away good money, but all in the nature of insurance against that bankruptcy which would no longer hang over him if only the divorce went through; and he questioned Winifred rigorously until she could assure him that the money had been sent. Poor woman!—it cost her many a pang to send what must find its way into the vanity-bag of 'that creature'! Soames, hearing of it, shook his head. They were not dealing with a Forsyte, reasonably tenacious of his purpose. It was very risky without knowing how the land lay out there. Still, it would look well with the Court; and he would see that Dreamer brought it out. "I wonder," he said suddenly, "where that ballet goes after the Argentine"; never omitting a chance of reminder; for he knew that Winifred still had a weakness, if not for Dartie, at least for not laundering him in public. Though not good at showing admiration, he admitted that she was behaving extremely well, with all her children at home gaping like young birds for news of their father—Imogen just on the point of coming out, and Val very restive about the whole thing. He felt that Val was the real heart of the matter to Winifred, who certainly loved him beyond her other children. The boy could spoke the wheel of this divorce yet if he set his mind to it. And Soames was very careful to keep the proximity of the preliminary proceedings from his nephew's ears. He did more. He asked him to dine at the Remove, and over Val's cigar introduced the subject which he knew to be nearest to his heart.

"I hear," he said, "that you want to play polo up at Oxford."

Val became less recumbent in his chair.

"Rather!" he said.

"Well," continued Soames, "that's a very expensive business. Your grandfather isn't likely to consent to it unless he can make sure that he's not got any other drain on him." And he paused to see whether the boy understood his meaning.

Val's thick dark lashes concealed his eyes, but a slight grimace appeared on his wide mouth, and he muttered:

"I suppose you mean my Dad!"

"Yes," said Soames; "I'm afraid it depends on whether he continues to be a drag or not"; and said no more, letting the boy dream it over.

But Val was also dreaming in those days of a silver-roan palfrey and a girl riding it. Though Crum was in town and an introduction to Cynthia Dark to be had for the asking, Val did not ask; indeed, he shunned Crum and lived a life strange even to himself, except in so far as accounts with tailor and livery stable were concerned. To his mother, his sisters, his young brother, he seemed to spend this Vacation in 'seeing fellows,' and his evenings sleepily at home. They could not propose anything in daylight that did not meet with the one response: "Sorry; I've got to see a fellow"; and he was put to extraordinary shifts to get in and out of the house unobserved in riding clothes; until, being made a member of the Goat's Club, he was able to transport them there, where he could change unregarded and slip off on his hack to Richmond Park. He kept his growing sentiment religiously to himself. Not for a world would he breathe to the 'fellows,' whom he was not 'seeing,' anything so ridiculous from the point of view of their creed and his. But he could not help its destroying his other appetites. It was coming between him and the legitimate pleasures of youth at last on its own in a way which must, he knew, make him a milksop in the eyes of Crum. All he cared for was to dress in his last-created riding togs, and steal away to the Robin Hill Gate, where presently the silver roan would come demurely sidling with its slim and dark-haired rider, and in the glades bare of leaves they would go off side by side, not talking very much, riding races sometimes, and sometimes holding hands. More than once of an evening, in a moment of expansion, he had been tempted to tell his mother how this shy sweet cousin had stolen in upon him and wrecked his 'life.' But bitter experience, that all persons above thirty-five were spoil-sports, prevented him. After all, he supposed he would have to go through with College, and she would have to 'come out,' before they could be married; so why complicate things, so long as he could see her? Sisters were teasing and unsympathetic beings, a brother worse, so there was no one to confide in. Ah! And this beastly divorce business! What a misfortune to have a name which other people hadn't! If only he had been called Gordon or Scott or Howard or something fairly common! But Dartie—there wasn't another in the directory! One might as well have been named Morkin for all the covert it afforded! So matters went on, till one day in the middle of January the silver-roan palfrey and its rider were missing at the tryst. Lingering in the cold, he debated whether he should ride on to the house. But Jolly might be there, and the memory of their dark encounter was still fresh within him. One could not be always fighting with her brother! So he returned dismally to town and spent an evening plunged in gloom. At breakfast next day he noticed that his mother had on an unfamiliar dress and was wearing her hat. The dress was black with a glimpse of peacock blue, the hat black and large—she looked exceptionally well. But when after breakfast she said to him, "Come in here, Val," and led the way to the drawing-room, he was at once beset by qualms. Winifred carefully shut the door and passed her handkerchief over her lips; inhaling the violette de Parme with which it had been soaked, Val thought: 'Has she found out about Holly?'

Her voice interrupted:

"Are you going to be nice to me, dear boy?"

Val grinned doubtfully.

"Will you come with me this morning——"

"I've got to see——" began Val, but something in her face stopped him. "I say," he said, "you don't mean——"

"Yes, I have to go to the Court this morning."

Already!—that d—-d business which he had almost succeeded in forgetting, since nobody ever mentioned it. In self-commiseration he stood picking little bits of skin off his fingers. Then noticing that his mother's lips were all awry, he said impulsively: "All right, mother; I'll come. The brutes!" What brutes he did not know, but the expression exactly summed up their joint feeling, and restored a measure of equanimity.

"I suppose I'd better change into a 'shooter,' " he muttered, escaping to his room. He put on the 'shooter,' a higher collar, a pearl pin, and his neatest grey spats, to a somewhat blasphemous accompaniment. Looking at himself in the glass, he said, "Well, I'm damned if I'm going to show anything!" and went down. He found his grandfather's carriage at the door, and his mother in furs, with the appearance of one going to a Mansion House Assembly. They seated themselves side by side in the closed barouche, and all the way to the Courts of Justice Val made but one allusion to the business in hand. "There'll be nothing about those pearls, will there?"

The little tufted white tails of Winifred's muff began to shiver.

"Oh, no," she said, "it'll be quite harmless to-day. Your grandmother wanted to come too, but I wouldn't let her. I thought you could take care of me. You look so nice, Val. Just pull your coat collar up a little more at the back—that's right."

"If they bully you——" began Val.

"Oh! they won't. I shall be very cool. It's the only way."

"They won't want me to give evidence or anything?"

"No, dear; it's all arranged." And she patted his hand. The determined front she was putting on it stayed the turmoil in Val's chest, and he busied himself in drawing his gloves off and on. He had taken what he now saw was the wrong pair to go with his spats; they should have been grey, but were deerskin of a dark tan; whether to keep them on or not he could not decide. They arrived soon after ten. It was his first visit to the Law Courts, and the building struck him at once.

"By Jove!" he said as they passed into the hall, "this'd make four or five jolly good racket courts."

Soames was awaiting them at the foot of some stairs.

"Here you are!" he said, without shaking hands, as if the event had made them too familiar for such formalities. "It's Happerly Browne, Court I. We shall be on first."

A sensation such as he had known when going in to bat was playing now in the top of Val's chest, but he followed his mother and uncle doggedly, looking at no more than he could help, and thinking that the place smelled 'fuggy.' People seemed to be lurking everywhere, and he plucked Soames by the sleeve.

"I say, Uncle, you're not going to let those beastly papers in, are you?"

Soames gave him the sideway look which had reduced many to silence in its time.

"In here," he said. "You needn't take off your furs, Winifred."

Val entered behind them, nettled and with his head up. In this confounded hole everybody—and there were a good many of them—seemed sitting on everybody else's knee, though really divided from each other by pews; and Val had a feeling that they might all slip down together into the well. This, however, was but a momentary vision—of mahogany, and black gowns, and white blobs of wigs and faces and papers, all rather secret and whispery—before he was sitting next his mother in the front row, with his back to it all, glad of her violette de Parme, and taking off his gloves for the last time. His mother was looking at him; he was suddenly conscious that she had really wanted him there next to her, and that he counted for something in this business. All right! He would show them! Squaring his shoulders, he crossed his legs and gazed inscrutably at his spats. But just then an 'old Johnny' in a gown and long wig, looking awfully like a funny raddled woman, came through a door into the high pew opposite, and he had to uncross his legs hastily, and stand up with everybody else.

'Dartie *versus* Dartie!'

It seemed to Val unspeakably disgusting to have one's name called out like this in public! And, suddenly conscious that someone nearly behind him had begun talking about his family, he screwed his face round to see an old be-wigged buffer, who spoke as if he were eating his own words—queer-looking old cuss, the sort of man he had seen once or twice dining at Park Lane and punishing the port; he knew now where they 'dug them up.' All the same he found the old buffer quite fascinating, and would have continued to stare if his mother had not touched his arm. Reduced to gazing before him, he fixed his eyes on the Judge's face instead. Why should that old 'sportsman' with his sarcastic mouth and his quick-moving eyes have the power to meddle with their private affairs—hadn't he affairs of his own, just as many, and probably just as nasty? And there moved in Val, like an illness, all the deep-seated individualism of his breed. The voice behind him droned along: "Differences about money matters—extravagance of the respondent" (What a word! Was that his father?)—"strained situation—frequent absences on the part of Mr. Dartie. My client, very rightly, your Ludship will agree, was anxious to check a course—but lead to ruin—remonstrated—gambling at cards and on the race-course——" ('That's right!' thought Val, 'pile it on!') "Crisis early in October, when the respondent wrote her this letter from his Club." Val sat up and his ears burned. "I propose to read it with the emendations necessary to the epistle of a gentleman who has been—shall we say dining, me Lud?"

'Old brute!' thought Val, flushing deeper; 'you're not paid to make jokes!'

" 'You will not get the chance to insult me again in my own house. I am leaving the country to-morrow. It's played out'—an expression, your Ludship, not unknown in the mouths of those who have not met with conspicuous success."

'Sniggering owls!' thought Val, and his flush deepened.

" 'I am tired of being insulted by you.' My client will tell your Ludship that these so-called insults consisted in her calling him 'the limit'—a very mild expression, I venture to suggest, in all the circumstances."

Val glanced sideways at his mother's impassive face, it had a hunted look in the eyes. 'Poor mother,' he thought, and touched her arm with his own. The voice behind droned on.

" 'I am going to live a new life.—M. D.'

"And next day, me Lud, the respondent left by the steamship *Tuscarora* for Buenos Aires. Since then we have nothing from him but a cabled refusal in answer to the letter which my client wrote the following day in great distress, begging him to return to her. With your Ludship's permission, I shall now put Mrs. Dartie in the box."

When his mother rose, Val had a tremendous impulse to rise too and say: 'Look here! I'm going to see you jolly well treat her decently.' He subdued it, however; heard her saying, 'the truth, the whole truth, and nothing but the truth,' and looked up. She made a rich figure of it, in her furs and large hat, with a slight flush on her cheek-bones, calm, matter-of-fact; and he felt proud of her thus confronting all these 'confounded lawyers.' The examination began. Knowing that this was only the preliminary to divorce, Val followed with a certain glee the questions framed so as to give the impression that she really wanted his father back. It seemed to him that they were 'foxing Old Bagwigs finely.' And he received a most unpleasant jar when the Judge said suddenly:

"Now, why did your husband leave you—not because you called him 'the limit,' you know?"

Val saw his uncle lift his eyes to the witness box, without moving his face; he heard a shuffle of papers behind him; and instinct told him that the issue was in peril. Had Uncle Soames and the old buffer behind made a mess of it? His mother was speaking with a slight drawl.

"No, my Lord, but it had gone on a long time."

"What had gone on?"

"Our differences about money."

"But you supplied the money. Do you suggest that he left you to better his position?"

'The brute! The old brute, and nothing but the brute!' thought Val suddenly. 'He smells a rat—he's trying to get at the pastry!' And his heart stood still. If—if he did, then, of course, he would know that his mother didn't really want his father back. His mother spoke again, a thought more fashionably.

"No, my Lord, but you see I had refused to give him any more money. It took him a long time to believe that, but he did at last—and when he did——"

"I see, you had refused. But you've sent him some since."

"My Lord, I wanted him back."

"And you thought that would bring him?"

"I don't know, my Lord, I acted on my father's advice."

Something in the Judge's face, in the sound of the papers behind him, in the sudden crossing of his uncle's legs, told Val that she had made just the right answer. 'Crafty!' he thought; 'by Jove, what humbug it all is!'

The Judge was speaking:

"Just one more question, Mrs. Dartie. Are you still fond of your husband?"

Val's hands, slack behind him, became fists. What business had that Judge to make things human suddenly? To make his mother speak out of her heart, and say what, perhaps, she didn't know herself, before all these people! It wasn't decent. His mother answered, rather low: "Yes, my Lord." Val saw the Judge nod. 'Wish I could take a cock-shy at your head!' he thought irreverently, as his mother came back to her seat beside him. Witnesses to his father's departure and continued absence followed—one of their own maids even, which struck Val as particularly beastly; there was more talking, all humbug; and then the Judge pronounced the decree for restitution, and they got up to go. Val walked out behind his mother, chin squared, eyelids drooped, doing his level best to despise everybody. His mother's voice in the corridor roused him from an angry trance.

"You behaved beautifully, dear. It was such a comfort to have you. Your uncle and I are going to lunch."

"All right," said Val; "I shall have time to go and see that fellow." And, parting from them abruptly, he ran down the stairs and out into the air. He bolted into a hansom, and drove to the Goat's Club. His thoughts were on Holly and what he must do before her brother showed her this thing in to-morrow's paper.

When Val had left them Soames and Winifred made their way to the Cheshire Cheese. He had suggested it as a meeting place with Mr. Bellby. At that early Lour of noon they would have it to themselves, and Winifred had thought it would be 'amusing' to see this far-famed hostelry. Having ordered a light repast, to the consternation of the waiter, they awaited its arrival together with that of Mr. Bellby, in silent reaction after the hour and a half's suspense on the tenterhooks of publicity. Mr. Bellby entered presently, preceded by his nose, as cheerful as they were glum. Well! they had got the decree of restitution, and what was the matter with that!

"Quite," said Soames in a suitably low voice, "but we shall have to begin again to get evidence. He'll probably try the divorce—it will look fishy if it comes out that we knew of misconduct from the start. His questions showed well enough that he doesn't like this restitution dodge."

"Pho!" said Mr. Bellby cheerily, "he'll forget! Why, man, he'll have tried a hundred cases between now and then. Besides, he's bound by precedent to give ye your divorce, if the evidence is satisfactory. We won't let um know that Mrs. Dartie had knowledge of the facts. Dreamer did it very nicely—he's got a fatherly touch about um!"

Soames nodded.

"And I compliment ye, Mrs. Dartie," went on Mr. Bellby; "ye've a natural gift for giving evidence. Steady as a rock."

Here the waiter arrived with three plates balanced on one arm, and the remark: "I 'urried up the pudden, sir. You'll find plenty o' lark in it to-day."

Mr. Bellby applauded his forethought with a dip of his nose. But Soames and Winifred looked with dismay at their light lunch of gravified brown masses, touching them gingerly with their forks in the hope of distinguishing the bodies of the tasty little song-givers. Having begun, however, they found they were hungrier than they thought, and finished the lot, with a glass of port apiece. Conversation turned on the war. Soames thought Ladysmith would fall, and it might last a year. Bellby thought it would be over by the summer. Both agreed that they wanted more men. There was nothing for it but complete victory, since it was now a question of prestige. Winifred brought things back to more solid ground by saying that she did not want the divorce suit to come on till after the summer holidays had begun at Oxford, then the boys would have forgotten about it before Val had to go up again; the London season too would be over. The lawyers reassured her, an interval of six months was necessary—after that the earlier the better. People were now beginning to come in, and they parted—Soames to the city, Bellby to his chambers, Winifred in a hansom to Park Lane to let her mother know how she had fared. The issue had been so satisfactory on the whole that it was considered advisable to tell James, who never failed to say day after day that he didn't know about Winifred's affair, he couldn't tell. As his sands ran out, the importance of mundane matters became increasingly grave to him, as if he were feeling: 'I must make the most of it, and worry well; I shall soon have nothing to worry about.'

He received the report grudgingly. It was a new-fangled way of going about things, and he didn't know! But he gave Winifred a cheque, saying:

"I expect you'll have a lot of expense. That's a new hat you've got on. Why doesn't Val come and see us?"

Winifred promised to bring him to dinner soon. And, going home, she sought her bedroom where she could be alone. Now that her husband had been ordered back into her custody with a view to putting him away from her for ever, she would try once more to find out from her sore and lonely heart what she really wanted.

SUSAN GLASPELL

(1876–1948)

Susan Glaspell was known primarily as a playwright, although she also wrote novels, short stories, and a biography. She was born in Davenport, Iowa. Her husband, George Cram Cook, founded the first modern American theater company, the Provincetown Players, for which Glaspell and Eugene O'Neill were the principal playwrights. Of Glaspell's fourteen plays, eleven were written for the Players.

One of Glaspell's Provincetown plays was the one-act *Trifles*, produced in 1916. The following year she turned *Trifles* into a short story titled ''A Jury of Her Peers.'' This is her best-known story and is considered an early feminist classic. Seven decades later, Catherine MacKinnon wrote that ''The law sees and treats women the way men see and treat women.'' Here Glaspell portrays women rebelling against the exclusion of female voices, perceptions, and empathy from the patriarchal legal system.

The story is loosely based on a real-life case covered by Glaspell when she worked as a court reporter for the *Des Moines Daily News*. In December 1900, John Hossack, a wealthy Iowa farmer, was killed by ax blows to the head while asleep beside his wife, Margaret. Margaret Hossack was arrested during her husband's funeral and convicted of murder in a sensational trial. Glaspell herself played a major role in stirring public interest in the case, filing twenty-six lively stories marked by progressively greater sympathy for the defendant. By the day of the verdict, over two thousand spectators were packing the courthouse.

Immediately after the verdict, Glaspell left the newspaper and devoted herself full-time to imaginative writing. Hossack appealed her conviction to the Iowa Supreme Court, which granted her a new trial because of procedural errors. The second jury deadlocked, favoring conviction by a margin of nine to three, and Hossock was released with her guilt or innocence forever unresolved.

A JURY OF HER PEERS

— 1917 —

When Martha Hale opened the storm-door and got the north wind, she ran back for her big woollen scarf. As she hurriedly wound that round her head her eye made a scandalized sweep of her kitchen. It was no ordinary thing that called her away—it was probably farther from ordinary than anything that had ever happened in Dickson County. But her kitchen was in no shape for leaving: bread ready for mixing, half the flour sifted and half unsifted.

She hated to see things half done; but she had been at that when they stopped to get Mr. Hale, and the sheriff came in to say his wife wished Mrs. Hale would come too—adding, with a grin, that he guessed she was getting scarey and wanted another woman along. So she had dropped everything right where it was.

"Martha!" now came her husband's impatient voice. "Don't keep folks waiting out here in the cold."

She joined the three men and the one woman waiting for her in the sheriff's car.

After she had the robes tucked in she took another look at the woman beside her. She had met Mrs. Peters the year before, at the county fair, and the thing she remembered about her was that she didn't seem like a sheriff's wife. She was small and thin and didn't have a strong voice. Mrs. Gorman, sheriff's wife before Gorman went out and Peters came in, had a voice that seemed to be backing up the law wife every word. But if Mrs. Peters didn't look like a sheriff's wife, Peters made it up in looking like a sheriff—a heavy man with a big voice, who was particularly genial with the law-abiding, as if to make it plain that he knew the difference between criminals and non-criminals. And right there it came into Mrs. Hale's mind that this man who was so lively with all of them was going to the Wrights' now as a sheriff.

"The country's not very pleasant this time of year," Mrs. Peters at last ventured.

Mrs. Hale scarcely finished her reply, for they had gone up a little hill and could see the Wright place, and seeing it did not make her feel like talking. It looked very lonely this cold March morning. It had always been a lonesome-looking place. It was down in a hollow, and the poplar trees around it were lonely-looking trees. The men were looking at it and talking about what had happened. The county attorney was bending to one side, scrutinizing the place as they drew up to it.

"I'm glad you came with me," Mrs. Peters said nervously, as the two women were about to follow the men in through the kitchen door.

Even after she had her foot on the doorstep, Martha Hale had a moment of feeling she could not cross this threshold. And the reason it seemed she couldn't cross it now was because she hadn't crossed it before. Time and time again it had been in her mind, "I ought to go over and see Minnie Foster"—she still thought of her as Minnie Foster, though for twenty years she had been Mrs. Wright. And then there was always something to do and Minnie Foster would go from her mind. But *now* she could come.

The men went over to the stove. The women stood close together by the door. Young Henderson, the county attorney, turned around and said, "Come up to the fire, ladies."

Mrs. Peters took a step forward, then stopped. "I'm not—cold," she said.

And so the two women stood by the door, at first not even so much as looking around the kitchen.

The men talked about what a good thing it was the sheriff had sent his deputy out that morning to make a fire for them, and then Sheriff Peters stepped back from the stove, unbuttoned his outer coat, and leaned his hands on the kitchen table in a way that seemed to mark the beginning of official business. "Now, Mr. Hale," he said in a sort of semi-official voice, "before we move things about, you tell Mr. Henderson just what it was you saw when you came here yesterday morning."

The county attorney was looking around the kitchen.

"By the way," he asked, "has anything been moved?" He turned to the sheriff. "Are things just as you left them yesterday?"

Peters looked from cupboard to sink; to a small worn rocker a little to one side of the kitchen table.

"It's just the same."

"Well, Mr. Hale," said the county attorney, "tell just what happened when you came here yesterday morning."

Mrs. Hale, still leaning against the door, had that sinking feeling of the mother whose child is about to speak a piece. Lewis often wandered along and got things mixed up in a story. She hoped he would tell this straight and plain, and not say unnecessary things that would make it harder for Minnie Foster. He didn't begin at once, and she noticed that he looked queer, as if thinking of what he had seen here yesterday.

"Yes, Mr. Hale?" the county attorney reminded.

"Harry and I had started to town with a load of wood," Mrs. Hale's husband began.

Harry was Mrs. Hale's oldest boy. He wasn't with them now, for the wood never got to town yesterday and he was taking it this morning, so he hadn't been home when the sheriff stopped to say he wanted Mr. Hale to come over to the Wright place and tell the county attorney his story there, where he could point it all out. With all Mrs. Hale's other emotions came the fear Harry wasn't dressed warm enough—they hadn't any of them realized how that north wind did bite.

"We come along this road," Hale was going on, "and as we got in sight of the house I says to Harry, 'I'm goin' to see if I can't get John Wright to take a telephone.' You see," he explained to Henderson, "unless I can get somebody to go in with me they won't come out this branch road except for a price *I* can't pay. I'd spoke to Wright about it before; but he put me off, saying folks talked too much anyway, and all he asked was peace and quiet—guess you know about how much he talked himself. But I thought maybe if I went to the house and talked about it before his wife, and said all the women-folks liked the telephones, and that in this lonesome stretch of road it would be a good thing—well, I said to Harry that that was what I was going to say—though I said at the same time that I didn't know as what his wife wanted made much difference to John——"

Now, there he was!—saying things he didn't need to say. Mrs. Hale tried to catch her husband's eye, but fortunately the county attorney interrupted with:

"Let's talk about that a little later, Mr. Hale. I do want to talk about that, but I'm anxious now to know just what happened when you got here."

When he began this time, it was deliberately, as if he knew it were important.

"I didn't see or hear anything. I knocked at the door. And still it was all quiet inside. I knew they must be up—it was past eight o'clock. So I knocked again, louder, and I thought I heard somebody say, 'Come in.' I wasn't sure—I'm not sure yet. But I opened the door—this door," jerking a hand toward the door by which the two women stood, "and there, in that rocker"—pointing to it—"sat Mrs. Wright."

Everyone in the kitchen looked at the rocker. It came into Mrs. Hale's mind that this chair didn't look in the least like Minnie Foster—the Minnie Foster of twenty years before. It was a dingy red, with wooden rungs up the back, and the middle rung gone; the chair sagged to one side.

"How did she—look?" the county attorney was inquiring.

"Well," said Hale, "she looked—queer."

"How do you mean—queer?"

He took out note-book and pencil. Mrs. Hale did not like the sight of that pencil. She kept her eye on her husband, as if to keep him from saying unnecessary things that would go into the book and make trouble.

Hale spoke guardedly: "Well, as if she didn't know what she was going to do next. And kind of—done up."

"How did she seem to feel about your coming?"

"Why, I don't think she minded—one way or other. She didn't pay much attention. I said, 'Ho' do, Mrs. Wright. It's cold, ain't it?' And she said, 'Is it?'—and went on pleatin' of her apron.

"Well, I was surprised. She didn't ask me to come up to the stove, but just set there, not even lookin' at me. And so I said, 'I want to see John.'

"And then she—laughed. I guess you would call it a laugh.

"I thought of Harry and the team outside, so I said, a little sharp, 'Can I see John?' 'No,' says she—kind of dull like. 'Ain't he home?' says I. Then she looked at me. 'Yes,' says she, 'he's home.' 'Then why can't I see him?' I asked her, out of patience with her now. ' 'Cause he's dead,' says she, just as quiet and dull—and fell to pleatin' her apron. 'Dead?' says I, like you do when you can't take in what you've heard.

"She just nodded her head, not getting a bit excited, but rockin' back and forth.

" 'Why—where is he?' says I, not knowing *what* to say.

"She just pointed upstairs—like this"—pointing to the room above.

"I got up, with the idea of going up there myself. By this time I—didn't know what to do. I walked from there to here, then I says, 'Why, what did he die of?'

" 'He died of a rope around his neck,' says she; and just went on pleatin' at her apron."

Hale stopped speaking, staring at the rocker. Nobody spoke; it was as if all were seeing the woman who had sat there the morning before.

"And what did you do then?" the attorney asked.

"I went out and called Harry. I thought I might—need help. I got Harry in, and we went upstairs." His voice fell almost to a whisper. "There he was—lying over the——"

"I think I'd rather have you go into that upstairs," the county attorney interrupted, "where you can point it all out. Just go on now with the rest of the story."

"Well, my first thought was to get that rope off. It looked——"

He stopped; he did not say how it looked.

"But Harry, he went up to him and he said, 'No, he's dead all right, and we'd better not touch anythin''. So we went downstairs.

"She was still sitting that same way. 'Has anybody been notified?' I asked. 'No,' says she, unconcerned.

" 'Who did this, Mrs. Wright?' said Harry. He said it business-like, and she stopped pleatin' at her apron. 'I don't know,' she says. 'You don' *know*?' says Harry. 'Weren't you sleepin' in the bed with him?' 'Yes,' says she, 'but I was on the inside.' 'Somebody slipped a rope round his neck and strangled him, and you didn't wake up?' says Harry. 'I didn't wake up,' she said after him.

"We may have looked as if we didn't see how that could be, for after a minute she said, 'I sleep sound.'

"Harry was going to ask her more questions, but I said maybe that weren't our business; maybe we ought to let her tell her story first to the coroner or the sheriff. So Harry went fast as he could over to High Road—the Rivers' place, where there's a telephone."

"And what did she do when she knew you had gone for the coroner?"

"She moved from that chair to this one over here, and just sat there with her hands held together and looking down. I got a feeling that I ought to make some conversation, so I said I had come in to see if John wanted to put in a telephone; and at that she started to laugh, and then she stopped and looked at me—scared."

At sound of a moving pencil the man who was telling the story looked up.

"I dunno—maybe it wasn't scared; I wouldn't like to say it was. Soon Harry got back, and then Dr. Lloyd came, and you, Mr. Peters, and so I guess that's all I know that you don't."

He said this with relief, moved as if relaxing. The county attorney walked to the stair door.

"I guess we'll go upstairs first—then out to the barn and around there."

He paused and looked around the kitchen.

"You're convinced there was nothing important here?" he asked the sheriff. "Nothing that would—point to any motive?"

The sheriff too looked all around. "Nothing here but kitchen things," he said, with a little laugh for the insignificance of kitchen things.

The county attorney was looking at the cupboard. He opened the upper part and looked in. After a moment he drew his hand away sticky.

"Here's a nice mess," he said resentfully.

The two women had drawn nearer, and now the sheriff's wife spoke.

"Oh—her fruit," she said, looking to Mrs. Hale for understanding. "She worried about that when it turned so cold last night. She said the fire would go out and her jars might burst."

Mrs. Peters' husband broke into a laugh.

"Well, can you beat the women! Held for murder, and worrying about her preserves!"

The young attorney set his lips.

"I guess before we're through with her she may have something more serious than preserves to worry about."

"Oh, well," said Mrs. Hale's husband, with good-natured superiority, "women are used to worrying over trifles."

The two women moved a little closer together. Neither of them spoke. The county attorney seemed to remember his manners—and think of his future.

"And yet," said he, with the gallantry of a young politician, "for all their worries, what would we do without the ladies?"

The women did not speak. He went to the sink to wash his hands, turned to wipe them on the roller towel, pulled it for a cleaner place.

"Dirty towels! Not much of a house-keeper, would you say, ladies?" He kicked his foot against some dirty pans under the sink.

"There's a great deal of work to be done on a farm," said Mrs. Hale stiffly.

"To be sure. And yet"—with a little bow to her—"I know there are some Dickson County farm-houses that do not have such roller towels."

"Those towels get dirty awful quick. Men's hands aren't always as clean as they might be."

"Ah, loyal to your sex, I see," he laughed. He gave her a keen look. "But you and Mrs. Wright were neighbours. I suppose you were friends too."

Martha Hale shook her head.

"I've seen little enough of her of late years. I've not been in this house—it's more than a year."

"And why was that? You didn't like her?"

"I liked her well enough," she replied with spirit. "Farmers' wives have their hands full, Mr. Henderson. And then——" She looked around the kitchen.

"Yes?" he encouraged.

"It never seemed a very cheerful place," said she, more to herself than to him.

"No," he agreed; "I don't think anyone would call it cheerful. I shouldn't say she had the home-making instinct.

"Well, I don't know as Wright had either," she muttered.

"You mean they didn't get on very well?"

"No; I don't mean anything," she answered, with decision. "But I don't think a place would be any the cheerfuler for John Wright's bein' in it."

"I'd like to talk to you about that a little later, Mrs. Hale." He moved towards the stair door, followed by the two men.

"I suppose anything Mrs. Peters does 'll be all right?" the sheriff inquired. "She was to take in some clothes for her, you know—and a few little things. We left in such a hurry yesterday."

The county attorney looked at the two women they were leaving alone among the kitchen things.

"Yes—Mrs. Peters," he said, his glance resting on the woman who was not Mrs. Peters, the big farmer woman who stood behind the sheriff's wife. "Of course Mrs. Peters is one of us," he added in a manner of entrusting responsibility. "And keep your eye out, Mrs. Peters, for anything that might be of use. No telling; you women might come upon a clue to the motive—and that's the thing we need."

Mr. Hale rubbed his face in the fashion of a slow man getting ready for a pleasantry. "But would the women know a clue if they did come upon it?" he said. Having delivered himself of this, he followed the others through the stair door.

The women stood motionless, listening to the footsteps, first upon the stairs, then in the room above them.

Then, as if releasing herself from something too strange, Mrs. Hale began to arrange the dirty pans under the sink, which the county attorney's disdainful push of the foot had upset.

"I'd hate to have men coming into my kitchen, snoopin' round and criticizing."

"Of course it's no more than their duty," said the sheriff's wife, in her timid manner.

"Duty's all right, but I guess that deputy sheriff that come out to make the fire might have got a little of this on." She gave the roller towel a pull. "Wish I'd thought of that sooner! Seems mean to talk about her for not having things slicked up, when she had to come away in such a hurry."

She looked around the kitchen. Certainly it was not "slicked up." Her eye was held by a bucket of sugar on a low shelf. The cover was off the wooden bucket, and beside it was a paper bag—half full.

Mrs. Hale moved towards it.

"She was putting this in there," she said to herself—slowly.

She thought of the flour in her kitchen at home—half sifted, half not sifted. She had been interrupted, and had left things half done. What had interrupted Minnie Foster? Why had that work been left half done? She made a move as if to finish it—unfinished things always bothered her, and then she saw that Mrs. Peters was watching her, and she didn't want Mrs. Peters to get that feeling she had of work begun and then—for some reason—not finished.

"It's a shame about her fruit," she said, going to the cupboard. "I wonder if it's all gone.

"Here's one that's all right," she said at last. She held it towards the light. "This is cherries, too." She looked again. "I declare I believe that's the only one.

"She'll feel awful bad, after all her hard work in the hot weather. I remember the afternoon I put up my cherries last summer."

She put the bottle on the table, and was about to sit down in the rocker. But something kept her from sitting in that chair. She stood looking at it, seeing the woman who had sat there "pleatin' at her apron."

The thin voice of the sheriff's wife broke in upon her: "I must be getting those things from the front room closet." She opened the door into the other room, started in, stepped back. "You coming with me, Mrs. Hale?" she asked nervously. "You—you could help me get them."

They were soon back. "My!" said Mrs. Peters, dropping the things on the table and hurrying to the stove.

Mrs. Hale stood examining the clothes the woman who was being detained in town had said she wanted.

"Wright was close!" she exclaimed, holding up a shabby black skirt that bore the marks of much making over. "I think maybe that's why she kept so much to herself. I s'pose she felt she couldn't do her part; and then, you don't enjoy things when you feel shabby. She used to wear pretty clothes and be lively—when she was Minnie Foster, one of the town girls, singing in the choir. But that—oh, that was twenty years ago."

With a carefulness in which there was something tender, she folded the shabby clothes and piled them at one corner of the table. She looked up at Mrs. Peters, and there was something in the other woman's look that irritated her.

"She don't care," she said to herself. "Much difference it makes to her whether Minnie Foster had pretty clothes when she was a girl."

Then she looked again, and she wasn't so sure; in fact, she hadn't at any time been sure about Mrs. Peters. She had that shrinking manner, and yet her eyes looked as if they could see a long way into things.

"This all you was to take in?" asked Mrs. Hale.

"No," said the sheriff's wife; "she said she wanted an apron. Funny thing to want," she ventured in her nervous way, "for there's not much to get you dirty in jail, goodness knows. But I suppose just to make her feel more natural. She said they were in the bottom drawer of this cupboard. Yes—here they are. And then her little shawl that always hung on the stair door."

She took the small grey shawl from behind the door leading upstairs.

Suddenly Mrs. Hale took a quick step towards the other woman.

"Mrs. Peters!"

"Yes, Mrs. Hale?"

"Do you think she—did it?"

Mrs. Peters looked frightened. "Oh, I don't know," she said, in a voice that seemed to shrink from the subject.

"Well, I don't think she did," affirmed Mrs. Hale. "Asking for an apron, and her little shawl. Worryin' about her fruit."

"Mr. Peters says——" Footsteps were heard in the room above; she stopped, looked up, then went on in a lowered voice: "Mr. Peters says—it looks bad for her. Mr. Henderson is awful sarcastic in a speech, and he's going to make fun of her saying she didn't wake up."

For a moment Mrs. Hale had no answer. Then, "Well, I guess John Wright didn't wake up—when they was slippin' that rope under his neck," she muttered.

"No, it's *strange*," breathed Mrs. Peters. "They think it was such a—funny way to kill a man."

"That's just what Mr. Hale said," said Mrs. Hale, in a resolutely natural voice. "There was a gun in the house. He says that's what he can't understand."

"Mr. Henderson said, coming out, that what was needed for the case was a motive. Something to show anger—or sudden feeling."

"Well, I don't see any signs of anger around here," said Mrs. Hale. "I don't——"

She stopped. Her eye was caught by a dish-towel in the middle of the kitchen table. Slowly she moved towards the table. One half of it was wiped clean, the other half untidy. Her eyes made a slow, almost unwilling turn to the bucket of sugar and the half-empty bag beside it. Things begun—and not finished.

She stepped back. "Wonder how they're finding things upstairs? I hope she had it in better shape up there. Seems kind of *sneaking*, locking her up in town and coming out here to get her own house to turn against her!"

"But, Mrs. Hale," said the sheriff's wife, "the law is the law."

"I s'pose it is," answered Mrs. Hale shortly.

She turned to the stove, saying something about that fire not being much to brag of.

"The law is the law—and a bad stove is a bad stove. How'd you like to cook on this?" with the poker pointing to the broken lining. She opened the oven door. The thought of Minnie Foster trying to bake in that oven—and the thought of her never going over to see Minnie Foster——

She was startled by hearing Mrs. Peters say, "A person gets discouraged—and loses heart."

The sheriff's wife had looked from the stove to the sink—the pail of water which had been carried in from outside. The two women stood there silent, above them the footsteps of the men who were looking for evidence against the woman who had worked in that kitchen. That look of seeing into things, of seeing through a thing to something else, was in the eyes of the sheriff's wife now. When Mrs. Hale next spoke to her, it was gently.

"Better loosen up your things, Mrs. Peters. We'll not feel them when we go out."

Mrs. Peters went to the back of the room to hang up the fur tippet she was wearing. "Why, she was piecing a quilt," she exclaimed, and held up a large sewing basket piled high with quilt pieces.

Mrs. Hale spread some of the blocks on the table.

"It's log-cabin pattern," she said, putting several of them together. "Pretty, isn't it?"

They were so engaged with the quilt that they did not hear the footsteps on the stairs. As the stair door opened Mrs. Hale was saying, "Do you suppose she was going to quilt it, or just knot it?"

The sheriff threw up his hands.

"They wonder whether she was going to quilt it, or just knot it!"

There was a laugh for the ways of women, a warming of hands over the stove, and then the county attorney said briskly, "Well, let's go right out to the barn and get that cleared up."

"I don't see as there's anything so strange," Mrs. Hale said resentfully, after the outside door had closed on the three men—"our taking up our time with little things while we're waiting for them to get the evidence. I don't see as it's anything to laugh about."

"Of course they've got awful important things on their minds," said the sheriff's wife apologetically.

They returned to an inspection of the blocks for the quilt. Mrs. Hale was looking at the fine, even sewing, preoccupied with thoughts of the woman who had done that sewing, when she heard the sheriff's wife say, in a startled tone, "Why, look at this one."

"The sewing," said Mrs. Peters, in a troubled way. "All the rest of them have been so nice and even—but—this one. Why, it looks as if she didn't know what she was about!"

Their eyes met—something flashed to life, passed between them; then, as if with an effort, they seemed to pull away from each other. A moment Mrs. Hale sat there, her fingers upon those stitches so unlike the rest of the sewing. Then she had pulled a knot and drawn the threads.

"Oh, what are you doing, Mrs. Hale?" asked the sheriff's wife.

"Just pulling out a stitch or two that's not sewed very good," said Mrs. Hale mildly.

"I don't think we ought to touch things," Mrs. Peters said.

"I'll just finish up this end," answered Mrs. Hale.

She threaded a needle and started to replace bad sewing with good. Then in that thin, timid voice, she heard: "Mrs. Hale!"

"Yes, Mrs. Peters?"

"What do you suppose she was so—nervous about?"

"Oh, *I* don't know," said Mrs. Hale, as if dismissing a thing not important enough to spend much time on. "I don't know as she was—nervous. I sew awful queer sometimes when I'm just tired."

"Well, I must get these clothes wrapped. They may be through sooner than we think. I wonder where I could find a piece of paper—and string."

"In that cupboard, maybe," suggested Mrs. Hale.

One piece of the crazy sewing remained unripped. Mrs. Peters' back turned, Martha Hale scrutinized that piece, compared it with the dainty, accurate stitches of the other blocks. The difference was startling. Holding this block it was hard to remain quiet, as if the distracted thoughts of the woman who had perhaps turned to it to try and quiet herself were communicating themselves to her.

"Here's a bird-cage," Mrs. Peters said. "Did she have a bird, Mrs. Hale?"

"Why, I don't know whether she did or not." She turned to look at the cage Mrs. Peters was holding up. "I've not been here in so long." She sighed. "There was a man round last year selling canaries cheap—but I don't know as she took one. Maybe she did. She used to sing real pretty herself."

"Seems kind of funny to think of a bird here. But she must have had one—or why would she have a cage? I wonder what happened to it."

"I suppose maybe the cat got it," suggested Mrs. Hale, resuming her sewing.

"No; she didn't have a cat. She's got that feeling some people have about cats—being afraid of them. When they brought her to our house yesterday, my cat got in the room, and she was real upset and asked me to take it out."

"My sister Bessie was like that," laughed Mrs. Hale.

The sheriff's wife did not reply. The silence made Mrs. Hale turn. Mrs. Peters was examining the bird-cage.

"Look at this door," she said slowly. "It's broke. One hinge has been pulled apart."

Mrs. Hale came nearer.

"Looks as if someone must have been—rough with it."

Again their eyes met—startled, questioning, apprehensive. For a moment neither spoke nor stirred. Then Mrs. Hale, turning away, said brusquely, "If they're going to find any evidence, I wish they'd be about it. I don't like this place."

"But I'm awful glad you came with me, Mrs. Hale." Mrs. Peters put the bird-cage on the table and sat down. "It would be lonesome for me—sitting here alone."

"Yes, it would, wouldn't it?" agreed Mrs. Hale. She had picked up the sewing, but now it dropped to her lap, and she murmured: "But I tell you what I *do* wish, Mrs. Peters. I wish I had come over sometimes when she was here. I wish—I had."

"But of course you were awful busy, Mrs. Hale. Your house—and your children."

"I could've come. I stayed away because it weren't cheerful—and that's why I ought to have come. I"—she looked around—"I've never liked this place. Maybe because it's down in a hollow and you don't see the road. I don't know what it is, but it's a lonesome place, and always was. I wish I had come over to see Minnie Foster sometimes. I can see now——"

"Well, you mustn't reproach yourself. Somehow we just don't see how it is with other folks till—something comes up."

"Not having children makes less work," mused Mrs. Hale, "but it makes a quiet house. And Wright out to work all day—and no company when he did come in. Did you know John Wright, Mrs. Peters?"

"Not to know him. I've seen him in town. They say he was a good man."

"Yes—good," conceded John Wright's neighbour grimly. "He didn't drink, and kept his word as well as most, I guess, and paid his debts. But he was a hard man, Mrs. Peters. Just to pass the time of day with him——" She shivered. "Like a raw wind that gets to the bone." Her eye fell upon the cage on the table before her, and she added, "I should think she would've wanted a bird!"

Suddenly she leaned forward, looking intently at the cage. "But what do you s'pose went wrong with it?"

"I don't know," returned Mrs. Peters; "unless it got sick and died."

But after she said this she reached over and swung the broken door. Both women watched it.

"You didn't know—her?" Mrs. Hale asked.

"Not till they brought her yesterday," said the sheriff's wife.

"She—come to think of it, she was kind of like a bird herself. Real sweet and pretty, but kind of timid and—flutterly. How—she—did—change."

Finally, as if struck with a happy thought and relieved to get back to every-day things: "Tell you what, Mrs. Peters, why don't you take the quilt in with you? It might take up her mind."

"Why, I think that's a real nice idea, Mrs. Hale. There couldn't possibly be any objection to that, could there? Now, just what will I take? I wonder if her patches are in here?" They turned to the sewing basket.

"Here's some red," said Mrs. Hale, bringing out a roll of cloth. Underneath this was a box. "Here, maybe her scissors are in here—and her things." She held it up. "What a pretty box! I'll warrant that was something she had a long time ago—when she was a girl."

She held it in her hand a moment; then, with a little sigh, opened it.

Instantly her hand went to her nose. "Why!"

Mrs. Peters drew nearer—then turned away.

"There's something wrapped up in this piece of silk," faltered Mrs. Hale.

"This isn't her scissors," said Mrs. Peters, in a shrinking voice.

Mrs. Hale raised the piece of silk. "Oh, Mrs. Peters!" she cried. "It's——"

Mrs. Peters bent closer.

"It's the bird," she whispered.

"But, Mrs. Peters!" cried Mrs. Hale. "*Look* at it! Its *neck*—look at its neck! It's all—other side *to*."

The sheriff's wife again bent closer.

"Somebody wrung its neck," said she, in a voice that was slow and deep.

The eyes of the two women met—this time clung together in a look of dawning comprehension, of growing horror. Mrs. Peters looked from the dead bird to the broken door of the cage. Again their eyes met. And just then there was a sound at the outside door.

Mrs. Hale slipped the box under the quilt pieces in the basket. The country attorney and sheriff came in.

"Well, ladies," said the attorney, as one turning from serious things to little pleasantries, "have you decided whether she was going to quilt it or knot it?"

"We think," said the sheriff's wife hastily, "that she was going to knot it."

"Well, that's very interesting, I'm sure." He caught sight of the cage. "Has the bird flown?"

"We think the cat got it," said Mrs. Hale in a prosaic voice.

He was walking up and down, as if thinking something out.

"Is there a cat?" he asked absently.

Mrs. Hale shot a look up at the sheriff's wife.

"Well, not *now*," said Mrs. Peters. "They're superstitious, you know; they leave."

The county attorney did not heed her. "No sign at all of anyone having come in from the outside," he said to Peters, continuing an interrupted conversation. "Their own rope. Now let's go upstairs again and go over it, piece by piece. It would have to have been someone who knew just the——"

The stair door closed behind them and their voices were lost.

The two women sat motionless, not looking at each other, but as if peering into something and at the same time holding back. When they spoke now it was as if they were afraid of what they were saying, but could not help saying it.

"She liked the bird," said Martha Hale. "She was going to bury it in that pretty box."

"When I was a girl," said Mrs. Peters, under her breath, "my kitten—there was a boy took a hatchet, and before my eyes—before I could get there——" She covered her face an instant. "If they hadn't held me back I would have"—she caught herself, and finished weakly—"hurt him."

Then they sat without speaking or moving.

"I wonder how it would seem," Mrs. Hale began, as if feeling her way over strange ground—"never to have had any children around." Her eyes made a sweep of the kitchen. "No, Wright wouldn't like the bird—a thing that sang. She used to sing. He killed that too."

Mrs. Peters moved. "Of course we don't know who killed the bird."

"I knew John Wright," was the answer.

"It was an awful thing was done in this house that night, Mrs. Hale," said the sheriff's wife. "Killing a man while he slept—slipping a thing round his neck that choked the life out of him."

Mrs. Hale's hand went to the bird-cage. "His neck. Choked the life out of him."

"We don't *know* who killed him," whispered Mrs. Peters wildly. "We don't *know*."

Mrs. Hale had not moved. "If there had been years and years of nothing, then a bird to sing to you, it would be awful—still, after the bird was still."

"I know what stillness is," whispered Mrs. Peters. "When we homesteaded in Dakota, and my first baby died—after he was two years old—and me with no other then——"

Mrs. Hale stirred. "How soon do you suppose they'll be through looking for the evidence?"

"I know what stillness is," repeated Mrs. Peters. Then she too pulled back. "The law has got to punish crime, Mrs. Hale."

"I wish you'd seen Minnie Foster when she wore a white dress with blue ribbons, and stood up there in the choir and sang."

The picture of that girl, the thought that she had lived neighbour to her for twenty years, and had let her die for lack of life, was suddenly more than the woman could bear.

"Oh, I *wish* I'd come over here once in a while!" she cried. "That was a crime! That was a crime! Who's going to punish *that*?"

"We mustn't—take on," said Mrs. Peters, with a frightened look towards the stairs.

"I might 'a' *known* she needed help! I tell you, it's *queer*, Mrs. Peters. We live close together, and we live far apart. We all go through the same things—it's all just a different kind of the same thing! If it weren't—why do you and I *know*—what we know this minute?"

Seeing the jar of fruit on the table, she reached for it. "If I was you I wouldn't *tell* her her fruit was gone! Tell her it *ain't*. Tell her it's all right—all of it. Here—take this in to prove it to her! She—she may never know whether it was broke or not."

Mrs. Peters took the bottle of fruit as if glad to take it—as if touching a familiar thing, having something to do, could keep her from something else. She looked about for something to wrap the fruit in, took a petticoat from the pile of clothes she had brought from the front room, nervously started winding that round the bottle.

"My!" she began, in a high voice, "it's a good thing the men couldn't hear us! Getting all stirred up over a little thing like a—dead canary. As if that could have anything to do with—with——My, wouldn't they *laugh*?"

There were footsteps on the stairs.

"Maybe they would," muttered Mrs. Hale—"maybe they wouldn't."

"No, Peters," said the county attorney, "it's all perfectly clear, except the reason for doing it. But you know juries when it comes to women. If there was some definite thing—something to *show*. Something to make a story about. A thing that would connect up with this clumsy way of doing it."

Mrs. Hale looked at Mrs. Peters. Mrs. Peters was looking at her. Quickly they looked away from one another. The outer door opened and Mr. Hale came in.

"I've nailed back that board we ripped off," he said.

"Much obliged, Mr. Hale," said the sheriff. "We'll be getting along now."

"I'm going to stay here awhile by myself," the county attorney suddenly announced. "You can send Frank out for me, can't you?" he asked the sheriff. "I want to go over everything. I'm not satisfied we can't do better."

Again, for one brief moment, the women's eyes met.

The sheriff came up to the table.

"Did you want to see what Mrs. Peters was going to take in?"

The county attorney picked up the apron. He laughed.

"Oh, I guess they're not very dangerous things the ladies have picked out."

Mrs. Hale's hand was on the sewing basket in which the box was concealed. She felt that she ought to take her hand off the basket. She did not seem able to. She picked up one of the quilt blocks she had piled on to cover the box. She had a fear that if he took up the basket she would snatch it from him.

But he did not take it. With another laugh he turned away, saying, "No, Mrs. Peters doesn't need supervising. For that matter, a sheriff's wife is married to the law. Ever think of it that way, Mrs. Peters?"

Mrs. Peters had turned her face away. "Not—just that way," she said.

"Married to the law!" chuckled Mrs. Peters' husband. He moved towards the door into the front room, and said to the county attorney, "I just want you to come here a minute, George. We ought to take a look at these windows."

"Oh—windows!" scoffed the county attorney.

"We'll be leaving in a second, Mr. Hale," Mr. Peters told the farmer, as he followed the county attorney into the other room.

"Can't be leavin' too soon to suit me," muttered Hale, and went out.

Again, for one final moment, the two women were alone in that kitchen.

Martha Hale sprang up, her hands tight together, looking at that other woman, with whom it rested. At first she could not see her eyes, for the sheriff's wife had not turned back since she turned away at that suggestion of being married to the law. Slowly, unwillingly, Mrs. Peters turned her head until her eyes met the eyes of the other woman. There was a moment when they held each other in a steady, burning look in which there was no evasion nor flinching. Then Martha Hale's eyes pointed the way to the basket in which was hidden the thing that would convict the third woman—that woman who was not there, and yet who had been there with them through that hour.

For a moment Mrs. Peters did not move. And then she did it. Threw back the quilt pieces, got the box, tried to put it in her hand-bag. It was too big. Desperately she opened it, started to take the bird out. But there she broke—she could not touch the bird. She stood there helpless, foolish.

There was a sound at the door. Martha Hale snatched the box from the sheriff's wife and got it in the pocket of her big coat just as the sheriff and the county attorney came back into the kitchen.

"Well, Henry," said the county attorney, facetiously, "at least we found out that she was not going to quilt it. She was going to—what is it you call it, ladies?"

Mrs. Hale's hand was against the pocket of her coat.

"We call it—knot it," was her answer.

AGATHA CHRISTIE

(1890–1976)

Born in Torquay, Devon, Agatha Mary Clarissa Miller never attended school, but wrote short stories and poems from an early age. In 1914 she married Colonel Archibald Christie, from whom she was later divorced after a sensational episode in which she disappeared for ten days. Agatha Christie's first foray into mystery writing, *The Mysterious Affair at Styles* (1920), introduced private detective Hercule Poirot and ushered in the golden age of mystery fiction.

Publishing some seventy novels and twice as many short stories, Christie became the most popular crime writer of all time, indeed the best-selling fiction author in world history, with some two billion copies sold in more than a hundred languages. Many of her novels were in series featuring the sleuths Poirot, Miss Jane Marple, or Tommy and Tuppence Beresford. Her typical plot is the intellectual puzzle of a murder with many suspects, each of whom is eliminated until one is left to be arrested or die. In addition, Christie wrote the longest-running play ever, *The Mousetrap* (playing in London from 1952 to the present), as well as other successful dramas. She was made a Dame Commander of the Order of the British Empire in 1971.

"The Witness for the Prosecution" was first published in *Munsey's Magazine* in 1924 and was then reprinted in Christie's collections, *The Hound of Death* (1933) and *Witness for the Prosecution and Other Stories* (1948). This is an ingenious, highly suspenseful tale in which a solicitor, Mr. Mayherne, takes the central role usually reserved for detectives in Christie's writing. Some critics rank "Witness" as Christie's finest short story.

With the initial word in the title dropped, *Witness for the Prosecution* was adapted by Christie for the stage in 1953 and won the New York Drama Critics' Circle Award for best foreign play. In 1957 a movie version was released, starring Charles Laughton, Marlene Dietrich, and Tyrone Power. During filming, all visitors to the studio were made to sign a "Secrecy Pledge" not to reveal the ending. The play and film actually conclude differently from the short story, tacking on to the story's superb denouement an additional and unsatisfactory twist.

THE WITNESS FOR THE PROSECUTION

— 1924 —

Mr. Mayherne adjusted his pince-nez and cleared his throat with a little dry-as-dust cough that was wholly typical of him. Then he looked again at the man opposite him, the man charged with willful murder.

Mr. Mayherne was a small man, precise in manner, neatly, not to say foppishly dressed, with a pair of very shrewd and piercing gray eyes. By no means a fool. Indeed, as a solicitor, Mr. Mayherne's reputation stood very high. His voice, when he spoke to his client, was dry but not unsympathetic.

"I must impress upon you again that you are in very grave danger, and that the utmost frankness is necessary."

Leonard Vole, who had been staring in a dazed fashion at the blank wall in front of him, transferred his glance to the solicitor.

"I know," he said hopelessly. "You keep telling me so. But I can't seem to realize yet that I'm charged with murder—*murder*. And such a dastardly crime, too."

Mr. Mayherne was practical, not emotional. He coughed again, took off his pince-nez, polished them carefully, and replaced them on his nose. Then he said, "Yes, yes, yes. Now, my dear Mr. Vole, we're going to make a determined effort to get you off—and we shall succeed—we shall succeed. But I must have all the facts. I must know just how damaging the case against you is likely to be. Then we can fix upon the best line of defense."

Still the young man looked at him in the same dazed, hopeless fashion. To Mr. Mayherne the case had seemed black enough, and the guilt of the prisoner assured. Now, for the first time, he felt a doubt.

"You think I'm guilty," said Leonard Vole, in a low voice. "But I swear I'm not! It looks pretty black against me, I know that. I'm like a man caught in a net—the meshes of it all round me, entangling me whichever way I turn. But I didn't do it, Mr. Mayherne, I didn't do it!"

In such a position a man was bound to protest his innocence. Mr. Mayherne knew that. Yet, in spite of himself, he was impressed. It might be, after all, that Leonard Vole was innocent.

"You are right, Mr. Vole," he said gravely. "The case does look very black against you. Nevertheless, I accept your assurance. Now, let us get to facts. I want you to tell me in your own words exactly how you came to make the acquaintance of Miss Emily French."

"It was one day in Oxford Street. I saw an elderly lady crossing the road.

She was carrying a lot of parcels. In the middle of the street she dropped them, tried to recover them, found a bus was almost on top of her, and just managed to reach the curb safely, dazed and bewildered by people having shouted at her. I recovered her parcels, wiped the mud off them as best I could, retied the string of one, and returned them to her."

"There was no question of your having saved her life?"

"Oh, dear me, no! All I did was to perform a common act of courtesy. She was extremely grateful, thanked me warmly, and said something about my manners not being those of most of the younger generation—I can't remember the exact words. Then I lifted my hat and went on. I never expected to see her again. But life is full of coincidences. That very evening I came across her at a party at a friend's house. She recognized me at once and asked that I should be introduced to her. I then found out that she was a Miss Emily French and that she lived at Cricklewood. I talked to her for some time. She was, I imagine, an old lady who took sudden and violent fancies to people. She took one to me on the strength of a perfectly simple action which anyone might have performed. On leaving, she shook me warmly by the hand and asked me to come and see her. I replied, of course, that I should be very pleased to do so, and she then urged me to name a day. I did not want particularly to go, but it would have seemed churlish to refuse, so I fixed on the following Saturday. After she had gone, I learned something about her from my friends. That she was rich, eccentric, lived alone with one maid, and owned no less than eight cats."

"I see," said Mr. Mayherne. "The question of her being well off came up as early as that?"

"If you mean that I inquired—" began Leonard Vole hotly, but Mr. Mayherne stilled him with a gesture.

"I have to look at the case as it will be presented by the other side. An ordinary observer would not have supposed Miss French to be a lady of means. She lived poorly, almost humbly. Unless you had been told the contrary, you would in all probability have considered her to be in poor circumstances—at any rate to begin with. Who was it exactly who told you that she was well off?"

"My friend, George Harvey, at whose house the party took place."

"Is he likely to remember having done so?"

"I really don't know. Of course it is some time ago now."

"Quite so, Mr. Vole. You see, the first aim of the prosecution will be to establish that you were in low water financially—that is true, is it not?"

Leonard Vole flushed.

"Yes," he said, in a low voice. "I'd been having a run of infernal bad luck just then."

"Quite so," said Mr. Mayherne again. "That being, as I say, in low water financially, you met this rich old lady and cultivated her acquaintance assiduously. Now if we are in a position to say that you had no idea she was well off, and that you visited her out of pure kindness of heart—"

"Which is the case."

"I dare say. I am not disputing the point. I am looking at it from the outside point of view. A great deal depends on the memory of Mr. Harvey. Is he likely to remember that conversation or is he not? Could he be confused by counsel into believing that it took place later?"

Leonard Vole reflected for some minutes. Then he said steadily enough, but with a rather pale face, "I do not think that that line would be successful, Mr. Mayherne. Several of those present heard his remark, and one or two of them chaffed me about my conquest of a rich old lady."

The solicitor endeavored to hide his disappointment with a wave of the hand.

"Unfortunate," he said. "But I congratulate you upon your plain speaking, Mr. Vole. It is to you I look to guide me. Your judgment is quite right. To persist in the line I spoke of would have been disastrous. We must leave that point. You made the acquaintance of Miss French, you called upon her, the acquaintanceship progressed. We want a clear reason for all this. Why did you, a young man of thirty-three, good-looking, fond of sport, popular with your friends, devote so much of your time to an elderly woman with whom you could hardly have anything in common?"

Leonard Vole flung out his hands in a nervous gesture.

"I can't tell you—I really can't tell you. After the first visit, she pressed me to come again, spoke of being lonely and unhappy. She made it difficult for me to refuse. She showed so plainly her fondness and affection for me that I was placed in an awkward position. You see, Mr. Mayherne, I've got a weak nature—I drift—I'm one of those people who can't say no. And believe me or not, as you like, after the third or fourth visit I paid her I found myself getting genuinely fond of the old thing. My mother died when I was young, an aunt brought me up, and she, too, died before I was fifteen. If I told you that I genuinely enjoyed being mothered and pampered, I dare say you'd only laugh."

Mr. Mayherne did not laugh. Instead he took off his prince-nez again and polished them, a sign with him that he was thinking deeply.

"I accept your explanation, Mr. Vole," he said at last. "I believe it to be psychologically probable. Whether a jury would take that view of it is another matter. Please continue your narrative. When was it that Miss French first asked you to look into her business affairs?"

"After my third or fourth visit to her. She understood very little of money matters, and was worried about some investments."

Mr. Mayherne looked up sharply.

"Be careful, Mr. Vole. The maid, Janet Mackenzie, declares that her mistress was a good woman of business and transacted all her own affairs, and this is borne out by the testimony of her bankers."

"I can't help that," said Vole earnestly. "That's what she said to me."

Mr. Mayherne looked at him for a moment or two in silence. Though he had no intention of saying so, his belief in Leonard Vole's innocence was at that moment strengthened. He knew something of the mentality of elderly ladies. He saw Miss French, infatuated with the good-looking young man, hunting about for pretexts that would bring him to the house. What more likely than that she would plead ignorance of business, and beg him to help her with her money affairs? She was enough of a woman of the world to realize that any man is slightly flattered by such an admission of his superiority. Leonard Vole had been flattered. Perhaps, too, she had not been averse to letting this young man know that she was wealthy. Emily French had been a strong-willed old woman, willing to pay her price for what she wanted. All this passed rapidly through Mr. Mayherne's mind, but he gave no indication of it, and asked instead a further question.

"And did you handle her affairs for her at her request?"

"I did."

"Mr. Vole," said the solicitor, "I am going to ask you a very serious question, and one to which it is vital I should have a truthful answer. You were in low water financially. You had the handling of an old lady's affairs—an old lady who, according to her own statement, knew little or nothing of business. Did you at any time, or in any manner, convert to your own use the securities which you handled? Did you engage in any transaction for your own pecuniary advantage which will not bear the light of day?" He quelled the other's response. "Wait a minute before you answer. There are two courses open to us. Either we can make a feature of your probity and honesty in conducting her affairs while pointing out how unlikely it is that you would commit murder to obtain money which you might have obtained by such infinitely easier means. If, on the other hand, there is anything in your dealings which the prosecution will get hold of—if, to put it badly, it can be proved that you swindled the old lady in any way, we must take the line that you had no motive for the murder, since she was already a profitable source of income to you. You perceive the distinction. Now, I beg of you, take your time before you reply."

But Leonard Vole took no time at all.

"My dealings with Miss French's affairs were all perfectly fair and above board. I acted for her interests to the very best of my ability, as anyone will find who looks into the matter."

"Thank you," said Mr. Mayherne. "You relieve my mind very much. I pay you the compliment of believing that you are far too clever to lie to me over such an important matter."

"Surely," said Vole eagerly, "the strongest point in my favor is the lack of motive. Granted that I cultivated the acquaintanceship of a rich old lady in the hopes of getting money out of her—that, I gather, is the substance of what you have been saying—surely her death frustrates all my hopes?"

The solicitor looked at him steadily. Then, very deliberately, he repeated his unconscious trick with his pince-nez. It was not until they were firmly replaced on his nose that he spoke.

"Are you not aware, Mr. Vole, that Miss French left a will under which you are the principal beneficiary?"

"What?" The prisoner sprang to his feet. His dismay was obvious and unforced. "What are you saying? She left her money to me?"

Mr. Mayherne nodded slowly. Vole sank down again, his head in his hands.

"You pretend you know nothing of this will?"

"Pretend? There's no pretense about it. I knew nothing about it."

"What would you say if I told you that the maid, Janet Mackenzie, swears that you *did* know? That her mistress told her distinctly that she had consulted you in the matter, and told you of her intentions?"

"Say? That she's lying! No, I go too fast. Janet is an elderly woman. She was a faithful watchdog to her mistress, and she didn't like me. She was jealous and suspicious. I should say that Miss French confided her intentions to Janet, and that Janet either mistook something she said, or else was convinced in her own mind that I had persuaded the old lady into doing it. I dare say that she herself believes now that Miss French actually told her so."

"You don't think she dislikes you enough to lie deliberately about the matter?"

Leonard Vole looked shocked and startled.

"No, indeed! Why should she?"

"I don't know," said Mr. Mayherne thoughtfully. "But she's very bitter against you."

The wretched young man groaned again.

"I'm beginning to see," he muttered. "It's frightful. I made up to her, that's what they'll say, I got her to make a will leaving her money to me, and then I go there that night, and there's nobody in the house—they find her the next day—oh, it's awful!"

"You are wrong about there being nobody in the house," said Mr. Mayherne. "Janet, as you remember, was to go out for the evening. She went, but about half past nine she returned to fetch the pattern of a blouse sleeve which she had promised to a friend. She let herself in by the back door, went upstairs and fetched it, and went out again. She heard voices in the sitting-room, though she could not distinguish what they said, but she will swear that one of them was Miss French's and one was a man's."

"At half past nine," said Leonard Vole. "At half past nine—" He sprang to his feet. "But then I'm saved—saved—"

"What do you mean, saved?" cried Mr. Mayherne, astonished.

"By half past nine I was at home again! My wife can prove that. I left Miss French about five minutes to nine. I arrived home about twenty past nine. My wife was there waiting for me. Oh, thank God—thank God! And bless Janet Mackenzie's sleeve pattern."

In his exuberance, he hardly noticed that the grave expression on the solicitor's face had not altered. But the latter's words brought him down to earth with a bump.

"Who, then, in your opinion, murdered Miss French?"

"Why, a burglar, of course, as was thought at first. The window was forced, you remember. She was killed with a heavy blow from a crowbar, and the crowbar was found lying on the floor beside the body. And several articles were missing. But for Janet's absurd suspicions and dislike of me, the police would never have swerved from the right track."

"That will hardly do, Mr. Vole," said the solicitor. "The things that were missing were mere trifles of no value, taken as a blind. And the marks on the window were not at all conclusive. Besides, think for yourself. You say you were no longer in the house by half past nine. Who, then, was the man Janet heard talking to Miss French in the sitting-room? She would hardly be having an amicable conversation with a burglar."

"No," said Vole. "No—" He looked puzzled and discouraged. "But, anyway" he added with reviving spirit, "it lets me out. I've got an alibi, You must see Romaine—my wife—at once."

"Certainly," acquiesced the lawyer. "I should already have seen Mrs. Vole but for her being absent when you were arrested. I wired to Scotland at once, and I understand that she arrives back tonight. I am going to call upon her immediately I leave here."

Vole nodded, a great expression of satisfaction settling down over his face.

"Yes, Romaine will tell you. It's a lucky chance that."

"Excuse me, Mr. Vole, but you are very fond of your wife?"

"Of course."

"And she of you?"

"Romaine is devoted to me. She'd do anything in the world for me."

He spoke enthusiastically, but the solicitor's heart sank a little lower. The testimony of a devoted wife—would it gain credence?

"Was there anyone else who saw you return at nine-twenty. A maid, for instance?"

"We have no maid."

"Did you meet anyone in the street on the way back?"

"Nobody I knew. I rode part of the way in a bus. The conductor might remember."

Mr. Mayherne shook his head doubtfully.

"There is no one, then, who can confirm your wife's testimony?"

"No. But it isn't necessary, surely?"

"I dare say not. I dare say not," said Mr. Mayherne hastily. "Now there's just one thing more. Did Miss French know that you were a married man?"

"Oh, yes."

"Yet you never took your wife to see her. Why was that?"

For the first time, Leonard Vole's answer came halting and uncertain.

"Well—I don't know."

"Are you aware that Janet Mackenzie says her mistress believed you to be single, and contemplated marrying you in the future?"

Vole laughed. "Absurd! There was forty years' difference in age between us."

"It has been done," said the solicitor dryly. "The fact remains. Your wife never met Miss French?"

"No—" Again the constraint.

"You will permit me to say," said the lawyer, "that I hardly understand your attitude in the matter."

Vole flushed, hesitated, and then spoke.

"I'll makc a clean breast of it. I was hard up, as you know. I hoped that Miss French might lend me some money. She was fond of me, but she wasn't at all interested in the struggles of a young couple. Early on, I found that she had taken it for granted that my wife and I didn't get on—were living apart. Mr. Mayherne—I wanted the money—for Romaine's sake. I said nothing, and allowed the old lady to think what she chose. She spoke of my being an adopted son to her. There was never any question of marriage—that must be just Janet's imagination."

"And that is all?"

"Yes—that is all."

Was there just a shade of hesitation in the words? The lawyer fancied so. He rose and held out his hand.

"Good-by, Mr. Vole." He looked into the haggard young face and spoke with an unusual impulse. "I believe in your innocence in spite of the multitude of facts arrayed against you. I hope to prove it and vindicate you completely."

Vole smiled back at him.

"You'll find the alibi is all right," he said cheerfully.

Again he hardly noticed that the other did not respond.

"The whole thing hinges a good deal on the testimony of Janet Mackenzie," said Mr. Mayherne. "She hates you. That much is clear."

"She can hardly hate me," protested the young man.

The solicitor shook his head as he went out. *Now for Mrs. Vole,* he said to himself. He was seriously disturbed by the way the thing was shaping.

The Voles lived in a small shabby house near Paddington Green. It was to this house that Mr. Mayherne went.

In answer to his ring, a big slatternly woman, obviously a charwoman, answered the door.

"Mrs. Vole? Has she returned yet?"

"Got back an hour ago. But I dunno if you can see her."

"If you will take my card to her," said Mr. Mayherne quietly. "I am quite sure that she will do so."

The woman looked at him doubtfully, wiped her hand on her apron, and took the card. Then she closed the door in his face and left him on the step outside.

In a few minutes, however, she returned with a slightly altered manner.

"Come inside, please."

She ushered him into a tiny drawing-room. Mr. Mayherne, examining a drawing on the wall, started up suddenly to face a tall, pale woman who had entered so quietly that he had not heard her.

"Mr. Mayherne? You are my husband's solicitor, are you not? You have come from him? Will you please sit down?"

Until she spoke he had not realized that she was not English. Now, observing her more closely, he noticed the high cheekbones, the dense blue-black of the hair, and an occasional very slight movement of the hands that was distinctly foreign. A strange woman, very quiet. So quiet as to make one uneasy. From the very first Mr. Mayherne was conscious that he was up against something that he did not understand.

"Now, my dear Mrs. Vole," he began, "you must not give way—"

He stopped. It was so very obvious that Romaine Vole had not the slightest intention of giving way. She was perfectly calm and composed.

"Will you please tell me about it?" she said. "I must know everything. Do not think to spare me. I want to know the worst." She hesitated, then repeated in a lower tone, with a curious emphasis which the lawyer did not understand, "I want to know the worst."

Mr. Mayherne went over his interview with Leonard Vole. She listened attentively, nodding her head now and then.

"I see," she said, when he had finished. "He wants me to say that he came in at twenty minutes past nine that night?"

"He did come in at that time?" said Mr. Mayherne sharply.

"That is not the point," she said coldly. "Will my saying so acquit him? Will they believe me?"

Mr. Mayherne was taken aback. She had gone so quickly to the core of the matter.

"That is what I want to know," she said. "Will it be enough? Is there anyone else who can support my evidence?"

There was a suppressed eagerness in her manner that made him vaguely uneasy.

"So far there is no one else," he said reluctantly.

"I see," said Romaine Vole.

She sat for a minute or two perfectly still. A little smile played over her lips.

The lawyer's feeling of alarm grew stronger and stronger.

"Mrs. Vole—" he began. "I know what you must feel—"

"Do you?" she asked. "I wonder."

"In the circumstances—"

"In the circumstances—I intend to play a lone hand."

He looked at her in dismay.

"But, my dear Mrs. Vole—you are overwrought. Being so devoted to your husband—"

"I beg your pardon?"

The sharpness of her voice made him start. He repeated in a hesitating manner, "Being so devoted to your husband—"

Romaine Vole nodded slowly, the same strange smile on her lips.

"Did he tell you that I was devoted to him?" she asked softly. "Ah! yes, I can see he did. How stupid men are! Stupid—stupid—stupid—"

She rose suddenly to her feet. All the intense emotion that the lawyer had been conscious of in the atmosphere was now concentrated in her tone.

"I hate him, I tell you! I hate him. I hate him. I hate him! I would like to see him hanged by the neck till he is dead."

The lawyer recoiled before her and the smoldering passion in her eyes.

She advanced a step nearer and continued vehemently.

"Perhaps I shall see it. Supposing I tell you that he did not come in that night at twenty past nine, but at twenty past ten? You say that he tells you he knew nothing about the money coming to him. Supposing I tell you he knew all about it, and counted on it, and committed murder to get it? Supposing I tell you that he admitted to me that night when he came in what he had done? That there was blood on his coat? What then? Supposing that I stand up in court and say all these things?"

Her eyes seemed to challenge him. With an effort he concealed his growing dismay, and endeavored to speak in a rational tone.

"You cannot be asked to give evidence against your husband—"

"I should like you to tell me one thing," said Mr. Mayherne. He contrived to appear as cool and unemotional as ever. "Why are you so bitter against Leonard Vole?"

She shook her head, smiling a little.

"Yes, you would like to know. But I shall not tell you. I will keep my secret."

Mr. Mayherne gave his dry little cough and rose.

"There seems no point in prolonging this interview," he remarked. "You will hear from me again after I have communicated with my client."

She came closer to him, looking into his eyes with her own wonderful dark ones.

"Tell me," she said, "did you believe—honestly—that he was innocent when you came here today?"

"I did," said Mr. Mayherne.

"You poor little man." She laughed.

"And I believe so still," finished the lawyer. "Good evening, madam."

He went out of the room, taking with him the memory of her startled face. *This is going to be the devil of a business,* said Mr. Mayherne to himself as he strode along the street.

Extraordinary, the whole thing. An extraordinary woman. A very dangerous woman. Women were the devil when they got their knife into you.

What was to be done? That wretched young man hadn't a leg to stand upon. Of course, possibly he did commit the crime.

No, said Mr. Mayherne to himself. *No—there's almost too much evidence against him. I don't believe this woman. She was trumping up the whole story. But she'll never bring it into court.*

He wished he felt more conviction on the point.

The police court proceedings were brief and dramatic. The principal witnesses for the prosecution were Janet Mackenzie, maid to the dead woman, and Romaine Heilger.

Mr. Mayherne sat in court and listened to the damning story that the latter told. It was on the lines she had indicated to him in their interview.

The prisoner reserved his defense and was committed for trial.

Mr. Mayherne was at his wits' end. The case against Leonard Vole was black beyond words. Even the famous K.C. who was engaged for the defense held out little hope.

"If we can shake that woman's testimony, we might do something," he said dubiously. "But it's a bad business."

Mr. Mayherne had concentrated his energies on one single point. Assuming Leonard Vole to be speaking the truth, and to have left the murdered woman's house at nine o'clock, who was the man Janet heard talking to Miss French at half past nine?

The only ray of light was in the shape of a scapegrace nephew who had in bygone days cajoled and threatened his aunt out of various sums of money. Janet Mackenzie, the solicitor learned, had always been attached to this young man, and had never ceased urging his claims upon her mistress. It certainly seemed possible that it was this nephew who had been with Miss French after Leonard Vole left, especially as he was not to be found in any of his old haunts.

In all other directions, the lawyer's researches had been negative in their result. No one had seen Leonard Vole entering his own house, or leaving that of Miss French. No one had seen any other man enter or leave the house in Cricklewood. All inquiries drew blank.

It was the eve of the trial when Mr. Mayherne received the letter which was to lead his thoughts in an entirely new direction.

It came by the six-o'clock post. An illiterate scrawl, written on common paper and enclosed in a dirty envelope with the stamp stuck on crooked.

Mr. Mayherne read it through once or twice before he grasped its meaning.

Dear Mister:

Youre the lawyer chap wot acts for the young feller. If you want that painted foreign hussy showd up for wot she is an her pack of lies you come to 16 Shaw's Rents Stepney tonight It ull cawst you 2 hundred quid Arsk for Missis Mogson.

The solicitor read and reread this strange epistle. It might, of course, be a hoax, but when he thought it over, he became increasingly convinced that it was genuine, and also convinced that it was the one hope for the prisoner. The evidence of Romaine Heilger damned him completely, and the line the defense meant to pursue, the line that the evidence of a woman who had admittedly lived an immoral life was not to be trusted, was at best a weak one.

Mr. Mayherne's mind was made up. It was his duty to save his client at all costs. He must go to Shaw's Rents.

He had some difficulty in finding the place, a ramshackle building in an evil-smelling slum, but at last he did so, and on inquiry for Mrs. Mogson was sent up to a room on the third floor. On this door he knocked, and getting no answer, knocked again.

At this second knock, he heard a shuffling sound inside, and presently the door was opened cautiously half an inch and a bent figure peered out.

Suddenly the woman, for it was a woman, gave a chuckle and opened the door wider.

"So it's you, dearie," she said, in a wheezy voice. "Nobody with you, is there? No playing tricks? That's right. You can come in—you can come in."

With some reluctance the lawyer stepped across the threshold into the small, dirty room, with its flickering gas jet. There was an untidy unmade bed in a corner, a plain deal table, and two rickety chairs. For the first time Mr. Mayherne had a full view of the tenant of this unsavory apartment. She was a woman of middle age, bent in figure, with a mass of untidy gray hair and a scarf wound tightly round her face. She saw him looking at this and laughed again, the same curious, toneless chuckle.

"Wondering why I hide my beauty, dear? He, he, he. Afraid it may tempt you, eh? But you shall see—you shall see."

She drew aside the scarf, and the lawyer recoiled involuntarily before the almost formless blur of scarlet. She replaced the scarf again.

"So you're not wanting to kiss me, dearie? He, he, I don't wonder. And yet I was a pretty girl once—not so long ago as you'd think, either. Vitriol, dearie, vitriol—that's what did that. Ah! but I'll be even with 'em—"

She burst into a hideous torrent of abuse which Mr. Mayherne tried vainly to quell. She fell silent at last, her hands clenching and unclenching themselves nervously.

"Enough of that," said the lawyer sternly. "I've come here because I have reason to believe you can give me information which will clear my client, Leonard Vole. Is that the case?"

Her eyes leered at him cunningly.

"What about the money, dearie?" she wheezed. "Two hundred quid, you remember."

"It is your duty to give evidence, and you can be called upon to do so."

"That won't do, dearie. I'm an old woman, and I know nothing. But you give me two hundred quid, and perhaps I can give you a hint or two. See?"

"What kind of hint?"

"What should you say to a letter? A letter from *her*. Never mind how I got hold of it. That's my business. It'll do the trick. But I want my two hundred quid."

Mr. Mayherne looked at her coldly, and made up his mind.

"I'll give you ten pounds, nothing more. And only that if this letter is what you say it is."

"Ten pounds?" She screamed and raved at him.

"Twenty," said Mr. Mayherne, "and that's my last word."

He rose as if to go. Then, watching her closely, he drew out a pocket-book, and counted out twenty one-pound notes.

"You see," he said. "That is all I have with me. You can take it or leave it."

But already he knew that the sight of the money was too much for her. She cursed and raved impotently, but at last she gave in. Going over to the bed, she drew something from beneath the tattered mattress.

"Here you are," she snarled. "It's the top one you want."

It was a bundle of letters that she threw to him, and Mr. Mayherne untied them and scanned them in his usual cool, methodical manner. The woman, watching him eagerly, could gain no clue from his impassive face.

He read each letter through, then returned again to the top one and read it a second time. Then he tied the whole bundle up again carefully.

They were love letters, written by Romaine Heilger, and the man they were written to was not Leonard Vole. The top letter was dated the day of the latter's arrest.

"I spoke true, dearie, didn't I?" whined the woman. "It'll do for her, that letter?"

Mr. Mayherne put the letters in his pocket, then he asked a question.

"How did you get hold of this correspondence?"

"That's telling," she said with a leer. "But I know something more. I heard in court what that hussy said. Find out where she was at twenty past ten, the time she says she was at home. Ask at the Lion Road Cinema. They'll remember—a fine upstanding girl like that—curse her!"

"Who is the man?" asked Mr. Mayherne. "There's only a Christian name here."

The other's voice grew thick and hoarse, her hands clenched and unclenched. Finally she lifted one to her face.

"He's the man that did this to me. Many years ago now. She took him away from me—a chit of a girl she was then. And when I went after him—and went for him, too—he threw the cursed stuff at me! And she laughed! I've had it in for her for years. Followed her, I have, spied upon her. And now I've got her! She'll suffer for this, won't she, Mr. Lawyer? She'll suffer?"

"She will probably be sentenced to a term of imprisonment for perjury," said Mr. Mayherne quietly.

"Shut away—that's what I want. You're going, are you? Where's my money? Where's that good money?"

Without a word, Mr. Mayherne put down the notes on the table. Then, drawing a deep breath, he turned and left the squalid room. Looking back, he saw the old woman crooning over the money.

He wasted no time. He found the cinema in Lion Road easily enough, and, shown a photograph of Romaine Heilger, the commissionaire recognized her at once. She had arrived at the cinema with a man some time after ten o'clock on the evening in question. He had not noticed her escort particularly, but he remembered the lady who had spoken to him about the picture that was showing. They stayed until the end, about an hour later.

Mr. Mayherne was satisfied. Romaine Heilger's evidence was a tissue of lies from beginning to end. She had evolved it out of her passionate hatred. The lawyer wondered whether he would ever know what lay behind that hatred. What had Leonard Vole done to her? He had seemed dumfounded when the solicitor had reported her attitude to him. He had declared earnestly that such a thing was incredible—yet it had seemed to Mr. Mayherne that after the first astonishment his protests had lacked sincerity.

He did know. Mr. Mayherne was convinced of it. He knew, but he had no intention of revealing the fact. The secret between those two remained a secret. Mr. Mayherne wondered if some day he should come to learn what it was.

The solicitor glanced at his watch. It was late, but time was everything. He hailed a taxi and gave an address.

"Sir Charles must know of this at once," he murmured to himself as he got in.

The trial of Leonard Vole for the murder of Emily French aroused widespread interest. In the first place the prisoner was young and good-looking, then he was accused of a particularly dastardly crime, and there was the further interest of Romaine Heilger, the principal witness for the prosecution. There had been pictures of her in many papers, and several fictitious stories as to her origin and history.

The proceedings opened quietly enough. Various technical evidence came first. Then Janet Mackenzie was called. She told substantially the same story as before. In cross-examination counsel for the defense succeeded in getting her to contradict herself once or twice over her account of Vole's association with Miss French; he emphasized the fact that though she had heard a man's voice in the sitting-room that night, there was nothing to show that it was Vole who was there, and he managed to drive home a feeling that jealousy and dislike of the prisoner were at the bottom of a good deal of her evidence.

Then the next witness was called.

"Your name is Romaine Heilger?"

"Yes."

"You are an Austrian subject?"

"Yes."

"For the last three years you have lived with the prisoner and passed yourself off as his wife?"

Just for a moment Romaine Heilger's eyes met those of the man in the dock. Her expression held something curious and unfathomable.

"Yes."

The questions went on. Word by word the damning facts came out. On the night in question the prisoner had taken out a crowbar with him. He had returned at twenty minutes past ten, and had confessed to having killed the old lady. His cuffs had been stained with blood, and he had burned them in the kitchen stove. He had terrorized her into silence by means of threats.

As the story proceeded, the feeling of the court which had, to begin with, been slightly favorable to the prisoner, now set dead against him. He himself sat with downcast head and moody air, as though he knew he were doomed.

Yet it might have been noted that her own counsel sought to restrain Romaine's animosity. He would have preferred her to be more unbiased.

Formidable and ponderous, counsel for the defense arose.

He put it to her that her story was a malicious fabrication from start to finish, that she had not even been in her own house at the time in question, that she was in love with another man and was deliberately seeking to send Vole to his death for a crime he did not commit.

Romaine denied these allegations with superb insolence.

Then came the surprising denouement, the production of the letter. It was read aloud in court in the midst of a breathless stillness.

> *"Max, beloved, the Fates have delivered him into our hands! He has been arrested for murder—but, yes, the murder of an old lady! Leonard, who would not hurt a fly! At last I shall have my revenge. The poor chicken! I shall say that he came in that night with blood upon him—that he confessed to me. I shall hang him, Max—and when he hangs he will know and realize that it was Romaine who sent him to his death. And then—happiness, Beloved! Happiness at last!"*

There were experts present ready to swear that the handwriting was that of Romaine Heilger, but they were not needed. Confronted with the letter, Romaine broke down utterly and confessed everything. Leonard Vole had returned to the house at the time he said, twenty past nine. She had invented the whole story to ruin him.

With the collapse of Romaine Heilger, the case for the Crown collapsed also. Sir Charles called his few witnesses, the prisoner himself went into the box and told his story in a manly straightforward manner, unshaken by cross-examination.

The prosecution endeavored to rally, but without great success. The judge's summing up was not wholly favorable to the prisoner, but a reaction had set in and the jury needed little time to consider their verdict.

"We find the prisoner not guilty."

Leonard Vole was free!

Little Mr. Mayherne hurried from his seat. He must congratulate his client.

He found himself polishing his pince-nez vigorously, and checked himself. His wife had told him only the night before that he was getting a habit of it. Curious things, habits. People themselves never knew they had them.

An interesting case—a very interesting case. That woman, now, Romaine Heilger.

The case was dominated for him still by the exotic figure of Romaine Heilger. She had seemed a pale, quiet woman in the house at Paddington, but in court she had flamed out against the sober background, flaunting herself like a tropical flower.

If he closed his eyes he could see her now, tall and vehement, her exquisite body bent forward a little, her right hand clenching and unclenching itself unconsciously all the time.

Curious things, habits. That gesture of hers with the hand was her habit, he supposed. Yet he had seen someone else do it quite lately. Who was it now? Quite lately—

He drew in his breath with a gasp as it came back to him. The woman in Shaw's Rents—

He stood still, his head whirling. It was impossible—impossible—Yet, Romaine Heilger was an actress.

The K.C. came up behind him and clapped him on the shoulder.

"Congratulated our man yet? He's had a narrow shave, you know. Come along and see him."

But the little lawyer shook off the other's hand.

He wanted one thing only—to see Romaine Heilger face to face.

He did not see her until some time later, and the place of their meeting is not relevant.

"So you guessed," she said, when he had told her all that was in his mind. "The face? Oh! that was easy enough, and the light of that gas jet was too bad for you to see the makeup."

"But why—why—"

"Why did I play a lone hand?" She smiled a little, remembering the last time she had used the words.

"Such an elaborate comedy!"

"My friend—I had to save him. The evidence of a woman devoted to him would not have been enough—you hinted as much yourself. But I know something of the psychology of crowds. Let my evidence be wrung from me, as an admission, damning me in the eyes of the law, and a reaction in favor of the prisoner would immediately set in."

"And the bundle of letters?"

"One alone, the vital one, might have seemed like a—what do you call it?—put-up job."

"Then the man called Max?"

"Never existed, my friend."

"I still think," said little Mr. Mayherne, in an aggrieved manner, "that we could have got him off by the—er—normal procedure."

"I dared not risk it. You see you thought he was innocent—"

"And you knew it? I see," said little Mr. Mayherne.

"My dear Mr. Mayherne," said Romaine, "you do not see at all. I knew—he was guilty!"

W. SOMERSET MAUGHAM

(1874–1965)

William Somerset Maugham was born in Paris at the British Embassy, the son of Robert Ormond Maugham, an English lawyer with a Paris law firm and solicitor to the Embassy. The author's grandfather, Robert Maugham, was a distinguished barrister, the founder of the Incorporated Law Society and the *Legal Observer* (later the *Solicitor's Journal*), for which he was dubbed the "Father of Legal Journalism." Somerset Maugham's three brothers all pursued careers in law, one of them (Frederic Herbert) rising to the rank of Lord Chancellor.

Somerset Maugham learned to read English from the criminal court reports in newspapers. Breaking with his ancestral vocation, however, he received an M.D. degree from St. Thomas's Hospital in London in 1897, the same year that his first novel, *Liza of Lambeth*, was published. In 1917 he was the chief agent in Russia for British and American intelligence, attempting to prevent the Bolshevik coup. Maugham's major novels included *Of Human Bondage* (his most celebrated work), *The Moon and Sixpence*, *Cakes and Ale*, and *The Razor's Edge*. He was also acclaimed as a short-story writer and playwright.

A frequent traveler to Asia and the Pacific, indeed perhaps the most widely traveled writer of his time, Maugham based many of his works on his journeys. While visiting Singapore in 1921, he stayed at the home of a lawyer, Courtenay Dickinson, where he heard the story of a sensational Malayan scandal, the trial of Mrs. Ethel Mabel Proudlock. In 1911 Proudlock had shot William Crozier Steward on the veranda of her home, claiming that he tried to kiss her. Proudlock was convicted of murder and sentenced to be hanged, but the European community in Malaya petitioned for and obtained a pardon for her. She returned to England without her husband and died in an asylum, having gone insane during her month on death row.

Maugham's story "The Letter" appeared in *International Magazine*, April 1924, and then in his collection *The Casuarina Tree* (1926), and was also adapted as a successful play and as a hit movie starring Bette Davis. Maugham took the plot of "The Letter" from the Proudlock trial testimony, adding only the element of the letter itself. As in several of his other murder stories, Maugham focuses here on a character who takes the law into his or her own hands. The most intriguing legal aspect of the story is the problem of professional ethics posed by the conduct of the defense lawyer, Mr. Joyce.

THE LETTER

— 1924 —

Outside on the quay the sun beat fiercely. A stream of motors, lorries and buses, private cars and hirelings, sped up and down the crowded thoroughfare, and every chauffeur blew his horn; rickshaws threaded their nimble path amid the throng, and the panting coolies found breath to yell at one another; coolies, carrying heavy bales, sidled along with their quick jog-trot and shouted to the passer-by to make way; itinerant vendors proclaimed their wares. Singapore is the meeting-place of a hundred peoples; and men of all colours, black Tamils, yellow Chinks, brown Malays, Armenians, Jews and Bengalis, called to one another in raucous tones. But inside the office of Messrs. Ripley, Joyce and Naylor it was pleasantly cool; it was dark after the dusty glitter of the street and agreeably quiet after its unceasing din. Mr. Joyce sat in his private room, at the table, with an electric fan turned full on him. He was leaning back, his elbows on the arms of the chair, with the tips of the outstretched fingers of one hand resting neatly against the tips of the outstretched fingers of the other. His gaze rested on the battered volumes of the Law Reports which stood on a long shelf in front of him. On the top of a cupboard were square boxes of japanned tin, on which were painted the names of various clients.

There was a knock at the door.

"Come in."

A Chinese clerk, very neat in his white ducks, opened it.

"Mr. Crosbie is here, sir."

He spoke beautiful English, accenting each word with precision, and Mr. Joyce had often wondered at the extent of his vocabulary. Ong Chi Seng was a Cantonese, and he had studied law at Gray's Inn. He was spending a year or two with Messrs. Ripley, Joyce and Naylor in order to prepare himself for practice on his own account. He was industrious, obliging, and of exemplary character.

"Show him in," said Mr. Joyce.

He rose to shake hands with his visitor and asked him to sit down. The light fell on him as he did so. The face of Mr. Joyce remained in shadow. He was by nature a silent man, and now he looked at Robert Crosbie for quite a minute without speaking. Crosbie was a big fellow, well over six feet high, with broad shoulders, and muscular. He was a rubber-planter, hard with the constant exercise of walking over the estate, and with the tennis which was his relaxation when the day's work was over. He was deeply sunburned. His hairy hands, his feet in clumsy boots were enormous, and Mr. Joyce found himself thinking that a blow of that great fist would easily kill the fragile Tamil. But there was no fierceness in his blue eyes; they were confiding and gentle; and his face, with its big, undistinguished features, was open, frank and honest. But at this moment it bore a look of deep distress. It was drawn and haggard.

"You look as though you hadn't had much sleep the last night or two," said Mr. Joyce.

"I haven't."

Mr. Joyce noticed now the old felt hat, with its broad double brim, which Crosbie had placed on the table; and then his eyes travelled to the khaki shorts he wore, showing his red hairy thighs, the tennis shirt open at the neck, without a tie, and the dirty khaki jacket with the ends of the sleeves turned up. He looked as though he had just come in from a long tramp among the rubber trees. Mr. Joyce gave a slight frown.

"You must pull yourself together, you know. You must keep your head."

"Oh, I'm all right."

"Have you seen your wife to-day?"

"No, I'm to see her this afternoon. You know, it is a damned shame that they should have arrested her."

"I think they had to do that," Mr. Joyce answered in his level, soft tone.

"I should have thought they'd have let her out on bail."

"It's a very serious charge."

"It is damnable. She did what any decent woman would do in her place. Only, nine women out of ten wouldn't have the pluck. Leslie's the best woman in the world. She wouldn't hurt a fly. Why, hang it all, man, I've been married to her for twelve years, do you think I don't know her? God, if I'd got hold of the man I'd have wrung his neck, I'd have killed him without a moment's hesitation. So would you."

"My dear fellow, everybody's on your side. No one has a good word to say for Hammond. We're going to get her off. I don't suppose either the assessors or the judge will go into court without having already made up their minds to bring in a verdict of not guilty."

"The whole thing's a farce," said Crosbie violently. "She ought never to have been arrested in the first place, and then it's terrible, after all the poor girl's gone through, to subject her to the ordeal of a trial. There's not a soul I've met since I've been in Singapore, man or woman, who hasn't told me that Leslie was absolutely justified. I think it's awful to keep her in prison all these weeks."

"The law is the law. After all, she confesses that she killed the man. It is terrible, and I'm dreadfully sorry for both you and for her."

"It don't matter a hang," interrupted Crosbie.

"But the fact remains that murder has been committed, and in a civilised community a trial is inevitable."

"Is it murder to exterminate noxious vermin? She shot him as she would have shot a mad dog."

Mr. Joyce leaned back again in his chair and once more placed the tips of his ten fingers together. The little construction he formed looked like the skeleton of a roof. He was silent for a moment.

"I should be wanting in my duty as your legal adviser," he said at last, in an even voice, looking at his client with his cool, brown eyes, "if I did not tell you that there is one point which causes me just a little anxiety. If your wife had only shot Hammond once, the whole thing would be absolutely plain sailing. Unfortunately she fired six times."

"Her explanation is perfectly simple. In the circumstances anyone would have done the same."

"I dare say," said Mr. Joyce, "and of course I think the explanation is very reasonable. But it's no good closing our eyes to the facts. It's always a good plan to put yourself in another man's place, and I can't deny that if I were prosecuting for the Crown that is the point on which I should centre my enquiry."

"My dear fellow, that's perfectly idiotic."

Mr. Joyce shot a sharp glance at Robert Crosbie. The shadow of a smile hovered over his shapely lips. Crosbie was a good fellow, but he could hardly be described as intelligent.

"I dare say it's of no importance," answered the lawyer, "I just thought it was a point worth mentioning. You haven't got very long to wait now, and when it's all over I recommend you to go off somewhere with your wife on a trip, and forget all about it. Even though we are almost dead certain to get an acquittal, a trial of that sort is anxious work, and you'll both want a rest."

For the first time Crosbie smiled, and his smile strangely changed his face. You forgot the uncouthness and saw only the goodness of his soul.

"I think I shall want it more than Leslie. She's borne up wonderfully. By God, there's a plucky little woman for you."

"Yes, I've been very much struck by her self-control," said the lawyer. "I should never have guessed that she was capable of such determination."

His duties as her counsel had made it necessary for him to have a good many interviews with Mrs. Crosbie since her arrest. Though things had been made as easy as could be for her, the fact remained that she was in gaol, awaiting her trial for murder, and it would not have been surprising if her nerves had failed her. She appeared to bear her ordeal with composure. She read a great deal, took such exercise as was possible, and by favour of the authorities worked at the pillow lace which had always formed the entertainment of her long hours of leisure. When Mr. Joyce saw her, she was neatly dressed in cool, fresh, simple frocks, her hair was carefully arranged, and her nails were manicured. Her manner was collected. She was able even to jest upon the little inconveniences of her position. There was something casual about the way in which she spoke of the tragedy, which suggested to Mr. Joyce that only her good breeding prevented her from finding something a trifle ludicrous in a situation which was eminently serious. It surprised him, for he had never thought that she had a sense of humour.

He had known her off and on for a good many years. When she paid visits to Singapore she generally came to dine with his wife and himself, and once or twice she had passed a week-end with them at their bungalow by the sea. His wife had spent a fortnight with her on the estate, and had met Geoffrey Hammond several times. The two couples had been on friendly, if not on intimate, terms, and it was on this account that Robert Crosbie had rushed over to Singapore immediately after the catastrophe and begged Mr. Joyce to take charge personally of his unhappy wife's defence.

The story she told him the first time he saw her she had never varied in the smallest detail. She told it as coolly then, a few hours after the tragedy, as she told it now. She told it connectedly, in a level, even voice, and her only sign of confusion was when a slight colour came into her cheeks as she described one or two of its incidents. She was the last woman to whom one would have expected such a thing to happen. She was in the early thirties, a fragile creature, neither short nor tall, and graceful rather than pretty. Her wrists and ankles were very delicate, but she was extremely thin, and you could see the bones of her hands through the white skin, and the veins were large and blue. Her face was colourless, slightly sallow, and her lips were pale. You did not notice the colour of her eyes. She had a great deal of light brown hair, and it had a slight natural wave; it was the sort of hair that with a little touching-up would have been very pretty, but you could not imagine that Mrs. Crosbie would think of resorting to any such device. She was a quiet, pleasant, unassuming woman. Her manner was engaging, and if she was not very popular it was because she suffered from a certain shyness. This was comprehensible enough, for the planter's life is lonely, and in her own house, with people she knew, she was in her quiet way charming. Mrs. Joyce, after her fortnight's stay, had told her husband that Leslie was a very agreeable hostess. There was more in her, she said, than people thought; and when you came to know her you were surprised how much she had read and how entertaining she could be.

She was the last woman in the world to commit murder.

Mr. Joyce dismissed Robert Crosbie with such reassuring words as he could find and, once more alone in his office, turned over the pages of the brief. But it was a mechanical action, for all its details were familiar to him. The case was the sensation of the day, and it was discussed in all the clubs, at all the dinner tables, up and down the Peninsula, from Singapore to Penang. The facts that Mrs. Crosbie gave were simple. Her husband had gone to Singapore on business, and she was alone for the night. She dined by herself, late, at a quarter to nine, and after dinner sat in the sitting-room working at her lace. It opened on the verandah. There was no one in the bungalow, for the servants had retired to their own quarters at the back of the compound. She was surprised to hear a step on the gravel path in the garden, a booted step, which suggested a white man rather than a native, for she had not heard a motor drive up, and she could not imagine who could be coming to see her at that time of night. Someone ascended the few stairs that led up to the bungalow, walked across the verandah, and appeared at the door of the room in which she sat. At the first moment she did not recognise the visitor. She sat with a shaded lamp, and he stood with his back to the darkness.

"May I come in?" he said.

She did not even recognise the voice.

"Who is it?" she asked.

She worked with spectacles, and she took them off as she spoke.

"Geoff. Hammond."

"Of course. Come in and have a drink."

She rose and shook hands with him cordially. She was a little surprised to see him, for though he was a neighbour neither she nor Robert had been lately on very intimate terms with him, and she had not seen him for some weeks. He was the manager of a rubber estate nearly eight miles from theirs, and she wondered why he had chosen this late hour to come and see them.

"Robert's away," she said. "He had to go to Singapore for the night."

Perhaps he thought his visit called for some explanation, for he said:

"I'm sorry. I felt rather lonely to-night, so I thought I'd just come along and see how you were getting on."

"How on earth did you come? I never heard a car."

"I left it down the road. I thought you might both be in bed and asleep."

This was natural enough. The planter gets up at dawn in order to take the roll-call of the workers, and soon after dinner he is glad to go to bed. Hammond's car was in point of fact found next day a quarter of a mile from the bungalow.

Since Robert was away there was no whisky and soda in the room. Leslie did not call the boy, who was probably asleep, but fetched it herself. Her guest mixed himself a drink and filled his pipe.

Geoff. Hammond had a host of friends in the colony. He was at this time in the late thirties, but he had come out as a lad. He had been one of the first to volunteer on the outbreak of war, and had done very well. A wound in the knee caused him to be invalided out of the army after two years, but he returned to the Federated Malay States with a D.S.O. and an M.C. He was one of the best billiard-players in the colony. He had been a beautiful dancer and a fine tennis-player, but though able no longer to dance, and his tennis, with a stiff knee, was not so good as it had been, he had the gift of popularity and was universally liked. He was a tall, good-looking fellow, with attractive blue eyes and a fine head of black, curling hair. Old stagers said his only fault was that he was too fond of the girls, and after the catastrophe they shook their heads and vowed that they had always known this would get him into trouble.

He began now to talk to Leslie about the local affairs, the forth-coming races in Singapore, the price of rubber, and his chances of killing a tiger which had been lately seen in the neighbourhood. She was anxious to finish by a certain date the piece of lace on which she was working, for she wanted to send it home for her mother's birthday, and so put on her spectacles again, and drew towards her chair the little table on which stood the pillow.

"I wish you wouldn't wear those great horn-spectacles," he said. "I don't know why a pretty woman should do her best to look plain."

She was a trifle taken aback at this remark. He had never used that tone with her before. She thought the best thing was to make light of it.

"I have no pretensions to being a raving beauty, you know, and if you ask me point-blank, I'm bound to tell you that I don't care two pins if you think me plain or not."

"I don't think you're plain. I think you're awfully pretty."

"Sweet of you," she answered, ironically. "But in that case I can only think you half-witted."

He chuckled. But he rose from his chair and sat down in another by her side.

"You're not going to have the face to deny that you have the prettiest hands in the world," he said.

He made a gesture as though to take one of them. She gave him a little tap.

"Don't be an idiot. Sit down where you were before and talk sensibly, or else I shall send you home."

He did not move.

"Don't you know that I'm awfully in love with you?" he said.

She remained quite cool.

"I don't. I don't believe it for a minute, and even if it were true I don't want you to say it."

She was the more surprised at what he was saying, since during the seven years she had known him he had never paid her any particular attention. When he came back from the war they had seen a good deal of one another, and once when he was ill Robert had gone over and brought him back to their bungalow in his car. He had stayed with them for a fortnight. But their interests were dissimilar, and the acquaintance had never ripened into friendship. For the last two or three years they had seen little of him. Now and then he came over to play tennis, now and then they met him at some planter's who was giving a party, but it often happened that they did not set eyes on him for a month at a time.

Now he took another whisky and soda. Leslie wondered if he had been drinking before. There was something odd about him, and it made her a trifle uneasy. She watched him help himself with disapproval.

"I wouldn't drink any more if I were you," she said, good-humouredly still.

He emptied his glass and put it down.

"Do you think I'm talking to you like this because I'm drunk?" he asked abruptly.

"That is the most obvious explanation, isn't it?"

"Well, it's a lie. I've loved you ever since I first knew you. I've held my tongue as long as I could, and now it's got to come out. I love you, I love you, I love you."

She rose and carefully put aside the pillow.

"Good-night," she said.

"I'm not going now."

At last she began to lose her temper.

"But, you poor fool, don't you know that I've never loved anyone but Robert, and even if I didn't love Robert you're the last man I should care for."

"What do I care? Robert's away."

"If you don't go away this minute I shall call the boys, and have you thrown out."

"They're out of earshot."

She was very angry now. She made a movement as though to go on to the verandah, from which the house-boy would certainly hear her, but he seized her arm.

"Let me go," she cried furiously.

"Not much. I've got you now."

She opened her mouth and called "Boy, boy," but with a quick gesture he put his hand over it. Then before she knew what he was about he had taken her in his arms and was kissing her passionately. She struggled, turning her lips away from his burning mouth.

"No, no, no," she cried. "Leave me alone. I won't."

She grew confused about what happened then. All that had been said before she remembered accurately, but now his words assailed her ears through a mist of horror and fear. He seemed to plead for her love. He broke into violent protestations of passion. And all the time he held her in his tempestuous embrace. She was helpless, for he was a strong, powerful man, and her arms were pinioned to her sides; her struggles were unavailing, and she felt herself grow weaker; she was afraid she would faint, and his hot breath on her face made her feel desperately sick. He kissed her mouth, her eyes, her cheeks, her hair. The pressure of his arms was killing her. He lifted her off her feet. She tried to kick him, but he only held her more closely. He was carrying her now. He wasn't speaking any more, but she knew that his face was pale and his eyes hot with desire. He was taking her into the bedroom. He was no longer a civilised man, but a savage. And as he ran he stumbled against a table which was in the way. His stiff knee made him a little awkward on his feet, and with the burden of the woman in his arms he fell. In a moment she had snatched herself away from him. She ran round the sofa. He was up in a flash, and flung himself towards her. There was a revolver on the desk. She was not a nervous woman, but Robert was to be away for the night, and she had meant to take it into her room when she went to bed. That was why it happened to be there. She was frantic with terror now. She did not know what she was doing. She heard a report. She saw Hammond stagger. He gave a cry. He said something, she didn't know what. He lurched out of the room on to the verandah. She was in a frenzy now, she was beside herself, she followed him out, yes, that was it, she must have followed him out, though she remembered nothing of it, she followed firing automatically, shot after shot, till the six chambers were empty. Hammond fell down on the floor of the verandah. He crumpled up into a bloody heap.

When the boys, startled by the reports, rushed up, they found her standing over Hammond with the revolver still in her hand and Hammond lifeless. She looked at them for a moment without speaking. They stood in a frightened, huddled bunch. She let the revolver fall from her hand, and without a word turned and went into the sitting-room. They watched her go into her bedroom and turn the key in the lock. They dared not touch the dead body, but looked at it with terrified eyes, talking excitedly to one another in undertones. Then the head-boy collected himself; he had been with them for many years, he was Chinese and a level-headed fellow. Robert had gone into Singapore on his motor-cycle, and the car stood in the garage. He told the seis to get it out; they must go at once to the Assistant District Officer and tell him what had happened. He picked up the revolver and put it in his pocket. The A.D.O., a man called Withers, lived on the outskirts of the nearest town, which was about thirty-five miles away. It took them an hour and a half to reach him. Everyone was asleep, and they had to rouse the boys. Presently Withers came out and they told him their errand. The head-boy showed him the revolver in proof of what he said. The A.D.O. went into his room to dress, sent for his car, and in a little while was following them back along the deserted road. The dawn was just breaking as he reached the Crosbies' bungalow. He ran up the steps of the verandah, and stopped short as he saw Hammond's body lying where he fell. He touched the face. It was quite cold.

"Where's mem?" he asked the house-boy.

The Chinese pointed to the bedroom. Withers went to the door and knocked. There was no answer. He knocked again.

"Mrs. Crosbie," he called.

"Who is it?"

"Withers."

There was another pause. Then the door was unlocked and slowly opened. Leslie stood before him. She had not been to bed, and wore the tea-gown in which she had dined. She stood and looked silently at the A.D.O.

"Your house-boy fetched me," he said. "Hammond. What have you done?"

"He tried to rape me, and I shot him."

"My God. I say, you'd better come out here. You must tell me exactly what happened."

"Not now. I can't. You must give me time. Send for my husband."

Withers was a young man, and he did not know exactly what to do in an emergency which was so out of the run of his duties. Leslie refused to say anything till at last Robert arrived. Then she told the two men the story, from which since then, though she had repeated it over and over again, she had never in the slightest degree diverged.

The point to which Mr. Joyce recurred was the shooting. As a lawyer he was bothered that Leslie had fired not once, but six times, and the examination of the dead man showed that four of the shots had been fired close to the body. One might almost have thought that when the man fell she stood over him and emptied the contents of the revolver into him. She confessed that her memory, so accurate for all that had preceded, failed her here. Her mind was blank. It pointed to an uncontrollable fury; but uncontrollable fury was the last thing you would have expected from this quiet and demure woman. Mr. Joyce had known her a good many years, and had always thought her an unemotional person; during the weeks that had passed since the tragedy her composure had been amazing.

Mr. Joyce shrugged his shoulders.

"The fact is, I suppose," he reflected, "that you can never tell what hidden possibilities of savagery there are in the most respectable of women."

There was a knock at the door.

"Come in."

The Chinese clerk entered and closed the door behind him. He closed it gently, with deliberation, but decidedly, and advanced to the table at which Mr. Joyce was sitting.

"May I trouble you, sir, for a few words private conversation?" he said.

The elaborate accuracy with which the clerk expressed himself always faintly amused Mr. Joyce, and now he smiled.

"It's no trouble, Chi Seng," he replied.

"The matter on which I desire to speak to you, sir, is delicate and confidential."

"Fire away."

Mr. Joyce met his clerk's shrewd eyes. As usual Ong Chi Seng was dressed in the height of local fashion. He wore very shiny-patent-leather shoes and gay silk socks. In his black tie was a pearl and ruby pin, and on the fourth finger of his left hand a diamond ring. From the pocket of his neat white coat protruded a gold fountain pen and a gold pencil. He wore a gold wrist-watch and on the bridge of his nose invisible pince-nez. He gave a little cough.

"The matter has to do with the case R. *v.* Crosbie, sir."

"Yes?"

"A circumstance has come to my knowledge, sir, which seems to me to put a different complexion on it."

"What circumstance?"

"It has come to my knowledge, sir, that there is a letter in existence from the defendant to the unfortunate victim of the tragedy."

"I shouldn't be at all surprised. In the course of the last seven years I have no doubt that Mrs. Crosbie often had occasion to write to Mr. Hammond."

Mr. Joyce had a high opinion of his clerk's intelligence and his words were designed to conceal his thoughts.

"That is very probable, sir. Mrs. Crosbie must have communicated with the deceased frequently, to invite him to dine with her for example, or to propose a tennis game. That was my first thought when the matter was brought to my notice. This letter, however, was written on the day of the late Mr. Hammond's death."

Mr. Joyce did not flicker an eyelash. He continued to look at Ong Chi Seng with the smile of faint amusement with which he generally talked to him.

"Who has told you this?"

"The circumstances were brought to my knowledge, sir, by a friend of mine."

Mr. Joyce knew better than to insist.

"You will no doubt recall, sir, that Mrs. Crosbie has stated that until the fatal night she had had no communication with the deceased for several weeks."

"Have you got the letter?"

"No, sir."

"What are its contents?"

"My friend gave me a copy. Would you like to peruse it, sir?"

"I should."

Ong Chi Seng took from an inside pocket a bulky wallet. It was filled with papers, Singapore dollar notes and cigarette cards. From the confusion he presently extracted a half-sheet of thin notepaper and placed it before Mr. Joyce. The letter read as follows:—

R. will be away for the night. I absolutely must see you. I shall expect you at eleven. I am desperate, and if you don't come I won't answer for the consequences. Don't drive up.—L.

It was written in the flowing hand which the Chinese were taught at the foreign schools. The writing, so lacking in character, was oddly incongruous with the ominous words.

"What makes you think that this note was written by Mrs. Crosbie?"

"I have every confidence in the veracity of my informant, sir," replied Ong Chi Seng. "And the matter can very easily be put to the proof. Mrs.

Crosbie will, no doubt, be able to tell you at once whether she wrote such a letter or not."

Since the beginning of the conversation Mr. Joyce had not taken his eyes off the respectable countenance of his clerk. He wondered now if he discerned in it a faint expression of mockery.

"It is inconceivable that Mrs. Crosbie should have written such a letter," said Mr. Joyce.

"If that is your opinion, sir, the matter is of course ended. My friend spoke to me on the subject only because he thought, as I was in your office, you might like to know of the existence of this letter before a communication was made to the Deputy Public Prosecutor."

"Who has the original?" asked Mr. Joyce sharply.

Ong Chi Seng made no sign that he perceived in this question and its manner a change of attitude.

"You will remember, sir, no doubt, that after the death of Mr. Hammond it was discovered that he had had relations with a Chinese woman. The letter is at present in her possession."

That was one of the things which had turned public opinion most vehemently against Hammond. It came to be known that for several months he had had a Chinese woman living in his house.

For a moment neither of them spoke. Indeed everything had been said and each understood the other perfectly.

"I'm obliged to you, Chi Seng. I will give the matter my consideration."

"Very good, sir. Do you wish me to make a communication to that effect to my friend?"

"I dare say it would be as well if you kept in touch with him," Mr. Joyce answered with gravity.

"Yes, sir."

The clerk noiselessly left the room, shutting the door again with deliberation, and left Mr. Joyce to his reflections. He stared at the the copy, in its neat, impersonal writing, of Leslie's letter. Vague suspicions troubled him. They were so disconcerting that he made an effort to put them out of his mind. There must be a simple explanation of the letter, and Leslie without doubt could give it at once, but, by heaven, an explanation was needed. He rose from his chair, put the letter in his pocket, and took his topee. When he went out Ong Chi Seng was busily writing at his desk.

"I'm going out for a few minutes, Chi Seng," he said.

"Mr. George Reed is coming by appointment at twelve o'clock, sir. Where shall I say you've gone?"

Mr. Joyce gave him a thin smile.

"You can say that you haven't the least idea."

But he knew perfectly well that Ong Chi Seng was aware that he was going to the gaol. Though the crime had been committed in Belanda and the trial was to take place at Belanda Bharu, since there was in the gaol no convenience for the detention of a white woman Mrs. Crosbie had been brought to Singapore.

When she was led into the room in which he waited she held out her thin, distinguished hand, and gave him a pleasant smile. She was as ever neatly and simply dressed, and her abundant, pale hair was arranged with care.

"I wasn't expecting to see you this morning," she said, graciously.

She might have been in her own house, and Mr. Joyce almost expected to hear her call the boy and tell him to bring the visitor a gin pahit.

"How are you?" he asked.

"I'm in the best of health, thank you." A flicker of amusement flashed across her eyes. "This is a wonderful place for a rest cure."

The attendant withdrew and they were left alone.

"Do sit down," said Leslie.

He took a chair. He did not quite know how to begin. She was so cool that it seemed almost impossible to say to her the thing he had come to say. Though she was not pretty there was something agreeable in her appearance. She had elegance, but it was the elegance of good breeding in which there was nothing of the artifice of society. You had only to look at her to know what sort of people she had and what kind of surroundings she had lived in. Her fragility gave her a singular refinement. It was impossible to associate her with the vaguest idea of grossness.

"I'm looking forward to seeing Robert this afternoon," she said, in her good-humoured, easy voice. (It was a pleasure to hear her speak, her voice and her accent were so distinctive of her class.) "Poor dear, it's been a great trial to his nerves. I'm thankful it'll all be over in a few days."

"It's only five days now."

"I know. Each morning when I awake I say to myself, 'one less.' " She smiled then. "Just as I used to do at school and the holidays were coming."

"By the way, am I right in thinking that you had no communication whatever with Hammond for several weeks before the catastrophe?"

"I'm quite positive of that. The last time we met was at a tennis-party at the MacFarrens. I don't think I said more than two words to him. They have two courts, you know, and we didn't happen to be in the same sets."

"And you haven't written to him?"

"Oh, no."

"Are you quite sure of that?"

"Oh, quite," she answered, with a little smile. "There was nothing I should write to him for except to ask him to dine or to play tennis, and I hadn't done either for months."

"At one time you'd been on fairly intimate terms with him. How did it happen that you had stopped asking him to anything?"

Mrs. Crosbie shrugged her thin shoulders.

"One gets tired of people. We hadn't anything very much in common. Of course, when he was ill Robert and I did everything we could for him, but the last year or two he'd been quite well, and he was very popular. He had a good many calls on his time, and there didn't seem to be any need to shower invitations upon him."

"Are you quite certain that was all?"

Mrs. Crosbie hesitated for a moment.

"Well, I may just as well tell you. It had come to our ears that he was living with a Chinese woman, and Robert said he wouldn't have him in the house, I had seen her myself."

Mr. Joyce was sitting in a straight-backed arm-chair, resting his chin on his hand, and his eyes were fixed on Leslie. Was it his fancy that, as she made this remark, her black pupils were filled on a sudden, for the fraction of a second, with a dull red light? The effect was startling. Mr. Joyce shifted in his chair. He placed the tips of his ten fingers together. He spoke very slowly, choosing his words.

"I think I should tell you that there is in existence a letter in your handwriting to Geoff. Hammond."

He watched her closely. She made no movement, nor did her face change colour, but she took a noticeable time to reply.

"In the past I've often sent him little notes to ask him to something or other, or to get me something when I knew he was going to Singapore."

"This letter asks him to come and see you because Robert was going to Singapore."

"That's impossible. I never did anything of the kind."

"You'd better read it for yourself."

He took it out of his pocket and handed it to her. She gave it a glance and with a smile of scorn handed it back to him.

"That's not my handwriting."

"I know, it's said to be an exact copy of the original."

She read the words now, and as she read a horrible change came over her. Her colourless face grew dreadful to look at. It turned green. The flesh seemed on a sudden to fall away and her skin was tightly stretched over the bones. Her lips receded, showing her teeth, so that she had the appearance of making a grimace. She stared at Mr. Joyce with eyes that started from their sockets. He was looking now at a gibbering death's head.

"What does it mean?" she whispered.

Her mouth was so dry that she could utter no more than a hoarse sound. It was no longer a human voice.

"That is for you to say," he answered.

"I didn't write it. I swear I didn't write it."

"Be very careful what you say. If the original is in your handwriting it would be useless to deny it."

"It would be a forgery."

"It would be difficult to prove that. It would be easy to prove that it was genuine."

A shiver passed through her lean body. But great beads of sweat stood on her forehead. She took a handkerchief from her bag and wiped the palms of her hands. She glanced at the letter again and gave Mr. Joyce a sidelong look.

"It's not dated. If I had written it and forgotten all about it, it might have been written years ago. If you'll give me time, I'll try and remember the circumstances."

"I noticed there was no date. If this letter were in the hands of the prosecution they would cross-examine the boys. They would soon find out whether someone took a letter to Hammond on the day of his death."

Mrs. Crosbie clasped her hands violently and swayed in her chair so that he thought she would faint.

"I swear to you that I didn't write that letter."

Mr. Joyce was silent for a little while. He took his eyes from her distraught face, and looked down on the floor. He was reflecting.

"In these circumstances we need not go into the matter further," he said slowly, at last breaking the silence. "If the possessor of this letter sees fit to place it in the hands of the prosecution you will be prepared."

His words suggested that he had nothing more to say to her, but he made no movement of departure. He waited. To himself he seemed to wait a very long time. He did not look at Leslie, but he was conscious that she sat very still. She made no sound. At last it was he who spoke.

"If you have nothing more to say to me I think I'll be getting back to my office."

"What would anyone who read the letter be inclined to think that it meant?" she asked then.

"He'd know that you had told a deliberate lie," answered Mr. Joyce sharply.

"When?"

"You have stated definitely that you had had no communication with Hammond for at least three months."

"The whole thing has been a terrible shock to me. The events of that dreadful night have been a nightmare. It's not very strange if one detail has escaped my memory."

"It would be unfortunate, when your memory has reproduced so exactly every particular of your interview with Hammond, that you should have forgotten so important a point as that he came to see you in the bungalow on the night of his death at your express desire."

"I hadn't forgotten. After what happened I was afraid to mention it. I thought you'd none of you believe my story if I admitted that he'd come at my invitation. I dare say it was stupid of me; but I lost my head, and after I'd said once that I'd had no communication with Hammond I was obliged to stick to it."

By now Leslie had recovered her admirable composure, and she met Mr. Joyce's appraising glance with candour. Her gentleness was very disarming.

"You will be required to explain, then, *why* you asked Hammond to come and see you when Robert was away for the night."

She turned her eyes full on the lawyer. He had been mistaken in thinking them insignificant, they were rather fine eyes, and unless he was mistaken they were bright now with tears. Her voice had a little break in it.

"It was a surprise I was preparing for Robert. His birthday is next month. I knew he wanted a new gun and you know I'm dreadfully stupid about sporting things. I wanted to talk to Geoff, about it. I thought I'd get him to order it for me."

"Perhaps the terms of the letter are not very clear to your recollection. Will you have another look at it?"

"No, I don't want to," she said quickly.

"Does it seem to you the sort of letter a woman would write to a somewhat distant acquaintance because she wanted to consult him about buying a gun?"

"I dare say it's rather extravagant and emotional. I do express myself like that, you know. I'm quite prepared to admit it's very silly." She smiled. "And after all, Geoff. Hammond wasn't quite a distant acquaintance. When he was ill I'd nursed him like a mother. I asked him to come when Robert was away, because Robert wouldn't have him in the house."

Mr. Joyce was tired of sitting so long in the same position. He rose and walked once or twice up and down the room, choosing the words he proposed to say; then he learned over the back of the chair in which he had been sitting. He spoke slowly in a tone of deep gravity.

"Mrs. Crosbie, I want to talk to you very, very seriously. This case was comparatively plain sailing. There was only one point which seemed to me to require explanation: as far as I could judge, you had fired no less than four shots into Hammond when he was lying on the ground. It was hard to accept the possibility that a delicate, frightened, and habitually self-controlled woman, of gentle nature and refined instincts, should have surrendered to an absolutely uncontrolled frenzy. But of course it was admissible. Although Geoffrey Hammond was much liked and on the whole thought highly of, I was prepared to prove that he was the sort of man who might be guilty of the crime which in justification of your act you accused him of. The fact, which was discovered after his death, that he had been living with a Chinese woman gave us something very definite to go upon. That robbed him of any sympathy which might have been felt for him. We made up our minds to make use of the odium which such a connection cast upon him in the minds of all respectable people. I told your husband this morning that I was certain of an acquittal, and I wasn't just telling him that to give him heart. I do not believe the assessors would have left the court."

They looked into one another's eyes. Mrs. Crosbie was strangely still. She was like a little bird paralysed by the fascination of a snake. He went on in the same quiet tones.

"But this letter has thrown an entirely different complexion on the case. I am your legal adviser, I shall represent you in court. I take your story as you tell it me, and I shall conduct your defence according to its terms. It may be that I believe your statements, and it may be that I doubt them. The duty of counsel is to persuade the court that the evidence placed before it is not such as to justify it in bringing in a verdict of guilty, and any private opinion he may have of the guilt or innocence of his client is entirely beside the point."

He was astonished to see in Leslie's eyes the flicker of a smile. Piqued, he went on somewhat dryly:

"You're not going to deny that Hammond came to your house at your urgent, and I may even say, hysterical invitation?"

Mrs. Crosbie, hesitating for an instant, seemed to consider.

"They can prove that the letter was taken to his bungalow by one of the house-boys. He rode over on his bicycle."

"You mustn't expect other people to be stupider than you. The letter will put them on the track of suspicions which have entered nobody's head. I will not tell you what I personally thought when I saw the copy. I do not wish you to tell me anything but what is needed to save your neck."

Mrs. Crosbie gave a shrill cry. She sprang to her feet, white with terror.

"You don't think they'd hang me?"

"If they came to the conclusion that you hadn't killed Hammond in self-defence, it would be the duty of the assessors to bring in a verdict of guilty. The charge is murder. It would be the duty of the judge to sentence you to death."

"But what can they prove?" she gasped.

"I don't know what they can prove. You know. I don't want to know. But if their suspicions are aroused, if they begin to make inquiries, if the natives are questioned—what is it that can be discovered?"

She crumpled up suddenly. She fell on the floor before he could catch her. She had fainted. He looked round the room for water, but there was none there, and he did not want to be disturbed. He stretched her out on the floor, and kneeling beside her waited for her to recover. When she opened her eyes he was disconcerted by the ghastly fear that he saw in them.

"Keep quite still," he said. "You'll be better in a moment."

"You won't let them hang me," she whispered.

She began to cry, hysterically, while in undertones he sought to quieten her.

"For goodness sake pull yourself together," he said.

"Give me a minute."

Her courage was amazing. He could see the effort she made to regain her self-control, and soon she was once more calm.

"Let me get up now."

He gave her his hand and helped her to her feet. Taking her arm, he led her to the chair. She sat down wearily.

"Don't talk to me for a minute or two," she said.

"Very well."

When at last she spoke it was to say something which he did not expect. She gave a little sigh.

"I'm afraid I've made rather a mess of things," she said.

He did not answer, and once more there was a silence.

"Isn't it possible to get hold of the letter?" she said at last.

"I do not think anything would have been said to me about it if the person in whose possession it is was not prepared to sell it."

"Who's got it?"

"The Chinese woman who was living in Hammond's house."

A spot of colour flickered for an instant on Leslie's cheek-bones.

"Does she want an awful lot for it?"

"I imagine that she has a very shrewd idea of its value. I doubt if it would be possible to get hold of it except for a very large sum."

"Are you going to let me be hanged?"

"Do you think it's so simple as all that to secure possession of an unwelcome piece of evidence? It's no different from suborning a witness. You have no right to make any such suggestion to me."

"Then what is going to happen to me?"

"Justice must take its course."

She grew very pale. A little shudder passed through her body.

"I put myself in your hands. Of course I have no right to ask you to do anything that isn't proper."

Mr. Joyce had not bargained for the little break in her voice which her habitual self-restraint made quite intolerably moving. She looked at him with humble eyes, and he thought that if he rejected their appeal they would haunt him for the rest of his life. After all, nothing could bring poor Hammond back to life again. He wondered what really was the explanation of that letter. It was not fair to conclude from it that she had killed Hammond without provocation. He had lived in the East a long time and his sense of professional honour was not perhaps so acute as it had been twenty years before. He stared at the floor. He made up his mind to do something which he knew was unjustifiable, but it stuck in his throat and he felt dully resentful towards Leslie. It embarrassed him a little to speak.

"I don't know exactly what your husband's circumstances are?"

Flushing a rosy red, she shot a swift glance at him.

"He has a good many tin shares and a small share in two or three rubber estates. I suppose he could raise money."

"He would have to be told what it was for."

She was silent for a moment. She seemed to think.

"He's in love with me still. He would make any sacrifice to save me. Is there any need for him to see the letter?"

Mr. Joyce frowned a little, and, quick to notice, she went on.

"Robert is an old friend of yours. I'm not asking you to do anything for me, I'm asking you to save a rather simple, kind man who never did you any harm from all the pain that's possible."

Mr. Joyce did not reply. He rose to go and Mrs. Crosbie, with the grace that was natural to her, held out her hand. She was shaken by the scene, and her look was haggard, but she made a brave attempt to speed him with courtesy.

"It's so good of you to take all this trouble for me. I can't begin to tell you how grateful I am."

Mr. Joyce returned to his office. He sat in his own room, quite still, attempting to do no work, and pondered. His imagination brought him many strange ideas. He shuddered a little. At last there was the discreet knock on the door which he was expecting. Ong Chi Seng came in.

"I was just going out to have my tiffin, sir," he said.

"All right."

"I didn't know if there was anything you wanted before I went, sir."

"I don't think so. Did you make another appointment for Mr. Reed?"

"Yes, sir. He will come at three o'clock."

"Good."

Ong Chi Seng turned away, walked to the door, and put his long slim fingers on the handle. Then, as though on an afterthought, he turned back.

"Is there anything you wish me to say to my friend, sir?"

Although Ong Chi Seng spoke English so admirably he had still a difficulty with the letter R, and he pronounced it "fliend."

"What friend?"

"About the letter Mrs. Crosbie wrote to Hammond deceased, sir."

"Oh! I'd forgotten about that. I mentioned it to Mrs. Crosbie and she denies having written anything of the sort. It's evidently a forgery."

Mr. Joyce took the copy from his pocket and handed it to Ong Chi Seng. Ong Chi Seng ignored the gesture.

"In that case, sir, I suppose there would be no objection if my fliend delivered the letter to the Deputy Public Prosecutor."

"None. But I don't quite see what good that would do your friend."

"My fliend, sir, thought it was his duty in the interests of justice."

"I am the last man in the world to interfere with anyone who wishes to do his duty, Chi Seng."

The eyes of the lawyer and of the Chinese clerk met. Not the shadow of a smile hovered on the lips of either, but they understood each other perfectly.

"I quite understand, sir," said Ong Chi Seng, "but from my study of the case R. *v*. Crosbie I am of opinion that the production of such a letter would be damaging to our client."

"I have always had a very high opinion of your legal acumen, Chi Seng."

"It has occurred to me, sir, that if I could persuade my fliend to induce the Chinese woman who had the letter to deliver it into our hands it would save a great deal of trouble."

Mr. Joyce idly drew faces on his blotting-paper.

"I suppose your friend is a business man. In what circumstances do you think he would be induced to part with the letter?"

"He has not got the letter. The Chinese woman has the letter. He is only a relation of the Chinese woman. She is an ignorant woman; she did not know the value of that letter till my fliend told her."

"What value did he put on it?"

"Ten thousand dollars, sir."

"Good God! Where on earth do you suppose Mrs. Crosbie can get ten thousand dollars! I tell you the letter's a forgery."

He looked up at Ong Chi Seng as he spoke. The clerk was unmoved by the outburst. He stood at the side of the desk, civil, cool and observant.

"Mr. Crosbie owns an eighth share of the Betong Rubber Estate and a sixth share of the Selantan River Rubber Estate. I have a fliend who will lend him the money on the security of his property."

"You have a large circle of acquaintance, Chi Seng."

"Yes sir."

"Well, you can tell them all to go to hell. I would never advise Mr. Crosbie to give a penny more than five thousand for a letter that can be very easily explained."

"The Chinese woman does not want to sell the letter, sir. My fliend took a long time to persuade her. It is useless to offer her less than the sum mentioned."

Mr. Joyce looked at Ong Chi Seng for at least three minutes. The clerk bore the searching scrutiny without embarrassment. He stood in a respectful attitude with downcast eyes. Mr. Joyce knew his man. Clever fellow, Chi Seng, he thought, I wonder how much he's going to get out of it.

"Ten thousand dollars is a very large sum."

"Mr. Crosbie will certainly pay it rather than see his wife hanged, sir."

Again Mr. Joyce paused. What more did Chi Seng know than he had said? He must be pretty sure of his ground if he was obviously so unwilling to bargain. That sum had been fixed because whoever it was that was managing the affair knew it was the largest amount that Robert Crosbie could raise.

"Where is the Chinese woman now?" asked Mr. Joyce.

"She is staying at the house of my fliend, sir."

"Will she come here?"

"I think it more better if you go to her, sir. I can take you to the house to-night and she will give you the letter. She is a very ignorant woman, sir, and she does not understand cheques."

"I wasn't thinking of giving her a cheque. I will bring bank-notes with me."

"It would only be waste of valuable time to bring less than ten thousand dollars, sir."

"I quite understand."

"I will go and tell my fliend after I have had my tiffin, sir."

"Very good. You'd better meet me outside the club at ten o'clock to-night."

"With pleasure, sir," said Ong Chi Seng.

He gave Mr. Joyce a little bow and left the room. Mr. Joyce went out to have luncheon, too. He went to the club and here, as he had expected, he saw Robert Crosbie. He was sitting at a crowded table, and as he passed him, looking for a place, Mr. Joyce touched him on the shoulder.

"I'd like a word or two with you before you go," he said.

"Right you are. Let me know when you're ready."

Mr. Joyce had made up his mind how to tackle him. He played a rubber of bridge after luncheon in order to allow time for the club to empty itself. He did not want on this particular matter to see Crosbie in his office. Presently Crosbie came into the card-room and looked on till the game was finished. The other players went on their various affairs, and the two were left alone.

"A rather unfortunate thing has happened, old man," said Mr. Joyce, in a tone which he sought to render as casual as possible. "It appears that your wife sent a letter to Hammond asking him to come to the bungalow on the night he was killed."

"But that's impossible," cried Crosbie. "She's always stated that she had had no communication with Hammond. I know from my own knowledge that she hadn't set eyes on him for a couple of months."

"The fact remains that the letter exists. It's in the possession of the Chinese woman Hammond was living with. Your wife meant to give you a present on your birthday, and she wanted Hammond to help her to get it. In the emotional excitement that she suffered from after the tragedy, she forgot all about it, and having once denied having any communication with Hammond she was afraid to say that she had made a mistake. It was, of course, very unfortunate, but I dare say it was not unnatural."

Crosbie did not speak. His large, red face bore an expression of complete bewilderment, and Mr. Joyce was at once relieved and exasperated by his lack of comprehension. He was a stupid man, and Mr. Joyce had no patience with stupidity. But his distress since the catastrophe had touched a soft spot in the lawyer's heart; and Mrs. Crosbie had struck the right note when she asked him to help her, not for her sake, but for her husband's.

"I need not tell you that it would be very awkward if this letter found its way into the hands of the prosecution. Your wife has lied, and she would be asked to explain the lie. It alters things a little if Hammond did not intrude, an unwanted guest, but came to your house by invitation. It would be easy to arouse in the assessors a certain indecision of mind."

Mr. Joyce hesitated. He was face to face now with his decision. If it had been a time for humour, he could have smiled at the reflection that he was taking so grave a step, and that the man for whom he was taking it had not the smallest conception of its gravity. If he gave the matter a thought, he probably imagined that what Mr. Joyce was doing was what any lawyer did in the ordinary run of business.

"My dear Robert, you are not only my client, but my friend. I think we must get hold of that letter. It'll cost a good deal of money. Except for that I should have preferred to say nothing to you about it."

"How much?"

"Ten thousand dollars."

"That's a devil of a lot. With the slump and one thing and another it'll take just about all I've got."

"Can you get it at once?"

"I suppose so. Old Charlie Meadows will let me have it on my tin shares and on those two estates I'm interested in."

"Then will you?"

"Is it absolutely necessary?"

"If you want your wife to be acquitted."

Crosbie grew very red. His mouth sagged strangely.

"But . . ." he could not find words, his face now was purple. "But I don't understand. She can explain. You don't mean to say they'd find her guilty? They couldn't hang her for putting a noxious vermin out of the way."

"Of course they wouldn't hang her. They might only find her guilty of manslaughter. She'd probably get off with two or three years."

Crosbie started to his feet and his red face was distraught with horror.

"Three years."

Then something seemed to dawn in that slow intelligence of his. His mind was darkness across which shot suddenly a flash of lightning, and though the succeeding darkness was as profound, there remained the memory of something not seen but perhaps just descried. Mr. Joyce saw that Crosbie's big red hands, coarse and hard with all the odd jobs he had set them to, trembled.

"What was the present she wanted to make me?"

"She says she wanted to give you a new gun."

Once more that great red face flushed a deeper red.

"When have you got to have the money ready?"

There was something odd in his voice now. It sounded as though he spoke with invisible hands clutching at his throat.

"At ten o'clock to-night. I thought you could bring it to my office at about six."

"Is the woman coming to you?"

"No, I'm going to her."

"I'll bring the money. I'll come with you."

Mr. Joyce looked at him sharply.

"Do you think there's any need for you to do that? I think it would be better if you left me to deal with this matter by myself."

"It's my money, isn't it? I'm going to come."

Mr. Joyce shrugged his shoulders. They rose and shook hands. Mr. Joyce looked at him curiously.

At ten o'clock they met in the empty club.

"Everything all right?" asked Mr. Joyce.

"Yes. I've got the money in my pocket."

"Let's go then."

They walked down the steps. Mr. Joyce's car was waiting for them in the square, silent at that hour, and as they came to it Ong Chi Seng stepped out of the shadow of a house. He took his seat beside the driver and gave him a direction. They drove past the Hotel de l'Europe and turned up by the Sailor's Home to get into Victoria Street. Here the Chinese shops were still open, idlers lounged about, and in the roadway rickshaws and motor-cars and gharries gave a busy air to the scene. Suddenly their car stopped and Chi Seng turned round.

"I think it more better if we walk here, sir," he said.

They got out and he went on. They followed a step or two behind. Then he asked them to stop.

"You wait here, sir. I go in and speak to my fliend.'

He went into a shop, open to the street, where three or four Chinese were standing behind the counter. It was one of those strange shops where nothing was on view, and you wondered what it was they sold there. They saw him address a stout man in a duck suit with a large gold chain across his breast, and the man shot a quick glance out into the night. He gave Chi Seng a key and Chi Seng came out. He beckoned to the two men waiting and slid into a doorway at the side of the shop. They followed him and found themselves at the foot of a flight of stairs.

"If you wait a minute I will light a match," he said, always resourceful. "You come upstairs, please."

He held a Japanese match in front of them, but it scarcely dispelled the darkness and they groped their way up behind him. On the first floor he unlocked a door and going in lit a gas-jet.

"Come in, please," he said.

It was a small square room, with one window, and the only furniture consisted of two low Chinese beds covered with matting. In one corner was a large chest, with an elaborate lock, and on this stood a shabby tray with an opium pipe on it and a lamp. There was in the room the faint, acrid scent of the drug. They sat down and Ong Chi Seng offered them cigarettes. In a moment the door was opened by the fat Chinaman whom they had seen behind the counter. He bade them good-evening in very good English, and sat down by the side of his fellow-countryman.

"The Chinese woman is just coming," said Chi Seng.

A boy from the shop brought in a tray with a teapot and cups and the Chinaman offered them a cup of tea. Crosbie refused. The Chinese talked to one another in undertones, but Crosbie and Mr. Joyce were silent. At last there was the sound of a voice outside; someone was calling in a low tone; and the Chinaman went to the door. He opened it, spoke a few words, and ushered a woman in. Mr. Joyce looked at her. He had heard much about her since Hammond's death, but he had never seen her. She was a stoutish person, not very young, with a broad, phlegmatic face, she was powdered and rouged and her eyebrows were a thin black line, but she gave you the impression of a woman of character. She wore a pale blue jacket and a white skirt, her costume was not quite European nor quite Chinese, but on her feet were little Chinese silk slippers. She wore heavy gold chains round her neck, gold bangles on her wrists, gold ear-rings and elaborate gold pins in her black hair. She walked in slowly, with the air of a woman sure of herself, but with a certain heaviness of tread, and sat down on the bed beside Ong Chi Seng. He said something to her and nodding she gave an incurious glance at the two white men.

"Has she got the letter?" asked Mr. Joyce.

"Yes, sir."

Crosbie said nothing, but produced a roll of five-hundred-dollar notes. He counted out twenty and handed them to Chi Seng.

"Will you see if that is correct?"

The clerk counted them and gave them to the fat Chinaman.

"Quite correct, sir."

The Chinaman counted them once more and put them in his pocket. He spoke again to the woman and she drew from her bosom a letter. She gave it to Chi Seng who cast his eyes over it.

"This is the right document, sir," he said, and was about to give it to Mr. Joyce when Crosbie took it from him.

"Let me look at it," he said.

Mr. Joyce watched him read and then held out his hand for it.

"You'd better let me have it."

Crosbie folded it up deliberately and put it in his pocket.

"No, I'm going to keep it myself. It's cost me enough money."

Mr. Joyce made no rejoinder. The three Chinese watched the little passage, but what they thought about it, or whether they thought, it was impossible to tell from their impassive countenances. Mr. Joyce rose to his feet.

"Do you want me any more to-night, sir?" said Ong Chi Seng.

"No." He knew that the clerk wished to stay behind in order to get his agreed share of the money, and he turned to Crosbie. "Are you ready?"

Crosbie did not answer, but stood up. The Chinaman went to the door and opened it for them. Chi Seng found a bit of candle and lit it in order to light them down, and the two Chinese accompanied them to the street. They left the woman sitting quietly on the bed smoking a cigarette. When they reached the street the Chinese left them and went once more upstairs.

"What are you going to do with that letter?" asked Mr. Joyce.

"Keep it."

They walked to where the car was waiting for them and here Mr. Joyce offered his friend a lift. Crosbie shook his head.

"I'm going to walk." He hesitated a little and shuffled his feet. "I went to Singapore on the night of Hammond's death partly to buy a new gun that a man I knew wanted to dispose of. Good-night."

He disappeared quickly into the darkness.

Mr. Joyce was quite right about the trial. The assessors went into court fully determined to acquit Mrs. Crosbie. She gave evidence on her own behalf. She told her story simply and with straightforwardness. The D.P.P. was a kindly man and it was plain that he took no great pleasure in his task. He asked the necessary questions in a deprecating manner. His speech for the prosecution might really have been a speech for the defence, and the assessors took less than five minutes to consider their popular verdict. It was impossible to prevent the great outburst of applause with which it was received by the crowd that packed the courthouse. The judge congratulated Mrs. Crosbie and she was a free woman.

No one had expressed a more violent disapprobation of Hammond's behaviour than Mrs. Joyce; she was a woman loyal to her friends and she had insisted on the Crosbies staying with her after the trial, for she in common with everyone else had no doubt of the result, till they could make arrangements to go away. It was out of the question for poor, dear, brave Leslie to return to the bungalow at which the horrible catastrophe had taken place. The trial was over by half-past twelve and when they reached the Joyces' house a grand luncheon was awaiting them. Cocktails were ready, Mrs. Joyce's million-dollar cocktail was celebrated through all the Malay States, and Mrs. Joyce drank Leslie's health. She was a talkative, vivacious woman, and now she was in the highest spirits. It was fortunate, for the rest of them were silent. She did not wonder; her husband never had much to say, and the other two were naturally exhausted from the long strain to which they had been subjected. During luncheon she carried on a bright and spirited monologue. Then coffee was served.

"Now, children," she said in her gay, bustling fashion, "you must have a rest and after tea I shall take you both for a drive to the sea."

Mr. Joyce, who lunched at home only by exception, had of course to go back to his office.

"I'm afraid I can't do that, Mrs. Joyce," said Crosbie. "I've got to get back to the estate at once."

"Not to-day?" she cried.

"Yes, now. I've neglected it for too long and I have urgent business. But I shall be very grateful if you will keep Leslie until we have decided what to do."

Mrs. Joyce was about to expostulate, but her husband prevented her.

"If he must go, he must, and there's an end of it."

There was something in the lawyer's tone which made her look at him quickly. She held her tongue and there was a moment's silence. Then Crosbie spoke again.

"If you'll forgive me, I'll start at once so that I can get there before dark." He rose from the table. "Will you come and see me off, Leslie?"

"Of course."

They went out of the dining-room together.

"I think that's rather inconsiderate of him," said Mrs. Joyce. "He must know that Leslie wants to be with him just now."

"I'm sure he wouldn't go if it wasn't absolutely necessary."

"Well, I'll just see that Leslie's room is ready for her. She wants a complete rest, of course, and then amusement."

Mrs. Joyce left the room and Joyce sat down again. In a short time he heard Crosbie start the engine of his motor-cycle and then noisily scrunch over the gravel of the garden path. He got up and went into the drawing-room. Mrs. Crosbie was standing in the middle of it, looking into space, and in her hand was an open letter. He recognised it. She gave him a glance as he came in and he saw that she was deathly pale.

"He knows," she whispered.

Mr. Joyce went up to her and took the letter from her hand. He lit a match and set thc paper afire. She watched it burn. When he could hold it no longer he dropped it on the tiled floor and they both looked at the paper curl and blacken. Then he trod it into ashes with his foot.

"What does he know?"

She gave him a long, long stare and into her eyes came a strange look. Was it contempt or despair? Mr. Joyce could not tell.

"He knows that Geoff, was my lover."

Mr. Joyce made no movement and uttered no sound.

"He'd been my lover for years. He became my lover almost immediately after he came back from the war. We knew how careful we must be. When we became lovers I pretended I was tired of him, and he seldom came to the house when Robert was there. I used to drive out to a place we knew and he met me, two or three times a week, and when Robert went to Singapore he used to come to the bungalow late, when the boys had gone for the night. We saw one another constantly, all the time, and not a soul had the smallest suspicion of it. And then lately, a year ago, he began to change. I didn't know what was the matter. I couldn't believe that he didn't care for me any more. He always denied it. I was frantic. I made him scenes. Sometimes I thought he hated me. Oh, if you knew what agonies I endured. I passed through hell. I knew he didn't want me any more and I wouldn't let him go. Misery! Misery! I loved him. I'd given him everything. He was my life. And then I heard he was living with a Chinese woman. I couldn't believe it. I wouldn't believe it. At last I saw her, I saw her with my own eyes, walking in the village, with her gold bracelets and her necklaces, an old, fat, Chinese woman. She was older than I was. Horrible! They all knew in the kampong that she was his mistress. And when I passed her, she looked at me and I knew that she knew I was his mistress too. I sent for him. I told him I must see him. You've read the letter. I was mad to write it. I didn't know what I was doing. I didn't care. I hadn't seen him for ten days. It was a lifetime. And when last we'd parted he took me in his arms and kissed me, and told me not to worry. And he went straight from my arms to hers."

She had been speaking in a low voice, vehemently, and now she stopped and wrung her hands.

"That damned letter. We'd always been so careful. He always tore up any word I wrote to him the moment he'd read it. How was I to know he'd leave that one? He came, and I told him I knew about the China-woman. He denied it. He said it was only scandal. I was beside myself. I don't know what I said to him. Oh, I hated him then. I tore him limb from limb. I said everything I could to wound him. I insulted him. I could have spat in his face. And at last he turned on me. He told me he was sick and tired of me and never wanted to see me again. He said I bored him to death. And then he acknowledged that it was true about the China-woman. He said he'd known her for years, before the war, and she was the only woman who really meant anything to him, and the rest was just pastime. And he said he was glad I knew and now at last I'd leave him alone. And then I don't know what happened, I was beside myself, I saw red. I seized the revolver and I fired. He gave a cry and I saw I'd hit him. He staggered and rushed for the verandah. I ran after him and fired again. He fell and then I stood over him and I fired and fired till the revolver went click, click, and I knew there were no more cartridges."

At last she stopped, panting. Her face was no longer human, it was distorted with cruelty, and rage and pain. You would never have thought that this quiet, refined woman was capable of such fiendish passion. Mr. Joyce took a step backwards. He was absolutely aghast at the sight of her. It was not a face, it was a gibbering, hideous mask. Then they heard a voice calling from another room, a loud, friendly, cheerful voice. It was Mrs. Joyce.

"Come along, Leslie darling, your room's ready. You must be dropping with sleep."

Mrs. Crosbie's features gradually composed themselves. Those passions, so clearly delineated, were smoothed away as with your hand you would smooth a crumpled paper, and in a minute the face was cool and calm and unlined. She was a trifle pale, but her lips broke into a pleasant, affable smile. She was once more the well-bred and even distinguished woman.

"I'm coming, Dorothy dear. I'm sorry to give you so much trouble."

FRANK O'CONNOR

(1903–1966)

Michael Francis O'Donovan, who assumed the pen name Frank O'Connor, was born into an impoverished family in Cork, Ireland. He left school at age fourteen. In 1918 he joined the Irish Republican Army, in the service of which he was imprisoned for a year. O'Connor taught himself literature and Gaelic culture, and by the 1930s was involved with the nationalistic Irish literary revival. During this time he associated with such towering figures as George Russell, Sean O'Casey, and William Butler Yeats, serving with Yeats as co-director of the Abbey Theatre in Dublin.

After trying his hand at poetry, novels, and drama, O'Connor concentrated on short stories. In this medium he realized his gifts and became one of the acknowledged modern masters. Yeats has said that O'Connor, by employing realism and humor, "(did) for Ireland what Chekhov did for Russia." Ultimately, however, O'Connor reacted against Irish parochialism and censorship by accepting academic appointments in the United States. He returned to his homeland for the last five years of his life.

O'Connor wrote in a number of his stories about provincial folk defying the law. Best known among these is "The Majesty of the Law," originally published in the *Fortnightly Review*, August 1935, and included in the collection *Bones of Contention* (1936). In this tale O'Connor comically celebrates an ancient code opposed to the legalities of the modern world. The old man, Dan, embodies individuality and irresponsibility, while the police sergeant is torn between the old system and the new.

THE MAJESTY OF THE LAW

— 1935 —

Old Dan Bride was breaking brosna for the fire when he heard a step on the path. He paused, a bundle of saplings on his knee.

Dan had looked after his mother while the life was in her, and after her death no other woman had crossed his threshold. Signs on it, his house had that look. Almost everything in it he had made with his own hands in his own way. The seats of the chairs were only slices of log, rough and round and thick as the saw had left them, and with the rings still plainly visible through the grime and polish that coarse trouser-bottoms had in the course of long years imparted. Into these Dan had rammed stout knotted ash-boughs that served alike for legs and back. The deal table, bought in a shop, was an inheritance from his mother and a great pride and joy to him though it rocked whenever he touched it. On the wall, unglazed and fly-spotted, hung in mysterious isolation a Marcus Stone print, and beside the door was a calendar with a picture of a racehorse. Over the door hung a gun, old but good, and in excellent condition, and before the fire was stretched an old setter who raised his head expectantly whenever Dan rose or even stirred.

He raised it now as the steps came nearer and when Dan, laying down the bundle of saplings, cleaned his hands thoughtfully on the seat of his trousers, he gave a loud bark, but this expressed no more than a desire to show off his own watchfulness. He was half human and knew people thought he was old and past his prime.

A man's shadow fell across the oblong of dusty light thrown over the half-door before Dan looked round.

"Are you alone, Dan?" asked an apologetic voice.

"Oh, come in, come in, sergeant, come in and welcome," exclaimed the old man, hurrying on rather uncertain feet to the door which the tall policeman opened and pushed in. He stood there, half in sunlight, half in shadow, and seeing him so, you would have realized how dark the interior of the house really was. One side of his red face was turned so as to catch the light, and behind it an ash tree raised its boughs of airy green against the sky. Green fields, broken here and there by clumps of red-brown rock, flowed downhill, and beyond them, stretched all across the horizon, was the sea, flooded and almost transparent with light. The sergeant's face was fat and fresh, the old man's face, emerging from the twilight of the kitchen, had the color of wind and sun, while the features had been so shaped by the struggle with time and the elements that they might as easily have been found impressed upon the surface of a rock.

"Begor, Dan," said the sergeant, " 'tis younger you're getting."

"Middling I am, sergeant, middling," agreed the old man in a voice which seemed to accept the remark as a compliment of which politeness would not allow him to take too much advantage. "No complaints."

"Begor, 'tis as well because no one would believe them. And the old dog doesn't look a day older."

The dog gave a low growl as though to show the sergeant that he would remember this unmannerly reference to his age, but indeed he growled every time he was mentioned, under the impression that people had nothing but ill to say of him.

"And how's yourself, sergeant?"

"Well, now, like the most of us, Dan, neither too good nor too bad. We have our own little worries, but, thanks be to God, we have our compensations."

"And the wife and family?"

"Good, praise be to God, good. They were away from me for a month, the lot of them, at the mother-in-law's place in Clare."

"In Clare, do you tell me?"

"In Clare. I had a fine quiet time."

The old man looked about him and then retired to the bedroom, from which he returned a moment later with an old shirt. With this he solemnly wiped the seat and back of the log-chair nearest the fire.

"Sit down now, sergeant. You must be tired after the journey. 'Tis a long old road. How did you come?"

"Teigue Leary gave me the lift. Wisha now, Dan, don't be putting yourself out. I won't be stopping. I promised them I'd be back inside an hour."

"What hurry is on you?" asked Dan. "Look, your foot was only on the path when I made up the fire."

"Arrah, Dan, you're not making tea for me?"

"I am not making it for you, indeed; I'm making it for myself, and I'll take it very bad of you if you won't have a cup."

"Dan, Dan, that I mightn't stir, but 'tisn't an hour since I had it at the barracks!"

"Ah, whisht, now, whisht! Whisht, will you! I have something here to give you an appetite."

The old man swung the heavy kettle onto the chain over the open fire, and the dog sat up, shaking his ears with an expression of the deepest interest. The policeman unbuttoned his tunic, opened his belt, took a pipe and a plug of tobacco from his breast pocket, and crossing his legs in an easy posture, began to cut the tobacco slowly and carefully with his pocket knife. The old man went to the dresser and took down two handsomely decorated cups, the only cups he had, which, though chipped and handleless, were used at all only on very rare occasions; for himself he preferred his tea from a basin. Happening to glance into them, he noticed that they bore signs of disuse and had collected a lot of the fine white turf-dust that always circulated in the little smoky cottage. Again he thought of the shirt, and, rolling up his sleeves with a stately gesture, he wiped them inside and out till they shone. Then he bent and opened the cupboard. Inside was a quart bottle of pale liquid, obviously untouched. He removed the cork and smelt the contents, pausing for a moment in the act as though to recollect where exactly he had noticed that particular smoky smell before. Then, reassured, he stood up and poured out with a liberal hand.

"Try that now, sergeant," he said with quiet pride.

The sergeant, concealing whatever qualms he might have felt at the idea of drinking illegal whiskey, looked carefully into the cup, sniffed, and glanced up at old Dan.

"It looks good," he commented.

"It should be good," replied Dan with no mock modesty.

"It tastes good too," said the sergeant.

"Ah, sha," said Dan, not wishing to praise his own hospitality in his own house, " 'tis of no great excellence."

"You'd be a good judge, I'd say," said the sergeant without irony.

"Ever since things became what they are," said Dan, carefully guarding himself against a too-direct reference to the peculiarities of the law administered by his guest, "liquor isn't what it used to be."

"I've heard that remark made before now, Dan," said the sergeant thoughtfully. "I've heard it said by men of wide experience that it used to be better in the old days."

"Liquor," said the old man, "is a thing that takes time. There was never a good job done in a hurry."

" 'Tis an art in itself."

"Just so."

"And an art takes time."

"And knowledge," added Dan with emphasis. "Every art has its secrets, and the secrets of distilling are being lost the way the old songs were lost. When I was a boy there wasn't a man in the barony but had a hundred songs in his head, but with people running here, there and everywhere, the songs were lost. . . . Ever since things became what they are," he repeated on the same guarded note, "there's so much running about the secrets are lost."

"There must have been a power of them."

"There was. Ask any man today that makes whiskey do he know how to make it out of heather."

"And was it made of heather?" asked the policeman.

"It was."

"You never drank it yourself?"

"I didn't, but I knew old men that did, and they told me that no whiskey that's made nowadays could compare with it."

"Musha, Dan, I think sometimes 'twas a great mistake of the law to set its hand against it."

Dan shook his head. His eyes answered for him, but it was not in nature for a man to criticize the occupation of a guest in his own home.

"Maybe so, maybe not," he said noncommittally.

"But sure, what else have the poor people?"

"Them that makes the laws have their own good reasons."

"All the same, Dan, all the same, 'tis a hard law."

The sergeant would not be outdone in generosity. Politeness required him not to yield to the old man's defense of his superiors and their mysterious ways.

"It is the secrets I'd be sorry for," said Dan, summing up. "Men die and men are born, and where one man drained another will plow, but a secret lost is lost forever."

"True," said the sergeant mournfully. "Lost forever."

Dan took his cup, rinsed it in a bucket of clear water by the door and cleaned it again with the shirt. Then he placed it carefully at the sergeant's elbow. From the dresser he took a jug of milk and a blue bag containing sugar; this he followed up with a slab of country butter and—a sure sign that he had been expecting a visitor—a round cake of homemade bread, fresh and uncut. The kettle sang and spat and the dog, shaking his ears, barked at it angrily.

"Go away, you brute!" growled Dan, kicking him out of his way.

He made the tea and filled the two cups. The sergeant cut himself a large slice of bread and buttered it thickly.

"It is just like medicines," said the old man, resuming his theme with the imperturbability of age. "Every secret there was is lost. And leave no one tell me that a doctor is as good a man as one that had the secrets of old times."

"How could he be?" asked the sergeant with his mouth full.

"The proof of that was seen when there were doctors and wise people there together."

"It wasn't to the doctors the people went, I'll engage?"

"It was not. And why?" With a sweeping gesture the old man took in the whole world outside his cabin. "Out there on the hillsides is the sure cure for every disease. Because it is written"—he tapped the table with his thumb—"it is written by the poets 'wherever you find the disease you will find the cure.' But people walk up the hills and down the hills and all they see is flowers. Flowers! As if God Almighty—honor and praise to Him!—had nothing better to do with His time than be making old flowers!"

"Things no doctor could cure the wise people cured," agreed the sergeant.

"Ah, musha, 'tis I know it," said Dan bitterly. "I know it, not in my mind but in my own four bones."

"Have you the rheumatics at you still?" the sergeant asked in a shocked tone.

"I have. Ah, if you were alive, Kitty O'Hara, or you, Nora Malley of the Glen, 'tisn't I'd be dreading the mountain wind or the sea wind; 'tisn't I'd be creeping down with my misfortunate red ticket for the blue and pink and yellow dribble-drabble of their ignorant dispensary."

"Why then indeed," said the sergeant, "I'll get you a bottle for that."

"Ah, there's no bottle ever made will cure it."

"That's where you're wrong, Dan. Don't talk now till you try it. It cured my own uncle when he was that bad he was shouting for the carpenter to cut the two legs off him with a handsaw."

"I'd give fifty pounds to get rid of it," said Dan magniloquently. "I would and five hundred."

The sergeant finished his tea in a gulp, blessed himself and struck a match which he then allowed to go out as he answered some question of the old man. He did the same with a second and third, as though titillating his appetite with delay. Finally he succeeded in getting his pipe alight and the two men pulled round their chairs, placed their toes side by side in the ashes, and in deep puffs, lively bursts of conversation, and long, long silences, enjoyed their smoke.

"I hope I'm not keeping you?" said the sergeant, as though struck by the length of his visit.

"Ah, what would you keep me from?"

"Tell me if I am. The last thing I'd like to do is waste another man's time."

"Begor, you wouldn't waste my time if you stopped all night."

"I like a little chat myself," confessed the policeman.

And again they became lost in conversation. The light grew thick and colored and, wheeling about the kitchen before it disappeared, became tinged with gold; the kitchen itself sank into cool grayness with cold light on the cups and basins and plates of the dresser. From the ash tree a thrush began to sing. The open hearth gathered brightness till its light was a warm, even splash of crimson in the twilight.

Twilight was also descending outside when the sergeant rose to go. He fastened his belt and tunic and carefully brushed his clothes. Then he put on his cap, tilted a little to side and back.

"Well, that was a great talk," he said.

" 'Tis a pleasure," said Dan, "a real pleasure."

"And I won't forget the bottle for you."

"Heavy handling from God to you!"

"Good-bye now, Dan."

"Good-bye, sergeant, and good luck."

Dan didn't offer to accompany the sergeant beyond the door. He sat in his old place by the fire, took out his pipe once more, blew through it thoughtfully, and just as he leaned forward for a twig to kindle it, heard the steps returning. It was the sergeant. He put his head a little way over the half-door.

"Oh, Dan!" he called softly.

"Ay, sergeant?" replied Dan, looking round, but with one hand still reaching for the twig. He couldn't see the sergeant's face, only hear his voice.

"I suppose you're not thinking of paying that little fine, Dan?"

There was a brief silence. Dan pulled out the lighted twig, rose slowly and shambled towards the door, stuffing it down in the almost empty bowl of the pipe. He leaned over the half-door while the sergeant with hands in the pockets of his trousers gazed rather in the direction of the laneway, yet taking in a considerable portion of the sea line.

"The way it is with me, sergeant," replied Dan unemotionally, "I am not."

"I was thinking that, Dan; I was thinking you wouldn't."

There was a long silence during which the voice of the thrush grew shriller and merrier. The sunken sun lit up rafts of purple cloud moored high above the wind.

"In a way," said the sergeant, "that was what brought me."

"I was just thinking so, sergeant, it only struck me and you going out the door."

"If 'twas only the money, Dan, I'm sure there's many would be glad to oblige you."

"I know that, sergeant. No, 'tisn't the money so much as giving that fellow the satisfaction of paying. Because he angered me, sergeant."

The sergeant made no comment on this and another long silence ensued.

"They gave me the warrant," the sergeant said at last, in a tone which dissociated him from all connection with such an unneighborly document.

"Did they so?" exclaimed Dan, as if he was shocked by the thoughtlessness of the authorities.

"So whenever 'twould be convenient for you—"

"Well, now you mention it," said Dan, by way of throwing out a suggestion for debate, "I could go with you now."

"Ah, sha, what do you want going at this hour for?" protested the sergeant with a wave of his hand, dismissing the notion as the tone required.

"Or I could go tomorrow," added Dan, warming to the issue.

"Would it be suitable for you now?" asked the sergeant, scaling up his voice accordingly.

"But, as a matter of fact," said the old man emphatically, "the day that would be most convenient to me would be Friday after dinner, because I have some messages to do in town, and I wouldn't have the journey for nothing."

"Friday will do grand," said the sergeant with relief that this delicate matter was now practically disposed of. "If it doesn't they can damn well wait. You could walk in there yourself when it suits you and tell them I sent you."

"I'd rather have yourself there, sergeant, if it would be no inconvenience. As it is, I'd feel a bit shy."

"Why then, you needn't feel shy at all. There's a man from my own parish there, a warder; one Whelan. Ask for him; I'll tell him you're coming, and I'll guarantee when he knows you're a friend of mine he'll make you as comfortable as if you were at home."

"I'd like that fine," Dan said with profound satisfaction. "I'd like to be with friends, sergeant."

"You will be, never fear. Good-bye again now, Dan. I'll have to hurry."

"Wait now, wait till I see you to the road."

Together the two men strolled down the laneway while Dan explained how it was that he, a respectable old man, had had the grave misfortune to open the head of another old man in such a way as to require his removal to hospital, and why it was that he couldn't give the old man in question the satisfaction of paying in cash for an injury brought about through the victim's own unmannerly method of argument.

"You see, sergeant," Dan said, looking at another little cottage up the hill, "the way it is, he's there now, and he's looking at us as sure as there's a glimmer of sight in his weak, wandering, watery eyes, and nothing would give him more gratification than for me to pay. But I'll punish him. I'll lie on bare boards for him. I'll suffer for him, sergeant, so that neither he nor any of his children after him will be able to raise their heads for the shame of it."

On the following Friday he made ready his donkey and butt and set out. On his way he collected a number of neighbors who wished to bid him farewell. At the top of the hill he stopped to send them back. An old man, sitting in the sunlight, hastily made his way indoors, and a moment later the door of his cottage was quietly closed.

Having shaken all his friends by the hand, Dan lashed the old donkey, shouted: "Hup there!" and set out alone along the road to prison.

GEORGE ORWELL

(1903–1950)

George Orwell was the pen name of Eric Arthur Blair. Born in Motihari, India, Orwell was the son of a British official in India's Opium Department. He attended schools in England, including Eton, then served from 1922 to 1927 with the India Imperial Police in Burma (now Myanmar). The next phase of Orwell's life, during which he began to write, is aptly described by the title of his book about it: *Down and Out in Paris and London*. Other books followed, including *Burmese Days, Keep the Aspidistra Flying, The Road to Wigan Pier*, and *Homage to Catalonia*, the last of these based on Orwell's experiences fighting on the Loyalist side in the Spanish Civil War.

During the 1930s and 1940s Orwell was also a prolific essayist and journalist. His masterworks, however, are the novels *Animal Farm* (1945) and *1984* (1949), perhaps the most trenchant analyses ever produced of the totalitarian madness of the twentieth century. Six months after *1984* was published, Orwell died of tuberculosis at the age of forty-six.

Orwell was only nineteen years old when he chose Burma as the province of India in which to serve as an Imperial Policeman. After initial training, he was given a succession of provincial assignments as an Assistant Superintendent of Police. Orwell initially shared the anti-Burmese prejudices of his British colleagues, but toward the end of his stay he became more sympathetic to the growing Burmese nationalistic movement, seeing himself as "a cog in the machine of imperialism," and resigned his commission.

Orwell's masterful essay "Shooting an Elephant," really a documentary short story that may or may not have been based on detailed fact, was published in *New Writing*, Autumn 1936. In it Orwell describes an incident from this darkest period of his life, when "I was hated by large numbers of people—the only time in my life that I have been important enough for this to happen to me." The story adroitly portrays the impact of law on the magistrate, the person entrusted with the burden of enforcement (a burden compounded here by the weight of imperialism). Unlike most officials, Orwell admits to the powerful motivation of wishing to avoid looking like a fool.

SHOOTING AN ELEPHANT

— 1936 —

In Moulmein, in lower Burma, I was hated by large numbers of people—the only time in my life that I have been important enough for this to happen to me. I was sub-divisional police officer of the town, and in an aimless, petty kind of way anti-European feeling was very bitter. No one had the guts to raise a riot, but if a European woman went through the bazaars alone somebody would probably spit betel juice over her dress. As a police officer I was an obvious target and was baited whenever it seemed safe to do so. When a nimble Burman tripped me up on the football field and the referee (another Burman) looked the other way, the crowd yelled with hideous laughter. This happened more than once. In the end the sneering yellow faces of young men that met me everywhere, the insults hooted after me when I was at a safe distance, got badly on my nerves. The young Buddhist priests were the worst of all. There were several thousands of them in the town and none of them seemed to have anything to do except stand on street corners and jeer at Europeans.

All this was perplexing and upsetting. For at that time I had already made up my mind that imperialism was an evil thing and the sooner I chucked up my job and got out of it the better. Theoretically—and secretly, of course—I was all for the Burmese and all against their oppressors, the British. As for the job I was doing, I hated it more bitterly than I can perhaps make clear. In a job like that you see the dirty work of Empire at close quarters. The wretched prisoners huddling in the stinking cages of the lock-ups, the grey, cowed faces of the long-term convicts, the scarred buttocks of the men who had been flogged with bamboos—all these oppressed me with an intolerable sense of guilt. But I could get nothing into perspective. I was young and ill-educated and I had had to think out my problems in the utter silence that is imposed on every Englishman in the East. I did not even know that the British Empire is dying, still less did I know that it is a great deal better than the younger empires that are going to supplant it. All I knew was that I was stuck between my hatred of the empire I served and my rage against the evil-spirited little beasts who tried to make my job impossible. With one part of my mind I thought of the British Raj as an unbreakable tyranny, as something clamped down, in *saecula saeculorum*, upon the will of prostrate peoples; with another part I thought that the greatest joy in the world would be to drive a bayonet into a Buddhist priest's guts. Feelings like these are the normal by-products of imperialism; ask any Anglo-Indian official, if you can catch him off duty.

One day something happened which in a roundabout way was enlightening. It was a tiny incident in itself, but it gave me a better glimpse than I had had before of the real nature of imperialism—the real motives for which despotic governments act. Early one morning the sub-inspector at a police station the other end of the town rang me up on the 'phone and said that an elephant was ravaging the bazaar. Would I please come and do something about it? I did not know what I could do, but I wanted to see what was happening and I got on to a pony and started out. I took my rifle, an old .44 Winchester and much too small to kill an elephant, but I thought the noise might be useful *in terrorem*. Various Burmans stopped me on the way and told me about the elephant's doings. It was not, of course, a wild elephant, but a tame one which had gone "must." It had been chained up, as tame elephants always are when their attack of "must" is due, but on the previous night it had broken its chain and escaped. Its mahout, the only person who could manage it when it was in that state, had set out in pursuit, but had taken the wrong direction and was now twelve hours' journey away, and in the morning the elephant had suddenly reappeared in the town. The Burmese population had no weapons and were quite helpless against it. It had already destroyed somebody's bamboo hut, killed a cow and raided some fruit-stalls and devoured the stock; also it had met the municipal rubbish van and, when the driver jumped out and took to his heels, had turned the van over and inflicted violences upon it.

The Burmese sub-inspector and some Indian constables were waiting for me in the quarter where the elephant had been seen. It was a very poor quarter, a labyrinth of squalid bamboo huts, thatched with palm-leaf, winding all over a steep hillside. I remember that it was a cloudy, stuffy morning at the beginning of the rains. We began questioning the people as to where the elephant had gone and, as usual, failed to get any definite information. That is invariably the case in the East; a story always sounds clear enough at a distance, but the nearer you get to the scene of events the vaguer it becomes. Some of the people said that the elephant had gone in one direction, some said that he had gone in another, some professed not even to have heard of any elephant. I had almost made up my mind that the whole story was a pack of lies, when we heard yells a little distance away. There was a loud, scandalized cry of "Go away, child! Go away this instant!" and an old woman with a switch in her hand came round the corner of a hut, violently shooing away a crowd of naked children. Some more women followed, clicking their tongues and exclaiming; evidently there was something that the children ought not to have seen. I rounded the hut and saw a man's dead body sprawling in the mud. He was an Indian, a black Dravidian coolie, almost naked, and he could not have been dead many minutes. The people said that the elephant had come suddenly upon him round the corner of the hut, caught him with its trunk, put its foot on his back and ground him into the earth. This was the rainy season and the ground was soft, and his face had scored a trench a foot deep and a couple of yards long. He was lying on his belly with arms crucified and head sharply twisted to one side. His face was coated with mud, the eyes wide open, the teeth bared and grinning with an expression of unendurable agony. (Never tell me, by the way, that the dead look peaceful. Most of the corpses I have seen looked devilish.) The friction of the great beast's foot had stripped the skin from his back as neatly as one skins a rabbit. As soon as I saw the dead man I sent an orderly to a friend's house nearby to borrow an elephant rifle. I had already sent back the pony, not wanting it to go mad with fright and throw me if it smelt the elephant.

The orderly came back in a few minutes with a rifle and five cartridges, and meanwhile some Burmans had arrived and told us that the elephant was in the paddy fields below, only a few hundred yards away. As I started forward practically the whole population of the quarter flocked out of the houses and followed me. They had seen the rifle and were all shouting excitedly that I was going to shoot the elephant. They had not shown much interest in the elephant when he was merely ravaging their homes, but it was different now that he was going to be shot. It was a bit of fun to them, as it would be to an English crowd; besides they wanted the meat. It made me vaguely uneasy. I had no intention of shooting the elephant—I had merely sent for the rifle to defend myself if necessary—and it is always unnerving to have a crowd following you. I marched down the hill, looking and feeling a fool, with the rifle over my shoulder and an ever-growing army of people jostling at my heels. At the bottom, when you got away from the huts, there was a metalled road and beyond that a miry waste of paddy fields a thousand yards across, not yet ploughed but soggy from the first rains and dotted with coarse grass. The elephant was standing eight yards from the road, his left side towards us. He took not the slightest notice of the crowd's approach. He was tearing up bunches of grass, beating them against his knees to clean them and stuffing them into his mouth.

I had halted on the road. As soon as I saw the elephant I knew with perfect certainty that I ought not to shoot him. It is a serious matter to shoot a working elephant—it is comparable to destroying a huge and costly piece of machinery—and obviously one ought not to do it if it can possibly be avoided. And at that distance, peacefully eating, the elephant looked no more dangerous than a cow. I thought then and I think now that his attack of "must" was already passing off; in which case he would merely wander harmlessly about until the mahout came back and caught him.

Moreover, I did not in the least want to shoot him. I decided that I would watch him for a little while to make sure that he did not turn savage again, and then go home.

But at that moment I glanced round at the crowd that had followed me. It was an immense crowd, two thousand at the least and growing every minute. It blocked the road for a long distance on either side. I looked at the sea of yellow faces above the garish clothes—faces all happy and excited over this bit of fun, all certain that the elephant was going to be shot. They were watching me as they would watch a conjurer about to perform a trick. They did not like me, but with the magical rifle in my hands I was momentarily worth watching. And suddenly I realized that I should have to shoot the elephant after all. The people expected it of me and I had got to do it; I could feel their two thousand wills pressing me forward, irresistibly. And it was at this moment, as I stood there with the rifle in my hands, that I first grasped the hollowness, the futility of the white man's dominion in the East. Here was I, the white man with his gun, standing in front of the unarmed native crowd—seemingly the leading actor of the piece; but in reality I was only an absurd puppet pushed to and fro by the will of those yellow faces behind. I perceived in this moment that when the white man turns tyrant it is his own freedom that he destroys. He becomes a sort of hollow, posing dummy, the conventionalized figure of a sahib. For it is the condition of his rule that he shall spend his life in trying to impress the "natives," and so in every crisis he has got to do what the "natives" expect of him. He wears a mask, and his face grows to fit it. I had got to shoot the elephant. I had committed myself to doing it when I sent for the rifle. A sahib has got to act like a sahib; he has got to appear resolute, to know his own mind and do definite things. To come all that way, rifle in hand, with two thousand people marching at my heels, and then to trail feebly away, having done nothing—no, that was impossible. The crowd would laugh at me. And my whole life, every white man's life in the East, was one long struggle not to be laughed at.

But I did not want to shoot the elephant. I watched him beating his bunch of grass against his knees, with that preoccupied grandmotherly air that elephants have. It seemed to me that it would be murder to shoot him. At that age I was not squeamish about killing animals, but I had never shot an elephant and never wanted to. (Somehow it always seems worse to kill a *large* animal.) Besides, there was the beast's owner to be considered. Alive, the elephant was worth at least a hundred pounds; dead, he would only be worth the value of his tusks, five pounds, possibly. But I had got to act quickly. I turned to some experienced-looking Burmans who had been there when we arrived, and asked them how the elephant had been behaving. They all said the same thing: he took no notice of you if you left him alone, but he might charge if you went too close to him.

It was perfectly clear to me what I ought to do. I ought to walk up to within, say, twenty-five yards of the elephant and test his behavior. If he charged, I could shoot; if he took no notice of me, it would be safe to leave him until the mahout came back. But also I knew that I was going to do no such thing. I was a poor shot with a rifle and the ground was soft mud into which one would sink at every step. If the elephant charged and I missed him, I should have about as much chance as a toad under a steam-roller. But even then I was not thinking particularly of my own skin, only of the watchful yellow faces behind. For at that moment, with the crowd watching me, I was not afraid in the ordinary sense, as I would have been if I had been alone. A white man mustn't be frightened in front of "natives"; and so, in general, he isn't frightened. The sole thought in my mind was that if anything went wrong those two thousand Burmans would see me pursued, caught, trampled on and reduced to a grinning corpse like that Indian up the hill. And if that happened it was quite probable that some of them would laugh. That would never do. There was only one alternative. I shoved the cartridges into the magazine and lay down on the road to get a better aim.

The crowd grew very still, and a deep, low, happy sigh, as of people who see the theatre curtain go up at last, breathed from innumerable throats. They were going to have their bit of fun after all. The rifle was a beautiful German thing with cross-hair sights. I did not then know that in shooting an elephant one would shoot to cut an imaginary bar running from ear-hole to ear-hole. I ought, therefore, as the elephant was sideways on, to have aimed straight at his ear-hole; actually I aimed several inches in front of this, thinking the brain would be further forward.

When I pulled the trigger I did not hear the bang or feel the kick—one never does when a shot goes home—but I heard the devilish roar of glee that went up from the crowd. In that instant, in too short a time, one would have thought, even for the bullet to get there, a mysterious, terrible change had come over the elephant. He neither stirred nor fell, but every line of his body had altered. He looked suddenly stricken, shrunken, immensely old, as though the frightful impact of the bullet had paralysed him without knocking him down. At last, after what seemed a long time—it might have been five seconds, I dare say—he sagged flabbily to his knees. His mouth slobbered. An enormous senility seemed to have settled upon him. One could have imagined him thousands of years old. I fired again into the same spot. At the second shot he did not collapse but climbed with desperate slowness to his feet and stood weakly upright, with legs sagging and head drooping. I fired a third time. That was the shot that did for him. You could see the agony of it jolt his whole body and knock the last remnant of strength from his legs. But in falling he seemed for a moment to rise, for as his hind legs collapsed beneath him he seemed to tower upward like a huge rock toppling, his trunk reaching skywards like a tree. He trumpeted, for the first and only time. And then down he came, his belly towards me, with a crash that seemed to shake the ground even where I lay.

I got up. The Burmans were already racing past me across the mud. It was obvious that the elephant would never rise again, but he was not dead. He was breathing very rhythmically with long rattling gasps, his great mound of a side painfully rising and falling. His mouth was wide open—I could see far down into caverns of pale pink throat. I waited a long time for him to die, but his breathing did not weaken. Finally I fired my two remaining shots into the spot where I thought his heart must be. The thick blood welled out of him like red velvet, but still he did not die. His body did not even jerk when the shots hit him, the tortured breathing continued without a pause. He was dying, very slowly and in great agony, but in some world remote from me where not even a bullet could damage him further. I felt that I had got to put an end to that dreadful noise. It seemed dreadful to see the great beast lying there, powerless to move and yet powerless to die, and not even to be able to finish him. I sent back for my small rifle and poured shot after shot into his heart and down his throat. They seemed to make no impression. The tortured gasps continued as steadily as the ticking of a clock.

In the end I could not stand it any longer and went away. I heard later that it took him half an hour to die. Burmans were bringing dahs and baskets even before I left, and I was told they had stripped his body almost to the bones by the afternoon.

Afterwards, of course, there were endless discussions about the shooting of the elephant. The owner was furious, but he was only an Indian and could do nothing. Besides, legally I had done the right thing, for a mad elephant has to be killed, like a mad dog, if its owner fails to control it. Among the Europeans opinion was divided. The older men said I was right, the younger men said it was a damn shame to shoot an elephant for killing a coolie, because an elephant was worth more than any damn Coringhee coolie. And afterwards I was very glad that the coolie had been killed; it put me legally in the right and it gave me a sufficient pretext for shooting the elephant. I often wondered whether any of the others grasped that I had done it solely to avoid looking a fool.

WILLIAM FAULKNER

(1897–1962)

A striking amount of William Harrison Faulkner's fiction plays out against a backdrop of law and justice. His works are richly peopled with lawyers, judges, justices of the peace, and law students. Faulkner's grandfather, John Wesley Thompson Falkner, practiced law and served as deputy United States District Attorney and Lafayette County Attorney, and other members of his family had distinguished legal careers going back five generations.

A more immediate legal influence on Faulkner was his close friend, literary agent, and mentor Phil Stone. Stone was a Yale Law School graduate who practiced law in Oxford, Mississippi, and became president of the state bar association. Faulkner's most important fictional lawyer, Gavin Stevens, may have been based on Stone. Appearing in many of the author's books, including *Intruder in the Dust, Knight's Gambit, Requiem for a Nun*, and *The Town*, Stevens is Faulkner's most articulate character, and among his most humane.

One of the short stories involving Gavin Stevens is "Tomorrow," first published by Faulkner in the *Saturday Evening Post*, November 23, 1940, and later included in the collection *Knight's Gambit* (1949). This is the account of Stevens's first case out of law school, a murder trial. Beyond functioning as an advocate, however, the lawyer here is also a detective, a listener, and a man of compassion. He uncovers the story of a victim, cruelly mistreated by the legal system, who salvages his dignity in the only way that he can.

Faulkner's birthplace was New Albany, Mississippi, but he moved at an early age to the nearby town of Oxford. Oxford became, under the name of Jefferson, the seat of Yoknapatawpha County, the locus of most of his fiction. Among his major novels are *The Sound and the Fury, As I Lay Dying, Sanctuary, Light in August, Absalom, Absalom!, The Wild Palms*, and *The Hamlet*. Only with the publication of *The Portable Faulkner* in 1946 did his reputation become secure; three years later, he was awarded the Nobel Prize in Literature.

TOMORROW

— 1940 —

Uncle Gavin had not always been county attorney. But the time when he had not been was more than twenty years ago and it had lasted for such a short period that only the old men remembered it, and even some of them did not. Because in that time he had had but one case.

He was a young man then, twenty-eight, only a year out of the state-university law school where, at grandfather's instigation, he had gone after his return from Harvard and Heidelberg; and he had taken the case voluntarily, persuaded grandfather to let him handle it alone, which grandfather did, because everyone believed the trial would be a mere formality.

So he tried the case. Years afterward he still said it was the only case, either as a private defender or a public prosecutor, in which he was convinced that right and justice were on his side, that he ever lost. Actually he did not lose it—a mistrial in the fall court term, an acquittal in the following spring term—the defendant a solid, well-to-do farmer, husband and father, too, named Bookwright, from a section called Frenchman's Bend in the remote southeastern corner of the county; the victim a swaggering bravo calling himself Buck Thorpe and called Bucksnort by the other young men whom he had subjugated with his fists during the three years he had been in Frenchman's Bend; kinless, who had appeared overnight from nowhere, a brawler, a gambler, known to be a distiller of illicit whiskey and caught once on the road to Memphis with a small drove of stolen cattle, which the owner promptly identified. He had a bill of sale for them, but none in the country knew the name signed to it.

And the story itself was old and unoriginal enough: The country girl of seventeen, her imagination fired by the swagger and the prowess and the daring and the glib tongue; the father who tried to reason with her and got exactly as far as parents usually do in such cases; then the interdiction, the forbidden door, the inevitable elopement at midnight; and at four o'clock the next morning Bookwright waked Will Varner, the justice of the peace and the chief officer of the district, and handed Varner his pistol and said, 'I have come to surrender. I killed Thorpe two hours ago.' And a neighbor named Quick, who was first on the scene, found the half-drawn pistol in Thorpe's hand; and a week after the brief account was printed in the Memphis papers, a woman appeared in Frenchman's Bend who claimed to be Thorpe's wife, and with a wedding license to prove it, trying to claim what money or property he might have left.

I can remember the surprise that the grand jury even found a true bill;

when the clerk read the indictment, the betting was twenty to one that the jury would not be out ten minutes. The district attorney even conducted the case through an assistant, and it did not take an hour to submit all the evidence. Then Uncle Gavin rose, and I remember how he looked at the jury—the eleven farmers and storekeepers and the twelfth man, who was to ruin his case—a farmer, too, a thin man, small, with thin gray hair and that appearance of hill farmers—at once frail and work-worn, yet curiously imperishable—who seem to become old men at fifty and then become invincible to time. Uncle Gavin's voice was quiet, almost monotonous, not ranting as criminal-court trials had taught us to expect; only the words were a little different from the ones he would use in later years. But even then, although he had been talking to them for only a year, he could already talk so that all the people in our country—the Negroes, the hill people, the rich flatland plantation owners—understood what he said.

'All of us in this country, the South, have been taught from birth a few things which we hold to above all else. One of the first of these—not the best; just one of the first—is that only a life can pay for the life it takes; that the one death is only half complete. If that is so, then we could have saved both these lives by stopping this defendant before he left his house that night; we could have saved at least one of them, even if we had had to take this defendant's life from him in order to stop him. Only we didn't know in time. And that's what I am talking about—not about the dead man and his character and the morality of the act he was engaged in; not about self-defense, whether or not this defendant was justified in forcing the issue to the point of taking life, but about us who are not dead and what we don't know—about all of us, human beings who at bottom want to do right, want not to harm others; human beings with all the complexity of human passions and feelings and beliefs, in the accepting or rejecting of which we had no choice, trying to do the best we can with them or despite them—this defendant, another human being with that same complexity of passions and instincts and beliefs, faced by a problem—the inevitable misery of his child who, with the headstrong folly of youth—again that same old complexity which she, too, did not ask to inherit— was incapable of her own preservation—and solved that problem to the best of his ability and beliefs, asking help of no one, and then abode by his decision and his act.'

He sat down. The district attorney's assistant merely rose and bowed to the court and sat down again. The jury went out and we didn't even leave the room. Even the judge didn't retire. And I remember the long breath, something, which went through the room when the clock hand above the bench passed the ten-minute mark and then passed the half-hour mark, and the judge beckoned a bailiff and whispered to him, and the bailiff went out and returned and whispered to the judge, and the judge rose and banged his gavel and recessed the court.

I hurried home and ate my dinner and hurried back to town. The office was empty. Even grandfather, who took his nap after dinner, regardless of who hung and who didn't, returned first; after three o'clock then, and the whole town knew now that Uncle Gavin's jury was hung by one man, eleven to one for acquittal; then Uncle Gavin came in fast, and grandfather said, 'Well, Gavin, at least you stopped talking in time to hang just your jury and not your client.'

'That's right, sir,' Uncle Gavin said. Because he was looking at me with his bright eyes, his thin, quick face, his wild hair already beginning to turn white. 'Come here, Chick,' he said. 'I need you for a minute.'

'Ask Judge Frazier to allow you to retract your oration, then let Charley sum up for you,' grandfather said. But we were outside then, on the stairs, Uncle Gavin stopping halfway down, so that we stood exactly halfway from anywhere, his hand on my shoulder, his eyes brighter and intenter than ever.

'This is not cricket,' he said. 'But justice is accomplished lots of times by methods that won't bear looking at. They have moved the jury to the back room in Mrs. Rouncewell's boardinghouse. The room right opposite that mulberry tree. If you could get into the back yard without anybody seeing you, and be careful when you climb the tree—'

Nobody saw me. But I could look through the windy mulberry leaves into the room, and see and hear, both—the nine angry and disgusted men sprawled in chairs at the far end of the room; Mr. Holland, the foreman, and another man standing in front of the chair in which the little, worn, dried-out hill man sat. His name was Fentry. I remembered all their names, because Uncle Gavin said that to be a successful lawyer and politician in our country you did not need a silver tongue nor even an intelligence; you needed only an infallible memory for names. But I would have remembered his name anyway, because it was Stonewall Jackson—Stonewall Jackson Fentry.

'Don't you admit that he was running off with Bookwright's seventeen-year-old daughter?' Mr. Holland said. 'Don't you admit that he had a pistol in his hand when they found him? Don't you admit that he wasn't hardly buried before that woman turned up and proved she was already his wife? Don't you admit that he was not only no-good but dangerous, and that if it hadn't been Bookwright, sooner or later somebody else would have had to, and that Bookwright was just unlucky?'

'Yes,' Fentry said.

'Then what do you want?' Mr. Holland said. 'What do you want?'

'I can't help it,' Fentry said. 'I ain't going to vote Mr. Bookwright free.'

And he didn't. And that afternoon Judge Frazier discharged the jury and set the case for retrial in the next term of court; and the next morning Uncle Gavin came for me before I had finished breakfast.

'Tell your mother we might be gone overnight,' he said. 'Tell her I promise not to let you get either shot, snake-bit or surfeited with soda pop. . . . Because I've got to know,' he said. We were driving fast now, out the northeast road, and his eyes were bright, not baffled, just intent and eager. 'He was born and raised and lived all his life out here at the very other end of the country, thirty miles from Frenchman's Bend. He said under oath that he had never even seen Bookwright before, and you can look at him and see that he never had enough time off from hard work to learn how to lie in. I doubt if he ever even heard Bookwright's name before.'

We drove until almost noon. We were in the hills now, out of the rich flat land, among the pine and bracken, the poor soil, the little tilted and barren patches of gaunt corn and cotton which somehow endured, as the people they clothed and fed somehow endured; the roads we followed less than lanes, winding and narrow, rutted and dust choked, the car in second gear half the time. Then we saw the mailbox, the crude lettering: G. A. FENTRY; beyond it, the two-room log house with an open hall, and even I, a boy of twelve, could see that no woman's hand had touched it in a lot of years. We entered the gate.

Then a voice said, 'Stop! Stop where you are!' And we hadn't even seen him—an old man, barefoot, with a fierce white bristle of mustache, in patched denim faded almost to the color of skim milk, smaller, thinner even than the son, standing at the edge of the worn gallery, holding a shotgun across his middle and shaking with fury or perhaps with the palsy of age.

'Mr Fentry—' Uncle Gavin said.

'You've badgered and harried him enough!' the old man said. It was fury; the voice seemed to rise suddenly with a fiercer, an uncontrollable blaze of it: 'Get out of here! Get off my land! Go!'

'Come,' Uncle Gavin said quietly. And still his eyes were only bright, eager, intent and grave. We did not drive fast now. The next mailbox was within the mile, and this time the house was even painted, with beds of petunias beside the steps, and the land about it was better, and this time the man rose from the gallery and came down to the gate.

'Howdy, Mr. Stevens,' he said. 'So Jackson Fentry hung your jury for you.'

'Howdy, Mr. Pruitt,' Uncle Gavin said. 'It looks like he did. Tell me.'

And Pruitt told him, even though at that time Uncle Gavin would forget now and then and his language would slip back to Harvard and even to Heidelberg. It was as if people looked at his face and knew that what he asked was not just for his own curiosity or his own selfish using.

'Only ma knows more about it than I do,' Pruitt said. 'Come up to the gallery.'

We followed him to the gallery, where a plump, whitehaired old lady in a clean gingham sunbonnet and dress and a clean white apron sat in a low rocking chair, shelling field peas into a wooden bowl. 'This is Lawyer Stevens,' Pruitt said. 'Captain Stevens' son, from town. He wants to know about Jackson Fentry.'

So we sat, too, while they told it, the son and the mother talking in rotation.

'That place of theirs,' Pruitt said. 'You seen some of it from the road. And what you didn't see don't look no better. But his pa and his grandpa worked it, made a living for themselves and raised families and paid their taxes and owed no man. I don't know how they done it, but they did. And Jackson was helping from the time he got big enough to reach up to the plow handles. He never got much bigger than that neither. None of them ever did. I reckon that was why. And Jackson worked it, too, in his time, until he was about twenty-five and already looking forty, asking no odds of nobody, not married and not nothing, him and his pa living alone and doing their own washing and cooking, because how can a man afford to marry when him and his pa have just one pair of shoes between them. If it had been worth while getting a wife a tall, since that place had already killed his ma and his grandma both before they were forty years old. Until one night—'

'Nonsense,' Mrs. Pruitt said. 'When your pa and me married, we didn't even own a roof over our heads. We moved into a rented house, or rented land—'

'All right,' Pruitt said. 'Until one night he come to me and said how he had got him a sawmilling job down at Frenchman's Bend.'

'Frenchman's Bend?' Uncle Gavin said, and now his eyes were much brighter and quicker than just intent. 'Yes,' he said.

'A day-wage job,' Pruitt said. 'Not to get rich; just to earn a little extra money maybe, risking a year or two to earn a little extra money, against the life his grandpa led until he died between the plow handles one day, and that his pa would lead until he died in a corn furrow, and then it would be his turn, and not even no son to come and pick him up out of the dirt. And that he had traded with a nigger to help his pa work their place while he was gone, and would I kind of go up there now and then and see that his pa was all right.'

'Which you did,' Mrs. Pruitt said.

'I went close enough,' Pruitt said. 'I would get close enough to the field to hear him cussing at the nigger for not moving fast enough and to watch the nigger trying to keep up with him, and to think what a good thing it was Jackson hadn't got two niggers to work the place while he was gone, because if that old man—and he was close to sixty then—had had to spend one full day sitting in a chair in the shade with nothing in his hands to chop or hoe with, he would have died before sundown. So Jackson left. He walked. They didn't have but one mule. They ain't never had but one mule. But it ain't but about thirty miles. He was gone about two and a half years. 'Then one day—'

'He come home that first Christmas,' Mrs. Pruitt said.

'That's right,' Pruitt said. 'He walked them thirty miles home and spent Christmas Day, and walked them other thirty miles back to the sawmill.'

'Whose sawmill?' Uncle Gavin said.

'Quick's,' Pruitt said. 'Old Man Ben Quick's. It was the second Christmas he never come home. Then, about the beginning of March, about when the river bottom at Frenchman's Bend would be starting to dry out to where you could skid logs through it and you would have thought he would be settled down good to his third year of sawmilling, he come home to stay. He didn't walk this time. He come in a hired buggy. Because he had the goat and the baby.'

'Wait,' Uncle Gavin said.

'We never knew how he got home,' Mrs. Pruitt said. 'Because he had been home over a week before we even found out he had the baby.'

'Wait,' Uncle Gavin said.

They waited, looking at him, Pruitt sitting on the gallery railing and Mrs. Pruitt's fingers still shelling the peas out of the long brittle hulls, looking at Uncle Gavin. His eyes were not exultant now any more than they had been baffled or even very speculative before; they had just got brighter, as if whatever it was behind them had flared up, steady and fiercer, yet still quiet, as if it were going faster than the telling was going.

'Yes,' he said. 'Tell me.'

'And when I finally heard about it and went up there,' Mrs. Pruitt said, 'that baby wasn't two weeks old. And how he had kept it alive, and just on goat's milk—'

'I don't know if you know it,' Pruitt said. 'A goat ain't like a cow. You milk a goat every two hours or so. That means all night too.'

'Yes,' Mrs. Pruitt said. 'He didn't even have diaper cloths. He had some split floursacks the midwife had showed him how to put on. So I made some cloths and I would go up there; he had kept the nigger on to help his pa in the field and he was doing the cooking and washing and nursing that baby, milking the goat to feed it; and I would say, "Let me take it. At least until he can be weaned. You come stay at my house, too, if you want," and him just looking at me—little, thin, already wore-out something that never in his whole life had ever set down to a table and et all he could hold—saying, "I thank you, ma'am. I can make out." '

'Which was correct,' Pruitt said. 'I don't know how he was at sawmilling, and he never had no farm to find out what kind of a farmer he was. But he raised that boy.'

'Yes,' Mrs. Pruitt said. 'And I kept on after him: "We hadn't even heard you was married," I said. "Yessum," he said. "We was married last year. When the baby come, she died." "Who was she?" I said. "Was she a Frenchman Bend girl?" "No'm," he said. "She come from downstate." "What was her name?" I said. "Miss Smith," he said.'

'He hadn't even had enough time off from hard work to learn how to lie either,' Pruitt said. 'But he raised that boy. After their crops were in in the fall, he let the nigger go, and next spring him and the old man done the work like they use to. He had made a kind of satchel, like they say Indians does, to carry the boy in. I would go up there now and then while the ground was still cold and see Jackson and his pa plowing and chopping brush, and that satchel hanging on a fence post and that boy asleep bolt upright in it like it was a feather bed. He learned to walk that spring, and I would stand there at the fence and watch that durn little critter out there in the middle of the furrow, trying his best to keep up with Jackson, until Jackson would stop the plow at the turn row and go back and get him and set him straddle of his neck and take up the plow and go on. In the late summer he could walk pretty good. Jackson made him a little hoe out of a stick and a scrap of shingle, and you could see Jackson chopping in the middle-thigh cotton, but you couldn't see the boy at all; you could just see the cotton shaking where he was.'

'Jackson made his clothes,' Mrs. Pruitt said. 'Stitched them himself, by hand. I made a few garments and took them up there. I never done it but once though. He took them and he thanked me. But you could see it. It was like he even begrudged the earth itself for what the child had to eat to keep alive. And I tried to persuade Jackson to take him to church, have him baptized. "He's already named," he said. "His name is Jackson and Longstreet Fentry. Pa fit under both of them." '

'He never went nowhere,' Pruitt said. 'Because where you saw Jackson, you saw that boy. If he had had to steal that boy down there at Frenchman's Bend, he couldn't 'a' hid no closer. It was even the old man that would ride over to Haven Hill store to buy their supplies, and the only time Jackson and that boy was separated as much as one full breath was once a year when Jackson would ride in to Jefferson to pay their taxes, and when I first seen the boy I thought of a setter puppy, until one day I knowed Jackson had gone to pay their taxes and I went up there and the boy was under the bed, not making any fuss, just backed up into the corner, looking out at me. He didn't blink once. He was exactly like a fox or a wolf cub somebody had caught just last night.'

We watched him take from his pocket a tin of snuff and tilt a measure of it into the lid and then into his lower lip, tapping the final grain from the lid with delicate deliberation.

'All right,' Uncle Gavin said, 'Then what?'

'That's all,' Pruitt said. 'In the next summer him and the boy disappeared.'

'Disappeared?' Uncle Gavin said.

'That's right. They were just gone one morning. I didn't know when. And one day I couldn't stand it no longer, I went up there and the house was empty, and I went on to the field where the old man was plowing, and at first I thought the spreader between his plow handles had broke and he had tied a sapling off, and it was that shotgun, and I reckon what he said to me was about what he said to you this morning when you stopped there. Next year he had the nigger helping him again. Then, about five years later, Jackson come back. I don't know when. He was just there one morning. And the nigger was gone again, and him and his pa worked the place like they use to. And one day I couldn't stand it no longer, I went up there and I stood at the fence where he was plowing, until after a while the land he was breaking brought him up to the fence, and still he hadn't never looked at me; he plowed right by me, not ten feet away, still without looking at me, and he turned and come back, and I said, "Did he die, Jackson?" and then he looked at me. "The boy," I said. And he said, "What boy?" '

They invited us to stay for dinner.

Uncle Gavin thanked them. 'We brought a snack with us,' he said. 'And it's thirty miles to Varner's store, and twenty-two from there to Jefferson. And our roads ain't quite used to automobiles yet.'

So it was just sundown when we drove up to Varner's store in Frenchman's Bend Village; again a man rose from the deserted gallery and came down the steps to the car.

It was Isham Quick, the witness who had first reached Thorpe's body—a tall, gangling man in the middle forties, with a dreamy kind of face and near-sighted eyes, until you saw there was something shrewd behind them, even a little quizzical.

'I been waiting for you,' he said 'Looks like you made a water haul.' He blinked at Uncle Gavin. 'That Fentry.'

'Yes,' Uncle Gavin said. 'Why didn't you tell me?'

'I didn't recognize it myself,' Quick said. 'It wasn't until I heard your jury was hung, and by one man, that I associated them names.'

'Names?' Uncle Gavin said. 'What na—Never mind. Just tell it.'

So we sat on the gallery of the locked and deserted store while the cicadas shrilled and rattled in the trees and the lightning bugs blinked and drifted above the dusty road, and Quick told it, sprawled on the bench beyond Uncle Gavin, loose-jointed, like he would come all to pieces the first time he moved, talking in a lazy sardonic voice, like he had all night to tell it in and it would take all night to tell it. But it wasn't that long. It wasn't long enough for what was in it. But Uncle Gavin says it don't take many words to tell the sum of any human experience; that somebody has already done it in eight: He was born, he suffered and he died.

'It was pap that hired him. But when I found out where he had come from, I knowed he would work, because folks in that country hadn't never had time to learn nothing but hard work. And I knowed he would be honest for the same reason: that there wasn't nothing in his country a man could want bad enough to learn how to steal it. What I seem to have underestimated was his capacity for love. I reckon I figured that, coming from where he come from, he never had none a-tall, and for that same previous reason—that even the comprehension of love had done been lost out of him back down the generations where the first one of them had had to take his final choice between the pursuit of love and the pursuit of keeping on breathing.

'So he come to work, doing the same work and drawing the same pay as the niggers done. Until in the late fall, when the bottom got wet and we got ready to shut down for the winter, I found out he had made a trade with pap to stay on until spring as watchman and caretaker, with three days out to go home Christmas. And he did, and the next year when we started up, he had done learned so much about it and he stuck to it so, that by the middle of summer he was running the whole mill hisself, and by the end of summer pap never went out there no more a-tall and I just went when I felt like it, maybe once a week or so; and by fall pap was even talking about building him a shack to live in in place of that shuck mattress and a old broke-down cookstove in the boiler shed. And he stayed through that winter too. When he went home that Christmas we never even knowed it, when he went or when he come back, because even I hadn't been out there since fall.

'Then one afternoon in February—there had been a mild spell and I reckon I was restless—I rode out there. The first thing I seen was her, and it was the first time I had ever done that—a woman, young, and maybe when she was in her normal health she might have been pretty, too; I don't know. Because she wasn't just thin, she was gaunted. She was sick, more than just starved-looking, even if she was still on her feet, and it wasn't just because she was going to have that baby in a considerable less than another month. And I says, "Who is that?" and he looked at me and says, "That's my wife," and I says, "Since when? You never had no wife last fall. And that child ain't a month off." And he says, "Do you want us to leave?" and I says, "What do I want you to leave for?" I'm going to tell this from what I know now, what I found out after them two brothers showed up here three years later with their court paper, not from what he ever told me, because he never told nobody nothing.'

'All right,' Uncle Gavin said. 'Tell.'

'I don't know where he found her. I don't know if he found her somewhere, or if she just walked into the mill one day or one night and he looked up and seen her, and it was like the fellow says—nobody knows where or when love or lightning either is going to strike, except that it ain't going to strike there twice, because it don't have to. And I don't believe she was hunting for the husband that had deserted her—likely he cut and run soon as she told him about the baby—and I don't believe she was scared or ashamed to go back home just because her brothers and father had tried to keep her from marrying the husband, in the first place. I believe it was just some more of that same kind of black-complected and not extra-intelligent and pretty durn ruthless blood pride that them brothers themselves was waving around here for about a hour that day.

'Anyway, there she was, and I reckon she knowed her time was going to be short, and him saying to her, "Let's get married," and her saying, "I can't marry you. I've already got a husband." And her time come and she was down then, on that shuck mattress, and him feeding her with a spoon, likely, and I reckon she knowed she wouldn't get up from it, and he got the midwife, and the baby was born, and likely her and the midwife both knowed by then she would never get up from that mattress and maybe they even convinced him at last, or maybe she knowed it wouldn't make no difference nohow and said yes, and he taken the mule pap let him keep at the mill and rid seven miles to Preacher Whitfield's and brung Whitfield back about daylight, and Whitfield married them and she died, and him and Whitfield buried her. And that night he come to the house and told pap he was quitting, and left the mule, and I went out to the mill a few days later and he was gone—just the shuck mattress and the stove, and the dishes and skillet mammy let him have, all washed and clean and set on the shelf. And in the third summer from then, them two brothers, them Thorpes—'

'Thorpes,' Uncle Gavin said. It wasn't loud. It was getting dark fast now, as it does in our country, and I couldn't see his face at all any more. 'Tell,' he said.

'Black-complected like she was—the youngest one looked a heap like her—coming up in the surrey, with the deputy or bailiff or whatever he was, and the paper all wrote out and stamped and sealed all regular, and I says, "You can't do this. She come here of her own accord, sick and with nothing, and he taken her in and fed her and nursed her and got help to born that child and a preacher to bury her; they was even married before she died. The preacher and the midwife both will prove it." And the oldest brother says, "He couldn't marry her. She already had a husband. We done already attended to him." And I says, "All right. He taken that boy when nobody come to claim him. He has raised that boy and clothed and fed him for two years and better." And the oldest one drawed a money purse half outen his pocket and let it drop back again. "We aim to do right about that, too—when we have seen the boy," he says. "He is our kin. We want him and we aim to have him." And that wasn't the first time it ever occurred to me that this world ain't run like it ought to be run a heap of more times than what it is, and I says, "It's thirty miles up there. I reckon you all will want to lay over here tonight and rest your horses." And the oldest one looked at me and says, "The team ain't tired. We won't stop." "Then I'm going with you," I says. "You are welcome to come," he says.

'We drove until midnight. So I thought I would have a chance then, even if I never had nothing to ride. But when we unhitched and laid down on the ground, the oldest brother never laid down. "I ain't sleepy," he says. "I'll set up a while." So it wasn't no use, and I went to sleep and then the sun was up and it was too late then, and about middle morning we come to that mailbox with the name on it you couldn't miss, and the empty house with nobody in sight or hearing neither, until we heard the ax and went around to the back, and he looked up from the woodpile and seen what I reckon he had been expecting to see every time the sun rose for going on three years now. Because he never even stopped. He said to the little boy, "Run. Run to the field to grandpap. Run," and come straight at the oldest brother with the ax already raised and the down-stroke already started, until I managed to catch it by the haft just as the oldest brother grabbed him and we lifted him clean off the ground, holding him, or trying to. "Stop it, Jackson!" I says. "Stop it! They got the law!"

'Then a puny something was kicking and clawing me about the legs; it was the little boy, not making a sound, just swarming around me and the brother both, hitting at us as high as he could reach with a piece of wood Fentry had been chopping. "Catch him and take him on to the surrey," the oldest one says. So the youngest one caught him; he was almost as hard to hold as Fentry, kicking and plunging even after the youngest one had picked him up, and still not making a sound, and Fentry jerking and lunging like two men until the youngest one and the boy was out of sight. Then he collapsed. It was like all his bones had turned to water, so that me and the oldest brother lowered him down to the chopping block like he never had no bones a-tall, laying back against the wood he had cut, panting, with a little froth of spit at each corner of his mouth. "It's the law, Jackson," I says. "Her husband is still alive."

' "I know it," he says. It wasn't much more than whispering. "I been expecting it. I reckon that's why it taken me so by surprise. I'm all right now."

' "I'm sorry for it," the brother says. "We never found out about none of it until last week. But he is our kin. We want him home. You done well by him. We thank you. His mother thanks you. Here," he says. He taken the money purse outen his pocket and puts it into Fentry's hand. Then he turned and went away. After a while I heard the carriage turn and go back down the hill. Then I couldn't hear it any more. I don't know whether Fentry ever heard it or not.

' "It's the law, Jackson," I says. "But there's two sides to the law. We'll go to town and talk to Captain Stevens. I'll go with you."

'Then he set up on the chopping block, setting up slow and stiff. He wasn't panting so hard now and he looked better now, except for his eyes, and they was mostly just dazed looking. Then he raised the hand that had the money purse in it and started to mop his face with the money purse, like it was a handkerchief; I don't believe he even knowed there was anything in his hand until then, because he taken his hand down and looked at the money purse for maybe five seconds, and then he tossed it—he didn't fling it; he just tossed it like you would a handful of dirt you had been examining to see what it would make—over behind the chopping block and got up and walked across the yard toward the woods, walking straight and not fast, and not looking much bigger than that little boy, and into the woods. "Jackson," I says. But he never looked back.

'And I stayed that night as Rufus Pruitt's and borrowed a mule from him; I said I was just looking around, because I didn't feel much like talking to nobody, and the next morning I hitched the mule at that gate and started up the path, and I didn't see old man Fentry on the gallery a-tall at first.

'When I did see him he was moving so fast I didn't even know what he had in his hands until it went "boom!" and I heard the shot rattling in the leaves overhead and Rufus Pruitt's mule trying his durn best either to break the hitch rein or hang hisself from the gatepost.

'And one day about six months after he had located here to do the balance of his drinking and fighting and sleight-of-hand with other folks' cattle, Bucksnort was on the gallery here, drunk still and running his mouth, and about a half dozen of the ones he had beat unconscious from time to time by foul means and even by fair on occasion, as such emergencies arose, laughing every time he stopped to draw a fresh breath. And I happened to look up, and Fentry was setting on his mule out there in the road.

'He was just setting there, with the dust of them thirty miles caking into the mule's sweat, looking at Thorpe. I don't know how long he had been there, not saying nothing, just setting there and looking at Thorpe; then he turned the mule and rid back up the road toward them hills he hadn't ought to never have left. Except maybe it's like the fellow says, and there ain't nowhere you can hide from either lightning or love. And I didn't know why then. I hadn't associated them names. I knowed that Thorpe was familiar to me, but that other business had been twenty years ago and I had forgotten it until I heard about that hung jury of yourn. Of course he wasn't going to vote Bookwright free. . . . It's dark. Let's go to supper.'

But it was only twenty-two miles to town now, and we were on the highway now, the gravel; we would be home in an hour and a half, because sometimes we could make thirty and thirty-five miles an hour, and Uncle Gavin said that someday all the main roads in Mississippi would be paved like the streets in Memphis and every family in America would own a car. We were going fast now.

'Of course he wasn't,' Uncle Gavin said. 'The lowly and invincible of the earth—to endure and endure and then endure, tomorrow and tomorrow and tomorrow. Of course he wasn't going to vote Bookwright free.'

'I would have,' I said. 'I would have freed him. Because Buck Thorpe was bad. He—'

'No, you wouldn't,' Uncle Gavin said. He gripped my knee with one hand even though we were going fast, the yellow light beam level on the yellow road, the bugs swirling down into the light beam and ballooning away. 'It wasn't Buck Thorpe, the adult, the man. He would have shot that man as quick as Bookwright did, if he had been in Bookwright's place. It was because somewhere in that debased and brutalized flesh which Bookwright slew there still remained, not the spirit maybe, but at least the memory, of that little boy, that Jackson and Longstreet Fentry, even though the man the boy had become didn't show it, and only Fentry did. And you wouldn't have freed him either. Don't ever forget that. Never.'

STERLING A. BROWN
(1901–1989)

The poet, critic, and folklorist Sterling Allen Brown was born in Washington, D.C., and raised on the campus of Howard University, where his father, the Reverend Sterling N. Brown, was dean of religion. After graduating Phi Beta Kappa from Williams College, Brown earned an M.A. from Harvard. He taught at Virginia Seminary, Lincoln University, and Fisk University, collecting rural African American folklore wherever he went. In 1929 Brown returned to Howard, where he taught English until 1969.

Drawing upon the language, personalities, and spirit of African American folk culture, Brown's book *Southern Road* (1932) and later poems established him as the "African American poet laureate," although he smarted from a perceived lack of recognition of his poetic gifts for much of his life. Brown also became the dean of African American literary critics, publishing several groundbreaking studies and serving in important capacities in the Federal Writers' Project during the New Deal. His anthology, *The Negro Caravan* (1941), co-edited with Arthur P. Davis and Ulysses S. Lee, helped to define African American literature as an academic field.

In addition, Brown exerted great influence as a teacher. His students at Howard included LeRoi Jones, Kenneth B. Clark, and Ossie Davis, among many others. Henry Louis Gates, Jr., has written of Brown: "Such a prolific output in a life that spans the era of Booker T. Washington and the era of Black Power makes him not only the bridge between 19th-and 20th-century black literature, but also the last of the great 'race men,' the Afro-American men of letters, a tradition best epitomized by W. E. B. Du Bois."

Brown wrote only a few short stories. The story presented here, "And/Or," originally appeared in 1946. One of the earliest works of fiction to face squarely the legal issues of civil rights, it recounts a college student's efforts to vote in segregated Alabama.

African Americans' right to vote was guaranteed by the Fifteenth Amendment to the Constitution in 1870, but in the South, intimidation, poll taxes, property qualifications, and literacy tests were used to effectively disenfranchise blacks. Tests often consisted of reading, understanding, and interpreting the state or federal constitution to the satisfaction of election officials. It was not until the Voting Rights Act of 1965 that knowledge and literacy tests were outlawed.

AND/OR

— 1946 —

For safety's sake, though he is a lieutenant in the army now and may never come back to the South, let us call him Houston. He was short and frail, with a dark brown sensitive face. I first met him at the FEPC hearings in Birmingham when, on short acquaintance, he revealed to me how he was burned up by conditions in Dixie. To judge from his twang, he was southern-born, and he was Tuskegee trained, but he had the rather dicty restaurant on edge when he went into his tirades. The brown burghers, some of them a bit jittery anyway at FEPC and especially at the influx of a bunch of young "foreign" and radical Negroes into dynamite-loaded Birmingham, eyed him carefully over their glasses of iced tea.

I ran into him again in the small Alabama town where he was teaching. He was still quite a talker, in his high-pitched voice with a quaver in it—though he didn't quaver in other respects. He was brimming over with facts and consequent bitterness, deeper than I expected in a graduate of Tuskegee. To him, as to so many college men, the Negro's great need was the ballot. He had made a thoughtful study of the disenfranchising techniques and political shenanigans of Alabama in general. He laughed sardonically at the Negro's being asked to interpret such "constitutional" questions as "What is *non compos mentis* when it is applied to a citizen in legal jeopardy?" But he knew also how deeply engraved was the symbol at the head of the Democratic column on the official ballot used in all elections in Alabama: a rooster with the words "White Supremacy" arched over its head, and the words under it: "For the Right." White supremacy was well symbolized by the rooster, he thought; and he was afraid that Negro purposefulness was too well symbolized by a chicken. And a chicken with pip, lethargic, gaping, and trembling. He was determined to vote himself, and he told me with gusto the tragicomedy, at times the farce, of his experiences with the county board of registrars.

Knowing the ropes, Houston's first strategic step to get the vote was to buy a radio at a white store and charge it. This was his first charge account in the town, but it meant a possible white sponsor to vouch for him when the polls opened. Two weeks later he applied to the Board of Registrars. He was asked, "Do you have three hundred dollars worth of taxable property?"

Houston said no, but added that he understood that the property qualification was alternative to the literacy qualification. He was told that he was wrong: he had to have three hundred dollars worth of property or forty acres of land. That seemed to end the matter as far as the Board was concerned. Houston waited a few minutes and then asked if he would be permitted to make out an application. He was granted permission with the warning that the Board would have to pass on his case, and that as he did not have the property qualification, the chances were against him. He was also told that he needed two residents of the town to vouch for his character. He named the merchant from whom he had bought the radio and a clothing merchant.

When approached, the first merchant said that he would be glad to go over and sign, but that he couldn't leave his store just then. He would go over late that afternoon. Houston thanked him. The next day he telephoned the merchant, who hadn't quite managed it the day before but would try to get over some time that day. Houston thanked him again. The next day the merchant hadn't seen his way clear, either, things being so busy, but he gave his word that he wouldn't let the polls close on Houston. Three days later, the merchant told Houston that he had just got tied up and the polls had closed. A week later, Houston went to the store and paid the balance on the radio. The merchant said that he was sorry; he just hadn't been able to get around to doing that little favor, but he gave his word again that he would be glad indeed to go over when the polls opened again. Yessir, glad. That would be just the next month, Houston told him.

When the polls opened the next month, Houston called the merchant, who made an appointment with him for "about 2 P.M." At the store on the dot, Houston was told that the merchant was out of town. Yessir, a quick trip.

Houston then applied to the second merchant, with whom he had had even more dealings, but on a cash basis. The run-around here was also efficient. He didn't know Houston well enough "to take an oath about his character," but he promised that if men at the Post Office and Bank said O.K., he would vouch for him. Every time the Post Office superintendent called, the merchant was out. Finally, the banker caught him, and the appointment was made.

"I understand you have an application for R. T. Houston, who has been working out at the school for the last three years or so." The board informed the merchant that investigation showed that Houston did not have either three hundred dollars worth of property or forty acres of land. The merchant said, "Oh, I don't know anything about that." He wanted to get out of there quick. Houston stated again his understanding about the alternative literacy qualification.

"It doesn't make any difference whether you graduated from Harvard.

If you don't have the property, you can't register," the merchant offered. Houston remembered that he seemed to cheer up, saying it.

The merchant and Houston left the office, Houston thanking him for his time, and the merchant saying jocularly, "Well, you got to get your three hundred dollars worth of property or forty acres of land somewhere. What are you going to do?"

"I'm going to register," said Houston. "There is a provision in the Constitution for having your qualifications determined." Houston was partly compensated for the long runaround by the look of amazement on the merchant's face.

With two other colleagues, both acquainted with the law, Houston approached the Board again to thresh out the matter of qualifications. The registrar, a woman, stated that somebody else had asked the same question and that she had "marked it in the book." She was told that the property qualification was an alternative.

"No," she said, "you must have the property."

"When was the amendment passed making both qualifications necessary?"

This question was ignored. In triumph, the registrar read the second qualification. ". . . owner or husband of woman who is owner . . . of forty acres of land, or personal property or real estate assessed . . . at value of three hundred dollars or more," etc.

She was then asked to read the first qualification. She complied, hesitantly. Another registrar horned in: "This board will have to pass on you, and we register who we want to register."

The first qualification set up the requirement of "reading and writing any article of the Constitution of the United States in the English language . . ." and of being "regularly engaged in some lawful employment the twelve months next preceding the time they offer to register . . . etc." The word linking this to the second qualification is *or*.

On being asked what the word *or* meant, the registrar said that it meant *in addition to*, based on an interpretation from the Attorney General. Houston and his colleagues asked for this ruling, but it was not produced. Instead the three trouble-makers were shunted across the hall to the Probate Judge's office. The Judge was asked point blank if "or" in the state constitution meant "and." The Judge replied point-blank that it did. "You must have both the property as well as the literacy qualification," he said. The registrars got their ruling from the Attorney General; the Judge knew nothing of any law that had been made. Questioned closely on whether all the list of voters owned three hundred dollars worth of property, the Judge hedged. He complained that his questioners were only trying to get him into an argument with the Board of Registrars.

"What steps should we take to get an interpretation of the disputed passage?" was the straw breaking the camel's back.

"Find out for yourself," the Judge yelled, and stormed out of his office.

A few hours later, while preparing papers for an appeal to the Circuit Court to clarify the problem of qualification, Houston learned that the Board of Registrars had been busy telephoning him. Another call, unidentified but "from someone in touch with the Judge," informed Houston that he would get his registration papers.

When he walked into the office, there was a decided stir. One of the women on the Board said, "Here he is now." The spokesman of the Board was polite. "We decided to let you register," he said.

"Thank you very much," said Houston. The certificate was signed and dated as of the preceding day, when the Judge had ruled on "And / Or."

Houston was told that it would be wise to get two good people of the town to vouch for him.

He named colleagues of his at the school.

"We mean white people," said the registrar. "Don't you know two good white people?"

"Nossir," said Houston politely. "I don't know two good white people . . . to vouch for me."

NADINE GORDIMER

(1923–)

Nadine Gordimer was born near Johannesburg, South Africa, the daughter of emigrés from Lithuania and Britain. Her mother took her out of school when she was eleven and arranged for her to be tutored privately until she was sixteen. Gordimer was twenty-one and already a published writer of short stories when she completed a year of general studies at the University of Witwatersrand. Her first collection of stories, *Face to Face*, was published in 1949.

In 1948 the Afrikaner National Party came to power in South Africa and established the regime of apartheid. From the beginning Gordimer was a passionate witness against apartheid's injustice and brutality. Her novels *A World of Strangers* (1958) and *The Late Bourgeois World* (1966) were banned by the government for twelve and ten years respectively, and *Burger's Daughter* (1979) was banned temporarily, but Gordimer remained in her homeland to work as South Africa's most famous writer and outspoken critic. Her many writing awards include the Booker Prize (joint winner, 1974, for *The Conservationist*) and the Nobel Prize for Literature in 1991.

As well as commenting on the political situation, Gordimer's writing explores the complexity of the human condition, illuminating both the public and the private realms of people's lives and and the relation of each to the other. Gordimer has said with amusement that since apartheid has ended, some people fear that she will have nothing to write about anymore.

"Happy Event" was published in *The Forum* (Johannesburg) in November 1953 and appeared in Gordimer's 1956 collection of short stories, *Six Feet of the Country*. Both Ella, the privileged white mistress, and her African servant, Lena, find themselves with unwanted pregnancies, and each chooses a different solution.

HAPPY EVENT

— 1953 —

There were so many things in life you couldn't ever imagine yourself doing, Ella Plaistow told herself. Once or twice she had said it aloud, too, to Allan. But mostly it grew, forced its way up out of the silences that fell upon her like a restraining hand during those first few days after she had come home from the nursing home. It seemed to burst through her mouth in a sudden irresistible germination, the way a creeper shoots and uncurls into leaf and stem in one of those films which telescope plant growth into the space of a few terrifying vital seconds.

Silence followed it again. In her mind, if she had spoken inwardly, to herself; in the room, if she had spoken aloud. The silence that covers the endless inward activity of shuffling for a foothold, making out of a hundred-and-one past justifications and pressures the accommodations of a new position for oneself. It was true, of course. You start off as a child, pretending to think the blonde doll prettier than the brunette, so that your loved sister may fall into the trap of choosing the one you don't want for yourself. You go on by one day finding your own tongue glibly acquiescing to a discussion of your best friend's temperament with someone whom you know to be her disliked enemy. And before you know where you are, you have gone through all the sidlings and inveiglings of taking somebody's work for less than it is worth, throwing someone into an agony of jealousy for the sake of a moment's vanity, pretending not to see an old lover lest he should not seem impressive enough in the eyes of the new one. It is impossible to imagine yourself doing any of these; but once done . . . Like ants teeming to repair a broken anthill, like white corpuscles rushing to a wound, all the forces that protect oneself from oneself have already begun their quick, sure, furtive, uneasy juggling for a new stance, a rearrangement for comfort into which amorphous life seems to have edged you.

'It's your *body* that objects,' said Allan. 'Remember that. That's all. There's some sort of physical protest that's got nothing to do with you at all, really. You must expect it. It'll pass off in a week or so.'

And of course he was quite right. She certainly didn't have any regrets. They had two children, a girl and a boy (the wrong way round, as they said—the girl was the elder—but it's dangerous to have everything too much the way you want it!) who were just old enough to be left with their grandmother. Allan's new partner was thoroughly reliable, the bond on the house was almost paid off; at last there was nothing to stop Allan and Ella: they had booked to go to Europe, in the spring of next year. So to have allowed themselves to be stopped by this—! To be, instead, this time next year, caught up in chemists' bills and napkins and wakeful nights all over again! No, they had brought up their babies, had loved and resented them and were content with them, and all through eight years had planned for this time when they would suddenly lift themselves clear of whatever it was that their lives had settled into, and land, free of it, lightly in another country.

Because it was something that Ella could never have dreamed she would ever do, in a week or two the trip to the nursing home slipped away into the unimportance of things that might never have happened. She was busy planning next winter's clothes for the children—it would be in winter in South Africa while she and Allan were in spring in Europe—and getting the garden into shape because they hoped to let the house for the period they were to be away, and if they wanted a decent tenant the place must look attractive. She was just beginning to feel really strong again—undoubtedly that business had left her a little weak—and it was just as well, since she had so much to do, when, of course, servant trouble started.

The old house-cum-garden boy, Thomasi, began quarrelling with Lena, the native maid whom Ella had thought herself lucky to engage two months ago. Lena, a heavy, sullen, light-coloured Basuto, represented in her closed-in solemnity something that challenged irritation in Thomasi. Thomasi was a Basuto himself—Ella had the vague conviction that it was best to have servants who belonged to the same tribe, rather as she would have felt that it would be better to have two Siamese cats instead of one Siamese and one tabby, or two fan-tailed goldfish rather than one plain and one fancy. She always felt puzzled and rather peevish, then, when, as had happened often before, she found that her two Basutos or two Zulus or two Xhosas did not necessarily get on any better than one would have expected two Frenchmen to get on simply because both were French, or two Englishmen simply because both were English.

Now Thomasi, barely five feet tall and with that charming, ancient, prehuman look of little dark-skinned men with bandy legs, was maddened by the very presence of Lena, like an insect circling angrily around the impassive head of some great slow animal. He quarrelled with her over dusters, over the state of the kitchen sink, over the bones for the dog; he went about his work shaking his head and rumbling with volcanic mutterings.

'If you've got anything to say, come out and say it,' Ella said to him, irritated herself. 'What's the matter now?'

'That woman is too lazy, madam,' he said in his high, philosophical, exasperated voice.

It was difficult to think of old Thomasi as something quite like oneself, when he rose to his hind legs. (Yes, one had the feeling that this was *exactly* what happened when he got up from polishing the floor. Of course, if he had been dressed in a tailored American-drape hopsack instead of the regulation 'kitchen boy' outfit that was a cross between a small boy's cotton sailor suit and a set of underwear, he might not have looked any funnier than any of the small, middle-aged Johannesburg men behind their directors' desks.) 'Look, Thomasi, she does her work. I'm satisfied with her. I don't want you to go making trouble. I'm the missus, and she works for me, not you, you understand?'

Then, later in the day, Ella would relent. Having shown Thomasi the hand of authority, she could approach him on the other level of their association: that of common concern for the house that they had 'run' together for nearly six years, and whose needs and prides and inanimate quirks both understood perfectly.

'Thomasi?'

'Missus?' She might be strolling in the garden, pretending that she was not seeking him out. He would go on wielding the grass shears, widening and snapping like the sharp bill of some great bird imprisoned in his hands.

'What has she done?'

'Well, I tell her the dog he mustn't have the small bone. Yesterday I tell her. Now she doesn't say nothing when I tell her. This morning I see she give the chicken bone to the dog. All that small bone, you know, the missus keep for the cats. Now when I say why you give that bone to the dog, the dog he's going to get sick, she just look me . . . '

The coffee cups left unwashed from the night before.

The iron left switched on while she went to her room after lunch.

And too many friends in her room at night, too many.

'I think she makes the kaffir beer,' said Thomasi.

But at this complaint Ella was ready to discredit all the others, again. This was Thomasi trying to cook something up. If the girl brewed kaffir beer in her room, Thomasi would be her first customer, not the informant seeking to get her into trouble.

'Listen, Thomasi, I don't want to hear any more of these tales and grumbles, you understand? I'll see if Lena works properly or not, and I don't want you interfering with her.'

As she would give her children a handful of sweets each to equalize some difference between them, Ella cleared out a cupboard that needed clearing anyway, and gave Thomasi an old shirt of Allan's, Lena a cheap blue satin nightgown that she had bought to take to the nursing home and that she somehow felt she didn't want to wear again. 'I must keep the peace,' she said to Allan. 'I'm not going to go training another new girl now. I must stick it out with this one until we go. She's a perfectly nice girl, really—a bit sulky, that's all. But you know what an old devil he can be when he wants to. I shouldn't be surprised if what's behind it is that he fancies her, and she's not interested. Shame, he looks such a little old wizened imp of a thing next to her, she's such a hulking, big-breasted Juno.'

But the gifts did not quiet for long whatever it was that inflamed Thomasi's malice. The following month, on a Monday morning, Ella found Thomasi alone in the kitchen, cooking the greasy, metallic-tasting fried eggs that were his idea of a white man's breakfast. Lena, he said, bearing his message from across that neat stretch of grass and crisscross washing line that was the no-man's-land between the lives of the white people in the house and the black people in their back-yard quarters, said she was sick this morning. She would do the washing tomorrow.

'Are those for the master . . . ?' Ella indicated the eggs but lacked the courage to complain. 'What's wrong with Lena?'

Over the frying pan, Thomasi gave a great shrug of disbelief and contempt.

'What does she say?'

Thomasi turned around to the young woman in the soiled pink dressing-gown, the dark line of her plucked and dyed white-woman's eyebrows showing like pen strokes on the pastel of her fair-skinned face, unmade-up, faintly greasy with the patina of sleep. His brow drew in, intricately lined, over his little yellowish eyes; he said with exaggerated poise and indifference, 'I don't know how she's sick. I can't say how a person she's sick when there's noise in her room all night. When people is talking there, late. Sometime I think: She got someone staying there, or something? Talking, and late, late, a baby crying.'

Ella went out, over the stones and the grass, across the yard to the native girl's room. The grass was crisp with dew and the chill struck through the old sandals she liked to wear instead of slippers; long threads of spider-web danced between the clothes-line. She knocked on the door of the little brick room; the window was closed and curtained. She knocked again and called softly, 'Lena?'

'Ma'm?' The voice came after a pause.

Ella opened the door with difficulty—natives usually tampered with the doorknobs of their rooms, making them removable as an added protection against intruders—and, finding it would open only halfway, edged her way in. The room had a warm animal smell, like the inside of the cupboard where old Lixi, the tabby, lay with her kittens at her belly, purring and licking, purring and licking. The air in here had nothing to do with that other air, wet and sharp with morning, just outside: it was a creature air, created by breathing beings. Although the room was small, Lena in her bed seemed far away. The bed was raised high on bricks, and it was half-curtained, like a homemade four-poster. Some sort of design worked in red and purple thread trailed round the hems of the material. Lena lay, her head turned to the angle of her raised arm on the pillow. She seemed to be taking some communion of comfort from her own tender exposed armpit, close to her face.

'Are you sick, Lena?' said the white woman gently.

The black woman turned her head back and forth once, quickly, on the pillow. She swallowed and said, 'Yes.'

'What do you feel?' said Ella, still at the door, which she now saw could not open properly because of a cupboard made of boxes which was pushed half against it.

'My stomach, ma'm.' She moved under the fringed travelling rug that was her blanket.

'Do you think you've eaten something that's made you sick?' said Ella.

The girl did not answer. Ella saw her big slow eyes and the white of her teeth come out of the gloom.

'Sometime I've got a cold in my stomach,' the girl said at last.

'Is it pain?' said Ella.

'I can do the washing tomorrow,' said the voice from the great, hemmed-in agglomerate of the bed.

'Oh, it doesn't matter,' said Ella. 'I'll send Thomasi out with something for you to take. And do you want something to eat?'

'Only tea, thank you ma'm.'

'All right then.'

She felt the woman's slow eyes watching her out of that room, which curiously, despite its poverty, its soapbox cupboards fretted with cut-out newspaper edgings, the broken china ducks, and the sword-fern draped in stained crêpe paper (the ornaments and the fern were discards from the house), had something of the richly charged air of grand treasure-filled rooms of old houses heavy with association, rooms much used, thick with the overlaid echoes of human concourse. She thought, for some reason, of the kind of room in which one expects to find a Miss Havishman. And how ridiculous! These two whitewashed servants' rooms neatly placed out of the way between the dustbin and the garage! What had they to do with Dickens or flights of fancy or anything else, in fact, except clean, weatherproof, and fairly decent places for the servants to sleep? They belonged to nothing and nobody, merely were thrown in along with the other conditions of work.

On the kitchen step Ella stopped and shook each foot like a cat; her feet were sopping. She made a little exclamation of irritation with herself.

And when she had dressed, she sent Thomasi out to the room with a dose of chlorodyne ready-mixed with water in one of the old kitchen-glasses. She got her younger child Pip ready for Allan to take to nursery school and saw that her daughter Kathie had some cake to take for her school lunch in place of the sandwiches Lena usually made.

'Darned nuisance, mmh?' Allan said (suppressing a belch, with distaste, after the eggs).

'Can't be helped, I suppose,' Ella said. 'I wouldn't mind so much if only it wasn't Monday. You know how it is when the washing isn't done on the right day. It puts the whole of the rest of the week out. Anyway, she should be all right by tomorrow.'

The next morning when Ella got up, Lena was already doing the washing. 'Girl appeared again?' called Allan from the bathroom. Ella came in, holding one of Pip's vests to her cheek to see if it was quite dry. 'She doesn't look too good, poor thing. She's moving terribly slowly between the tub and the line.'

'Well she's never exactly nimble is she?' murmured Allan, concentrating on the slight dent in his chin, always a tricky place to shave. They smiled at each other; when they smiled at each other these days, they had the conspiring look of children who have discovered where the Christmas presents are hidden: Europe, leisure, and the freedom of the money they had saved up were unspoken between them.

Ella and Allan Plaistow lived in one of the pleasantest of Johannesburg suburbs: gently rolling country to the north of the city, where the rich had what amounted to country estates, and the impecunious possessors of good taste had small houses in an acre or two of half-cultivated garden. Some of the younger people, determined not to be forced back into real suburbia through lack of money, kept chickens or bred dogs to supplement the upkeep of their places, and one couple even had a small Jersey herd. Ella was one of their customers, quite sure she could taste the difference between their, and what she called 'city' milk.

One morning about a week after the native girl Lena had delayed Ella's wash-day, the milk delivery cart was bowling along the ruts it had made for itself along the track between the dairy and the houses in the Plaistows' direction, when the horse swerved and one wheel bowed down the tall grasses at the side of the track. There was a tinny clang; the wheel slithered against something. Big Charlie, the milk 'boy', growled softly at the horse, and climbed down to see. There, as if it had made a bed for itself in the long grass the way an animal turns round and round before sinking to rest, was a paraffin tin. Big Charlie stubbed at it once with his boot, as if to say, oh, well, if that's all . . . But it gave back the resistance of a container that has something inside it; through his toes, there came to him the realization that this was not merely an empty tin. It was upside down, the top pressed to the ground. He saw an edge of blue material, stained with dew and earth, just showing. Still with his foot, he pushed hard—too hard, for whatever was inside was light—and the tin rocked over. There spilled out of it a small bundle, the naked decaying body of what had been a newborn child, rolled, carelessly as one might roll up old clothing, in a blue satin nightgown.

It did not seem for a moment to Big Charlie that the baby was dead. He gave a kind of aghast cluck, as at some gross neglect—one of his own five doubled up with a bellyache after eating berries, or the youngest with flies settling on his mouth because the mother had failed to wipe the milk that trickled down his chin from her abundance when she fed him—and knelt down to make haste to do whatever it was that the little creature needed. And then he saw that this was hardly a child at all; was now closer to those kittens he was sometimes ordered by his employers to drown in a bucket of water or closer still to one of those battered fledglings found lying beneath the mimosa trees the night after a bad summer storm.

So now he stood back and did not want to touch it. With his mouth lifted over his teeth in a superstitious horror at the coldness of what had been done, he took the crumpled satin in the tips of his fingers and folded it over the body again, then dropped the bundle back into the paraffin tin and lifted the tin onto the cart beside him.

As he drove, he looked down now and then, swiftly, in dismay to see it there still beside him. The bodice of the nightgown was uppermost and lifted in the firm currents of the morning air. It was inside out, and showed a sewn-on laundry label. Big Charlie could neither read or write so he did not know that it said in the neat letters devised for the nursing home, E. PLAISTOW.

That, of course, was how Ella came to find herself in court.

When she opened the door to the plainclothes detective that afternoon, she had the small momentary start, a kind of throb in some organ one didn't know one had, of all people who do not steal and who have paid their taxes: an alarm at the sight of a policeman that is perhaps rooted in the memory of childhood threats. The man was heavily built and large-footed and he had a very small, well-brushed moustache, smooth as the double flick of a paintbrush across his broad lip. He said in Afrikaans, '*Goeie middag. Mevrou Plaistow?*' And when she answered in English, he switched to slow, stilted English. She led him into the living room with a false air of calm and he sat on the edge of the sofa. When he told her that the Evans's milk boy had found a dead native baby in a paraffin tin on the veld, she made a polite noise of horror and even felt a small shudder, just back of her jaws, at the idea, but her face kept its look of strained patience: what had this gruesome happening to do with *her?* Then he told her that the child was found wrapped in a blue satin nightgown bearing her name, and she rose instantly from her chair in alarm, as if there had been a sudden jab inside her.

'*In my nightgown?*' she accused, standing over the man.

'Yes, I'm afraid so, lady.'

'But are you sure?' she said, withdrawing into anger and hauteur.

He opened a large brief-case he had brought with him and which she had imagined as much a part of his equipment as his official English or the rolled-gold signet ring on his little finger. Carefully he spread out the blue satin, which still kept, all refracted by creases, the sheen of satin, despite the earth stains and some others caused by something that had dried patchily—perhaps that birth fluid, *vernix caseosa*, in which a baby is coated when it slips into the world. The sight filled her with revulsion: 'Oh, put it away!' she said with difficulty.

'You recognize it?' he said—pronouncing the word as if it were spelled 'racognize'.

'It's mine all right,' she said. 'It's the one I gave to Lena a few weeks ago. But good God—?'

'It's a native girl, of course, the one you gave it to?' He had taken out his notebook.

Now all sorts of things were flooding into her mind. 'That's right! She was sick, she stayed in bed one day. The boy said he heard a baby cry in the night—' She appealed to the policeman: 'But it couldn't be!'

'Now if you'll just tal me, lady, what was the date when you gave the girl the nightgown . . . ' Out of the disorder of her quicker mind, his own slow one stolidly sorted this recollection from that; her confused computation of dates and times through the measure of how much time had passed between the day Pip chipped a tooth at nursery school (that, she remembered distinctly, happened on the same day that she had given Thomasi a shirt and Lena the nightgown) and the morning the washing had not been done, became a statement. Then she went, haltingly because of her nervousness, into the kitchen to call Lena and Thomasi. 'Thomasi!' she called. And then, after a pause: 'Lena.' And she watched for her, coming across the yard.

But the two Africans met the fact of the policeman far more calmly than she herself had done. For Africans there is no stigma attached to any involvement with the forces of the law; the innumerable restrictions by which their lives are hedged from the day they are born make transgressions commonplace and punishment inevitable. To them a few days in prison is no more shaming than an attack of the measles. After all, there are few people who could go through a lifetime without at least once forgetting to carry the piece of paper which is their 'pass' to free movement about the town, or without getting drunk, or without sitting on a bench which looks just like every other bench but happens to be provided exclusively for the use of people with a pale skin. All these things keep Africans casually going in and out of prison, hardly the worse—since it is accepted that this is the ways things are—for a cold, buggy night in the cells or a kick from a warder.

Lena has not a pleasant face, thought Ella, but thought too that perhaps she was merely reading this into the face, now. The woman simply stood there, answering, in an obedient Afrikaans, the detective's questions about her identity. The detective had hitched his solid rump onto the kitchen table, and his manner had changed to the impatient one customarily used for Africans by all white persons in authority. The woman appeared weary, more than anything else; she did not look at the detective when he spoke to her or she answered. And she spoke coldly, as was her custom; just as she said, 'Yes madam no madam,' when Ella reproached her for some neglected chore. She was an untidy woman, too; now she had on her head a woollen *doek* again, instead of the maid's cap Ella provided for her to wear. Ella looked at her, from the *doek* to the coloured sandals with the cut thongs where they caught the toes; looked at her in a kind of fascination, and tried to fit with her the idea of the dead baby, rolled in a nightgown and thrust into a paraffin tin. It was neither credible nor did it inspire revulsion. Because she is not a *motherly* figure, Ella thought—that is it. One cannot imagine her mother to anything. She is the sort of woman, white or black, who is always the custodian of other people's children; she washes their faces and wipes their noses, but they throw their arms around somebody else's neck.

And just then the woman looked at her, suddenly, directly, without a flicker of escape, without dissimulation or appeal, not as a woman looks to another woman, or even a human being to another human being; looked at her out of those wide-set, even-lidded eyes and did not move a muscle of her face.

Oh, but I don't know her, I know nothing about her . . . Ella recoiled, retracting to herself.

'She'll have to come along with me,' the detective was saying, and as the woman stood a moment, as if awaiting some permission, he told her in Afrikaans that she could go to her room if she wanted anything, but she must be quick.

Ella stood near the door watching her servant go slowly across the yard to the little brick room. Her own heart was pounding slowly. She felt a horrible conflict of agitation and shame—for what, she did not know. But if I go after her, she seemed to answer herself, what can I say to her? Behind Ella, the detective was questioning Thomasi, and Thomasi was enjoying it; she could hear from the quick, meaningful, confidential tones of Thomasi's voice that he was experiencing all the relish of a gossip who finds himself at last in the powerful position of being able to influence the lives of those who have forced him out into the cold of a vicarious recorder.

Ella said suddenly to the detective, 'Will you excuse me now, please—' and went away through the house to her bedroom. She was standing there still, some minutes later, when the detective called from the front door, 'Thank you very much, lady, hey? We'll let you know—' and she did not come out but called back, as if she were at some task she could not leave for a moment, 'I'm sorry—will you find your way out . . . '

But she could not forbear to bend apart the slats of the venetian blind in time to see the back of Lena, in one of those cheap short coats—jeep coats, they were called, beloved of suburban African girls—getting into the police car. It's unbelievable, she told herself; she didn't look any fatter than she does now . . . And she did the whole week's washing . . .

The moment Ella heard the car drive away, she went to telephone Allan. As she dialled, she noticed that her fingers were fumbling and damp. I'm really upset, she thought; I'm really upset about this thing.

By the time the court case came to be heard, the quiet, light-coloured Lena lying in her bed that day with her head turned to her arm for comfort, standing obediently before the questioning of the detective in the kitchen, was changed in Ella Plaistow's mind into the ghoulish creature who emerged out of discussion of the affair with friends and neighbours. A woman who could kill her own baby! A murderer, nothing less! It's quite awful to think that she handled Pip and Kathie, other women sympathized. It just shows you, you never know who you're taking into your home . . . You never know, with *them* . . . You can send them to a doctor to make sure you aren't harbouring someone who's diseased, but you've no way of finding out what sort of person a servant is. Well, Thomasi didn't like her from the first, you know, Ella always said at this point. Ah, Thomasi, someone would murmur, now he's a good old thing.

So that when Ella saw the woman Lena in court, there was something disquieting and unexpected about the ordinariness, the naturalness of her appearance: this was simply the woman who had stood so often at the stove in Ella's red-and-white kitchen. And where was the other, that creature who had abandoned her own newborn child to the cold of the veld?

Embarrassment precluded all other feelings, once the white woman found herself in the witness stand. Ella had never, she said again and again afterward, felt such a fool in her whole life.

'You are, of course, a married woman?' said the magistrate.

'Yes,' said Ella.

'How long have you been married?'

'Eight years.'

'I see. And you have children?'

'Yes, two children.'

'Mrs. Plaistow, am I to understand that you, a woman who has been married for eight years and has herself borne two children, were not aware that this woman in your employ was on the point of giving birth to a child?'

Of course, the man must have thought her quite moronic! But how to explain that one didn't go measuring one's servant's waistline, that she was a very big well-built woman in any case, and that since she must have been well into her pregnancy when she started work, any further changes in her figure were not noticed?

He made such a *fool* of me, Ella protested; you can't imagine how *idiotic* I felt.

The case dragged on through two days. The woman herself said that the child had been born dead, and that since no one knew that she was pregnant, she had been 'frightened' and had hidden the body and then left it on the veld, but post-mortem findings showed strong evidence that the child might have lived some hours after birth, and had not died naturally. Then there was Thomasi's statement that he had heard an infant cry in the night.

'In your opinion, Doctor,' the magistrate asked the government medical officer, in an attempt to establish how much time had elapsed between the birth and death of the infant, 'would it be possible for a woman to resume her normal day's work thirty-six hours after confinement? This women did her employer's household washing the following day.'

The doctor smiled slightly. 'Were the woman in question a European, I should, of course, say this would be most unlikely. Most unlikely. But of a native woman, I should say yes—yes, it would be possible.' In the silence of the court, the reasonableness, the validity of this statement had the air of clinching the matter. After all, everyone knew, out of a mixture of hearsay and personal observation, the physical stamina of the African. Hadn't everyone heard of at least one native who had walked around for three days with a fractured skull, merely complaining of a headache? And of one who had walked miles to a hospital, carrying, Van Gogh-like, in a piece of newspaper, his own ear—sliced off in a faction fight?

Lena got six months' hard labour. Her sentence coincided roughly with the time Ella and Allan spent in Europe, but though she was out of prison by the time they returned, she did not go back to work for them again.

REBECCA WEST

(1892–1983)

The passages printed below are excerpted from Rebecca West's report of the Nuremberg trials, "Greenhouse with Cyclamens I." First published in *The New Yorker*, Sept. 7, 1946, under the title "Extraordinary Exiles," the essay was later reprinted along with accounts of other court cases in West's book *A Train of Powder* (1955). In the Nuremberg trials, a series of prosecutions convened in the German city of the same name from 1945 to 1946, an International Military Tribunal representing the Allied powers of World War II tried leaders of Nazi Germany for war crimes, crimes against peace, and crimes against humanity. Some have viewed these prosecutions as illegal applications, by the victors to the vanquished, of *ex post facto* standards. Others have seen them as unprecedentedly idealistic attempts to hold individuals responsible for heinous crimes against international law.

Assigned to cover the closing sessions of Nuremberg, West arrived in the eleventh month of the oppressive proceedings. "Greenhouse with Cyclamens I" (the title is a metaphor for the German imagination) conflates her own experiences at Nuremberg with the larger significance of the trials. West strongly supported affirming the rule of law by punishing the Nazi war criminals, and her portrayal of the defendants and what they stood for is sharp and unforgiving.

"Greenhouse with Cyclamens I" is included in this anthology as a penetrating and vivid chronicle of the people and issues implicated in an extraordinary trial. West is concerned with the reactions of individuals, whether defendants or spectators, to the drama and tedium of the Nuremberg courtroom. Underlying her analysis of personalities is the theme of law groping to find meaning from atrocities by fashioning a new international order.

Rebecca West was born Cicily Isabel Fairfield. At the age of nine she moved from London to Edinburgh, where she was educated at George Watson's Ladies' College. Adopting her *nom de plume* from the heroine in Henrik Ibsen's play *Rosmersholm*, she began her writing career on the staffs of feminist and socialist periodicals. In 1913 West commenced a decade-long affair with H. G. Wells, with whom she had a son. She wrote six novels, including *The Fountain Overflows* and *The Birds Fall Down*. West is best remembered, however, for her nonfiction, particularly her books *Black Lamb and Grey Falcon*, a two-volume 1941 work on Yugoslavia, and *The Meaning of Treason*, a 1947 study of the trials of wartime traitors who deserted Britain for Germany.

GREENHOUSE WITH CYCLAMENS I

— 1955 —

There rushed up towards the plane the astonishing face of the world's enemy: pine woods on little hills, grey-green glossy lakes, too small ever to be anything but smooth, gardens tall with red-tongued beans, fields striped with copper wheat, russet-roofed villages with headlong gables and pumpkin-steeple churches that no architect over seven could have designed. Another minute and the plane dropped to the heart of the world's enemy: Nuremberg. It took not many more minutes to get to the courtroom where the world's enemy was being tried for his sins; but immediately those sins were forgotten in wonder at a conflict which was going on in that court, though it had nothing to do with the indictments considered by it. The trial was then in its eleventh month, and the courtroom was a citadel of boredom. Every person within its walk was in the grip of extreme tedium. This is not to say that the work in hand was being performed languidly. An iron discipline met that tedium head on and did not yield an inch to it. But all the same the most spectacular process in the court was by then a certain tug-of-war concerning time. Some of those present were fiercely desiring that that tedium should come to an end at the first possible moment, and the others were as fiercely desiring that it should last for ever and ever.

The people in court who wanted the tedium to endure eternally were the twenty-one defendants in the dock, who disconcerted the spectator by presenting the blatant appearance that historical characters, particularly in distress, assume in bad pictures. They looked what they were as crudely as Mary Queen of Scots at Fotheringay or Napoleon on St. Helena in a mid-Victorian Academy success. But it was, of course, an unusually ghastly picture. They were wreathed in suggestions of death. Not only were they in peril of the death sentence, there was constant talk about millions of dead and arguments whether these had died because of these men or not; knowing so well what death is, and experiencing it by anticipation, these men preferred the monotony of the trial to its cessation. So they clung to the procedure through their lawyers and stretched it to the limits of its texture; and thus they aroused in the rest of the court, the people who had a prospect of leaving Nuremberg and going back to life, a savage impatience. This the iron discipline of the court prevented from finding an expression for itself. But it made the air more tense.

It seemed ridiculous for the defendants to make any effort to stave off the end, for they admitted by their appearance that nothing was to go well with them again on this earth. These Nazi leaders, self-dedicated to the breaking of all rules, broke last of all the rule that the verdict of a court must not be foretold. Their appearance announced what they believed. The Russians had asked for the death penalty for all of them, and it was plain that the defendants thought that wish would be granted. Believing that they were to lose everything, they forgot what possession had been. Not the slightest trace of their power and their glory remained; none of them looked as if he could ever have exercised any valid authority. Göring still used imperial gestures, but they were so vulgar that they did not suggest that he had really filled any great position; it merely seemed probable that in certain bars the frequenters had called him by some such nickname as "The Emperor." These people were also surrendering physical characteristics which might have been thought inalienable during life, such as the colour and texture of their skins and the moulding of their features. Most of them, except Schacht, who was white-haired, and Speer, who was black like a monkey, were neither dark nor fair any more; and there was amongst them no leanness that did not sag and no plumpness that seemed more than inflation by some thin gas. So diminished were their personalities that it was hard to keep in mind which was which, even after one had sat and looked at them for days; and those who stood out defined themselves by oddity rather than character.

Hess was noticeable because he was so plainly mad: so plainly mad that it seemed shameful that he should be tried. His skin was ashen, and he had that odd faculty, peculiar to lunatics, of falling into strained positions which no normal person could maintain for more than a few minutes, and staying fixed in contortion for hours. He had the classless air characteristic of asylum inmates; evidently his distracted personality had torn up all clues to his past. He looked as if his mind had no surface, as if every part of it had been blasted away except the depth where the nightmares live. Schacht was as noticeable because he was so far from mad, so completely his ordinary self in these extraordinary circumstances. He sat twisted in his seat so that his tall body, stiff as a plank, was propped against the end of the dock, which ought to have been at his side. Thus he sat at right angles to his fellow defendants and looked past them and over their heads: it was always his argument that he was far superior to Hitler's gang. Thus, too, he sat at right angles to the judges on the bench confronting him: it was his argument that he was a leading international banker, a most respectable man, and no court on earth could have the right to try him. He was petrified by rage because this court was pretending to have this right. He might have been a corpse frozen by rigor mortis, a disagreeable corpse who had contrived to aggravate the process so that he should be specially difficult to fit into his coffin.

A few others were still individuals. Streicher was pitiable, because it was plainly the community and not he who was guilty of his sins. He was a dirty old man of the sort that gives trouble in parks, and a sane Germany would have sent him to an asylum long before. Baldur von Schirach, the Youth Leader, startled because he was like a woman in a way not common among men who looked like women. It was as if a neat and mousy governess sat there, not pretty, but with never a hair out of place, and always to be trusted never to intrude when there were visitors: as it might be Jane Eyre. And though one had read surprising news of Göring for years, he still surprised. He was so very soft. Sometimes he wore a German Air Force uniform, and sometimes a light beach suit in the worst of playful taste, and both hung loosely on him, giving him an air of pregnancy. He had thick brown young hair, the coarse bright skin of an actor who has used grease paint for decades, and the preternaturally deep wrinkles of the drug addict. It added up to something like the head of a ventriloquist's dummy. He looked infinitely corrupt, and acted naïvely. When the other defendants' lawyers came to the door to receive instructions, he often intervened and insisted on instructing them himself, in spite of the evident fury of the defendants, which, indeed, must have been poignant, since most of them might well have felt that, had it not been for him, they never would have had to employ these lawyers at all. One of these lawyers was a tiny little man of very Jewish appearance, and when he stood in front of the dock, his head hardly reaching to the top of it, and flapped his gown in annoyance because Göring's smiling wooden mask was bearing down between him and his client, it was as if a ventriloquist had staged a quarrel between two dummies.

Göring's appearance made a strong but obscure allusion to sex. It is a matter of history that his love affairs with women played a decisive part in the development of the Nazi party at various stages, but he looked as one who would never lift a hand against a woman save in something much more peculiar than kindness. He did not look like any recognized type of homosexual, yet he was feminine. Sometimes, particularly when his humour was good, he recalled the madam of a brothel. His like are to be seen in the late morning in doorways along the steep streets of Marseille, the professional mask of geniality still hard on their faces though they stand relaxed in leisure, their fat cats rubbing against their spread skirts. Certainly there had been a concentration on appetite, and on elaborate schemes for gratifying it; and yet there was a sense of desert thirst. No matter what aqueducts he had built to bring water to his encampment, some perversity in the architecture had let it run out and spill on the sands long before it reached him. Sometimes even now his wide lips smacked together as if he were a well-fed man who had heard no news as yet that his meals were to stop. He was the only one of all these defendants who, if he had the chance, would have walked out of the Palace of Justice and taken over Germany again, and turned it into the stage for the enactment of the private fantasy which had brought him to the dock.

As these men gave up the effort to be themselves, they joined to make a common pattern which simply reiterated the plea of not guilty. All the time they made quite unidiosyncratic gestures expressive of innocence and outraged common sense, and in the intervals they stood up and chatted among themselves, forming little protesting groups, each one of which, painted as a mural, would be instantly recognized as a holy band that had tried to save the world but had been frustrated by mistaken men. But this performance they rendered more weakly every day. They were visibly receding from the field of existence and were, perhaps, no longer conscious of the recession. It is possible that they never thought directly of death or even of imprisonment, and there was nothing positive in them at all except their desire to hold time still. They were all praying with their sharp-set nerves: "Let this trial never finish, let it go on for ever and ever, without end."

The nerves of all others present in the Palace of Justice were sending out a counter-prayer: the eight judges on the bench, who were plainly dragging the proceedings over the threshold of their consciousness by sheer force of will; the lawyers and the secretaries who sat sagged in their seats at the tables in the well of the court; the interpreters twittering unhappily in their glass box like cage-birds kept awake by a bright light, feeding the microphones with French and Russian and English versions of the proceedings for the spectators' earphones; the guards who stood with their arms gripping their white truncheons behind their backs, all still and hard as metal save their childish faces, which were puffy with boredom. All these people wanted to leave Nuremberg as urgently as a dental patient enduring the drill wants to up and leave the chair; and they would have had as much difficulty as the dental patient in explaining the cause of that urgency. Modern drills do not inflict real pain, only discomfort. But all the same the patients on whom they are used feel that they will go mad if that grinding does not stop. The people at Nuremberg were all well fed, well clothed, well housed, and well cared for by their organizations, on a standard well above their recent experience. This was obviously true of the soldiers who had campaigned in the war, and of the British and French civilians at work in the court; and it was, to an extent that would have surprised most Europeans, true of the American civilians. It never crossed the Atlantic, the news of just how uncomfortable life became in the United States during the war: what the gasoline shortage did to make life untenable in the pretty townships planned on the supposition that every householder had an automobile; how the titanic munitions programme had often to plant factories in little towns that could not offer a room apiece to the incoming workers; what it was like to live in an all-electric house when electric equipment was impossible to replace or repair. By contrast, what Nuremberg gave was the life of Riley, but it was also the water-torture, boredom falling drop by drop on the same spot on the soul.

What irked was the isolation in a small area, cut off from normal life by the barbed wire of army regulations; the perpetual confrontation with the dreary details of an ugly chapter in history which the surrounding rubble seemed to prove to have been torn out of the book and to require no further discussion; the continued enslavement by the war machine. To live in Nuremberg was, even for the victors, in itself physical captivity. The old town had been destroyed. There was left the uninteresting new town, in which certain grubby hotels improvised accommodation for Allied personnel, and were the sole places in which they might sleep and eat and amuse themselves. On five days a week, from ten to five, and often on Saturday mornings, their duties compelled them to the Palace of Justice of Nuremberg, an extreme example of the German tendency to overbuild, which has done much to get them into the recurring financial troubles that make them look to war for release. Every German who wanted to prove himself a man of substance built himself a house with more rooms than he needed and put more bricks into it than it needed; and every German city put up municipal buildings that were as much demonstrations of solidity as for use. Even though the Nuremberg Palace of Justice housed various agencies we would not find in a British or American or French law court, such as a Labour Exchange, its mass could not be excused, for much of it was a mere waste of masonry and an expense of shame, in obese walls and distended corridors. It recalled Civil War architecture but lacked the homeliness; and it made the young American heart sicken with nostalgia for the clean-run concrete and glass and plastic of modern office buildings. From its clumsy tripes the personnel could escape at the end of the working day to the tennis courts and the swimming pools, provided that they were doing only routine work. Those who were more deeply involved had to go home and work on their papers, with little time for any recreation but dinner parties, which themselves, owing to the unique character of the Nuremberg event, were quite unrefreshing. For the guests at these parties had either to be co-workers grown deadly familiar with the passing months or VIPs come to see the show, who, as most were allowed to stay only two days, had nothing to bring to the occasion except the first superficial impressions, so apt to be the same in every case. The symbol of Nuremberg was a yawn.

The Allies reacted according to their histories. The French, many of whom had been in concentration camps, rested and read; no nation has endured more wars, or been more persistent in its creation of a culture, and it has been done this way. The British reconstituted an Indian hill station; anybody who wants to know what they were like in Nuremberg need only read the early works of Rudyard Kipling. In villas set among the Bavarian pines, amid German modernist furniture, each piece of which seemed to have an enormous behind, a triple feat of reconstitution was performed: people who were in Germany pretended they were people in the jungle who were pretending they were in England. The Americans gave those huge parties of which the type was fixed in pioneering days, when the folks in the scattered homesteads could meet so rarely that it would have been tiring out the horses for nothing not to let geniality go all up the scale; and for the rest they contended with disappointment. Do what you will with America, it remains vast, and it follows that most towns are small in a land where the people are enthralled by the conception of the big town. Here were children of that people, who had crossed a great ocean in the belief that they were going to see the prodigious, and were back in a small town smaller than any of the small towns they had fled.

. . .

It might seem that this is only to say that at Nuremberg people were bored. But this was boredom on a huge historic scale. A machine was running down, a great machine, the greatest machine that has ever been created: the war machine, by which mankind, in spite of its infirmity of purpose and its frequent desire for death, has defended its life. It was a hard machine to operate; it was the natural desire of all who served it, save those rare creatures, the born soldiers, that it should become scrap. There was another machine which was warming up: the peace machine, by which mankind lives its life. Since enjoyment is less urgent than defence it is more easily served. All over the world people were sick with impatience because they were bound to the machine that was running down, and they wanted to be among the operators of the machine that was warming up. They did not want to kill and be grimly immanent over conquered territory; they wanted to eat and drink and be merry and wise among their own kind. It maddened them further that some had succeeded in getting their desire and had made their transfer to peace. By what trickery did these lucky bastards get their priority of freedom? Those who asked themselves that bitter question grew frenzied in the asking, because their conditions became more and more exasperating. The prisoners who guarded the prisoners of Nuremberg were always finding themselves flaring up into rage because they were using equipment that had been worn out and could not be replaced because of the strain on the supply lines. It could not be credited how often, by 1946, the Allies' automobiles broke down on German roads. What was too old was enraging; and who was too new was exasperating too. The commonest sight in a Nuremberg office was a man lifting a telephone, giving a number, speaking a phrase with the slurred and confident ease that showed he had used it a thousand times before to set some routine in motion, and breaking off in a convulsion of impatience. "Smith isn't there? He's *gawn*? And you don't know anything about it? Too bad. . . ." All very inconvenient, and inconvenient too that it is impossible to imagine how, after any future war, just this will not happen—unless that war is so bad that after it nothing will happen any more.

The situation would have been more tolerable if these conquerors had taken the slightest interest in their conquest; but they did not. They were even embarrassed by it. "Pardon my mailed glove," they seemed to murmur as they drove in the American automobiles, which were all the Nuremberg roads then carried save for the few run by the British and French, past the crowds of Germans who waited for the streetcars beside the round black Nuremberg towers, which were hollow ruins; or on Sundays, as they timidly strolled about the villages, bearing themselves like polite people who find themselves intruding on a bereaved family; or as they informed their officers, if they were GIs, that such and such a garage proprietor or doorman was a decent fellow, really he was, though he was a kraut. Here were men who were wearing the laurels of the vastest and most improbable military victory in history, and all they wanted was to be back doing well where they came from, whether this was New York or the hick towns which comedians name to raise a laugh at the extreme of American provincialism. Lines on a young soldier's brow proclaimed that he did not care what decoration he won in the Ardennes; he wanted to go home and pretend Pearl Harbor had never been troubled and get in line for the partnership which should be open for the right man in a couple of years' time. A complexion beyond the resources of the normal bloodstream, an ambience of perfume amounting almost to a general anaesthetic for the passer-by, showed that for the female the breaking of traditional shackles and participation in the male glory of military triumph cannot give the pleasure to be derived from standing under a bell of white flowers while the family friends file past.

Considering this huge and urgent epidemic of nostalgia, the behaviour of these exiles was strangely sweet. They raged against things rather than against one another. At breakfast in the Grand Hotel they uttered such cries as, "Christ, am I allergic to powdered eggs with a hair in 'em!" with a passion that seemed excessive even for such ugly provocation; but there was very little spite. The nicknames were all good-humoured, and were imparted to the stranger only on that understanding. When it was divulged that one of the most gifted of the interpreters, a handsome young person from Wisconsin, was known as the Passionate Haystack, care was taken to point out that no reflection on her was implied, but only a tribute to a remarkable hair-do. This kindliness could show itself as imaginative and quick-witted. The Russians in Nuremberg never mixed with their Allies except at large parties, which they attended in a state of smiling taciturnity. Once a young Russian officer, joyously drunk, walked into the ballroom of the Grand Hotel, which was crowded with American personnel, and walked up to a pretty stenographer and asked her to dance. The band was not playing, and there was a sudden hush. Someone told the band to strike up again, the floor was crowded with dancing couples, a group gathered round the Russian boy and rushed him away to safety, out of the hotel and into an automobile; and he was dumped on the sidewalk as soon as his captors found an empty street. It is encouraging that those men would take so much trouble to save from punishment a man of whom they knew nothing save that he belonged to a group which refused all intercourse with them.

This sweetness of atmosphere was due chiefly to the American tradition of pleasantness in superficial social relations, though many of the exiles were constrained to a special tenderness by their personal emotions. For some of them sex was here what it was anywhere else. There is an old story which describes a native of Cincinnati, returned from a trip to Europe, telling a fellow townsman of an encounter with a beautiful girl which had brightened a night he had spent in Paris. On and on the story goes, dwelling on the plush glories of the restaurant, the loveliness of the girl and her jewels and her dress, the magic of a drive in the Bois de Boulogne, the discreet luxury of the house to which she took him, till it rises to a climax in a bedroom carpeted with bear skins and lined with mirrors. "And then?" "Well—then it was very much like what it is in Cincinnati." To many, love in Nuremberg was just as they had known it in Cincinnati, but for others the life of the heart was lived, in this desolate place given over to ruin and retributive law, with a special poignancy.

Americans marry young. There was hardly a man in the town who had not a wife in the United States, who was not on the vigorous side of middle age, and who was not spiritually sick from a surfeit of war and exile. To the desire to embrace was added the desire to be comforted and to comfort; and the delights of gratification were heart-rending, like spring and sunset and the breaking wave, because they could not last. The illusion was strong that if these delights could go on for ever they would always remain perfect. It seemed to many lovers that whatever verdicts were passed on the Nazis at the end of the trial, much happiness that might have been immortal would then be put to death. Those wives who were four thousand miles away haunted Nuremberg like phantasms of the living and proved the sacredness of what was to be killed. "He loves me, but he is going back to her out of old affection and a sense of duty to his children. Ah, what I am losing in this man who can still keep a woman in his heart, when passion is gone, who is a good father." These temporary loves were often noble, though there were some who would not let them be so. There were men who said, "You are a good kid, but of course it is my wife I really love," when these terms were too perfunctory, considering his plight and the help he had been given. There were also women who despised the men who needed them. Through the Bavarian forests, on Saturdays and Sundays, there often drove one of the more exalted personalities of Nuremberg, accompanied by a lovely and odious female child, whom he believed, since he was among the more elderly exiles and was taking exile badly, not to be odious and to be kind. She seemed to be sucking a small jujube of contempt; by waving her eyelashes and sniffing as the automobile passed those likely to recognize its occupants, she sought to convey that she was in company that bored her.

Those who loved the trial for the law's sake also found the course of their love running not too smoothly. This was not because they were uncomfortably impressed by the arguments brought forward by the declared opponents of the Nuremberg prosecutions. None of these was really effective when set against the wholeness of the historical crisis which had provoked it. It was absurd to say that the defendants were being tried for *ex post facto* crimes when the Briand-Kellogg Pact of 1928 had made aggressive warfare a crime by renouncing the use of war as an instrument of policy; and it was notable that even those opponents who had a special insight into that pact because they had helped to frame it were unable to meet this point, save by pleading that it had not been designed to be used as a basis for the prosecution of war criminals. But that plea was invalid, for in 1928 the necessary conditions for such prosecutions did not exist. There was then no country that seemed likely to wage war which was not democratic in its government, since the only totalitarian powers in Europe, the Soviet Union and Italy, were still weak. It would not be logical to try the leaders of a democracy for their governmental crimes, since they had been elected by the people, who thereby took the responsibility for all their actions. If a democracy breaks the Briand-Kellogg Pact, it must pay by taxation and penalties that fall on the whole people. But the leaders of a totalitarian state seize political power and continually declare that they, and not the people, are responsible for all governmental acts, and if these be crimes according to international law, their claim to responsibility must make them subject to trial before what tribunal international law decrees. This argument is so much in accordance with reality that, in the courtroom itself, it was never doubted. All the defendants, with one exception, seemed to think that the Allies were right in indicting not the German people, but the officers and instruments of the Nazi Government, for conspiring together to commit crimes against peace and the rules of war and humanity; and in most cases their line of defence was that not they, but Hitler or some other members of the party, had taken the actual decisions which led to these crimes. This line of defence, by its references to Hitler alone, concedes the basis of the Nuremberg trials. The one dissenter who would not make this concession was Schacht, who behaved as if there had been a democratic state superimposed on the Nazi state, and that this had been the scene of his activities.

There was obviously more in the other argument used by the opponents of the trial: that even if it were right to persecute the Nazi leaders on charges of conspiracy to commit crimes against peace and the rules of war and humanity, it could not be right to have a Soviet judge on the bench, since the Soviet Union had convicted itself of these crimes by its public rape of Finland and Poland and the Baltic Provinces. Truly there was here often occasion for shame. The English judges sat without their wigs, in plain gowns like their American colleagues, as a sign that this was a tribunal above all local tribunals. The Russian judges sat in military uniform as a sign that this was no tribunal at all, and when Vishinsky visited Nuremberg in the early months of the trial, he attended a banquet at which the judges were present, and proposed a toast to the conviction of the accused, a cantrip which would have led to the quashing of the trial in any civilized country.

This incident appeared to recommend the obvious idealistic prescription of trying the Nazi leaders before a tribunal which should exclude all representatives of the belligerent powers and find all its judges in the neutral countries. But that prescription loses its appeal when it is considered with what a laggard step would, say, the Swedish judge have gone home from

Nuremberg, after having concurred in a verdict displeasing to the Soviet Union. But that there had to be a trial cannot be doubted. It was not only that common sense could predict that if the Nazis were allowed to go free the Germans would not have believed in the genuineness of the Allies' expressed disapproval of them, and that the good Germans would have been cast down in spirit, while the bad Germans would have wondered how long they need wait for the fun and jobbery to start again. It was that, there in Germany, there was a call for punishment. This is something that no one who was not there in 1946 will ever know, and perhaps one had to be at Nuremberg to learn it fully. It was written on the tired, temporizing faces and the bodies, nearly dead with the desire for life, of the defendants in the dock. It was written also on the crowds that waited for the streetcars and never looked at the Allied personnel as they drove past, and it was written on Nuremberg itself, in many places: on the spot just within the walls of the old town, outside the shattered Museum of Gothic Art, where a vast stone head of Jehovah lay on the pavement. Instead of scrutinizing the faces of men, He stared up at the clouds, as if to ask what He himself could be about; and the voices of the German children, bathing in the chlorinated river that wound through the faintly stinking rubble, seemed to reproach Him, because they sounded the same as if they had been bathing in a clear river running between meadows. There was a strange pattern printed on this terrain; and somehow its meaning was that the people responsible for the concentration camps and the deportations and the attendant evocation of evil must be tried for their offences.

It might seem possible that Britain and America might have limited their trials to the criminals they had found in the parts of Germany and Austria which they had conquered, and thus avoided the embarrassment of Soviet judges on the bench. But had they done so the Soviet Union would have represented them to its own people as dealing with the Nazi leaders too gently, to the Germans in the Eastern Zone as dealing with them too harshly. So there had to be an international tribunal at Nuremberg, and the Americans and the British and the French had to rub along with it as best they could. The Nuremberg judges realized the difficulty of the situation and believed that the imperfection could be remedied by strict adherence to a code of law, which they must force themselves to apply as if they were not victors but representatives of a neutral power. It was an idealistic effort, but the cost was immense. However much a man loved the law he could not love so much of it as wound its sluggish way through the Palace of Justice at Nuremberg. For all who were there, without exception, this was a place of sacrifice, of boredom, of headache, of homesickness.

Here was a paradox. In the courtroom these lawyers had to think day after day at the speed of whirling dervishes, yet were living slowly as snails, because of the boredom that pervaded all Nuremberg and was at its thickest in the Palace of Justice. They survived the strain. The effect on the defendants could be tested by their response to the cross-examinations of Göring. They were frightened when Sir David Maxwell Fyfe, the chief acting British prosecutor, cross-examined him and in a businesslike way got him against the wall and extorted from him admissions of vast crime; and they were amused when Mr. Justice Jackson, the chief American prosecutor, could not cross-examine Göring at all well, because he had a transatlantic prepossession that a rogue who had held high office would be a solemn and not a jolly rogue, and was disconcerted by his impudence. But to the Russian cross-examination of Göring neither they nor anyone else in the court could bend their attention, because it was childish; it might have been part of a mock trial organized by a civics teacher in a high school. This was perhaps a superficial impression. It might be that the Russians were pursuing a legal aim other than ours. "It seems to me, when I look back on the last few months," said one of the journalists who sat through the whole trial, "that again and again I have seen the Russians do the most mysterious things. I don't think I dreamed that one of the leading Russian lawyers, all togged up in his military uniform, stepped up to the rostrum and squared his shoulders as if he were going to do some weight-lifting and shouted at whatever defendant it was in the box, 'Did you conspire to wage an aggressive war against the peace-loving democracies? Answer yes or no.' When the defendant said 'No,' the Russian lawyer thought for a long time and said, 'I accept your answer.' I cannot work that one out." The men in the dock did not try.

But they were inert before the French. These were veiled from us by a misleading familiarity, an old and false association of images. They wore the round caps and white jabots and black gowns we have seen all our lives in Daumier drawings, and we expected them to be the wolves and sharks and alligators that Daumier drew. But they were civilized and gentle people, who gave a token of strength in their refusal to let what had happened to them of late years leave marks on their French surface. The judge, Monsieur Donnedieu de Vabres, was like many men that are to be seen all over France, and in many old French pictures, and in the plays of Molière and Marivaux: small and stocky, with a white moustache, and a brow kept wrinkled by the constant offences against logic perpetrated by this chaotic universe; a man whom one might have suspected of being academic and limited and pedantic, though sensible and moderate; a man whom one would not have suspected of having been, only two years before, released from a term of imprisonment in a German jail, which would have left many of us incapable and fanatic. From the slightly too elegant speeches of all these French lawyers it could be divined that when they were little boys they were made to learn Lamartine's *Le Lac* by heart. From the speeches of none of them could it be divined that France had lately been shamed and starved and tortured. But they could not press their case so that the men in the dock found themselves forced to listen to it. They were too familiar with that case; they had known all about it before the Nazis ever existed, from the lips of their fathers and their grandfathers; they had been aware that if the Germans practised habitually the brutalizing business of invasion they would strengthen the criminal element in their souls till they did such things as were now being proved against the men in the dock. Their apprehensions had been realized through their own agony. They had been so right that they had suffered wrongs for which no court could ever compensate them. The chief French prosecutor, Auguste Champetier de Ribes, had been the chief anti-Munich minister in Daladier's cabinet, and had followed his conscience before the war in full knowledge of what might happen to him after the war. The fire of their resentment was now burned to ashes. It did not seem worth while to say over again what they had said so often and so vainly; and the naïve element in the Nazis noted the nervelessness of their attack and wrote them off as weaklings. It was here that the Americans and the British found themselves possessed of an undeserved advantage. Through the decades they had refused to listen to the French point of view. Now they were like the sailor who was found beating a Jew because the Jews had crucified Christ. When he was reminded that that had happened a long time ago, he answered that that might be, but he had just heard about it.

So the Germans listened to the closing speeches made by Mr. Justice Jackson and Sir Hartley Shawcross, and were openly shamed by their new-minted indignation. When Mr. Justice Jackson brought his speech to an end by pointing a forefinger at each of the defendants in turn and denouncing his specific share in the Nazi crime, all of them winced, except old Streicher, who munched and mumbled away in some private and probably extremely objectionable dream, and Schacht, who became stiffer than ever, stiff as an iron stag in the garden of an old house. It was not surprising that all the rest were abashed, for the speech showed the civilized good sense against which they had conspired, and it was patently admirable, patently a pattern of the material necessary to the salvation of peoples. It is to be regretted that one phrase in it may be read by posterity as falling beneath the level of its context; for it has a particular significance to all those who attended the Nuremberg trial. "Göring," said Mr. Justice Jackson, "stuck a pudgy finger in every pie." The courtroom was not small, but it was full of Göring's fingers. His soft and white and spongy hands were for ever smoothing his curiously abundant brown hair, or covering his wide mouth while his plotting eyes looked facetiously around, or weaving impudent gestures of innocence in the air. The other men in the dock broke into sudden and relieved laughter at the phrase; Göring was plainly angered, though less by the phrase than by their laughter.

The next day, when Sir Hartley Shawcross closed the British case, there was no laughter at all. His speech was not so shapely and so decorative as Mr. Justice Jackson's, for English rhetoric has crossed the Atlantic in this century and is now more at home in the United States than on its native ground, and he spoke at greater length and stopped more legal holes. But his words were full of a living pity, which gave the men in the box their worst hour. The feminine Shirach achieved a gesture that was touching. He listened attentively to what Sir Hartley had to say of his activities as a Youth Leader; and when he heard him go on to speak of his responsibility for the deportation of forty thousand Soviet children he put up his delicate hand and lifted off the circlet of his headphones, laying it down very quietly on the ledge before him. It seemed possible that he had indeed the soul of a governess, that he was indeed Jane Eyre and had been perverted by a Mr. Rochester, who, disappearing into self-kindled flames, had left him disenchanted and the prey of a prim but inextinguishable remorse. And when Sir Hartley quoted the deposition of a witness who had described a Jewish father who, standing with his little son in front of a firing squad, "pointed to the sky, stroked his head, and seemed to explain something to the boy," all the defendants wriggled on their seats, like children rated by a schoolmaster, while their faces grew old.

There was a mystery there: that Mr. Prunes and Prisms should have committed such a huge, cold crime. But it was a mystery that girt all Nuremberg. It was most clearly defined in a sentence spoken by the custodian of the room in the Palace of Justice that housed all the exhibits relating to atrocities. Certain of these were unconvincing; some, though not all, of the photographs purporting to show people being shot and tortured had a posed and theatrical air. This need not have indicated conscious fraud. It might well have been that these photographs represented attempts to reconstruct incidents which had really occurred, made at the instigation of officials as explanatory glosses to evidence provided by eyewitnesses, and that they had found their way into the record by error. But there was much stuff that was authentic. Somebody had been collecting tattooed human skin, and it is hard to think where such a connoisseur could find his pieces unless he had power over a concentration camp. Some of these pelts were infinitely pathetic, because of their obscenity. Through the years came the memory of the inconveniently high-pitched voice of an English child among a crowd of tourists watching a tournament of water-jousting in a French port: "Mummy, come and look, there's a sailor who's got no shirt on, and he has the funniest picture on his back—there's a lady with no clothes on upside down on a St. Andrew's Cross, and there's a snake crawling all over her and somebody with a whip." There had been men who had thought they could make a pet of cruelty, and the grown beast had flayed them.

But it was astonishing that there had been so much sadism. The French doctor in charge of these exhibits pondered, turning in his hand a lamp-shade made of tattooed human skin, "These people where I live send me in my breakfast tray strewn with pansies, beautiful pansies. I have never seen more beautiful pansies, arranged with exquisite taste. I have to remind myself that they belong to the same race that supplied me with my exhibits, the same race that tortured me month after month, year after year, at Mauthausen." And, indeed, flowers were the visible sign of that mystery, flowers that were not only lovely but beloved. In the windowboxes of the high-gabled houses the pink and purple petunias were bright like lamps. In the gardens of the cottages bordering a road which was no longer there, which was a torn trench, the phloxes shone white and clear pink and mauve, as under harsh heat they will not do, unless they are well watered. It is tedious work, training clematis over low posts, so that its beauty does not stravaig up the walls but lies open under the eye; but on the edge of the town many gardeners grew it thus. The countryside beyond continued this protestation of innocence. A path might mount the hillside, through the lacework of light and shadow the pine trees cast over the soft reddish bed of the pine needles, to the upland farm where the wedding party poured out of the door, riotous with honest laughter, but freezing before a camera into honest solemnity; it might fall to the valley and follow the trout stream, where the dragonflies drew iridescent patterns just above the cloudy green water, to the edge of the millpond, where the miller's flax-haired little son played with the grey kittens among the meadowsweet; it would not lead to any place where it seemed other than plain that Germany was a beautiful country, inhabited by a people who loved all pleasant things and meant no harm.

Yet the accusations that were made against the leaders in the Palace of Justice at Nuremberg were true. They were proved true because the accusers did not want to make them. They would much rather have gone home. That could be seen by those who shamefully evaded the rules of the court and found a way into one of the offices in the Palace of Justice which overlooked the orchard which served as exercise ground of the jail behind it. There, at certain hours, the minor Nazi prisoners not yet brought to trial padded up and down, sullen and puffy, with a look of fierceness, as if they were missing the opportunity for cruelty as much as the company of women or whatever their fancy might be. They were watched by American military guards, who stood with their young chins dropped and their hands clasped behind them, slowly switching their white truncheons backwards and forwards, in the very rhythm of boredom itself. If an apple fell from the tree beside them they did not bend to pick it up. Nothing that happened there could interest them. It was not easy to tell that these guards were not the prisoners, so much did they want to go home. Never before can conquerors in charge of their captives have been less furious, more innocent of vengeance. A history book opened in the mind; there stirred a memory that Alexander the Great had had to turn back on the Hydaspes because his soldiers were homesick.

. . .

Monday, September 30, 1946, was one of those glorious days that autumn brings to Germany, heavy and golden, yet iced, like an iced drink. By eight o'clock a fleet of Allied automobiles, collected from all over Western Germany, was out in the countryside picking up the legal personnel and the visitors from their billets and bringing them back to the Palace of Justice. The Germans working in the fields among the early mists did not raise their heads to look at the unaccustomed traffic, though the legal personnel, which had throughout the trial gone about their business unattended, now had armed military police with screaming sirens in jeeps as outriders.

This solemn calm ended on the doorstep of the Palace of Justice. Within there was turbulence. The administration of the court had always aroused doubts, by a certain tendency toward the bizarre, which manifested itself especially in the directions given to the military police in charge of the gallery where the VIPs sat. The ventilation of the court was bad, and the warm air rose to the gallery, so in the afternoon the VIPs were apt to doze. This struck the commandant, Colonel Andrus, as disrespectful to the court, though the gallery was so high that what went on there was unlikely to be noticed. Elderly persons of distinction, therefore, enjoyed the new experience of being shaken awake by young military policemen under a circle of amused stares. If they were sitting in the front row of the gallery an even odder experience might overtake them. The commandant had once looked up at the gallery and noted a woman who had crossed her ankles and was showing her shins and a line of petticoat, and he conceived that this might upset the sex-starved defendants, thus underestimating both the length of time it takes for a woman to become a VIP and the degree of the defendants' preoccupations. But, out of a further complication of delicacy, he forbade both men and women to cross their ankles. Thus it happened that one of the most venerable of English judges found himself, one hot summer afternoon, being tapped on the shoulder with a white club by a young military policeman and told to wake up, stay awake, and uncross his legs.

These rules were the subject of general mirth in Nuremberg, but the higher American authorities neither put an end to them nor took their existence as a warning that perhaps the court should be controlled on more sensible lines. An eccentricity prevailed which came to its climax in the security arrangements for these two final days. There was a need for caution. Certainly in Berlin nobody would have lifted a finger to avenge the Nazis, but here in Bavaria there were still some people who had never had any reason to feel that the Nazi regime had been a bad thing for them, and among them there must have been some boys who had been too young for military service and had enjoyed their time with Hitler Youth. It might also have been that Martin Bormann, who at the end of the war had replaced Göring, and who was said to have been killed by Russian fire after escaping from the Chancellery, and who was being indicted *in absentia* at this trial, might now choose to reappear.

It therefore seemed obvious that there would be stringent precautions to see that no unauthorized person entered the Palace of Justice, and we had imagined that we would have to queue up before a turnstile, by which competent persons would sit and examine our passes under a strong light. There was a rumour that there was a mark on the passes which would show only under X-rays. But, instead, authority jammed the vast corridors of the Palace of Justice with a mass of military police, who, again and again, demanded the passes of the entrants and peered at them in a half-light. It was extremely unlikely that these confused male children could have detected the grossest forgery, but the question was never posed, for the corridor was so dark that it was difficult to read large print. No attempt had been made to clarify the situation by posting at strategic points men who could recognize the legal personnel; and thus it happened that, outside the judges' entrance to the courtroom, a military policeman, switching his white club, savagely demanded, "And how the hell did you get in here?" of a person who was in fact one of the judges. In the midst of this muddle certain precautionary measures were taken which were at once not strict enough and too strict and quite ineffectual.

Men were forbidden to take briefcases into court, and women were forbidden to carry handbags or wear long coats. These prohibitions were undignified and futile. Women's suits are not made with pockets large enough to hold passes, script, fountain pens, notebooks, and spectacle cases, and few women went into court without a certain amount of their possessions packed away inside their brassieres or stocking tops. One French woman journalist, obedient to the ban on long coats, came in a padded jacket which she had last worn on an assignment in the Asiatic theatre of war, and when she was sitting in court discovered that in the holster pocket over her ribs she had left a small loaded revolver. It may look on paper as if those responsible for the security arrangements at Nuremberg could justify themselves by pointing to the fact that the Palace of Justice was not blown up. But those who were there know that there was just one reason for this: nobody wanted to blow it up. But although the problem raised by Nuremberg security need not have been approached so eccentrically, it never could have been brought to a satisfactory solution. There were no persons qualified by experience to take control at a high level, for there had never been a like occasion; and there was not such a superfluity of customs officials and police workers that a large number of them could have been abstracted from their usual duties and seconded to special duties without harm; and if there had been, the business of transporting them and housing them would have created fresh problems. This was a business badly done, but it could have been done no better.

It seemed natural enough that nobody should have been very anxious to blow up the Palace of Justice when the defendants came into the dock that Monday. The court had not sat for a month, while the judges were considering their verdicts, and during that time the disease of uniformity which had attacked the prisoners during the trial had overcome them. Their pale and lined faces all looked alike; their bodies sagged inside their clothes, which seemed more alive than they were. They were gone. They were finished. It seemed strange that they could ever have excited loyalty; it was plainly impossible that they should ever attract it again. It was their funeral which the Germans were attending as they looked down on the ground when they walked in the streets of the city. Those Germans thought of them as dead.

They were not abject. These ghosts gathered about them the rags of what had been good in them during their lives. They listened with decent composure to the reading of the judgments, and, as on any other day, they found amusement in the judges' pronunciation of the German names. That is something pitiable which those who do not attend trials never see: the eagerness with which people in the dock snatch at any occasion for laughter. Sometimes it seems from the newspaper reports that a judge has been too facetious when trying a serious case, and the fastidious shudder. But it can be taken for granted that the accused person did not shudder, he welcomed the little joke, the small tear in the tent of grimness that enclosed him. These defendants laughed when they could, and retained their composure when it might well have cracked. On Monday afternoon the darkened mind of Hess passed through some dreadful crisis. He ran his hands over his brows again and again as if he were trying to brush away cobwebs, but the blackness covered him. All humanity left his face; it became an agonized muzzle. He began to swing backwards and forwards on his seat with the regularity of a pendulum. His head swung forward almost to his knees. His skin became blue. If one could pity Ribbentrop and Göring, then was the time. They had to sit listening to the judgment upon them while a lunatic swayed and experienced a nameless evil in the seat beside them. He was taken away soon, but it was as if the door of hell had swung ajar. It was apparent now, as on many occasions during the trial, that the judges found it repulsive to try a man in such a state; but the majority of the psychiatrists consulted by the court had pronounced him sane.

The first part of the judgment did not refer to the defendants but to bodies they had formed. It had been argued by the prosecution that the seven Nazi organizations—the Gestapo, SD, SS, Reich Cabinet, Corps of Political Leaders, General Staff and OKW, and Storm Troops—should be declared criminal in nature and that membership in them should by itself be the subject of a criminal charge. The judges admitted this in the cases of the first three, on the grounds that at an early date these organizations had so openly aimed at the commission of violence and the preaching of race hatred that no man could have joined them without criminal intent. The image of a rat in a trap often crossed the mind at Nuremberg, and it was evoked then. No man who had ever been an SS member could deny it. The initials and the number of his blood group were tattooed under his arm. But, of course, that trap did not spring. There were too many SS men, too many armpits, for any occupying force to inspect. The Storm Troopers were not put in the same category, because they were assessed as mere hooligans and bullies, too brutish to be even criminals. Of the others it was recognized that many persons must have joined them or consented to remain within them without realizing what Hitler was going to make of them. This was reasonable enough, for it meant that members of this organization could still be prosecuted if there was reason to believe they had committed crimes as a result of their membership.

But the refusal to condemn all the seven organizations was greatly resented by some of the spectators. It was felt to be a sign that the tribunal was soft and not genuinely anti-Nazi. This was partly due to temperamental and juristic differences among the nations. The four judges took turns at reading the judgment, and this section was read by the English member judge, Lord Oaksey. His father before him was a judge, who was Lord Chief Justice in the twenties; and he had the advantage which the offspring of an old theatrical family have over other actors. He had inherited the technique and he refined on it, and could get his effects economically. He read this passage of the judgment in a silver voice untarnished by passion, with exquisite point; but to a spectator who was not English it might have seemed that this was just one of the committee of an English club explaining to his colleagues that it was necessary to expel a member. The resemblance need not have been disquieting. People who misbehave in such clubs really do get expelled by their committees, and they remain expelled; whereas the larger gestures and rhetoric of history have often been less effective. But this was not understood by those whose national habit it is to cross-breed their judges with prosecutors or to think that the law should have its last say with a moralist twang.

There was, in other quarters, a like unease about the verdicts on the Service defendants, on Field Marshal Keitel and General Jodl and Admirals Doenitz and Raeder. Keitel and Jodl were found guilty on all four counts of the indictment: first, of conspiracy to commit the crimes alleged in the other counts, which were crimes against peace, crimes in war, and crimes against humanity. Raeder was found guilty on the three counts, and Doenitz was found guilty on the second. There was some feeling among those who attended only the end of the trial, and a very great deal of strong feeling among people all over the world who did not attend the court, that these defendants had been put into the dock for carrying out orders as soldiers and sailors must. But there is a great deal in the court's argument that the only orders a soldier or a sailor is bound to obey are those which are recognized practice in the Services of the time. It is obvious that if an admiral were ordered by a demented First Sea Lord to serve broiled babies in the officers' mess he ought to disobey; and it was shown that these generals and admirals had exhibited very little reluctance to carry out orders of Hitler which tended towards baby-broiling. Here was another point at which there was a split between the people who had attended the trial, or long stints of it, and the people who had not. Much evidence came up during the hearings which proved these men very different from what the products of Sandhurst and Dartmouth, West Point and Annapolis, are hoped to be. Doenitz, for example, exhorted his officers to be inspired by the example of some of their comrades who, confined in a camp in Australia, found that there were a few Communists among the other captured troops, managed to distract the attention of the guards, and murdered these wretched men.

But it was in the case of the admirals that the court made a decision which proved Nuremberg to be a step farther on the road to civilization. They were charged with violating the Naval Protocol of 1936, which reaffirmed the rules of submarine warfare laid down in the London Naval Agreement of 1930. They had, and there was no doubt about it, ordered their submarines to attack all merchant ships without warning and not stop to save the survivors. But the tribunal acquitted them on this charge on the grounds that the British and the Americans had committed precisely the same offence. On May 8, 1940, the British Admiralty ordered all vessels in the Skagerrak to be sunk on sight. Also Admiral Nimitz stated in answer to interrogatories that unrestricted submarine warfare had been carried on by the American Navy in the Pacific Ocean from the first day that the campaign opened. The fact was that we and the Germans alike had found the protocol unworkable. Submarines cannot be used at all if they are to be obliged to hang about after they have made a killing and throw away their own security. The Allies admitted this by acquitting the admirals, and the acquittal was not only fair dealing between victors and vanquished, it was a step towards honesty. It was written down for ever that submarine warfare cannot be carried on without inhumanity, and that we have found ourselves able to be inhumane. We have to admit that we are in this trap before we can get out of it. This *nostra culpa* of the conquerors might well be considered the most important thing that happened at Nuremberg. But it evoked no response at the time, and it has been forgotten.

But in this court nothing could be clear-cut, and nothing could have a massive effect, because it was international, and international law, as soon as it escapes from the sphere of merchandise (in which, were men good, it would alone need to be busy), is a mist with the power to make solids as misty as itself. It was true that the Nazi crimes of cruelty demanded punishment. There in Nuremberg the Germans, pale among the rubble, were waiting for that punishment as a purification, after which they might regain their strength and rebuild their world; and it was obvious that the tribunal must sit to disprove Job's lament that the houses of the wicked are safe from fear. A tyrant had suspended the rule of law in his country and no citizen could seek legal protection from personal assault, theft, or imprisonment; and he had created so absolute a state of anarchy that when he fell from power the courts themselves had disappeared and could not be reconstituted to do justice on him and his instruments. Finally he had invaded other territories and reproduced this ruin there. Plainly some sort of emergency tribunal had to take over the work of the vanished tribunals when it was possible, if the Nazis were not to enjoy a monstrous immunity simply because they had included among their crimes the destruction of the criminal courts. It was only just that the Nazis should pay the due penalty for the offences they had committed against the laws of their own land, the millions of murders, kidnappings and wrongful imprisonments, and thefts. "Of course," people said then and still say, "it was right that the Nazis should have been punished for what they did to the Jews. To the left wing. To the religious dissidents. To the Poles. To the Czechs. To the French deportees. To half Europe. But aggressive war, that was a new crime, invented for the occasion, which had never been written on the statute books before." They spoke the very reverse of the truth. The condemnation of aggressive war as a crime was inherent in the Kellogg-Briand Pact; whereas no international body has ever given its sanction to a mechanism by which crimes committed in one nation which had gone unpunished because of a collapse of civil order could subsequently be punished by other nations. It is to be doubted whether the most speculative mind had ever drawn up the specification for such a mechanism.

Here one sees the dangers of international law. It would seem entirely reasonable to give nations which had remained at the common level of civilization the right to exercise judicial powers in nations which have temporarily fallen below that level and are unable to guarantee their citizens justice. But we can all remember how Hitler prefaced his invasions by pretences that civil order had been destroyed wherever there was a German minority, how it was roared at the world over the radio that Germans in Czechoslovakia and Poland and Yugoslavia were being beaten in the streets and driven out of their houses and farms and were denied all police protection. Such an article of international law would give both knight-errantry and tyranny their marching orders. This, at Nuremberg, was not a remote consideration, though Germany seemed to lie dead around us. Each of the judges read some part of the judgment; and when the Russian had his turn there was a temptation not to give the earphones the right switch to the English version, for the Russian language rolled forth from the firm fleshy lips of this strong man like a river of life, a river of genius, inexhaustible and unpredictable genius. To listen to Slav oratory is to feel that Aksakov and Dostoevski and Bishop Peter Nyegosh had half their great work done for them by the language they used. But soon the desire to know what he was talking about proved irresistible. It turned out that the Russian was reading the part of the judgment that condemned the Germans for their deportations: for taking men and women away from their homes and sending them to distant camps where they worked as slave labour in conditions of great discomfort, and were often unable to communicate with their families. There was here a certain irony, and a certain warning.

. . .

The next day, the last day of the trial, there was something like hatred to be seen on the faces of many Germans in the street. The Palace of Justice was even fuller than before, the confusion engendered in the corridors by the inefficient scrutiny system was still more turbulent. There were some bad officials at Nuremberg, and that day they got completely out of hand. One of them, an American, male and a colonel, had always been remarkable for having the drooping bosom and resentful expression of a nursing mother who has had a difficult parturition, and for having throughout the trial nagged at the correspondents as if they were the staff of the maternity ward that had failed him. Hitherto he had not been arresting; the mind had simply noted him as infringing a feminine patent. But standing this day at the entrance of the gallery, staring at obviously valid passes, minute after minute, with the moonish look of a stupid woman trying to memorize the pattern of a baby's bootee, he was strangely revolting in his epicene distress.

The defendants were, however, quiet and cool. They were feeling the relief that many of us had known in little, when we had waited all through an evening for an air raid and at last heard the sirens, and, ironically, they even looked better in health. In the morning session they learned which of them the court considered guilty and which innocent, and why; and they listened to the verdicts with features decently blank except when they laughed. And, miraculously enough, they found the standing joke of the judges' pronunciation of German names just as funny today as before; and the acquittals amused them no end. Three of the defendants were found not guilty. One of these was a negative matter which caused no reaction except comradely satisfaction: that Hans Fritzsche, the radio chief of Goebbels' Propaganda Ministry, should have been found innocent recalled the case of poor Elmer in the classic American comedy, *Three Men on a Horse*. Elmer, it may be remembered, was a gentle creature, who neither smoked nor drank nor used rough words, and when he was found in a compromising attitude with a gangster's moll, and the gangster was wroth, one of the gang inquired, "But even if the worst was true, what would that amount to, in the case of Elmer?"

But the acquittals of von Papen and Schacht were richly positive. The two old foxes had got away again. They had tricked and turned and doubled on their tracks and lain doggo at the right time all their lives, which their white hairs showed had not been brief; and they had done it this time too. And it was absolutely right that they should have been acquitted. It would only have been possible to get them by stretching the law, and it is better to let foxes go and leave the law unstretched. Von Papen had never performed an official act, not even to the initialling of a faintly dubious memorandum, which could be connected with the commission of a war crime or a crime against humanity. He had intrigued and bullied his way through artificially provoked diplomatic crises with the weaker powers, he had turned the German Embassy in Vienna into a thieves' kitchen where the downfall of Schuschnigg was planned and executed; but this skulduggery could not be related to the planning of aggressive warfare, and if he had been found guilty there would have been grounds for a comparison, which would have been quite unfair but very difficult to attack on logical grounds, with Sir Neville Henderson. As for Schacht, he had indeed found the money for the Nazis' rearmament programme, but rearmament itself had never been pronounced a crime; and it is impossible to conceive an article of international law which would have made him a criminal for his doings and not given grounds for a comparison with Lord Keynes. Indeed, the particular jiggery-pokery he had invented to make Germany's foreign trade a profitable racket, particularly in the Balkans, was so gloriously successful, and would have produced such staggering returns if it had been uninterrupted, that he cannot have wished for war.

But, all the same, these were not children of light, and the association of innocence with their names was entertaining. When the verdict on von Papen was pronounced the other defendants gave him good-natured, rallying glances of congratulation; and he looked just as any Foreign Office man would look on acquittal, modest and humorous and restrained. But when the defendants heard that Schacht was to go free, Göring laughed, but all the rest looked grim. A glance at Schacht showed that in this they were showing no unpardonable malice. He was sitting in his customary twisted attitude, to show that he had nothing to do with the defendants sitting beside him and was paying no attention to the proceedings of the court, his long neck stretched up as if to give him the chance to breathe the purer upper air, his face red with indignation. As he heard the verdict of not guilty he looked more indignant than ever, and he tossed his white hairs. Had anyone gone to him and congratulated him on his acquittal he would certainly have replied that he considered it insulting to suppose that any other verdict could have been passed on him, and that he was meditating an action for wrongful imprisonment. There was, to be sure, nothing unnatural or illogical in his attitude. The court had cleared him with no compliments but with no qualifications, and the charges which had been brought against him were definitely part of the more experimental side of Nuremberg. Why should he feel grateful for the acquittal that was his right? There was no reason at all. But it must have been trying to be incarcerated over months in the company of one whose reason was quite so net and dry, who was capable of such strictly logical behaviour as Schacht was to show over the affair of the orange.

This was quite a famous affair, for it amused the other defendants, who laughed at it as they had not been able to laugh at his acquittal, and told their wives. That was how it got known, long before one of the court psychiatrists told it in his book. Each defendant was given an orange with his lunch; and of the three acquitted men two had the same inspiration to perform a symbolic act of sympathy with their doomed comrades by giving their oranges away. Von Papen sent his to von Neurath, and Fritzsche sent his to von Schirach. But Schacht ate his own orange. And why not? Why should a man give up an orange which he had a perfect right to eat and send it to somebody else, just because he had been acquitted of crimes that he had committed? The laughter of his fellow prisoners was manifestly unjust. But surely they earned the right to be a little unjust, to laugh illogically, by what happened to them later at the afternoon session.

Something had happened to the architecture of the court which might happen in a dream. It had always appeared that the panelled wall behind the dock was solid. But one of the panels was really a door. It opened, and the convicted men came out one by one to stand between two guards and hear what they had earned. Göring, in his loose suit, which through the months had grown looser and looser, came through that door and looked surprised, like a man in pajamas who opens a door out of his hotel room in the belief that it leads to his bathroom and finds that he has walked out into a public room. Earphones were handed to him by the guard and he put them on, but at once made a gesture to show that they were not carrying the sound. They had had to put on a longer flex to reach from the ground to the ear of a standing man, and the adjustment had been faulty. His guards knelt down and worked on them. On the faces of all the judges there was written the thought, "Yes, this is a nightmare. This failure of the earphones proves it," and it was written on his face too. But he bent down and spoke to them and took a hand in the repair. This man of fifty-three could see the fine wires without spectacles. When the earphones were repaired he put them on with a steady hand and learned that this was not a nightmare, he was not dreaming. He took them off with something like a kingly gesture and went out, renouncing the multitudinous words and gesture that must have occurred to him at this moment. He was an inventive man and could not have had to look far for a comment which, poetic, patriotic, sardonic, or obscene, would certainly have held the ear of the court and sounded in history; and he was a man without taste. Yet at this moment he had taste enough to know that the idea of his death was more impressive than any of his own ideas.

A great mercy was conferred upon him. At this last moment that he would be seen by his fellow men it was not evident that he was among the most evil of human beings that have ever been born. He simply appeared as a man bravely sustaining the burden of fear. This mercy was extended to all the prisoners. It must be recorded that there was not a coward among them. Even Ribben-trop, who was white as stone because of his terror, showed a hard dignity, and Kaltenbrunner, who looked like a vicious horse and gave no promise of restraint, bowed quietly to the bench. Frank, the governor of Poland, he who had repented and become a good Catholic and wore black glasses more constantly than any of the others, gave an odd proof of his complete perturbation. He lost his sense of direction and stood with his back to the bench until he was spun round by the guards. But then he listened courageously enough to his sentence of death.

There was a deep unity in their behavior as there was a unity in their appearance. The only diversion was the mad little slap Hess gave the guards when they tried to hand him his earphones. He would not wear them, so he did not hear his sentence. The Service defendants, too, were distinct in their bearing, for they had experience of courts-martial and knew the protocol, and bowed and went out when their sentences were delivered. The others seemed to believe that the judge would add to their sentences some phrase of commination, and waited for it, looking straight in front of them; and, curiously enough, they seemed to be disappointed when the commination did not come. Perhaps they hoped that it would also be an explanation. That was what all in the court required: an explanation. We were going to hang eleven of these eighteen men, and imprison the other seven for ten, fifteen, twenty years, or for life; but we had no idea why they had done what they did. All but Streicher had Intelligence Quotients far above the average, and most of them had not been unfavoured in their circumstances. We had learned what they did, beyond all doubt, and that is the great achievment of the Nuremberg trial. No literate person can now pretend that these men were anything but abscesses of cruelty. But we learned nothing about them that we did not know before, except that they were capable of heroism to which they had no moral right, and that there is nothing in the legend that a bully is always a coward.

Then the court rose. It did so in the strict physical sense of the word. Usually when a court rises it never enjoys a foot of real elevation; the judge stalks from the bench, the lawyers and spectators debouch through the corridors, their steps heavy by reason of what they have just heard. But this court rose as a plane takes off, as gulls wheel off the sea when a siren sounds, as if it were going to fly out of the window, to soar off the roof. The courtroom was empty in a minute or two, and the staff hurried along the corridors into one another's offices, saying good-bye, good-bye to each other, good-bye to the trial, good-bye to the feeling of autumn that had grown so melancholy in these latter days, because of the reddening creepers and the ice in the sunshine, and these foreseen sentences of death.

The great left at once, that very day, if they were great enough, and so did some who were not so very great, but who, avid for home, had plotted for precedence as addicts plot to get drugs. The less great and the less farseeing had to wait their turn, for again transport could not meet the demands of the occasion, and the going was worse than the coming. Fog took a hand, and it was usually noon before the planes could leave the ground. Visitors and correspondents waited at the airport for days, some of them for a week, and more and more people tried to go away by train, and some who succeeded ran into awkward currency difficulties. And in the Palace of Justice there were packing cases on the floor of every office: the typewriters had to go home, the files had to go home, the stationery had to go home. Those who had finished and were free ran in and bent down beaming to say good-bye to those still on their knees beside these packing cases, who beamed up at them because they were to be free themselves quite soon, and cried happy thanks for the parting gift, which if they were to remain any time was often a pot of those prodigious cyclamens grown by the one-legged gardener in the greenhouse at the press camp. It was a party, it was like going off for a cruise, only instead of leaving home, you were going home, going home, going home.

JOHN BARTH

(1930–)

John Barth is considered a founder of the "postmodernist novel," a genre known for its irony and playfulness. His most famous works include *The Sot-Weed Factor* (1960), *Giles Goat-Boy* (1966), *Lost in the Funhouse* (1968), and *Chimera* (1972), which won the National Book Award in 1973. Born in Cambridge, Maryland, Barth attended the University of Maryland. From 1973 to 1991 he taught creative writing at Johns Hopkins University, where he is now Emeritus Professor. Most of Barth's fiction is set close to home in the tidewater Maryland area, including his first novel, *The Floating Opera*, written when he was only twenty-four and later nominated for the National Book Award.

While the excerpt is a wonderful example of Barth's comedic powers, *The Floating Opera* is also a philosophical novel. Its principal action takes place in the 1930s. Todd Andrews is a lawyer and self-proclaimed "cosmic cynic" who views his practice as a mere livelihood: "I consider it no more my career than a hundred other things." One of those other things is writing an *Inquiry* into his father's suicide and the question of whether he should follow suit. For years Todd has been having an affair with Jane, the wife of his best friend, Harrison Mack.

This excerpt recounts Todd's legal representation of Harrison in Harrison's claim to his late father's estate. The case, which takes a scatological turn, is a wickedly funny parody of the lengths to which clients and lawyers can go in their legal maneuvers. At stake is $3 million, bequeathed to various individuals and organizations in seventeen different wills. The contest narrows to a battle between Harrison and his mother, with Mrs. Mack eventually winning. However, Todd will later appeal the decision and devise a scheme that delays the appeal until one of the conservative judges on the Court of Appeals is replaced by a liberal (making a majority sympathetic to Harrison's politics), and the judgment will be reversed.

from THE FLOATING OPERA

— 1956 —

The law

That will-o'-the-wisp, the law: where shall I begin to speak of it? Is the law the legal rules, or their interpretations by judges, or by juries? Is it the precedent or the present fact? The norm or the practice? I think I'm not interested in what the law is.

Surely, though, I am curious about things that the law can be made to do, but this disinterestedly, without involvement. A child encounters a toy tractor, winds it up, and sets it climbing over a book. The tractor climbs well. The child puts another book here, so, and angles the first. The tractor surmounts them, with difficulty. The child opens the pages of the first book, leans the second obliquely against it, and places his shoe behind the two. The tractor tries, strains, spins, whirrs, and falls like a turtle on its back, treads racing uselessly. The child moves on to his crayons and picture puzzles, no expression on his face. I don't know what you mean, sir, when you speak of justice.

It may be that, like Capt. Osborn, you have come to believe that I have opinions about everything, absurd ones at that. Very well. But of most things about which people hold some sort of opinion, I have none at all, except by implication. What I mean is this: the law, for example, prescribes certain things that shall not be done, or certain ways in which things shall be done, but of most specific human acts it has nothing to say one way or the other. Yet these extralegal acts, or most of them, are certainly influenced and conditioned, implicitly, by the laws pertaining to other things. People, for example, aren't allowed to kill us while we're performing our extralegal acts. In the same way, though I have no opinion one way or the other on whether suicide, for instance, is a sin, I have certain opinions on a few other things that made it possible for me to contemplate suicide in 1937, and actually to resolve to destroy myself.

All right. I have no general opinions about the law, or about justice, and if I sometimes set little obstacles, books and slants, in the path of the courts, it is because I'm curious, merely, to see what will happen. On those occasions when the engine of the law falls impotently sprawling, I make a mental note of it, and without a change of expression, go on to my boat or my *Inquiry*. Winning or losing litigations is of no concern to me, and I think I've never made a secret of that fact to my clients. They come to me, and they come before the law, because *they* think they have a case. The law and I are uncommitted.

One more thing, before I explain the contest over Harrison Mack Senior's will: if you have followed this chapter so far, you might sensibly ask, "Doesn't your attitude—which is, after all, irresponsible—allow for the defeat, even the punishment, of the innocent, and at times the victory of the guilty? And does this not concern you?" It does indeed allow for the persecution of innocence—though perhaps not so frequently as you might imagine. And this persecution *concerns* me, in the sense that it holds my attention, but not especially in the sense that it bothers me. Under certain circumstances, to be explained later, I am not averse to pillorying the innocent, to throwing my stone, with the crowd, at some poor martyr. Irresponsibility, yes: I affirm, I insist upon my basic and ultimate irresponsibility. Yes indeed.

It did not deeply concern me, as I said before, whether Harrison received his inheritance or not, though I stood to profit by some fifty thousand dollars or more if he did. In any world but ours, the case of the Mack estate would be fantastic; even in ours, it received considerable publicity from the Maryland press.

Old man Mack, whom I've come to admire tremendously though I never met him, died in 1935, after years of declining physical and mental health. He left a large estate: stock in the Mack Pickle Co. amounting to 58 per cent of the total shares, and worth perhaps two million dollars in fairly good times; stock in various other business concerns, some more prosperous than others; a large house in Ruxton, another in West Palm Beach, and cottages in Nova Scotia and Maryland (including the one I was seduced in); extensive farmlands, especially cucumber farms, the crop from which was bought by the Mack Pickle Co.; perhaps a hundred thousand dollars in cash; assorted automobiles, cabin cruisers, horses, and dogs, and, through the majority stockholdings, the potential presidency of the pickle company, which office carried a salary of twenty-five thousand dollars a year. It was, undeniably, an estate that many people would consider worth going to court about.

Now of the several characteristics of Harrison *père*, three were important to the case: he was in the habit of using his wealth as a club to keep his kin in line; he was, apparently, addicted to the drawing up of wills; and, especially in his last years, he was obsessively jealous of the products of his mind and body, and permitted none to be destroyed.

You perhaps recall my saying that when I first met Harrison Junior, in 1925, he was undergoing an attack of communism, and had been disinherited as a result? It seems that disinheritance, or the threat of it, was the old man's favorite disciplinary measure, not only for his son, but also for his wife. When young Harrison attended Dartmouth rather than Johns

Hopkins; when he studied journalism rather than business; when he became a communist rather than a Republican; he was disinherited until such time as he mended his ways. When Mother Mack went to Europe rather than to West Palm Beach; when she chose sparkling burgundy over highballs, Dulaney Valley over Ruxton, Roosevelt and Garner over Hoover and Curtis; she was disinherited until such time as she recanted her heresies.

All these falls from and reinstatements to grace, of course, required emendations of Father Mack's will, and a number of extrafamiliar circumstances also demanded frequent revision of his bequests. His country club admits someone he doesn't like: the club must be disinherited. A pickle-truck driver runs down a state policeman checking on overloaded vehicles: the driver must be defended in court and provided for explicitly in the will. After the old man's death, when his safe was opened, a total of seventeen complete and distinct testamentary instruments was found, chronologically arranged, each beginning with a revocation of the preceding one. He hadn't been able to throw any of his soul-children into the fire.

Now this situation, though certainly unusual, would in itself have presented no particular problem of administration, because the law provides that where there are several wills, the last shall be considered representative of the testator's real intentions, other things being equal. And each of these wills explicitly revoked the preceding one. But alas, with Mr. Mack all other things weren't equal. Not only did his physical well-being deteriorate in his last years, through arthritis to leukemia to the grave; his sanity deteriorated also, gradually, along the continuum from relative normalcy through marked eccentricity to jibbering idiocy. In the first stages he merely inherited and disinherited his relatives and his society; in the second he no longer went to work, he required entertainment as well as care from his nurses, and he allowed nothing of his creation-including hair-and nail-clippings, urine, feces, and wills—to be thrown away; in the last stages he could scarcely move or talk, had no control whatever over his bodily functions, and recognized no one. To be sure, the stages were not dramatically marked, but blended into one another imperceptibly.

Of the seventeen wills (which represented by no means all the wills Mack had written, merely those written since he acquired his mania for preserving things), only the first two were composed during the time when the old man's sanity was pretty much indisputable; that is, prior to 1933. The first left about half the state to Harrison Junior and the other half to Mother Mack, provided it could not be demonstrated to the court that she had drunk any sparkling burgundy since 1920. This one was dated 1924. The other, dated 1932, left about half the estate to Mrs. Mack unconditionally and the rest to Harrison, provided it could not be demonstrated to the court that during a five-year probationary period, 1932–37, Harrison had done, written, or said anything that could reasonably be construed as evidence of communist sympathies. This clause, incidentally, ran through most of the subsequent testaments as well.

Of the other fifteen documents, ten were composed in 1933 and 1934, years when the testator's sanity was open to debate. The last five, all written in the first three months of 1935, could be established without much difficulty, in court, as being the whims of a lunatic: one left everything to Johns Hopkins University on condition that the University's name be changed to Hoover College (the University politely declined); others bequeathed the whole shebang to the Atlantic Ocean or the A.F.L.

Luckily for the majesty of Maryland's law, there were only two primary and four secondary contestants for the estate. Elizabeth Sweetman Mack, the testator's widow, was interested in having Will #6, a product of late 1933, adjudged the last testament: it bequeathed her virtually the entire estate, on the sparkling-burgundy condition described above. Harrison Junior preferred #8, the fruit of early 1934; it bequeathed *him* virtually the whole works, on the clean-skirts condition also described above. Misses Janice Kosko, Shirley Mae Greene, and Berenice Silverman, registered nurses all, who had attended old Mack during the first, second, and third stages, respectively, of his physical invalidity, liked Wills #3, 9, and 12, in that order: therein, apparently, their late employer provided them remuneration for services beyond the line of duty. The final contestant was the pastor of the Macks' neighborhood church: in Will #13 the bulk of the estate was to pass to that church, with the express hope that the richer and more influential organized religion became, the sooner it would be cast off by the people.

It was an edifying spectacle. Mrs. Mack retained Messrs. Dugan, Froebel & Kemp, of Baltimore, to defend her legal rights; her son retained Andrews, Bishop, & Andrews, of Cambridge; the nurses and the minister retained separate attorneys. Everyone was a little afraid to carry the thing to court immediately, and for several months there was a welter of legal nonsense, threats, and counterthreats, among the six firms involved. Five of us joined forces to oust the clergyman from the sweepstakes—it was enough for the three nurses to agree that Mack was definitely insane by the time Will #13 was composed. A month later, by pretty much the same technique, Misses Kosko and Greene induced Miss Silverman to withdraw, on the solemnly contracted condition that should either of them win, she would get 20 per cent of the loot. Then, in a surprise maneuver, Bill Froebel, of Dugan, Froebel & Kemp, produced sworn affidavits from two Negro maids of the Mack household, to the effect that they had seen Miss Greene indulging in "unnatural and beastly" practices with the deceased—the practices were described in toothsome detail—and suggested to that young lady that, should she not decide the contest wasn't worth the trouble, he would release the affidavits to the newspapers. I never learned for certain whether the affidavits were true or false, but in either case they were effective: the additional attraction of several thousand dollars, payable when Mrs. Mack won the case, induced Miss Greene to seek her happiness outside the courts.

The field was cleared, then, in 1936, of half the entries, before the race even began. Only Miss Kosko, Harrison Junior, and Mrs. Mack remained. Each of them, of necessity, must attempt to prove two things: that Father Mack was still legally sane when the will of their choice was written, and that by the time the subsequent wills were written, he no longer could comprehend what he was about. On this basis, Miss Kosko, I should say, had the strongest case, since her will (dated February 1933) was the earliest of the three. But love was her undoing: she retained as her attorney her boy friend, a lad fresh out of law school, none too bright. After our initial out-of-court sparring I was fairly confident that he was no match for either Froebel or myself, and when, late in 1936, he refused on ethical grounds a really magnanimous bribe from Froebel, I was certain.

And sure enough, when the first swords clashed in Baltimore Probate Court, in May of 1936, Froebel was able, with little trouble, to insinuate that the young lawyer was an ass; that the nurse Miss Kosko was a hussy out to defraud poor widows of their honest legacies by seducing old men in their dotage; that Mrs. Mack, out of the kindness of her bereaved heart, had already offered the trollop a gratuity more munificent than she deserved (this news was ruled out as incompetent evidence, of course); and that even to listen tolerantly to such ill-concealed avariciousness was a tribute to the patience and indulgence of long-suffering judges. In addition, Froebel must have offered some cogent arguments, for surrogate courts, even in Baltimore, are notoriously competent, and the judge ruled in his favor. When Froebel then offered Miss Kosko another settlement, considerably smaller than the first, the young barrister accepted it humbly, coming as it did on the heels of his defeat, and didn't even think of appealing the judgment until it was too late.

Then, in June of the same year, Froebel filed suit for Mrs. Mack, charging flatly that Mr. Mack had been of unsound mind when he wrote Will #8, Harrison's will, and never again regained his sanity. If the court so ruled, then Mrs. Mack's will, #6, would become the authentic testamentary instrument, since Miss Kosko was out of the running. If the court ruled against him, then our document, #8, would automatically revoke his.

There was not much difference between Mack's mental state in late 1933 and his mental state in early 1934. I introduced statements from Misses Kosko and Greene that in both years he required them to save the contents of his bedpan in dill-pickle jars, which were then stored in the wine cellar, and I got the impression that the judge—a staid fellow—believed Mack had been insane from the beginning. The newspapers, too, expressed the opinion that there was no particular evidence on either side, and that, besides, it was a disgraceful thing for a mother and her son to squabble so selfishly. All the pressure was for out-of-court settlement on a fifty-fifty basis, but both Harrison and his mother—who had never especially liked each other—refused, on the advice of their attorneys. Froebel thought he could win, and wanted the money; I thought I could win, and wanted to see.

Will #6, remember, gave all the estate to Mrs. Mack, provided she hadn't tasted sparkling burgundy since 1920. Our will left the money and property to Harrison, if he had steered clear of Moscow since 1932, and in addition, bequeathed to Mrs. Mack the several hundred pickle jars just mentioned. Both documents included the extraordinary provision that, should the separate conditions not be fulfilled, the terms were to be reversed.

Froebel's arguments, essentially, were two: (*1*) That a man has not necessarily lost his business sense if he provides once for a complete reversal of bequests, of the sort seen in Will #6, assuming he is really dead set against sparkling burgundy; but then to reverse himself completely in the space of a few months indicates that something has snapped in his head, since there were no dramatic external changes to account for the new will. (2) That the bequest of the pickle jars appeared in no wills before #8, and in all the wills from #8 through #16, and that such a bequest is evidence tending to show that Mack no longer understood the nature of his estate.

"Not necessarily," I suggested. "Suppose he didn't love his wife?"

"Ah," Froebel replied quickly, "but he left the pickle jars to a different person each time, not to Mrs. Mack every time."

"But remember," I said, "he saved the mess because he liked it; the bequest of it, then, is an act of love. Would you call love insane?"

"Indeed not," Froebel answered. "But if he'd loved her, he'd have given her the property as well as the—excrement."

"No indeed," I countered. "Remember that in one will he bequeathed all his money to the church because he disliked the church. Couldn't the bequest to my client be such an act, and the bequest to yours the real gift?"

"It could indeed," Froebel grinned. "Will you say that that's the case?"

"No, I shan't," I said. "I merely suggested the possibility."

"And in doing so," Froebel declared, "you suggest the possibility that Will Number Eight is as insane as Will Number Thirteen, the church will you mentioned. Anyone who bequeaths three millions of dollars as a punishment, I suggest, is out of perspective."

Oh, Bill Froebel was a lawyer. When it came to impromptu legal sophistry, he and I had no equals at the Maryland Bar.

My arguments were (*1*) that the inclusion of the pickle jars was hardly sufficient evidence of a sudden loss of understanding, when Mack had been collecting them since Will #3 or 4; (2) that therefore the testator was either sane when he composed both instruments or insane when he composed them; (3) that if he was sane both times, Will #8 was official; (4) that if insane both times, some earlier will was official and must be brought forward, or otherwise Mack could be deemed to have died intestate (in which case Harrison would get all the money, Mrs. Mack retaining only dower).

The judge, Frank Lasker of the Baltimore bench, agreed. Froebel appealed the decision through the Court of Appeals to the Maryland Supreme Court, and both appellate courts affirmed the lower court's judgment. It seemed as if Harrison were a wealthy man: all that remained was to wait until January of 1937—the end of his probationary period—and then to demonstrate that Harrison had kept clear of communist sympathy since 1932. He assured me that nothing could be suggested which could be called fellow-traveling, even remotely. Froebel threatened for a while to institute a new suit, in favor of Will #2, but nothing came of his threat.

The final test was in the form of a hearing. Harrison and I appeared at the Baltimore courthouse early in January; Judge Lasker read the terms of Will #8 and declared that if no one present could offer evidence of such sympathies as were therein interdicted, he was prepared to declare the matter settled and to order the will executed. Froebel then appeared, much to my surprise, and announced that he had such evidence, enough to warrant the reversal of bequests provided for by our will, and was ready to offer it to the court.

"You told me there wasn't anything," I reminded Harrison, who had turned white.

"I swear there isn't!" he whispered back, but nevertheless he began perspiring and trembling a little. I sat back to see what Froebel had cooked up.

"What will you attempt to prove?" the Judge asked him.

"That as recently as last year, your honor, while his poor father was in the grave—perhaps speeded there (who knows?) by his son's regrettable irresponsibility—that just last year, your honor, this son, who is now so eager to take from his mother what is rightfully hers, was aiding and abetting actively, with large gifts of money, that doctrine against which his father's entire life was such an eloquent argument; confident, I doubt not, that he could conceal his surreptitious Bolshevism until such time as he was in a position to devote the whole of the Mack estate toward overthrowing the way of life that made its accumulation possible!"

Froebel was a past master of the detached noun clause: judge and spectators were stirred.

"For heaven's sake!" Harrison whispered. "You don't think he means my Spanish donations!"

"If you were silly enough to make any, then I daresay he does," I replied, appalled anew at Harrison's innocence.

And indeed, the "Spanish donations" were precisely what Froebel had in mind. He offered in evidence photostated checks, four of them, for one thousand dollars each, made out to an American subscription agency representing the Spanish Loyalist government. They were dated March 10, May 19, September 2, and October 7, and all were signed *Harrison A. Mack, Jr.*

Judge Lasker examined the photostats and frowned. "Did you write these checks?" he asked Harrison, passing the pictures to him.

"Of course!" Harrison yelled. "What the hell's that—"

"Order!" suggested the Judge. "Aren't you aware that the Loyalist movement is run by the Communist Party? Directed from the Kremlin?"

"Aw, come on!" Harrison pleaded, until I poked him and he sat down.

"May I point out," Froebel continued blandly, "that not only is a gift to the Loyalists in essence a gift to Moscow, but this particular subscription agency is a Party organization under FBI surveillance. A man may donate to the Loyalists through honest, if vague, liberalism, I daresay; but one doesn't send checks to this subscription outfit unless one is sympathetic with the Comintern. Young Mr. Mack, like too many of our idle aristocrats, is, I fear, a blue blood with a Red heart."

I believe it was this final metaphor that won Froebel the judgment. I saw the newspaper people virtually doff their hats in tribute, and scribble the immortal words for the next editions of their papers. Even the Judge smiled benignly upon the trope: I could see that it struck him square in the prejudices, and found a welcome there.

There was some further discussion, but no one listened closely; everyone was repeating to himself, with a self-satisfied smile, that too many young aristocrats are blue bloods with Red hearts. *Blue bloods with Red hearts!* How could mere justice cope with poetry? Men, I think, are ever attracted to the *bon mot* rather than the *mot juste*, and judges, no less than other men, are often moved by considerations more aesthetic than judicial. Even I was not a little impressed, and regretted only that we had no jury to be overwhelmed by such a purple plum from the groves of advocacy. A *blue blood with a Red heart!* How brandish reasonableness against music? Should I hope to tip the scale with puny logic, when Froebel had Parnasus in his pan? In vain might I warn Judge Lasker that, through the press, all America was watching, and Europe as well, for his decision.

"My client, a lover of freedom and human dignity," I declared, "made his contributions to the oppressed Loyalists as a moral obligation, proper to every good American, to fight those Rebels who would crush the independence of the human spirit, and trample liberty under hobnailed boots! How can you charge him with advocating anarchy and violent overthrow, when in a single year he gives four thousand dollars to support the Spanish Government against those who would overthrow it?"

And on I went for some minutes, trying to make capital out of the Spanish confusion, wherein the radicals were the *status quo* and the reactionaries the rebels. It was an admirable bit of casuistry, but I knew my cause was lost. Only Froebel, I think, had ears for my rhetoric; the rest of the room was filled with *blue bloods with Red hearts*.

And Judge Lasker, as I think I mentioned, was famously conservative. Though by no means a fascist himself-he was probably uncommitted in the Spanish revolution-he epitomized the unthinking antagonism of his class toward anything pinker than the blue end of the spectrum: a familiar antagonism that used to infuriate me when, prior to 1924, I was interested in such things as social justice. When finally he ruled, he ruled in Froebel's favor.

"It does not matter whether there is a difference between the Moscow and Madrid varieties of communism," he declared, "or whether the Court or anyone else approves or disapproves of the defendant's gifts or the cause for which they were intended. The fact is that the subscription agency involved is a communist organization under government surveillance, and a gift to that agency is a gift to communism. There can be no question of the donor's sympathy with what the agency represented, and what it represented was communism. The will before me provides that should such sympathy be demonstrated, as it has been here, the terms of the document are to be reversed. The Court here orders such a reversal."

Well, we were poor again. Harrison went weak, and when I offered him a cigar he came near to vomiting.

"It's incredible!" he croaked, actually perspiring from the shock of it.

"Do you give up?" I asked him. "Or shall I appeal?"

He clutched at the hope. "Can we appeal?"

"Sure," I said. "Don't you see how unlogical Lasker's reasoning is?"

"Unlogical! It was so logical it overwhelmed me!"

"Not at all. He said the subscription agency was sympathetic to communism. You give money to the agency; therefore you're sympathetic to communism. It's like saying that if you give money to a Salvation Army girl who happens to be a vegetarian you're sympathetic to vegetarians. The communists support the Loyalists; you support the Loyalists; therefore you're a communist."

Harrison was tremendously relieved, but so weak he could scarcely stand. He laughed shortly.

"Well! That puts us back in the race, doesn't it? Ha, I'd thought there for a while—Christ, Toddy, you've saved my ass again! Damned judge! We've got it now, boy!"

I shook my head, and he went white again.

"What the hell's wrong?"

"I'll appeal," I said, "but we'll lose again, I guess."

"How's that? Lose again!" He laughed, and sucked in his breath.

"Forget about the logic," I said. "Nobody really cares about the logic. They make up their minds by their prejudices about Spain. I think you'd have lost here even without Froebel's metaphor. I'd have to talk Lasker into liberalism to win the case."

I went on to explain that of the seven judges of the Court of Appeals who would review the decision, three were Republicans with a pronounced anti-liberal bias, two were fairly liberal Democrats, one was a reactionary "Southern Democrat," more anti-liberal than the Republicans, and the seventh, an unenthusiastic Democrat, was relatively unbiased.

"I know them all," I said. "Abrams, Moore, and Stevens, the Republicans, will vote against you. Forrester, the Southern Democrat, would vote for you if it were a party issue, but it's not; he'll go along with the Republicans. Stedman and Barnes, the liberals, will go along with you, and I think Haddaway will too, because he likes me and because he dislikes Lasker's bad logic."

"But hell, that's four to three!" Harrison cried. "That means I lose!"

"As I said."

"How about the Maryland Supreme Court?"

"That's too much to predict," I said. "I don't know that they've declared themselves on Spain, and I don't know them personally. But they've affirmed almost every important verdict of the Court of Appeals in three years."

Harrison was crushed. "It's unjust!"

I smiled. "You know how these things are."

"Aw, but what the hell!" He shook his head, tapped his feet impatiently, pursed his lips, sighed in spasms. I expected him to faint, but he held on tightly, though he could scarcely talk. The truth was, of course, that it is one thing—an easy thing—to give what Cardinal Newman calls "notional" assent to a proposition such as "There is no justice"; quite another and more difficult matter to give it "real" assent, to learn it stingingly, to the heart, through involvement. I remember hoping that Harrison was strong enough at least to be educated by his expensive loss.

I appealed the judgment of the Court.

"Just to leave the door open," I explained. "I might think of something."

That evening, before I left Baltimore with Harrison, we had dinner at Bill Froebel's club, as his guests. I praised his inspiration, and he my logic-twisting. Harrison was morose, and although he drank heavily, he refused to join in the conversation. He couldn't drive home. On the way, he would clutch my arm and groan, "Three million bucks, Toddy!"

I looked coldly at him.

"Hell, man," he protested, "I know what you're thinking, but you should know me better. I don't want the money like another man might, just to go crazy on. Think what we could do on three million bucks, the three of us!"

It was the first time since Jane and I had resumed our affair in 1935 that Harrison had spoken again of "the three of us," as he had used to do.

"A million apiece?" I asked. "Or a joint account?"

Harrison felt the bristles and flinched, and all the way home he felt constrained to pretend that the loss of three million dollars touched his philosophical heart not at all. I watched the effort from the corner of my eye, and marveled sadly at his disorientation.

Finally he broke down, as we were crossing the Choptank River bridge, pulling into Cambridge. The water was white-capped and cold-looking. Dead ahead, at the end of the boulevard that the bridge ran onto, Morton's Marvelous Tomatoes, Inc., spread its red neon banner across the sky, and I smiled. The town lights ran in a flat string along the water's edge, from Hambrooks Bar Lighthouse, flashing on the right, to the Macks' house in East Cambridge, its ground-floor windows still lit, where Jane was waiting.

"I give up, Toddy," he said tersely. "I'm no philosopher. I can't say I wouldn't have been happy at one time without the money—I *did* get myself disinherited a few times, you know. But once it came so close and seemed so sure—"

"What is it?" I demanded.

"Ah, Christ—Janie and I had plans." He choked on his plans. "How the hell can I say it? I just don't feel like living any more."

"You *what?*" I sneered. "What'll you do—hang yourself in the cellar? There's a twentypenny nail right there, in a joist—you'll find it. It's already been broken in. And I know an undertaker who can turn black faces white again."

"All right, all right," Harrison said. "I don't care what you think. I said I'm no philosopher."

"Forget about philosophy," I said. "You don't lack philosophy; you lack guts. I suppose you're going to ask me to marry Jane afterwards, so the two of us can remember you? You're wallowing, Harrison. It's swinish."

"I'm weak, Toddy," he said. "I can't help it. Don't think I'm not ashamed of it."

"Then cut it out."

"You can't just cut it out," Harrison protested, and I sensed that he was growing stronger. "I'm past believing that people can change."

"You don't want to cut it out."

"Sure I do. It doesn't matter whether I do or not; I can't do it. I'm weak in some ways, Toddy. You don't understand that."

I flicked my cigarette out of the ventilator in a shower of sparks. We were off the bridge then, coasting along the dual highway in the Macks' big automobile.

"I know what weakness is. But you make your own difficulties, Harrison. It's hard because you never thought of it as easy. Listen. An act of will is the easiest thing there is—so easy it's laughable how people make mountains of it."

Harrison had by this time actually put aside the idea of his loss and was following the thought.

"You know better," he said. "You can't discount psychology."

"I'm not saying anything about psychology," I maintained. "Psychology doesn't interest me. We act as if we could choose, and so we can, in effect. All you have to do to be strong is stop being weak."

"Impossible."

"You never tried it."

Nor, alas, did he want to just then: I could see that plainly enough. We went into the house for a last drink. Jane had heard the news, of course, by telephone, and she cried awhile. I told her flatly that I had no sympathy for either of them while they behaved like that.

"What would *you* do, damn it!" she cried impatiently.

I laughed. "I've never lost three million bucks," I said, "but I'll tell you what I did once, after Dad hanged himself for losing a few thousand."

I told them then, for the first time, the story of my adventures with Col. Henry Morton—which story, reader, I'll pause to tell you, too, sooner or later, but not just now. I had decided that I didn't want Harrison to brood over his money: he wasn't ready to be strong of his own choosing yet, apparently, and so I opened the way toward turning him into a cynic, in emulation of me. He was ripe for it anyhow, it seemed to me, and even the one story might do the trick.

There's little need for weakness, reader: you are freer, perhaps, than you'd be comfortable knowing.

As I left, Jane asked me: "You don't have anything up your sleeve, Toddy?"

"I shan't commit myself," I said. "But Harrison might as well believe he's out three million bucks, at least for a while."

"What will he do?" she asked anxiously. "Did he say anything to you coming home?"

"He'll either grow stronger or hang himself," I predicted. "If he grows stronger it won't matter to him whether he gets the money or not, really, and then I wouldn't mind seeing him get it. If he kills himself over it, I'll be just as glad he's dead, frankly. Sissies make me uncomfortable. That goes for you, too. You're not ready for three million bucks yet. You don't deserve it."

Then I left. I suppose if *I* ever lost three million dollars I'd holler like a stuck hero. Or perhaps not: one really can't tell until the thing is upon one.

Well, the will case dropped out of the papers then; the Court of Appeals wouldn't hear the appeal for at least six months, though I doubted that they'd wait much longer than that. In the meantime, Lizzie Mack, Harrison's mother, couldn't use up the old man's estate (except for running expenses for the house), though it was temporarily hers.

I conducted, during the next few months, a rather intensive investigation into the characters of the appellate court judges—my findings confirmed my original estimate of the situation. As far as one with much information could guess, the decision would be four to three for Lizzie if the hearing were held when tentatively scheduled.

And if it weren't? I considered that question, sitting in my office, staring at my staring-wall opposite the desk. What advantage was there in delay, if any? And how could one delay the appeal? The advantage was negative: that is, I was certain of defeat if there were no delay; if there were any, I might very possibly still be defeated, but there would be more time for something to turn up. So, I suppose, a condemned man snatches at a day's reprieve, still hoping for a god on wires to fetch him off, and on the very gibbet, his neck roped, pleads eye-to-sky for the saving car. Who knows? Perhaps, hooded and dropped, he yet awaits in a second's agony for God's hands on him, till the noose cracks neck and hope in one sick snap. To be sure, ours was but a matter of money, but the principle was the same. By September the Loyalists might be winning, or it might become dangerous over here to like the fascists, the way Hitler was behaving. By October Franco might win, and the poor crushed Loyalists be pitied, then when they were no longer a threat. Anything could happen to swing one more vote our way. November was an off-year election month: perhaps some party issue would ally John Forrester, the reactionary Democrat, with his more liberal colleagues. Perhaps—

I smiled, moved my feet off the desk, and went to the file. I looked up each of the judges, checking the length of their incumbencies and the number of years in office remaining to each.

"Ah, Freddie Barnes, you old whoremonger," I cooed; "so you're up to the post again this year, are you?"

That fact mattered little, since Roosevelt was going great guns and Barnes was a popular figure in Maryland: he'd be re-elected without difficulty. Of the other Democrats, Forrester had two years to go, Haddaway had four, and Stedman had six. I checked the Republicans: Abrams had two years yet; Stevens, six; Moore—

"Well, well, well!" I grinned. "You rascal, Rollo! Time to run again, eh?"

Mrs. Lake, at my request, spent the rest of her afternoon telephoning various Baltimorians for me, some eminent and some shady, some honest and some flexible, some friendly and some employable. By quitting time I was one of perhaps seven people who knew as a fact, beyond puny speculation, that Judge Rollo Moore, despite the backing of Maryland republicanism, was going to lose his coming election by a well-insured margin to Joseph Singer, who, bless his heart, was a chronic if somewhat fuzzy liberal—a man after Harrison's own heart.

We would win, by God, almost certainly, if we could hold off the appeal until November!

PHILIP ROTH
(1933–)

"Eli, the Fanatic" first appeared in *Commentary* in April 1959 and was one of five stories published that same year in the collection *Goodbye, Columbus.* This book, Philip Roth's first, won considerable popular and critical acclaim, including the National Book Award.

Throughout his career Roth has been both reviled and admired as a quintessentially Jewish American writer. After the publication in *The New Yorker* in 1957 of a story that would appear in *Goodbye, Columbus,* some Jews criticized Roth's writing as anti-Semitic. Roth wrote, "At my lunch meeting about 'Defender of the Faith' with two representatives from the Anti-Defamation League, I said that being interviewed by them as an alleged purveyor of material harmful and defamatory to the Jews was particularly disorienting since, as a high school senior thinking about studying law, I had sometimes imagined working on their staff, defending the civil and legal rights of Jews." Roth has said that being charged with defamation at the start of his career probably gave his writing a direction and emphasis that it might not have had otherwise, and caused him to do two things: to explain himself and to defend himself.

Set in postwar New York suburbia, "Eli, The Fanatic" presents the dilemma of American Jews who long to be assimilated and accepted but, in attaining this goal, risk betraying not only those who suffered, but themselves. The title character is a nervous young Jewish lawyer who is called upon by fellow Jews in his affluent community to do something about the orthodox yeshiva that has opened in their midst, which is run by displaced persons from the war and becomes an embarrassment to the community. When Eli visits Rabbi Tzuref and invokes the town zoning laws, the rabbi tells him, "What you call law, I call shame. The heart, Mr. Peck, the heart is law!"

Philip Milton Roth was born in Newark, New Jersey, and educated at Bucknell and the University of Chicago. His best-known novel is *Portnoy's Complaint,* which was the best-selling fiction book of 1969 and became notorious for its sexual explicitness. Roth's prolific output also includes *The Ghost Writer* (1979), *The Counterlife* (1987; winner of the National Book Critics Circle Award), *Patrimony* (1991; National Book Critics Circle Award for biography/autobiography), *Operation Shylock* (1993; PEN/Faulkner Award), and *Sabbath's Theater* (1995; National Book Award).

ELI, THE FANATIC

— 1959 —

Leo Tzuref stepped out from back of a white column to welcome Eli Peck. Eli jumped back, surprised; then they shook hands and Tzuref gestured him into the sagging old mansion. At the door Eli turned, and down the slope of lawn, past the jungle of hedges, beyond the dark, untrampled horse path, he saw the street lights blink on in Woodenton. The stores along Coach House Road tossed up a burst of yellow—it came to Eli as a secret signal from his townsmen: "Tell this Tzuref where we stand, Eli. This is a modern community, Eli, we have our families, we pay taxes . . ." Eli, burdened by the message, gave Tzuref a dumb, weary stare.

"You must work a full day," Tzuref said, steering the attorney and his briefcase into the chilly hall.

Eli's heels made a racket on the cracked marble floor, and he spoke above it. "It's the commuting that's killing," he said, and entered the dim room Tzuref waved open for him. "Three hours a day . . . I came right from the train." He dwindled down into a harp-backed chair. He expected it would be deeper than it was and consequently jarred himself on the sharp bones of his seat. It woke him, this shiver of the behind, to his business. Tzuref, a bald shaggy-browed man who looked as if he'd once been very fat, sat back of an empty desk, halfway hidden, as though he were settled on the floor. Everything around him was empty. There were no books in the bookshelves, no rugs on the floor, no draperies in the big casement windows. As Eli began to speak Tzuref got up and swung a window back on one noisy hinge. "May and it's like August," he said, and with his back to Eli, he revealed the black circle on the back of his head. The crown of his head was missing! He returned through the dimness—the lamps had no bulbs—and Eli realized all he'd seen was a skullcap. Tzuref struck a match and lit a candle, just as the half-dying shouts of children at play rolled in through the open window. It was as though Tzuref had opened it so Eli could hear them.

"Aah, now," he said. "I received your letter."

Eli poised, waiting for Tzuref to swish open a drawer and remove the letter from his file. Instead the old man leaned forward onto his stomach, worked his hand into his pants pocket, and withdrew what appeared to be a week-old handkerchief. He uncrumpled it; he unfolded it; he ironed it on the desk with the side of his hand. "So," he said.

Eli pointed to the grimy sheet which he'd gone over word-by-word with his partners, Lewis and McDonnell. "I expected an answer," Eli said. "It's a week."

"It was so important, Mr. Peck, I knew you would come."

Some children ran under the open window and their mysterious babble—not mysterious to Tzuref, who smiled—entered the room like a third person. Their noise caught up against Eli's flesh and he was unable to restrain a shudder. He wished he had gone home, showered and eaten dinner, before calling on Tzuref. He was not feeling as professional as usual—the place was too dim, it was too late. But down in Woodenton they would be waiting, his clients and neighbors. He spoke for the Jews of Woodenton, not just himself and his wife.

"You understood?" Eli said.

"It's not hard."

"It's a matter of zoning . . ." and when Tzuref did not answer, but only drummed his fingers on his lips, Eli said, "We didn't make the laws . . ."

"You respect them."

"They protect us . . . the community."

"The law is the law," Tzuref said.

"Exactly!" Eli had the urge to rise and walk about the room.

"And then of course"—Tzuref made a pair of scales in the air with his hands—"The law is not the law. When is the law that is the law not the law?" He jiggled the scales. "And vice versa."

"Simply," Eli said sharply. "You can't have a boarding school in a residential area." He would not allow Tzuref to cloud the issue with issues. "We thought it better to tell you before any action is undertaken."

"But a house in a residential area?"

"Yes. That's what residential means." The DP's English was perhaps not as good as it seemed at first. Tzuref spoke slowly, but till then Eli had mistaken it for craft—or even wisdom. "Residence means home," he added.

"So this is my residence."

"But the children?"

"It is their residence."

"*Seventeen* children?"

"Eighteen," Tzuref said.

"But you *teach* them here."

"The Talmud. That's illegal?"

"That makes it school."

Tzuref hung the scales again, tipping slowly the balance.

"Look, Mr. Tzuref, in America we call such a place a boarding school."

"Where they teach the Talmud?"

"Where they teach period. You are the headmaster, they are the students."

Tzuref placed his scales on the desk. "Mr. Peck," he said, "I don't believe it . . ." but he did not seem to be referring to anything Eli had said.

"Mr. Tzuref, that is the law. I came to ask what you intend to do."

"What I *must* do?"

"I hope they are the same."

"They are." Tzuref brought his stomach into the desk. "We stay." He smiled. "We are tired. The headmaster is tired. The students are tired."

Eli rose and lifted his briefcase. It felt so heavy packed with the grievances, vengeances, and schemes of his clients. There were days when he carried it like a feather—in Tzuref's office it weighed a ton.

"Goodbye, Mr. Tzuref."

"Sholom," Tzuref said.

Eli opened the door to the office and walked carefully down the dark tomb of a corridor to the door. He stepped out on the porch and, leaning against a pillar, looked down across the lawn to the children at play. Their voices whooped and rose and dropped as they chased each other round the old house. The dusk made the children's game look like a tribal dance. Eli straightened up, started off the porch, and suddenly the dance was ended. A long piercing scream trailed after. It was the first time in his life anyone had run at the sight of him. Keeping his eyes on the lights of Woodenton, he headed down the path.

And then, seated on a bench beneath a tree, Eli saw him. At first it seemed only a deep hollow of blackness—then the figure emerged. Eli recognized him from the description. There he was, wearing the hat, that hat which was the very cause of Eli's mission, the source of Woodenton's upset. The town's lights flashed their message once again: "Get the one with the hat. What a nerve, what a nerve . . ."

Eli started towards the man. Perhaps he was less stubborn than Tzuref, more reasonable. After all, it was the law. But when he was close enough to call out, he didn't. He was stopped by the sight of the black coat that fell down below the man's knees, and the hands which held each other in his lap. By the round-topped, wide-brimmed Talmudic hat, pushed onto the back of his head. And by the beard, which hid his neck and was so soft and thin it fluttered away and back again with each heavy breath he took. He was asleep, his sidelocks curled loose on his cheeks. His face was no older than Eli's.

Eli hurried towards the lights.

The note on the kitchen table unsettled him. Scribblings on bits of paper had made history this past week. This one, however, was unsigned. "Sweetie," it said, "I went to sleep. I had a sort of Oedipal experience with the baby today. Call Ted Heller."

She had left him a cold soggy dinner in the refrigerator. He hated cold soggy dinners, but would take one gladly in place of Miriam's presence. He was ruffled, and she never helped that, not with her infernal analytic powers. He loved her when life was proceeding smoothly—and that was when she loved him. But sometimes Eli found being a lawyer surrounded him like quicksand—he couldn't get his breath. Too often he wished he were pleading for the other side; though if he were on the other side, then he'd wish he were on the side he was. The trouble was that sometimes the law didn't seem to be the answer, *law* didn't seem to have anything to do with what was aggravating everybody. And that, of course, made him feel foolish and unnecessary . . . Though that was not the situation here—the townsmen had a case. But not *exactly*, and if Miriam were awake to see Eli's upset, she would set about explaining his distress to him, understanding him, forgiving him, so as to get things back to Normal, for Normal was where they loved one another. The difficulty with Miriam's efforts was they only upset him more; not only did they explain little to him about himself or his predicament, but they convinced him of *her* weakness. Neither Eli nor Miriam, it turned out, was terribly strong. Twice before he'd faced this fact, and on both occasions had found solace in what his neighbors forgivingly referred to as "a nervous breakdown."

Eli ate his dinner with his briefcase beside him. Halfway through, he gave in to himself, removed Tzuref's notes, and put them on the table, beside Miriam's. From time to time he flipped through the notes, which had been carried into town by the one in the black hat. The first note, the incendiary:

To whom it may concern:

Please give this gentleman the following: Boys shoes with rubber heels and soles.

5 prs size 6c
3 prs size 5c
3 prs size 5b
2 prs size 4a
3 prs size 4c
1 pr size 7b
1 pr size 7c

Total 18 prs. boys shoes. This gentleman has a check already signed. Please fill in correct amount.

L. TZUREF
Director, Yeshivah of Woodenton, N.Y.
(5/8/48)

"Eli, a regular greenhorn," Ted Heller had said. "He didn't say a word. Just handed me the note and stood there, like in the Bronx the old guys who used to come around selling Hebrew trinkets."

"A Yeshivah!" Artie Berg had said. "Eli, in Woodenton, a Yeshivah! If I want to live in Brownsville, Eli, I'll live in Brownsville."

"Eli," Harry Shaw speaking now, "the old Puddington place. Old man Puddington'll roll over in his grave. Eli, when I left the city, Eli, I didn't plan the city should come to me."

Note number two:

Dear Grocer:

Please give this gentleman ten pounds of sugar. Charge it to our account, Yeshivah of Woodenton, NY—which we will now open with you and expect a bill each month. The gentleman will be in to see you once or twice a week.

L. TZUREF, *Director*
(5/10/48)

P.S. Do you carry kosher meat?

"He walked right by my window, the greenie," Ted had said, "and he nodded, Eli. He's my *friend* now."

"Eli," Artie Berg had said, "he handed the damn thing to a *clerk* at Stop N' Shop—and in that hat yet!"

"Eli," Harry Shaw again, "it's not funny. Someday, Eli, it's going to be a hundred little kids with little *yamalkahs* chanting their Hebrew lessons on Coach House Road, and then it's not going to strike you funny."

"Eli, what goes on up there—my kids hear strange sounds."

"Eli, this is a modern community."

"Eli, we pay taxes."

"Eli."

"Eli!"

"*Eli!*"

At first it was only another townsman crying in his ear; but when he turned he saw Miriam, standing in the doorway, behind her belly.

"Eli, sweetheart, how was it?"

"He sai'd no."

"Did you see the other one?" she asked.

"Sleeping, under a tree."

"Did you let him know how people feel?"

"He was sleeping."

"Why didn't you wake him up? Eli, this isn't an everyday thing."

"He was tired!"

"Don't shout, please," Miriam said.

" 'Don't shout. I'm pregnant. The baby is heavy.' " Eli found he was getting angry at nothing she'd said yet; it was what she was going to say.

"He's a very heavy baby the doctor says," Miriam told him.

"Then sit *down* and make my dinner." Now he found himself angry about her not being present at the dinner which he'd just been relieved that she wasn't present at. It was as though he had a raw nerve for a tail, that he kept stepping on. At last Miriam herself stepped on it.

"Eli, you're upset. I understand."

"You *don't* understand."

She left the room. From the stairs she called, "I do, sweetheart."

It was a trap! He would grow angry knowing she would be "understanding." She would in turn grow more understanding seeing his anger. He would in turn grow angrier . . . The phone rang.

"Hello," Eli said.

"Eli, Ted. So?"

"So nothing."

"Who is Tzuref? He's an American guy?"

"No. A DP. German."

"And the kids?"

"DP's too. He teaches them."

"What? What subjects?" Ted asked.

"I don't know."

"And the guy with the hat, you saw the guy with the hat?"

"Yes. He was sleeping."

"Eli, he sleeps with the *hat?*"

"He sleeps with the hat."

"Goddam fanatics," Ted said. "This is the twentieth century, Eli. Now it's the guy with the hat. Pretty soon all the little Yeshivah boys'll be spilling down into town."

"Next thing they'll be after our daughters."

"Michele and Debbie wouldn't look at them."

"Then," Eli mumbled, "you've got nothing to worry about, Teddie," and he hung up.

In a moment the phone rang. "Eli? We got cut off. We've got nothing to worry about? You worked it out?"

"I have to see him again tomorrow. We can work something out."

"That's fine, Eli. I'll call Artie and Harry."

Eli hung up.

"I thought you said *nothing* worked out." It was Miriam.

"I did."

"Then why did you tell Ted *something* worked out?"

"It did."

"Eli, maybe you should get a little more therapy."

"That's enough of that, Miriam."

"You can't function as a lawyer by being neurotic. That's no answer."

"You're ingenious, Miriam."

She turned, frowning, and took her heavy baby to bed.

The phone rang.

"Eli, Artie. Ted called. You worked it out? No trouble?"

"Yes."

"When are they going?"

"Leave it to me, will you, Artie? I'm tired. I'm going to sleep."

In bed Eli kissed his wife's belly and laid his head upon it to think. He laid it lightly, for she was that day entering the second week of her ninth month. Still, when she slept, it was a good place to rest, to rise and fall with her breathing and figure things out. "If that guy would take off that crazy hat. I know it, what eats them. If he'd take off that crazy hat everything would be all right."

"What?" Miriam said.

"I'm talking to the baby."

Miriam pushed herself up in bed. "Eli, please, baby, shouldn't you maybe stop in to see Dr. Eckman, just for a little conversation?"

"I'm fine."

"Oh, sweetie!" she said, and put her head back on the pillow.

"You know what your mother brought to this marriage—a sling chair and a goddam New School enthusiasm for Sigmund Freud."

Miriam feigned sleep, he could tell by the breathing.

"I'm telling the kid the truth, aren't I, Miriam? A sling chair, three months to go on a *New Yorker* subscription, and *An Introduction to Psychoanalysis*. Isn't that right?"

"Eli, must you be aggressive?"

"That's all you worry about, is your insides. You stand in front of the mirror all day and look at yourself being pregnant."

"Pregnant mothers have a relationship with the fetus that fathers can't understand."

"Relationship my ass. What is my liver doing now? What is my small intestine doing now? Is my island of Lagerhans on the blink?"

"Don't be jealous of a little fetus, Eli."

"I'm jealous of your island of Lagerhans!"

"Eli, I can't argue with you when I know it's not me you're really angry with. Don't you see, sweetie, you're angry with yourself."

"You and Eckman."

"Maybe he could help, Eli."

"Maybe he could help you. You're practically lovers as it is."

"You're being hostile again," Miriam said.

"What do you care—it's only *me* I'm being hostile towards."

"Eli, we're going to have a beautiful baby, and I'm going to have a perfectly simple delivery, and you're going to make a fine father, and there's absolutely no reason to be obsessed with whatever is on your mind. All we have to worry about—" she smiled at him "—is a name."

Eli got out of bed and slid into his slippers. "We'll name the kid Eckman if it's a boy and Eckman if it's a girl."

"Eckman Peck sounds terrible."

"He'll have to live with it," Eli said, and he went down to his study where the latch on his briefcase glinted in the moonlight that came through the window.

He removed the Tzuref notes and read through them all again. It unnerved him to think of all the flashy reasons his wife could come up with for his reading and rereading the notes. "Eli, why are you so *preoccupied* with Tzuref?" "Eli, stop getting *involved*. Why do you think you're getting *involved*, Eli?" Sooner or later, everybody's wife finds their weak spot. His goddam luck he had to be neurotic! Why couldn't he have been born with a short leg.

He removed the cover from his typewriter, hating Miriam for the edge she had. All the time he wrote the letter, he could hear what she would be saying about his not being *able* to let the matter drop. Well, her trouble was that she wasn't *able* to face the matter. But he could hear her answer already: clearly, he was guilty of "a reaction formation." Still, all the fancy phrases didn't fool Eli: all she wanted really was for Eli to send Tzuref and family on their way, so that the community's temper would quiet, and the calm circumstances of their domestic happiness return. All she wanted were order and love in her private world. Was she so wrong? Let the world bat its brains out—in Woodenton there should be peace. He wrote the letter anyway:

Dear Mr. Tzuref:

Our meeting this evening seems to me inconclusive. I don't think there's any reason for us not to be able to come up with some sort of compromise that will satisfy the Jewish community of Woodenton and the Yeshivah and yourself. It seems to me that what most disturbs my neighbors are the visits to town by the gentleman in the black hat, suit, etc. Woodenton is a progressive suburban community whose members, both Jewish and Gentile, are anxious that their families live in comfort and beauty and serenity. This is, after all, the twentieth century, and we do not think it too much to ask that the members of our community dress in a manner appropriate to the time and place.

Woodenton, as you may not know, has long been the home of well-to-do Protestants. It is only since the war that Jews have been able to buy property here, and for Jews and Gentiles to live beside each other in amity. For this adjustment to be made, both Jews and Gentiles alike have had to give up some of their more extreme practices in order not to threaten or offend the other. Certainly such amity is to be desired. Perhaps if such conditions had existed in prewar Europe, the persecution of the Jewish people, of which you and those 18 children have been victims, could not have been carried out with such success—in fact, might not have been carried out at all.

Therefore, Mr. Tzuref, will you accept the following conditions? If you can, we will see fit not to carry out legal action against the Yeshivah for failure to comply with township Zoning ordinances No. 18 and No. 23. The conditions are simply:

1. The religious, educational, and social activities of the Yeshivah of Woodenton will be confined to the Yeshivah grounds.

2. Yeshivah personnel are welcomed in the streets and stores of Woodenton provided they are attired in clothing usually associated with American life in the 20th century.

If these conditions are met, we see no reason why the Yeshivah of Woodenton cannot live peacefully and satisfactorily with the Jews of Woodenton—as the Jews of Woodenton have come to live with the Gentiles of Woodenton. I would appreciate an immediate reply.

Sincerely,

ELI PECK, *Attorney*

Two days later Eli received his immediate reply:

Mr. Peck:
The suit the gentleman wears is all he's got.

Sincerely,
Leo Tzuref, Headmaster

Once again, as Eli swung around the dark trees and onto the lawn, the children fled. He reached out with his briefcase as if to stop them, but they were gone so fast all he saw moving was a flock of skullcaps.

"Come, come . . ." a voice called from the porch. Tzuref appeared from behind a pillar. Did he *live* behind those pillars? Was he just watching the children at play? Either way, when Eli appeared, Tzuref was ready, with no fore-warning.

"Hello," Eli said.

"Sholom."

"I didn't mean to frighten them."

"They're scared, so they run."

"I didn't do anything."

Tzuref shrugged. The little movement seemed to Eli strong as an accusation. What he didn't get at home, he got here.

Inside the house they took their seats. Though it was lighter than a few evenings before, a bulb or two would have helped. Eli had to hold his briefcase towards the window for the last gleamings. He removed Tzuref's letter from a manila folder. Tzuref removed Eli's letter from his pants pocket. Eli removed the carbon of his own letter from another manila folder. Tzuref removed Eli's first letter from his back pocket. Eli removed the carbon from his briefcase. Tzuref raised his palms. ". . . It's all I've got . . ."

Those upraised palms, the mocking tone—another accusation. It was a crime to keep carbons! Everybody had an edge on him—Eli could do no right.

"I offered a compromise, Mr. Tzuref. You refused."

"Refused, Mr. Peck? What is, is."

"The man could get a new suit."

"That's all he's got."

"So you told me," Eli said.

"So I told you, so you know."

"It's not an insurmountable obstacle, Mr. Tzuref. We have stores."

"For that too?"

"On Route 12, a Robert Hall—"

"To take away the one thing a man's got?"

"Not take away, *replace.*"

"But I tell you he has nothing. *Nothing.* You have that word in English? *Nicht? Gornisht?*"

"Yes, Mr. Tzuref, we have the word."

"A mother and a father?" Tzuref said. "No. A wife? No. A baby? A little ten-month-old baby? No! A village full of friends? A synagogue where you knew the feel of every seat under your pants? Where with your eyes closed you could smell the cloth of the Torah?" Tzuref pushed out of his chair, stirring a breeze that swept Eli's letter to the floor. At the window he leaned out, and looked, beyond Woodenton. When he turned he was shaking a finger at Eli. "And a medical experiment they performed on him yet! That leaves nothing, Mr. Peck. Absolutely nothing!"

"I misunderstood."

"No news reached Woodenton?"

"About the suit, Mr. Tzuref. I thought he couldn't afford another."

"He can't."

They were right where they'd begun. "Mr. Tzuref!" Eli demanded. "*Here?*" He smacked his hand to his billfold.

"Exactly!" Tzuref said, smacking his own breast.

"Then we'll buy him one!" Eli crossed to the window and taking Tzuref by the shoulders, pronounced each word slowly. "We-will-pay-for-it. All right?"

"Pay? What, diamonds!"

Eli raised a hand to his inside pocket, then let it drop. Oh stupid! Tzuref, father to eighteen, had smacked not what lay under his coat, but deeper, under the ribs.

"Oh . . ." Eli said. He moved away along the wall. "The suit is all he's got then."

"You got my letter," Tzuref said.

Eli stayed back in the shadow, and Tzuref turned to his chair. He swished Eli's letter from the floor, and held it up. "You say too much . . . all this reasoning . . . all these conditions . . ."

"What can I do?"

"You have the word 'suffer' in English?"

"We have the word suffer. We have the word law too."

"Stop with the law! You have the word suffer. Then try it. It's a little thing."

"They won't," Eli said.

"But you, Mr. Peck, how about you?"

"I am them, they are me, Mr. Tzuref."

"Aach! You are us, we are you!"

Eli shook and shook his head. In the dark he suddenly felt that Tzuref might put him under a spell. "Mr. Tzuref, a little light?"

Tzuref lit what tallow was left in the holders. Eli was afraid to ask if they couldn't afford electricity. Maybe candles were all they had left.

"Mr. Peck, who made the law, may I ask you that?"

"The people."

"No."

"Yes."

"Before the people."

"No one. Before the people there was no law." Eli didn't care for the conversation, but with only candlelight, he was being lulled into it.

"Wrong," Tzuref said.

"We make the law, Mr. Tzuref. It is our community. These are my neighbors. I am their attorney. They pay me. Without law there is chaos."

"What you call law, I call shame. The heart, Mr. Peck, the heart is law! God!" he announced.

"Look, Mr. Tzuref, I didn't come here to talk metaphysics. People use the law, it's a flexible thing. They protect what they value, their property, their well-being, their happiness—"

"Happiness? They hide their shame. And you, Mr. Peck, you are shameless?"

"We do it," Eli said, wearily, "for our children. This is the twentieth century . . ."

"For the goyim maybe. For me the Fifty-eighth." He pointed at Eli. "That is too old for shame."

Eli felt squashed. Everybody in the world had evil reasons for his actions. Everybody! With reasons so cheap, who buys bulbs. "Enough wisdom, Mr. Tzuref. Please. I'm exhausted."

"Who isn't?" Tzuref said.

He picked Eli's papers from his desk and reached up with them. "What do you intend for us to do?"

"What you must," Eli said. "I made the offer."

"So he must give up his suit?"

"Tzuref, Tzuref, leave me be with that suit! I'm not the only lawyer in the world. I'll drop the case, and you'll get somebody who won't talk compromise. Then you'll have no home, no children, nothing. Only a lousy black suit! Sacrifice what you want. I know what I would do."

To that Tzuref made no answer, but only handed Eli his letters.

"It's not me, Mr. Tzuref, it's them."

"They are you."

"No," Eli intoned, "I am me. They are them. You are you."

"You talk about leaves and branches. I'm dealing with under the dirt."

"Mr. Tzuref, you're driving me crazy with Talmudic wisdom. This is that, that is the other thing. Give me a straight answer."

"Only for straight questions."

"Oh, God!"

Eli returned to his chair and plunged his belongings into his case. "Then, that's all," he said angrily.

Tzuref gave him the shrug.

"Remember, Tzuref, you called this down on yourself."

"*I* did?"

Eli refused to be his victim again. Double-talk proved nothing.

"Goodbye," he said.

But as he opened the door leading to the hall, he heard Tzuref.

"And your wife, how is she?"

"Fine, just fine." Eli kept going.

"And the baby is due when, any day?"

Eli turned. "That's right."

"Well," Tzuref said, rising. "Good luck."

"You know?"

Tzuref pointed out the window—then, with his hands, he drew upon himself a beard, a hat, a long, long coat. When his fingers formed the hem they touched the floor. "He shops two, three times a week, he gets to know them."

"He *talks* to them?"

"He sees them."

"And he can tell which is my wife?"

"They shop at the same stores. He says she is beautiful. She has a kind face. A woman capable of love . . . though who can be sure."

"*He* talks about *us*, to *you?*" demanded Eli.

"You talk about us, to her?"

"Goodbye, Mr. Tzuref."

Tzuref said, "Sholom. And good luck—I know what it is to have children. Sholom," Tzuref whispered, and with the whisper the candles went out. But the instant before, the flames leaped into Tzuref's eyes, and Eli saw it was not luck Tzuref wished him at all.

Outside the door, Eli waited. Down the lawn the children were holding hands and whirling around in a circle. At first he did not move. But he could not hide in the shadows all night. Slowly he began to slip along the front of the house. Under his hands he felt where bricks were out. He moved in the shadows until he reached the side. And then, clutching his briefcase to his chest, he broke across the darkest spots of the lawn. He aimed for a distant glade of woods, and when he reached it he did not stop, but ran through until he was so dizzied that the trees seemed to be running beside him, fleeing not towards Woodenton but away. His lungs were nearly ripping their seams as he burst into the yellow glow of the Gulf station at the edge of town.

"Eli, I had pains today. Where were you?"

"I went to Tzuref."

"Why didn't you call? I was worried."

He tossed his hat past the sofa and onto the floor. "Where are my winter suits?"

"In the hall closet. Eli, it's May."

"I need a strong suit." He left the room, Miriam behind him.

"Eli, talk to me. Sit down. Have dinner. Eli, what are you doing? You're going to get moth balls all over the carpet."

He peered out from the hall closet. Then he peered in again—there was a zipping noise, and suddenly he swept a greenish tweed suit before his wife's eyes.

"Eli, I love you in that suit. But not now. Have something to eat. I made dinner tonight—I'll warm it."

"You've got a box big enough for this suit?"

"I got a Bonwit's box, the other day. Eli, *why*?"

"Miriam, you see me doing something, let me do it."

"You haven't eaten."

"I'm *doing* something." He started up the stairs to the bedroom.

"Eli, would you please tell me what it is you want, and why?"

He turned and looked down at her. "Suppose this time you give me the reasons *before* I tell you what I'm doing. It'll probably work out the same anyway."

"Eli, I want to help."

"It doesn't concern you."

"But I want to help *you*," Miriam said.

"Just be quiet, then."

"But you're upset," she said, and she followed him up the stairs, heavily, breathing for two.

"Eli, what now?"

"A shirt." He yanked open all the drawers of their new teak dresser. He extracted a shirt.

"Eli, batiste? With a tweed suit?" she inquired.

He was at the closet now, on his knees. "Where are my cordovans?"

"Eli, why are you doing this so compulsively? You look like you *have* to do something."

"Oh, Miriam, you're supersubtle."

"Eli, stop this and talk to me. Stop it or I'll call Dr. Eckman."

Eli was kicking off the shoes he was wearing. "Where's the Bonwit box?"

"Eli, do you want me to have the baby right *here!*"

Eli walked over and sat down on the bed. He was draped not only with his own clothing, but also with the greenish tweed suit, the batiste shirt, and under each arm a shoe. He raised his arms and let the shoes drop onto the bed. Then he undid his necktie with one hand and his teeth and added that to the booty.

"Underwear," he said. "He'll need underwear."

"Who!"

He was slipping out of his socks.

Miriam kneeled down and helped him ease his left foot out of the sock. She sat with it on the floor. "Eli, just lie back. Please."

"Plaza 9-3103."

"What?"

"Eckman's number," he said. "It'll save you the trouble."

"Eli—"

"You've got that goddam tender 'You need help' look in your eyes, Miriam, don't tell me you don't."

"I don't."

"I'm not flipping," Eli said.

"I know, Eli."

"Last time I sat in the bottom of the closet and chewed on my bedroom slippers. That's what I did."

"I know."

"And I'm not doing that. This is not a nervous breakdown, Miriam, let's get that straight."

"Okay," Miriam said. She kissed the foot she held. Then, softly, she asked, "What *are* you doing?"

"Getting clothes for the guy in the hat. Don't tell me why, Miriam. Just let me do it."

"That's all?" she asked.

"That's all."

"You're not leaving?"

"No."

"Sometimes I think it gets too much for you, and you'll just leave."

"What gets too much?"

"I don't *know*, Eli. Something gets too much. Whenever everything's peaceful for a long time, and things are nice and pleasant, and we're expecting to be even happier. Like now. It's as if you don't think we *deserve* to be happy."

"Damn it, Miriam! I'm giving this guy a new suit, is that all right? From now on he comes into Woodenton like everybody else, is that all right with you?"

"And Tzuref moves?"

"I don't even know if he'll take the suit, Miriam! What do you have to bring up moving!"

"Eli, I didn't bring up moving. Everybody did. That's what everybody wants. Why make everybody un*happy*. It's even a law, Eli."

"Don't tell me what's the law."

"All right, sweetie. I'll get the box."

"*I'll* get the box. Where is it?"

"In the basement."

When he came up from the basement, he found all the clothes neatly folded and squared away on the sofa: shirt, tie, shoes, socks, underwear, belt, and an old gray flannel suit. His wife sat on the end of the sofa, looking like an anchored balloon.

"Where's the green suit?" he said.

"Eli, it's your loveliest suit. It's my favorite suit. Whenever I think of you, Eli, it's in that suit."

"Get it out."

"Eli, it's a Brooks Brothers suit. You say yourself how much you love it."

"Get it out."

"But the gray flannel's more practical. For shopping."

"Get it out."

"You go overboard, Eli. That's your trouble. You won't do anything in moderation. That's how people destroy themselves."

"I do *everything* in moderation. That's my trouble. The suit's in the closet again?"

She nodded, and began to fill up with tears. "Why docs it have to be *your* suit? Who are you even to decide to give a suit? What about the others?" She was crying openly, and holding her belly. "Eli, I'm going to have a baby. Do we need all *this?*" and she swept the clothes off the sofa to the floor.

At the closet Eli removed the green suit. "It's a J. Press," he said, looking at the lining.

"I hope to hell he's happy with it!" Miriam said, sobbing.

A half hour later the box was packed. The cord he'd found in the kitchen cabinet couldn't keep the outfit from popping through. The trouble was there was too much: the gray suit *and* the green suit, an oxford shirt as well as the batiste. But let him have two suits! Let him have three, four, if only this damn silliness would stop! And a hat—of course! God, he'd almost forgotten the hat. He took the stairs two at a time and in Miriam's closet yanked a hatbox from the top shelf. Scattering hat and tissue paper to the floor, he returned downstairs, where he packed away the hat he'd worn that day. Then he looked at his wife, who lay outstretched on the floor before the fireplace. For the third time in as many minutes she was saying, "Eli, this is the real thing."

"Where?"

"Right under the baby's head, like somebody's squeezing oranges."

Now that he'd stopped to listen he was stupefied. He said, "But you have two more weeks . . ." Somehow he'd really been expecting it was to go on not just another two weeks, but another nine months. This led him to suspect, suddenly, that his wife was feigning pain so as to get his mind off delivering the suit. And just as suddenly he resented himself for having such a thought. God, what had he become! He'd been an unending bastard towards her since this Tzuref business had come up—just when her pregnancy must have been most burdensome. He'd allowed her no access to him, but still, he was sure, for good reasons: she might tempt him out of his confusion with her easy answers. He could be tempted all right, it was why he fought so hard. But now a sweep of love came over him at the thought of her contracting womb, and his child. And yet he would not indicate it to her. Under such splendid marital conditions, who knows but she might extract some promise from him about his concern with the school on the hill.

Having packed his second bag of the evening, Eli sped his wife to Woodenton Memorial. There she proceeded not to have her baby, but to lie hour after hour through the night having at first oranges, then bowling balls, then basketballs, squeezed back of her pelvis. Eli sat in the waiting room, under the shattering African glare of a dozen rows of fluorescent bulbs, composing a letter to Tzuref.

Dear Mr. Tzuref:

The clothes in this box are for the gentleman in the hat. In a life of sacrifice what is one more? But in a life of no sacrifices even one is impossible. Do you see what I'm saying, Mr. Tzuref? I am not a Nazi who would drive eighteen children, who are probably frightened at the sight of a firefly, into homelessness. But if you want a home here, you must accept what we have to offer. The world is the world, Mr. Tzuref. As you would say, what is, is. All we say to this man is change your clothes. Enclosed are two suits and two shirts, and everything else he'll need, including a new hat. When he needs new clothes let me know.

We await his appearance in Woodenton, as we await friendly relations with the Yeshivah of Woodenton.

He signed his name and slid the note under a bursting flap and into the box. Then he went to the phone at the end of the room and dialed Ted Heller's number.

"Hello."

"Shirley, it's Eli."

"Eli, we've been calling all night. The lights are on in your place, but nobody answers. We thought it was burglars."

"Miriam's having the baby."

"At home?" Shirley said. "Oh, Eli, what a fun-idea!"

"Shirley, let me speak to Ted."

After the ear-shaking clatter of the phone whacking the floor, Eli heard footsteps, breathing, throat-clearing, then Ted. "A boy or a girl?"

"Nothing yet."

"You've given Shirley the bug, Eli. Now she's going to have *our* next one at home."

"Good."

"That's a terrific way to bring the family together, Eli."

"Look, Ted, I've settled with Tzuref."

"When are they going?"

"They're not exactly going, Teddie. I settled it—you won't even know they're there."

"A guy dressed like 1000 B.C. and I won't know it? What are you thinking about, pal?"

"He's changing his clothes."

"Yeah, to what? Another funeral suit?"

"Tzuref promised me, Ted. Next time he comes to town, he comes dressed like you and me."

"What! Somebody's kidding somebody, Eli."

Eli's voice shot up. "If he says he'll do it, he'll do it!"

"And, Eli," Ted asked, "he said it?"

"He said it." It cost him a sudden headache, this invention.

"And suppose he doesn't change, Eli. Just suppose. I mean that *might* happen, Eli. This might just be some kind of stall or something."

"No," Eli assured him.

The other end was quiet a moment. "Look, Eli," Ted said, finally, "he changes. Okay? All right? But they're still up there, aren't they? *That* doesn't change."

"The point is you won't know it."

Patiently Ted said, "Is this what we asked of you, Eli? When we put our faith and trust in you, is that what we were asking? We weren't concerned that this guy should become a Beau Brummel, Eli, believe me. We just don't think this is the community for them. And, Eli, we isn't me. The Jewish members of the community appointed me, Artie, and Harry to see what could be done. And we appointed you. And what's happened?"

Eli heard himself say, "What happened, happened."

"Eli, you're talking in crossword puzzles."

"My wife's having a baby," Eli explained, defensively.

"I realize that, Eli. But this is a matter of zoning, isn't it? Isn't that what we discovered? You don't abide by the ordinance, you go. I mean I can't raise mountain goats, say, in my backyard—"

"This isn't so simple, Ted. People are involved—"

"People? Eli, we've been through this and through this. We're not just dealing with people—these are religious fanatics is what they are. Dressing like that. What I'd really like to find out is what goes on up there. I'm getting more and more skeptical, Eli, and I'm not afraid to admit it. It smells like a lot of hocus-pocus abracadabra stuff to me. Guys like Harry, you know, they think and they think and they're afraid to admit what they're thinking. I'll tell you. Look, I don't even know about this Sunday school business. Sundays I drive my oldest kid all the way to Scarsdale to learn Bible stories . . . and you know what she comes up with? This Abraham in the Bible was going to kill his own kid for a sacrifice. She gets nightmares from it, for God's sake! You call that religion? Today a guy like that they'd lock him up. This is an age of science, Eli. I size people's feet with an X-ray machine, for God's sake. They've disproved all that stuff, Eli, and I refuse to sit by and watch it happening on my own front lawn."

"Nothing's happening on your front lawn, Teddie. You're exaggerating, nobody's sacrificing their kid."

"You're damn right, Eli—I'm not sacrificing mine. You'll see when you have your own what it's like. All the place is, is a hideaway for people who can't face life. It's a matter of *needs*. They have all these superstitions, and why do you think? Because they can't face the world, because they can't take their place in society. That's no environment to bring kids up in, Eli."

"Look, Ted, see it from another angle. We can convert them," Eli said, with half a heart.

"What, make a bunch of Catholics out of them? Look, Eli—pal, there's a good healthy relationship in this town because it's modern Jews and Protestants. That's the point, isn't it, Eli? Let's not kid each other, I'm not Harry. The way things are now are fine—like human beings. There's going to be no pogroms in Woodenton. Right? 'Cause there's no fanatics, no crazy people—" Eli winced, and closed his eyes a second—"just people who respect each other, and leave each other be. Common sense is the ruling thing, Eli. I'm for common sense. Moderation."

"Exactly, exactly, Ted. I agree, but common sense, maybe, says make this guy change his clothes. Then maybe—"

"Common sense says that? Common sense says to me they go and find a nice place somewhere else, Eli. New York is the biggest city in the world, it's only 30 miles away—why don't they go there?"

"Ted, give them a chance. Introduce them to common sense."

"Eli, you're dealing with *fanatics*. Do they display common sense? Talking a dead language, that makes sense? Making a big thing out of suffering, so you're going oy-oy-oy all your life, that's common sense? Look, Eli, we've been through all this. I don't know if you know—but there's talk that *Life* magazine is sending a guy out to the Yeshivah for a story. With pictures."

"Look, Teddie, you're letting your imagination get inflamed. I don't think *Life*'s interested."

"But I'm interested, Eli. And we thought you were supposed to be."

"I am," Eli said, "I am. Let him just change the clothes, Ted. Let's see what happens."

"They live in the medieval ages, Eli—it's some superstition, some *rule*."

"Let's just *see*," Eli pleaded.

"Eli, every day—"

"One more day," Eli said. "If he doesn't change in one more day. . . ."

"What?"

"Then I get an injunction first thing Monday. That's that."

"Look, Eli—it's not up to me. Let me call Harry—"

"You're the spokesman, Teddie. I'm all wrapped up here with Miriam having a baby. Just give me the day—them the day."

"All right, Eli. I want to be fair. But tomorrow, that's all. Tomorrow's the judgment day, Eli, I'm telling you."

"I hear trumpets," Eli said, and hung up. He was shaking inside—Teddie's voice seemed to have separated his bones at the joints. He was still in the phone booth when the nurse came to tell him that Mrs. Peck would positively not be delivered of a child until the morning. He was to go home and get some rest, he looked like *he* was having the baby. The nurse winked and left.

But Eli did not go home. He carried the Bonwit box out into the street with him and put it in the car. The night was soft and starry, and he began to drive the streets of Woodenton. Square cool windows, apricot-colored, were all one could see beyond the long lawns that fronted the homes of the townsmen. The stars polished the permanent baggage carriers atop the station wagons in the driveways. He drove slowly, up, down, around. Only his tires could be heard taking the gentle curves in the road.

What peace. What incredible peace. Have children ever been so safe in their beds? Parents—Eli wondered—so full in their stomachs? Water so warm in its boilers? Never. Never in Rome, never in Greece. Never even did walled cities have it so good! No wonder then they would keep things just as they were. Here, after all, were peace and safety—what civilization had been working toward for centuries. For all his jerkiness, that was all Ted Heller was asking for, peace and safety. It was what his parents had asked for in the Bronx, and his grandparents in Poland, and theirs in Russia or Austria, or wherever else they'd fled to or from. It was what Miriam was asking for. And now they had it—the world was at last a place for families, even Jewish families. After all these centuries, maybe there just had to be this communal toughness—or numbness—to protect such a blessing. Maybe that was the trouble with the Jews all along—too soft. Sure, to live takes guts . . . Eli was thinking as he drove on beyond the train station, and parked his car at the darkened Gulf station. He stepped out, carrying the box.

At the top of the hill one window trembled with light. What *was* Tzuref doing up there in that office? Killing babies—probably not. But studying a language no one understood? Practicing customs with origins long forgotten? Suffering sufferings already suffered once too often? Teddie was right—why keep it up! However, if a man chose to be stubborn, then he couldn't expect to survive. The world is give-and-take. What sense to sit and brood over a suit. Eli would give him one last chance.

He stopped at the top. No one was around. He walked slowly up the lawn, setting each foot into the grass, listening to the shh shhh shhhh his shoes made as they bent the wetness into the sod. He looked around. Here there was nothing. Nothing! An old decaying house—and a suit.

On the porch he slid behind a pillar. He felt someone was watching him. But only the stars gleamed down. And at his feet, off and away, Woodenton glowed up. He set his package on the step of the great front door.

Inside the cover of the box he felt to see if his letter was still there. When he touched it, he pushed it deeper into the green suit, which his fingers still remembered from winter. He should have included some light bulbs. Then he slid back by the pillar again, and this time there was something on the lawn. It was the second sight he had of him. He was facing Woodenton and barely moving across the open space towards the trees. His right fist was beating his chest. And then Eli heard a sound rising with each knock on the chest. What a moan! It could raise hair, stop hearts, water eyes. And it did all three to Eli, plus more. Some feeling crept into him for whose deepness he could find no word. It was strange. He listened—it did not hurt to hear this moan. But he wondered if it hurt to make it. And so, with only stars to hear, he tried. And it did hurt. Not the bumblebee of noise that turned at the back of his throat and winged out his nostrils. What hurt buzzed down. It stung and stung inside him, and in turn the moan sharpened. It became a scream, louder, a song, a crazy song that whined through the pillars and blew out to the grass, until the strange hatted creature on the lawn turned and threw his arms wide, and looked in the night like a scarecrow.

Eli ran, and when he reached the car the pain was only a bloody scratch across his neck where a branch had whipped back as he fled the greenie's arms.

The following day his son was born. But not till one in the afternoon, and by then a great deal had happened.

First, at nine-thirty the phone rang. Eli leaped from the sofa—where he'd dropped the night before—and picked it screaming from the cradle. He could practically smell the hospital as he shouted into the phone, "Hello, yes!"

"Eli, it's Ted. Eli, he *did* it. He just walked by the store. I was opening the door, Eli, and I turned around and I swear I thought it was you. But it was him. He still walks like he did, but the clothes, Eli, the clothes."

"Who?"

"The greenie. He has on man's regular clothes. And the suit, it's a beauty."

The suit barreled back into Eli's consciousness, pushing all else aside. "What color suit?"

"Green. He's just strolling in the green suit like it's a holiday. Eli . . . is it a Jewish holiday?"

"Where is he now?"

"He's walking straight up Coach House Road, in this damn tweed job. Eli, it worked. You were right."

"We'll see."

"What next?"

"We'll see."

He took off the underwear in which he'd slept and went into the kitchen where he turned the light under the coffee. When it began to perk he held his head over the pot so it would steam loose the knot back of his eyes. It still hadn't when the phone rang.

"Eli, Ted again. Eli, the guy's walking up and down every street in town. Really, he's on a tour or something. Artie called me, Herb called me. Now Shirley calls that he just walked by our house. Eli, go out on the porch you'll see."

Eli went to the window and peered out. He couldn't see past the bend in the road, and there was no one in sight.

"Eli?" He heard Ted from where he dangled over the telephone table. He dropped the phone into the hook, as a few last words floated up to him—"Eliyousawhim . . . ?" He threw on the pants and shirt he'd worn the night before and walked barefoot on to his front lawn. And sure enough, his apparition appeared around the bend: in a brown hat a little too far down on his head, a green suit too far back on the shoulders, an unbuttoned-down button-down shirt, a tie knotted so as to leave a two-inch tail, trousers that cascaded onto his shoes—he was shorter than that black hat had made him seem. And moving the clothes was that walk that was not a walk, the tiny-stepped shlumpy gait. He came round the bend, and for all his strangeness—it clung to his whiskers, signaled itself in his locomotion—he looked as if he belonged. Eccentric, maybe, but he belonged. He made no moan, nor did he invite Eli with wide-flung arms. But he did stop when he saw him. He stopped and put a hand to his hat. When he felt for its top, his hand went up too high. Then it found the level and fiddled with the brim. The fingers fiddled, fumbled, and when they'd finally made their greeting, they traveled down the fellow's face and in an instant seemed to have touched each one of his features. They dabbed the eyes, ran the length of the nose, swept over the hairy lip, until they found their home in the hair that hid a little of his collar. To Eli the fingers said, *I have a face, I have a face at least*. Then his hand came through the beard and when it stopped at his chest it was like a pointer—and the eyes asked a question as tides of water shifted over them. *The face is all right, I can keep it?* Such a look was in those eyes that Eli was still seeing them when he turned his head away. They were the hearts of his jonquils, that only last week had appeared—they were the leaves on his birch, the bulbs in his coach lamp, the droppings on his lawn: those eyes were the eyes in his head. They were his, he had made them. He turned and went into his house and when he peeked out the side of the window, between shade and molding, the green suit was gone.

The phone rang.

"Eli, Shirley."

"I saw him, Shirley," and he hung up.

He sat frozen for a long time. The sun moved around the windows. The coffee steam smelled up the house. The phone began to ring, stopped, began again. The mailman came, the cleaner, the bakery man, the gardener, the ice cream man, the League of Women Voters lady. A Negro woman spreading some strange gospel calling for the revision of the Food and Drug Act knocked at the front, rapped the windows, and finally scraped a half-dozen pamphlets under the back door. But Eli only sat, without underwear, in last night's suit. He answered no one.

Given his condition, it was strange that the trip and crash at the back door reached his inner ear. But in an instant he seemed to melt down into the crevices of the chair, then to splash up and out to where the clatter had been. At the door he waited. It was silent, but for a fluttering of damp little leaves on the trees. When he finally opened the door, there was no one there. He'd expected to see green, green, green, big as the doorway, topped by his hat, waiting for him with those eyes. But there was no one out there, except for the Bonwit's box which lay bulging at his feet. No string tied it and the top rode high on the bottom.

The coward! He couldn't do it! He couldn't!

The very glee of that idea pumped fuel to his legs. He tore out across his back lawn, past his new spray of forsythia, to catch a glimpse of the bearded one fleeing naked through yards, over hedges and fences, to the safety of his hermitage. In the distance a pile of pink and white stones—which Harriet Knudson had painted the previous day—tricked him. "Run," he shouted to the rocks, "Run, you . . ." but he caught his error before anyone else did, and though he peered and craned there was no hint anywhere of a man about his own size, with white, white, terribly white skin (how white must be the skin of his body!) in cowardly retreat. He came slowly, curiously, back to the door. And while the trees shimmered in the light wind, he removed the top from the box. The shock at first was the shock of having daylight turned off all at once. Inside the box was an eclipse. But black soon sorted from black, and shortly there was the glassy black of lining, the coarse black of trousers, the dead black of fraying threads, and in the center the mountain of black: the hat. He picked the box from the doorstep and carried it inside. For the first time in his life he *smelled* the color of blackness: a little stale, a little sour, a little old, but nothing that could overwhelm you. Still, he held the package at arm's length and deposited it on the dining room table.

Twenty rooms on a hill and they store their old clothes with me! What am I supposed to do with them? Give them to charity? That's where they came from. He picked up the hat by the edges and looked inside. The crown was smooth as an egg, the brim practically threadbare. There is nothing else to do with a hat in one's hands but put it on, so Eli dropped the thing on his head. He opened the door to the hall closet and looked at himself in the full-length mirror. The hat gave him bags under the eyes. Or perhaps he had not slept well. He pushed the brim lower till a shadow touched his lips. Now the bags under his eyes had inflated to become his face. Before the mirror he unbuttoned his shirt, unzipped his trousers, and then, shedding his clothes, he studied what he was. What a silly disappointment to see yourself naked in a hat. Especially in that hat. He sighed, but could not rid himself of the great weakness that suddenly set on his muscles and joints, beneath the terrible weight of the stranger's strange hat.

He returned to the dining room table and emptied the box of its contents: jacket, trousers, and vest (*it* smelled deeper than blackness). And under it all, sticking between the shoes that looked chopped and bitten, came the first gleam of white. A little fringed serape, a gray piece of semi-underwear, was crumpled at the bottom, its thready border twisted into itself. Eli removed it and let it hang free. What is it? For warmth? To wear beneath underwear in the event of a chest cold? He held it to his nose but it did not smell from Vick's or mustard plaster. It was something special, some Jewish thing. Special food, special language, special prayers, why not special BVD's? So fearful was he that he would be tempted back into wearing his traditional clothes—reasoned Eli—that he had carried and buried in Woodenton everything, including the special underwear. For that was how Eli now understood the box of clothes. The greenie was saying, Here, I give up. I refuse even to be tempted. We surrender. And that was how Eli continued to understand it until he found he'd slipped the white fringy surrender flag over his hat and felt it clinging to his chest. And now, looking at himself in the mirror, he was momentarily uncertain as to who was tempting who into what. Why *did* the greenie leave his clothes? Was it even the greenie? Then who was it? And why? But, Eli, for Christ's sake, in an age of science things don't happen like that. Even the goddam pigs take drugs . . .

Regardless of who was the source of the temptation, what was its end, not to mention its beginning, Eli, some moments later, stood draped in black, with a little white underneath, before the full-length mirror. He had to pull down on the trousers so they would not show the hollow of his ankle. The greenie, didn't he wear socks? Or had he forgotten them? The mystery was solved when Eli mustered enough courage to investigate the trouser pockets. He had expected some damp awful thing to happen to his fingers should he slip them down and out of sight—but when at last he jammed bravely down he came up with a khaki army sock in each hand. As he slipped them over his toes, he invented a genesis: a G.I.'s present in 1945. Plus everything else lost between 1938 and 1945, he had also lost his socks. Not that he had lost the socks, but that he'd had to stoop to accepting these, made Eli almost cry. To calm himself he walked out the back door and stood looking at his lawn.

On the Knudson back lawn, Harriet Knudson was giving her stones a second coat of pink. She looked up just as Eli stepped out. Eli shot back in again and pressed himself against the back door. When he peeked between the curtain all he saw were paint bucket, brush, and rocks scattered on the Knudsons' pink-spattered grass. The phone rang. Who was it—Harriet Knudson? Eli, there's a Jew at your door. *That's me.* Nonsense, Eli, I saw him with my own eyes. *That's me, I saw you too, painting your rocks pink.* Eli, you're having a nervous breakdown again. Jimmy, Eli's having a nervous breakdown again. Eli, this is Jimmy, hear you're having a little breakdown, anything I can do, boy? Eli, this is Ted, Shirley says you need help. Eli, this is Artie, you need help. Eli, Harry, you need help you need help . . . The phone rattled its last and died.

"God helps them who help themselves," intoned Eli, and once again he stepped out the door. This time he walked to the center of his lawn and in full sight of the trees, the grass, the birds, and the sun, revealed that it was he, Eli, in the costume. But nature had nothing to say to him, and so stealthily he made his way to the hedge separating his property from the field beyond and he cut his way through, losing his hat twice in the underbrush. Then, clamping the hat to his head, he began to run, the threaded tassels jumping across his heart. He ran through the weeds and wild flowers, until on the old road that skirted the town he slowed up. He was walking when he approached the Gulf station from the back. He supported himself on a huge tireless truck rim, and among tubes, rusted engines, dozens of topless oil cans, he rested. With a kind of brainless cunning, he readied himself for the last mile of his journey.

"How are you, Pop?" It was the garage attendant, rubbing his greasy hands on his overalls, and hunting among the cans.

Eli's stomach lurched and he pulled the big black coat round his neck.

"Nice day," the attendant said and started around to the front.

"Sholom," Eli whispered and zoomed off towards the hill.

The sun was directly overhead when Eli reached the top. He had come by way of the woods, where it was cooler, but still he was perspiring beneath his new suit. The hat had no sweatband and the cloth clutched his head. The children were playing. The children were always playing, as if it was that alone that Tzuref had to teach them. In their shorts, they revealed such thin legs that beneath one could see the joints swiveling as they ran. Eli waited for them to disappear around a corner before he came into the open. But something would not let him wait—his green suit. It was on the porch, wrapped around the bearded fellow, who was painting the base of a pillar. His arm went up and down, up and down, and the pillar glowed like white fire. The very sight of him popped Eli out of the woods onto the lawn. He did not turn back, though his insides did. He walked up the lawn, but the children played on; tipping the black hat, he mumbled, "Shhh . . . shhhh," and they hardly seemed to notice.

At last he smelled paint.

He waited for the man to turn to him. He only painted. Eli felt suddenly that if he could pull the black hat down over his eyes, over his chest and belly and legs, if he could shut out all light, then a moment later he would be home in bed. But the hat wouldn't go past his forehead. He couldn't kid himself—he was there. No one he could think of had forced him to do this.

The greenie's arm flailed up and down on the pillar. Eli breathed loudly, cleared his throat, but the greenie wouldn't make life easier for him. At last, Eli had to say "Hello."

The arm swished up and down; it stopped—two fingers went out after a brush hair stuck to the pillar.

"Good day," Eli said.

The hair came away; the swishing resumed.

"Sholom," Eli whispered and the fellow turned.

The recognition took some time. He looked at what Eli wore. Up close, Eli looked at what he wore. And then Eli had the strange notion that he was two people. Or that he was one person wearing two suits. The greenie looked to be suffering from a similar confusion. They stared long at one another. Eli's heart shivered, and his brain was momentarily in such a mixed-up condition that his hands went out to button down the collar of his shirt that somebody else was wearing. What a mess! The greenie flung his arms over his face.

"What's the matter . . ." Eli said. The fellow had picked up his bucket and brush and was running away. Eli ran after him.

"I wasn't going to hit . . ." Eli called. "Stop . . ." Eli caught up and grabbed his sleeve. Once again, the greenie's hands flew up to his face. This time, in the violence, white paint spattered both of them.

"I only want to . . ." But in that outfit Eli didn't really know what he wanted. "To talk . . ." he said finally. "For you to look at me. Please, just *look* at me . . ."

The hands stayed put, as paint rolled off the brush onto the cuff of Eli's green suit.

"Please . . . please," Eli said, but he did not know what to do. "Say something, speak *English*," he pleaded.

The fellow pulled back against the wall, back, back, as though some arm would finally reach out and yank him to safety. He refused to uncover his face.

"Look," Eli said, pointing to himself. "It's your suit. I'll take care of it."

No answer—only a little shaking under the hands, which led Eli to speak as gently as he knew how.

"We'll . . . we'll moth-proof it. There's a button missing"—Eli pointed—"I'll have it fixed. I'll have a zipper put in . . . Please, please—just look at me . . ." He was talking to himself, and yet how could he stop? Nothing he said made any sense—that alone made his heart swell. Yet somehow babbling on, he might babble something that would make things easier between them. "Look . . ." He reached inside his shirt to pull the frills of underwear into the light. "I'm wearing the special underwear, even . . . Please," he said, "*please, please, please*" he sang, as as if it were some sacred word. "Oh, *please* . . ."

Nothing twitched under the tweed suit—and if the eyes watered, or twinkled, or hated, he couldn't tell. It was driving him crazy. He had dressed like a fool, and for what? For this? He reached up and yanked the hands away.

"There!" he said—and in that first instant all he saw of the greenie's face were two white droplets stuck to each cheek.

"Tell me—" Eli clutched his hands down to his sides—"Tell me, what can I do for you, I'll do it . . ."

Stiffly, the greenie stood there, sporting his two white tears.

"Whatever I can do . . . Look, look, what I've done *already*." He grabbed his black hat and shook it in the man's face.

And in exchange, the greenie gave him an answer. He raised one hand to his chest, and then jammed it, finger first, towards the horizon. And with what a pained look! As though the air were full of razors! Eli followed the finger and saw beyond the knuckle, out past the nail, Woodenton.

"What do you want?" Eli said. "I'll bring it!"

Suddenly the greenie made a run for it. But then he stopped, wheeled, and jabbed that finger at the air again. It pointed the same way. Then he was gone.

And then, all alone, Eli had the revelation. He did not question his understanding, the substance or the source. But with a strange, dreamy elation, he started away.

On Coach House Road, they were double-parked. The Mayor's wife pushed a grocery cart full of dog food from Stop N' Shop to her station wagon. The President of the Lions Club, a napkin around his neck, was jamming pennies into the meter in front of the Bit-in-Teeth Restaurant. Ted Heller caught the sun as it glazed off the new Byzantine mosaic entrance to his shoe shop. In pinkened jeans, Mrs. Jimmy Knudson was leaving Halloway's Hardware, a paint bucket in each hand. Roger's Beauty Shoppe had its doors open—women's heads in silver bullets far as the eye could see. Over by the barbershop the pole spun, and Artie Berg's youngest sat on a red horse, having his hair cut; his mother flipped through *Look*, smiling: the greenie had changed his clothes.

And into this street, which seemed paved with chromium, came Eli Peck. It was not enough, he knew, to walk up one side of the street. That was not enough. Instead he walked ten paces up one side, then on an angle, crossed to the other side, where he walked ten more paces, and crossed back. Horns blew, traffic jerked, as Eli made his way up Coach House Road. He spun a moan high up in his nose as he walked. Outside no one could hear him, but he felt it vibrate the cartilage at the bridge of his nose.

Things slowed around him. The sun stopped rippling on spokes and hubcaps. It glowed steadily as everyone put on brakes to look at the man in black. They always paused and gaped, whenever he entered the town. Then in a minute, or two, or three, a light would change, a baby squawk, and the flow continue. Now, though lights changed, no one moved.

"He shaved his beard," Eric the barber said.

"Who?" asked Linda Berg.

"The . . . the guy in the suit. From the place there."

Linda looked out the window.

"It's Uncle Eli," little Kevin Berg said, spitting hair.

"Oh, God," Linda said, "Eli's having a nervous breakdown."

"A nervous breakdown!" Ted Heller said, but not immediately. Immediately he had said "Hoooly . . ."

Shortly, everybody in Coach House Road was aware that Eli Peck, the nervous young attorney with the pretty wife, was having a breakdown. Everybody except Eli Peck. He knew what he did was not insane, though he felt every inch of its strangeness. He felt those black clothes as if they were the skin of his skin—the give and pull as they got used to where he bulged and buckled. And he felt eyes, every eye on Coach House Road. He saw headlights screech to within an inch of him, and stop. He saw mouths: first the bottom jaw slides forward, then the tongue hits the teeth, the lips explode, a little thunder in the throat, and they've said it: Eli Peck Eli Peck Eli Peck Eli Peck. He began to walk slowly, shifting his weight down and forward with each syllable: E-li-Peck-E-li-Peck-E-li-Peck. Heavily he trod, and as his neighbors uttered each syllable of his name, he felt each syllable shaking all his bones. He knew who he was down to his marrow—they were telling him. Eli Peck. He wanted them to say it a thousand times, a million times, he would walk forever in that black suit, as adults whispered of his strangeness and children made "Shame . . . shame" with their fingers.

"It's going to be all right, pal . . ." Ted Heller was motioning to Eli from his doorway. "C'mon, pal, it's going to be all right . . ."

Eli saw him, past the brim of his hat. Ted did not move from his doorway, but leaned forward and spoke with his hand over his mouth. Behind him, three customers peered through the doorway. "Eli, it's Ted, remember Ted . . ."

Eli crossed the street and found he was heading directly towards Harriet Knudson. He lifted his neck so she could see his whole face.

He saw her forehead melt down to her lashes. "Good morning, Mr. Peck."

"Sholom," Eli said, and crossed the street where he saw the President of the Lions.

"Twice before . . ." he heard someone say, and then he crossed again, mounted the curb, and was before the bakery, where a delivery man charged past with a tray of powdered cakes twirling above him. "Pardon me, Father," he said, and scooted into his truck. But he could not move it. Eli Peck had stopped traffic.

He passed the Rivoli Theater, Beekman Cleaners, Harris' Westinghouse, the Unitarian Church, and soon he was passing only trees. At Ireland Road he turned right and started through Woodenton's winding streets. Baby carriages stopped whizzing and creaked—"Isn't that . . ." Gardeners held their clipping. Children stepped from the sidewalk and tried the curb. And Eli greeted no one, but raised his face to all. He wished passionately that he had white tears to show them . . . And not till he reached his own front lawn, saw his house, his shutters, his new jonquils, did he remember his wife. And the child that must have been born to him. And it was then and there he had the awful moment. He could go inside and put on his clothes and go to his wife in the hospital. It was not irrevocable, even the walk wasn't. In Woodenton memories are long but fury short. Apathy works like forgiveness. Besides, when you've flipped, you've flipped—it's Mother Nature.

What gave Eli the awful moment was that he turned away. He knew exactly what he could do but he chose not to. To go inside would be to go halfway. There was more . . . So he turned and walked towards the hospital and all the time he quaked an eighth of an inch beneath his skin to think that perhaps he'd chosen the crazy way. To think that he'd *chosen* to be crazy! But if you chose to be crazy, then you weren't crazy. It's when you didn't choose. No, he wasn't flipping. He had a child to see.

"Name?"

"Peck."

"Fourth floor." He was given a little blue card.

In the elevator everybody stared. Eli watched his black shoes rise four floors.

"Four."

He tipped his hat, but knew he couldn't take it off.

"Peck," he said. He showed the card.

"Congratulations," the nurse said. ". . . the grandfather?"

"The father. Which room?"

She led him to 412. "A joke on the Mrs?" she said, but he slipped in the door without her.

"Miriam?"

"Yes?"

"Eli."

She rolled her white face towards her husband. "Oh, Eli . . . Oh, Eli."

He raised his arms. "What could I do?"

"You have a son. They called all morning."

"I came to see him."

"Like *that*!" she whispered harshly. "Eli, you can't go around like that."

"I have a son. I want to see him."

"Eli, why are you doing this to me!" Red seeped back into her lips. "*He's* not your fault," she explained. "Oh, Eli, sweetheart, why do you feel guilty about everything. Eli, change your clothes. I forgive you."

"Stop forgiving me. Stop understanding me."

"But I love you."

"That's something else."

"But, sweetie, you *don't* have to dress like that. You didn't do anything. You don't have to feel guilty because . . . because everything's all right. Eli, can't you see that?"

"Miriam, enough reasons. Where's my son?"

"Oh, please, Eli, don't flip now. I need you now. Is that why you're flipping—because I need you?"

"In your selfish way, Miriam, you're very generous. I want my son."

"Don't flip now. I'm afraid, now that he's out." She was beginning to whimper. "I don't know if I love him, now that he's out. When I look in the mirror, Eli, he won't be there . . . Eli, Eli, you look like you're going to your own funeral. Please, can't you leave well enough *alone*? Can't we just have a family?"

"No."

In the corridor he asked the nurse to lead him to his son. The nurse walked on one side of him, Ted Heller on the other.

"Eli, do you want some help? I thought you might want some help."

"No."

Ted whispered something to the nurse; then to Eli he whispered, "Should you be walking around like this?"

"Yes."

In his ear Ted said, "You'll . . . you'll frighten the kid . . ."

"There," the nurse said. She pointed to a bassinet in the second row and looked, puzzled, to Ted. "Do I go in?" Eli said.

"No," the nurse said. "She'll roll him over." She rapped on the enclosure full of babies. "Peck," she mouthed to the nurse on the inside.

Ted tapped Eli's arm. "You're not thinking of doing something you'll be sorry for . . . are you, Eli? Eli—I mean you know you're still Eli, don't you?"

In the enclosure, Eli saw a bassinet had been wheeled before the square window.

"Oh, Christ . . ." Ted said. "You don't have this Bible stuff on the brain—" And suddenly he said, "You wait, pal." He started down the corridor, his heels tapping rapidly.

Eli felt relieved—he leaned forward. In the basket was what he'd come to see. Well, now that he was here, what did he think he was going to say to it? I'm your father, Eli, the Flipper? I am wearing a black hat, suit, and fancy underwear, all borrowed from a friend? How could he admit to this reddened ball—*his* reddened ball—the worst of all: that Eckman would shortly convince him he wanted to take off the whole business. He couldn't admit it! He wouldn't do it!

Past his hat brim, from the corner of his eye, he saw Ted had stopped in a doorway at the end of the corridor. Two interns stood there smoking, listening to Ted. Eli ignored it.

No, even Eckman wouldn't make him take it off! No! He'd wear it, if he chose to. He'd make the kid wear it! Sure! Cut it down when the time came. A smelly hand-me-down, whether the kid liked it or not!

Only Teddie's heels clacked; the interns wore rubber soles—for they were there, beside him, unexpectedly. Their white suits smelled, but not like Eli's.

"Eli," Ted said, softly, "visiting time's up, pal."

"How are you feeling, Mr. Peck? First child upsets everyone. . . ."

He'd just pay no attention; nevertheless, he began to perspire, thickly, and his hat crown clutched his hair.

"Excuse me—Mr. Peck. . . ." It was a new rich bass voice. "Excuse me, rabbi, but you're wanted . . . in the temple." A hand took his elbow, firmly; then another hand, the other elbow. Where they grabbed, his tendons went taut.

"Okay, rabbi. Okay okay okay okay okay okay. . . ." He listened; it was a very soothing word, that okay. "Okay okay everything's going to be okay." His feet seemed to have left the ground some, as he glided away from the window, the bassinet, the babies. "Okay easy does it everything's all right all right—"

But he rose, suddenly, as though up out of a dream, and flailing his arms, screamed: "*I'm the father!*"

But the window disappeared. In a moment they tore off his jacket—it gave so easily, in one yank. Then a needle slid under his skin. The drug calmed his soul, but did not touch it down where the blackness had reached.

HARPER LEE

(1926–)

Nelle Harper Lee was born in the small Alabama town of Monroeville, also home to her lifelong friend Truman Capote. Lee's father, A. C. Lee, was a lawyer, newspaper editor, and legislator, and her sister Alice became an attorney as well. Harper Lee herself attended the University of Alabama Law School, leaving only six months short of a degree to attempt a literary career in New York City.

Lee began by writing short stories and essays, and eventually quit her job as an airline reservations clerk to expand one of her stories into a novel. After years of rewriting by Lee, *To Kill a Mockingbird* was published in 1960 and became a sensational success; its sales of more than 16 million copies have made it one of the best-selling books of the century. Awards included the 1961 Pulitzer Prize for Fiction and the National Conference of Christian and Jews Brotherhood Award. Lee has published no other books since.

To Kill a Mockingbird is the story of the trial of a black man falsely accused of raping a young white woman. Although the trial is not explicitly based on any real event, it resembles countless actual prosecutions of Southern black men on similar charges, such as the Scottsboro case of 1931. The novel's setting, a small town in Alabama named Maycomb, clearly resembles Lee's Monroeville. The narrator, Scout, is the daughter of the attorney who is assigned to defend the accused, Tom Robinson. That attorney, Atticus Finch, is modelled on A. C. Lee.

This excerpt includes Atticus's closing argument. Despite his knowledge that in the racist world of the 1930s South an erroneous conviction is inevitable, the lawyer musters considerable eloquence and humanity in an attempt to appeal to the jurors' best instincts. Tom is convicted and is then killed trying to escape from jail. (The characters Jem and Dill are Scout's brother and friend.)

Atticus's speech is melodramatic, but so is most of the poetry of law. This speech, and Atticus's words and actions throughout the book, have been impressed upon the popular mind by Gregory Peck's memorable portrayal of the character in the Academy Award–winning movie based on the novel. As a result, Atticus Finch has become the preeminent icon of the good lawyer in contemporary America. His courage and passion for justice have inspired many young people to become lawyers, and many lawyers to become socially responsible advocates.

from TO KILL A MOCKINGBIRD

— 1960 —

We raced back to the courthouse, up the steps, up two flights of stairs, and edged our way along the balcony rail. Reverend Sykes had saved our seats.

The courtroom was still, and again I wondered where the babies were. Judge Taylor's cigar was a brown speck in the center of his mouth; Mr. Gilmer was writing on one of the yellow pads on his table, trying to outdo the court reporter, whose hand was jerking rapidly. "Shoot," I muttered, "we missed it."

Atticus was halfway through his speech to the jury. He had evidently pulled some papers from his briefcase that rested beside his chair, because they were on his table. Tom Robinson was toying with them.

". . . absence of any corroborative evidence, this man was indicted on a capital charge and is now on trial for his life. . . ."

I punched Jem. "How long's he been at it?"

"He's just gone over the evidence," Jem whispered, "and we're gonna win, Scout. I don't see how we can't. He's been at it 'bout five minutes. He made it as plain and easy as—well, as I'da explained it to you. You could've understood it, even."

"Did Mr. Gilmer—?"

"Sh-h. Nothing new, just the usual. Hush now."

We looked down again. Atticus was speaking easily, with the kind of detachment he used when he dictated a letter. He walked slowly up and down in front of the jury, and the jury seemed to be attentive: their heads were up, and they followed Atticus's route with what seemed to be appreciation. I guess it was because Atticus wasn't a thunderer.

Atticus paused, then he did something he didn't ordinarily do. He unhitched his watch and chain and placed them on the table, saying, "With the court's permission—"

Judge Taylor nodded, and then Atticus did something I never saw him do before or since, in public or in private: he unbuttoned his vest, unbuttoned his collar, loosened his tie, and took off his coat. He never loosened a scrap of his clothing until he undressed at bedtime, and to Jem and me, this was the equivalent of him standing before us stark naked. We exchanged horrified glances.

Atticus put his hands in his pockets, and as he returned to the jury, I saw his gold collar button and the tips of his pen and pencil winking in the light.

"Gentlemen," he said. Jem and I again looked at each other: Atticus might have said, "Scout." His voice had lost its aridity, its detachment, and he was talking to the jury as if they were folks on the post office corner.

"Gentlemen," he was saying, "I shall be brief, but I would like to use my remaining time with you to remind you that this case is not a difficult one, it requires no minute sifting of complicated facts, but it does require you to be sure beyond all reasonable doubt as to the guilt of the defendant. To begin with, this case should never have come to trial. This case is as simple as black and white.

"The state has not produced one iota of medical evidence to the effect that the crime Tom Robinson is charged with ever took place. It has relied instead upon the testimony of two witnesses whose evidence has not only been called into serious question on cross-examination, but has been flatly contradicted by the defendant. The defendant is not guilty, but somebody in this courtroom is.

"I have nothing but pity in my heart for the chief witness for the state, but my pity does not extend so far as to her putting a man's life at stake, which she has done in an effort to get rid of her own guilt.

"I say guilt, gentlemen, because it was guilt that motivated her. She has committed no crime, she has merely broken a rigid and time-honored code of our society, a code so severe that whoever breaks it is hounded from our midst as unfit to live with. She is the victim of cruel poverty and ignorance, but I cannot pity her: she is white. She knew full well the enormity of her offense, but because her desires were stronger than the code she was breaking, she persisted in breaking it. She persisted, and her subsequent reaction is something that all of us have known at one time or another. She did something every child has done—she tried to put the evidence of her offense away from her. But in this case she was no child hiding stolen contraband: she struck out at her victim—of necessity she must put him away from her—he must be removed from her presence, from this world. She must destroy the evidence of her offense.

"What was the evidence of her offense? Tom Robinson, a human being. She must put Tom Robinson away from her. Tom Robinson was her daily reminder of what she did. What did she do? She tempted a Negro.

"She was white, and she tempted a Negro. She did something that in our society is unspeakable: she kissed a black man. Not an old Uncle, but a strong young Negro man. No code mattered to her before she broke it, but it came crashing down on her afterwards.

"Her father saw it, and the defendant has testified as to his remarks. What did her father do? We don't know, but there is circumstantial evidence to indicate that Mayella Ewell was beaten savagely by someone who led almost exclusively with his left. We do know in part what Mr. Ewell did: he did what any God-fearing, persevering, respectable white man would do under the circumstances—he swore out a warrant, no doubt signing it with his left hand, and Tom Robinson now sits before you, having taken the oath with the only good hand he possesses—his right hand.

"And so a quiet, respectable, humble Negro who had the unmitigated temerity to 'feel sorry' for a white woman has had to put his word against two white people's. I need not remind you of their appearance and conduct on the stand—you saw them for yourselves. The witnesses for the state, with the exception of the sheriff of Maycomb County, have presented themselves to you gentlemen, to this court, in the cynical confidence that their testimony would not be doubted, confident that you gentlemen would go along with them on the assumption—the evil assumption—that *all* Negroes lie, that *all* Negroes are basically immoral beings, that *all* Negro men are not to be trusted around our women, an assumption one associates with minds of their caliber.

"Which, gentlemen, we know is in itself a lie as black as Tom Robinson's skin, a lie I do not have to point out to you. You know the truth, and the truth is this: some Negroes lie, some Negroes are immoral, some Negro men are not to be trusted around women—black or white. But this is a truth that applies to the human race and to no particular race of men. There is not a person in this courtroom who has never told a lie, who has never done an immoral thing, and there is no man living who has never looked upon a woman without desire."

Atticus paused and took out his handkerchief. Then he took off his glasses and wiped them, and we saw another "first": we had never seen him sweat—he was one of those men whose faces never perspired, but now it was shining tan.

"One more thing, gentlemen, before I quit. Thomas Jefferson once said that all men are created equal, a phrase that the Yankees and the distaff side of the Executive branch in Washington are fond of hurling at us. There is a tendency in this year of grace, 1935, for certain people to use this phrase out of context, to satisfy all conditions. The most ridiculous example I can think of is that the people who run public education promote the stupid and idle along with the industrious—because all men are created equal, educators will gravely tell you, the children left behind suffer terrible feelings of inferiority. We know all men are not created equal in the sense some people would have us believe—some people are smarter than others, some people have more opportunity because they're born with it, some men make more money than others, some ladies make better cakes than others—some people are born gifted beyond the normal scope of most men.

"But there is one way in this country in which all men are created equal—there is one human institution that makes a pauper the equal of a Rockefeller, the stupid man the equal of an Einstein, and the ignorant man the equal of any college president. That institution, gentlemen, is a court. It can be the Supreme Court of the United States or the humblest J. P. court in the land, or this honorable court which you serve. Our courts have their faults, as does any human institution, but in this country our courts are the great levelers, and in our courts all men are created equal.

"I'm no idealist to believe firmly in the integrity of our courts and in the jury system—that is no ideal to me, it is a living, working reality. Gentlemen, a court is no better than each man of you sitting before me on this jury. A court is only as sound as its jury, and a jury is only as sound as the men who make it up. I am confident that you gentlemen will review without passion the evidence you have heard, come to a decision, and restore this defendant to his family. In the name of God, do your duty."

Atticus's voice had dropped, and as he turned away from the jury he said something I did not catch. He said it more to himself than to the court. I punched Jem. "What'd he say?"

" 'In the name of God, believe him,' I think that's what he said."

Dill suddenly reached over me and tugged at Jem. "Looka yonder!"

We followed his finger with sinking hearts. Calpurnia was making her way up the middle aisle, walking straight toward Atticus.

She stopped shyly at the railing and waited to get Judge Taylor's attention. She was in a fresh apron and she carried an envelope in her hand.

Judge Taylor saw her and said, "It's Calpurnia, isn't it?"

"Yes sir," she said. "Could I just pass this note to Mr. Finch, please sir? It hasn't got anything to do with—with the trial."

Judge Taylor nodded and Atticus took the envelope from Calpurnia. He opened it, read its contents and said, "Judge, I—this note is from my sister. She says my children are missing, haven't turned up since noon . . . I . . . could you—"

"I know where they are, Atticus." Mr. Underwood spoke up. "They're right up yonder in the colored balcony—been there since precisely one-eighteen P.M."

Our father turned around and looked up. "Jem, come down from there," he called. Then he said something to the Judge we didn't hear. We climbed across Reverend Sykes and made our way to the staircase.

Atticus and Calpurnia met us downstairs. Calpurnia looked peeved, but Atticus looked exhausted.

Jem was jumping in excitement. "We've won, haven't we?"

"I've no idea," said Atticus shortly. "You've been here all afternoon? Go home with Calpurnia and get your supper—and stay home."

"Aw, Atticus, let us come back," pleaded Jem. "Please let us hear the verdict, *please* sir."

"The jury might be out and back in a minute, we don't know—" but we could tell Atticus was relenting. "Well, you've heard it all, so you might as well hear the rest. Tell you what, you all can come back when you've eaten your supper—eat slowly, now, you won't miss anything important—and if the jury's still out, you can wait with us. But I expect it'll be over before you get back."

"You think they'll acquit him that fast?" asked Jem.

Atticus opened his mouth to answer, but shut it and left us.

I prayed that Reverend Sykes would save our seats for us, but stopped praying when I remembered that people got up and left in droves when the jury was out—tonight, they'd overrun the drugstore, the O.K. Café and the hotel, that is, unless they had brought their suppers too.

Calpurnia marched us home: "—skin every one of you alive, the very idea, you children listenin' to all that! Mister Jem, don't you know better'n to take your little sister to that trial? Miss Alexandra'll absolutely have a stroke of paralysis when she finds out! Ain't fittin' for children to hear . . ."

The streetlights were on, and we glimpsed Calpurnia's indignant profile as we passed beneath them. "Mister Jem, I thought you was gettin' some kinda head on your shoulders—the very idea, she's your little sister! The very *idea*, sir! You oughta be perfectly ashamed of yourself—ain't you got any sense at all?"

I was exhilarated. So many things had happened so fast I felt it would take years to sort them out, and now here was Calpurnia giving her precious Jem down the country—what new marvels would the evening bring?

Jem was chuckling. "Don't you want to hear about it, Cal?"

"Hush your mouth, sir! When you oughta be hangin' your head in shame you go along laughin'—" Calpurnia revived a series of rusty threats that moved Jem to little remorse, and she sailed up the front steps with her classic, "If Mr. Finch don't wear you out, I will—get in that house, sir!"

Jem went in grinning, and Calpurnia nodded tacit consent to having Dill in to supper. "You all call Miss Rachel right now and tell her where you are," she told him. "She's run distracted lookin' for you—you watch out she don't ship you back to Meridian first thing in the mornin'."

Aunt Alexandra met us and nearly fainted when Calpurnia told her where we were. I guess it hurt her when we told her Atticus said we could go back, because she didn't say a word during supper. She just rearranged food on her plate, looking at it sadly while Calpurnia served Jem, Dill and me with a vengeance. Calpurnia poured milk, dished out potato salad and ham, muttering, " 'shamed of yourselves," in varying degrees of intensity. "Now you all eat slow," was her final command.

Reverend Sykes had saved our places. We were surprised to find that we had been gone nearly an hour, and were equally surprised to find the courtroom exactly as we had left it, with minor changes: the jury box was empty, the defendant was gone; Judge Taylor had been gone, but he reappeared as we were seating ourselves.

"Nobody's moved, hardly," said Jem.

"They moved around some when the jury went out," said Reverend Sykes. "The menfolk down there got the womenfolk their suppers, and they fed their babies."

"How long have they been out?" asked Jem.

" 'bout thirty minutes. Mr. Finch and Mr. Gilmer did some more talkin', and Judge Taylor charged the jury."

"How was he?" asked Jem.

"What say? Oh, he did right well. I ain't complainin' one bit—he was mighty fair-minded. He sorta said if you believe this, then you'll have to return one verdict, but if you believe this, you'll have to return another one. I thought he was leanin' a little to our side—" Reverend Sykes scratched his head.

Jem smiled. "He's not supposed to lean, Reverend, but don't fret, we've won it," he said wisely. "Don't see how any jury could convict on what we heard—"

"Now don't you be so confident, Mr. Jem, I ain't ever seen any jury decide in favor of a colored man over a white man. . . ." But Jem took exception to Reverend Sykes, and we were subjected to a lengthy review of the evidence with Jem's ideas on the law regarding rape: it wasn't rape if she let you, but she had to be eighteen—in Alabama, that is—and Mayella was nineteen. Apparently you had to kick and holler, you had to be overpowered and stomped on, preferably knocked stone cold. If you were under eighteen, you didn't have to go through all this.

"Mr. Jem," Reverend Sykes demurred, "this ain't a polite thing for little ladies to hear . . ."

"Aw, she doesn't know what we're talkin' about," said Jem. "Scout, this is too old for you, ain't it?"

"It most certainly is not, I know every word you're saying." Perhaps I was too convincing, because Jem hushed and never discussed the subject again.

"What time is it, Reverend?" he asked.

"Gettin' on toward eight."

I looked down and saw Atticus strolling around with his hands in his pockets: he made a tour of the windows, then walked by the railing over to the jury box. He looked in it, inspected Judge Taylor on his throne, then went back to where he started. I caught his eye and waved to him. He acknowledged my salute with a nod, and resumed his tour.

Mr. Gilmer was standing at the windows talking to Mr. Underwood. Bert, the court reporter, was chain-smoking: he sat back with his feet on the table.

But the officers of the court, the ones present—Atticus, Mr. Gilmer, Judge Taylor sound asleep, and Bert, were the only ones whose behavior seemed normal. I had never seen a packed courtroom so still. Sometimes a baby would cry out fretfully, and a child would scurry out, but the grown people sat as if they were in church. In the balcony, the Negroes sat and stood around us with biblical patience.

The old courthouse clock suffered its preliminary strain and struck the hour, eight deafening bongs that shook our bones.

When it bonged eleven times I was past feeling: tired from fighting sleep, I allowed myself a short nap against Reverend Sykes's comfortable arm and shoulder. I jerked awake and made an honest effort to remain so, by looking down and concentrating on the heads below: there were sixteen bald ones, fourteen men that could pass for redheads, forty heads varying between brown and black, and—I remembered something Jem had once explained to me when he went through a brief period of psychical research: he said if enough people—a stadium full, maybe—were to concentrate on one thing, such as setting a tree afire in the woods, that the tree would ignite of its own accord. I toyed with the idea of asking everyone below to concentrate on setting Tom Robinson free, but thought if they were as tired as I, it wouldn't work.

Dill was sound asleep, his head on Jem's shoulder, and Jem was quiet.

"Ain't it a long time?" I asked him.

"Sure is, Scout," he said happily.

"Well, from the way you put it, it'd just take five minutes."

Jem raised his eyebrows. "There are things you don't understand," he said, and I was too weary to argue.

But I must have been reasonably awake, or I would not have received the impression that was creeping into me. It was not unlike one I had last winter, and I shivered, though the night was hot. The feeling grew until the atmosphere in the courtroom was exactly the same as a cold February morning, when the mockingbirds were still, and the carpenters had stopped hammering on Miss Maudie's new house, and every wood door in the neighborhood was shut as tight as the doors of the Radley Place. A deserted, waiting, empty street, and the courtroom was packed with people. A steaming summer night was no different from a winter morning. Mr. Heck Tate, who had entered the courtroom and was talking to Atticus, might have been wearing his high boots and lumber jacket. Atticus had stopped his tranquil journey and had put his foot onto the bottom rung of a chair; as he listened to what Mr. Tate was saying, he ran his hand slowly up and down his thigh. I expected Mr. Tate to say any minute, "Take him, Mr. Finch. . . ."

But Mr. Tate said, "This court will come to order," in a voice that rang with authority, and the heads below us jerked up. Mr. Tate left the room and returned with Tom Robinson. He steered Tom to his place beside Atticus, and stood there. Judge Taylor had roused himself to sudden alertness and was sitting up straight, looking at the empty jury box.

What happened after that had a dreamlike quality; in a dream I saw the jury return, moving like underwater swimmers, and Judge Taylor's voice came from far away, and was tiny. I saw something only a lawyer's child could be expected to see, could be expected to watch for, and it was like watching Atticus walk into the street, raise a rifle to his shoulder and pull the trigger, but watching all the time knowing that the gun was empty.

A jury never looks at a defendant it has convicted, and when this jury came in, not one of them looked at Tom Robinson. The foreman handed a piece of paper to Mr. Tate who handed it to the clerk who handed it to the judge. . . .

I shut my eyes. Judge Taylor was polling the jury: "Guilty . . . guilty . . . guilty . . . guilty . . ." I peeked at Jem: his hands were white from gripping the balcony rail, and his shoulders jerked as if each "guilty" was a separate stab between them.

Judge Taylor was saying something. His gravel was in his fist, but he wasn't using it. Dimly, I saw Atticus pushing papers from the table into his briefcase. He snapped it shut, went to the court reporter and said something, nodded to Mr. Gilmer, and then went to Tom Robinson and whispered something to him. Atticus put his hand on Tom's shoulder as he whispered. Atticus took his coat off the back of his chair and pulled it over his shoulder. Then he left the courtroom, but not by his usual exit.

He must have wanted to go home the short way, because he walked quickly down the middle aisle toward the south exit. I followed the top of his head as he made his way to the door. He did not look up.

Someone was punching me, but I was reluctant to take my eyes from the people below us, and from the image of Atticus's lonely walk down the aisle.

"Miss Jean Louise?"

I looked around. They were standing. All around us and in the balcony on the opposite wall, the Negroes were getting to their feet. Reverend Sykes's voice was as distant as Judge Taylor's:

"Miss Jean Louise, stand up. Your father's passin'."

It was Jem's turn to cry. His face was streaked with angry tears as we made our way through the cheerful crowd. "It ain't right," he muttered, all the way to the corner of the square where we found Atticus waiting. Atticus was standing under the street light looking as though nothing had happened: his vest was buttoned, his collar and tie were neatly in place, his watch-chain glistened, he was his impassive self again.

"It ain't right, Atticus," said Jem.

"No son, it's not right."

We walked home.

Aunt Alexandra was waiting up. She was in her dressing gown, and I could have sworn she had on her corset underneath it. "I'm sorry, brother," she murmured. Having never heard her call Atticus "brother" before, I stole a glance at Jem, but he was not listening. He would look up at Atticus, then down at the floor, and I wondered if he thought Atticus somehow responsible for Tom Robinson's conviction.

"Is he all right?" Aunty asked, indicating Jem.

"He'll be so presently," said Atticus. "It was a little too strong for him." Our father sighed. "I'm going to bed," he said. "If I don't wake up in the morning, don't call me."

"I didn't think it wise in the first place to let them—"

"This is their home, sister," said Atticus. "We've made it this way for them, they might as well learn to cope with it."

"But they don't have to go to the courthouse and wallow in it—"

"It's just as much Maycomb County as missionary teas."

"Atticus—" Aunt Alexandra's eyes were anxious. "You are the last person I thought would turn bitter over this."

"I'm not bitter, just tired. I'm going to bed."

"Atticus—" said Jem bleakly.

He turned in the doorway. "What, son?"

"How could they do it, how could they?"

"I don't know, but they did it. They've done it before and they did it tonight and they'll do it again and when they do it—seems that only children weep. Good night."

But things are always better in the morning. Atticus rose at his usual ungodly hour and was in the livingroom behind the *Mobile Register* when we stumbled in. Jem's morning face posed the question his sleepy lips struggled to ask.

"It's not time to worry yet," Atticus reassured him, as we went to the diningroom. "We're not through yet. There'll be an appeal, you can count on that. Gracious alive, Cal, what's all this?" He was staring at his breakfast plate.

Calpurnia said, "Tom Robinson's daddy sent you along this chicken this morning. I fixed it."

"You tell him I'm proud to get it—bet they don't have chicken for breakfast at the White House. What are these?"

"Rolls," said Calpurnia. "Estelle down at the hotel sent 'em."

Atticus looked up at her, puzzled, and she said, "You better step out here and see what's in the kitchen, Mr. Finch."

We followed him. The kitchen table was loaded with enough food to bury the family: hunks of salt pork, tomatoes, beans, even scuppernongs. Atticus grinned when he found a jar of pickled pigs' knuckles. "Reckon Aunty'll let me eat these in the diningroom?"

Calpurnia said, "This was all 'round the back steps when I got here this morning. They—they 'preciate what you did, Mr. Finch. They—they aren't oversteppin' themselves, are they?"

Atticus's eyes filled with tears. He did not speak for a moment. "Tell them I'm very grateful," he said. "Tell them—tell them they must never do this again. Times are too hard. . . ."

He left the kitchen, went in the diningroom and excused himself to Aunt Alexandra, put on his hat and went to town.

We heard Dill's step in the hall, so Calpurnia left Atticus's uneaten breakfast on the table. Between rabbit-bites Dill told us of Miss Rachel's reaction to last night, which was: if a man like Atticus Finch wants to butt his head against a stone wall it's his head.

"I'da got her told," growled Dill, gnawing a chicken leg, "but she didn't look much like tellin' this morning. Said she was up half the night wonderin' where I was, said she'da had the sheriff after me but he was at the hearing."

"Dill, you've got to stop goin' off without tellin' her," said Jem. "It just aggravates her."

Dill sighed patiently. "I told her till I was blue in the face where I was goin'—she's just seein' too many snakes in the closet. Bet that woman drinks a pint for breakfast every morning—know she drinks two glasses full. Seen her."

"Don't talk like that, Dill," said Aunt Alexandra. "It's not becoming to a child. It's—cynical."

"I ain't cynical, Miss Alexandra. Tellin' the truth's not cynical, is it?"

"The way you tell it, it is."

Jem's eyes flashed at her, but he said to Dill, "Let's go. You can take that runner with you."

When we went to the front porch, Miss Stephanie Crawford was busy telling it to Miss Maudie Atkinson and Mr. Avery. They looked around at us and went on talking. Jem made a feral noise in his throat. I wished for a weapon.

"I hate grown folks lookin' at you," said Dill. "Makes you feel like you've done something."

Miss Maudie yelled for Jem Finch to come there.

Jem groaned and heaved himself up from the swing. "We'll go with you," Dill said.

Miss Stephanie's nose quivered with curiosity. She wanted to know who all gave us permission to go to court—she didn't see us but it was all over town this morning that we were in the Colored balcony. Did Atticus put us up there as a sort of—? Wasn't it right close up there with all those—? Did Scout understand all the—? Didn't it make us mad to see our daddy beat?

"Hush, Stephanie." Miss Maudie's diction was deadly. "I've not got all the morning to pass on the porch—Jem Finch, I called to find out if you and your colleagues can eat some cake. Got up at five to make it, so you better say yes. Excuse us, Stephanie. Good morning, Mr. Avery."

There was a big cake and two little ones on Miss Maudie's kitchen table. There should have been three little ones. It was not like Miss Maudie to forget Dill, and we must have shown it. But we understood when she cut from the big cake and gave the slice to Jem.

As we ate, we sensed that this was Miss Maudie's way of saying that as far as she was concerned, nothing had changed. She sat quietly in a kitchen chair, watching us.

Suddenly she spoke: "Don't fret, Jem. Things are never as bad as they seem."

Indoors, when Miss Maudie wanted to say something lengthy she spread her fingers on her knees and settled her bridgework. This she did, and we waited.

"I simply want to tell you that there are some men in this world who were born to do our unpleasant jobs for us. Your father's one of them."

"Oh," said Jem. "Well."

"Don't you oh well me, sir," Miss Maudie replied, recognizing Jem's fatalistic noises, "you are not old enough to appreciate what I said."

Jem was staring at his half-eaten cake. "It's like bein' a caterpillar in a cocoon, that's what it is," he said. "Like somethin' asleep wrapped up in a warm place. I always thought Maycomb folks were the best folks in the world, least that's what they seemed like."

"We're the safest folks in the world," said Miss Maudie. "We're so rarely called on to be Christians, but when we are, we've got men like Atticus to go for us."

Jem grinned ruefully. "Wish the rest of the county thought that."

"You'd be surprised how many of us do."

"Who?" Jem's voice rose. "Who in this town did one thing to help Tom Robinson, just who?"

"His colored friends for one thing, and people like us. People like Judge Taylor. People like Mr. Heck Tate. Stop eating and start thinking, Jem. Did it ever strike you that Judge Taylor naming Atticus to defend that boy was no accident? That Judge Taylor might have had his reasons for naming him?"

This was a thought. Court-appointed defenses were usually given to Maxwell Green, Maycomb's latest addition to the bar, who needed the experience. Maxwell Green should have had Tom Robinson's case.

"You think about that," Miss Maudie was saying. "It was no accident. I was sittin' there on the porch last night, waiting. I waited and waited to see you all come down the sidewalk, and as I waited I thought, Atticus Finch won't win, he can't win, but he's the only man in these parts who can keep a jury out so long in a case like that. And I thought to myself, well, we're making a step—it's just a baby-step, but it's a step."

" 't's all right to talk like that—can't any Christian judges an' lawyers make up for heathen juries," Jem muttered. "Soon's I get grown—"

"That's something you'll have to take up with your father," Miss Maudie said.

We went down Miss Maudie's cool new steps into the sunshine and found Mr. Avery and Miss Stephanie Crawford still at it. They had moved down the sidewalk and were standing in front of Miss Stephanie's house. Miss Rachel was walking toward them.

"I think I'll be a clown when I get grown," said Dill.

Jem and I stopped in our tracks.

"Yes sir, a clown," he said. "There ain't one thing in this world I can do about folks except laugh, so I'm gonna join the circus and laugh my head off."

"You got it backwards, Dill," said Jem. "Clowns are sad, it's folks that laugh at them."

"Well I'm gonna be a new kind of clown. I'm gonna stand in the middle of the ring and laugh at the folks. Just looka yonder," he pointed. "Every one of 'em oughta be ridin' broomsticks. Aunt Rachel already does."

Miss Stephanie and Miss Rachel were waving wildly at us, in a way that did not give the lie to Dill's observation.

"Oh gosh," breathed Jem. "I reckon it'd be ugly not to see 'em."

Something was wrong. Mr. Avery was red in the face from a sneezing spell and nearly blew us off the sidewalk when we came up. Miss Stephanie was trembling with excitement, and Miss Rachel caught Dill's shoulder. "You get on in the back yard and stay there," she said. "There's danger a'comin'."

" 's matter?" I asked.

"Ain't you heard yet? It's all over town—"

At that moment Aunt Alexandra came to the door and called us, but she was too late. It was Miss Stephanie's pleasure to tell us: this morning Mr. Bob Ewell stopped Atticus on the post office corner, spat in his face, and told him he'd get him if it took the rest of his life.

"I wish Bob Ewell wouldn't chew tobacco," was all Atticus said about it.

According to Miss Stephanie Crawford, however, Atticus was leaving the post office when Mr. Ewell approached him, cursed him, spat on him, and threatened to kill him. Miss Stephanie (who, by the time she had told it twice was there and had seen it all—passing by from the Jitney Jungle, she was)—Miss Stephanie said Atticus didn't bat an eye, just took out his handkerchief and wiped his face and stood there and let Mr. Ewell call him names wild horses could not bring her to repeat. Mr. Ewell was a veteran of an obscure war; that plus Atticus's peaceful reaction probably prompted him to inquire, "Too proud to fight, you nigger-lovin' bastard?" Miss Stephanie said Atticus said, "No, too old," put his hands in his pockets and strolled on. Miss Stephanie said you had to hand it to Atticus Finch, he could be right dry sometimes.

Jem and I didn't think it entertaining.

"After all, though," I said, "he was the deadest shot in the county one time. He could—"

"You know he wouldn't carry a gun, Scout. He ain't even got one—" said Jem. "You know he didn't even have one down at the jail that night. He told me havin' a gun around's an invitation to somebody to shoot you."

"This is different," I said. "We can ask him to borrow one."

We did, and he said, "Nonsense."

Dill was of the opinion that an appeal to Atticus's better nature might work: after all, we would starve if Mr. Ewell killed him, besides be raised exclusively by Aunt Alexandra, and we all knew the first thing she'd do before Atticus was under the ground good would be to fire Calpurnia. Jem said it might work if I cried and flung a fit, being young and a girl. That didn't work either.

But when he noticed us dragging around the neighborhood, not eating, taking little interest in our normal pursuits, Atticus discovered how deeply frightened we were. He tempted Jem with a new football magazine one night; when he saw Jem flip the pages and toss it aside, he said, "What's bothering you, son?"

Jem came to the point: "Mr. Ewell."

"What has happened?"

"Nothing's happened. We're scared for you, and we think you oughta do something about him."

Atticus smiled wryly. "Do what? Put him under a peace bond?"

"When a man says he's gonna get you, looks like he means it."

"He meant it when he said it," said Atticus. "Jem, see if you can stand in Bob Ewell's shoes a minute. I destroyed his last shred of credibility at that trial, if he had any to begin with. The man had to have some kind of comeback, his kind always does. So if spitting in my face and threatening me saved Mayella Ewell one extra beating, that's something I'll gladly take. He had to take it out on somebody and I'd rather it be me than that houseful of children out there. You understand?"

Jem nodded.

Aunt Alexandra entered the room as Atticus was saying, "We don't have anything to fear from Bob Ewell, he got it all out of his system that morning."

"I wouldn't be so sure of that, Atticus," she said. "His kind'd do anything to pay off a grudge. You know how those people are."

"What on earth could Ewell do to me, sister?"

"Something furtive," Aunt Alexandra said. "You may count on that."

"Nobody has much chance to be furtive in Maycomb," Atticus answered.

After that, we were not afraid. Summer was melting away, and we made the most of it. Atticus assured us that nothing would happen to Tom Robinson until the higher court reviewed his case, and that Tom had a good chance of going free, or at least of having a new trial. He was at Enfield Prison Farm, seventy miles away in Chester County. I asked Atticus if Tom's wife and children were allowed to visit him, but Atticus said no.

"If he loses his appeal," I asked one evening, "what'll happen to him?"

"He'll go to the chair," said Atticus, "unless the Governor commutes his sentence. Not time to worry yet, Scout. We've got a good chance."

Jem was sprawled on the sofa reading *Popular Mechanics*. He looked up. "It ain't right. He didn't kill anybody even if he was guilty. He didn't take anybody's life."

"You know rape's a capital offense in Alabama," said Atticus.

"Yessir, but the jury didn't have to give him death—if they wanted to they could've gave him twenty years."

"Given," said Atticus. "Tom Robinson's a colored man, Jem. No jury in this part of the world's going to say, 'We think you're guilty, but not very,' on a charge like that. It was either a straight acquittal or nothing."

Jem was shaking his head. "I know it's not right, but I can't figure out what's wrong—maybe rape shouldn't be a capital offense. . . ."

Atticus dropped his newspaper beside his chair. He said he didn't have any quarrel with the rape statute, none whatever, but he did have deep misgivings when the state asked for and the jury gave a death penalty on purely circumstantial evidence. He glanced at me, saw I was listening, and made it easier. "—I mean, before a man is sentenced to death for murder, say, there should be one or two eyewitnesses. Someone should be able to say, 'Yes, I was there and saw him pull the trigger.' "

"But lots of folks have been hung—hanged—on circumstantial evidence," said Jem.

"I know, and lots of 'em probably deserved it, too—but in the absence of eye-witnesses there's always a doubt, sometimes only the shadow of a doubt. The law says 'reasonable doubt,' but I think a defendant's entitled to the shadow of a doubt. There's always the possibility, no matter how improbable, that he's innocent."

"Then it all goes back to the jury, then. We oughta do away with juries." Jem was adamant.

Atticus tried hard not to smile but couldn't help it. "You're rather hard on us, son. I think maybe there might be a better way. Change the law. Change it so that only judges have the power of fixing the penalty in capital cases."

"Then go up to Montgomery and change the law."

"You'd be surprised how hard that'd be. I won't live to see the law changed, and if you live to see it you'll be an old man."

This was not good enough for Jem. "No sir, they oughta do away with juries. He wasn't guilty in the first place and they said he was."

"If you had been on that jury, son, and eleven other boys like you, Tom would be a free man," said Atticus. "So far nothing in your life has interfered with your reasoning process. Those are twelve reasonable men in everyday life, Tom's jury, but you saw something come between them and reason. You saw the same thing that night in front of the jail. When that crew went away, they didn't go as reasonable men, they went because we were there. There's something in our world that makes men lose their heads—they couldn't be fair if they tried. In our courts, when it's a white man's word against a black man's, the white man always wins. They're ugly, but those are the facts of life."

"Doesn't make it right," said Jem stolidly. He beat his fist softly on his knee. "You just can't convict a man on evidence like that—you can't."

"You couldn't, but they could and did. The older you grow the more of it you'll see. The one place where a man ought to get a square deal is in a courtroom, be he any color of the rainbow, but people have a way of carrying their resentments right into a jury box. As you grow older, you'll see white men cheat black men every day of your life, but let me tell you something and don't you forget it—whenever a white man does that to a black man, no matter who he is, how rich he is, or how fine a family he comes from, that white man is trash."

Atticus was speaking so quietly his last word crashed on our ears. I looked up, and his face was vehement. "There's nothing more sickening to me than a low-grade white man who'll take advantage of a Negro's ignorance. Don't fool yourselves—it's all adding up and one of these days we're going to pay the bill for it. I hope it's not in you children's time."

MICHAEL GILBERT

(1912–)

Michael Gilbert is one of the preeminent postwar detective-story writers. He has written over twenty novels, hundreds of short stories, and plays for the stage, television, and radio. Of particular interest to readers of this anthology, he also edited *The Oxford Book of Legal Anecdotes.*

Gilbert was born in Billinghay, Lincolnshire. Under the influence of his uncle, Sir Maurice Gwyer, Lord Chief Justice of India, he earned a law degree from the University of London. Gilbert was captured by the Germans in Italy during World War II; while imprisoned, he was inspired by reading Cecil Hare's legal mystery novel, *Tragedy at Law,* to become a crime writer. In 1947, he joined a firm of solicitors, Trower, Still and Keeling, later becoming a partner. His legal work included serving as legal advisor to the government of Bahrain and drafting Raymond Chandler's will. Gilbert did his writing while commuting between his Kent home and his London office.

Gilbert's knowledge of law is evident in his plots; indeed, in his fiction, the law is second only to the police in importance. His first acclaimed novel, *Smallbone Deceased* (1950), is a satire on law offices. Another popular book, *Death Has Deep Roots* (1951), is a courtroom novel featuring a French law firm with ties to the wartime Resistance. Enough of Gilbert's novels and short stories have lawyers as protagonists that he was able to publish a collection, *Stay of Execution and Other Stories of Legal Practice* (1971).

Among Gilbert's "stories of legal practice" is "Mr. Portway's Practice." This was first published as "The Income Tax Mystery" in *Ellery Queen's Mystery Magazine,* May 1958, and nicely illustrates the author's characteristic dry wit.

MR. PORTWAY'S PRACTICE

— 1958 —

I qualified as a solicitor before the war, and in 1937 I bought a share in a small partnership in the City. Then the war came along and I joined the Infantry. I was already thirty-five and it didn't look as if I was going to see much active service, so I cashed in on my knowledge of German and joined the Intelligence Corps. That was fun, too.

When the war finished I got back to London and found our old office bombed and the other partner dead. As far as a legal practice can do, it had disappeared. I got a job without any difficulty in a firm in Bedford Row, but I didn't enjoy it. The work was easy enough but there was no real future in it. So I quit and joined the Legal Branch of Inland Revenue.

This may seem even duller than private practice, but in fact it wasn't. As soon as I had finished the subsidiary training in accountancy that all Revenue officials have to take, I was invited to join a very select outfit known as I.B.A. or Investigation Branch (Active).

If you ask a Revenue official about I.B.A. he'll tell you it doesn't exist. This may simply mean that he hasn't heard of it. Most ordinary Revenue investigation is done by accountants who examine balance sheets and profit and loss accounts and vouchers and receipts and ask questions and go on asking questions until the truth emerges.

Some cases can't be treated like that. They need active investigation. Someone has got to go and find out the facts. That's where I.B.A. comes in.

It isn't all big cases involving millions of pounds. The Revenue reckons to achieve the best results by making a few shrewd examples in the right places. One of our most spectacular coups was achieved when a member of the department opened a greengrocer's shop in Crouch End—but that's by the way.

When the name of Mr. Portway cropped up in I.B.A. records it was natural that the dossier should get pushed across to me. For Mr. Portway was a solicitor. I can't remember precisely how he first came to our notice. You'd be surprised what casual items can set I.B.A. in motion. A conversation in a railway carriage; a hint from an insurance assessor; a bit of loud-voiced boasting in a pub. We don't go in for phone tapping. It's inefficient, and, from our point of view, quite unnecessary.

The thing about Mr. Portway was simply this. That he seemed to make a very substantial amount of money without working for it.

The first real confirmation came from a disgruntled girl who had been hired to look after his books and fired for inefficiency. Mr. Portway ran a good car, she said. Dressed well. Spent hundreds of pounds at the wine merchant (she'd seen one of his bills) and conducted an old-fashioned one-man practice which, by every law of economics, should have left him broke.

Some days he had no clients at all, she said, and spent the morning in his room reading a book (detective stories chiefly); then took two hours for lunch, snoozed a little on his return, had a cup of tea, and went home. Other days, a client or two would trickle in. The business was almost entirely buying and selling of houses and leases and mortgages and sale agreements. Mr. Portway did it all himself. He had one girl to do the typing and look after the outer office, and another (our informant) to keep the books.

I don't suppose you know anything about solicitors' accounting, and I'm not proposing to give you a dissertation on it, but the fact is that solicitors are bound by very strict rules indeed. Rules imposed by Act of Parliament and jealously enforced by the Law Society. And quite right, too. Solicitors handle a lot of other people's money.

When we'd made a quiet check to see if Mr. Portway had any private means of his own (he didn't), we decided that this was the sort of case we ought to have a look at. It wasn't difficult. Mr. Portway knew nothing about figures. However small his staff, he had to have someone with the rudiments of accountancy, or he couldn't have got through his annual audit. We watched the periodicals until we saw his advertisement, and I applied for the job.

I don't know if there were any other applicants, but I'm sure I was the only one who professed both law and book-keeping and who was prepared to accept the mouse-like salary that he was offering.

Mr. Portway was a small, round, pink-checked, white-haired man. One would have said Pickwickian, except that he didn't wear glasses, nor was there anything in the least owl-like about his face. So far as any comparison suggested itself he looked like a tortoise. It was a sardonic, leathery, indestructible face, with the long upper lip of a philosopher.

He greeted me warmly and showed me my room. The office occupied the ground floor and basement of the house. On the right as you came in, and overlooking the paved courtyard and fountain which is all that remains of the old Lombards Inn, was Mr. Portway's sanctum, a very nice room on the small side, and made smaller by the rows of bookcases full of bound reports. In fact, the whole suite of offices was tiny, a box-like affair.

I have given you some idea of the scale of things so that you can gather how easy I thought my job was going to be. My guess was that a week would be quite enough for me to detect any funny business that was going on.

I was quite wrong.

A week was enough to convince me that something was wrong. But by the end of a month I hadn't got a step nearer to finding out what it was.

My predecessor hadn't kept the books awfully well, but that was inefficiency, not dishonesty.

I reported my findings to my superiors.

"Mr. Portway," I said, "has a business which appears to produce, in costs, just about enough to pay the salaries of his two assistants, the rent, rates, lighting and other outgoings, and to leave him no personal profit at all. Indeed, in some instances, he has had to make up, from his own pocket, small deficiencies in the office account. Nor does this money come from private means. It is part of my duty as accountant to make Mr. Portway's own private tax returns"—(this, it is fair to him to say, was at his own suggestion)—"and apart from a very small holding in War Stock and occasional casual earnings for articles on wine, on which he is an acknowledged expert, he has—or at least declares—no outside resources at all. Nevertheless, enjoying as he does a 'minus' income, he lives well, appears to deny himself little in the way of comfort. He is not extravagant, but I could not estimate his expenditure on himself at less than two thousand pounds per annum."

My masters found this report so unsatisfactory that I was summoned to an interview. The head of the department at that time, Dai Evans, was a tubby and mercurial Welshman, like Lloyd George without the moustache. He was on Christian-name terms with all his staff; but he wasn't a good man to cross.

"Are you asking me to believe in miracles, Michael?" he said. "How can a man have a wallet full of notes to spend on himself each week if he doesn't earn them from somewhere?"

"Perhaps he makes them," I suggested.

Dai elected to take this seriously. "A forger, you mean. I wouldn't have thought it likely."

"No," I said. "I didn't quite mean that." (I knew as well as anyone that the skill and organization, to say nothing of the supplies of special paper, necessary for bank-note forgery were far beyond the resources of an ordinary citizen.) "I thought he might have a hoard. Some people do, you know. There's nothing intrinsically illegal in it."

Dai grunted. "Why should he trouble to keep up an office? You say it costs him money. Why wouldn't he shift his hoard to a safe deposit? That way he'd save himself money and work. I don't like it, Michael. We're on to something here, boy. Don't let it go."

So I returned to Lombards Inn, and kept my eyes and ears open. And as the weeks passed the mystery grew more irritating and more insoluble.

I made a careful calculation during the month which ensued. In the course of it Mr. Portway acted in the purchase of one house for £5,000, and the sale of another at about the same price. He drafted a lease of an office in the City. And fixed up a mortgage for an old lady with a Building Society. The costs he received for these transactions totalled £171 5s. And that was around five pounds less than he paid out, to keep the office going for the same period.

One day, about three o'clock in the afternoon, I took some papers in to him. I found him sitting in the chair beside the fireplace, *The Times* (which he read every day from cover to cover) in one hand, and in the other a glass.

He said, "You find me indulging in my secret vice. I'm one of the old school, who thinks that claret should be drunk after lunch, and burgundy after dinner."

I am fond of French wines myself and he must have seen the quick glance I gave at the bottle.

"It's a Pontet Canet," he said. "Of 1943. Certainly the best of the war years, and almost the best Château of that year. You'll find a glass in the filing cabinet."

You can't drink wine standing up. Before I knew what I was doing, we were seated on either side of the fireplace with the bottle between us. After a second glass Mr. Portway fell into a mood of reminiscence. I kept my ears open, of course, for any useful information, but only half of me, at that moment, was playing the spy. The other half was enjoying an excellent claret, and the company of a philosopher.

It appeared that Mr. Portway had come late to the law. He had studied art under Bertolozzi, the great Florentine engraver, and had spent a couple of years in the workshops of Herr Groener, who specialized in intaglios and metal relief work. He took down from the mantel-shelf a beautiful little reproduction in copper of the Papal Colophon which he had made himself. Then the first world war, most of which he had spent in Egypt and Palestine, had disoriented him.

"I felt need," he said, "of something a little more tangible in my life than the art of metal relievo." He had tried, and failed, to become an architect. And had then chosen law, to oblige an uncle who had no son.

"There have been Portways," he said, "in Lombards Inn for two centuries. I fear I shall be the last."

Then the telephone broke up our talk, and I went back to my room.

As I thought about things that night, I came to the conclusion that Mr. Portway had presented me with the answer to one problem, in the act of setting me another. I was being driven, step by step, to the only logical conclusion. That he had found some method, some perfectly safe and private method, of manufacturing money.

But not forgery, as the word is usually understood. Despite his bland admission of an engraver's training, the difficulties were too great. Where could he get his paper? And such notes as I had seen did not look in the least like forgeries.

I had come to one other conclusion. The heart of the secret lay in the strong-room. This was the one room that no one but Mr. Portway ever visited; the room of which he alone had the key. Try as I would I had never ever seen inside the door. If he wanted a deed out of it, Mr. Portway would wait until I was at lunch before he went in to fetch it. And he was always last away from the office when we closed.

The door of the strong-room was a heavy old-fashioned affair, and if you have time to study it, and are patient enough, you can get the measure of any lock in the end. I had twice glimpsed the actual key, too, and that is a great help. It wasn't long before I had equipped myself with keys which I was pretty sure would open the door. The next thing was to find an opportunity to use them.

In the end I hit on quite a simple plan.

At about three o'clock one afternoon I announced that I had an appointment with the local Inspector of Taxes. I thought it would take an hour or ninety minutes. Would it be all right if I went straight home? Mr. Portway agreed. He was in the middle of drafting a complicated conveyance, and looked safely anchored in his chair.

I went back to my room, picked up my hat, raincoat and brief-case, and tiptoed down to the basement. The secretarial staff was massacring a typewriter in the outer office.

Quietly I opened the door of one of the basement storage rooms; I had used my last few lunch breaks, when I was alone in the office, to construct myself a hideaway, by moving a rampart of deed boxes a couple of feet out from the wall, and building up the top with bundles of old papers. Now I shut the door behind me, and squeezed carefully into my lair. Apart from the fact that the fresh dust I had disturbed made me want to sneeze, it wasn't too bad. Soon the dust particles resettled themselves, and I fell into a state of somnolence.

It was five o'clock before I heard Mr. Portway moving. His footsteps came down the passage outside, and stopped. I heard him open the door of the other strong-room opposite. A pause. The door shut again. The next moment my door opened and the lights sprang on.

I held my breath. The lights went out and the door shut. I heard the click of the key in the lock. Then the footsteps moved away.

He was certainly thorough. I even heard him look into the lavatory. (My first plan had been to lock myself in it. I was glad now that I had not.) At last the steps moved away upstairs; more pottering about, the big outer door slammed shut, and silence came down like a blanket.

I let it wait for an hour or two. The trouble was the cleaner, an erratic lady called Gertie. She had a key of her own and sometimes she came in the evening and sometimes early in the morning. I had studied her movements for several weeks. The latest she had ever left the premises was a quarter to eight at night.

By half-past eight I felt it was safe for me to start moving.

The room door presented no difficulties. The lock was on my side, and I simply unscrewed it. The strong-room door was a different matter. I had got what is known in the trade as a set of 'approximates'; which are blank keys of the type and, roughly, the shape to open a given lock. My job was to find the one that worked best, and then file it down and fiddle it until it would open the lock. (You can't do this with a modern lock, which is tooled to a hundredth of an inch, but old locks, which rely on complicated convolutions and strong springs, though they look formidable, are actually much easier.)

By half-past ten I heard the sweet click which means success, and I swung the steel door open, turned on the light switch and stepped in.

It was a small vault with walls of whitewashed brick, with a run of wooden shelves round two of the sides, carrying a line of black deed boxes. I didn't waste much time on them. I guessed the sort of things they would contain.

On the left, behind the door, was a table. On the table stood a heavy, brass-bound, teak box; the sort of thing that might have been built to contain a microscope, only larger. It was locked, and this was a small, Bramah-type lock, which none of my implements were really designed to cope with.

I worked for some time at it, but without a lot of hope. The only solution seemed to be to lug the box away with me—it was very heavy, but just portable—and get someone to work on it. I reflected that I should look pretty silly if it did turn out to be a valuable microscope that one of old Portway's clients had left with him for safe keeping.

Then I had an idea. On the shelf inside the door was a small black tin box with 'E. Portway. Personal' painted on the front. It was the sort of thing a careful man might keep his War Savings Certificates and passport in. It too was locked, but with an ordinary deed-box lock, which one of the keys on my ring fitted. I opened it, and, sure enough, lying on top of the stacked papers in it, the first thing that caught my eye was a worn leather keyholder containing a single, brass Bramah key.

I suddenly felt a little breathless. Perhaps the ventilation in that underground room was not all that it should have been. Moving with deliberation I fitted the brass key into the tiny keyhole, pressed home, and twisted.

Then I lifted the top of the box. And came face to face with Mr. Portway's secret.

At first sight it was disappointing. It looked like nothing more than a handpress. The sort of thing you use for impressing a company seal, only larger. I lifted it out, picked up a piece of clean white paper off the shelf, slid it in and pressed down the handle. Then I released it and extracted the paper.

Imprinted on it was a neat, orange Revenue stamp for £20. I went back to the box. Inside was a tray, and arranged in it stamps of various denominations, starting at 10s., £1, £2 and £5 and so on upwards. The largest was for £100.

I picked one out and held it up to the light. It was beautifully made. Mr. Portway had not wasted his time at Bertolozzi's Florentine atelier. There was even an arrangement of cogs behind each stamp by which the three figures of the date could be set; tiny, delicate wheels, each a masterpiece of the watchmaker's art.

I heard the footsteps crossing the courtyard, and Mr. Portway was through the door before I even had time to put down the seal I was holding.

"What are you doing here?" I said stupidly.

"When anyone turns on the strong-room light," he said, "it turns on the light in my office, too. I've got a private arrangement with the caretaker of the big block at the end who keeps an eye open for me. If she sees my light on, she telephones me."

"I see," I said. Once I had got over the actual shock of seeing him there I wasn't alarmed. I was half his age and twice his size. "I've been admiring your homework. Every man his own stamp office. A lovely piece of work."

"Is it not?" agreed Mr. Portway, blinking at me under the strong light. I could read in his Chelonian face neither fear nor anger. Rather a sardonic amusement at the turn of affairs. "Are you a private detective, by any chance?"

I told him who I was.

"You have been admiring my little machine?"

"My only real surprise is that no one has thought of it before."

"Yes," he said. "It's very useful. To a practising solicitor, of course. I used to find it a permanent source of irritation that my clients should pay more to the Government—who, after all, hadn't raised a finger to earn it—than they did to me. Do you realise that if I act for the purchase of a London house for £5,000, I get about £43, whilst the Government's share is £100?"

"Scandalous," I agreed. "And so you devised this little machine to adjust the balance. Such a simple and fool-proof form of forgery, when you come to think of it." The more I thought of it the more I liked it. "Just think of the effort you would have to expend—to say nothing of stocks of special paper—if you set out to forge a hundred one-pound notes. Whereas with this machine—a small die—a simple pressure."

"Oh, there's more to it than that," said Mr. Portway. "A man would be a fool to forge Treasury notes. They have to be passed into circulation, and each one is a potential danger to its maker. Here, when I have stamped a document, it goes into a deed box. It may not be looked at again for twenty years. Possibly never."

"As a professional accountant," I said, "I am not sure that that angle is not the one that appeals to me most. Let me see. Take that purchase you were talking about. Your client would give you two cheques, one for your costs, which goes through the books in the ordinary way, and a separate one for the stamp duty."

"Made out to cash."

"Made out to cash, of course. Which you would yourself cash at the bank. Then come back here——"

"I always took the trouble to walk through the Stamp Office in case anyone should be watching me."

"Very sound," I said. "Then you came back here, stamped the document yourself that evening, and put the money in your pocket. It never appeared in your books at all."

"That's right," said Mr. Portway. He seemed gratified at the speed with which I had perceived the finer points of his arrangements.

"There's only one thing I can't quite see," I said. "You're a bachelor, a man with simple tastes. Could you not—I don't want to sound pompous—by working a little harder, have made sufficient money legitimately for your reasonable needs?"

Mr. Portway looked at me for a moment, his smile broadening.

"I see," he said, "that you have not had time to examine the rest of my strong-room. My tastes are far from simple, and owing to the scandalous and confiscatory nature of modern taxation—oh, I beg your pardon. I was forgetting for the moment——"

"Don't apologize," I said. "I have often thought the same thing myself. You were speaking of expensive tastes."

Mr. Portway stepped over to a large, drop-fronted deed box, labelled 'Lord Lampeter's Settled Estate', and unlocked it with a key from a chain. Inside was a rack, and in the rack I counted the dusty ends of two dozen bottles.

"Château Margaux. The 1934 vintage. I shouldn't say that even now it has reached its peak. Now here"—he unlocked 'The Dean of Melchester. Family Affairs'—"I have a real treasure. A Mouton Rothschild of 1924."

"1924!"

"In magnums. I know that you appreciate a good wine. Since this may perhaps be our last opportunity——"

"Well——"

Mr. Portway took a corkscrew, a decanter, and two glasses from a small cupboard labelled 'Estate Duty Forms. Miscellaneous', drew the cork of the Mouton Rothschild with care and skill, and decanted it with a steady hand. Then he poured two glasses. We both held it up to the single unshaded light to note the dark, rich, almost black colour, and took our first, ecstatic mouthful. It went down like oiled silk.

"What did you say you had in the other boxes?" I enquired reverently.

"My preference has been for the clarets," said Mr. Portway. "Of course, as I only really started buying in 1945 I have nothing that you could call a museum piece. But I picked up a small lot of 1927 Château Talbot which has to be tasted to be believed. And if a good burgundy was offered, I didn't say no to it." He gestured towards the Marchioness of Gravesend in the corner. "There's a 1937 Romanée Conti—but your glass is empty. . . ."

As we finished the Mouton Rothschild in companionable silence I looked at my watch. It was two o'clock in the morning.

"You will scarcely find any transport to get you home now," said Mr. Portway. "Might I suggest that the only thing to follow a fine claret is a noble burgundy."

"Well——" I said.

I was fully aware that I was compromising my official position, but it hardly seemed to matter. Actually I think my mind had long since been made up. As dawn was breaking, and the Romanée Conti was sinking in the bottle, we agreed provisional articles of partnership.

The name of the firm is Portway & Gilbert of 7 Lombards Inn.

If you are thinking, by any chance, of buying a house——

LOUIS AUCHINCLOSS

(1917–   )

When his first novel was rejected, the young Louis Stanton Auchincloss left Yale College before graduating and entered law school at the University of Virginia. There he made *Law Review*, and after receiving his LL.B. in 1941, he joined the firm of Sullivan and Cromwell in New York.

After his novel *The Indifferent Children* was published in 1947, Auchincloss considered leaving the law to pursue a Ph.D. in English, but decided against it and continued to write fiction while practicing law. In 1951, however, after publishing a number of short stories, he resigned to write full-time. Three years later, finding that he missed the stimulation of legal work, Auchincloss joined the firm of Hawkins, Delafield and Wood. From then on he had a productive career as both lawyer and writer. He was made a partner in 1958 and remained with the firm as a specialist in trusts and estates until his retirement in 1986.

Auchincloss's literary output includes twenty-five novels and thirteen books of short stories. Gore Vidal has said that Auchincloss knows "banking and law, power and money," and these are indeed central themes in his fiction. His most highly regarded novels include *The House of Five Talents* (1960), *Portrait in Brownstone* (1962), *The Rector of Justin* (1964), and *The Embezzler* (1966).

"The Senior Partner's Ghosts" was first published in the *Virginia Law Review* in March 1964 as part of its fiftieth-anniversary commemoration, and may have been the first piece of fiction to appear in the pages of a law review. It is the wry story of a proper senior attorney, Sylvaner Price, who embarks on a project to write a biography of his firm's eminent and esteemed founder, the late Guthrie Arnold. When Price employs the method of free association, an evil genius torments him with tales of his subject's unethical behavior.

THE SENIOR PARTNER'S GHOSTS

— 1964 —

The wife of the youngest partner of Arnold & Degener, who had married her husband after his promotion and so had not shared with him the restraining influences of the long clerkship years, had once said of the firm's offices at One Chase Manhattan Plaza that they were as austere as the Escorial and that Mr. Price reminded her, in the center of his dreary labyrinth of closed doors and gray corridors, of a watching, spidery Philip II. A troublemaker repeated the remark to Mr. Price, but the effect was not at all what the troublemaker had sought. Sylvaner Price neither grunted nor frowned; for all his interlocutor could see he might not even have heard the comment. Yet, deep within, his heart had quivered with pleasure, and ever after he liked his youngest partner's wife. For she alone had divined that he was a romantic and that the key to open the high dark gates of his heart's stronghold was not to be found in Blackstone or in Maitland, in Pollock, or in Holmes, but quite simply in Victor Hugo.

Yet, if simple, it was nonetheless a difficult fact to divine, and the young woman's remark might have been a chance shot. Certainly to the world Sylvaner Price created the ever consistent impression of a man who had no existence outside of the famous law firm which had been forged by Guthrie Arnold to be the indispensable tool of the greatest corporations and kept sharp and polished by his more than worthy successor. For although Lloyd Degener had succeeded to the position of "senior partner," being the public and political figure, it was Price who held the old man's clients and still dominated the private councils of the firm. He was a tall, thin, spare figure with a small round belly and a round, almost bald head down the center of which ran a few long dark hairs. His face, too, was round and bore in the center a small hook nose on the thin bridge of which were fastened his spectacles, constantly glittering in the head-shaking movement that expressed his constant chagrin with human perversity. He was a man of no accessories, no appendages, no stray bits or loose ends. His mild, nervous wife and her little infirm boy had been converted, years before, into two large manila folders marked "Estates of——," and his big bare Fifth Avenue apartment, with its large dark furniture and small dull prints was simply an annex to One Chase Manhattan Plaza, traveling between which twice a day, in the back seat of his old Pierce Arrow, he made his sole brief contacts with the outside world through window and newspaper.

No, the romantic in Sylvaner Price could not have been surprised by the youngest partner's wife, or indeed by anyone else, unless that person had chanced to observe the furtive little gesture that he made with his right hand every morning when he came into the office, just as he passed the Lazlo portrait of his predecessor. He would glance quickly up at it and quickly down again, and then pass his hand in a rapid half-concealed clutching motion across his chest. One might have almost thought that he was crossing himself. The gesture was certainly reverent, but, more importantly, it implied, unlike any of his others, a certain depth of feeling.

The huge picture hung in the dark paneled reception hall, whose tables, bare of magazines or even newspapers, testified to the sobriety of a client's wait. The late Guthrie Arnold was depicted, standing up, seemingly tall, in a pink coat and top hat, one hand holding a riding crop, the other raised to the bridle of a magnificent bay whose head and front legs occupied more than half of the canvas. One might have assumed that it was an English eighteenth-century portrait, a Romney earl or Lawrence baronet, had it not been for the long oblong countenance of the subject, as equine as its supposed mount, which suggested, with its high intelligent brow, its magisterially dry, thin lips, and its general air of looking down more from a bench than a saddle, the learned profession practiced in the long bare corridors that met at the foot of the frame. One might even have speculated that Mr. Arnold had posed for the artist in unfamiliar garb, with unaccustomed props, that he had, like a visitor in an old photographer's gallery, stuck his head through a hole in a backdrop on which was painted a gaudy scene, had not the lighted glass cases on either side of the portrait and their rows of silver trophy cups testified to indubitable accomplishments in field and stream. The whole group of picture and cases brought to mind a shrine in some barbarous land to a pagan god to whom a greater latitude of behavior was allowed than to his austere and merely mortal votaries. If Mr. Arnold had enjoyed life, that tightly gripped riding crop seemed to imply, it was because Mr. Arnold had been unique. Did any clerk presume to do likewise? Speak up!

Oh, yes, *there* was the romance of Sylvaner Price's life, his memory of Guthrie Arnold, or, more accurately, what he planned to do with that memory. Like all dry, impersonal men, Price was intensely aware that he was dry and impersonal, but this did not mean that he was not proud of the long-hidden imagination which was at last, well past his seventieth year, to explode before a gaping world in all the colors of the rainbow. For what he now planned was nothing less than a sublime work of art—a work of art in the form of a book, a first volume to Lloyd Degener's proposed history of the firm, which would contain a separate biography of the founder that he hoped would rock the downtown world back in its chairs and make it speculate of the author: "Is this our old Sylvaner Price? This Melville, this Whitman, this *peacock*?"

It would be done, too, without the least cheapness, without smirking revelations of discreditable litigations or puerile boastings, in a government-policed era, of what clients used to do in braver, buccaneer days. No, his book would be made glorious simply by its characterization of the great man who had founded and given his name to the firm, a characterization that would reveal him in all the splendor of an individual to an age that had forgotten what such a thing was. Guthrie Arnold in Sylvaner Price's pages would *live,* as a man as well as a lawyer, as a sportsman as well as a philanthropist, as a connoisseur in porcelains as well as in horseflesh, as a wit, as a dandy, as a lady killer, as an iconoclast, in short, as a holy terror. Oh, yes, everyone would gape that Sylvaner Price even *knew* of such things, but that would be just the wonderful fun of it! He had not slaved for his predecessor for four decades without knowing him. And if he, like his other colleagues, had been a worker in the hive all his days and nights, he would prove at least that he had been a worker who had witnessed the flight of the queen bee.

And now, at last, he had actually started on the great work. His mornings from ten o'clock to noon were consecrated to the task. In this hallowed period he was alone with his dictaphone, and Miss Ives, on guard outside his closed door, saw that no calls or callers shattered his peace. Leaning back in his chair and touching the tips of his long fingers together, his eyes resting on the silver-framed photograph of the Lazlo portrait, he would try to achieve what he had heard described as "free association." He would imagine his mind as a white sheet and wait until the unrelated slides of his unconscious memory were projected upon it. As soon as they began to cohere into any definite subject he would turn on his machine. But one day in the third week of his project, an anecdote that he was dictating came out in a very different shape from what he had planned. Indeed, it was so different that the experience quite shook him up.

"Clients," he had started. "Clients and the getting of clients. Mr. Arnold always said that a job well done was worth a hundred chats on a hundred golf courses. He scorned the idea of the public relations partner to act as a decoy to bring customers to the less charming experts behind the scene. 'Would you go to a dentist because you found his partner good company?' he would ask. The only way, he insisted, that a lawyer could use a social occasion to attract business was by showing off his expertise. And to do that one had to *be* an expert. Mr. Arnold would don his white tie as another man might don his overalls—for work. After dinner, over the brandies with the men, slipping into a seat by the chairman of the biggest company, he might let the talk glide into the channels of the latter's current reorganization. 'I was interested to see in the paper that you didn't use a Section 15 subsidiary. I suppose you wouldn't have qualified under 14-C. Too bad.' When promptly challenged as to the advantages of such a course and informed, perhaps a bit tartly, that the company was represented by Able Fine, Mr. Arnold would raise both hands in prompt disclaimer. 'Ah, my dear fellow, if Able Fine is guiding you, you're all right. Of course, he has some excellent reason for doing as he has done. Depend upon it.' Yet he would shake his head from time to time, as if troubled with a secret, stubborn doubt, and in departing he might reassail his disconcerted fellow guest with the solicitous query: 'Able made a complete recovery from that heart attack, didn't he? Oh, good, good.' "

Price closed his teeth together with a little click as he slowly straightened in his chair. Had *he* said all that? Quickly he adjusted the machine to play back his tape, and there, indubitably, were the scratchy words. Appalled, he took the disc from its pin and dropped it in his wastebasket. Where had such a memory come from? *Memory*? It was no memory, but the rankest fairy tale! Obviously, he was tired or strained or showing his age. He shivered and rang for Miss Ives to tell her that he would start his ordinary day's work and leave the book until the morrow.

But on the morrow the same thing happened. He had chosen for the morning's "free association" the seemingly safe topic of estate administration, and after a rambling start had got into his stride along the following line:

"If there was one thing Mr. Arnold liked it was what he called a 'clean' estate. He maintained that when one had elderly testators it was a duty to start 'cleaning up' in their lifetimes. 'Get rid of foreign property,' he would enjoin me; 'sweep up odd bits of oil ventures, liquidate unnecessary partnerships. When an estate is ripe, it should come off the bough into your hands with hardly a pluck.' Sometimes he carried out his theories with a logic and a matter-of-factness that was a bit disconcerting to his associates. When we got word of his brother Jay's death in Paris, I recall his rubbing his hands briskly together and exclaiming: 'Isn't it luck that we sold that North African mine?' And he actually whistled a tune!"

Price rose slowly to his feet and pressed the tips of his fingers against his lowered lids. There was no need this time to play back the tape; he simply removed the disc and placed it, like its predecessor, in the basket. Then he pulled out his silk handkerchief, carefully daubed his gleaming brow and walked out to the reception hall and over to the portrait of Mr. Arnold.

"What is it, sir?" he whispered under his breath. "Don't you *want* me to write my book?"

He continued to stare until it almost seemed to him that one of those small gray eyes had winked. A mean, mocking, glinting wink. He turned quickly to the receptionist, but she was not minding him. Two messengers, sitting on the bench beside her, looked vacantly at the ceiling. When he glanced back at the portrait, it was as it had always been. The wink had been imagined; he was even conscious of having consciously imagined it. But had he imagined the sudden atmosphere, at once cold and fetid, of the big room?

That day he presided, in Lloyd Degener's absence in Washington, at the partners' weekly lunch, seated at the end of the long oval table in the private dining room of the Merchants' Club. He was as silent as he decently could be, but he felt jumpy all during the meal and could hardly endure listening to the department heads as they reported, with lawyers' prolixity, on the business in their respective charges. At the end of the meal he hit the table sharply with the little gavel that was always left at his place and made a speech that he had no memory of either preparing or conceiving. He could only listen in a kind of stupor to his own harsh voice as it angrily made point after point.

"We've heard, gentlemen, a lot about what's going on *inside* the office, but not a word of what's going on outside. Yet I suppose you all know about Frank Schrader in Dunlap, Schrader & Todd. It's cancer, and only a matter of months. Now I don't think I need to tell anyone, at least anyone in the corporate and securities line, that Frank Schrader is the one man who's been holding that firm together. But on the skids or not, they've still got some beautiful business: Seaboard Trust, Angus Chemicals, and the Stutz family. A lot of that business *belongs* here. Old man Stutz, for example, is a natural for the Arnold & Degener roster. We're perfectly set up for him, and he for us. Now I want to see you fellows move in on that business. Review all your friends in those companies. Check their boards of directors. See which of you belong to what clubs they belong to. Arrange opportunities to meet them. Sometimes I think you fellows think clients grow on trees. Must I do *all* the work around here?"

Wonderingly, as he heard his voice cease, he glanced about the silent, shocked table. They were all staring at him.

"*Well*, gentlemen?" his voice demanded.

"I've been away for six weeks," came at last the mild, impertinent Southern drawl of the youngest partner, he with the clever wife, the brilliant "boy" with ruffled hair and freckles. "And so perhaps I haven't heard. Have the Canons of Professional Ethics been suspended? Has the Bar Association officially endorsed ambulance chasing?"

Price felt his hand reach for the gavel as the spurt of rebellious laughter started around the table, and he struck the table harder than he had ever heard it struck before. "You can talk to me about ethics when you've paid the rent!" his voice cried out. "There's not one of you who'd be where you are without me. I can hire as many brains as I want, but where do I get the clients? Where, gentlemen? I repeat: on *trees*?" He rose now and tossed the gavel contemptuously on the table. "The meeting is adjourned."

Walking back to the office, Jack Keating, an estates partner, earnest and heavy-jawed, Price's principal pupil, kept up a rather breathless pace with him. "You were terrific, sir," he said. "A reminder like that is a tonic to us all. We get so smug about our big larder of business. Do you know, if I had closed my eyes, I would have sworn it was old Mr. Arnold himself talking!"

Price closed his eyes and gave a little moan. "Oh, don't, Jack, please don't," he murmured.

That evening he worked late, and when he emerged from his office the reception hall was empty. He switched on the light above the portrait and went over to stand beneath it, glancing cautiously to each side to be sure that he was alone. Then he fixed his eyes on the eyes of Mr. Arnold's likeness.

"What do you want?" he asked.

The aspect of the portrait did not change. To his infinite relief it remained an inanimate canvas. But as he continued to stare at it, he felt again that distinct chill in the air about him, a chill that he now associated with this strange communion between himself and the dead. An idea took sudden shape from the misty corners of his mind, flowing together out of Lord knows what long-locked compartments, that there existed an evil spirit imprisoned and imprisoned by *him* right here, where he was now standing, hemmed in to a corner of the great reception room, bound down, so to speak, with the gilded frame of the portrait, with the glass of the trophy cases, confined to that single spot as too dangerous to be allowed to roam. But if it was there, if it always had been there, why was it now felt for the first time and why by him, Sylvaner Price? Why indeed, by all that was unholy, unless it was because he was doing something that he had never done before, and what was that but writing the story of Guthrie Arnold?

"So that's it!" he cried. "I'm letting you out. Letting you out at last. And you think you'll come on your own terms! You think that *you*, the evil genius of Guthrie Arnold, will now prevail—as you never could in his lifetime—over his good, his noble, his magnificent spirit. Well, you won't, that's all I can tell you, my hearty! You'll come into my book, but in your proper place. You want to be wicked, but you'll be only witty. You want to be savage, but you'll be only severe. You want to be slippery, but you'll be merely ingenious. You want to be heartless, but you'll be only just. Oh, I'll *fix* you now, for what you've done to me!"

He was suddenly aware that he was no longer alone, and turning with a little jump he saw a law clerk staring at him with an astonishment that he made no effort to conceal.

"Well, what are you gaping at?" Price demanded testily. "Go on about your business. I'm rehearsing a skit we're putting on at the Bar Association. That's all."

"Yes, sir."

"That's all, I tell you!" he shouted, and the young man fled.

The next morning Price spent his allotted two hours alone with his machine dictating an account of Mr. Arnold's technique in domestic matters. This was to be the basis for what he hoped would be the liveliest chapter of the book, for the late senior partner had known perfectly how to expose fortune hunters, how to keep family money out of the hands of in-laws and incompetents, but it was also the section of Price's proposed book that seemed most to bristle with opportunities for the antic spirit that had now visited him thrice. Price enunciated his words in a hard, graveled tone, as though in uttering them he was nonetheless holding them under his domination, so that he might have resembled some grim old dog-walker in Central Park, moving slowly ahead in the midst of a tumbling mass of canines, each firmly attached by leash to his clenched fist. But everything came out as he had wished, and at twelve o'clock, when Miss Ives knocked, he had completed a full disc of anecdote without the interpolation of his unsought collaborator.

"Is there anything up, Miss Ives?"

"Oh, yes, sir. I almost interrupted you, but I remembered how strict your orders were. Dr. Salter called at eleven. Miss Jenkins died."

"Miss Jenkins! Good heavens, of course, you should have called me. Have you got the will out of the vault?"

"Here it is, sir."

Alone again behind his closed door, he adjusted his features to a fitting solemnity. It was impossible altogether to repress Mr. Arnold's image of the falling of a ripe piece of fruit. Miss Jenkins had approached the perfect client; for eighty-five years she seemed to have been preparing for a neat and orderly demise. Her houses, in town and country, were deeded to her church, subject only to her life estate, and her jewelry and artifacts of any value had been parceled out in her lifetime among her nephews and nieces. There remained, indeed, little enough to bother her faithful counsel: little, that is, but a custodian account at the Standard Trust Company containing fifteen millions of "blue chip" securities. In only one respect had she fallen short of perfection: in her last will (she had made them annually) she had omitted Sylvaner Price as her co-executor with her bank.

"You'll have your counsel fees, Sylvaner," she had gruffly pointed out. "There's really no need for commissions, too, is there? One executor should be quite enough to handle this estate."

He had assured her that it should, but now, as he turned to the last page and contemplated the testatrix's tall strong signature beside the red wafer seal that was stamped over the two ends of the red ribbon that bound the pages together, he felt with his sudden regret a curious itching in his fingertips. Dropping the will to the desk he held up his hands, the palms toward him, and was startled to see his fingers twitching like the legs of two overturned crabs. Repulsed, he let his hands fall to the desk, one on either side of the will and contemplated with shock their immediately quickened movements.

"What do you want?" he cried. "Do you want me to tear *that* up? Do you want to deprive me of my prize estate? Well, go ahead, do your damndest!"

Hypnotized, he continued to watch his waving extremities. His right hand now turned itself over on its palm and slid along the surface of the desk to the drawers on the right and, dropping to the lowest, pulled it open to disclose the pages of another will. For a moment Price stared, and then with a start he recognized it as the next-to-last will that he had prepared for Miss Jenkins and which she had declined to execute because it had provided for two executors. His busy right hand, now flipping the pages expertly, pulled out page eight and brought it up, with the help of his suddenly cooperating arm, to toss it beside the executed instrument. Oh, how he *saw* it now, of course! Page eight was identical in all respects in each will except that the earlier one appointed as executors Sylvaner Price and Standard Trust Company while the later appointed only Standard.

"But what can you do about it?" he demanded, as much now in fascination as in fear of his suddenly quiet hands. "Can you break the seal? Are you trying to put me in jail?"

For answer his right hand soared into the air and then plunged into his vest pocket to extract the gold knife at the end of his watch chain. His left hand moved immediately to open the fine blade, and Price, transfixed, watched as the knife, held between his right forefinger and thumb, deftly and speedily scraped off the red paper seal. Next the ribbon was cut and pulled out and page eight removed and thrown, with the remnants of the seal, into the wastebasket. And all the while his mind kept up with his appendages, explaining, anticipating, almost gloating.

"But there'll be a copy of the executed will in Miss Jenkins' apartment. Oh, no there won't! I remember now, she wouldn't keep a copy. She said the servants might pry. But if I attach a new seal, a chemical test would show that the old one had been removed. Yes, but there won't *be* a chemical test. That's just the point! Who would ever question the fact that Miss Jenkins wanted two executors? Had she not appointed two in thirty previous wills? How it fits! How it all fits!"

His hands appeared to be suddenly at a loss. They sank to the blotter, more like tired doves now than crabs, but the fingers continued to flutter. They seemed to be appealing to him, to be trying to communicate that they had done all they could. . . .

"But naturally!" he cried with near hysteria. "You want ribbon and a new seal. You shall have them!"

He hurried to his door, opened it and found that Miss Ives was not at her desk. Pulling open the drawer where she kept her office supplies, he snatched the ribbon and red paper seal and returned to his room. In a few moments, with a deftness as amazing as the skill with which the first seal had been removed, Miss Jenkins' will with its new page eight had been reribboned and a new seal affixed carefully in the exact place of the old. Price stared with wonder at the completed document. Nobody would have dreamed that it had been tampered with. It would be probated without a murmur from a single relative, a single legatee. And yet the work of ten minutes would operate to bring to him and his firm, by simple operation of law, a statutory commission of three hundred thousand dollars! It was the perfect crime.

The perfect . . . ! Price came at last to his old senses as he stared, with perfectly immobile body and slowly blinking eyes at the will. The *will*! But it was not a will; it was no more Miss Jenkins' will than his own, lying untampered with in the office vault. It was a rank forgery, and the forger, ghost or no ghost, should be put behind bars. His round gleaming forehead was pimpled again with drops of sweat as he contemplated *who* it would be to stand in that criminal docket. But it was absurd, macabre, unholy! Ghosts could not be allowed to administer estates according to the concealed wickedness of long buried men. What was done could be undone. He started from his chair to reach in the basket for the removed, the desecrated, the *real* page eight and uttered a little shriek when he saw that he had torn it in two. He snatched up the forged will to rip it likewise in twain but paused just in time. After all, it was, if forged, still the client's only will, and the client was dead!

Sylvaner Price raised his eyes to the ceiling and his guilty fists above his eyes and shook them as he cursed the memory of Guthrie Arnold. But the words were no sooner uttered than his chest was struck by what seemed the impact of a thousand needles, and he fell forward unconscious over his desk and the creamy white red-ribboned parchment on which Miss Ives had so carefully typed the posthumous wishes of the late Miss Jenkins.

In the white hygienic serenity of his hospital room Price enjoyed a dull, doped peace. The proximity to death in which his coronary attack had briefly placed him had left him totally indifferent. He had even been capable of a small smile when Jack Keating, obviously warned to bring to his troubled mind no office news except of the most consoling character, had murmured into his oxygen tent that Miss Jenkins' will had been admitted to probate only two days after her demise, creating what was deemed an office record. It was all right, Price reassured himself. He would know what to do about that. If he should die, he would not have earned the commissions, and if he lived he could renounce them. If there were an afterlife, he could explain to Miss Jenkins, and if not . . . well, he did not really think he believed in anything but nothingness. The nothingness that meant absence of all need of lawyers. The nothingness of total rest.

As he recuperated he began, little by little, to resume his work on the biography, but not at all according to his original plan. Back in his apartment, seated on a couch by a window looking over a wintry Central Park, he dictated for a lengthening period each day to Miss Ives. As the doctor said he was not to exert himself, he consulted no notebooks or records. With his eyes closed and his now innocent hands folded tranquilly on his diminished abdomen, he spoke from memory. From memory or imagination? What did it matter? There were to be no further vividnesses. He was to put Guthrie Arnold back into the legend of the firm, and for this he needed only to consult his own high principles. What did it matter if his history would be like every other firm history? Was there not something restful, dignified, even rather noble about the well-prepared, the well-documented, the well-printed, the well-bound, and the unread?

"Mr. Arnold in his later years was able to delegate some of the detail of his burdensome practice to the shoulders of his younger partners and associates." Price's usual sharp, staccato voice had evened itself out into what was almost a sonorous flow. "This did not mean, however, that he shortened his hours. Whenever he saved time it was to contribute it to the many charitable enterprises on whose boards he so assiduously served. It was the function of younger men, he always maintained, to dedicate themselves wholly to their profession. Every young lawyer, he insisted, should have a hobby—law. But it was the duty of older men to begin to consider the community as a whole. . . ."

Oh, yes, it had all the effect that he knew it would. That other spirit, no longer manifested in the pricking of his brow or the wagging of his fingers, seemed quite at rest, and thinking of the altar of reliquaries in the office reception hall, he wondered if the *cordon sanitaire* with which he was now binding it off might not have manifested itself in the actual apparition of the kind of looped cord used in art galleries to keep back crowds. But evidently not, for nothing untoward was reported from downtown.

When Jack Keating came to report on the administration of the Jenkins estate, Price told him that he had decided to waive his commissions. Keating looked surprised, but it immediately struck Price that there was something factitious about his expression.

"I had a conversation with Miss Jenkins shortly before she died," Price explained gruffly. "She told me she had decided to have only one executor—the bank. Unfortunately I did not have time to prepare a new will. Naturally, under the circumstances, I cannot take commissions."

"Naturally." There was something too quickly conciliatory in Keating's tone, something almost medically professional, nurse-like. "One wouldn't expect you to. Was it perhaps like the conversation young Smedburg saw you having one night in the reception hall with the portrait of Mr. Arnold?"

Price gave him a long, hard stare. "Perhaps."

"They're expensive, Mr. Price, your chats with spirits."

In twenty years Keating had never been so familiar. His tone was friendly, as was his rueful laugh, but they were the tone and the laugh that one used to the senile. How well Price knew them!

"You don't believe I had that talk with Miss Jenkins," he said quietly.

"I believe *you* believe it," Keating insisted eagerly. "All of us believe that. All your partners, I mean."

"But you think I've lost my mind."

"Never!" Keating shook his head with a slow, irritating solemnity. "Never. We simply believe you've been under a strain. My God, man, you're not made of iron! You have been running the shop by day and by night, in all seasons, for how many years? How could you expect to get through a lifetime without one crack on the surface?"

A faint smile appeared on Price's thin lips. "What then must Humpty Dumpty do?"

As Keating looked down now at the floor, both hands on his knees, Price suddenly realized that he was embarrassed, mortally embarrassed. All his chuckles and his slow nods had been but a tattered façade to cover his misery. The poor man was suffering as *he* had suffered when he had had to guide old Arnold in his senility. "Tell me," Price said in a gentler tone.

"I want to know. I will do anything the firm suggests. What do they think I should do? Resign?"

Keating looked up, his face aglow with relief. "Oh, no, never!" he exclaimed warmly. "We need you much too much. But would you consider . . ." He faltered, wretched again. "Would you consider seeing a psychiatrist?"

"Certainly. Whomever you wish. Whenever you wish."

"There's Dr. Haven. He's the head man at St. Andrew's." Keating's voice shivered with the desire to get it over with. "He's not one of your bearded Freudians. He knows what it's all about. He . . ."

"Make me an appointment, Keating. My doctor says I may go out on Monday. I shall go to Dr. Haven."

"Thank you, sir!" Keating was a clerk again as he jumped gratefully to his feet. "I'm sure it's nothing serious. A couple of talks, and you'll be all squared away."

"Very likely." He coughed, the older partner again, as Keating made his way hastily to the door. "Oh, and Keating," he called.

"Yes, sir?"

"Send me up a renunciation of commissions in the Jenkins estate. And one of the clerks who's a notary with it. He can file it in the Surrogate's Court on his way back."

Keating's face was pathetic in its disappointment. "Won't you wait, sir, until you've seen Dr. Haven?"

"Do as I say, Keating," Price said gravely, "or I shall go to court myself."

He smiled a bit grimly as he heard the whispers in the corridor and knew that Keating was consulting with Miss Ives. But it was all right. His authority still held. Keating would do as he was told.

Dr. Haven made things very easy for him. He was, as promised, not in the least Freudian-looking; he might have come off the golf course, so round, so bald, so tweeded was he, yet withal so friendly, so sympathetic, so oddly wonderful. There was no idea, he quickly reassured Price, of any lying on couches or talking of sex. Price could simply sit, as stiffly as he liked, for all the world as if he were a client in his own office, and tell his story to an auditor whose unique virtue would be his complete attention.

"We're not even thinking of analysis," the doctor frankly told him. "It's not really feasible with older patients. Let's see first what we can do with a patchwork job."

Vastly reassured, Price told him, with less embarrassment than he would have believed possible, of his strange visitations. Haven seemed not in the least surprised; he nodded as understandingly as if he, too, were constantly bothered by such mischievous sprites as haunted his patient. Yet nonetheless it came as a reassurance and not a disappointment, when, after only four sessions in which they had covered, with a disillusioning speed, the salient events in Sylvaner Price's life, the doctor announced his personal disbelief in the evil spirit of Guthrie Arnold.

"The anecdotes that you dictated were all within your own conscious or unconscious memory," he pointed out. "If they were not actually said by Arnold, they could have been said about him. Or said about someone else and associated by you unconsciously with Arnold. And what happened to the Jenkins will—well, you *saw* what happened to the Jenkins will."

"You think, then, I'm a horror?" Price asked sadly.

"I think, my friend, that you've been a victim of your own deepest fears. All your life you have identified pleasure with sin. That has been very clear from what you have told me of your past. Mr. Arnold was to you a godlike figure who enjoyed a special exemption. He could frolic without incurring the penalties that Sylvaner Price would have incurred. The only way *you* could frolic was by somehow creeping under his exemption. But the moment you tried this, by putting yourself as a biographer in the shoes of your subject—a clever device, I admit—well, of course, you had immediately to sin and immediately to suffer. Clever as it is, the subconscious can't escape itself."

Price considered this for a full minute. "So Mr. Arnold wasn't, after all, that way?"

"What way?"

"Wasn't a crook."

"My dear fellow, I have no doubt that he was every bit as distinguished a member of your profession as your great firm has always proudly claimed!"

"And do you have no doubt, by like token, that, once I have accepted your diagnosis, I may continue my book in the spirit in which it was originally conceived?"

"No doubt whatever."

Price nodded several times and then, abruptly rising, bade his doctor good day and asked him to send his bill.

"Oh, your firm has taken care of that."

Price looked down at him with the faintest trace of a smile. "I hope they find me worth it."

The next morning, once more in his office, he told Miss Ives that he would revive his isolated biographical sessions, and he addressed himself once more to his dictaphone. Warily, with an eye occasionally cocked at the closed door that led out to the reception hall and its portrait, he began to describe Mr. Arnold as an administrator.

"One of the greatest pitfalls in building a large firm is accommodation business. Every client thinks you can turn over his minor headaches—his wife's fight with the department store, his niece's divorce, his son's traffic violations—to some young clerk and have them lost in the ocean of office overhead. But Mr. Arnold understood perfectly not only that the accumulation of these matters can seriously clog the operation of a law firm, but that being dipped in human spite and perversity they frequently resulted, even when competently handled, in client dissatisfaction. And so he developed his great art of referral. Never has it been carried to more Olympian heights! He could make the unhappy lawyer to whom he entrusted the garrulous old maid with the tangled leasehold think that he was getting a green shoot, the precursor of new business, and not, as in fact he was, a dead branch lopped off the healthy tree of the Arnold roster. 'Don't forget, Price,' he used to remind me with his cackling laugh, 'that a wise referral should accomplish two things: it should clean up your own yard and make a dump of your neighbor's lawn!' "

Price was on his feet now, his fists clenched, his eyes closed in the old agony. Would there be no end to these hideous anecdotes? Would the fiend never let him be? Where would his itching fingers lead him next? Their tips were burning again now, and, opening his hands, he stared at them in terror. Across the white spread sheet of his stunned mind a series of horrible slides were projected, succeeding each other with little clicks. There was the locked drawer of the office files, then the heavy round knob of the office safe. He had a sensation of metal on his finger tips, but *why?* Why in the name of Beelzebub? What horrors could he be seeking there? His right hand began to move up and down, like a dog at the end of a leash, wanting to be taken out, wanting . . .

No, no, what a hell, was there no keeping it out? "Miss Ives!" With a desperate effort he turned and sent the dictaphone crashing to the floor.

Pale and staring, she loomed through the slowly opened door.

"Come in, come in. I've smashed that damn machine. Yes, come in and leave my door open. Always, please, Miss Ives, from now on, leave my door open. I shall dictate only to you. In fact, I'll start right now. Are you ready?"

Miss Ives was always ready. Price walked rapidly back and forth across his room as he continued his reminiscences, and each time that he reached the open door he cast his eyes suspiciously toward the great portrait at the end of the reception hall that gazed so superciliously down at small waiting clients, clutching like immigrants' bundles their small heaps of problems.

"Mr. Arnold," he dictated in his most rasping tone, "always insisted that the Code of Professional Ethics should be more strictly interpreted. Unlike so many of his contemporaries, he never held a share of stock in a corporation that he represented. He would not even allow the firm's telephone number to appear on our letterhead, and it was only with the greatest difficulty that we persuaded him to enter it in the directory."

He paused to glance boldly now for a longer interval at the portrait. Innocuous again, mild, showy, even faintly vulgar, it had dwindled to the more fitting proportions of a piece of interior decoration. Well, if that was the only way! Bitter, dry, determined, Price picked up again his narrative. As he intoned the names of civic institutions and civic honors, as he listed honorary degrees and quoted from testimonials, as he delivered anecdotes to illustrate the wisdom, the common sense, the humanity, the lovableness of his subject, he might have been an undertaker driving in, one by one, the nails of the coffin of Guthrie Arnold—his Guthrie Arnold, Satan's Guthrie Arnold, the firm's Guthrie Arnold, anybody's Guthrie Arnold—what did it matter so long as there was peace?

QUENTIN CRISP

(1908–)

Born Denis Pratt in Surrey, England, Quentin Crisp worked in his early years as a commercial artist and artist's model. *The Naked Civil Servant* is the chronicle of his first forty years of life as a homosexual. "It seemed to me that there were few homosexuals in the world," he writes. "I felt that the entire strength of the club must be prepared to show its membership card at any time, and, to a nature as dramatic as mine, not to deny rapidly became to protest. By the time I was twenty-three I had made myself into a test case." With wit and grace, Crisp describes how he cultivated and flaunted an effeminate appearance at a time when homosexuality was not only scandalous but illegal. In this excerpt Crisp recounts the harassment to which the London police subjected gay men in the 1930s and 1940s, and his trial after he was arrested for alleged solicitation.

In England homosexuality has come under the scrutiny of the legal system for hundreds of years. Buggery (the corresponding American term is *sodomy*) was made a felony punishable by death in 1533, and the death sentence was not repealed and replaced with life imprisonment until 1861. Beginning in 1885, *any* homosexual act was subject to a two-year prison term under the Criminal Law Amendment Act. (It was under this act that Oscar Wilde was sentenced ten years later.) In 1898 sexual solicitation of any kind was also made punishable with up to two years' imprisonment. Although this statute was actually drafted with pimps in mind, it was widely used against homosexual solicitation and was the legal basis for Crisp's arrest. With the passage of the Sexual Offences Act in 1967, homosexuality between consenting adults aged twenty-one and older finally become immune from legal punishment.

In 1982 Crisp left London for New York, where he resides today. In addition to numerous books, including *Love Made Easy* (1977), *Chog, A Gothic Fantasy* (1979), *Quentin Crisp's Book of Quotations* (1989), and *Resident Alien: The New York Diaries* (1996), he has published articles both in the United States and abroad. He has also made film appearances, most recently as Queen Elizabeth I in *Orlando* (1994).

from THE NAKED CIVIL SERVANT

— 1968 —

It was while I was in Mr. MacQueen's employ that I was arrested. . . . This was an eventuality that I and my enemies had expected ever since the far-off days when I had first been questioned by the police. A young man called Bermondsey Lizzie had once said, 'You'll get years one of these days, girl, but you'll tell them everything, won't you?—when you come up for trial, I mean. I'll never forgive you if you don't.'

Being in a display firm is like working for the movie industry. When you are not coping with a crisis you are wondering how on earth to fill in your time. During one of these lulls I was given a day off. I decided to spend this buying a pair of shoes. This was always a difficult and dangerous mission for me. If I wanted to use the longest words for the shortest thing I would say that I was a passive foot fetishist. My feet were smaller than an ordinary mortal's and I wanted everyone to know this. As time went by I wore shorter and shorter shoes, not because the length of my feet decreased but because the amount of discomfort I could bear became greater. Finally I was able to endure footwear that was hardly visible to the naked eye. For me, as for Hans Andersen's little mermaid, every step was agony but as she had finally been rewarded by dancing with a prince, I never gave up. Almost as uncomfortable as wearing the shoes was buying them. Both I and the shop assistant needed all the fortitude we could summon. I would describe the shoes I had in mind and ask for a size four. The salesman or woman (according to what sex the management had decided I was) would measure my foot and bring me a shoe that fitted me perfectly. This immediately aroused my suspicion. When I ripped it off and looked at the sole, I found it to be a six. Moving down the scale in semitones, I would try on successive sizes until my toes were folded inside the shoe like the leaves of an artichoke. Then I would say, 'Now lift me up.' If I could stand in them, those were the shoes I bought. Tottering into the street, I screamed for a taxi. To this day my feet are two mis-shapen plinths of twisted bone.

Since I knew what an ordeal awaited me once I had entered a shoe shop, I did not do so lightly. I scrutinized the goods in the window until I was sure what I wanted was inside. This was what I was doing on the fatal afternoon. I had already systematically searched all the likely windows in Oxford Street and was just starting on Charing Cross Road when I was stopped by two policemen disguised as human beings. They demanded to see my exemption papers. As always I showed them the one that said that I suffered from sexual perversion. When my inquisitors had retrieved their eyebrows from the roots of their hair, they gave me back this by now rather grubby document and I moved on.

Outside the Hippodrome Theatre I met by chance a certain part-time hooligan called Mr. Palmer. I slapped on to his plate his ration of eternal wisdom for the day and turned into Coventry Street. Almost immediately I was stopped a second time by the same two men. 'Just a moment, you,' they said. 'We are taking you in for soliciting.'

I marched before them following the instructions they muttered to me from behind. These led to Savile Row police station where I was searched by one man while others stood round saying, 'Mind how you go.' I was not stripped, but my pockets were emptied and I was sufficiently unzipped for it to be seen that I was not wearing women's underclothes. Then I was asked if I minded having my finger-prints taken. I replied that it couldn't matter less. To this day, my prints lie in the files of Scotland Yard and just beyond them there are ten little squiggles that I expect Edgar Lustgarten sits up nights pondering over. They are the marks of my fingernails, which it had not been possible to keep out of the ink.

The police did not start to be really irritating until the question arose of finding someone to go bail for me. This was necessary so that I could by telephone distribute my most immediate bookings in the schools among the various models and warn Mr. MacQueen that I would not be at work the next day or possibly for six months to come. If all this had not been necessary, I would quite contentedly have spent the night in the police station. I can sleep anywhere. I offered to supply a list of names, addresses and telephone numbers and the money for making the calls so that someone might quickly be found who was free to come to Savile Row. This they would not allow me to do. 'Just give us one name,' they said stubbornly. So I gave the ballet teacher, on whom they called several times without finding her in. At about ten at night they asked me for the name of another person and I gave them that of the man who had written the Kangaroo limerick. Fortunately he arrived almost immediately. I dashed through the blacked-out streets of London, first to Mr Palmer. He was the young man to whom I had been seen speaking in the street during the afternoon. I asked him (if he could get time off from work) to come to court the following morning and say that he knew me. Then I went on to Toni's to tell the world in case anyone was interested in seeing foul play. Finally I reached home and made countless telephone calls, some offering speaking parts to friends of long standing who could act as character witnesses, and others to people who might like to appear as crowd artists. The next day, dressed in black so as to maintain the great tradition, I set out with my entourage for Bow Street.

As soon as I stepped into the courtroom, I was assailed by two contrary feelings. The first was that here was the long awaited fully involving situation to which I could summon all my capacity for survival. The second was that I might fall on the floor in a dead faint and that it might be just as well if I did.

In the days when I knew the Irish and the Scottish boys, I was often in police courts to act as a chorus to them or their friends and to cry 'Woe unto Ilium' if an unfair verdict was given, but as soon as I, myself, was on trial, I found that I knew nothing of the judicial ritual. I had not, for instance, remembered that the magistrate sits in a state of patient trance while the case against you is conducted by his clerk.

I marvelled at the benignity of the magistrate, who himself instructed me in the procedure of the court, and I was appalled by his clerk's bitchiness. He played the whole scene for laughs, turning slowly towards the public, with his hands in the air like George Sanders uttering his best lines. These included, 'You are a male person, I presume.' This total abandonment of dignity reminded me of the collapse of Harley Street at my medical examination four years earlier.

The police behaved in the perfectly conventional way that I remembered well. They rattled off their evidence as though it were the litany. They said that between the hours of this and that, they had observed the accused stopping and speaking to various people who had looked horrified and torn themselves away. At one moment they included in this great work of fiction a touch of realism. They mentioned the young man with whom I had talked outside the Hippodrome.

When the police had completed their evidence, the magistrate asked me if I would prefer to reply from the dock or go into the witness box where I would have to take the oath. I chose the latter, not because I hoped to gain anything from invoking the aid of You-Know-Who but because it would raise me to a higher vantage point and, like posing on a rostrum in an art school, lend me a spurious nobility. It also meant that I did not have my back to the audience for the whole of my big scene, which I had decided to play dead straight like Imogen in Cymbeline.

I forbore to state that the two policemen who had arrested me were inveterate liars. I humbly put forward the opinion that they had drawn mistaken conclusions from what they saw and that their error had been prompted by their having read my exemption paper which described me as homosexual. This they had not mentioned in their evidence. I also suggested that they might have misinterpreted my appearance. I said that I dressed and lived in such a way that the whole world could see that I was homosexual but that this set me apart from the rest of humanity rather than making it easy for me to form contacts with it. Who, I asked the magistrate, could possibly hope to solicit anybody in broad daylight in a crowded London street looking as I did?

At this point, I was later told by one of my friends who was sitting in the court, a stranger whispered, 'They can't do nothing with 'im. He can't 'elp 'isself. You can see that.'

This we all agreed marked the dawn of a new day.

Various kind people gave evidence as to the irreproachability of my character and, to my relief, Mr. Palmer went into the witness box to declare that he had spoken to me the previous afternoon because he knew me. He was nervous, but he spoke clearly and without hesitation. That he had secret reserves of courage I did not at that time know. I only discovered that ten years later when, at about the age of thirty-two, he committed suicide. Everyone who spoke on my behalf was asked by the magistrate's clerk if he knew that I was homosexual and replied that he did. This question was in each case followed immediately by the words, uttered in a voice hoarse with incredulity, 'And yet you describe him as respectable?' All said, 'Yes.'

When the magistrate tired of this recital of my praises he said that the evidence against me was insufficient to convict me. I was dismissed. He meant that the evidence was a lie. If it had been true, it could have caused the downfall of an archbishop.

Everyone who was present at my trial or who was told about it later was amazed at my acquittal. One friend, fearing the worst, had advised me to try to have my case postponed while I engaged the services of a lawyer. This would incidentally have brought up one of the nastier points of the law. If I did this and then lost my case, I must take it for granted that my sentence would be heavier. In other words Justice revenges herself not only on those who commit crimes but also on those who take up her time. I decided against seeking legal aid not because I feared that my time in jail might be prolonged but because my case did not seem to require the help of 'my learned friend'. There were no subtle legal points to be argued. Unless the accused produces an alibi there never can be evidence of a person not speaking to strangers. I felt that if I clearly protested my innocence it should be effective. I also feared that a lawyer might deliberately blur the issue of my being homosexual on the quite logical ground that it was not the point. Whether it was relevant or not, my one desire was to state in a court of law that I was homosexual and as stainless as Sheffield steel. This was a distinction that, ten years earlier, would have been very difficult to make, but this magistrate at least had seen that this might be so.

The police, as usual, merely wanted a conviction. They thought that their case simply could not go wrong once I had been seen in court. This scramble to gain promotion by securing a large number of arrests is an unpleasant part of the police system, but I could not say that, either in this case in particular or throughout my life generally, the police have treated me badly. What made me feel so unremittingly hostile towards them was their facetiousness and the insulting manner displayed by a group of people who should at all costs remain neutral.

When they arrested me they could only be accused of stating a little more than they could prove. They followed a known homosexual who stopped several times (possibly pretending) to look in shop windows. Whenever I stopped a small crowd collected. I don't remember the details of that afternoon but it would be safe to assume that a few remarks were made to me or at me. Unless constables were standing between me and whoever was speaking they would not be able to say for certain whether I replied or not. Their crime was that they swore I had and implied that I had spoken first. I could swear that I did not speak first to anyone because I never did. I could be fairly certain that I did not answer at all because remarks uttered by strangers, unless they are made in an American accent, always contained a veiled or a naked insult. So I was technically not guilty and, at the time, felt appropriately outraged. Yet if there are degrees of innocence, I would not now claim to have won first class honours. My thoughts on this subject are vague because I am not sure what the laws against soliciting are framed to prevent. If soliciting is a crime because it is a nuisance to those who do not wish to be importuned, then not only I but most homosexuals are guiltless. Very few men would dare to annoy strangers by detaining them against their will or even continuing to speak to them if the slightest irritation were evinced. Is soliciting criminal because it is the first step in the procedure of prostitution? This can less be taken for granted in a homosexual context than in any other. Many men make overtures to others without any thought of receiving or parting with money.

Of all these charges I would claim to be not guilty but how innocent am I?

I do not solicit for immoral purposes because it would be unfeminine—

and risky—but perhaps my very existence is a form of importuning. I no longer ask strange men for money because I do not think I would get it but, if it were offered to me, I would not feel ashamed to take it. In the last analysis I cannot say that I have ever refrained from taking any course of action on the ground that it was wrong or illegal or immoral.

JOHN FOWLES

(1926–   )

Set in Victorian England, *The French Lieutenant's Woman* evokes the sooty tumult and dislocation of London and the untrammelled natural beauty and provincialism of Lyme Regis. The twentieth-century narrator pauses throughout the novel to reflect on social, political, and literary currents of the Victorian Age (one of his digressions analyzes an 1835 French rape trial) and to juxtapose them against their modern counterparts.

Sarah Woodruff, the enigmatic character for whom the novel is named, is a lady's companion and former governess who is reputed to have lost her virtue to a French sailor. She forms an erotic attachment to a wealthy and discontented bachelor, Charles Smithson, leading him to break his engagement to the rich but conventional Ernestina Freeman. After breaking off his engagement, however, Charles finds that Sarah has mysteriously disappeared, and he hires a private detective to find her. Meanwhile, the aggrieved father of the jilted fiancée threatens to files suit against Charles for breach of promise of marriage.

''Breach of promise'' can be traced in England back to the ecclesiastical courts, although most cases were recorded between 1850 and 1900. (*The French Lieutenant's Woman* is set in 1867.) Breach-of-promise actions were regarded as vulgar by the upper classes. They were largely resorted to by lower-middle-class women (and, to a lesser extent, men), who were commonly awarded sizeable damages either by juries or by out-of-court settlements. In this excerpt, the Freemans do not ultimately go to court or seek any monetary awards, but the fact that they contemplate such an action may indicate their slightly lower social status: while Charles is heir to a baronetcy, Freeman's fortune was made by his father through commercial success and the establishment of a store in London's West End.

John Fowles was born in Essex, England, and graduated from Oxford in 1950. He has written poetry and essays as well as fiction, the latter including *The Collector* (1963), *The Magus* (1966), *The Ebony Tower* (1974), and, most recently, *A Maggot* (1985).

from THE FRENCH LIEUTENANT'S WOMAN

— 1969 —

Ah Christ, that it were possible
For one short hour to see
The souls we loved, that they might tell us
What and where they be.

TENNYSON, *Maud* (1855)

Private Inquiry Office, Patronized by the Aristocracy, and under the sole direction of Mr. Pollaky himself. Relations with both the British and the Foreign Detective Police. DELICATE AND CONFIDENTIAL INQUIRIES INSTITUTED WITH SECRECY AND DISPATCH IN ENGLAND, THE CONTINENT AND THE COLONIES. EVIDENCE COLLECTED FOR CASES IN THE DIVORCE COURT, &C.

MID-VICTORIAN ADVERTISEMENT

A *week might pass, two, but then she would stand before him* . . . The third week begins, and she has not stood before him. Charles cannot be faulted; he has been here, there, everywhere.

He had achieved this ubiquity by hiring four detectives—whether they were under the sole direction of Mr. Pollaky, I am not sure, but they worked hard. They had to, for they were a very new profession, a mere eleven years old, and held in general contempt. A gentleman in 1866 who stabbed one to death was considered to have done a very proper thing. "If people go about got up as garrotters," warned *Punch*, "they must take the consequences."

Charles's men had first tried the governess agencies, without success; they had tried the Educational Boards of all the denominations that ran Church schools. Hiring a carriage, he had himself spent fruitless hours patroling, a pair of intent eyes that scanned each younger female face that passed, the genteel-poor districts of London. In one such Sarah must be lodging: in Peckham, in Pentonville, in Putney; in a dozen similar districts of neat new roads and one-domestic houses he searched. He also helped his men to investigate the booming new female clerical agencies. A generalized hostility to Adam was already evident in them, since they had to bear the full brunt of masculine prejudice and were to become among the most important seedbeds of the emancipation movement. I think these experiences, though fruitless in the one matter he cared about, were not all wasted on Charles. Slowly he began to understand one aspect of Sarah better: her feeling of resentment, of an unfair because remediable bias in society.

One morning he had woken to find himself very depressed. The dreadful possibility of prostitution, that fate she had once hinted at, became a certainty. That evening he went in a state of panic to the same Haymarket area he visited earlier. What the driver imagined, I cannot suppose; but he must certainly have thought his fare the most fastidious man who ever existed. They drove up and down those streets for two hours. Only once did they stop; the driver saw a red-haired prostitute under a gaslight. But almost at once two taps bade him drive on again.

Other consequences of his choice of freedom had meanwhile not waited to exact their toll. To his finally achieved letter to Mr. Freeman he received no answer for ten days. But then he had to sign for one, delivered ominously by hand, from Mr. Freeman's solicitors.

Sir,

In re Miss Ernestina Freeman

We are instructed by Mr. Ernest Freeman, father of the above-mentioned Miss Ernestina Freeman, to request you to attend at these chambers at 3 o'clock this coming Friday. Your failure to attend will be regarded as an acknowledgement of our client's right to proceed.

AUBREY & BAGGOTT

Charles took the letter to his own solicitors. They had handled the Smithson family affairs since the eighteenth century. And the present younger Montague, facing whose desk the confessed sinner now shamefacedly sat, was only a little older than Charles himself. The two men had been at Winchester together; and without being close friends, knew and liked each other well enough.

"Well, what does it mean, Harry?"

"It means, my dear boy, that you have the devil's own luck. They have cold feet."

"Then why should they want to see me?"

"They won't let you off altogether, Charles. That is asking too much. My guess is that you will be asked to make a *confessio delicti.*"

"A statement of guilt?"

"Just so. I am afraid you must anticipate an ugly document. But I can only advise you to sign it. You have no case."

On that Friday afternoon Charles and Montague were ushered into a funereal waiting room in one of the Inns of Court. Charles felt it was something like a duel; Montague was his second. They were made to cool their heels until a quarter past three. But since this preliminary penance had been predicted by Montague, they bore it with a certain nervous amusement.

At last they were summoned. A short and choleric old man rose from behind a large desk. A little behind him stood Mr. Freeman. He had no eyes but for Charles, and they were very cold eyes indeed; all amusement vanished. Charles bowed to him, but no acknowledgment was made. The two solicitors shook hands curtly. There was a fifth person present: a tall, thin, balding man with penetrating dark eyes, at the sight of whom Montague imperceptibly flinched.

"You know Mr. Serjeant Murphy?"

"By reputation only."

A serjeant-at-law was in Victorian times a top counsel; and Serjeant Murphy was a killer, the most feared man of his day.

Mr. Aubrey peremptorily indicated the chairs the two visitors were to take, then sat down himself again. Mr. Freeman remained implacably standing. Mr. Aubrey shuffled papers, which gave Charles time he did not want to absorb the usual intimidating atmosphere of such places: the learned volumes, the rolls of sheepskin bound in green ferret, the mournful box-files of dead cases ranged high around the room like the urns of an overpopulated *columbarium*.

The old solicitor looked severely up.

"I think, Mr. Montague, that the facts of this abominable breach of engagement are not in dispute. I do not know what construction your client has put upon his conduct to you. But he has himself provided abundant evidence of his own guilt in this letter to Mr. Freeman, though I note that with the usual impudence of his kind he has sought to—"

"Mr. Aubrey, such language in these circumstances—"

Serjeant Murphy pounced. "Would you prefer to hear the language *I* should use, Mr. Montague—and in open court?"

Montague took a breath and looked down. Old Aubrey stared at him with a massive disapproval. "Montague, I knew your late grandfather well. I fancy he would have thought twice before acting for such a client as yours—but let that pass for the nonce. I consider this letter . . ." and he held it up, as if with tongs ". . . I consider this disgraceful letter adds most impertinent insult to an already gross injury, both by its shameless attempt at self-exoneration and the complete absence from it of any reference to the criminal and sordid liaison that the writer well knows is the blackest aspect of his crime." He glowered at Charles. "You may, sir, have thought Mr. Freeman not to be fully cognizant of your amours. You are wrong. We know the name of the female with whom you have entered into such base conversation. We have a witness to circumstances I find too disgusting to name."

Charles flushed red. Mr. Freeman's eyes bored into him. He could only lower his head; and curse Sam. Montague spoke.

"My client did not come here to defend his conduct."

"Then you would not defend an action?"

"A person of your eminence in our profession must know that I cannot answer that question."

Serjeant Murphy intervened again. "You would not defend an action if one were brought?"

"With respect, sir, I must reserve judgment on that matter."

A vulpine smile distorted the serjeant-at-law's lips.

"The judgment is not at issue, Mr. Montague."

"May we proceed, Mr. Aubrey?"

Mr. Aubrey glanced at the serjeant, who nodded grim assent.

"This is not an occasion, Mr. Montague, when I should advise too much standing upon plea." He shuffled papers again. "I will be brief. My advice to Mr. Freeman has been clear. In my long experience, my very long experience, this is the vilest example of dishonorable behavior I have ever had under my survey. Even did not your client merit the harsh judgment he would inevitably receive, I believe firmly that such vicious conduct should be exhibited as a warning to others." He left a long silence, then, for the words to sink deep. Charles wished he could control the blood in his cheeks. Mr. Freeman at least was now looking down; but Serjeant Murphy knew very well how to use a flushing witness. He put on what admiring junior counsel called his basilisk quiz, in which irony and sadism were nicely prominent.

Mr. Aubrey, in a somber new key, went on. "However, for reasons I shall not go into, Mr. Freeman has elected to show a mercy the case in no way warrants. He does not, upon conditions, immediately have it in mind to proceed."

Charles swallowed, and glanced at Montague.

"I am sure my client is grateful to yours."

"I have, with esteemed advice . . ." Mr. Aubrey bowed briefly towards the serjeant, who bobbed his head without taking his eyes off the wretched Charles ". . . prepared an admission of guilt. I should instruct you that Mr. Freeman's decision not to proceed immediately is most strictly contingent upon your client's signing, on this occasion and in our presence, and witnessed by all present, this document."

And he handed it to Montague, who glanced at it, then looked up.

"May I request five minutes' discussion in private with my client?"

"I am most surprised you should find discussion necessary." He puffed up a little, but Montague stood firm. "Then very well, very well. If you must."

So Harry Montague and Charles found themselves back in the funereal waiting room. Montague read the document, then handed it drily to Charles.

"Well, here's your medicine. You've got to take it, dear boy."

And while Montague stared out at the window, Charles read the admission of guilt.

I, Charles Algernon Henry Smithson, do fully, freely and not upon any consideration but my desire to declare the truth, admit that:

1. I contracted to marry Miss Ernestina Freeman;
2. I was given no cause whatsoever by the innocent party (the said Miss Ernestina Freeman) to break my solemn contract with her;
3. I was fully and exactly apprised of her rank in society, her character, her marriage portion and future prospects before my engagement to her hand and that nothing I learned subsequently of the aforesaid Miss Ernestina Freeman in any way contradicted or denied what I had been told;
4. I did break that contract without just cause or any justification whatsoever beyond my own criminal selfishness and faithlessness;
5. I entered upon a clandestine liaison with a person named Sarah Emily Woodruff, resident at Lyme Regis and Exeter, and I did attempt to conceal this liaison;
6. My conduct throughout this matter has been dishonorable, and by it I have forever forfeited the right to be considered a gentleman.

Furthermore, I acknowledge the right of the injured party to proceed against me *sine die* and without term or condition.

Furthermore, I acknowledge that the injured party may make whatsoever use she desires of this document.

Furthermore, my signature hereto appended is given of my own free will, in full understanding of the conditions herein, in full confession of my conduct, and under no duress whatsoever, upon no prior or posterior consideration whatsoever and no right of redress, rebuttal, demurral or denial in any particular, now and henceforth under all the abovementioned terms.

"Have you no comment on it?"

"I fancy that there must have been a dispute over the drafting. No lawyer would happily put in that sixth clause. If it came to court, one might well argue that no gentleman, however foolish he had been, would make such an admission except under duress. A counsel could make quite a lot of that. It is really in our favor. I'm surprised Aubrey and Murphy have allowed it. My guess is that it is Papa's clause. He wants you to eat humble pie."

"It is vile."

He looked for a moment as if he would tear it to pieces.

Montague gently took it from him. "The law is not concerned with truth, Charles. You should know that by now."

"And that 'may make whatsoever use she desires'—what in heaven's name does that mean?"

"It could mean that the document is inserted in *The Times*. I seem to recall something similar was done some years ago. But I have a feeling old Freeman wants to keep this matter quiet. He would have had you in court if he wanted to put you in the stocks."

"So I must sign."

"If you like I can go back and argue for different phrases—some form that would reserve to you the right to plead extenuating circumstances if it came to trial. But I strongly advise against. The very harshness of this as it stands would argue far better for you. It pays us best to pay their price. Then if needs be we can argue the bill was a deuced sight too stiff."

Charles nodded, and they stood.

"There's one thing, Harry. I wish I knew how Ernestina is. I cannot ask him."

"I'll see if I can have a word with old Aubrey afterwards. He's not such a bad old stick. He has to play it up for Papa."

So they returned; and the admission was signed, first by Charles, then by each of the others in turn. All remained standing. There was a moment's awkward silence. Then at last Mr. Freeman spoke.

"And now, you blackguard, never darken my life again. I wish I were a younger man. If—"

"My dear Mr. Freeman!"

Old Aubrey's sharp voice silenced his client. Charles hesitated, bowed to the two lawyers, then left followed by Montague.

But outside Montague said, "Wait in the carriage for me."

A minute or two later he climbed in beside Charles.

"She is as well as can be expected. Those are his words. He also gave me to understand what Freeman intends to do if you go in for the marriage game again. Charles, he will show what you have just signed to the next father-in-law to be. He means you to remain a bachelor all your life."

"I had guessed as much."

"Old Aubrey also told me, by the way, to whom you owe your release on parole."

"To her? That too I had guessed."

"He would have had his pound of flesh. But the young lady evidently rules that household."

The carriage rolled on for a hundred yards before Charles spoke.

"I am marked and defiled to the end of my life."

"My dear Charles, if you play the Muslim in a world of Puritans, you can expect no other treatment. I am as fond as the next man of a pretty ankle. I don't blame you. But don't tell me that the price is not fairly marked."

The carriage rolled on. Charles stared gloomily out at the sunny street.

"I wish I were dead."

"Then let us go to Verrey's and demolish a lobster or two. And you shall tell me about the mysterious Miss Woodruff before you die."

JAMES ALAN McPHERSON
(1943–   )

James Alan McPherson was born in Savannah, Georgia, in what he has described as a "lower-class black community." After attending segregated public schools, he went on to Morris Brown College at the same time that the civil-rights movement swept the South. He proceeded to Harvard Law School, graduating in 1968.

Continuing a long tradition of Harvard Law School writers (among them Richard Henry Dana, James Russell Lowell, Henry James, Owen Wister, Arthur Train, Archibald MacLeish, and Scott Turow), McPherson pursued a literary rather than a legal career. He has published two books of short stories, *Hue and Cry* (1969) and *Elbow Room* (1977), the second of which won the 1978 Pulitzer Prize for Fiction. McPherson is also Professor of English at the University of Iowa Writers' Workshop and a contributing editor of the *Atlantic Monthly.*

Although he chose a nonlegal path after graduating, McPherson's experience at Harvard Law School was formative. Of Paul Freund's Constitutional Law class, McPherson wrote, "I began to see the outlines of a new identity. . . . I saw that through the protean uses made of the Fourteenth Amendment, in the gradual elaboration of basic rights to be protected by federal authority, an outline of something much more complex than 'black' or 'white' had been begun." Later, on Albion W. Tourgée's brief to the United States Supreme Court in the 1896 "separate but equal" case, *Plessy v. Ferguson,* McPherson wrote that Tourgée (another lawyer-writer) "was proposing . . . that each United States citizen would attempt to approximate the ideals of the nation, be on at least conversant terms with all its diversity, carry the mainstream of the culture inside himself. As an American, by trying to wear these clothes he would be a synthesis of high and low, black and white, city and country, provincial and universal. . . . This was the model I was aiming for in my book of stories (*Elbow Room*)."

Legal themes figure prominently in both *Elbow Room* and *Hue and Cry.* The latter begins with an epigraph quoting Pollock and Maitland, in their *History of English Law,* about the need to raise a "hue and cry" against criminal outrages, and its stories all concern outrages such as racial prejudice or age discrimination. In "An Act of Prostitution," taken from this collection, the injustices occur in a courtroom where the accused hooker is by no means the only prostitute.

AN ACT OF PROSTITUTION

— 1969 —

When he saw the woman the lawyer put down his pencil and legal pad and took out his pipe.

"Well," he said. "How do you want to play it?"

"I wanna get outta here," the whore said. "Just get me outta here."

"Now get some sense," said the lawyer, puffing on the pipe to draw in the flame from the long wooden match he had taken from his vest pocket. "You ain't got a snowball's chance in hell."

"I just want out," she said.

"You'll catch hell in there," he said, pointing with the stem of his pipe to the door which separated them from the main courtroom. "Why don't you just get some sense and take a few days on the city."

"I can't go up there again," she said. "Those dike matrons in Parkville hate my guts because I'm wise to them. They told me last time they'd really give it to me if I came back. I can't do no time up there again."

"Listen," said the lawyer, pointing the stem of his pipe at her this time, "you ain't got a choice. Either you cop a plea or I don't take the case."

"*You* listen, you two-bit Jew shyster." The whore raised her voice, pointing her very chubby finger at the lawyer. "*You* ain't got no choice. The judge told you to be my lawyer and you got to do it. I ain't no dummy, you know that?"

"Yeah," said the lawyer. "You're a real smarty. That's why you're out on the streets in all that snow and ice. You're a real smarty all right."

"You chickenshit," she said. "I don't want you on my case anyway, but I ain't got no choice. If you was any good, you wouldn't be working the sweatboxes in this court. I ain't no dummy."

"You're a real smarty," said the lawyer. He looked her up and down: a huge woman, pathetically blonde, big-boned and absurd in a skirt sloppily crafted to be mini. Her knees were ruddy and the flesh below them was thick and white and flabby. There was no indication of age about her. Like most whores, she looked at the same time young but then old, possibly as old as her profession. Sometimes they were very old but seemed to have stopped aging at a certain point so that ranking them chronologically, as the lawyer was trying to do, came hard. He put his pipe on the table, on top of the police affidavit, and stared at her. She sat across the room, near the door in a straight chair, her flesh oozing over its sides. He watched her pull her miniskirt down over the upper part of her thigh, modestly, but with the same hard, cold look she had when she came in the room. "You're a real smarty," he commented, drawing on his pipe and exhaling the smoke into the room.

The fat woman in her miniskirt still glared at him. "Screw you, Yid!" she said through her teeth. "Screw your fat mama and your chubby sister with hair under her arms. Screw your brother and your father and I hope they should go crazy playing with themselves in pay toilets."

The lawyer was about to reply when the door to the consultation room opened and another man came into the small place. "Hell, Jimmy," he said to the lawyer, pretending to ignore the woman, "I got a problem here."

"Yeah?" said Jimmy.

The other man walked over to the brown desk, leaned closer to Jimmy so that the woman could not hear and lowered his voice. "I got this kid," he said. "A nice I-talian boy that grabbed this Cadillac outta a parking lot. Now he only done it twice before and I think the Judge might go easy if he got in a good mood before the kid goes on, this being Monday morning and all."

"So?" said Jimmy.

"So I was thinking," the other lawyer said, again lowering his voice and leaning much closer and making a sly motion with his head to indicate the whore on the chair across the room. "So I was thinking. The Judge knows Philomena over there. She's here almost every month and she's always good for a laugh. So I was thinking, this being Monday morning and all and with a cage-load of nigger drunks out there, why not put her on first, give the old man a good laugh and then put my I-talian boy on. I know he'd get a better deal that way."

"What's in it for me?" said Jimmy, rapping the ashes from his pipe into an ashtray.

"Look, I done *you* favors before. Remember that Chinaman? Remember the tip I gave you?"

Jimmy considered while he stuffed tobacco from a can into his pipe. He lit the pipe with several matches from his vest pocket and considered some more. "I don't mind, Ralph," he said. "But if she goes first the Judge'll get a good laugh and then he'll throw the book at her."

"*What the hell, Jimmy?*" said Ralph. He glanced over at the whore who was eying them hatefully. "Look, buddy," he went on, "you know who that is? Fatso Philomena Brown. She's up here almost every month. Old Bloom knows her. I tell you, she's good for a laugh. That's all. Besides, she's married to a nigger anyway."

"Well," said Jimmy. "So far she ain't done herself much good with me. She's a real smarty. She thinks I'm a Jew."

"There you go," said Ralph. "Come on, Jimmy. I ain't got much time before the Clerk calls my kid up. What you say?"

Jimmy looked over at his client, the many pounds of her rolled in great logs of meat under her knees and around her belly. She was still sneering. "O.K." He turned his head back to Ralph. "O.K., I'll do it."

"Now look," said Ralph, "this is how we'll do. When they call me up I'll tell the Clerk I need more time with my kid for consultation. And since you follow me on the docket you'll get on pretty soon, at least before I will. Then after everybody's had a good laugh, I'll bring my I-talian on."

"Isn't *she* Italian?" asked Jimmy, indicating the whore with a slight movement of his pipe.

"Yeah. But she's married to a nigger."

"O.K.," said Jimmy, "we'll do it."

"What's that?" said the whore, who had been trying to listen all this time. "What are you two kikes whispering about anyway? What the hell's going on?"

"Shut up," said Jimmy, the stem of his pipe clamped far back in his mouth so that he could not say it as loud as he wanted. Ralph winked at him and left the room. "Now listen," he said to Philomena Brown, getting up from his desk and walking over to where she still sat against the wall. "If you got a story, you better tell me quick because we're going out there soon and I want you to know I ain't telling no lies for you."

"I don't want you on my case anyway, kike," said Philomena Brown.

"It ain't what *you* want. It's what the old man out there says you gotta do. Now if you got a story let's have it *now*."

"I'm a file clerk. I was just looking for work."

"Like *hell!* Don't give *me* that shit. When was the last time you had your shots?"

"I ain't never had none," said Mrs. Brown.

Now they could hear the Clerk, beyond the door, calling the Italian boy into court. They would have to go out in a few minutes. "Forget the story," he told her. "Just pull your dress down some and wipe some of that shit off your eyes. You look like hell."

"I don't want you on the case, Moses," said Mrs. Brown.

"Well you got me," said Jimmy. "You got me whether you want me or not." Jimmy paused, put his pipe in his coat pocket, and then said: "And my name is *Mr. Mulligan!*"

The woman did not say anything more. She settled her weight in the chair and made it creak.

"Now let's get in there," said Jimmy.

The Judge was in his Monday morning mood. He was very ready to be angry at almost anyone. He glared at the Court Clerk as the bald, seemingly consumptive man called out the names of six defendants who had defaulted. He glared at the group of drunks and addicts who huddled against the steel net of the prisoners' cage, gazing toward the open courtroom as if expecting mercy from the rows of concerned parties and spectators who sat in the hot place. Judge Bloom looked as though he wanted very badly to spit. There would be no mercy this Monday morning and the prisoners all knew it.

"*Willie Smith!* Willie Smith! Come into Court!" the Clerk barked.

Willie Smith slowly shuffled out of the prisoners' cage and up to the dirty stone wall, which kept all but his head and neck and shoulders concealed from the people in the musty courtroom.

From the bench the Judge looked down at the hungover Smith.

"You know, I ain't never seen him sitting down in that chair," Jimmy said to one of the old men who came to court to see the daily procession, filling up the second row of benches, directly behind those reserved for court-appointed lawyers. There were at least twelve of these old men, looking almost semi-professional in faded gray or blue or black suits with shiny knees and elbows. They liked to come and watch the fun. "Watch old Bloom give it to this nigger," the same old man leaned over and said into Jimmy Mulligan's ear. Jimmy nodded without looking back at him. And after a few seconds he wiped his ear with his hand, also without looking back.

The Clerk read the charges: Drunkenness, Loitering, Disorderly Conduct.

"You want a lawyer, Willie?" the Judge asked him. Judge Bloom was now walking back and forth behind his bench, his arms gravely folded behind his back, his belly very close to pregnancy beneath his black robe. "The Supreme Court says I have to give you a lawyer. You want one?"

"No sir," the hung-over Smith said, very obsequiously.

"Well, what's your trouble?"

"Nothing."

"You haven't missed a Monday here in months."

"Yes sir."

"All that money you spend on booze, how do you take care of your family?"

Smith moved his head and shoulders behind the wall in a gesture that might have been a shuffle.

"When was the last time you gave something to your wife?"

"Last Friday."

"You're a liar. Your wife's been on the City for years."

"I help," said Smith, quickly.

"You help, all right. You help her raise her belly and her income every year."

The old men in the second row snickered and the Judge eyed them in a threatening way. They began to stifle their chuckles. Willie Smith smiled.

"If she has one more kid she'll be making more than me," the Judge observed. But he was not saying it to Smith. He was looking at the old men.

Then he looked down at the now bashful, smiling Willie Smith. "You want some time to sleep it off or you want to pay?"

"I'll take the time."

"How much you want, Willie?"

"I don't care."

"You want to be out for the weekend, I guess."

Smith smiled again.

"Give him five days," the Judge said to the Clerk. The Clerk wrote in his papers and then said in a hurried voice: "Defendant Willie Smith, you have been found guilty by this court of being drunk in a public place, of loitering while in this condition, and of disorderly conduct. This court sentences you to five days in the House of Correction at Bridgeview and one month's suspended sentence. You have, however, the right to appeal in which case the suspended sentence will not be allowed and the sentence will then be thirty-five days in the House of Correction."

"You want to appeal, Willie?"

"Naw sir."

"See you next week," said the Judge.

"Thank you," said Willie Smith.

A black fellow in a very neatly pressed Army uniform came on next. He stood immaculate and proud and clean-shaven with his cap tucked under his left arm while the charges were read. The prosecutor was a hard-faced black police detective, tieless, very long-haired in a short-sleeved white shirt with wet armpits. The detective was tough but very nervous. He looked at his notes while the Clerk read the charges. The Judge, bald and wrinkled and drooping in the face, still paced behind his bench, his nose twitching from time to time, his arms locked behind the back. The soldier was charged with assault and battery with a dangerous weapon on a police officer; he remained standing erect and silent, looking off into the space behind the Judge until his lawyer, a plump, greasy black man in his late fifties, had heard the charge and motioned for him to sit. Then he placed himself beside his lawyer and put his cap squarely in front of him on the table.

The big-bellied black detective managed to get the police officer's name, rank and duties from him, occasionally glancing over at the table where the defendant and his lawyer sat, both hard-faced and cold. He shuffled through his notes, paused, looked up at the Judge, and then said to the white officer: "Now, Officer Bergin, would you tell the Court in your own words what happened?"

The white policeman put his hands together in a prayer-like gesture on the stand. He looked at the defendant whose face was set and whose eyes were fixed on the officer's hands. "We was on duty on the night of July twenty-seventh driving around the Lafayette Street area when we got a call to proceed to the Lafayette Street subway station because there was a crowd gathering there and they thought it might be a riot. We proceeded there, Officer Biglow and me, and when we got there sure enough there was a crowd of colored people running up and down the street and making noise and carrying on. We didn't pull our guns because they been telling us all summer not to do that. We got out of the car and proceeded to join the other officers there in forming a line so's to disperse the crowd. Then we spotted that fellow in the crowd."

"Who do you mean?"

"That fellow over there." Officer Bergin pointed to the defendant at the table. "That soldier, Irving Williams."

"Go on," said the black detective, not turning to look at the defendant.

"Well, he had on this red costume and a cape, and he was wearing this big red turban. He was also carrying a big black shield right outta Tarzan and he had that big long cane waving it around in the air."

"Where is that cane now?"

"We took it off him later. That's it over there."

The black detective moved over to his own table and picked up a long brown leather cane. He pressed a small button beneath its handle and then drew out from the interior of the cane a thin, silver-white rapier, three feet long.

"Is this the same cane?"

"Yes sir," the white officer said.

"Go on, Officer."

"Well, he was waving it around in the air and he had a whole lot of these colored people behind him and it looked to me that he was gonna charge the police line. So me and Tommy left the line and went in to grab him before he could start something big. That crowd was getting mean. The looked like they was gonna try something big pretty soon."

"Never mind," said the Judge. He had stopped walking now and stood at the edge of his elevated platform, just over the shoulder of the officer in the witness box. "Never mind what you thought, just get on with it."

"Yes sir." The officer pressed his hands together much tighter. "Well, Tommy and me, we tried to grab him and he swung the cane at me. Caught me right in the face here." He pointed his finger to a large red and black mark under his left eye. "So then we hadda use force to subdue him."

"What did you do, Officer?" the black detective asked.

"We hadda use the sticks. I hit him over the head once or twice, but not hard. I don't remember. Then Tommy grabbed his arms and we hustled him over to the car before these other colored people with him tried to grab us."

"Did he resist arrest?"

"Yeah. He kicked and fought us and called us lewd and lascivious names. We hadda handcuff him in the car. Then we took him down to the station and booked him for assault and battery.

"Your witness," said the black detective without turning around to face the other lawyer. He sat down at his own table and wiped his forehead and hands with a crumpled white handkerchief. He still looked very nervous but not as tough.

"May it please the Court," the defendant's black lawyer said slowly, standing and facing the pacing Judge. "I move . . ." And then he stopped because he saw that the Judge's small eyes were looking over his head, toward the back of the courtroom. The lawyer turned around and looked, and saw that everyone else in the room had also turned their heads to the back of the room. Standing against the back walls and along the left side of the room were twenty-five or so stern-faced, cold-eyed black men, all in African dashikies, all wearing brightly colored hats, and all staring at the Judge and the black detective. Philomena Brown and Jimmy Mulligan, sitting on the first bench, turned to look too, and the whore smiled but the lawyer said, "Oh hell," aloud. The men, all big, all bearded and tight-lipped, now locked hands and formed a solid wall of flesh around almost three-quarters of the courtroom. The Judge looked at the defendant and saw that he was smiling. Then he looked at the defendant's lawyer, who still stood before the Judge's bench, his head down, his shoulders pulled up towards his head. The Judge began to pace again. The courtroom was very quiet. The old men filling the second rows on both sides of the room leaned forward and exchanged glances with each other up and down the row. "Oh hell," Jimmy Mulligan said again.

Then the Judge stopped walking. "Get on with it," he told the defendant's lawyer. "There's justice to be done here."

The lawyer, whose face was now very greasy and wet, looked up at the officer, still standing in the witness box, but with one hand now at his right side, next to his gun.

"Officer Bergin," said the black lawyer. "I'm not clear about something. Did the defendant strike you *before* you asked him for the cane or *after* you attempted to take it from him?"

"Before. It was before. Yes sir."

"You *did* ask him for the cane, then?"

"Yes sir. I asked him to turn it over."

"And what did he do?"

"He hit me."

"But if he hit you before you asked for the cane, then it must be true that you asked him for the cane *after* he had hit you. Is that right?"

"Yes sir."

"In other words, after he had struck you in the face you were still polite enough to keep your hands off him and ask for the weapon."

"Yes sir. That's what I did."

"In other words, he hit you twice. Once, *before* you requested the cane and once *after* you requested it."

The officer paused. "No sir," he said quickly. "He only hit me once."

"And when was that again?"

"I thought it was before I asked for the cane but I don't know now."

"But you did ask for the cane before he hit you?"

"Yeah." The officer's hands were in prayer again.

"Now, Officer Bergin, did he hit you *because* you asked for the cane or did he hit you in the process of giving it to you?"

"He just hauled off and hit me with it."

"He made no effort to hand it over?"

"No, no sir. He hit me."

"In other words, he struck you the moment you got close enough for him to swing. He did not hit you as you were taking the cane from him?"

The officer paused again. Then he said: "No sir," He touched his face again, then put his right hand down to the area near his gun again. "I asked him for the cane and he hauled off and hit me in the face."

"Officer, are you telling this court that you did not get hit until you tried to take the cane away from this soldier, this Vietnam veteran, or that he saw you coming and immediately began to swing the cane?"

"He swung on me."

"Officer Bergin, did he swing on you, or did the cane accidentally hit you while you were trying to take it from him?"

"All I know is that he *hit me*." The officer was sweating now.

"Then you don't know just when he hit you, before or after you tried to take the cane from him, do you?"

The black detective got up and said in a very soft voice: "I object."

The black lawyer for the defendant looked over at him contemptuously. The black detective dropped his eyes and tightened his belt, and sat down again.

"That's all right," the oily lawyer said. Then he looked at the officer again. "One other thing," he said. "Was the knife still inside the cane or drawn when he hit you?"

"We didn't know about the knife till later at the station."

"Do you think that a blow from the cane by itself could kill you?"

"Object!" said the detective. But again his voice was low.

"*Jivetime Uncle Tom motherfucker!*" someone said from the back of the room. "Shave that Afro off your head!"

The Judge's eyes moved quickly over the men in the rear, surveying their faces and catching what was in all their eyes. But he did not say anything.

"The prosecution rests," the black detective said. He sounded very tired.

"The defense calls the defendant, Irving Williams," said the black lawyer.

Williams took the stand and waited, head high, eyes cool, mouth tight, militarily, for the Clerk to swear him in. He looked always toward the back of the room.

"Now Mr. Williams," his lawyer began, "tell this court in your own words the events of the night of July twenty-seventh of this year."

"I had been to a costume party." William's voice was slow and deliberate and resonant. The entire courtroom was tense and quiet. The old men stared, stiff and erect, at Irving Williams from their second-row benches. Philomena Brown settled her flesh down next to her lawyer, who tried to edge away from touching her fat arm with his own. The tight-lipped Judge Bloom had reassumed the pacing behind his bench.

"I was on leave from the base," Williams went on, "and I was coming from the party when I saw this group of kids throwing rocks. Being in the military and being just out of Vietnam, I tried to stop them. One of the kids had that cane and I took it from him. The shield belongs to me. I got it in Taiwan last year on R and R. I was trying to break up the crowd with my shield when this honkie cop begins to beat me over the head with his club. Police brutality. I tried to tell . . ."

"That's enough," the Judge said. "That's all I want to hear." He eyed the black men in the back of the room. "This case isn't for my court. Take it upstairs."

"If Your Honor pleases," the black lawyer began.

"I don't," said the Judge. "I've heard enough. Mr. Clerk, make out the papers. Send it upstairs to Cabot."

"This court has jurisdiction to hear this case," the lawyer said. He was very close to being angry. "This man is in the service. He has to ship out in a few weeks. We want a hearing today."

"Not in my court you don't get it. Upstairs, and that's *it!*"

Now the blacks in the back of the room began to berate the detective. "Jivetime cat! Handkerchief-head flunky! Uncle Tom motherfucker!" they called. "We'll get *you*, baby!"

"Get them out of here," the Judge told the policeman named Bergin. "Get them the hell out!" Bergin did not move. "Get them the hell out!"

At that moment Irving Williams, with his lawyer behind him, walked out of the courtroom. And the twenty-five bearded black men followed them. The black detective remained sitting at the counsel table until the Clerk asked him to make way for counsel on the next case. The detective got up slowly, gathered his few papers, tightened his belt again and moved over, his head held down, to a seat on the right side of the courtroom.

"Philomena Brown!" the Clerk called. "Philomena Brown! Come into Court!"

The fat whore got up from beside Jimmy Mulligan and walked heavily over to the counsel table and lowered herself into one of the chairs. Her lawyer was talking to Ralph, the Italian boy's counsel.

"Do a good job, Jimmy, please," Ralph said. "Old Bloom is gonna be awful mean now."

"Yeah," said Jimmy. "I got to really work on him."

One of the old men on the second row leaned over the back of the bench and said to Jimmy: "Ain't that the one that's married to a nigger?"

"That's her," said Jimmy.

"She's gonna catch hell. Make sure they give her hell."

"Yeah," said Jimmy. "I don't see how I'm gonna be able to try this with a straight face."

"Do a good job for me, please, Jimmy," said Ralph. "The kid's name is Angelico. Ain't that a beautiful name? He ain't a bad kid."

"Don't you worry, I'll do it." Then Jimmy moved over to the table next to his client.

The defendant and the arresting officer were sworn in. The arresting officer acted for the state as prosecutor and its only witness. He had to refer to his notes from time to time while the Judge paced behind his bench, his head down, ponderous and impatient. Then Philomena Brown got in the witness box and rested her great weight against its sides. She glared at the Judge, at the Clerk, at the officer in the box on the other side, at Jimmy Mulligan, at the old men smiling up and down the second row, and at everyone in the courtroom. Then she rested her eyes on the officer.

"Well," the officer read from his notes. "It was around one-thirty A.M. on the night of July twenty-eighth. I was working the night duty around the combat zone. I come across the defendant there soliciting cars. I had seen the defendant there soliciting cars on previous occasions in the same vicinity. I had then on previous occasions warned the defendant there about such activities. But she kept on doing it. On that night I come across the defendant soliciting a car full of colored gentlemen. She was standing on the curb with her arm leaning up against the door of the car and talking with these two colored gentlemen. As I came up they drove off. I then arrested her, after informing her of her rights, for being a common streetwalker and a public nuisance. And that's all I got to say."

Counsel for the whore waived cross-examination of the officer and proceeded to examine her.

"What's your name?"

"Mrs. Philomena Brown."

"Speak louder so the Court can hear you, Mrs. Brown."

She narrowed her eyes at the lawyer.

"What is your religion, Mrs. Brown?"

"I am a Roman Catholic. Roman Catholic born."

"Are you presently married?"

"Yeah."

"What is your husband's name?"

"Rudolph Leroy Brown, Jr."

The old men in the second row were beginning to snicker and the Judge lowered his eyes to them. Jimmy Mulligan smiled.

"Does your husband support you?"

"Yeah. We get along all right."

"Do *you* work, Mrs. Brown?"

"Yeah. That's how I make my living."

"What do you do for a living?"

"I'm a file clerk."

"Are you working now?"

"No. I lost my job last month on account of a bad leg I got. I couldn't move outta bed."

The men in the second row were grinning and others in the audience joined them in muffled guffaws and snickerings.

"What were you doing on Beaver Avenue on the night of July twenty-eighth?"

"I was looking for a job."

Now the entire court was laughing and the Judge glared out at them from behind his bench as he paced, his arms clasped behind his back.

"Will you please tell this court, Mrs. Brown, how you intended to find a job at that hour?"

"These two guys in a car told me they knew where I could find some work."

"As a file clerk?"

"Yeah. What the hell else do you think?"

There was here a roar of laughter from the court, and when the Judge visibly twitched the corners of his usually severe mouth, Philomena Brown saw it and began to laugh too.

"Order! Order!" the Clerk shouted above the roar. But he was laughing.

Jimmy Mulligan bit his lip. "Now, Mrs. Brown, I want you to tell me the truth. Have you ever been arrested before for prostitution?"

"Hell no!" she fired back. "They had me in here a coupla times but it was all a fluke. They never got nothing on me. I was framed, right from the start."

"How old are you, Mrs. Brown?"

"Nineteen."

Now the Judge stopped pacing and stood next to his chair. His face was dubious: very close and very far away from smiling. The old men in the second row saw this and stopped laughing, awaiting a cue from him.

"That's enough of this," said the Judge. "I know you. You've been up here seven times already this year and it's still summer. I'm going to throw the book at you." He moved over to the left end of the platform and leaned down to where a husky, muscular woman Probation Officer was standing. She had very short hair and looked grim. She had not laughed with the others. "Let me see her record," said the Judge. The manly Probation Officer handed it up to him and then they talked together in whispers for a few minutes.

"All right, *Mrs. Brown*," said the Judge, moving over to the right side of the platform near the defendant's box and pointing his finger at her. "You're still on probation from the last time you were up here. I'm tired of this."

"I don't wanna go back up there, Your Honor," the whore said. "They hate me up there."

"You're going back. That's it! You got six months on the State. Maybe while you're there you can learn how to be a file clerk so you can look for work during the day."

Now everyone laughed again.

"Plus you get a one-year suspended sentence on probation."

The woman hung her head with the gravity of this punishment.

"Maybe you can even learn a *good* profession while you're up there. Who knows? Maybe you could be a ballerina dancer."

The courtroom roared with laughter. The Judge could not control himself now.

"And another thing," he said. "When you get out, keep off the streets. You're obstructing traffic."

Such was the spontaneity of laughter from the entire courtroom after the remark that the lawyer Jimmy Mulligan had to wipe the tears from his eyes with his finger and the short-haired Probation Officer smiled, and even Philomena Brown had to laugh at this, her final moment of glory. The Judge's teeth showed through his own broad grin, and Ralph, sitting beside his Italian, a very pretty boy with clean, blue eyes, patted him on the back enthusiastically between uncontrollable bursts of laughter.

For five minutes after the smiling Probation Office led the fat whore in a miniskirt out of the courtroom, there was the sound of muffled laughter and occasional sniffles and movements in the seats. Then they settled down again and the Judge resumed his pacings and the Court Clerk, very slyly wiping his eyes with his sleeve, said in a very loud voice: "Angelico Carbone! Angelico Carbone! Come into Court!"

ELIZABETH JOLLEY

(1923–   )

Elizabeth Jolley's fiction blends satirical realism with dark humor. Her characters tend to be outsiders, often people who have been displaced from their homes. Many of these characters value ownership of land very highly, and they may turn to devious methods to obtain it. The short story printed here, "A Gentleman's Agreement," represents these themes.

In an Author's Note to her first short-story collection, *Five Acre Virgin and Other Stories*, Jolley explained that "A Gentleman's Agreement" belongs to a group "of twelve in which I have tried to present the human being overcoming the perplexities and difficulties of living. The collection is called 'The Discarders.' The characters appear to inhabit a crazy world. I think it is our world." "A Gentleman's Agreement," set in a context of property and contract law, is a tale of female self-sufficiency. It brings to mind novelist Diane Johnson's comment that "Men are generally more law-abiding than women. . . . Women have a feeling that since they didn't make the rules, the rules have nothing to do with them."

Born in Birmingham, England, Monica Elizabeth Jolley was trained as a nurse during World War II and has lived in Australia since 1959. She began writing in the early 1960s, but she endured years of rejections before publishing *Five Acre Virgin* (1976). Jolley was not recognized outside Australia until 1983, when her novels *Mr. Scobie's Riddle* and *Miss Peabody's Inheritance* appeared. Her other novels include *The Newspaper of Claremont Street* (1981), *Milk and Honey* (1984), *Foxybaby* (1985), *The Sugar Mother* (1988), *My Father's Moon* (1989), and *The George's Wife* (1993). Jolley is also a dramatist, scriptwriter, poet, and critic.

A GENTLEMAN'S AGREEMENT

— 1976 —

In the home science lesson I had to unpick my darts as Mrs Kay said they were all wrong and then I scorched the collar of my dress because I had the iron too hot. And then the sewing machine needle broke and there wasn't a spare and Mrs Kay got really wild and Peril Page cut all the notches off her pattern by mistake and that finished everything.

'I'm not ever going back to that school,' I said to Mother in the evening. 'I'm finished with that place!' So that was my brother and me both leaving school before we should have and my brother kept leaving jobs too, one job after another, sometimes not even staying long enough in one place to wait for his pay.

But Mother was worrying about what to get for my brother's tea.

'What about a bit of lamb's fry and bacon,' I said. She brightened up then and, as she was leaving to go up the terrace for her shopping, she said, 'You can come with me tomorrow then and we'll get through the work quicker.' She didn't seem to mind at all that I had left school.

Mother cleaned in a large block of luxury apartments. She had keys to the flats and she came and went as she pleased and as her work demanded. It was while she was working there that she had the idea of letting the people from down our street taste the pleasures rich people took for granted in their way of living. While these people were away to their offices or on business trips she let our poor neighbours in. We had wedding receptions and parties in the penthouse and the old folk came in to soak their feet and wash their clothes while Mother was doing the cleaning. As she said, she gave a lot of pleasure to people without doing anybody any harm, though it was often a terrible rush for her. She could never refuse anybody anything and, because of this, always had more work than she could manage and more people to be kind to than her time really allowed.

Sometimes at the weekends I went with Mother to look at Grandpa's valley. It was quite a long bus ride. We had to get off at the twenty-nine-mile peg, cross the Medulla brook and walk up a country road with scrub on either side till we came to some cleared acres of pasture which was the beginning of her father's land. She struggled through the wire fence hating the mud. She wept out loud because the old man hung on to his land and all his money was buried, as she put it, in the sodden meadows of cape weed and stuck fast in the outcrops of granite higher up where all the topsoil had washed away. She couldn't sell the land because Grandpa was still alive in a Home for the Aged, and he wanted to keep the farm though he couldn't do anything with it. Even sheep died there. They either starved or got drowned depending on the time of the year. It was either drought there or flood. The weatherboard house was so neglected it was falling apart, the tenants were feckless, and if a calf was born there it couldn't get up, that was the kind of place it was. When we went to see Grandpa he wanted to know about the farm and Mother tried to think of things to please him. She didn't say the fence posts were crumbling away and that the castor oil plants had taken over the yard so you couldn't get through to the barn.

There was an old apricot tree in the middle of the meadow, it was as big as a house and a terrible burden to us to get the fruit at just the right time. Mother liked to take some to the hospital so that Grandpa could keep up his pride and self-respect a bit.

In the full heat of the day I had to pick with an apron tied round me, it had deep pockets for the fruit. I grabbed at the green fruit when I thought Mother wasn't looking and pulled off whole branches so it wouldn't be there to be picked later.

'Don't take that branch!' Mother screamed from the ground. 'Them's not ready yet. We'll have to come back tomorrow for them.'

I lost my temper and pulled off the apron full of fruit and hurled it down but it stuck on a branch and hung there quite out of reach either from up the tree where I was or from the ground.

'Wait! Just you wait till I get a hold of you!' Mother pranced round the tree and I didn't come down till we had missed our bus and it was getting dark and all the dogs in the little township barked as if they were insane, the way dogs do in the country, as we walked through trying to get a lift home.

One Sunday in the winter it was very cold but Mother thought we should go all the same. We passed some sheep huddled in a natural fold of furze and withered grass all frost sparkling in the morning.

'Quick!' Mother said. 'We'll grab a sheep and take a bit of wool back to Grandpa.'

'But they're not our sheep,' I said.

'Never mind!' And she was in among the sheep before I could stop her. The noise was terrible but she managed to grab a bit of wool.

'It's terrible dirty and shabby,' she complained, pulling at the shreds with her cold fingers. 'I don't think I've ever seen such miserable wool.'

All that evening she was busy with the wool, she did make me laugh.

'How will modom have her hair done?' She put the wool on the kitchen table and kept walking all round it talking to it. She tried to wash it and comb it but it still looked awful so she put it round one of my curlers for the night.

'I'm really ashamed of the wool,' Mother said next morning.

'But it isn't ours,' I said.

'I know but I'm ashamed all the same,' she said. So when we were in the penthouse at South Heights she cut a tiny piece off the bathroom mat. It was so soft and silky. And later we went to visit Grandpa. He was sitting with his poor paralysed legs under his tartan rug.

'Here's a bit of the wool clip Dad,' Mother said, bending over to kiss him. His whole face lit up.

'That's nice of you to bring it, really nice.' His old fingers stroked the little piece of nylon carpet.

'It's very good, deep and soft.' He smiled at Mother.

'They do wonderful things with sheep these days Dad,' she said.

'They do indeed,' he said, and all the time he was feeling the bit of carpet.

'Are you pleased Dad?' Mother asked him anxiously. 'You are pleased aren't you?'

'Oh yes I am,' he assured her.

I thought I saw a moment of disappointment in his eyes, but the eyes of old people often look full of tears.

On the way home I tripped on the steps.

'Ugh! I felt your bones!' Really Mother was so thin it hurt to fall against her.

'Well what d'you expect me to be, a boneless wonder?'

Really Mother had such a hard life and we lived in such a cramped and squalid place. She longed for better things and she needed a good rest. I wished more than anything the old man would agree to selling his land. Because he wouldn't sell I found myself wishing he would die and whoever really wants to wish someone to die! It was only that it would sort things out a bit for us.

In the supermarket Mother thought and thought what she could get for my brother for his tea. In the end all she could come up with was fish fingers and a packet of jelly beans.

'You know I never eat fish! And I haven't eaten sweets in years.' My brother looked so tall in the kitchen. He lit a cigarette and slammed out and Mother was too tired and too upset to eat her own tea.

Grandpa was an old man and though his death was expected it was unexpected really and it was a shock to Mother to find she suddenly had eighty-seven acres to sell. And there was the house too. She had a terrible lot to do as she decided to sell the property herself and, at the same time, she did not want to let down the people at South Heights. There was a man interested to buy the land, Mother had kept him up her sleeve for years, ever since he had stopped once by the bottom paddock to ask if it was for sale. At the time Mother would have given her right arm to be able to sell it and she promised he should have first refusal if it ever came on the market.

We all three, Mother and myself and my brother, went out at the week-end to tidy things up. We lost my brother and then we suddenly saw him running and running and shouting, his voice lifting up in the wind as he raced up the slope of the valley.

'I do believe he's laughing! He's happy!' Mother just stared at him and she looked so happy too.

I don't think I ever saw the country look so lovely before.

The tenant was standing by the shed. The big tractor had crawled to the doorway like a sick animal and had stopped there, but in no time my brother had it going.

It seemed there was nothing my brother couldn't do. Suddenly after doing nothing in his life he was driving the tractor and making fire breaks, he started to paint the sheds and he told Mother what fencing posts and wire to order. All these things had to be done before the sale could go through. We all had a wonderful time in the country. I kept wishing we could live in the house, all at once it seemed lovely there at the top of the sunlit meadow. But I knew that however many acres you have, they aren't any use unless you have money too. I think we were all thinking this but no one said anything though Mother kept looking at my brother and the change in him.

There was no problem about the price of the land, this man, he was a doctor, really wanted it and Mother really needed the money.

'You might as well come with me,' Mother said to me on the day of the sale. 'You can learn how business is done.' So we sat in this lawyer's comfortable room and he read out from various papers and the doctor signed things and Mother signed. Suddenly she said to them, 'You know my father really loved his farm but he only managed to have it late in life and then he was never able to live there because of his illness.' The two men looked at her.

'I'm sure you will understand,' she said to the doctor, 'with your own great love of the land, my father's love for his valley. I feel if I could live there just to plant one crop and stay while it matures, my father would rest easier in his grave.'

'Well I don't see why not.' The doctor was really a kind man. The lawyer began to protest, he seemed quite angry.

'It's not in the agreement,' he began to say. But the doctor silenced him, he got up and came round to Mother's side of the table.

'I think you should live there and plant your one crop and stay while it matures,' he said to her. 'It's a gentleman's agreement,' he said.

'That's the best sort.' Mother smiled up at him and they shook hands.

'I wish your crop well,' the doctor said, still shaking her hand.

The doctor made the lawyer write out a special clause which they all signed. And then we left, everyone satisfied. Mother had never had so much money and the doctor had the valley at last but it was the gentleman's agreement which was the best part.

My brother was impatient to get on with improvements.

'There's no rush,' Mother said.

'Well one crop isn't very long,' he said.

'It's long enough,' she said.

So we moved out to the valley and the little weatherboard cottage seemed to come to life very quickly with the pretty things we chose for the rooms.

'It's nice whichever way you look out from these little windows,' Mother was saying and just then her crop arrived. The carter set down the boxes along the edge of the verandah and, when he had gone, my brother began to unfasten the hessian coverings. Inside were hundreds of seedlings in little plastic containers.

'What are they?' he asked.

'Our crop,' Mother said.

'Yes I know, but what is the crop? What are these?'

'Them,' said Mother, she seemed unconcerned, 'oh they're a jarrah forest,' she said.

'But that will take years and years to mature,' he said.

'I know,' Mother said. 'We'll start planting tomorrow. We'll pick the best places and clear and plant as we go along.'

'But what about the doctor?' I said, somehow I could picture him pale and patient by his car out on the lonely road which went through his valley. I seemed to see him looking with longing at his paddocks and his meadows and at his slopes of scrub and bush.

'Well he can come on his land whenever he wants to and have a look at us,' Mother said. 'There's nothing in the gentleman's agreement to say he can't.'

CHARLES A. REICH

(1928–   )

Charles Alan Reich is a unique figure in American culture and law. Born in New York City and educated at Yale Law School, he practiced at major law firms before becoming a law professor at Yale. His 1964 article "The New Property" was a strikingly original contribution to American legal thought and, along with another article he wrote, "Individual Rights and Social Welfare: The Emerging Legal Issues," revolutionized thinking about the welfare state. Six years later, in the landmark case of *Goldberg v. Kelly*, the United States Supreme Court explicitly adopted Reich's argument that welfare recipients have an "entitlement" to benefits.

Also in 1970, Reich published *The Greening of America*, heralding the coming of a new, revolutionary consciousness that would liberate the individual from an oppressive corporate state. The book became a definitive text of the youth culture and sold some three million copies. Suddenly the liberal law professor was a countercultural icon; in 1974 he resigned his professorship and moved to California.

A primary reason for Reich's move was his desire to write an autobiography. *The Sorcerer of Bolinas Reef* (the title refers to a Northern California reef that he uses as a metaphor for visionary self-discovery) is a painfully honest account of the personal costs of Reich's professional success. The second section of the book, "Young Lawyer," covers Reich's years at Arnold, Fortas and Porter, a prestigious corporate law firm in Washington, D.C. In the excerpt below, taken from "Young Lawyer," Reich describes the alienation of the lawyer's life and the conflicts between his or her public self and private identity.

from THE SORCERER OF BOLINAS REEF

— 1976 —

I remember a grey November day in Washington, D.C., in 1956. Our law firm had just won a famous victory. A corrupt official, who had brazenly stolen public funds and had been convicted, was freed on a technicality which I found in the statutes. The other lawyers who had worked on the case were going to have a victory dinner at the client's expense at Chez

Maxime, an exclusive French restaurant. I politely declined. I drove home through the miles of bleak apartment houses feeling no appetite and a hollow emptiness inside. At home I feasted on two hotdogs in solitary splendor and misery.

From 1953 to 1960 I was a young lawyer in Washington, D.C. I was close to the marble buildings where national decisions were made. I saw and was part of a world of high officials, lawyers, apartment houses, middle-class families, and single men and women—a world which all of us believed to be at the center, and yet typical, of American life. It was a world that confidently believed in itself. But for me, in my mid-twenties, something indefinable was always deeply wrong.

I never for one single moment meant to become a young lawyer. I never meant to be a young bachelor in Washington, D.C., with a job at a high-powered firm, an apartment on Connecticut Avenue, suits and ties from Brooks Brothers, dates with young women, and an open topped car. I still kept hold of very different dreams, and so in secret I was a spy from another world, able to see that world of Washington, D.C.—the people in it, and even myself in the role of a young lawyer—as a spy might see it, from the inside, but with an outsider's eye. I had not planned on this role of spy in alien territory, and once there, I could not be sure of ever getting away, or ever finding a different world beyond. So in a sense I was not a spy because this was my real life. And for all I know, other people were also spies, but I never found out. We could not open up to one another.

• • •

When I came to Washington it was under the most favorable circumstances imaginable. My personal dreams, my search for wisdom, and my plans for myself all came together in one perfect way: in 1953 I received an appointment as law clerk to Justice Hugo L. Black.

Along with David Vann, the other law clerk, I lived on the ground floor of the Justice's eighteenth-century house in Alexandria. We had breakfast with him in the kitchen, lunch with him in the public cafeteria at the Court, and dinner back home in the elegant old dining room. From early morning until bedtime we talked about the Constitution and the Bill of Rights. I found in Justice Black a person who had a total faith in the fundamental principles of justice. He carried the Constitution in his pocket as if it were the Bible. He was a warm and unpretentious man, and in a very profound way he made us two law clerks his sons for the year. He showed us how to wash dishes "right," but always did most of the dishes himself. He cooked steaks country-style on Sunday. He told us not to drink or smoke while pouring himself a drink—because liquor couldn't hurt a man at his age. He hinted that David could learn some new working habits from me and that I could learn a little about having fun from David. He was always trying tactfully to improve my driving. He made us look up words in the dictionary that we thought we knew the meaning of.

Hugo Black was an authentically great man. In a city that lived by display, power, gossip, and publicity, his way of life was simple and old-fashioned and wholly without artificial trappings. Each deputy assistant secretary of defense might have a chauffeur and a limousine; Justice Black drove his own old green Plymouth. He loved peace and quiet and a few choice friends. He did his own studying and thinking, and wrote his own opinions, sending to the Court library or the Library of Congress for books as he required them. If a phrase in the Constitution needed to be understood in the context of history or philosophy, he read or reread that history and philosophy. He thought every issue through from the beginning. In a world that was "realistic" about power, Justice Black was passionate about justice for each individual, no matter how inconsequential the person might seem to the world. He was utterly uncorrupted and incorruptible. He was powerful because he possessed the power of love—love of the Constitution, of justice, of democracy, of the people, of his family and friends, of his country. While other judges and lawyers often thought primarily about abstract rules and regulations, the first thing Justice Black saw in a case was the human being involved—the human factors, a particular man or woman's hopes and suffering; this became the focus of all his compassion and indignation.

How I gloried in that marvelous year. I knew that it was one of the greatest experiences that any person could ever have. I never stopped marveling that here I was, sitting at dinner with Justice Black and talking about freedom of speech while the Justice divided a steak three ways, and we passed the corn sticks and greens. I told myself: When you recognize a moment that is an authentic part of your dream, you have to give it all the passionate belief that it deserves.

We sat in the kitchen at breakfast, eating the eggs the Justice had cooked, while he read aloud from *The Washington Post* or talked about the Constitution. The sun streamed in through the windows of the small, low-ceilinged, old-fashioned room, that looked out on a garden. There sat the grand old man, in pajamas and bathrobe, his face serious and majestic, talking about the framers of the Constitution and the deep and terrible experience out of which had been born the protections of the Bill of Rights. He foresaw that we would become "a nation of clerks" if we could not remember what it meant to be a free people. And I knew this was my unique and magical moment to sit with the Prophet, the old man of the American Testament, and absorb his stern passion, his belief in truth, and carry it forward when I could.

After my clerkship ended, I wanted to stay in Washington. I went to work for a law office noted for its identification with Yale Law School, New Deal liberalism, and civil liberties.

The firm was an elegant place. I got a spirited greeting from the receptionist when I arrived; then I sat back in my swivel chair, feeling that I was able to cope with the world. It was in many ways a highly privileged existence. Lawyers arrived at work well after the early-morning rush. I would get myself some coffee from the large percolator down the hall and then enjoy the luxury of settling back with *The New York Times* and the *Post*—even reading the comics.

Sometimes, tilting in my chair, I doodled floor plans for a splendid office suite with a conference room and waiting room on one side, a private library and sitting room on the other—a magnificent corner sanctum for myself, the great man who must under no circumstances be disturbed.

The firm wanted its young men to assume a certain way of life. One was permitted and expected to take care of the necessary amenities of life on office time. I went for haircuts to the barber shop at the Mayflower Hotel. There was seldom a wait. The atmosphere was deferential and luxurious; one's shoes were shined during the haircut, and at the end a black attendant brushed one off from head to foot, helped one on with one's coat, and gratefully accepted a tip. It was easy to enjoy, and I did enjoy it. In a status-conscious city it felt good to feel so privileged.

There was a great sense of importance. Consider a conference with a high government official, along with two senior partners. I strode purposefully from the office, turning around at the door to say impressively, "We'll be at the Department of Justice." We hailed a taxi and got in. Then there was the monumental façade of the building on Constitution Avenue. The marble hallways, the elaborate reception room, the office of the official, an American flag behind his desk, a view of the Capitol Building from the long windows, portraits of predecessors in office and the official himself asking us to be seated. While the other men did most of the talking, and I returned their glances solemnly, I was inwardly telling myself, "This is what everyone wants! This is really living!" Where these men ate lunch, where they went for recreation, what they talked about, and what they wore was what everyone else wanted and tried to copy.

But even in these moments I could not keep up the pretense that everything from arriving in the morning to the haircut to such a conference was really a meaningful experience. What was happening at the conference was so detached from our real feelings as to make it an inhuman thing—no better, really, than listening to announcements by the stewardess on a coast-to-coast airplane trip. The participants spoke lines, they did not communicate. I wish I had dared look someone in the eye or smile at the high official or just yawn.

I liked to work; it was not self-punishment. I simply enjoyed functioning in a way that felt powerful and competent. And I liked the people I worked with in the firm. They were politically liberal, intelligent, sophisticated, lively, entertaining, and excellent lawyers. They were dedicated craftsmen, devoted to their profession. Yet I felt that they, and I, were all victims of our work.

Our work was detrimental to us, in the most profound way. The moments of enjoying work did not last very long. Something about the firm crept in to interfere. The most obvious forms of interference were interruptions, phone calls, distractions. But these had to be expected in a lawyer's life: a lawyer took whatever came along, without priority, form, turn, or order; he had to glory in his ability to play many parts instead of one. No, the trouble went beyond interruptions and multiple tasks.

The atmosphere in the firm was so often full of tension, overconcern, and uncomfortable pressure that it was hard to maintain a high style. More serious still, what I wrote usually met with some objections from the senior men and eventually ended up as a product different from what I had originally written. They always wanted everything put more strongly. I thought I could be powerful and convincing with a serene air, and I hated to see that sort of work turned into overemphasis. I liked to be the law journal scholar simply presenting my point of view.

The opposition were always "those sons of bitches" or "those bastards" or worse. I never felt the need to make the other side seem so evil. But such an objective memorandum would not do. "It isn't positive enough," they would object. "You can put our position more strongly." My own exact voice, then, was not what they wanted to hear. My expression, my thought, must fit larger objectives. I must present an argument with a conviction I did not necessarily feel, an eagerness that was not necessarily in me, a certainty that I might not possess.

Much of my work consisted of talking to people—colleagues, people from outside, public officials. It was much easier than writing, but was not completely satisfying either. All of these people had a professional, or public, self. They all represented a particular interest or point of view, and they took this position with what seemed to be their heart and soul. If positions had been taken in a purely detached manner, there might have been some zone for genuine human contact between the participants. But detachment did not win ball games; everyone must ring with seemingly true belief. After such a performance, there was little room left for a "real" person to show himself. One put one's entire self—writing, voice, manner, personality, personal appeal, even physical stance—at the service of the matter at hand. One coated over one's real self with a public self—every pore covered, if one were really professional, until the public self became first the only visible self, then the only real self.

Whatever they really felt, the other lawyers liked to adopt the appearance of being cynical about the law and its processes, the causes and clients for which they worked, and the firm itself. Deprecation of everything was almost a way of life with them. Winning and losing cases was a game. Questions of justice, wisdom or good policy were irrelevant for lawyers. They were, in one partner's memorable phrase, hired knife-throwers.

But they did not play it as if it were a game. At the heart of their conversations were tension, anxiety, and a total absorption in their work. I could not accept that lack of distance from work, that lack of a sense of irony or humor. They embraced it, they ate and drank it, they knew no moment away from it, it was life and love to them. It was a case of too much.

When I went to lunch with a couple of young lawyers from the firm, there was lots of animated talk, but I was deeply withdrawn. We talked about politics, but it seemed as if they were simply making an effort to sound clever and amusing. The young men waited eagerly for a chance to seize the center of the conversational stage. They did not really listen to each other, they prepared their own remarks for the moment when the person who was speaking finished. They listened only for the purpose of replying. What they said seemed always to be addressed not to the others at the table, but to some invisible judge or authority figure. So even at a casual moment, when there was no authority present, the conversation continued to be an oratory contest, the brilliant speakers impatiently waiting their chance to earn an A in Lunch.

But there was a worse kind of conversation at lunch. This was when some of the senior lawyers were present and the conversation concerned office cases. I disliked this sort of conversation on principle. I felt it breached an unspoken trust: to be a friend to the person with whom you have a meal. It spoiled the relaxaion of lunch or dinner, the chance of enjoying each other. Each man tried to get as much help as possible for his own work. "Let me pick your brains," they would say. It was upsetting to accept a friendly invitation to lunch only to have your companion suddenly turn into an intense interlocutor. I would become inwardly rigid at the violation, and the next day I would buy sandwiches, in a delicatessen and have lunch by myself on a park bench.

The lawyer's life had a fundamental lack of limits. This was even made into a virtue. You could be unexpectedly asked to work nights, Saturdays, Sundays. You might arrive in the office and be told to get on a plane and fly to New York. You might be fully occupied with one job and then abruptly put on another with both to be done in the time allotted for one. Work at the firm simply did not include a factor that showed respect for the needs of the individuals. That would have been considered an inexcusable form of softness.

I think that even worse than the violation of spirit was the destruction of consciousness. Few people respected my right to have my own thoughts and feelings for very long. Usually the whole day was one series of things that jangled the mind until it could no longer function. When I spent a long day at the office without access to my thoughts and feelings, I felt that every moment was one of outside pressure. And my real self was driven far inside. This destruction of thought and feeling plus the repressed anger that went with it made it impossible for me to regain any sense of self when the working day was over. You cannot strike your head all day with a hammer and then expect that the person within will want to come out when you get home.

All of this was epitomized when I was summoned to see one of the senior partners, Mr. Henderson. I entered his office and, in response to his gesture, sat down in a chair near the desk; he was writing something and did not look up for several minutes.

The office, beautifully decorated, was dominated by a huge and ornate desk. The desk was, more than anything else, a barrier. No one could sit *with* Mr. Henderson, only before him. From his fortress he could only watch human intercourse, not join in it.

Mr. Henderson asked about a point in a memorandum I had written. There was a sense of urgency about time, which forbade any personal comments. The urgency also meant that from his question to my answer there was supposed to be no pause or moment of thought, as if my response was to be produced electronically. My answer was received without acknowledgement; Mr. Henderson, however, allowed himself a long silence before his next question. The dialogue was edged with a feeling of competition, of scoring points. There was an acute tension I could feel viscerally.

The phone rang and I sat while he talked leisurely and graciously to some personage. This happened all the time. I felt tension within me—I could neither relax, think, nor leave.

The discussion of the memorandum resumed. His comments stressed words like "strategy," "our objective," "tactical." The other side was "the enemy." The judgments we were making took on an air of infinite precision and exactitude, as if every nuance and move could be calculated. The matter at hand grew in importance until it seemed like the world's most vital business, a matter for secrecy, discretion, gravity, and infinite concern.

The phone rang again, and this time the conversation lasted even longer. Feeling so hostile and so powerless, I sought to become an objective observer of the man at the desk. Mr. Henderson was a great liberal, a public-spirited lawyer, a man who had been a dedicated government official and now still helped in many progressive causes. He had started poor and was a self-made man, but he followed a newer pattern: not the business success story but success in college and law school; a climb up the meritocracy; a man of brains, ability, dedication. He was a pragmatist, but also a man of taste and sophistication. He could not be written off as an organization man, a dull man, or a conformist. Why, then, the harsh cynicism, the toughness, the oppressive self-control, the approach to everything by strategy, the need for power over people? The telephone conversation ceased, and his secretary came in to say that someone was waiting to see him. "Keep going on this," he told me, and the interview was ended.

Of all the lawyers at the firm, it was in Mr. Henderson that I sometimes imagined something, far below the surface, that was in some way like me. I am not talking about the Henderson that Washington knew or the other lawyers in the firm knew. I am talking about the person who could not really want the unutterable isolation of having all other people at a distance. Very simply, I imagined that we were people who could have been friends.

There was one part of me who walked through each day at the office with a tense, set determination, numb to the cries of pain or anger within myself. I could bear anything, endure anything, and do my job. The knowledge of this made me proud. I had volunteered to be in this play, and here I was. I could leave at any time. I told myself, accept whatever the job brings with it, so long as you work here. Then there was another part of me which actually felt pain, fear and anger, who could only take so much and then would go into a fury. There was so much pressure. Any of the partners could assign me work, and none checked with the others to see how much my work load totaled. It was up to me to tell a partner no if I was already too busy, but I never knew how much was expected of me, how much anyone else did, or whether my no would be believed or considered a form of malingering. There was so much boredom and waste of time, such as at long conferences where nothing of real substance happened. There was so much to cause anger, delays, explosive frustration, tension, anxiety, rebellion at what seemed to be stupid instructions, a work rhythm of undue hurry and undue delay, an ethic that required one to endure fools, bullies and petty tyrants with silence or even a pleasant smile. Under my tense and straining façade I boiled and seethed. But it was their firm, not mine.

When the invasion of my inner being became too great, I would disappear to one of my sanctuaries. At times I might go to the office library or any of three government libraries, one shabby-quiet in the typical government way, the second fluorescent and modern, the third the library of the Supreme Court. Also, lunch in out-of-the-way places—in a cafeteria within a large government building, in the fussy but delicious Methodist Building cafeteria near the Senate offices, in a restaurant, sometimes with an old friend from another line of work.

In the library of the Supreme Court—ornate, rich, magnificent, and hushed—I could have an immensely long and splendid wooden table to myself and the grave courtesy of attendants; even the washroom was of marble and scrupulously clean. Very few people used the library, and it was open only to former law clerks and members of the Supreme Court bar. It was like the interior of a place of worship, imposing a silence on everybody. Here I could feel like the privileged law clerk again, the private assistant to the Senior Justice, and not like some sweaty and harassed lawyer. Here I could work the way I liked to work, with moments of contemplation, short interruptions to glance idly at the shelved books or recent periodicals; here all was dignity, repose and silence, with ornamented chairs and table lamps, carpeted floor and carved woodwork.

Sometimes the ornate and solemn library invited a soliloquy. One day I opened *The New York Times* before starting work and saw that a woman I had been dating in New York had gotten married. I was sitting at this table, letting life pass me by, I thought to myself. A flood of emotions inundated my mind. With a great effort, I groped for the reassurance of my logical self. Wasn't this work what I should be doing? I asked myself. I did want public service, I did want to learn a craft, I did want to work on something important.

I was actually working on arguments to be presented to a government regulatory agency in a long-drawn-out proceeding involving a license to construct a dam on a navigable river. The problem was profoundly important: issues of conservation, recreation, natural beauty, preservation of salmon runs, electric rates to consumers, and private versus public power were in dispute. To work on this problem was, surely, to be involved in society in a meaningful way. It was the word "meaningful" that was the joke. The more one knew about how decisions were actually made, the more one felt one was laboring only with appearances.

Basically, the decision would be formed by the main forces that existed in the American polity. First, a set of values that put technology, economic progress, and private power high. Second, the organization and bureaucratic processes within the government agency. Third, political influences in the state and in Congress. Fourth, whatever private economic strength could be mustered. All of these were brought to the limited frame of reference and limited independence of a group of commissioners. This was by no means a corrupt process, in the ordinary sense of the word, but it was a process not amenable to mere reason. Reason, arguments, theories could only be of lesser importance in such a process, the sort of thing that would help to rationalize what was otherwise decided. The person who contributed intellect to such a process was helping to create and perpetuate a lie about how things really happened; he was an unintentional conspirator in the cover-up of social truth.

To see how little words meant, written or spoken, one need only visit a Washington hearing of some sort; a good starting place would be Capitol Hill. At a congressional committee hearing a torrent of words pour out, all for effect; Congressmen look and sound like automatons reading statements somebody else wrote; mountains of words pile up, few of them intended to have much meaning. To live among such people—senators, lawyers, officials—was to live in a world where the spoken word meant little and the written word still less (because it wasn't read); to survive meant either to pretend (which many succeeded in doing) or to live in the limbo of cynicism.

Many of my friends fell back on craftsmanship as a justification for their work, virtuosity for its own sake, a job that other professionals could appreciate. Medicine, painting, and physics were also crafts. But the craft must be morally and socially responsible—at least that is what I believed.

And a craft should be fulfilling as a form of self-expression. How could our craft be this when it was carried out, not only without concern for its social consequences, but also under tremendous pressure, urgency, drive—all of which produced not a work of art to be contemplated, but a product fed into the whirring wheels.

I couldn't help but feel the immense wastefulness of pouring so much energy, so many people's time, so much telephoning, typing, printing, traveling, into an activity that was fundamentally without direction. At the firm we spent by far the better part of our lives doing this work; how could that be justified? Was the society as a whole equally engaged in activities with little social value?

The truth was that I was spending my life in ways that were never what I really wanted to do. I did not want to be in Washington, I did not want to work for a law firm or even be a lawyer, I did not feel drawn toward the people I spent time with. I wanted to be somewhere else, doing something totally different, with people who were exciting and adventurous. No matter how hard I tried to believe that my work was a sign of my "maturity," I found myself full of yearning for something else.

Could one make a life out of this? Could one be a hired knife-thrower and enjoy it? For what pay or for what prestige could it make sense for a person to spend his days this way? There was no possibility of personal growth if there was no chance to experiment with life, to have new experiences, to grow in moral strength. In my law practice there was no grandeur, no public service, no commitment to a cause. No people to be close to. No sky, no sea, no forests, no mountains.

My soliloquy in the Supreme Court Library ended. My own little attempt to find pleasure in my work would begin to fail and I would gather up my papers, leave the splendor of the library, and take my work back to the busy and hectic office.

SUE MILLER
(1944–   )

Sue Miller's novel *The Good Mother* is the story of Anna Dunlap, the divorced mother of four-year-old Molly. In her love affair with an artist named Leo, Anna experiences a sexual and emotional awakening, but her joy turns quickly to despair when she is faced with the prospect of losing Molly as a result of the relaxed and open attitude that she and Leo adopt toward sex. When Molly reports an innocent, but inappropriate, incident to her father during a visit, he initiates a suit for sole custody that leads to a trial.

The chapter included here presents the beginning of Anna's ordeal. After she is served with a motion for temporary custody and notice of hearing, she and Leo meet with her lawyer, Muth, and Leo recounts the damning incident. Fearful that Leo will cause her to lose Molly, Anna experiences an abrupt change in her feelings for him.

In the book's acknowledgements, Miller thanks two attorneys who were "willing to enter my fictional world with their legal imagination" and who lent her treatises on family law. She also expresses her gratitude to Dr. David Hawkins, who "helped me understand the role of the *guardian ad litem* in custody cases."

A native of Chicago, Sue Miller received a B.A. from Radcliffe College in 1964, after which she obtained three master's degrees and held various jobs, including an eight-year position as a day-care teacher, before *The Good Mother,* her first novel, was published. Miller's subsequent books are *Inventing the Abbotts and Other Stories* (1987), *Family Pictures* (1990), *For Love* (1993), and *The Distinguished Guest* (1995).

from THE GOOD MOTHER
— 1986 —

When I called my lawyer on Monday, he was reassuring. This kind of thing happened all the time, he said. Threats about custody, they were like a post-divorce sport. It would probably turn out that Brian was negotiating for something—less money, more time, something like that—and was introducing the issue of custody as a red herring, just to soften me up.

"What I'd do if I were you," he said, "is just go on about my business.

You planning to go down there on Friday? Go on down there. My guess is no one'll say anything about any of this. The name of the game is intimidation."

"So you wouldn't worry about it?" I asked. I hadn't told him about Leo, and I was glad it seemed that now I wouldn't have to.

"I sure as hell wouldn't," he said. "In these kind of situations, don't worry about a thing till you're holding the papers in your hand. You get some kind of papers, then you call me back and we'll worry together. That's what I'm here for."

He was a heavyset, avuncular man, balding and oddly graceful in small things. I had met him only once, during the divorce proceedings, when I went downtown to his office to review the agreement with him. He had urged a few changes; had acted frustrated by my unresponsiveness. "You're not really getting your money's worth out of me," he'd said, shaking his big head. And I'd felt almost apologetic that I didn't want more from Brian.

He had come with me out to the elevator when I left, and as I watched him walk away, I was struck by his gait, something dainty and controlled in it, as though before he put on all the weight he'd been a dancer, an athlete.

I told Leo that Muth thought it was all right, didn't think we should worry.

"You told him about the thing with Molly," he said.

"No, but he said that it was most likely just a threat, anyway, that Brian would turn out to be working out something else, like less money or something."

"But you didn't tell him what happened," he persisted.

"Do you want to call him back?" I burst out. "I don't think we need to worry about it."

He looked at me. I'd been awake and dressed long before he'd gotten up, and had called the lawyer promptly at eight-thirty. We hadn't touched or kissed this morning. We'd moved around the kitchen getting our separate breakfasts, doing our separate chores, like an old married couple sunk deep in habitual solitude, but without that sense of comfort or familiarity.

"No, fine," he said. He was sitting at the table, wearing the same clothes he'd been wearing when we made love the night before. His white skin was puffy around his eyes. "Whatever you say."

"I say let's forget it," I said angrily.

"I hope we can."

On Wednesday morning, I was sitting alone in the living room in my nightgown—Leo was still asleep—when the guy came with the papers. As soon as the doorbell rang I knew what it was. I felt as though I'd gone through it already. I stood in the hallway and watched him below me slowly mounting the twisting stairway, as though he were a memory. I felt as distanced from the coming event as one does from a dream; but curious too: whose face would he wear? what words would he say?

He looked up at me from the landing below. "You Anna Dunlop?" he asked. He was young, wore a maroon jacket that read *Cambridge 1977 Babe Ruth All Stars* on its breast. On the arm that held out the envelope, the same gold script spelled *Bud.*

"Dunlap," I said.

He looked at the envelope as he moved up towards me. "Oh, right," he said, and grinned sheepishly. He was homely, with crusts of acne clustered beardlike around his mouth and chin. He held the envelope out. "This is for you," he said.

"Many thanks." I took it.

He shrugged, and immediately started down the stairs, moving backwards for the first few steps. "It's a job," he said. "What can I tell you." When he'd rounded the second landing and was more or less out of sight, he started taking the stairs two and three at a time, thundering down them like a child released from some social constraint.

I shut the door and walked down the dark hallway to the kitchen, tearing open the envelope as I went. I set it down for a moment to dial the telephone, but even as it began to ring, I was reading. The words on the papers before me also seemed familiar, but shocking. They leapt up: *complaint for modification of agreement . . . motion for temporary custody . . . sexual irregularities with minor child. . . .* I didn't want to see more. I folded the papers and put them back into the jagged envelope. The secretary was telling me that Muth hadn't arrived at the office yet. She took my number in a chirping, efficient voice.

I got another cup of coffee when I'd hung up, and took it out onto the back porch. I sat on the wooden chair there. After he had begun to spend his nights with us, Leo brought his galvanized tub over for Molly to use as a pool on the back porch. Now it leaned, empty and rimed with white, against the brown clapboards. Next to it was a milk crate full of plastic bottles and cups, tubes, toy boats, all the things she played with in the water.

Across the yard, my neighbor moved in her window, waved. I lifted my cup in response, as though it were just another day.

The phone shrilled. It was Muth. As I talked to him, I heard Leo groan, could imagine him stretching, in my room.

I told Muth that Brian had sent papers, that I had received them earlier this morning.

"*Aha*," he said. "Well, I was wrong. Down to business, huh?"

"I guess so," I said.

"Well, can you tell me, Mrs. Dunlap, I mean, is it clear from what he says, on what grounds he's making the motion? Or do you wanna read it to me, or what?" I heard Leo get up, his bare feet approaching the kitchen. I turned my body away from the open doorway.

"Sexual irregularities, he says."

"Sexual irregularities?"

"Yes," I said. Leo's steps had paused at the door.

"With who?" Muth asked.

"My lover," I said. "The man I've been seeing." Leo was motionless behind me.

"*Aha*," Muth said, and waited. I said nothing. Then: "Well, you wanna tell me where this is coming from, Mrs. Dunlap? I mean is this coming out of left field, or where?"

"Not exactly." My voice was low, my shoulders hunched away from the doorway.

"So you mean, this guy had some kind of contact, some kind of sexual contact, with, ah, the kid. With Molly?"

"Yes, in a certain sense, yes. Or it could be construed that way, yes." I heard Leo turn, pad away toward the bathroom.

"*Aha*," he said. And waited again. But I couldn't answer right away. I heard Leo down the hall, the rush of water, the singing of the pipes. I felt ashamed. *You* let it happen, Brian had said. It seemed as palpable a failure to me as the long swollen scratch on her dirty cheek at Sammy Brower's house.

"I'd like to come in and talk to you," I said finally.

"Yes," he said. "Yes, it's clear that that's what we'd better do. The sooner the better, I'd say. And, ah, can you bring your friend? He's going to have to, most likely, be included in all this. You know, there'll be a hearing, et cetera. You know, as a matter of fact, Mrs. Dunlap, maybe you could check these papers and see if there's a date, a date you're supposed to show up. Did you check for that?"

"No," I said.

"Well, you wanna do that now?" he asked.

"Sure," I said. I set the phone down, took the papers out again, leafed through them. There it was—August seventeenth. I picked the phone up. "It's here," I said.

"What do we get?" he asked. "A week, ten days?"

"It's Friday," I said. "A week from Friday."

"*Aha*," he said. "Well, I'll tell you, then, I'll give you to my secretary, and ask her to set you up pronto. I think I might have a space even today. Tomorrow for sure. We ought to get going on this, you know, figure out what angle we're going to take, that kinda jazz, pretty soon. As soon as possible, actually."

"Yes," I said, and he clicked off. After a moment, the secretary's flutey voice came on the line. Mr. Muth had time late in the morning tomorrow, she said. Was eleven-thirty all right? I agreed. She told me Mr. Muth wanted to be certain *both* of us were coming.

There was no problem, I told her. We'd both be there.

When Leo emerged from his shower, I was dressed, back in the kitchen, washing up. He stood in the doorway again and watched me, gripping a towel around his waist, his drooping curls raining silver drops on his shoulders. I looked at him. "That was my lawyer on the phone," I said.

"I wondered." He pulled the towel to the side, held it tighter at his hip. He would never have worn it before. It was like the sign of our mutual fall from grace; but I was, for the moment, glad not to see him naked.

"I got the papers today," I told him.

"Oh," he said. His face asked me how bad it was. "It's real then."

"It is," I said. I tried to keep my voice determined and cheerful.

He shook his head. "Jesus, Anna. I know you know it, but . . . I'm sorry." He stepped towards me, into the kitchen, but I raised my hand.

"I don't see this as *your fault*," I said. "I don't want you to tell me that." And I turned back to the counter, making big circles with the pink sponge.

"Muth can see us tomorrow," I said.

"Did he say anything?"

"About what?"

"Well, about what would happen. About whether this was . . . about getting Molly back."

"Not really. I didn't really talk to him in much detail."

"But you told him what happened?"

I looked at him. "Roughly, yes, but not in any detail."

He turned, as though he were going to leave the room. His arched footprints left a quickly fading steamy print on the linoleum, like the breath of his feet. At the door he stopped and said, without looking at me, "I'd like to be able to talk about this stuff, Anna. It's like you keep wishing it will go away if we don't discuss it. That's hard for me. It doesn't help me. Or *anything*."

I shook my head. "And I don't want to talk about it," I said. "I don't see how that would help. It's done. I don't *blame* you. That's not what it's about. But it's just that I feel like I'm holding on by a thread here, plus I've still got stuff I have to do at work. To keep going. These fucking rats."

I shrugged. "I just need to do this my way, I think. But I am sorry, I really am sorry, if it makes it worse for you."

"That's not it. It's not that I'm feeling sorry for myself. I . . . Jesus. That would be pretty self-indulgent. I just . . ." He looked at me. "I don't want to lose you."

"That's not the issue, is it?" I asked. "Your losing *me*?" And I turned away. In a moment I sensed, rather than heard, that he'd left the room. When I went to find him a few minutes later, to say I was sorry, he was gone. I imagined him swinging down the hall barefoot, partly dressed, as quickly and silently as he had in the spring when he'd wanted to get out before Molly heard him.

Leo wore a jacket and tie to Muth's office the next day. He'd had to borrow them from a friend, since he didn't own either. The jacket was a little tight, and Leo's cuffs, his big hands, stuck out. He looked like a farmboy visiting in town.

"That's very sweet of you," I said. "Wearing that." We were driving down Storrow Drive in light midmorning traffic. Summer school students lay reading, sunbathing on the green banks of the river. He looked at me quickly to be sure I was sincere. When he saw that I was, he thanked me. It struck me suddenly that much of our conversation for the last several days had been just this polite—apologies, thanks, careful backing away from demands or questions. Each of us was behaving as though the other was fragile, easily damaged. Nothing was natural between us. We hadn't made love since Sunday night, the night Leo returned; and as I remembered all that, it seemed to me that I had known, even as we did it, that it marked the end of something. Now we lay in the same bed together each night, sometimes touching each other lightly, without passion, before we turned away and sought sleep. But sex seemed unthinkable.

So did sleeping alone though. It was as though neither of us wanted to face himself. Even the night before, when I'd gone to his house just to apologize after I'd finished up at the lab, when I was sure each of us would want to be alone, we were unable to find a way to separate.

"I don't need to stay," I'd said, standing in his doorway. "I just came to say I was sorry for being so sharp this morning."

"No, no, that's O.K.," he said. "I understand. Come on in. I mean, I'd *like* you to stay." He stood back to make room for my entrance, then hesitated. "Unless you want to be alone or something." We looked at each other a moment. The thought of being alone terrified me.

"I'll stay," I said, and instantly felt how much I didn't want to, how much I *had* wanted to be alone. But I was already crossing his threshold,

I would hurt his feelings if I left, it was too late. And so we slept together another night with our backs curved towards each other, just as Brian and I had done in the last stages of our marriage.

In the morning, I'd gone home to change my clothes, then driven back over to Leo's to pick him up. He was waiting for me on the corner by his building, and I almost drove past him, he looked so unfamiliar in his costume. In the car, I kept looking over at him as I drove, but he seemed unconscious of me, lost in his own nervousness. His hands drummed on his knees. Once or twice he popped his knuckles.

We parked in an expensive lot downtown, and then, because we were early for the appointment with Muth, we stopped for coffee. The cafeteria was dim, functional, with small formica tables. The people around us were a curious combination of bums and businessmen. They seemed completely at home in one another's company. It was we who were out of place in this world—both wearing uniforms that seemed uncomfortable on us. My dress was a little too fancy, not secretarial enough. And when I saw the businessmen, dark and tailored, I realized that Leo looked worse in his attempt at respectability than he would have if he'd just worn a T-shirt and jeans. There was something that appeared nearly psychopathic to me abruptly, in the ill-fitting disguise. I sat across from him, sipping the burnt-tasting coffee and talking about what Muth was like, and I wanted to reach over and loosen the tie, wanted to ask him to take the jacket off. But I couldn't. He'd done it for me, to help me get Molly back.

Upstairs, when Muth approached us across the carpeted expanse of the firm's outer offices, I watched his face carefully for signs of his response to Leo; but it was unreadable, pleasant as ever. He was in shirtsleeves, rolled up, and a tie. He shook Leo's hand and mine as though we were perfectly respectable people.

In his office, he arranged the chairs for us, making small talk in his rambling way about the Red Sox. Once he'd got us settled, he sat down behind his desk, and asked me for the papers. I handed the torn envelope across to him. Leo and I sat in silence for three or four minutes while he read through them, neither of us looking at the other. I was intensely conscious of Leo though, of his restless shifting in his chair. I hoped he wouldn't be rude if Muth probed too deep.

Muth's face, bent over his desk, fell into a somber frowning pouchiness. Once or twice he ran his hand over his balding head. But when he looked up, he was neutral, boyishly middle-aged again.

"Well," he said. "The news is not good, I guess."

I found myself smiling politely, making some agreeable answer. Leo stared at me.

"I think what would help me right now," Muth said, extracting a pencil from a jar of them on his desk, "is to find out exactly what you think it is that's got Mr. Dunlap so fired up here. I think the phrase he uses is *sexual irregularities*, and I think *you* said on the phone, Mrs. Dunlap, that there *had* been some kind of contact between Mr. Cutter and . . . ah, Molly. That right?"

"Yes," I said. I nodded.

"Well, that's what I need to get straight then. Just what it was, when it happened, how often, that kind of thing." He looked up, expectantly, pleasantly.

"Once," Leo said.

"Once," he repeated, and wrote something down. He smiled at Leo. "Can you, ah, can you fill me in on it a bit, Mr. Cutter?"

I looked at Leo. He shifted forward in his chair, and without looking over at me, he started talking. As he began, I thought, *Why, he's practiced this.*

"It was sometime in June when it happened. Anna had left Molly and me alone for the evening. She was at the lab or something, I don't remember what, but she was supposed to get back in time to tuck Molly in. Molly and I had gone out to get ice cream. I'd given her a bath"—Muth's pencil whispered quickly on the page—"gotten her into her pj's, all that stuff. It was hot. I'd been working all day. Molly was in her room, playing, and she sounded happy, so I figured I'd take a shower. I told her I was going to, so she'd know where to find me, if she needed me." Leo's hands had been folded in his lap at first. Now, as he relaxed a little, they came to life, helped him tell the story.

"I, you know, got in the shower, and after a while, she came into the bathroom, started talking to me. It was like she just wanted company. She was just talking about this and that, the stories she'd picked out for her mother to read to her, some stuff that happened to her at day care. She was just sitting on the toilet seat, talking, the way she sometimes did."

"She'd come in before when you were in the shower?" Muth asked. He didn't look up.

"Me, or her mother, yeah. She liked the company."

Muth nodded.

"When I pushed the curtain back and started drying off, I noticed Molly was staring at me, at my"—there was the slightest hesitation as Leo chose the word—"penis. But she'd seen me naked before, I didn't think much of it. I was fooling around, you know, dancing."

"Dancing," Muth repeated.

"Yeah. I was dancing and singing actually." Leo's voice had begun to sound angry. I leaned forward. He looked up at me, then moved uncomfortably in his chair. When he spoke again, his voice was calm. "Singing 'Singin' in the Rain.' She liked that." He shrugged. "And then I finished, and I was just drying off, and she said, out of the blue, 'That's your penis?' " He cleared his throat. "You know, she was learning that stuff, those words. She had a book that talked about it, and they did the body parts at day care. Her mother—Anna—had talked about it some too, telling her the names of stuff." He shrugged again. "So I said yeah. She was, she was standing up, she'd gotten closer to the tub. I was, actually, a little uncomfortable about it. But I'd seen how relaxed Anna was about it all, and I didn't want to screw that up or anything. So I tried to seem natural, not cover up or anything.

"But then she said, 'Can I touch it?' "

Muth looked up sharply at Leo, his pencil still on the yellow pad.

"I honestly didn't think about it for more than a second. I just said sure. And, um, she did. She . . . held it for a second. And just the contact, I guess. The contact, and I think, the kind of . . . weirdness of the situation made me . . . that is, I started to get an erection. And I said, 'That's enough, Molly,' and I turned away. I put the towel on. She made some other comment, some question about my . . . about it getting big. And I told her that sometimes happened with men. And I went and got dressed." He looked at Muth, as if awaiting judgment.

"And that was that?" Muth asked.

"Yes. Pretty much." He paused. Then: "She did talk about it some more that night. She seemed a little anxious about it actually. She talked about the facts of life. Of sex. You know, she knew the purpose of an erection in a vague sense. She knew, sort of, what it was for, and I think it confused her. That I had one. So I tried to explain. I'm not sure how well I did."

"Aha," Muth said. "And did you discuss this with Mrs. Dunlap?"

"No." He shifted in his chair.

"Why not?"

"I was . . . To tell the truth, I was embarrassed. And I thought I'd handled it O.K. Or as well as anyone could've. So I didn't see that it was a problem."

"Aha," Muth said. Then he looked at Leo. "Can I just ask you, Mr., ah, Cutter, why you didn't just say no to the child. You said it made you uncomfortable. Why didn't you just tell her she couldn't touch you?"

"I didn't think that's what Anna—Mrs. Dunlap—would have wanted me to do."

"You didn't think Mrs. Dunlap would have wanted you to?" Suddenly Muth seemed lawyerlike to me, in a way he never had before. I could imagine him being mean in a courtroom.

"No," Leo said. "I thought she'd want me to be as relaxed, as natural with Molly, as she was. About her body and that kind of thing."

Muth made a note, then looked up again.

"So you might say you misunderstood the rules."

Leo shrugged. "I thought I understood them."

There was a long pause. Then Muth said, "I think when the time comes, Mr. Cutter, it'd be better for Mrs. Dunlap in the situation we've got here, if you just said you *mis*understood them."

After a moment Leo inclined his head slightly, stiffly.

Muth began to talk to me. He asked me what the rules were; how much Leo and I were naked around Molly; whether she'd been in bed with us; how much she knew about the facts of life. He asked me to describe the book I'd read to her, to describe the pictures in it. (They were cartoon figures, cheerful, dumpy, humorous.) He said he'd like me to bring the book in next time I came, that it might be helpful, depending on what Molly had said to Brian. He asked me how long Leo and I had been involved, how long he'd been spending nights at our house, how much Molly understood of our relationship, how often Leo had been alone with Molly. He took notes throughout, and sometimes as he wrote, his face took on the same frowning cast it had had when he bent over the papers from Brian; but whenever he lifted it to me and Leo, it was bland and open as a curious baby's.

Mostly I talked, though occasionally Leo offered an observation. Muth asked about how things had been when I'd been married to Brian, what his attitudes about sex had been, whether the patterns in the house had changed a lot since then, whether Molly had seemed at all disturbed by those changes. When finally he seemed to be running out of questions, I asked him what he thought would happen, what he thought Brian's chances were.

He shook his head. "This kind of thing is thought to call, Mrs. Dunlap. A lot depends on what Molly said, on how bothered she seems to be about it. But these judges, you know, they're by and large conservative. They don't like to hear anything about sexual stuff with kids." I sensed Leo moving slightly in his chair. "You know," Muth gestured with his slender fingers open, "they hear terrible stuff all the time. After a while, they lump everything like that together in their minds."

"What if . . ." I cleared my throat. "What if I said I wouldn't see Leo anymore. Would that make a difference?"

I could feel Leo snap to alertness, his eyes on me. My mouth parched. But Muth knew only strategy, seemed unconscious of anything that passed between us. He was already shaking his head.

"They hear it *all* the time. You can try it, for sure, but they don't believe it anyway. A promise, to them, is what someone is willing to say to get a kid back. Period."

The silence in the room was now explosive. Muth, unperturbed, looked from Leo to me. "O.K., then," he said. "If it's all right with you, Mr. Cutter, I'd like to talk to Mrs. Dunlap alone for a few minutes." He stood, Leo stood. "If you could just wait outside. . . ." He crossed to the door and opened it for Leo. "It was good to talk with you," Muth said, extending his hand. Leo reached out and shook it. "I appreciate your honesty."

Leo made a murmuring noise. Then without looking back at me, he left.

Even watching his stiff back out of the room, I was so focused on what all this meant for Molly, for Molly and me, that I didn't realize I could have managed not to ask my question in front of Leo by waiting only a few minutes longer. At the time, hurting him, alienating him, seemed inevitable, part of the price I had to pay.

Muth sat down. His tone was confidential. He invited me to share any doubts, any observations about aberrant behavior in Leo. I told him I had no doubts about him, that Leo had, except in this instance, behaved with Molly as I would have wanted him to.

"So it was just in this case that he misunderstood you?"

I waited a moment before I answered. "Yes," I said, feeling that I was betraying Leo as much by my agreement with Muth now, as I had by my question in front of him earlier.

Muth went on to talk about my work schedule, about how much Molly had seen Brian since the divorce, about how much she'd seen of him when we were still married, about who was taking care of Molly in Washington while Brian and Brenda worked. Three or four times he circled back around to Leo again, what I knew of his background, his sexual history before me. I tried to sound firm and confident, determined to try not to betray him any more than I felt I already had.

Finally he leaned back and tossed his pencil onto the pad.

"Okay," he said. "Now I think the approach here is gonna be to downpedal all this stuff about permissiveness. *You* know and *I* know that it's probably healthier for a kid to be pretty much open about this sexual stuff, right?"

I nodded.

"But what we're not gonna do here is, we're not gonna try to educate the judge about it, O.K.? Because that's not gonna work, right?"

I nodded.

"What we're gonna focus on is how happy she was, how much time you spent with her, how responsible you were. How Mr. Dunlap's a bit of a workaholic, how his wife has the same kind of job, how the choice is really between a loving mother and a paid babysitter. O.K.? Let them ask the stuff about this sexual thing with Cutter. It's gotta come out. But we're not gonna defend it or tie it in with the idea of sexual openness or anything. It's just gonna be a mistake *he* made. Got it?"

I nodded, ashamed. *You*, Brian's voice said, *you* let it happen.

"Now, let me tell you what I think we oughta do," Muth said. "See if you agree with me."

"O.K.," I said.

"I think that with what we've got here, our best chance is gonna be an expert, a shrink. See, you and Mr. Cutter both are clearly, you know, you come off, well—articulate, concerned with her, with Molly. With a guardian, a psychiatrist appointed by the court, you could talk, you know, the way you have with me here, and I think that would be our best shot. With their training, they look beyond just the bare facts. They're there to pick up, you know"—his hand circled in the air—"attitudes, feelings. My sense is, if we go with that, if I make a motion that we get a shrink to make a recommendation, that within a very short time he'd see what I've seen here: it was a mistake, it was, basically, Cutter's mistake, it's not about to happen again, right?"

"Right," I said.

"So, then he recommends she stays with you; and the judge, they give a lot of credence to that. I think . . . well, that's what I'd suggest anyway."

"That sounds reasonable to me," I said. And then, not to seem too passive, "Are there alternative strategies?"

He shook his head. "Not that readily come to mind. You have anything on the father?"

"What do you mean?"

"Well, like this." He gestured at the papers. "You know, like what he's got on you. Has he done anything you can point to where it's clearly bad judgment, incompetence?"

"Not really. He's very *busy*, as I've said. He always had trouble finding time for her."

"Sure, yeah, we'll *use* that, but in itself that's not enough."

"No, I really don't have anything."

"So," he said, and lifted his big shoulders. "Let's go with the shrink?"

"Yes," I said.

"Even with him though, I'd downpedal the specifics. But you could tell him, I mean he might be very interested that Mr. Dunlap was what you might say, *uptight* about sexual stuff. And it wouldn't hurt if you could remember, like, a scene where, if he might have frightened Molly a little with that strictness or something. But it will just be a more relaxed context, if you know what I mean. Less concerned with exactly *what* happened and more concerned with why, and that's to our advantage. You understand?"

I nodded. He came forward in his chair, leaned towards me.

"'Cause what happened, on the face of it, isn't good." He shook his head. "I mean, *I* can understand how it happened, *you* can understand how it happened, but I can also tell you how their attorney's going to present it, and it's not going to sound good." He shifted back again. "You know, there's a certain way of looking at this stuff—and I hate to tell you, but it's how a lot of the world sees it—and what we've got there is a guy, a guy kind of down and out, no regular job"—he raised his hand as I stirred, letting me know he knew it wasn't so. I was again struck by his hand's delicacy, the fingers that curved in slightly like a dancer's—"left alone with a kid, cavorting around in front of her, encouraging contact, aroused by her touch. They may suggest a lot worse, too, and he'll be the only one to deny it. You see what I mean. And depending on the judge, on how much he's able to imagine another context for that behavior, that'll be how it goes. That and the recommendation of the family service officer. So that's one thing potentially in your favor. That and Mr. Dunlap's pattern of fathering."

"And how soon will all this happen? When?"

He shrugged. "First there's this hearing, right?"

I nodded.

"O.K. The procedure there is we all make these motions, and then probably we get sent to the F.S.O."

"The F.S.O.?"

"Yeah, the family service officer. It'll be like an interview. It's usually a woman, a social worker, you know, young, bright. She'll sort of assess things, make sure this guardian deal with the shrink seems appropriate, work out the details. So, we oughta find out then, by Friday, a lot of stuff: approximately when you'll all see the shrink—and the kid will too, Molly, and the father—and maybe even, I think I'll push for it, a court date set."

"And that's when it'll get decided? The court date?"

"Right, the trial. Depending on how long it takes to see the shrink, that could be a couple of months. Maybe less. And that will take a couple of days, the trial. You know, you'll testify, your ex-husband will, the shrink, the whole thing."

"And is it true that I can't see Molly until then?"

"No way," he shook his head. "No. It's not true. Chances are your ex-husband will get *temporary* custody—he's moving for that, till the trial, you know, and that's pretty typical. But we'll fix you up with visitation, don't you worry. No," he said, and grinned, "he's just making points telling you that, showing everybody how seriously he takes all this. We'll have no trouble getting you visitation once he's done proving that."

We sat for a moment. He cleared his throat. "Now, about money," he said.

For a moment I didn't understand him, thought he was referring to some part of the financial arrangement between me and Brian. Brian had paid him for the divorce, so I'd never thought of a fee as part of this transaction.

"Oh," I said, and I couldn't keep the surprise out of my voice. "Of course."

"The retainer'll be twenty-five hundred. And it might be, I suppose, another thousand or so in the end."

I hoped my face wasn't registering the shock that I felt, the sharp sense of my idiocy. "I'm sorry, I don't know this, but *when* do I pay you?" I tried to keep my voice smooth, the question academic.

"Yesterday," he said, and grinned.

I looked quickly down at my hands. When I thought I had control of my face, I looked up at him and tried smiling back. "I'll have to make it tomorrow or the next day."

He nodded. "I understand," he said. "I won't say 'I told you so' about your divorce agreement, but I understand." He rose, and I did too. "But I will need it before the court date," he said, and he crossed to the door.

"You'll have it," I said, my mind already racing through my possibilities, turning down one dead-end corridor after another.

He walked me back to the reception area. Leo sat in one of the boxy upholstered chairs, and I was startled again at how the ill-fitting jacket robbed him of all his grace and poise. He seemed a liability, sitting there, and I felt a pulse of rage at him. I stood a little distant as Muth shook hands with him again.

We rode in silence in opposite corners of the carpeted elevator. Two women stood in front of us by the doors. One of them was talking about what sounded like her divorce. "My lawyer keeps saying 'Now, we're not out to punish anyone here, we just want what's right,' but I don't think he understands. I don't *care* what's right, I want to fucking *punish* the guy."

Her friend shook her head. "Sure you do. After what he's put you through?"

The doors opened. We crossed the marble lobby, stepped outside.

Muth's office, the reception room, the elevator, had all been windowless, lit by overhead spots. I was startled to see the sunshine, feel the light summer air push my dress against me. We walked the short block to the parking lot, and I paid the attendant. I was aware of the rigidity of Leo's presence, of his anger; but I was, in a serious way, preoccupied. And so I was startled, when I got into the car next to him and shut my door, that after a moment of inert silence, he violently struggled out of the jacket and threw it against the dashboard. Then he tore at the tie and pulled it off. He caught his collar yanking at it, and the button at the neck of the shirt pulled off, ripping the cloth, and ricocheting with a sharp snap off the windshield. We sat locked together among all the empty cars, the sound of Leo's panting rage filling the space between us, and I wondered how we'd get through the next ten days, two weeks, without damaging each other. In my several seconds of terror, when I thought he might be going to hurt me, what I had felt for Leo was a cold, welling hate.

TOM WOLFE

(1930–   )

Tom Wolfe has been called the ``stentorian spokesman and most flamboyant practioner'' of the New Journalism, which he defined as ``the use by people writing nonfiction of techniques which heretofore had been thought of as confined to the novel or the short story, to create in one form both the kind of objective reality of journalism and the subjective reality that people have always gone to the novel for.'' Wolfe's most famous examples of the New Journalism include *The Electric Kool-Aid Acid Test* (1968), *The Pump House Gang* (1968), *Radical Chic and Mau-Mauing the Flak Catchers* (1970), and *The Right Stuff* (1979).

The Bonfire of the Vanities (1987), Wolfe's first conventional novel, is a conscious attempt to recreate the nineteenth-century novel of social realism. In an essay titled ``Stalking the Billion-Footed Beast: A Literary Manifesto for the New Social Novel?'', Wolfe had stated that ``the future of the fictional novel would be in a highly detailed realism based on reporting . . . that would portray the individual in intimate and inextricable relation to the society around him.''

Bonfire is about the fall of Sherman McCoy, a million-dollar-a-year Wall Street investment banker and self-styled ``Master of the Universe.'' Sherman, well insulated against the ``other half,'' makes a wrong turn one night after crossing the Triborough Bridge with his mistress, Maria Ruskin. He ends up in the South Bronx and, ultimately, a lot of trouble; after a confrontation with two teenagers, he fatally injures one of them with his car and leaves the scene. Consequently he is forced to engage a street-smart criminal lawyer, Thomas Killian, whom he regards as ``a sharpie.'' These excerpts depict two scenes: Sherman's first meeting with Killian in his law office, and a later meeting at the Criminal Courts Building in which Killian describes the workings of the criminal justice system's ``Favor Bank.''

Tom Wolfe dedicated *Bonfire of the Vanities* to ``Counselor Eddie Hayes, who walked among the flames, pointing at the lurid lights.'' Hayes, a friend of Wolfe's and the model for Killian, was an assistant district attorney who later went into private practice, where his most publicized work was his controversial representation of artist Andy Warhol's estate.

Thomas Kennerly Wolfe, Jr., was born in Richmond, Virginia. After earning a Ph.D. in American Studies at Yale, he worked as a reporter for the *Springfield Union* (Massachusetts) and the *New York Herald Tribune*. He has served as a contributing editor to a number of publications, including *Esquire* and *Harper's.*

from THE BONFIRE OF THE VANITIES

— 1987 —

Reade Street was one of those old streets down near the courthouses and City Hall. It was a narrow street, and the buildings on either side, office building and light-industry lofts with cast-iron columns and architraves, kept it in a dismal gloaming, even on a bright spring day like this. Gradually the buildings in this area, which was known as TriBeCa, for "triangle below Canal Street," were being renovated as offices and apartments, but the area retained an irreducible grime. On the fourth floor of an old cast-iron building, Sherman walked down a corridor with a dingy tile floor.

Halfway down the corridor was a plastic plate incised with the names DERSHKIN, BELLAVITA, FISHBEIN & SCHLOSSEL. Sherman opened the door and found himself in a tiny and overpoweringly bright glassed-in vestibule tended by a Latin woman who sat behind a glass partition. He gave his name and asked to see Mr. Killian, and the woman pressed a buzzer. A glass door led to a larger, even brighter space with white walls. The lights overhead were so strong Sherman kept his head down. An orange industrial cord carpet covered the floor. Sherman squinted, trying to avoid the ferocious wattage. Just ahead, on the floor, he could make out the base of a couch. The base was made of white Formica. Pale tan leather cushions were on top of it. Sherman sat down, and his tailbone immediately slid forward. The seat seemed to tilt the wrong way. His shoulder blades hit the back cushions, which rested against a slab of Formica set perpendicular to the base. Gingerly he lifted his head. There was another couch across from him. On it were two men and a woman. One man had on a blue-and-white running suit with two big panels of electric-blue leather in front. The other man wore a trench coat made of some dull, dusty, grainy hide, elephant perhaps, with shoulders cut so wide he seemed gigantic. The woman wore a black leather jacket, also cut very large, black leather pants, and black boots that folded down below the knee like a pirate's. All three of them were squinting, just as Sherman was. They also kept sliding forward and then twitching and squirming back up, and their leather clothes rustled and squeaked. The Leather People. Jammed together on the couch, they resembled an elephant tormented by flies.

A man entered the reception area from an inner hallway, a tall thin bald man with bristling eyebrows. He wore a shirt and a tie but no jacket, and he had a revolver in a holster high on his left hip. He gave Sherman the sort of dead smile a doctor might give in a waiting room if he didn't want to be detained. Then he went back inside.

Voices from the inner hallway: a man and a woman. The man appeared to be pushing the woman forward. The woman took little steps and looked back at him over her shoulder. The man was tall and slender, probably in his late thirties. He wore a double-breasted navy-blue suit with a pale blue overplaid and a striped shirt with a stiff white collar. The collar had an exaggerated spread, very much a sharpie's look, to Sherman's way of thinking. He had a lean face, a delicate face, you might have said, had it not been for his nose, which appeared to have been broken. The woman was young, no more than twenty-five, all breasts, bright red lips, raging hair, and sultry makeup, popping out of a black turtleneck sweater. She wore black pants and teetered atop a pair of black spike-heel shoes.

At first their voices were muffled. Then the woman's voice became louder and the man's became lower. It was the classic case. The man wants to confine matters to a quiet private argument, but the woman decides to play one of her trump cards, which is Making a Scene. There is Making a Scene, and there is Tears. This was Making a Scene. The woman's voice became louder and louder, and at last the man's rose, too.

"But you gotta," the woman said.

"But I don't gotta, Irene."

"What am I suppose a do? Rot?"

"You suppose a pay your bills like everybody else," he said, mimicking her. "You already beat me for half my fee. And then you keep asking me to do things that could get me disbarred."

"You dun care."

"It ain't that I dun care, Irene. It's that I dun care anymore. You don't pay your bills. Don't look at me like that. You're on your own."

"But you gotta! What happens if they rearrest me?"

"You shoulda thoughta that, Irene. What did I tell you the first time you walked into this office? I told you two things. I told you, 'Irene, I'm not gonna be your friend. I'm gonna be your lawyer. But I'm gonna do more for you than your friends.' And I said, 'Irene, you know why I do this? I do it for money.' And then I said, 'Irene, remember those two things.' Idd'n'at right? Did'n I say that?"

"I can't go back there," she said. She lowered her heavy Tropical Twilight eyelids and then her whole head. Her lower lip trembled; her head and the raging hair shook, so did her shoulders.

The Tears.

"Oh, for Christ's sake, Irene. Come on!"

The Tears.

"All right. Look . . . I'll find out if they're going after you on a 220-31, and I'll represent you on rearraignment if they are, but that's it."

The Tears!—victorious even after these many millennia. The woman nodded like a penitent child. She walked out through the blazing waiting room. Her bottom bobbed in a glossy black shimmer. One of the Leather Men looked at Sherman and smiled, man to man, and said, "Ay, caramba."

On this alien terrain Sherman felt obliged to smile back.

The sharpie came into the reception room and said, "Mr. McCoy? I'm Tom Killian."

Sherman stood up and shook hands. Killian didn't shake hands very firmly; Sherman thought of the two detectives. He followed Killian down a hallway with more spotlights.

Killian's office was small, modern, and grim. It had no window. But at least it wasn't bright. Sherman looked at the ceiling. Of the nine recessed spotlights, seven had been unscrewed or allowed to burn out.

Sherman said, "The lights out there . . ." He shook his head and didn't bother to finish the sentence.

"Yeah, I know," said Killian. "That's what you get when you fuck your decorator. The guy who leased this place, he brought in this number, and she thought the building was gloomy. She put in, I mean, *lights*. The woman had watt fever. The place is supposed to remind you of Key Biscayne. That's what she said."

Sherman didn't hear anything after "fuck your decorator." As a Master of the Universe, he took a masculine pride in the notion that he could handle all sides of life. But now, like many respectable American males before him, he was discovering that All Sides of Life were colorful mainly when you were in the audience. *Fuck your decorator*. How could he let any decision affecting his life be made by this sort of person in this sort of atmosphere? He had called in sick—that lamest, weakest, most sniveling of life's small lies—to Pierce & Pierce; for this itching slum of the legal world.

Killian motioned toward a chair, a modern chair with a curved chrome frame and Chinese-red upholstery, and Sherman sat down. The back was too low. There was no way to get comfortable. Killian's chair, behind the desk, didn't look much better.

Killian let out a sigh and rolled his eyes again. "You heard me conferring with my client, Miss——" He made a curve in the air with his cupped hand.

"I did. Yes."

"Well, there you had criminal law in its basic form with all the elements." Well, theh you ed crim'nal lawr in its basic fawuhm wit'allee elements. At first Sherman thought the man was talking this way as further mimicry of the woman who had just left. Then he realized it wasn't her accent. It was Killian's own. The starched dandy who sat before him had a New York street accent, full of dropped consonants and tortured vowels. Nevertheless, he had lifted Sherman's spirits a notch or two by indicating that he knew Sherman was new to the world of criminal law and that he existed on a plateau far above it.

"What sort of case?" asked Sherman.

"Drugs. Who else can afford a trial lawyer for eight weeks?" Then, without any transition, he said: "Freddy told me your problem. I also been reading about the case in the tabloids. Freddy's a great man, but he has to much class to read the tabloids. I read 'em. So whyn't you tell me what actually happened."

To his surprise, once he got started, Sherman found it easy to tell his story in this place, to this man. Like a priest, his confessor, this dandy with a fighter's nose, was from another order.

Every now and then a plastic intercom box on Killian's desk would give an electronic beep, and the receptionist's faintly Latin voice would say, "Mr. Killian . . . Mr. Scannesi on 3-0" or "Mr. Rothblatt on 3-1," and Killian would say, "Tell 'im I'll call 'im back," and Sherman would resume. But then the machine beeped, and the voice said, "Mr. Leong on 3-0."

"Tell 'im—I'll take it." Killian gave his hand a deprecating flap in the air, as if to say. "This is nothing compared to what we're talking about, but I'll have to talk to this person for half a second."

"Ayyyyy, Lee," said Killian. "Whaddaya whaddaya? . . . No kiddin'? . . . Hey, Lee, I was just reading a book about you . . . Well, not about you but about you Leongs . . . Would I kid you? Whaddaya think, I want a hatchet in my back?"

Sherman grew increasingly irritated. At the same time, he was impressed. Apparently Killian was representing one of the defendants in the Chinatown voting scandal.

Finally Killian hung up and turned to Sherman and said, "So you took the car back to the garage and you exchanged a few words with the attendant and you walked home." This was no doubt to show that he hadn't been distracted by the interruption.

Sherman kept going, concluding with the visit of the two detectives, Martin and Goldberg, to his apartment.

Killian leaned forward and said, "Awright. The first thing you gotta understand is, from now on, you gotta keep your mouth shut. You understand? You got nothing to gain, *nothing*, by talking about this"—*tawkin*—"to anybody, I don't care who it is. All that's gonna happen is, you're gonna get jerked around some more like you did by these two cops."

"What *should* I have done? They were in the building. They knew I was upstairs. If I refused to talk to them, that would be like a clear indication I had something to hide."

"All you hadda do was tell them, 'Gentlemen, it's nice to meet you, you're conducting an investigation, I have absolutely no experience in this area, so I'm gonna turn you over to my attorney, good evening, don't let the doorknob hit you in the back on your way out.' "

"But even that—"

"It's better'n what happened, right? As a matter of fact, they woulda probably figured, Well, here's this Park Avenue swell who's too busy or too above-it-all to talk to characters like us. He's got people who do things like that for him. It wouldn't've prejudiced your case at all, probably. From now on, it sure as hell won't." He started chuckling. "The guy actually read your rights to you, hunh? I wish I coulda seen it. The dumb fuck probably lives in a two-family in Massapequa, and he's sitting there in an apartment on Park Avenue in the Seventies, and he's gotta inform you that if you are unable to afford a lawyer, the state will provide you one. He's gotta read you the whole thing."

Sherman was chilled by the man's detached amusement. "All right," he said, "but what does it mean?"

"It means they're trying to get evidence for a criminal charge."

"What kind?"

"What kinda evidence or what kinda charge?"

"What kind of charge."

"They have several possibilities. Assuming Lamb don't die"—*don't*—"there's reckless endangerment."

"Is that the same as reckless driving?"

"No, it's a felony. It's a fairly serious felony. Or if they really want to get hard-nosed about it, they could work on a theory of assault with a dangerous weapon, meaning the car. If Lamb dies, that creates two more possibilities. Manslaughter is one, and criminally negligent homicide is the other, although all the time I was in the D.A.'s office up there I never heard a charging anybody with criminally negligent homicide unless there was drunk driving involved. On top a that they got leaving the scene of an accident and failure to report an accident. Both felonies."

"But since I wasn't driving the car at the time this fellow was hit, can they bring any of these charges against *me*?"

"Before we get to that, let me explain something to you. Maybe they can't bring charges against *any*body."

"They can't?" Sherman felt his entire nervous system quicken at this first sign of hope.

"You looked your car over pretty carefully, right? No dents? No blood? No tissue? No broken glass? Right?"

"That's right."

"It's pretty obvious the kid wasn't hit very hard. The emergency room treated him for a broken wrist and let him go. Right?"

"Yes."

"The fact of the matter is, you don't even *know* if your car hit him, do you."

"Well, I did hear something."

"With all the shit that was going on at that moment, that coulda been anything. You *heard* something. You didn't see anything. You don't really *know*, do you?"

"Well . . . that's true."

"You beginning to see why I don't want you to talk to anybody?"

"Yes."

"And I mean *any*body. Okay? Now. Here's another thing. Maybe it wasn't your car that hit him. Did that possibility ever occur to you? Maybe it wasn't *any* car. You don't *know*. And *they* don't know, the cops don't know. These stories in the newspaper are very strange. Here's this big case, supposedly, but nobody knows where this cockamamie hit'n'run's supposed've taken place. *Bruckner Boulevard*. Bruckner Boulevard's five miles long! They got no witnesses. What the kid told his mother is hearsay. It don't"—*don't*—"mean a thing. They have no description of a driver. Even if they could establish that it was your car that hit him—they can't arrest a car. One a the garage attendants coulda loaned it to his sister-in-law's nephew so he could go up to Fordham Road to kiss his girlfriend good night. They don't know. And you don't know. As a matter of fact, stranger things have happened."

"But suppose the other boy comes forward? I swear to you, there was a second boy, a big powerful fellow."

"I believe you. It was a setup. They were gonna take you off. Yeah, he could come forward, but it sounds to me like he has his reasons not to. Judging by this story the mother tells, the kid didn't mention him, either."

"Yes," said Sherman, "but he could. I swear, I'm beginning to feel as if I should preempt the situation and take the initiative and go to the police with Maria—Mrs. Ruskin—and just tell them exactly what happened. I mean, I don't know about the law, but I feel morally certain that I did the right thing and that she did the right thing in the situation we were in."

"Ayyyyyy!" said Killian. "You Wall Street honchos really *are* gamblers! Ayyyyyy!! Whaddaya whaddaya!" Killian was grinning. Sherman stared at him in astonishment. Killian must have detected it, because he put on a perfectly serious face. "You got any idea what the D.A.'d do if you just walked in and said, 'Yeah, it was me and my girlfriend, who lives on Fifth Avenue, in my car'? They'd devour you—*de*-vour you."

"Why?"

"The case is already a political football, and they got *nothing* to go on. Reverend Bacon is yelling about it, it's on TV, *The City Light* has gone bananas over it, and it's putting a lot of pressure on Abe Weiss, who has an election coming up. I know Weiss very well. There is no real world to Abe Weiss. There's only what's on TV and in the newspapers. But I'll tell you something else. They wouldn't give you a break even if no one was watching."

"Why not?"

"You know what you do all day long when you work in the D.A.'s Office? You prosecute people named Tiffany Latour and LeBaron Courtney and Mestaffalah Shabazz and Camilio Rodriguez. You get so you're *dying* to get your hands on somebody with something on the ball. And if somebody gives you a couple like you and your friend Mrs. Ruskin—ayyyyyyyy, Biscuit City!"

The man seemed to have a horrible nostalgic enthusiasm for such a catch.

"What would happen?"

"For a start, there's no way in the world they wouldn't arrest you, and if I know Weiss, he'd make a big show of it. They might not be able to hold you very long, but it would be extremely unpleasant. That's guaranteed."

Sherman tried to imagine it. He couldn't. His spirits hit bottom. He let out a big sigh.

"*Now* you see why I don't want you to talk to anybody? You get the picture?"

"Yes."

"But look, I'm not trying to depress you. My job right now is not to defend you but to keep you from even having to be defended. I mean, that's assuming you decide to have me represent you. I'm not even gonna talk about a fee at this point, because I don't know what this is gonna involve. If you're lucky, I'll find out this is a bullshit case."

"How can you find out that?"

"The head of the Homicide Bureau in the Bronx D.A.'s Office is a guy I started out with up there, Bernie Fitzgibbon."

"And he'll tell you?"

"I think he will. We're friends. He's a Donkey, just like me."

"A donkey?"

"An Irishman."

"But is that wise, letting them know I've hired a lawyer and I'm worried? Won't that put ideas in their heads?"

"Christ, they already"—*awready*—"got ideas in their head, and they know you're worried. If you weren't worried after those two meatballs came to see you, there'd have to be something wrong with you. But I can take care a that. What you oughta start thinking about is your friend Mrs. Ruskin."

"That was what Freddy said."

"Freddy was right. If I'm gonna take this case, I wanna talk to her, and the sooner the better. You think she'd be willing to make a statement?"

"A statement?"

"A sworn statement we could have witnessed."

"Before I talked to Freddy, I would have said yes. Now I don't know. If I try to get her to make a sworn statement, in a legal setting, I don't know what she'll do."

"Well, one way or another, I'll want to talk to her. Can you get hold of her? I don't mind calling her myself, as far as that goes."

"No, it would be better if I did it."

"One thing is, you don't want her going around talking, either." *Tawkin tawkin tawkin.*

"Freddy tells me you went to the Yale Law School. When were you there?"

"The late seventies," said Killian.

"What did you think of it?"

"It was okay. Nobody there knew what the fuck I was talking about." *Tawkin.* "You might as well be from Afghanistan as Sunnyside, Queens. But I liked it. It's a nice place. It's easy, as law schools go. They don't try to bury you in details. They give you the scholarly view, the overview. You get the grand design. They're very good at giving you that. Yale is terrific for anything you wanna do, so long as it don't involve people with sneakers, guns, dope, lust, or sloth."

• • •

On Fridays the Taliaferro School discharged its students at 12:30 p.m. This was solely because so many of the girls came from families with weekend places in the country who wanted to get out of the city by 2:00 p.m., before the Friday-afternoon rush hour. So, as usual, Judy was going to drive out to Long Island with Campbell, Bonita, and Miss Lyons, the nanny, in the Mercury station wagon. As usual, Sherman would drive out in the Mercedes roadster that evening or the next morning, depending on how late he had to stay at Pierce & Pierce. Very convenient this arrangement had proved to be over the past few months. A leisurely visit with Maria in her little hideaway had become a regular Friday-night custom.

All morning, from his desk at Pierce & Pierce, he tried to reach Maria by telephone, at her apartment on Fifth Avenue and at the hideaway. No one answered at the hideaway. At the apartment a maid professed to know nothing of her whereabouts, not even what state or nation she was in. Finally he became desperate enough to leave his name and telephone number. She didn't call back.

She was avoiding him! At the Bavardages' she had told him to call her last night. He had called repeatedly; no answer at all. She was cutting off all contact! But for precisely what reason? Fear? She wasn't the fearful type . . . The crucial fact that would save him: *she was driving* . . . But if she vanished! That was crazy. She couldn't vanish. Italy! She could vanish in Italy! Awww . . . that was preposterous. He held his breath and opened his mouth. He could actually hear his heart beating . . . *tch, tch, tch, tch* . . . under his sternum. His eyes slid right off the computer terminals. Couldn't just sit here; he had to do something. The hell of it was, there was only one person he could turn to for advice, and that was someone he scarcely even knew, Killian.

About noon he called Killian. The receptionist said he was in court. Twenty minutes later Killian called from a noisy pay telephone and said he would meet him at one o'clock in the main lobby of the Criminal Courts Building at 100 Centre Street.

On the way out, Sherman told Muriel a mere half lie. He said he was going to see a lawyer named Thomas Killian, and he gave her Killian's telephone number. The half lie was in the offhand way he said it, which implied that Thomas Killian, Esq., was involved in Pierce & Pierce business.

On this balmy day in June, 100 Centre Street was an easy walk uptown from Wall Street. In all the years he had lived in New York and worked downtown, Sherman had never noticed the Criminal Courts Building, even though it was one of the biggest and grandest buildings in the City Hall area. An architect named Harvey Wiley Corbett had designed it in the

Moderne style, which was now called Art Deco. Corbett, once so famous, had been forgotten except by a handful of architectural historians; likewise, the excitement over the Criminal Courts Building when it was completed in 1933. The patterns of stone and brass and glass at the entrance were still impressive, but when Sherman reached the great lobby within, something put him on red alert. He could not have told you what. In fact, it was the dark faces, the sneakers and the warm-up jackets and the Pimp Rolls. To him it was like the Port Authority bus terminal. It was an alien terrain. Throughout the vast space, which had the soaring ceilings of an old-fashioned railroad station, were huddles of dark people, and their voices created a great nervous rumble, and around the edges of the dark people walked white men in cheap suits or sport jackets, watching them like wolves monitoring the sheep. More dark people, young men, walked through the lobby in twos and threes with a disconcerting pumping gait. Off to one side, in the gloom, a half dozen figures, black and white, leaned into a row of public telephones. On the other side, elevators swallowed up and disgorged more dark people, and the huddles of dark people broke up, and others formed, and the nervous rumble rose and fell and rose and fell, and the sneakers squeaked on the marble floors.

It wasn't hard to pick out Killian. He was near the elevators in another of his sharpie outfits, a pale gray suit with wide chalk stripes and a shirt with a white spread collar and maroon pinstripes. He was talking to a small middle-aged white man in a warm-up jacket. As Sherman walked up, he heard Killian say, "A discount for cash? Gedoudahere, Dennis. Whaddaya whaddaya?" The little man said something. "It's not a big thing, Dennis. Cash is all I get. Halfa my clients ain't been introduced to checking accounts, as it is. Besides, I pay my fucking taxes. That's one less thing to worry about." He saw Sherman walking up, nodded, then said to the little man: "What can I tell you? It's like I said. Get it to me by Monday. Otherwise I can't get started." The little man followed Killian's eyes toward Sherman, said something in a low voice, then walked off, shaking his head.

Killian said to Sherman, "How you doing?"

"Fine."

"You ever been here before?"

"No."

"The biggest law office in New York. You see those two guys over there?" He motioned toward two white men in suits and ties roaming among the huddles of dark people. "They're lawyers. They're looking for clients to represent."

"I don't understand."

"It's simple. They just walk up and say, 'Hey, you need a lawyer?' "

"Isn't that ambulance chasing?"

"That it is. See that guy over there?" He pointed to a short man in a loud, checked sport jacket standing in front of a bank of elevators. "His name is Miguel Escalero. They call him Mickey Elevator. He's a lawyer. He stands there half the morning, and every time somebody who looks Hispanic and miserable walks up, he says, '*¿Necesita usted un abogado*?' If the guy says, 'I can't afford a lawyer,' he says, 'How much you got in your pocket?' If the guy has fifty dollars, he's got himself a lawyer."

Sherman said, "What do you get for fifty dollars?"

"He'll walk the guy through a plea or an arraignment. If it actually involves working for the client, he don't want to know about it. A specialist. So how you doing?"

Sherman told him of his vain attempts to reach Maria.

"Sounds to me like she's got herself a lawyer," said Killian. As he spoke, he rolled his head around with his eyes half closed, like a boxer loosening up for a fight. Sherman found this rude but said nothing.

"And the lawyer's telling her not to talk to me."

"That's what I'd tell her if she was my client. Don't mind me. I did a buncha wrestler's bridges yesterday. I think I did something to my neck."

Sherman stared at him.

"I used to like to run," said Killian, "but all that pounding up and down screwed up my back. So now I go to the New York Athletic Club and lift weights. I see all these kids doing wrestler's bridges. I guess I'm too old for wrestler's bridges. I'm gonna try to get hold of her myself." He stopped rolling his head.

"How?"

"I'll think a something. Half a my practice consists of talking to people who are not anxious to talk." *Tawk.*

"To tell you the truth," said Sherman, "this really surprises me. Maria—Maria's not the cautious type. She's an adventuress. She's a gambler. This little Southern girl, from nowhere, who makes it to 962 Fifth Avenue . . . I don't know . . . And this may sound naive, but I think she genuinely . . . feels something for me. I think she loves me."

"I bet she loves 962 Fifth, too," said Killian. "Maybe she figures it's time to stop gambling."

"Perhaps," said Sherman, "but I just can't believe she would disappear on me. Of course, it's only been two days."

"If it comes to that," said Killian, "we have an investigator works right out of our office. Used to be a detective in Major Cases with the Police Department. But there's no point in running up expenses unless we really need to. And I don't think we gonna need to. Right now they got nothing.

I talked to Bernie Fitzgibbon. You remember the fellow I was talking to you about, in the Homicide Bureau of the Bronx D.A.'s Office?"

"You've already talked to him?"

"Yeah. The press has put pressure on them, so they're checking out cars. That's all 'at's happening. They got nothing."

"How can you be sure?"

"Whaddaya mean?"

"How can you be sure he'll tell you the truth?"

"Oh, he might not tell me everything he knows, but he's not gonna lie to me. He's not gonna mislead me."

"Why not?"

Killian looked out over the lobby of 100 Centre Street. Then he turned back to Sherman. "You ever hear of the Favor Bank?"

"The Favor Bank? No."

"Well, everything in this building, everything in the criminal justice system in New York"—*New Yawk*—"operates on favors. Everybody does favors for everybody else. Every chance they get, they make deposits in the Favor Bank. One time when I was just starting out as an assistant D.A., I was trying a case, and I was up against this lawyer, an older guy, and he was just tying trying me up in knots. The guy was Jewish. I didn't know how to handle him. So I talked it over with my supervisor, who was a Harp, like me. The next thing I know, he's taking me in to see the judge, in his chambers. The judge was a Harp, too, an old guy with white hair. I'll never forget it. We walk in, and he's standing beside his desk playing with one a these indoor putting sets. You hit the golf ball along the carpet, and instead of a hole there's this cup with a rim on it that slopes down. He don't"—*don't*—"even look up. He's lining up this putt. My bureau chief leaves the room, and I'm standing there, and the judge says, 'Tommy . . . 'He's still looking at the golf ball. Tommy, he calls me, and I never laid eyes on him except in the courtroom. 'Tommy,' he says, 'you seem like a good lad. I understand there's a certain Jew bastard been giving you a very hard time.' I'm fucking astounded. This is so irregular—you know, fuhgedaboudit. I can't even think a what to say. Then he says, 'I wouldn't worry about it anymore, Tommy.' He still don't look up. So I just said, 'Thank you, Judge,' and left the room. After that, it's the judge who's tying up this lawyer in knots. When I say 'Objection,' I can't get to the second syllable before he says 'Sustained.' All of a sudden I look like a genius. Now this was a pure deposit in the Favor Bank. There was absolutely nothing I could do for that judge—not then. A deposit in the Favor Bank is not *quid pro quo.* It's saving up for a rainy day. In criminal law there's a lotta gray areas, and you gotta operate in 'em, but if you make a mistake, you can be in a whole lotta trouble, and you're gonna need a whole lotta help in a hurry. I mean, look at these guys." He gestured toward the lawyers prowling among the people in the lobby and then toward Mickey Elevator. "They could be arrested. Without the Favor Bank, they'd be finished. But if you've been making your regular deposits in the Favor Bank, then you're in a position to make contracts. That's what they call big favors, contracts. You have to make good on contracts."

"You have to? Why?"

"Because everybody in the courthouse believes in a saying: 'What goes around comes around.' That means if you don't take care a me today, I won't take care a you tomorrow. When you got basically no confidence in your own abilities, that's a frightening idea."

"So you asked your friend Fitzgibbon for a contract? Is that the expression?"

"No, what I got from him was just an everyday favor, just your standard protocol. There's nothing to waste a contract on yet. My strategy is, things shouldn't reach that point. Right now, it seems to me, the loose cannon is your friend Mrs. Ruskin."

"I still think she'll get in touch with me."

"If she does, I tell you what you do. Set up a meeting with her and then call me. I'm never away from my telephone for more than an hour, not even on weekends. I think you ought to go wired."

"Wired?" Sherman sensed what he meant—and was appalled.

"Yeah. You ought to wear a recording device."

"A *recording device*?" Beyond Killian's shoulder Sherman became aware once more of the vast and bilious gloom of the lobby, of the dark shambling forms leaning into the telephone shells, wandering this way and that with their huge sneakers and curious rolling gaits, huddling together in their miserable *tête-à-têtes*, of Mickey Elevator cruising along the edges of this raggedy and miserable herd.

"Nothing to it," said Killian, apparently thinking that Sherman's concern was technological. "We tape the recorder to the small of your back. The microphone goes under your shirt. It's no bigger than the last joint of your little finger."

"Look, Mr. Killian—"

"Call me Tommy. Everybody else does."

Sherman paused and looked at the thin Irish face rising up from out of a British spread collar. All at once he felt as if he were on another planet. He would call him neither Mr. Killian nor Tommy.

"I'm worried about all this," he said, "but I'm not so worried that I would make a surreptitious recording of a conversation with someone I feel close to. So let's just forget about that."

"It's perfectly legal in the State of New York," said Killian, "and it's done all the time. You have every right to record your own conversations. You can do it on the telephone, you can do it in person."

"That's not the point," said Sherman. Involuntarily he thrust his Yale chin upward.

Killian shrugged. "Okay. All I'm saying is, it's kosher, and sometimes it's the only way to hold people to the truth."

"I . . ." Sherman started to enunciate a great principle but was afraid Killian might take it as an insult. So he settled for: "I couldn't do it."

"All right," said Killian. "We'll just see how things go. Try to get hold of her anyhow, and call me if you do. And I'm gonna take a shot at it myself."

As he left the building, Sherman noticed morose huddles of people on the steps. So many young men with stooped shoulders! So many dark faces! For an instant he could see the tall thin boy and the powerful brute. He wondered if it was entirely safe to be in the vicinity of a building that daily, hourly, brought together so many defendants in criminal cases.

JOYCE CAROL OATES
(1938–   )

Unlike many of her novels exploring the frankly violent lives of down-and-out or working-class people, *American Appetites*, Joyce Carol Oates's nineteenth novel, opens on the seemingly serene existence of affluent suburbanites. Ian McCullough, an intellectual at a prestigious research institution, leads an ordinary life until a young friend of his wife phones to ask him for help. Ian gives her money for an abortion. When his wife, Glynnis, finds the check, she jumps to the conclusion that Ian was the girl's lover. In the horrible argument that ensues, Glynnis brandishes a knife and Ian pushes her, leading her to trip and fall through a plate-glass window. Nineteen days later, she dies of the injuries.

Detectives visit the house to question Ian, and he realizes that he will need legal representation. He is summoned to the police station to answer further questions. Despite the reassurances of his lawyer, Nick Ottinger, Ian is charged and indicted not for manslaughter, but for second-degree murder. This excerpt contains Ian's discussions with Ottinger prior to the indictment and trial.

A writer since childhood, Joyce Carol Oates has published fiction, poetry, plays, nonfiction, and literary criticism. She has won numerous awards and prizes, including the 1970 National Book Award for *them*. She has taught at Princeton University since 1978 and is a co-editor of *The Ontario Review*.

from AMERICAN APPETITES
— 1989 —

It was nearly ten o'clock. The detectives had been questioning him for two hours.

Ian got abruptly to his feet, told Wentz and Holleran that he couldn't speak with them any longer; he had an appointment (it was true: he had an appointment) at the Institute, at ten o'clock. And he couldn't speak with them in any case, any longer, without an attorney.

So, affably enough, they put away their notebooks and thanked Ian for his trouble; and, at the door, which Ian opened for them, Wentz, unless it was Holleran, the one with the horn-rimmed glasses, shook Ian's hand, and smiled, and said, "You won't be leaving town of course; you'll be staying in this area, Dr. McCullough, for the foreseeable future, won't you."

And Ian said, furiously, "I'll go anywhere I damned want to go; in fact I am going to a conference in Frankfurt very soon"—though the Frankfurt conference was past; he'd missed it of course, had never even completed his paper.

"Well," Wentz said, still smiling, "I wouldn't, Dr. McCullough. If I were you."

He'd known at the time that he was making one blunder after another in talking to the detectives as he had: with so little premeditation or calculation; with such emotion, such a hope of making them see his innocence, even as he lied. His initial mistake, of course, was letting them into the house without a warrant.

Yet, as he was to tell his attorney, would an innocent man refuse to talk to the police? *Why* would an innocent man refuse to talk to the police?

"Because he's an amateur," Ian's attorney said. "And they are professionals."

After May 27 things happened swiftly.

As if a dike were unlocked, a great flood of water unleashed.

And there is no stopping it now, Ian thought.

He hired Nicholas Ottinger to represent him, upon the advice of his friends, for suddenly, within a space of twenty-four hours, it was obvious he would need representation; might even need, in time, "defense." Ottinger spoke cautiously yet optimistically; he thought the Hazelton police were probably just harassing Ian, trying to intimidate him with the possibility of pressing charges against him in Glynnis's death: involuntary manslaughter was the most they could try for, and that, without witnesses, would be very difficult to prove. There was no motive, for instance. There was no prior history of arrest, no criminal record. And Ian's position in the community, his professional reputation . . . all above reproach.

"It might be that the police have a grudge against you because of our ACLU campaign a few years ago," Ottinger said speculatively. "You remember: Thiel and Edwards. You and Glynnis were involved in the protest, weren't you?"

Ian was astonished and hurt. His political beliefs were so intimately allied with his sense of personal integrity—and his activism in such matters, in fact, so rare—it struck him as profoundly unjust that he should be punished for them. "They would harass me, make me the object of a criminal investigation, a suspect in the death of my own wife, because of . . . that?"

Ottinger said, in mild rebuke, "Of course, Ian. This is the real world, now. This isn't the Institute for Independent Research."

Nicholas Ottinger, a friendly acquaintance of the McCulloughs, though not in the strictest terms a friend, was a criminal lawyer with an excellent local reputation. A slender sinewy man in his mid-forties with a thin olive-pale skin and wiry black hair, quick, shrewd, inclined to impatience—Ian had admired his squash game over the years but would never have wanted to play with him—Ottinger had narrow opalescent eyes that looked as if they might shine in the dark. He was a graduate of Harvard Law who had, according to Ian's friends, distinguished himself in several criminal cases in recent years; he'd been involved since the 1960s in liberal-activist causes and in the American Civil Liberties Union; he knew, in the jargon of the trade, where the bodies were buried. Thus it should not have surprised Ian that he did not come cheaply. His fee was $200 an hour . . . for time out of court.

"And in court?" Ian asked.

"This will never go to trial," Ottinger said. "It will never get past a grand jury."

"But if it does?"

"A retainer of, say, thirty thousand against the two hundred dollars out of court, and three hundred and fifty an hour for time in. The balance to be returned if the jury doesn't indict." Ottinger spoke casually, as if he and Ian were discussing something quite innocuous. "But, as I say, this will never go to trial. They're just bluffing."

From all sides, so very suddenly, Ian began to hear of the police "making inquiries" of people: his friends, his neighbors, his associates at the Institute, even the secretarial staff, even his young assistants. What shame! What mortification! Like Glynnis, Ian found it painful to tolerate the very idea that other people were talking of him, forming opinions and judgments of him, enclosing him, it might be said, in a cocoon of words, a communal adjudication in which he had no role. Denis spoke with him, worriedly, and Amos Kuhn, and Dr. Max (who struck Ian as rather more embarrassed than sympathetic), and Malcolm Oliver, who warned him against incriminating himself in any way—"Don't give those bastards a crumb." Meika Cassity assured him, with a vehemence he found both touching and alarming, that she would "never give the police the slightest grounds for suspicion of *anything*."

He wondered if they had contacted Bianca, but the thought filled him with such sick dread he pushed it out of his mind at once.

He wondered what were the questions they asked. *Tell us what you know of Ian McCullough. Tell us what you know about his relationship with his wife. Tell us what you know about his character.*

He wondered what were the answers they were given.

On May 29 Ian was summoned to police headquarters for further questioning, as it was judiciously phrased: this time, of course, in the presence of "counsel." Entering the building, Ottinger beside him, passing through the revolving door—and stumbling as he maneuvered it, out of sheer nerves—Ian understood with a dreamy resignation that he was crossing the threshold into a new realm of being; had he any residual innocence, it was now to be shorn from him, as a sheep's clotted and soiled wool is shorn from it, to lie in tatters on the ground.

Awaiting Ian at headquarters, in a room resembling a seminar room, were Wentz and Holleran, old friends turned informants, and another detective, an older man, white-haired, ruddy-faced, with glacial blue eyes and a look of professional impatience, whose name Ian clearly heard and immediately forgot. The questions put to Ian were numbingly familiar: how had the "fatal" accident occurred . . . how could it have been an "accident," given the nature of Mrs. McCullough's skull fractures . . . had Ian and his wife been quarreling . . . what would account for the screams, "over a considerable period of time," reported by neighbors . . . why, if the McCulloughs were not, by Ian's own testimony, drinkers, had they been drinking on the night of the twenty-third of April . . . ?

"I don't know," Ian said, frequently.

Or: "I'm afraid I don't remember."

Nick Ottinger had coached Ian on how to respond to the detectives' questions, had assured him he need not answer any questions he didn't want to: or, indeed, any questions at all. If Ian did not know, he did not know; if he did not remember, he did not remember. He had after all freely confessed to having been drinking heavily . . . which the hospital report substantiated. ("Of course," Ottinger said, in warning, "you must know how residents in the area feel about people associated with the Institute," and Ian was moved to ask, naïvely and with dread, "No, how do they feel?" "Resentment, hostility, generally," Ottinger said. "You might say 'grudging admiration' if you wanted to stretch things a bit.")

Ian saw it now: resentment, hostility, thinly disguised contempt—the appellation "Dr." quickly acquired a certain mocking tone, as did "McCullough"—and, if admiration, very grudging indeed. It hurt him, and bewildered him, that he, of whom everyone was so fond, should be disliked generically; and that Wentz, whom Ian had thought an ally of a kind, stared at him with a peculiar intensity, as if he were a rare species of creature, like the unicorn, to be netted, entangled, trapped, brought down, his sides pierced with spears. . . . You are smart, Wentz seemed to be saying, but we are smarter.

It was not Wentz, however, but the older detective who, in the second hour, at about the time Ian thought the session might be ending, suddenly asked if the name "Sigrid Hunt" meant anything to him. The dramatic abruptness with which the question was posed, the misleading sense Ian had had of the session's coming to an end, suggested contrivance of a particularly clumsy and malevolent sort.

Quickly he said, "No," and then, his face heating, like a child caught in an obvious lie, "Yes. The name."

"But only the name, Dr. McCullough?"

Again Ian said, without quite thinking, as if, by answering so quickly, seemingly so spontaneously, he might deflect further questions of this kind, "Yes. She was a friend of my wife's."

" 'Was'?"

"My wife is no longer living."

"But Miss Hunt wasn't, or isn't, a friend of yours?"

Ian was staring at the tabletop, at its dull, scarified surface. For a long moment he could not speak. He felt physically ill yet dared give no sign; they were watching him too closely. "I loved my wife," he said.

"Excuse me, Dr. McCullough? What?"

"Nothing."

"What did you say?"

He sat mute, sick, sullen, staring at the tabletop. He thought, I will never forgive Glynnis for what she has done to me.

"Your name has been linked with a young woman named Sigrid Hunt," the detective said, with a schoolmasterly sternness, "yet you claim not to know her?"

Ian shook his head as if the question gave him pain.

"A young woman who resides in Poughkeepsie, a former dance instructor at Vassar College, her current whereabouts unknown. . . . Are you aware, Dr. McCullough, that Miss Hunt is missing, that a male friend of hers has reported her missing, and that the last time he spoke with her was on the very day of Mrs. McCullough's death?"

Ian looked up. "How is she missing? What do you mean?"

"Do you know her?"

"I . . . know of her," Ian said.

"Were you having an affair with her?"

"Where is she? What happened to her?"

"Were you having an affair with her, Dr. McCullough?"

"Excuse me," Ottinger interrupted, laying a restraining hand on Ian's arm. "My client has nothing further to say on the subject."

He cast Ian a fierce sidelong look; Ian had told him nothing about Sigrid Hunt.

Ian removed his glasses and rubbed, hard, at his eyes; he could not now recall a time when his eyes were not sore and when their soreness, with its acidic feel, did not give a kind of pleasure. The satisfaction of the penitent: I have cried my eyes out, what more do you want of me? While Ottinger and the white-haired detective spoke together, interrupting each other, two practiced professionals whose quarrel, Ian thought, did not interest him in the slightest, he thought of Sigrid, of how, so very oddly, he had not been thinking of her, in weeks: had not dared to think of her.

And so she was missing? And had her lover murdered her? And would Ian be blamed, too, for that?

He said quietly, "Sigrid Hunt was my wife's friend before she was my friend. I knew her, yes, but I didn't know her well. . . . I was not having a love affair with her." He paused, put his glasses back on, did not meet the detective's ironic look. "I was not having a love affair with her. And that's all I have to say on the subject."

"You have no idea, Dr. McCullough, where Miss Hunt is? You aren't concerned?"

Ottinger said sharply, "My client has nothing more to say on the subject."

Though in his own estimation Ian had betrayed himself, provoked to agitation before witnesses, and for the record—the interrogation, of course, had been taped—the police did not arrest him that morning. He and Ottinger left the station shortly before noon. In sheer nervous reaction Ian skipped down the steps and laughed. "I'm a free man!"

Ottinger said grimly, "You'd better tell me about this woman."

Ian, who had not yet eaten that day, drew a slow, deep, tremulous breath. It puzzled him that traffic passing in the street had the look of objects seen through water. He laughed again, and amended, "Temporarily. I'm a free man temporarily."

In as neutral a tone as possible, with exquisite tact, Nicholas Ottinger asked, "This woman, Sigrid Hunt—*is* she your lover?"

Ian said, "I have no lover."

"You'll have to tell me, you'll have to be frank with me," Ottinger said.

Ian said quietly, "I have no lover. I have not seen Sigrid Hunt in months. I know nothing of her being missing, and I know nothing of where she might be, and I know nothing of *her*, I assure you. Beyond that, it's really none of your business."

Ottinger said, "I see."

"My private life is none of your business, any more than it's their business, the goddamned police," Ian said, less quietly, beginning to get excited. "Intruding into our lives, putting us on public display. Poor Glynnis: she never meant all this! Never, never would she have meant all this!"

He could not bear another minute, another second, of Nicholas Ottinger's company; so shook hands with the man and walked off. The sunlight was dazzling: blinding. He was thinking he must call Bianca to warn her: Your father is being investigated in your mother's death. He must call Roberta Grinnell, whom he had not meant to frighten. And Sigrid Hunt, what of Sigrid Hunt? . . . He never wanted to see the woman again, or even speak with her, but he must know if something had happened to her; he must know where she was.

He went into a pub on South Street, sat at the bar, ordered a sandwich, beer, another beer, feeling, so very oddly, a measure of elation: he was free for the remainder of the day; hours opened up before him. He was free as anyone in Hazelton was free; that fact impressed him profoundly. He told himself, in Ottinger's well-chosen words, that the investigation was not serious, was merely a form of harassment, would come to nothing in the end: no one could prove it was not an accident. For there were no witnesses, and there was no motive. There were no witnesses, and there was no motive.

He told himself, swallowing down the last of his beer, Of course you are guilty; and of course you will be punished.

They arrested Ian on the morning of May 30, eighteen days after Glynnis's death. And informed him, in words that had the solemn ring of antiquity, that anything he said "can and will be used against you."

The formal charge was second-degree murder, not manslaughter as he and Ottinger had expected.

Preposterous, Ottinger said.

The grand jury will never indict, Ottinger said. He seemed to take the arrest as a personal insult; as, perhaps, it was intended.

Ian was served the warrant not in his home, or at the Institute—where, if they meant to be cruel, they might have surprised him—but in the Cattaraugus County courthouse, where Ottinger had arranged to "surrender" him privately: see him through the arraignment, post his bail bond, and get him released in a matter of minutes. Ottinger's strategy was to bring his client into the courthouse by way of a rear dock used for loading and unloading prisoners, that Ian might be spared a more public entry, and take him out, take him *quickly* out, the same way. As Ottinger told Ian, "You never know what sort of gauntlet you might have to run, in a case like this."

"Like this?"

"So much local publicity, rumors."

"Ah," said Ian humbly, with the air of a man who has a great deal to learn, "I hadn't known."

Before the arraignment, Ottinger telephoned the justice of the peace who had issued the arrest warrant, objecting strenuously to the $75,000 bonding fee, which he saw to be both excessive and insulting—"My client is hardly a man who would run away"; but the fee remained $75,000. Ian said, "Does it matter? Why does it matter?" The great shock was the charge itself, *murder*, that astonishing accusation *murder*; what did the rest of it matter? He had no difficulty meeting the 10 percent bail; $7,500 seemed a fair sum to him; after all, they were accusing him of having murdered his own wife.

Ottinger looked at his client, as he would, in the months to come, so frequently look at him: with patience, pity, some measure of sympathy, yet a measure too of contempt. You fool, he seemed to be saying. You asshole. "Of course it matters, everything matters; you must know you're fighting for your life," he said.

Startled, Ian laughed and said, "*My* life? Surely not."

· · ·

And then he was indicted, after all: Ian McCullough, who had wanted to believe that his destiny, legal and otherwise, was determined for him not by mere men, mortal like himself, and fallible—if not "shrewd," "manipulative," "opportunistic"—but by inhuman processes beautifully abstract as the rising and falling of the tides, the clockwork orbiting of planets, the ghostly trajectory of starlight across the void. But of course such thinking was, in the crude but accurate vernacular, bullshit. For the six women and nine men of the Cattaraugus County grand jury, June session, had simply voted to support Samuel S. Lederer's case against Ian McCullough: had found his narrative account of Glynnis McCullough's death persuasive. It was that, and nothing more.

And they had voted to indict not on lesser charges of manslaughter, criminally negligent homicide, but on charges of second-degree murder: had signed their names to the "true bill" of indictment, which charged that

> On the night of April 23 of this year, within the venue of Cattaraugus County, New York,
>
> Ian J. McCullough,
>
> defendant herein, did commit murder in the second degree in that he caused with force the death of Glynnis McCullough, his wife, thereby taking the life of the aforementioned Glynnis McCullough:
>
> In violation of Section 125:25 of the New York State Statutes.

And so he was arraigned in the Cattaraugus County courthouse another time, before another judge, his case to be sent to the docket of one Chief Superior Court Judge Benedict Harmon, of whom he had never heard, for motions and trial. The defense had fourteen days to file motions and the prosecution fourteen days in which to respond, at which point a date for the trial would be set, very likely in the fall. When Ian McCullough would have, as it's said, his day in court; when he might be exonerated of the crime lodged against him. When he might be publicly eviscerated, gutted like a fish.

Ian asked the assemblage, "If I were to plead guilty now, would this all come to an end?"

And they looked at him, to a man, as if he were mad. And Ottinger took him hastily aside and spoke with him: *What are you saying what on earth do you mean don't you understand have you no idea for Christ's sake Ian I'm not even open to pretrial conference for purposes of plea bargaining don't you know they have no case against you don't you understand a jury will never vote to convict*, and Ian sighed and acquiesced, or must have acquiesced, since the procedure, the talk, legal quibbling, paperwork, continued. It was lengthy and exhausting. His jaws ached from yawning. He thought, How could Glynnis have done this to me! I will grow to hate her, yet.

He thought, If I am guilty, I am guilty.

He thought, I will not lift a finger to defend myself. I will not play their contemptible game.

This time they were waiting for him; this time he could not contrive to elude them, reporters, photographers, "media" people with hand-held cameras and microphones jostling close, shouting questions at him: *Dr. McCullough? Dr. McCullough? Ian? How did you plead? What is your defense? When is the trial?* A crowd of thirty or more, men, women, all of them strangers, a proverbial pack, they seemed to him, like hyenas: yet with such enthusiasm for the hunt and, for the moment, for him, he stared at them with interest. *Dr. McCullough? Over here! Could you say a few words to our viewers—*

The contentious little crowd followed him to the sidewalk, where one of Ottinger's young assistants was waiting with a car; like any guilty man Ian ducked his head, shielded his face. He felt his sleeve plucked, a blow of sorts against his shoulder, heard Ottinger's raised voice, the startling fury of Ottinger's raised voice.

"I seem to be becoming a celebrity," Ian said, as they drove away, "without quite remembering what I did, still less why I did it."

Ottinger was not amused. "Just don't talk to those people," he said. "Any of them. *Any*one."

Ian, still cringing, nonetheless looked back at the crowd. It had grown alarmingly, within a few minutes, and was growing still. Women shoppers, men in business suits, boys on bicycles who slowed, stopped, straddled their bicycles, asking what was going on; who was in the Cadillac Seville as it sped away from the curb, why the cameras? In his rumpled seersucker suit, a tie of drab neutral colors knotted loosely about his throat, the object of the crowd's excited scrutiny looked like no murderer of distinction; certainly like no celebrity. Ian said shakily, but smiling, "It seems so easy, somehow."

"So easy? What is?" Ottinger asked. He was beginning to regard his client with a look of professional caution.

"Crossing over."

"Crossing over—?"

"To what's on the other side."

Ian was driven by a roundabout way to the Sheraton Motor Hotel by the Thruway, some six miles north of Hazelton-on-Hudson, a ten-story structure so new it was surrounded not by a carpet of perfectly trimmed green grass but by jagged rutted raw earth that gave it a startling, improvised look: the very place, Ian thought, for a murderer incognito. Ottinger had made a reservation for Ian and Bianca there under the pseudonymous identities of "Jonathan Hamilton" and his daughter "Veronica" until such time—it might be a few days, it might be two weeks—it was believed to be safe for them to return to 338 Pearce. If it would ever be safe.

When, on the morning of July 2, Nick Ottinger telephoned Ian to tell him the grand jury's decision—"Ian, I'm so sorry, I'm afraid I have bad news, preposterous bad news"—Ian felt a spasm of physical chill that left him weak and breathless. He had to grope for a place to sit down, telephone cord comically twisted around his legs, glasses skidding down his nose.

So extreme was his reaction, so stunned was he for hours afterward, like a steer struck a sledgehammer blow to the head, Ian realized that, yes, he had come to believe the grand jury would not indict; he had listened to Ottinger and his friends, had believed what they'd said. Not only that the grand jury would not indict but that it would not dare. I must have been desperate to believe, Ian thought. Even as I tried to convince myself I felt nothing.

Even as I tried to convince myself I am already a dead man.

Of course, capital punishment was not a possibility. The charge of murder in the first degree had been reserved in New York State for cases involving the killing of police officers or prison guards, but it was recently declared unconstitutional. Second-degree murder, as Ottinger explained, was a fairly general category, with which prosecutors might do as they wished; it yielded to three subcategories, which blurred and overlapped—"intentional" murder, "felony" murder, and "depraved indifference to human life." Such homicides ran the gamut from coolly premeditated gangland murders to crimes of passion to acts of self-defense, overzealously prosecuted. And there were those "murders" that were, at best, types of manslaughter or criminally negligent homicide.

"If I am convicted," Ian said, "what would be my sentence, and where?"

Ottinger winced. "You aren't going to be convicted, Ian. Lederer's case is so weak, I'm reasonably sure Harmon might dismiss it. I intend to—"

"Yes, of course," Ian said, "but if he doesn't, and if there is a trial, and if—?"

"It's impossible to say. The charges will probably be dropped to manslaughter-one or-two, for one thing. And there is the fourth degree of homicide, 'criminally negligent.' Which, at the discretion of the judge, could mean probation and no prison sentence at all. You have no prior record, your character witnesses will be impressive, your professional standing is extraordinary . . . and so forth. When you take the witness stand—"

"I'm not going to take the witness stand," Ian said.

Ottinger very carefully did not look at him. "That is your prerogative, of course."

"I have nothing to say in my 'defense.' It was an accident, and I don't remember its details. It was not my fault, nor was it Glynnis's fault, no one can prove it was not an accident, and I have nothing more to say." Ian paused. His voice had become high-pitched and defiant.

"As you like, Ian."

"Except for me, Glynnis would be alive today. I know that, and you know that; it is the single incontestable fact."

"Yes, perhaps. But—"

"If it had not been for me, for the very fact of me, not even taking into account any of my actions," Ian said, "my wife would be alive today."

"Perhaps. But you must not say such things."

"I will say such things," Ian said excitedly, "as I want to say. And I will not say such things as I do not want to say."

Again Ottinger spoke carefully, and tactfully. "You must understand, Ian, that the law is incapable of calibrating anything so subtle as metaphysical distinctions. It tries to measure intent, but it cannot measure what one might call the swerve, or the inclination, of the soul. . . . If you retain me as your defense attorney you will have to allow me to defend you as if I were defending—which indeed I am—an action, and not, in the most abstract terms, a man. Do you understand?"

Ian shrugged impatiently. "I'm not sure I want to understand."

"The law under which we operate, and cooperate, is adversarial in structure, as you know. It's a game of a kind, but unlike most games its boundaries are somewhat hazy. For instance, if the jury, however improbably, were to vote for conviction—"

"Yes, if the jury *were* to vote for conviction?"

"We would naturally appeal to the state supreme court. And there, of course, the game is radically altered: no jurors, for one thing; no emotion, or not much. I have had good luck," Ottinger said modestly, or was it in fact reluctantly—an acknowledgment of past success being simultaneously, in this instance, an acknowledgment of past failure—"with the state supreme court as it's presently constituted. But I won't go into that now. The point is—"

"But if I *am* convicted," Ian interrupted, "and if the supreme court upholds the conviction, what then? How long might I be sentenced to prison, and where?"

Ottinger said, almost irritably—how the man disliked being driven into a corner!—"It's difficult to answer, since sentencing is at the discretion of the judge. Murder-two, with which you're charged, carries with it a mandatory minimum of fifteen years; the maximum is twenty-five years to life. By minimum I mean that you would serve fifteen years before being eligible for parole."

"Fifteen years. That doesn't seem very long."

Ottinger stared at Ian as if he had said something not only mad but incomprehensible. He said, "In one of our state prison facilities, for instance at Sing Sing, a man like you—given your background, your profession, your temperament, your physical type, and, not least, the color of your skin—might discover that a single week is very long. A single day. A single hour. What *is* your field exactly? Demographics? It might be difficult to explain that to some of your fellow inmates."

"They would not like me, would they," Ian said slowly.

"They would not like you quite as you are accustomed to being liked."

"As, perhaps, I have not deserved being liked."

"*That* has nothing to do with the law," Ottinger said. "Very few of us are liked, still less loved, to the degree we imagine we deserve. The point is, Ian, for the sake of everyone in your life, particularly, I'd think, for your daughter's sake, you want to keep out of prison. Being physically humiliated, beaten, terrorized, sodomized, whatever, might have its theoretical appeal—"

"You think, then, it is only theory?"

"—but you are not a criminal in any reasonable sense of the word, and it's ridiculous to acquiesce to charges that you are. Keep in mind that 'Samuel S. Lederer' is no principle of wrathful justice but a run-of-the-mill backwoods prosecutor who went to a third-rate law school, hides his envy of more successful men inside a pose of moral rectitude, and would railroad his own grandmother into prison if it could help his faltering career. If you don't want to testify in your own behalf that is your decision; you can't be forced, and I won't try to coerce you, though I should say it's possible, in mid-trial, when you hear some of the prosecution's witnesses, you'll be moved to change your mind."

"I will never change my mind," Ian said. His voice was flat, icily uninflected. "There is no power on earth that can make me change my mind."

"Well. You make it a challenge, then," Ottinger said, smiling, "to defend you."

"Would you like me to find another attorney?"

"Of course not!" Ottinger said happily. "As I said, it's a challenge. *You* are a challenge."

"But if the trial drags on, if there's an appeal," Ian said thoughtfully, "there may be some problem about paying you. My finances are limited. My resources. With Bianca's college tuition and bills, and if I am forced to resign from the Institute—"

"You are not going to be forced to resign from the Institute," Ottinger said. "Put that thought out of your mind immediately."

"—and I'm not going to sell the house, because, you know, it was always, from the first, Glynnis's house; she loved it so, did so much to improve it, furnished it with such imagination, decorated it—well, you know. I would be killing her a second time if I sold the house . . . and for such a petty expediency, defending my*self*." Ian paused, looking at his hands. He spoke in the same flat dull dead voice, but his hands had begun to tremble. "I won't do it."

"Of course not," Ottinger said.

"I *won't* do it. She's so much more there, in the house, than she is at the cemetery . . . that's the main thing."

"You won't have to sell the house."

"Even as I know it's ridiculous to talk like that, as if a dead person 'were' anywhere at all, except in the memories of the living. Like the illustrious dead, our great mentors and ancestors—our fathers, you might say, if not, strictly speaking, *our* fathers. . . ." He paused; touched the back of a hand to his forehead, as if confused. "Still the house may, in time, be sold anyway," he said, "as my estate. If something happens to me, and Bianca inherits. Bianca *will* inherit, won't she, even if she is not yet twenty-one?"

"Don't think about the house, please," Ottinger said.

"You would help Bianca, wouldn't you, if something happened to me?"

"Of course," Ottinger said, managing, still, to smile, "but what are we talking about, exactly?"

Ian said, "The future."

"It might be better for you to leave the future to me," Ottinger said. "And not to think about the house, or your daughter, or going to prison, or—whatever. After all, you have indicated your faith in me, haven't you?" Ottinger's kindly, practical, eminently reasonable voice was so finely modulated as to suggest control achieved at some cost; he was regarding Ian as—was it Denis Grinnell, or Malcolm Oliver, or another of his friends?—had looked at him recently: a look of sympathy, pity, mild fear. Ian noticed for the first time a scattering of tiny scars around Ottinger's eyes, near-invisible, like stitches in the skin: an expression of perpetual squinting, and perpetual and intense thought. Had he had an accident? Slammed his head through a pane of glass?

Ottinger talked as Ottinger so brilliantly, and not inexpensively, did; and Ian nodded, as if knowing himself rebuked, chastised. He saw that his attorney was, as usual, handsomely dressed, in a powder-gray sharkskin suit with a silk polka-dot tie and matching silk handkerchief in his lapel pocket, dark polished shoes, white shirt, cuff links, clean close-trimmed nails. Of course he was smoothly shaven and gave off a subtle astringent odor, the very fragrance of sincerity. Beside him, or, rather, facing him—they were in Ottinger's inner office, a walnut-paneled and beautifully furnished room with a large disordered antique-looking desk behind which Ottinger sat erect and alert—Ian felt like a poor relation, an embarrassment: not yet shaven that day, or even showered, and dressed in clothes he'd pulled out of drawers and closets, groggy from another night's uneasy sleep. He was coatless, tieless, in a shirt and trousers surely in need of laundering, rundown and entirely too comfortable "moccasins," one frayed navy blue sock not quite the mate of the other. Help me, he thought.

Had Nick Ottinger been Glynnis's lover?—improbable, yet not impossible; not even, if one thought hard about it, improbable. Adulterous affairs were a matter (Ian gathered) of propinquity and opportunity; you drove out, if you were a woman, with the intention of shopping at the A & P, and *did* in fact shop at the A & P, but after a deftly orchestrated hour or so with your lover—in his office perhaps, if his office was private, or reasonably so; or in (this, upon reflection, more practical, and certainly more decorous) a room rented for that purpose, a motel room perhaps, miles away, the farther away the better (except of course for the logistics of time: marital life is bound together by a perpetual logic of time), one of the new Holiday Inns, Ramada Inns, Hilton Inns, Sheratons. Or one of those cheap, sleazy, *film noir* motels, older, grittier, possibly more evocative of sexual excess, sexual shame. Ian could not have said, the thought being so fresh and consequently so unnerving, whether he preferred Nick Ottinger to Denis Grinnell as Glynnis's lover: the one admittedly more stylish and attractive, the other frankly warmer, sweeter, more . . . fun. Did adulterous lovers have fun with each other's bodies, as, it might be presumed, married lovers often did not? Married lovers with a history of knowing too much, and too intimately, about each other's bodies? She'd scorned him for his impotence and of course it had been so, in his memory now, blurred as an underwater scene, decades of impotence, one after another episode of sexual failure and humiliation, the limp penis, the too-erect too-excitable too-quickly-ejaculating penis, so many ways of failing, like so many avenues of entropy, and so few of succeeding: a principle of the physical universe, as of civilization, that there was but one ideal standard of order beside which, falling away from which, all others were disorder. Ian tried to recall that year or two, so condensed in retrospect, when the Ottingers' daughter Rachel had been a friend of Bianca's, had drifted in and out of the McCulloughs' house in a pattern of tides, like most of Bianca's high school friends—*H'lo, Mrs. McCullough; H'lo, Dr. McCullough!*—pretty, smart, flirtatious, as brainy girls are flirtatious, all ironic nuances and ellipses, as difficult to interpret as a miniature poem of Emily Dickinson's. With her father's darkly bright eyes and his lawyerly interrogative manner, Rachel had been a favorite of Glynnis's, if Ian remembered correctly: a contrast, if not a rebuke, to their own daughter's less subtle style. Unless Ian had imagined it, he'd noticed the girl's level gaze sometimes lingering on him . . . unless he had imagined it. Oddly, his memory of Rachel's mother was less vivid, though the McCulloughs and the Ottingers, at one time new to Hazelton-on-Hudson, had been social acquaintances for a while: on the brink, one might have thought, of being friends. Each couple had entertained the other in their homes; for a while each had included the other in fairly small dinner parties; then, in obeisance to the law of tides of social life, of which Ian McCullough knew increasingly less with the passage of time, they had drifted apart. . . . Ian could not remember the last time he had been in the Ottingers' house; could not remember, in fact, the house itself. He wondered if Nick Ottinger was more familiar with his own.

All this while Ottinger had been talking, in that voice—of Ottinger's several voices—Ian thought teacherly, even avuncular: explaining to his client the differences, which seemed to Ian very difficult to grasp, between gradations of guilt, under the state statute. Why was "depraved indifference to human life" a murder-two charge instead of a manslaughter-one, or-two, or . . . Ian, who was not listening to much of this, interrupted—oddly, it must have seemed—to ask, "How is Stephanie these days? I don't think I've seen her in a long time."

"Stephanie? She's fine." Ottinger paused just long enough to allow Ian to know, as Ian perhaps did not quite know, that his question was both rude and inappropriate. "You may have heard," he said, "we've been divorced for about two years."

"No," Ian said, surprised. "I hadn't heard."

Ottinger, staring at papers before him, on the desk, said, "Well—I might have mentioned it to you, in fact, a while back; but there's no reason for you to remember."

Ian said, awkwardly, "You and Stephanie always struck me as such a . . . well-matched couple. And your daughter. Rachel. She always struck me as . . ." But why was he speaking of these people as if they were no longer living? "Is Stephanie in Hazelton? Or—?"

"No. Neither my wife nor my daughter is in Hazelton at the present time."

"I'm terribly sorry to hear it."

"*I'm* sorry," Ottinger said, coolly. "But, as you must know, these things happen."

"These things," Ian said sadly. "Or others."

With the precision of a finely calibrated machine, Ottinger reverted to his subject, to the exact sentence Ian had interrupted; but, now, nerved up as he was, oppressed by a new heaviness, as of a thickening of the air itself, Ian could not listen at all. Divorced! So that was it! He began to see, with hallucinatory vividness, Nick Ottinger (the vigorous hairy muscle-legged Nick Ottinger of the squash court, the locker room, the shower) making love to Glynnis, in the McCulloughs' very bedroom, luridly reflected by the several mirrors with which Glynnis had decorated the room. Their love affair would account for the atrophying of the McCulloughs' and the Ottingers' friendship; it would account for the Ottingers' divorce.

Ian wondered if there was, hidden away inside Ottinger's rather pretentiously impractical desk, in a folder at which no one but he was ever privileged to look, a sheaf of letters, cards, notes in Glynnis's handwriting.

Though, being a lawyer, the man would have them locked away. In a safety deposit box, perhaps.

Or would he, being a lawyer, have destroyed them systematically. . . .

Ian said, rather bluntly, "I never quite understood, Nick, why the four of us—that is, Glynnis and me, and you and Stephanie—didn't continue to see one another, as we were doing at one time. It was always something of a riddle to me"—though in truth, over the years, he'd only given the Ottingers a thought, and that fleeting, when he encountered them at Hazelton parties or ran into Nick at the gym—"our drifting apart."

"Well," Ottinger said reluctantly, clearly annoyed, or alarmed, at the turn their conversation was taking, "—these things happen too."

"Even our daughters, I think, aren't as close as they once were?"

"I wouldn't know."

"Glynnis, I'm sure, was very fond of you. Of you and Stephanie. I really can't understand—"

"Why don't we talk about this another time?"

"Another time?"

"*This* isn't, after all, the most felicitous time."

Ottinger smiled, to lessen the sharpness with which he'd spoken.

"Because I'm paying you two hundred dollars an hour, is that it?" Ian said, smiling too. He thought, You bastard.

And then, with no warning, he began to cry; tears astonished him, spilling hot and stinging from his eyes. He leapt to his feet and hid his face in his hands. "Christ, I'm sorry," he said. "I'd better leave."

Ottinger too was on his feet, as if outbursts of this sort, and his professional intervention, did not entirely surprise him. He said, "No. Don't leave. Use my lavatory, Ian, until you feel better."

So Ian used Ottinger's lavatory: a white-tiled, rather too coldly air-conditioned little room, with a light switch that tripped a waspish rattling fan. He ran water, washed his face, could not stop crying, angrily, helplessly, thinking that Nick Ottinger was the logical man to have been Glynnis's phantom lover, and that of course he had not been her lover; the idea was absurd. I am losing my mind, he thought. I must stop thinking of these things.

Beyond the noisy splash of the water in the bowl he heard a telephone ring in Ottinger's outer office, heard Ottinger's secretary put the call through to him, heard, through the wall, Ottinger's voice, a voice brotherly yet distant: close, familiar, intimate, yet muffled and indistinct. He felt a thrill of something very like passion, to realize that, at another time but in that room and at that desk, Nicholas Ottinger might have been speaking with Ian's own wife over the phone; while Ian McCullough, in blissful ignorance of being cuckolded, was at the Institute, knowing nothing of what they planned, what they did, with no recourse to him. How it fascinated him, even as it horrified him: the appetite and happiness of the lovers' lovemaking, the play of their bodies, without conscience or sentiment, mouths hungry for each other, hands grasping, clutching. . . . He remembered Glynnis's legs locked about his hips, her ankles snugly crossed; the quick tight hard rhythms of her body; the heat of her flesh: breasts, belly, thighs, vagina. At the peak of orgasm her body arched, convulsed, tightened frantically about him, racking him with pleasure so intense he could not bear it.

Yet he'd borne it; of course he'd borne it, so far as he could, in manly silence. Glynnis had screamed and screamed, but Ian had not.

On those occasions, that is, when he hadn't been impotent. When Glynnis had not turned aside from him, in hurt, or disappointment, or unarticulated rage.

Ottinger was promising Ian that he would get him through the arraignment in the morning as swiftly and as painlessly as possible. "Then Graham and I"—Graham was one of Ottinger's assistants, a young Harvard Law graduate—"will check you and Bianca in at the Sheraton. I'll put it on my Visa card; I'll take care of everything. Including a guard at your house, to protect your property." He walked Ian to the door, brisk, spirited, smiling, as if nothing out of the ordinary had happened a few minutes before; as if Ian had not suddenly broken down. He said, cheerfully, "It's expensive, of course, but it's worth it. Believe me, it's well worth it."

As if reluctant to give Ian up just yet, or doubtful of his ability to get down the stairs, Ottinger accompanied him out into the street. In the midday sun the smartly restored Georgian townhouse, muted red-brick, with black shutters and black wrought-iron grillwork, was striking as a stage set. Ian could not have said, staring at perfectly budded wax begonias in the window boxes and at the mica glint of the brick façade, why, on this warm midsummer day, he was here, on Chase Street, in the company of a man whom he did not much like; whom he'd always, for no reason he could name, distrusted.

"May I give you some final advice, Ian?" Ottinger asked. "At the risk of seeming presumptive? I would not, if I were you, try to contact that young woman, Sigrid Hunt, however tempting it might seem to do so. You have told me several times that you don't know where she is, that you have not spoken with her in months, and I believe you. But, still, it's crucial that you understand you'd be making a serious error if you try to contact her, or succeed in contacting her, and the prosecution finds out. They will subpoena the telephone company for your toll calls from your home or office, as I'm sure they already have, for past calls. Keep that in mind. If Lederer fails to locate Hunt to serve her a subpoena, we will hire a private investigator to see if *we* can't find her. But leave her to me!"

"Yes. Fine," Ian said indifferently. But thinking: Toll calls! The telephone company! Subpoena!

"And try not to become obsessed with your case, as, so often, men of your temperament do—*our* temperament, I should say; perfectionists, I mean: men who are accustomed to controlling their lives, not to being controlled. Remember that as your attorney I am going to 'defend' you; that is not your responsibility. My defense is an utterly simple one: no crime occurred, the death was an accident, purely and clearly an accident, as you have told me. So far as it's humanly possible, you should try to continue with your life and your work. You should *not* resign from the Institute. If you do so, that will be a victory for Lederer. *Mors tua, vita mea*—as the Romans said. 'Your death, my life.' "

"Yes," said Ian. "I know the Latin."

"But do you know the sentiment?"

Ottinger had the lawyer's instinctive habit of counterpunching: with him, you would never get the last word.

"The case, you know, may go on for a considerable period of time. It's in our interest to delay, until the excitement has quieted down. This inane Hazelton *notoriety*," Ottinger said.

He was smiling and squinting in the bright sunny air. The tiny scars around his eyes were clearly visible now: like stitches, thorns. The trauma to his head, Ian thought, and the bleeding must have been considerable.

"The fundamental thing is not to despair," Ottinger said. He shook Ian's hand, hard. "Not in private, and not in public."

As Ian turned away, he added, "Especially not in public."

ERNEST J. GAINES
(1933–)

Set in rural Louisiana in the 1940s, *A Lesson Before Dying* is, in Ernest Gaines's words, "the story of an uneducated young black condemned to death for a crime he did not commit and a black schoolteacher who restores his dignity before he dies." Originally intending to set the story in the late 1970s or early 1980s, Gaines wrote to the warden of Angola State Prison in Louisiana, explaining his plans for the novel and asking whether it would be possible for a schoolteacher to visit a prisoner. The warden wrote back: "I don't have the guards to protect you."

Although Gaines wrote again to clarify that his question was for research purposes, the warden didn't reply. Gaines says this was a blessing in disguise, because he then decided to set the novel in the 1940s: "In those days, executions could take place in the parish in which the crime was committed, so daily life would stop when the deputies drove in with a mobile electric chair the night before or early the morning of the execution. Like this story, you'd have cases where an all-white jury would convict a black man without hearing a defense—no call for change of venue, no witnesses, nothing."

This excerpt is the novel's opening chapter, which relates in spare prose Jefferson's hapless presence at a robbery-murder and the trial that finds him guilty. The narrator is Grant Wiggins, the teacher whose life intersects with Jefferson's after Jefferson's godmother requests that Wiggins help her godson die with the dignity denied him in the courtroom.

Ernest James Gaines was born on a plantation near Oscar, Louisiana, and worked for fifty cents a day picking potatoes when he was nine years old. After his parents separated he moved to California, graduated from San Francisco State College (where he began writing short stories), and then attended Stanford. Gaines is the author of six novels, the most famous of which are *The Autobiography of Miss Jane Pittman* (1971) and *A Lesson Before Dying* (1993), winner of the National Book Award and the National Book Critics Circle Award for fiction. Since 1983 he has been Writer-in-Residence at the University of Southwestern Louisiana.

from A LESSON BEFORE DYING

— 1993 —

I was not there, yet I was there. No, I did not go to the trial, I did not hear the verdict, because I knew all the time what it would be. Still, I was there. I was there as much as anyone else was there. Either I sat behind my aunt and his godmother or I sat beside them. Both are large women, but his godmother is larger. She is of average height, five four, five five, but weighs nearly two hundred pounds. Once she and my aunt had found their places—two rows behind the table where he sat with his court-appointed attorney—his godmother became as immobile as a great stone or as one of our oak or cypress stumps. She never got up once to get water or go to the bathroom down in the basement. She just sat there staring at the boy's clean-cropped head where he sat at the front table with his lawyer. Even after he had gone to await the jurors' verdict, her eyes remained in that one direction. She heard nothing said in the courtroom. Not by the prosecutor, not by the defense attorney, not by my aunt. (Oh, yes, she did hear one word—one word, for sure: "hog.") It was my aunt whose eyes followed the prosecutor as he moved from one side of the courtroom to the other, pounding his fist into the palm of his hand, pounding the table where his papers lay, pounding the rail that separated the jurors from the rest of the courtroom. It was my aunt who followed his every move, not his godmother. She was not even listening. She had gotten tired of listening. She knew, as we all knew, what the outcome would be. A white man had been killed during a robbery, and though two of the robbers had been killed on the spot, one had been captured, and he, too, would have to die. Though he told them no, he had nothing to do with it, that he was on his way to the White Rabbit Bar and Lounge when Brother and Bear drove up beside him and offered him a ride. After he got into the car, they asked him if he had any money. When he told them he didn't have a solitary dime, it was then that Brother and Bear started talking credit, saying that old Gropé should not mind crediting them a pint since he knew them well, and he knew that the grinding season was coming soon, and they would be able to pay him back then.

The store was empty, except for the old storekeeper, Alcee Gropé, who sat on a stool behind the counter. He spoke first. He asked Jefferson about his godmother. Jefferson told him his nannan was all right. Old Gropé nodded his head. "You tell her for me I say hello," he told Jefferson. He looked at Brother and Bear. But he didn't like them. He didn't trust them. Jefferson could see that in his face. "Do for you boys?" he asked. "A bottle of that Apple White, there, Mr. Gropé," Bear said. Old Gropé got the bottle off the shelf, but he did not set it on the counter. He could see that the boys had already been drinking, and he became suspicious. "You boys got money?" he asked. Brother and Bear spread out all the money they had in their pockets on top of the counter. Old Gropé counted it with his eyes. "That's not enough," he said. "Come on, now, Mr. Gropé," they pleaded with him. "You know you go'n get your money soon as grinding start." "No," he said. "Money is slack everywhere. You bring the money, you get your wine." He turned to put the bottle back on the shelf. One of the boys, the one called Bear, started around the counter. "You, stop there," Gropé told him. "Go back." Bear had been drinking, and his eyes were glossy, he walked unsteadily, grinning all the time as he continued around the counter. "Go back," Gropé told him. "I mean, the last time now—go back." Bear continued. Gropé moved quickly toward the cash register, where he withdrew a revolver and started shooting. Soon there was shooting from another direction. When it was quiet again, Bear, Gropé, and Brother were all down on the floor, and only Jefferson was standing.

He wanted to run, but he couldn't run. He couldn't even think. He didn't know where he was. He didn't know how he had gotten there. He couldn't remember ever getting into the car. He couldn't remember a thing he had done all day.

He heard a voice calling. He thought the voice was coming from the liquor shelves. Then he realized that old Gropé was not dead, and that it was he who was calling. He made himself go to the end of the counter. He had to look across Bear to see the storekeeper. Both lay between the counter and the shelves of alcohol. Several bottles had been broken, and alcohol and blood covered their bodies as well as the floor. He stood there gaping at the old man slumped against the bottom shelf of gallons and half gallons of wine. He didn't know whether he should go to him or whether he should run out of there. The old man continued to call: "Boy? Boy? Boy?" Jefferson became frightened. The old man was still alive. He had seen him. He would tell on him. Now he started babbling. "It wasn't me. It wasn't me, Mr. Gropé. It was Brother and Bear. Brother shot you. It wasn't me. They made me come with them. You got to tell the law that, Mr. Gropé. You hear me, Mr. Gropé?"

But he was talking to a dead man.

Still he did not run. He didn't know what to do. He didn't believe that this had happened. Again he couldn't remember how he had gotten there. He didn't know whether he had come there with Brother and Bear, or whether he had walked in and seen all this after it happened.

He looked from one dead body to the other. He didn't know whether he should call someone on the telephone or run. He had never dialed a telephone in his life, but he had seen other people use them. He didn't know what to do. He was standing by the liquor shelf, and suddenly he realized he needed a drink and needed it badly. He snatched a bottle off the shelf, wrung off the cap, and turned up the bottle, all in one continuous motion. The whiskey burned him like fire—his chest, his belly, even his nostrils. His eyes watered; he shook his head to clear his mind. Now he began to realize where he was. Now he began to realize fully what had happened. Now he knew he had to get out of there. He turned. He saw the money in the cash register, under the little wire clamps. He knew taking money was wrong. His nannan had told him never to steal. He didn't want to steal. But he didn't have a solitary dime in his pocket. And nobody was around, so who could say he stole it? Surely not one of the dead men.

He was halfway across the room, the money stuffed inside his jacket pocket, the half bottle of whiskey clutched in his hand, when two white men walked into the store.

That was his story.

The prosecutor's story was different. The prosecutor argued that Jefferson and the other two had gone there with the full intention of robbing the old man and then killing him so that he could not identify them. When the old man and the other two robbers were all dead, this one—it proved the kind of animal he really was—stuffed the money into his pockets and celebrated the event by drinking over their still-bleeding bodies.

The defense argued that Jefferson was innocent of all charges except being at the wrong place at the wrong time. There was absolutely no proof that there had been a conspiracy between himself and the other two. The fact that Mr. Gropé shot only Brother and Bear was proof of Jefferson's innocence. Why did Mr. Gropé shoot one boy twice and never shoot at Jefferson once? Because Jefferson was merely an innocent bystander. He took the whiskey to calm his nerves, not to celebrate. He took the money out of hunger and plain stupidity.

"Gentlemen of the jury, look at this—this—this boy. I almost said man, but I can't say man. Oh, sure, he has reached the age of twenty-one, when we, civilized men, consider the male species has reached manhood, but would you call this—this—this a man? No, not I. I would call it a boy and a fool. A fool is not aware of right and wrong. A fool does what others tell him to do. A fool got into that automobile. A man with a modicum of intelligence would have seen that those racketeers meant no good. But not a fool. A fool got into that automobile. A fool rode to the grocery store. A fool stood by and watched this happen, not having the sense to run.

"Gentlemen of the jury, look at him—look at him—look at this. Do you see a man sitting here? Do you see a man sitting here? I ask you, I implore, look carefully—do you see a man sitting here? Look at the shape of this skull, this face as flat as the palm of my hand—look deeply into those eyes. Do you see a modicum of intelligence? Do you see anyone here who could plan a murder, a robbery, can plan—can plan—can plan anything? A cornered animal to strike quickly out of fear, a trait inherited from his ancestors in the deepest jungle of blackest Africa—yes, yes, that he can do—but to plan? To plan, gentlemen of the jury? No, gentlemen, this skull here holds no plans. What you see here is a thing that acts on command. A thing to hold the handle of a plow, a thing to load your bales of cotton, a thing to dig your ditches, to chop your wood, to pull your corn. That is what you see here, but you do not see anything capable of planning a robbery or a murder. He does not even know the size of his clothes or his shoes. Ask him to name the months of the year. Ask him does Christmas come before or after the Fourth of July? Mention the names of Keats, Byron, Scott, and see whether the eyes will show one moment of recognition. Ask him to describe a rose, to quote one passage from the Constitution or the Bill of Rights. Gentlemen of the jury, this man planned a robbery? Oh, pardon me, pardon me, I surely did not mean to insult your intelligence by saying 'man'—would you please forgive me for committing such an error?

"Gentlemen of the jury, who would be hurt if you took this life? Look back to that second row. Please look. I want all twelve of you honorable men to turn your heads and look back to that second row. What you see there has been everything to him—mama, grandmother, godmother—everything. Look at her, gentlemen of the jury, look at her well. Take this away from her, and she has no reason to go on living. We may see him as not much, but he's her reason for existence. Think on that, gentlemen, think on it.

"Gentlemen of the jury, be merciful. For God's sake, be merciful. He is innocent of all charges brought against him.

"But let us say he was not. Let us for a moment say he was not. What justice would there be to take this life? Justice, gentlemen? Why, I would just as soon put a hog in the electric chair as this.

"I thank you, gentlemen, from the bottom of my heart, for your kind patience. I have no more to say, except this: We must live with our own conscience. Each and every one of us must live with his own conscience."

The jury retired, and it returned a verdict after lunch: guilty of robbery and murder in the first degree. The judge commended the twelve white men for reaching a quick and just verdict. This was Friday. He would pass sentence on Monday.

Ten o'clock on Monday, Miss Emma and my aunt sat in the same seats they had occupied on Friday. Reverend Mose Ambrose, the pastor of their church, was with them. He and my aunt sat on either side of Miss Emma. The judge, a short, red-faced man with snow-white hair and thick black eyebrows, asked Jefferson if he had anything to say before the sentencing. My aunt said that Jefferson was looking down at the floor and shook his head. The judge told Jefferson that he had been found guilty of the charges brought against him, and that the judge saw no reason that he should not pay for the part he played in this horrible crime.

Death by electrocution. The governor would set the date.

FURTHER READING

This volume is an anthology, not a work of theory. There is, however, a rapidly growing body of theoretical and critical writing about law and literature. To guide interested readers, we list below some of the more significant books in this field. The emphasis here is on law *in* literature, as opposed to law *as* literature or the use of interpretive techniques from literary criticism in analyzing legal texts.

Benjamin N. Cardozo, *Law and Literature and Other Essays and Addresses*, 1931.

Robert A. Ferguson, *Law and Letters in American Culture*, 1984.

Thomas C. Grey, *The Wallace Stevens Case: Law and the Practice of Poetry*, 1991.

Daniel Kornstein, *Kill All the Lawyers?: Shakespeare's Legal Appeal*, 1994.

Richard A. Posner, *Law and Literature: A Misunderstood Relation*, 1988.

Brook Thomas, *Cross-Examinations of Law and Literature: Cooper, Hawthorne, Stowe, and Melville*, 1987.

Richard H. Weisberg, *The Failure of the Word: The Protagonist as Lawyer in Modern Fiction*, 1984.

———, *Poethics, and Other Strategies of Law and Literature*, 1992.

James B. White, *The Legal Imagination: Studies in the Nature of Legal Thought and Expression*, 1973.

———, *When Words Lose Their Meaning: Constitutions and Reconstitutions of Language, Character, and Community*, 1984.

———, *Heracles' Bow: Essays on the Rhetoric and Poetry of Law*, 1985.

———, *Justice as Translation: An Essay in Cultural and Legal Criticism*, 1990.

CREDITS

Auchincloss, Louis: "The Senior Partner's Ghosts" from *Tales of Manhattan* by Louis Auchincloss. Copyright © 1964, 1966, 1967 by Louis Auchincloss. Reprinted by permission of Houghton Mifflin Company and Curtis Brown, Ltd. All rights reserved.

Barth, John: From *The Floating Opera* by John Barth. Copyright © 1967, 1968 by John Barth. Copyright © 1956 by John Barth. Used by permission of Doubleday, a division of Bantam, Doubleday Dell Publishing Group, Inc. and The Wylie Agency, Inc.

Brown, Sterling: "And/Or" by Sterling Brown. Copyright 1946 by Sterling Brown. Reprinted by permission of John L. Dennis for the Literary Estate of Sterling Brown.

Christie, Agatha: "The Witness for the Prosecution" from *The Witness for the Prosecution and Other Stories* by Agatha Christie. Copyright © 1924 by Agatha Christie Mallowan. Copyright 1933 by Agatha Christie Mallowan. Reprinted by permission of The Putnam Publishing Group and Hughes Massie Ltd.

Crisp, Quentin: From *The Naked Civil Servant* by Quentin Crisp. Copyright © 1968 by Quentin Crisp. Reprinted by permission of the publishers Dutton Signet, a division of Penguin Books USA and HarperCollins Publishers Limited.

Faulkner, William: "Tomorrow" from *Knight's Gambit* by William Faulkner. Copyright © 1940 and renewed 1968 by Estelle Faulkner and Jill Faulkner Summers. Copyright © 1949 by William Faulkner. Reprinted by permission of Random House, Inc. and Chatto & Windus.

Fowles, John: From *The French Lieutenant's Woman* by John Fowles. Copyright © 1969 by John Fowles. By permission of Little, Brown and Company and Sheil Land Associates Ltd.

Gaines, Ernest J.: From *A Lesson Before Dying* by Ernest J. Gaines. Copyright © 1993 by Ernest J. Gaines. Reprinted by permission of Alfred A. Knopf, Inc. and JCA Literary Agency.

Galsworthy, John: "Where Forsytes Fear to Tread" and "Dartie Versus Dartie" from *The Forsyte Saga* by John Galsworthy. Copyright © 1922 by Charles Scribner's Sons; copyright renewed 1950 by Ada Galsworthy. Reprinted with the permission of Scribner, a Division of Simon & Schuster and the Society of Authors as the literary representative of the Estate of John Galsworthy.

Gilbert, Michael: "Mr. Portway's Practice" by Michael Gilbert first appeared in *Ellery Queen's Mystery Magazine*, 1958. Copyright © 1958 by Michael Gilbert; renewed. Reprinted by permission of Curtis Brown, Ltd.

Glaspell, Susan: "A Jury of Her Peers" by Susan Glaspell first appeared in *Everyweek*. Copyright © 1917. Reprinted by permission of Curtis Brown, Ltd.

Gordimer, Nadine: "Happy Event" from *Selected Stories* by Nadine Gordimer. Copyright 1952, © 1956, 1957, 1959, 1960, 1961, 1964, 1965, 1968, 1969, 1971, 1975 by Nadine Gordimer. Used by permission of Viking Penguin, a division of Penguin Books USA Inc. and A.P. Watt Ltd. on behalf of Nadine Gordimer.

Jolley, Elizabeth: "A Gentleman's Agreement" from *Stories* by Elizabeth Jolley. Copyright © 1976, 1979, 1984 by Elizabeth Jolley. Used by permission of Viking Penguin, a division of Penguin Books USA Inc.

Lee, Harper: From *To Kill a Mockingbird* by Harper Lee. Copyright © 1960 by Harper Lee. Copyright renewed © 1988 by Harper Lee. Reprinted by permission of HarperCollins Publishers, Inc.

Maugham, W. Somerset: "The Letter" from *The Complete Short Stories* by W. Somerset Maugham first published by William Heinemann Ltd., now a division of Random House UK Ltd. Copyright © 1926 by The Royal Literary Fund. Reprinted by permission of A.P. Watt Ltd. on behalf of The Royal Literary Fund and Random House UK Ltd.

McPherson, James Alan: "An Act of Prostitution" from *Hue and Cry* by James Alan McPherson. Copyright © 1968, 1969 by James Alan McPherson. Reprinted by permission of Brandt & Brandt Literary Agents, Inc.

Miller, Sue: From *The Good Mother: A Novel* by Sue Miller. Copyright © 1986 by Sue Miller. Reprinted by permission of HarperCollins Publishers, Inc. and the author.

Oates, Joyce Carol: From *American Appetites* by Joyce Carol Oates. Copyright © 1989 by The Ontario Review Inc. Used by permission of Dutton Signet, a division of Penguin Books USA Inc. and Blanche C. Gregory, Inc.

O'Connor, Frank: "The Majesty of the Law" from *Collected Stories* by Frank O'Connor. Copyright 1952 by Frank O'Connor. Reprinted by permission of Alfred A. Knopf, Inc. and Writers House, Inc. as agent for the proprietor.

Orwell, George: "Shooting an Elephant" from *Shooting an Elephant and Other Essays* by George Orwell. Copyright 1950 by Sonia Brownell Orwell and renewed 1978 by Sonia Pitt-Rivers. Reprinted by permission of Harcourt Brace & Company. Rights outside the U.S. administrated by A.M. Heath. Copyright © Mark Hamilton as literary executor of the estate of the late Sonia Brownell Orwell and Martin Secker and Warburg Ltd. Used by permission.

Reich, Charles A.: From *The Sorcerer of Bolinas Reef* by Charles A. Reich is reprinted by permission of the author. Copyright © 1976 by Charles Reich.

Roth, Philip: "Eli, the Fanatic" from *Goodbye, Columbus* by Philip Roth. Copyright © 1959; renewed 1987 by Philip Roth. Reprinted by permission of Houghton Mifflin Co. All rights reserved.

West, Rebecca: From A *Train of Powder* by Rebecca West. Copyright 1946, 1947, 1950, 1953, 1955 by Rebecca West. Reprinted by permission of The Peters Fraser and Dunlop Group Limited.

Wolfe, Tom: Excerpts from *The Bonfires of the Vanities* by Tom Wolfe. Copyright © 1987 by Tom Wolfe. Reprinted by permission of Farrar, Straus & Giroux, Inc. and International Creative Management, Inc.

AUTHOR INDEX